MW00508911

Francis Hilliard

The Law of Torts

Vol. I

Francis Hilliard

The Law of Torts

Vol. I

Reprint of the original, first published in 1861.

1st Edition 2022 | ISBN: 978-3-37505-547-9

Verlag (Publisher): Salzwasser Verlag GmbH, Zeilweg 44, 60439 Frankfurt, Deutschland
Vertretungsberechtigt (Authorized to represent): E. Roepke, Zeilweg 44, 60439 Frankfurt, Deutschland
Druck (Print): Books on Demand GmbH, In de Tarpen 42, 22848 Norderstedt, Deutschland

THE

LAW OF TORTS

OR

PRIVATE WRONGS.

BY

FRANCIS HILLIARD,

AUTHOR OF "THE LAW OF MORTGAGES," "THE LAW OF VENDORS AND PURCHASERS," ETC.

SECOND EDITION, REVISED AND ENLARGED.

IN TWO VOLUMES.

VOL. I.

BOSTON:
LITTLE, BROWN AND COMPANY.
1861.

PREFACE TO THE FIRST EDITION.

THE following work has been prepared, to meet what has long seemed to me a manifest deficiency in the library of the law. *Torts,* or private wrongs, of course constitute a comprehensive and enlarged subject, among those with which jurisprudence has to deal. Indeed, this is one of the three great departments, into which the whole law is divided; Contracts, Torts, and Crimes, making up, in their broadest interpretation, an entire *corpus juris civilis.* In view of this obvious fact, it is not a little remarkable, that no elementary work has ever been compiled, either in Great Britain or the United States, exclusively devoted to the second of these great divisions, and embracing all the subordinate topics legitimately included therein. Contracts, as is well known, have been treated in numerous elaborate works. The same is true of crimes. But torts, so far as I am informed, have never, as such, been discussed in any treatise or abridgment. It is true, that most of the various wrongs recognized by the law are in some form or other found treated in legal compilations. But not in the mode demanded by the nature and importance of the general subject; as I think will appear from a brief view of the connections in which the learning relating thereto must be sought.

In the first place, works upon *Evidence* usually include quite a number of titles which fall under this comprehensive head. But I have never been able to understand upon what principle, in treatises of this description, some subjects are selected, and others wholly omitted. Being usually arranged alphabetically, it will readily occur to any one who runs over the headings of the pages, that there is no scientific basis for these collections, and that they do not purport to present a connected, systematic, or complete view of any one of the somewhat heterogeneous topics of which they promiscuously treat. For example, in a highly approved work of this nature, the following is the succession of subjects, under the first letter of the alphabet: *Account, Adultery, Agency, Arbitration, Assault, Assumpsit.* It would be difficult, perhaps, to explain, why *Action, Advancement, Agreement, Alien, Amendment, Auction,* were not added.

Moreover, although under the head of *proofs* may

naturally be comprehended a considerable portion of the whole law upon the subject to which such proofs relate, yet a certain degree of restriction is necessarily imposed upon the method of discussing that subject, by the formal and ostensible caption of the work itself — a work upon *Evidence*.

Another class of works, in which particular torts are treated, are those termed *Nisi Prius;* a designation, the precise origin of which, in this application, it is difficult to trace, and which has certainly long since lost all the significance that it ever possessed. Of these the same remark is true, as of the works on Evidence; that they select at discretion certain subordinate titles of the general subject, (if any such there be,) and intermingle them, alphabetically, with a variety of other topics, which fall under totally distinct branches of the law. For instance, a very voluminous work of this description occupies one entire, large volume with the following subjects: *Account, Adultery, Arbitration, Assault, Assumpsit, Attorney, Auction, Bankruptcy, Bills of Exchange.*

There is still a third class of elementary works, in which *Torts* are somewhat extensively treated, viz: those upon *Pleading* and *Practice.* And this leads me to speak of what I consider one of the prominent peculiarities of my own book, as distinguished from others on the same subject. By a singular process of inversion, in works of this class, as well as both the others already referred to, *remedies* have been substituted for *wrongs.* They treat, for example, not of the *act* of *trespass,* but of the *action* of trespass; not of the *conversion* of property, but of *trover,* as the *remedy* for such conversion; not of the miscellaneous omissions and commissions which constitute the comprehensive wrongs of *negligence* and *nuisance,* but of the *action on the case,* or, as it is usually termed with laconic and somewhat obscure brevity, simply *Case.* It is difficult to understand, how so obviously unphilosophical a practice became established, except that it grows out of the nature of the works, in which alone, as I have already explained, torts are treated. While not inappropriate in works upon pleading and practice, which in terms purport to discuss *remedies,* and rights and wrongs only as connected with remedies; the custom does not seem to be justified in the same way with reference to books either upon *Evidence* or *Nisi Prius,* which treat very largely of rights themselves, whether as connected with or separate from the actions brought to enforce them.

I make these remarks, not to disparage existing treatises or abridgments, of either of the classes referred to, each of which numbers works of the highest value and authority; but simply to explain the plan of my own book, and vindicate its departure from established precedents. To consider wrongs as merely incidental to remedies; to inquire for what injuries a particular action may be brought, instead of explaining the injuries themselves, and then asking what actions may be brought for their redress, seems to me to reverse the natural order of things; to give a false view of the law, as a system of forms rather than principles; to elevate the positive and conventional above the absolute and permanent. It is as if a writer upon astronomy should profess to discourse of the telescope; or a writer upon physiology, of the stethoscope; or a writer upon theology, of church architecture; — making in each of these cases the great truths of science a mere incidental appendage to the artificial instruments by which they are discovered or illustrated.

Without, however, attaching undue importance to mere titles or arrangements, I proceed to remark, that, in considering the extensive subject of private wrongs in the precise aspect which I have indicated; that is, in first looking at the wrong itself, its nature, its subject, its author, its recipient or *victim*, and subordinately its remedy; I have, at least to my own partial satisfaction, evolved a series of principles, far less fragmentary and disconnected, than they have always appeared to me when stated in connection with mere forms of action. In illustration of this remark, I take the liberty of referring to the first four chapters, occupying nearly one sixth part of the whole book, and treating successively of *Tort and Contract*, *Tort and Crime*, *General Nature and Elements of a Tort*, and the applications and limitations of the general principle *in pari delicto*. Also to the *eighteenth* chapter, which relates to *Possession*, as affecting the liability for a tort. From the very nature of these topics it may be inferred, and upon examination will be found, that they involve principles of great comprehensiveness, not modified or colored by diverse *forms of action*, and therefore not requiring to be disconnectedly set forth, as merely illustrative of such forms. I have myself been surprised to find, for example, how many general principles are common to the great *trio* of remedies, *trespass*, *case*, and *trover*; and also to injuries done, respectively, to the two grand divisions of property, real and personal.

Having thus attempted to vindicate my non-conformity to approved precedent and authority, I proceed briefly to explain the general plan of my own book. The first four chapters—in a certain sense *introductory*—I have already described. I then proceed with *Injuries to the Body*, including *Assault and Battery*, *False Imprisonment*, and *Injuries to Health*. Then follow *Injuries to Reputation*, including an extended view of the copious subject, *Libel and Slander*, (which are treated together, as being virtually one and the same, with only occasional variations,) and *Malicious*

Prosecution. Then follow — after two introductory chapters, one upon *Property*, as the subject of wrong, and the other, already referred to, upon *Possession*—*Injuries to Property*, consisting of *Nuisance*, (in the broad sense of the term,) which includes all *incorporeal rights; Trespass; Conversion; Waste; Fraud.* This completes the view of injuries to *absolute* rights. I proceed to those which grow out of the various *relations* recognized by the law. First, *public relations*, embracing all wrongs committed by *judicial and ministerial officers*, more especially *sheriffs* in the execution of civil process. Then *private relations*;—*Joint Ownership, Corporations, Master and Servant, Husband and Wife, Parent and Child, Bailment* (in its various forms) including *Innkeepers, Carriers*, and *Railroads.*

It will doubtless occur to every one, upon the reading of this *programme*, that the field is very extensive, and that many topics are brought together, which have little natural connection with one another. In answer to both these objections I would briefly say, that to consolidate *private wrongs* into one great subject, the unity of whose *nature* both admits and demands unity of *treatment*, is no daring attempt of mine, but is as old as *Blackstone*, or even as the *Civil Law*; that, although *contracts* of particular kinds have been often made the subjects of distinct treatises, yet no one ever doubted the propriety and value of the numerous works in which contracts in general are treated in connection; and that, if there is little in common, for example, between an *assault* and a *libel*, there is as little between a *bill of exchange* and a *lease*.

In conclusion, without assuming to have supplied the want referred to, I would suggest the great need of a comprehensive work upon *torts*, in consideration of the very large and increasing proportion of *actions of tort*, which are continually arising in our courts of justice. While the multiplying and extending relations of commerce, and facilities of communication, are constantly adding to the number and variety of *contracts*; the effect upon personal wrongs is still more marked. Men may contract together, as well by letter as by personal communication; but ordinarily a man slanders his *neighbor*, if any one; and actual *contact* is necessary, to cause one of those fearful disasters, which occasion so many protracted trials, and call for the application of so many nice and novel distinctions, in suits against railroad corporations.

With entire confidence in the *idea*, but much diffidence as to the *execution*, of the present work, I submit it to the candid consideration of the profession.

FRANCIS HILLIARD.

BOSTON, 1859.

PREFACE TO THE SECOND EDITION.

In this edition, for which the demand has proved unexpectedly and gratifyingly early, the work has been thoroughly revised and copiously enlarged. Many changes have been made in the arrangement, some entire new chapters added, and the substance of the very latest authorities incorporated into the body of the text or notes. The reflection and examination, which have only confirmed the author's confidence in the general plan of the book, have also brought to light many defects and errors in its execution; and these, so far as discovered, have now been supplied and corrected.

FRANCIS HILLIARD.

Boston, March, 1861.

CONTENTS.

CHAPTER I.

CHAPTER II.

CHAPTER III.

CHAPTER IV.

CHAPTER V.

CHAPTER VI.

CHAPTER VII.

CHAPTER VIII.

CHAPTER IX.

CHAPTER X.

CHAPTER XI.

CHAPTER XII.

CHAPTER XIII.

CHAPTER XIV.

CHAPTER XV.

CHAPTER XVI.

CHAPTER XVII.

CHAPTER XVIII.

CHAPTER XIX.

CHAPTER XX.

INDEX TO CASES CITED.

C.

D.

H.

N.

T.

THE LAW OF TORTS.

THE LAW OF TORTS.

CHAPTER I.

TORTS AS CONNECTED WITH CONTRACTS.

1. A TORT is a *private or civil wrong or injury*. (*a*) All acts or omissions, which the law recognizes as the subjects

---

(*a*) "A wrong independent of contract." Broom's Comm. 658; Com. Law Proc. Act, 1852.

The word is said to be derived from *tortus, tortum, (torqueo,) twisted* or *crooked*. Wrong; injury; the opposite of right (droit). So called, according to Lord Coke, because it is *wrested* or crooked, being contrary to that which is right and straight. Co. Lit. 158 *b;* Britt. c. 68, c. 107.

"De son *tort* demesne," is a phrase long known to the law. White's case, Cro. 20; Toml. L. D. 630.

The word *tort*, though, as above stated, originally derived from the Latin, is French, like many other terms which have long since become naturalized in the English law. It is somewhat remarkable, however, that, while transplanted into the jurisprudence of another country, it should have been

of its provision and application, are either *contracts*, *torts*, or *crimes*; (*a*) the first being *agreements*, express or implied; the second, *injuries* of omission or commission, done to individuals; (*b*) and the third, injuries done to the public or the State. Some elementary writers, indeed, have treated a breach of contract as a private wrong, and divided civil injuries into injuries to *things in possession*, meaning thereby what we have above designated as *torts*; and injuries to *things in action*, consisting in neglect or refusal to fulfil contracts and agreements, which are sometimes technically termed *things in action* or *choses in action*. (*c*) This classifi-

---

abandoned in the nation of its origin. In a late elaborate French work—"Traité Général de la Responsabilité, par M. A. Sourdat,"—relating exclusively to the subject of private wrongs, the word *tort* is not used, but *délit* and *quasi délit*.

(*a*) "Actiones in personam, quæ adversus eum intenduntur, qui ex contractu vel delicto obligatus est aliquid dare vel concedere." Inst. 4, 6, 15; 3 Bl. Comm. 117.

(*b*) Injuries may be by *nonfeasance*, not doing that which it was a legal obligation or contract to perform; *misfeasance*, the performance in an improper manner of an act which it was either the party's duty or his contract to perform, or which he had a right to do; and *malfeasance*, the unjustifiable performance of some act which the party had no right or which he had contracted not to do. 1 Chit. Gen. Prac. 8.

(*c*) "*Choses in possession* are such personal things of which one has possession; *choses in action* are such, of which the owner has not the possession, but merely a right of action for their possession." 2 Bl. Comm. 389, 397; Bouv. L. Dict. 1, 227.

"Another very leading distinction, in respect to goods and chattels, is the distribution of them into things in possession, and things in action. The latter are personal rights not reduced to possession, but recoverable by suit at law. Money due on bond, note, or other contract, damages due for breach of covenant, for the detention of chattels, *or for torts*, are included under this general head or title." 2 Kent, 351. See, also, 1 Pars. on Contr. 192 and n. *c*; Gillet *v*. Fairchild, 4 Denio, 80.

"In its most usual sense, wrong signifies an injury committed to the person or property of another, or to his relative rights, unconnected with contract, and these wrongs are committed with or without force. But in a more extended signification, wrong includes the violation of a contract; a failure by a man to perform his undertaking or promise, is a wrong or injury

cation, however, is far less simple and natural than the one above suggested.

2. In the course of our inquiries it will appear, under the appropriate heads or divisions, that there are certain prominent points of *distinction* between torts and contracts, as the subjects respectively of legal notice, enforcement or redress, to which in the present connection we need but briefly allude. Such are, *the several liability*, of parties jointly concerned in the same wrongful act, to the injured party, and the absence of such liability, as between themselves, for the purpose of *contribution;* the effect, upon the right of action, of *the death* of either party; the liability of parties under *personal disability* to contract, such as infants and married women; and the enforcement of the original claim or of a judgment recovered thereupon by attachment, arrest, or imprisonment. At present, however, we propose to consider more particularly the points of *connection* or *analogy* between torts and contracts.

3. A promise and a tort may be *coincident*, giving to the party injured by breach of the promise a remedy as for a simple wrong, without reference to the accompanying contract, as such. And in an action for such tort, (as in case of deceit,) it is not requisite to set forth the contract, or any consideration, but simply the fraud or deceit, and damages.[1] (*a*)

[1] Waterman *v.* Mattair, 5 Florida, 211.

---

to him to whom it is made." 2 Bouv. L. Dict. 667—*Wrong*. See 2 Sharsw. Black. 153, 2 *a*.

While non-payment of a debt is sometimes spoken of as a *wrong;* on the other hand, even criminal liability is rested upon the ground of the fundamental *contract* of society, whereby an individual is bound to obey the law, and pay the forfeiture prescribed for its transgression. 3 Sharsw. Black. 159.

It is remarked by a late writer (Sedgw. on Damages [3d ed.], 59), that by the forms of action of the common law, contracts and wrongs are intended to be kept wholly distinct.

(*a*) It is said, "Generally speaking, the law has endeavored to assimilate actions of tort arising out of contract with actions on contracts." Per Maule, J., Howard *v.* Shepherd, 9 C. B. 319. It is to be observed, however, that a mere executory contract, or an award founded thereon, will not so far

In other words, "The breach of a contract may be a wrong, in respect of which the party injured may sue in case, instead of suing upon the contract."[1]

[1] Per Cresswell, J., 9 C. B. 321. See Attwood v. Small, 6 C. & F. 232; Wilde v. Gibson, 1 H. L. Cas. 605; Comfort v. Fowke, 6 M. & W. 358; Polhill v. Walter, 3 B. & Ad. 114; Smout v. Ilbery, 10 M. & W. 1.

---

affect the title to property, as to justify an action of tort against the party who fails to carry such contract into effect. Under a submission to an arbitrator of all matters in difference between landlord and tenant, the arbitrator awarded, *inter alia*, that a stack of hay, left upon the premises by the tenant, should be delivered up by him to the landlord by a certain day, upon the tenant's being paid or allowed a certain sum in satisfaction for it. Held, that the property in the hay did not pass to the landlord on his tender of the money, by the mere force of the award, against the consent of the tenant, who refused to accept the money or deliver up the hay; and therefore that the landlord could not maintain trover for it, but his remedy was upon the award. Hunter v. Rice, 15 East, 52.

On the other hand, where the defendant purchased property of a party to whom the plaintiff's intestate conveyed it, his possession will be held to have commenced and to continue under the contract, and he cannot be made liable therefor in trover, without a demand and refusal, though the sale by the intestate may have been void. Stewart v. Spedder, 5 Md. 433.

The *connecting link*, or rather the *intermediate ground*, between tort and contract, may be said to be *fraud*. This will hereafter be more distinctly treated of, as a specific wrong. (See chap. 26.) In the present connection, we refer to it only as assimilating the two general classes of legal claim and liability. The ancient allegation, in the action on the case in assumpsit, of *an intent to defraud*, is significant of the sterner theory of former times, that violation of an express or implied promise is in and of itself a fraud.

It may be stated in general, that a false affirmation, made by the defendant *with intent to defraud* the plaintiff, whereby the plaintiff receives damage, is the ground of an action upon the case in the nature of deceit. Pasley v. Freeman, 3 T. R. 51. And more especially where a party intentionally misrepresents a material fact, or produces a false impression, in order to mislead another, or to entrap or cheat him, or to obtain an undue advantage over him; there is a positive fraud. Willink v. Vanderver, 1 Barb. 599.

And the still more stringent rule is laid down, that, if a man tells an untruth, knowing it to be such, in order to induce another to alter his condition, who does accordingly alter it, and thereby sustains damage, the former is liable in an action for deceit, although in making the false representation *no fraud or injury was intended by him.* Watson v. Poulson, 7 Eng. L. & Eq. 585; 1 Barb. 599.

4. Upon this principle, if a vendor, during the negotiation for the sale, makes a fraudulent representation in relation to

---

Fraud in obtaining a promissory note is a good defence to an action brought upon such note. Barber *v.* Kerr, 3 Barb. 149.

Thus, where the bookkeeper and cashier of a mercantile firm, by making false additions, and omitting to charge himself with large sums of money appropriated by him, had fraudulently made a balance to appear due to him upon the books of the firm, when he was in fact indebted to them; and had taken a note for the balance thus appearing; held, a good defence to an action upon the note. Ibid.

So, where a person's signature as surety is obtained by fraud and false pretences, this avoids the note as against one who has received it without consideration. Stewart *v.* Small, 2 Barb. 559.

In an action on the case, the declaration alleged that, the defendants having brought a bill for the foreclosure of a mortgage executed to them by the plaintiff to secure a note, it was agreed between the plaintiff and defendants before the decree thereon, that the time for redeeming should be limited to the first Monday of January, 1851, but that the defendants procured a decree thereon, that it should be redeemed previous to said day, viz.: on or before the first *day* of January, 1851, and that, after said decree was passed, the defendants falsely and fraudulently, and for the purpose of preventing the plaintiff from redeeming within the time so limited, represented to the plaintiff and thereby induced him to believe, that the time so limited was the first Monday of said January; that under said belief, and under an agreement between the plaintiff and the defendants, made after said first day of January, that the plaintiff might redeem on said first Monday of January, the plaintiff omitted to redeem until after said first day of January, but was prepared and offered to the defendants to do so on said first Monday, and on that day tendered to the defendants the amount due, which they refused to receive; and that by means thereof he was foreclosed, and, in order to have the foreclosure opened, and to obtain the privilege of redeeming, was obliged to and did bring his application therefor to said court, on which he was allowed to redeem, and that, in consequence of said wrongful conduct of the defendants, he was in the prosecution of said application subjected to great expense, trouble, vexation, and loss of time. Held, that such declaration disclosed a good ground of action. Raymond *v.* Sturges, 23 Conn. 134.

Recovery of judgment upon a contract is no bar to an action for deceit in procuring such contract. Wauzer *v.* De Baun, 1 E. D. Smith, 261. But a judgment for the defendant, in an action for a false representation of soundness in an exchange of horses, is a bar to a subsequent action of contract on the defendant's promise, at the time of exchange, that the horse was sound. Norton *v.* Doherty, 3 Gray, 372.

a material fact, and one on which the vendee has a right to rely, and the latter is thereby misled to his prejudice; the vendor is responsible in damages.[1] An action on the case is held to lie for a *false warranty*, even without fraud, and is governed by like rules, and is the same in its results, as *assumpsit* or *covenant* on the contract.[2] So an action of *deceit* lies, notwithstanding an express warranty.[3] And, on the other hand, an action on the case, in nature of deceit, will lie for the price of property sold, and which proved of no value, though there was no warranty.[4] The distinction is said to be, that, in an action founded upon deceit, the declaration must be in tort; but in case of warranty, may be either tort or assumpsit.[5] (*a*) Upon these grounds it has been held, that an action will lie against the seller of any interest in an estate, for affirming the rents to be more than they are, while he is in treaty, and prior to the sale; if the vendee relies upon such affirmation; although the seller was not then in possession.[6] So a vendor of real property is liable for false and fraudulent misdescription thereof;[7] or for false representation that a certain privilege is attached to the land, which is not included in the deed;[8] or for selling land which does not exist;[9] though not for fraudulent misrepresentation as to the land included in the boundaries of the deed;[10] or for a representation as to value.[11] So, where it was agreed between A. and B., that A. should buy a plantation for B., and that B. should pay A. whatever sum he should give for it, and B. paid to A. $3000 on A.'s representing to him that he paid that sum, when in fact he paid a less sum; an action on the case will lie in favor of B., against A., for the deceitful and false representation.[12] So,

[1] Pritchett *v.* Munroe, 22 Ala. 501; Howard *v.* Gould, 2 Williams, 524.

[2] Johnson *v.* McDaniel, 15 Ark. 109; Fowler *v.* Abrams, 3 E. D. Smith, 1.

[3] Cravens *v.* Grant, 4 Monr. 126.

[4] Waddill *v.* Chamberlayne, Jefferson, 10.

[5] Massie *v.* Crawford, 3 Monr. 218.

[6] Lysney *v.* Selby, 2 Ld. Raym. 1118.

[7] Clark *v.* Baird, 5 Seld. 183.

[8] Monell *v.* Colden, 13 Johns. 395.

[9] Wardell *v.* Fosdick, 13 Johns. 325.

[10] Lytle *v.* Bird, 3 Jones, Law, 222.

[11] Dupont *v.* Payton, 2 E. D. Smith, 424; Cronk *v.* Cole, 10 Ind. 485.

[12] Green *v.* Bryant, 2 Kelly, 66.

(*a*) See *Election*.

where property is sold on execution, the defendant is liable to the purchaser in an action for deceit, for false and fraudulent representations made by him at the sale.[1] And where a party, during a negotiation for the sale of property, stated that the other contracting party must take the property at his own risk, such statement, though negativing a warranty, will not exonerate the party from a liability for a suppression of the truth, or the suggestion of falsehood.[2] So, in an action on the case, for deceit, it appeared that the plaintiff purchased from the warehouse of the defendant, the manufacturer, copper for sheathing a ship. The defendant, who knew the object for which the copper was wanted, said, "I will supply you well." The copper, in consequence of some secret intrinsic defect, lasted only four months, four years being the average duration. Judgment for the plaintiff.[3]

5. An action for deceit may also be maintained for false and fraudulent verbal representations, whereby a party is induced to enter into a written agreement, and is thereby damnified.[4] Thus, in an action on the case for false representations on the sale of a ship, as to the timber of which she was built, whereby she was classed lower in Lloyd's books than she would have been, had she been built of such materials; held, although the sale took place under a written contract, minutely setting forth the build and dimensions of the vessel, (but omitting all mention of the materials,) the plaintiff might give in evidence prior verbal statements and declarations amounting to a warranty upon the point last mentioned.[5] (*a*) So, where the vendor of a public house made, pending the treaty, certain deceitful representations

[1] Minter *v.* Dent, 3 Rich. 205.
[2] George *v.* Johnson, 6 Humph. 36.
[3] Jones *v.* Bright, 5 Bing. 533.
[4] Dobell *v.* Stevens, 5 Dowl. & Ry. 490; Manes *v.* Kenyon, 18 Geo. 291; White *v.* Seaver, 25 Barb. 235; Sandford *v.* Handy, 23 Wend. 260.
[5] Wright *v.* Crookes, 1 Scott, N. 685.

(*a*) Such representations having been made by an agent without express authority; held, it was rightly left to the jury to infer from the subsequent conduct of the defendant, *ex. gr.* from his not having repudiated the warranty when apprised of it, that he was privy, or impliedly assented, to the misrepresentations. Wright *v.* Crookes, 1 Scott, N. 685.

respecting the amount of business done in the house, and the rent received for a part of the premises, whereby the plaintiff was induced to give a large sum for them; held, the latter might maintain an action on the case for the deceitful representations, although they were not noticed in the conveyance, or in a written memorandum of the bargain, drawn up after the representations were made.[1]

6. The fraud complained of may consist in acts rather than express deceit or misrepresentation; as in case of *fraudulent concealment.*[2] Thus the owner of a horse, which had the heaves and was worthless, in the course of a negotiation for an exchange, concealed the defect, and affirmed that the horse was worth $100, and the other party, not knowing of the defect, was thereby induced to make the exchange. Held, that this was sufficient to sustain an action on the case for deceit.[3] So, it being usual, in the sale by auction of drugs, if they are sea-damaged, to express it in the broker's catalogue, and drugs which are repacked, or the packages of which are discolored by sea-water, bearing an inferior price, although not damaged; the defendants, who had purchased some sea-damaged pimento, repacked it, and advertised it in catalogues which did not notice that it was sea-damaged or repacked, but referred it to be viewed, with little facility, however, of viewing it. They also exhibited impartial samples of the quality, and sold it by auction. Held, this was equivalent to a sale of the goods, as and for goods that were not sea-damaged, and that an action lay for the fraud; although the declaration stated, also, that it was sold as and for pimento of good quality and condition, whereas the samples showed that it was dusty and of inferior quality.[4] So, if a broker sell property, knowing it to be subject to the lien of a *fieri facias*, and conceal the fact, and send the buyer to investigate respecting incumbrances in a direction whence

[1] Dobell *v.* Stevens, 3 Barn. & Cress. 623.

[2] Nickley *v.* Thomas, 22 Barb. 652; McAdams *v.* Cates, 24 Mis. 223; Rossom *v.* Hancock, 3 Sneed, 434; Aortsen *v.* Ridgway, 18 Ill. 23.

[3] Stevens *v.* Fuller, 8 N. H. 463; Paddock *v.* Strobridge, 3 Williams, 470.

[4] Jones *v.* Bowden, 4 Taunt. 847.

he knows correct information cannot be obtained; although done by actions rather than words, he is liable to an action for deceit.[1] So, where one has given a deed of trust of his property, to be sold for the benefit of his creditors, and they have neither released their claim on him, nor assented to the deed; he has such an interest in a sale made by his trustee, that, if he stands by and sees property sold in which he knows that there is a latent defect, and does not disclose it; he makes himself liable to the purchaser in an action for deceit.[2] (*a*)

7. An action on the case as for a tort may sometimes be maintained, where another remedy would lie for or against *a third party* who is connected with the transaction in question. (*b*) As where one who represents the credit and char-

[1] Chisholm *v.* Gadsden, 1. Strobh. 220. [2] Case *v.* Edney, 4 Ired. 93.

(*a*) In relation to mere concealment, as affecting the validity of a contract, or furnishing a ground of action, a late writer remarks as follows: "If the seller knows of a defect in his goods which the buyer does not know, and if he had known would not have bought the goods, and the seller is silent, and only silent, his silence is nevertheless a moral fraud, and ought perhaps on moral grounds to avoid the transaction. But this *moral* fraud has not yet grown into a *legal* fraud. In cases of this kind there may be circumstances which cause this moral fraud to be a legal fraud, and give the buyer his action on the implied warranty, or on the deceit. And if the seller be not silent, but produce the sale by means of false representations, there the rule of *caveat emptor* does not apply, and the seller is answerable for his fraud. But the weight of authority requires that this should be *active fraud*. The common law does not oblige a seller to disclose all that he knows, which lessens the value of the property he would sell. He may be silent, leaving the purchaser to inquire and examine for himself, or to require a warranty. He may be silent, and be safe; but if he be more than silent—if by acts, and certainly if by words, he leads the buyer astray, inducing him to suppose that he buys with warranty, or otherwise preventing his examination or inquiry, this becomes a fraud of which the law will take cognizance. The distinction seems to be—and it is grounded upon the apparent necessity of leaving men to take some care of themselves in their business transactions—the seller may let the buyer cheat himself *ad libitum*, but must not actively assist him in cheating himself." 1 Pars. on Contr. 461. See Hilliard on Sales; *Fraud*, *Warranty*.

(*b*) And in this connection it may be remarked, as one of the leading points of distinction between actions of tort and of contract, that no *privity*

acter of a merchant, alleges that to be true which he knows to be false, or fraudulently conceals what he ought to have

---

is necessary, to sustain an action for tort. Gerhard *v.* Bates, 2 E. & B. 476; Langridge *v.* Tenny, 2 M. & W. 519. See Wright *v.* Defrees, 8 Ind. 298; Cazeaux *v.* Mali, 25 Barb. 578. But where a person, with a design to deceive and defraud another, makes a false representation of a matter, by which the party to whom the representation is made enters into a contract, and sustains an injury thereby; an action on the case, in the nature of deceit, will lie at the suit of the latter against the former, although a stranger to the contract. Weatherford *v.* Fishback, 3 Scam. 170. And, in such action, it is not necessary that the defendant should be benefitted by the deceit, or that he should collude with the person who is. Pasley *v.* Freeman, 3 T. R. 51.

Declaration, that the defendant and others had formed a company, upon a principle known as a *societé anonyme*, in the Kingdom of Spain, the capital of which was 96,000 shares of £1 each, out of which 12,000 were to be appropriated to the public, at 12*s.* 6*d.* per share, free from all further calls, and the said 12,000 shares were actually offered to the public; that the defendant, as such promoter and managing director, intending to deceive the public and to cause it to be publicly represented and advertised that the said company was likely to be a safe and profitable undertaking, and also to deceive the public who might become purchasers of the said 12,000 shares, and to induce them to become such purchasers, falsely, fraudulently, and deceitfully caused it to be publicly advertised and made known in and by a prospectus issued by the defendant as such director, (*inter alia,*) that the promoters of the said company, in proposing to issue to the public the said 12,000 shares at 12*s.* 6*d.* per share, free from all further calls, did not hesitate to guarantee to the bearers of the said 12,000 shares a minimum annual dividend of £33 per cent., payable in half-yearly dividends of £16 10*s.* per cent. each, and that the said guaranty should remain in force until the said 12*s.* 6*d.* per share should be thus repaid to the shareholder; that the defendant, by means of the said false, fraudulent, and deceitful representation, fraudulently induced the plaintiff to become, and the plaintiff by reason thereof became, the purchaser and bearer of 2500 of the said 12,000 shares at 12*s.* 6*d.* per share, and by means of the premises the plaintiff was induced to pay, and did pay 12*s.* 6*d.* for each of the said shares; whereas, in truth and in fact, at the time of making the said statement, the same was false and fraudulent to the knowledge of the defendant; and the defendant had no ground whatever for offering such guaranty to the public, as the defendant well knew; by means whereof the plaintiff had lost the money so paid by him as aforesaid. Held, that the count contained a sufficient allegation of a false representation by the defendant, and that the

revealed;[1] (a) and this, without showing an intent to defraud.[2] So the plaintiffs, being about to furnish the defendant's son

[1] Rumsey v. Lovell, Anthon, 17.

[2] Boyd v. Browne, 6 Barr, 310.

---

plaintiff was entitled to judgment upon it, as there was no necessity for any privity between the parties to support an action of tort for a false representation. Gerhard v. Bates, 20 Eng. L. & Eq. 129.

If A. makes inquiry of B. as to the circumstances of C., with respect to opening an account with him as a general customer, and B. fraudulently misrepresents him, in consequence of which A. sells C. goods from time to time, and is afterwards a loser by him; an action lies for the deceit, although the buyer paid for the first parcels of goods, on the purchase of which the reference is made. But only within a reasonable time and to a reasonable amount. Hutchinson v. Bell, 1 Taunt. 558.

The defendant, having had a credit lodged with him by a foreign house in favor of one W. T., to a certain amount, upon an express stipulation that W. T. should previously lodge in his hands goods to treble the amount; and being applied to by the plaintiffs, for information respecting the responsibility of W. T.; answered, that he knew nothing of W. T. himself, but what he had learned from his correspondent; but that he had a credit lodged with him for so much by a respectable house at H., which he held at W. T.'s disposal (omitting the condition); and that, upon a view of all the circumstances which had come to his (the defendant's) knowledge, the plaintiffs might execute W. T.'s order with safety, viz: an order for the sale and delivery of goods on credit. In an action on this representation, held, that there was a material suppression of the truth, and evidence sufficient for the jury to find fraud, which is the gist of the action; although the defendant had no immediate interest in making the false representation; and though, at the time when it was made, he added, that he gave the advice without prejudice to himself. Eyre v. Dunsford, 1 East, 318.

In an action on the case for giving a false character to a tradesman, whereby he was induced to trust an insolvent person, the Court held, that fraud was necessary to support the action; but set aside a verdict for the

(a) And other similar representations to other persons may be given in evidence. In such action, it is not necessary to attempt a literal recital, but only the substance of the representation. And the same amount of evidence is not necessary as in a criminal prosecution. But a declaration, that the defendant represented, in substance, that a purchaser of goods was a fit person to be trusted, and that goods might be safely sold to him on credit, is not supported by proof that the defendant said he was *doing a fair business*. Cutter v. Adams, 15 Verm. 237; Simmons v. Fay, 1 E. D. Smith, 107.

with goods on credit, inquired of the defendant, by letter, whether his son had, as he asserted, £300 of his own prop-

---

plaintiff, on payment of costs, though there were some circumstances in the case from which fraud might be inferred, on a suspicion that the inquiry was made of the defendant with a view to entrap him, and thereby obtain his guaranty for payment of the debt contracted by the insolvent. Tapp *v.* Lee, 3 Bos. & Pul. 367.

To an inquiry concerning the credit of another, who was recommended to deal with the plaintiff, a false representation by the defendant that the party might safely be credited, and that he spoke this from his own knowledge, and not from hearsay, will not sustain an action, if made *bonâ fide*, and with a belief of its truth. In such case, the word *knowledge* is to be construed *secundum subjectam materiam*, viz: the credit of another, and means only a strong belief, founded on what appeared to the defendant to be reasonable and certain grounds. Haycraft *v.* Creasy, 2 East, 92.

Declaration, that the defendant, employed as architect by A. and others, to superintend the building of a church, falsely and fraudulently represented and pretended, that he was authorized by A. to order, and did order, stone of the plaintiffs for the building of said church, for and on account of, and to be charged to A.; and that the plaintiffs, relying on that representation, and believing that the defendant had authority from A. to order the stone on his account, delivered the same, and the same was used in the building of the church; whereas, in truth and in fact, the defendant was not, as he well knew, authorized so to order the said stone; that, A. refusing to pay for the stone, the plaintiffs, trusting in the defendant's representation, sued A. for the price, and failed in their action, and had to pay A.'s costs, and also the costs incurred by their own attorneys. Held, the plaintiffs were entitled to recover not only the value of the stone, but also the costs of the former action. Randell *v.* Trimen, 37 Eng. L. & Eq. 275.

Although a liability of this nature is expressly required by statute to be created *in writing;* yet an action will lie for such false representation in writing, whereby the plaintiff was induced to give credit to a third person, although he might have been in part influenced by subsequent oral representations of the defendant; if he was substantially induced by the written representation. Tatton *v.* Wade, 18 Com. Bench, 371.

Under such statute, the representation must not only be in writing, but it must be made to the plaintiff by the defendant or with his knowledge and consent, and the damages recovered must be the result of the acts with reference to which the representation was made, and not consequential or remote, arising from transactions not in the contemplation and knowledge of both parties at the time the representation was made. Iasigi *v.* Brown, 17 How. U. S. 183.

erty. The defendant answered that he had; the fact being, that the defendant had lent his son £300 on his promissory note, payable with interest, on demand, and had received interest on the note. The son having afterwards become insolvent, held, a misrepresentation, for which the defendant was liable.[1] So, in an action on the case, the declaration stated that A., the father of the plaintiff, bargained with the defendant to buy of him a gun, for the use of himself and his sons; and the defendant, by falsely and fraudulently warranting the gun to have been made by B., and to be a good, safe, and secure gun, then sold the gun to A. for the use of himself and his sons for £24; whereas the defendant was guilty of great breach of duty, and of wilful deceit, negligence, and improper conduct, in this, that the gun was not made by B., nor was a good, safe, and secure gun, but was made by a very inferior maker to B., and was a bad, unsafe, ill-manufactured, and dangerous gun, and wholly unsound, and of very inferior materials; of all which the defendant, at the time of such warranty and sale, had notice; and that the plaintiff, knowing and confiding in the said warranty, used the gun, which but for the warranty he would not have done; and that the gun, being in the hands of the plaintiff, by reason and wholly in consequence of its weak, dangerous, and insufficient construction and materials, burst; whereby

[1] Corbett *v.* Brown, 8 Bing. 33.

The party *to* whom, as well as *by* whom, a promise is made in reference to a third person, may be guilty of a fraud which will avoid such promise. Thus where, on a composition between a debtor and creditor, they induced a third person to become security for the payment of one half the debt, by representing to him that this was to be in full of all demands, and the debtor, in pursuance of a previous arrangement of which the surety was unapprised, gave his own note for an additional sum; held, that the note having been given in fraud of the surety, the creditor could not enforce it. Weed *v.* Bentley, 6 Hill, 56.

On the other hand, where a creditor makes a compromise on the fraudulent representations of his debtor, and receives part of his debt, he may retain it, and maintain an action for the fraud. Jewett *v.* Petit, 4 Mich. 508.

the plaintiff was greatly wounded, &c., and wholly by means of the premises, breach of duty, &c., lost the use of his hand. Held, the action was maintainable.[1]

8. Upon similar ground, an action lies for knowingly and fraudulently transferring a promissory note, which had been paid and cancelled, as a valid and subsisting demand. The action may be either for the original consideration or for the damages sustained, and the measure of damages is *primâ facie* the amount of the note and interest; the ability of the maker to pay it being presumed, until the contrary is proved.[2] So, if a party transfer a promissory note upon a sufficient consideration, knowing it to be *usurious*, to one ignorant of that fact, he is instantly liable in an action on the case for the repayment of the consideration. But the statute of limitations will not begin to run till the fraud is discovered.[3]

9. It has been held, that an action of tort cannot be maintained in connection with a mere contract, unless the misrepresentation or deceit be *wilful;* that the *scienter* is an indispensable part of the allegation and proof. (*a*) It is said,

[1] Langridge *v.* Levy, 2 Mees. & Wels. 519.

[2] Neff *v.* Clute, 13 Barb. 466.

[3] Persons *v.* Jones, 12 Geo. 371.

(*a*) "If any one *knowingly* tells a falsehood, with intent to induce another to do an act which results in his loss, he is liable to that person in an action for deceit." Longmeid *v.* Holliday, 6 Exch. 761; acc. White *v.* Merritt, 3 Seld. 356.

For *latent* defects a seller generally is not liable. Paul *v.* Hadley, 23 Barb. 521.

Declaration, that the defendants falsely and fraudulently deceived the plaintiff in this, "that they, as brokers of the plaintiff, employed by him to purchase oil, falsely represented to him that they had purchased for him twenty-five tuns of palm oil, to arrive by The Celma, at the price of £30 per tun;" whereas, in fact, the defendants purchased the oil on the terms "that the said twenty-five tuns were sold, and would be delivered to the plaintiff after and subject to the prior delivery of eight hundred tuns of palm oil from the said vessel." Averments, that the vessel arrived with less than eight hundred tuns, and the consequent non-delivery to the plaintiff of the twenty-five tuns, and loss thereby. At the trial, the facts were proved as stated in the declaration, but it was conceded that there was no fraudulent

a fair and reasonably well-grounded belief, that the representations were true, is a sufficient defence, however unfounded they may turn out to be.[1] Thus in an old case it was held, that, if an action be brought for selling of oxen, affirming them to be the seller's when they were not, without laying *sciens* the same to be the goods of another, or that he sold them *fraudulenter* or *deceptivê;* it is bad upon demurrer, though good after verdict.[2] And where the vendor of a metal represents it to be copper, *knowing it to be only a composition*, and the vendee buys, relying on that representation, an action on the case will lie against the vendor for the deceit.[3] So, in order to maintain an action for a false representation of the credit of another, the representation must be shown to have been *fraudulent.*[4] If he was insolvent, the knowledge of his insolvency, as well as the fraudulent intent, must be proved.[5] Though an allegation of fraud implies knowledge.[6] But not the converse.[7] So an action does not lie for false representations, whereby the plaintiff, being induced to purchase from a third party, has sustained damage; the representations appearing to have been made *bonâ fide*, under a reasonable and well-grounded belief that they were true.[8] So in an action for deceit, in the sale of a slave, in respect to the title, it is not sufficient for the declaration to charge, that the defendant represented the slave to be an absolute slave, when he was in truth a slave only for a term of years; without charging fraud or deceit.[9] While, on the other hand, a declaration in trespass on the case, that the defendant falsely warranted a horse to be sound, knowing him at

[1] Shrewsbury *v.* Blount, 2 Scott, N. 588; Manes *v.* Kenyon, 18 Geo. 291; 2 Man. & G. 475; Eaves *v.* Twitty, 13 Ired. 468; Gatling *v.* Newell, 9 Ind. 572.

[2] Cross *v.* Garnet, 3 Mod. 261; acc. Turner *v.* Brent, 12 Mod. 245.

[3] Cornelius *v.* Molloy, 7 Barr, 293.

[4] Hopper *v.* Sisk, 1 Cart. 176. Bennett *v.* Terrill, 20 Geo. 83.

[5] Fooks *v.* Waples, 1 Harring. 131. See Savage *v.* Jackson, 19 Geo. 310.

[6] Terrell *v.* Bennet, 18 Geo. 404.

[7] Slade *v.* Little, 20 Geo. 371.

[8] Shrewsbury *v.* Blount, 2 Man. & G. 475; 2 Scott, N. 588.

[9] Brown *v.* Shields, 6 Leigh, 440.

---

intention on the part of the defendants. Held, the action was not maintainable. Thom *v.* Bigland, 20 Eng. L. & Eq. 467.

the time to be unsound, with proof of a representation of soundness, which, at the time of making it, *the defendant knew to be false;* is sufficient to entitle the plaintiff to a verdict.[1] If the declaration alleges an absolute representation of soundness, and a *scienter*, and the proof shows a representation "so far as he knew;" and also that the defendant in fact knew the unsoundness; this will be no variance. But, if the declaration allege an absolute warranty merely, and a breach, without alleging the *scienter*, this will not be supported by proof of a qualified warranty.[2] So, in order to sustain an action, to recover the consideration paid by the plaintiff upon the purchase of land, on the ground of fraud in the vendor, it must satisfactorily appear, that the defendant, in making the sale, misrepresented or intentionally concealed some material fact affecting his title.[3]

10. But on the other hand it is held, that, where a false and fraudulent warranty constitutes the gist of the action, it is not necessary to prove a *scienter*, although the plaintiff declares in tort.[4] (*a*) So, in an action on the case by the vendee against the vendor of land, for falsely representing that the tract embraced a certain portion of good land, whereby the vendee was induced to make the purchase, it is not necessary to prove that the vendor knew the representa-

[1] West *v.* Emery, 17 Verm. 583.
[2] Ibid.
[3] Camp *v.* Pulver, 5 Barb. 91.
[4] M'Leod *v.* Tutt, 1 How. (Miss.) 288.

(*a*) "I conceive that if a man, having no knowledge whatever on the subject, takes upon himself to represent a certain state of facts to exist, he does so at his peril; and, if it be done, either with a view to secure some benefit to himself or to deceive a third person, he is in law guilty of a fraud, for he takes upon himself to warrant his own belief of the truth of that which he so asserts. Although the person making the representation may have no knowledge of its falsehood, the representation may still have been fraudulently made." Per Maule, J., Evans *v.* Edmonds, 13 C. B. 786.

Upon a similar principle it has been sometimes held, that, in the sale of provisions for domestic use, the vendor, at his peril, is bound to know that they are sound and wholesome; and, if they are not so, he is liable to an action on the case, at the suit of the vendee. Van Bracklin *v.* Fonda, 12 Johns. 468. See Hilliard on Sales, *Warranty.*

tion to be false.[1] And the weight of authority now is, that actual misrepresentation avoids a sale of real property, even though made through ignorance of the seller himself; and that, if a party innocently and by mistake misrepresent a material fact, affecting the value of the property, upon which another party is ignorantly induced to act, it is as conclusive a ground for relief, more especially in equity, as a wilful and false assertion. Where one makes a representation positively, or professing to speak as of his own knowledge, without having any knowledge on the subject, the intentional falsehood is disclosed, and the intention to deceive is also inferred.[2]

11. A similar qualification of the vendor's liability is found in the principle, that the vendee must not have had knowledge or reasonable means of knowledge in regard to the subject-matter of the contract; that he must use diligence in discovering any defect, and not rely merely on his own judgment;[3] although it is not necessary that he should be governed *wholly* by the false representation.[4] Thus it is held, that at law an action may be maintained, for false representations made by a vendor to a purchaser, of matters *within the peculiar knowledge of the vendor*, whereby the purchaser is injured.[5] So case will lie for fraud in selling a blind horse for a sound price, though the purchaser examined the horse; if the blindness could not be discovered at first view.[6] So, in an action founded upon the defendant's falsely pretending to be owner of the thing sold; proof that the plaintiff knew, long before the trade, that the defendant did not own the thing sold, warrants a verdict for the defendant.[7] So, if a false representation be made, prior to, and not embodied in, a written sale, of the quality of the thing sold, with full opportunity for the purchaser to inspect and examine it; no

[1] Munroe *v.* Pritchett, 16 Ala. 785.

[2] See 1 Hilliard on Vendors, 325, 335-7.

[3] Fields *v.* Rouse, 3 Jones, Law, 72; Port *v.* Williams, 6 Ind. 219; Campbell *v.* Kinlock, 9 Rich. Law, 300; M'Daniel *v.* Strohecker, 19 Geo. 432; Gage *v.* Parker, 25 Barb. 141; Crouk *v.* Cole, 10 Ind. 485.

[4] Wade *v.* Tatton, 36 Eng. L. & Eq. 341.

[5] Shaeffer *v.* Sleade, 7 Blackf. 178.

[6] Hughes *v.* Robinson, 1 Monr. 215.

[7] Edeck *v.* Crim, 10 Barb. 445.

action for a deceit lies against the vendor, whether he knew of the defects or not.[1] (*a*) So, to maintain an action against the directors of a joint-stock company, for false and fraudulent representations contained in their prospectus and scrip-certificates, it must distinctly appear, that the plaintiff became the purchaser of shares upon the faith of such representations.[2]

12. While a vendee, in case of deceit, may claim as for a tort against the vendor, notwithstanding a contract or even a warranty; so, on the other hand, upon a similar ground, it is held that a fraudulent purchase does not vest a title to the property in the purchaser, but the vendor may sue for it in trover. (*b*) The general proposition is laid down, that he who

[1] Pickering *v.* Dowson, 4 Taunt. 779.

[2] Shrewsbury *v.* Blount, 2 Scott, N. 588.

(*a*) In an action on the case, brought by the buyer of cotton in bales against the seller, for a false and fraudulent packing thereof, without the knowledge of the latter; the defendant having shown a usage in the cotton trade, relative to the liability of the seller in such cases, held, in order to maintain the action, the plaintiff must prove notice given to the defendant of the fraud, as early as circumstances would admit, after the discovery of it; also an opportunity to examine the cotton, either in bulk or by sample; also have furnished him with evidence of the identity of the bags alleged to be so packed, and of the marks and numbers thereon. And, the plaintiff having used up the cotton without preserving the marks and numbers, or affording the defendant an opportunity to examine it, or giving him any notice of the false packing for six months; held, he could not recover. Casco Man. Co. *v.* Dixon, 3 Cush. 407.

(*b*) Whether a vendor, instead of thus repudiating the contract, may affirm it, and maintain an action for deceit against the vendee, is perhaps an unsettled point. It is said, though a vendor is liable in an action of deceit for false representations as to the title or qualities of a chattel sold by him, no action for a cheat has ever been maintained by a seller against a purchaser, for the misrepresentations of the latter upon these points. Setzart *v.* Wilson, 4 Ired. 501. See White *v.* Seaver, 25 Barb. 235.

But on the other hand it has been held, that, where false representations are made by a vendee, to induce the owner of the property to sell for a less price, and the sale is made at a reduced price in consequence of such false representations, and on the faith of their truth; it is a deceit for which an

has been induced to part with his property on a fraudulent contract may, on discovering the fraud, avoid the contract and claim a return of his property. Fraud destroys the contract, and the fraudulent purchaser acquires no title.[1] Thus a sale and delivery of goods, procured through the false representations of the vendee in regard to his solvency and credit, passes no title whatever to the property as between the parties; and the vendor may maintain an action therefor.[2] And if a purchase of goods is effected by means of fraudulent representations on the part of the vendee, the vendor may maintain trover for them against the vendee, without a previous demand.[3] Or if the vendee gives his own negotiable note for the price, the vendor may maintain such action without a previous tender of the note, provided the note has not been negotiated, and is produced at the trial, to be surrendered to the defendant.[4] So a vendor may maintain trover against a purchaser with notice from the first vendee, without a previous demand, and without restoring a note taken for the price from the first vendee.[5] More especially, where the defendant obtained merchandise from the plaintiff under fraudulent representations, paying part of the price in cash

1 Wheaton v. Baker, 14 Barb. 594.
2 Hunter v. The Hudson, &c. 20 Barb. 493.
3 Thurston v. Blanchard, 22 Pick. 18.
4 Ibid.
5 Stevens v. Austin, 1 Met. 557.

---

action on the case will lie. Oldham v. Bentley, 6 B. Mon. 428. See Lane v. Hogan, 5 Yerg. 290.

So it has been held, under some circumstances, that a remedy might be had by affirming and suing for breach of the contract, when it would not be competent to disaffirm it and claim title to the property sold. Thus, although an imposition on particular creditors, by false representations on the part of a father of the son's credit, might make him liable in a proper action; yet even an express fraud of that kind would not work a change of property, so as to render what was really the property of the father subject to an execution against the son. Hollowel v. Skinner, 4 Ired. 165.

Upon a somewhat reversed application of the general rule stated in the text, a special action on the case may be sustained against a debtor, for fraudulently representing himself *insolvent*, and thereby inducing his creditor to discharge a promissory note for less than its value. Edwards v. Owen, 15 Ohio, 500.

and giving his note for the balance; and, at the maturity of the note, could not be found, upon inquiry, at his last place of residence; held, trover would lie for the goods, without a tender of the money or note; the note being produced and tendered at the trial.[1] (*a*) And if A., under pretence of a purchase, obtains possession of B.'s goods, with a preconceived design not to pay for them, and absconds to avoid a suit for the value, and the sheriff seizes such goods in execution immediately after the delivery to A.; it seems that B. may lawfully rescue them out of the hands of the sheriff, even by stratagem; but the validity of the purchase by A. is a question for the jury.[2]

13. Upon the same principle, when one obtains credit upon the recommendation of some third party, whether written or verbal, he is responsible for the recommendation, as if he had made it himself; and, if false in material points, and known by him to be so, the seller may, upon obtaining knowledge of such falsehood, rescind the sale and recover the goods, so long as they remain in the hands of the vendee, or are not passed from him upon any new and valuable consideration.[3] Thus the creditors of a trader, who was insolvent, but who wished to purchase goods, being unwilling to extend to him further credit, told him that they did not like to sell to him if he could buy elsewhere; and gave him the name of another merchant, and authorized him to refer to them. He attempted to purchase of this merchant, and, being asked for references, gave the names of his original creditors, and was told to call again in half an hour. He did call again, in the course of the day, and the purchase was effected. No inquiry was made by the vendor of the purchaser as to his circumstances, nor did he give any assurances whatever relative thereto. On the same day, and after

[1] Ladd *v.* Moore, 3 Sandf. 589.

[2] Bristol *v.* Wilsmore, 2 Dowl. & Ry. 755.

[3] Fitzsimmons *v.* Joslin, 21 Vt. 129.

(*a*) In New York, trespass or replevin will also lie without a demand Schoeppel *v.* Corning, 5 Denio, 236.

the purchase was effected, the purchaser met one of his original creditors, who told him that he had been called upon by the vendor, and that "he had given as good an account of him as he could and not make himself liable;" "that he had told him that he (the purchaser) was a clever fellow, and was doing a thriving business in Vergennes, and that he (the creditor) had sold him goods, and he paid well, and he was ready to sell him more." At the time of this transaction, the purchaser was in arrears to the creditors for several hundred dollars each, and their demands had been placed in the hands of their attorney at Vergennes, where the purchaser resided, for collection; and, as soon as they learnt that this last purchase had been effected, they sent instructions to the attorney to attach the goods, as the property of the purchaser, upon their arrival at the place of destination. This was done; and as soon as the vendor was informed of the insolvency of the purchaser, which was within a week after the attachment, he demanded the goods of the sheriff, offering to pay freight; but the sheriff refused to surrender them. Held, the purchaser was responsible for the representations made by his creditor, and the vendor, having been thereby cheated and deceived, might sustain trover against the sheriff.[1]

14. But it has been held, that although, where a man, by giving a false account of himself, purchases and obtains possession of goods upon credit, the property continues in the vendor; yet, if goods are obtained by false pretences, and pawned without notice of the fraud, and, on the offender's being convicted of the cheat, the original owner obtains the goods, the pawnbroker may maintain trover against him.[2] So where A. by fraud induced B. to sell and deliver to him a chattel, and A. sold the same to C., a *bonâ fide* purchaser, without notice of the fraud, receiving in consideration other property in part payment, and applying the balance upon a preceding debt, and B. afterwards repossessed himself of the

[1] Fitzsimmons *v.* Joslin, 21 Vt. 129. [2] Anon. 6 Mod. 114.

chattel; it was held that C. could recover the value thereof of B. in trover.[1] But the mere possession of goods, fraudulently obtained, with no further *indicia* of title than a delivery order, is no defence, for a *bonâ fide* pawnee of the person fraudulently obtaining possession, against the original owner. Thus the plaintiffs, by their brokers, sold a quantity of tartaric acid, retaining possession of it, but delivering an invoice to the vendee. A. purchased the acid from the vendee, and received from him a delivery order on the plaintiffs. B., fraudulently pretending that he was buying for V. & Co., purchased the acid from A. through his broker, who received the delivery order, and indorsed it, making the acid specially deliverable to himself, and then delivered the order to B. for the purpose of his inspecting the acid. B. then sent the order to the plaintiffs, and, by his false representation that he had purchased the acid on his own account, obtained an order from the plaintiffs making the acid deliverable to his order. The plaintiffs also forwarded the goods, which B. then pledged for money *bonâ fide* advanced to him by the defendant. Held, in an action of trover to recover the goods, that the plaintiffs and B. had never stood in the relation of vendor and vendee; and, as B. had obtained the order for delivery by fraud, the plaintiffs were entitled to recover.[2]

15. More especially will the rule above stated be applied in favor of the vendor, where, in addition to the fraud of the purchaser, the sale and delivery are made *upon condition of immediate payment.* Thus, in an action to recover possession of a quantity of corn purchased by the defendant; it appeared that the defendant assured the vendor's agent, that the money to pay for the corn was arranged for, and that the vendor could have it as soon as the corn was delivered on board a ship. Upon that condition the corn was delivered; but the defendant on various pretexts avoided payment for several days, and the vessel sailed for Europe, with the corn on board; the defendant, on the day she sailed, executing a

[1] Kingsbury *v.* Smith, 13 N. H. 109.

[2] Kingsford *v.* Merry, 38 Eng. L. & Eq. 582. See 34 Ib. 607.

general assignment to trustees for the benefit of creditors, and being insolvent at that time, and at the time of the purchase, and having obtained advances upon the bills of lading, and applied them to other purposes. Held, both on the ground of fraud, and of a conditional sale and delivery, the plaintiff was entitled to recover.[1]

16. But, somewhat in conflict with cases already cited, it has been held that a sale procured by fraud is not absolutely void, but the seller may or may not avoid it at his option;[2] that a party who would disaffirm a fraudulent contract must act *promptly* upon discovering the fraud, and return or offer to return whatever he has received upon it, if of any value, in order to recover the property fraudulently purchased of him; that he must rescind the contract *in toto*, and thus place the purchaser in the position he was in before the sale.[3] And this rule has been applied to the case of a note given for the price. Thus the plaintiff sold to A. a quantity of stoves, and received in payment two notes made by B., for a part of the amount, and the note of A. for the balance; and A. subsequently sold part of the stoves to *bonâ fide* purchasers, and the defendant purchased the remainder. The plaintiffs then applied to B., and obtained four additional notes made by him, for a part of the purchase-money, and prosecuted two of them to judgment; and, after demanding the stoves of the defendant, brought this action to recover possession, on the ground that the purchase by A. was fraudulent; but without rescinding the contract, or returning or offering to return the notes. Held, the action could not be maintained.[4] So, where the notes of the purchaser have been received in part-payment, it has been held not sufficient to produce them at the trial, and offer to cancel them.[5] (*a*)

[1] Van Neste *v.* Conover, 20 Barb. 547.

[2] The Matteawan, &c. *v.* Bentley, 13 Barb. 641.

[3] Wheaton *v.* Baker, 14 Barb. 594; Denendorf *v.* Beardsley, 23 Barb. 656.

[4] Wheaton *v.* Baker, 14 Barb. 594.

[5] The Matteawan, &c. *v.* Bentley, 13 Barb. 641.

(*a*) The plaintiff being desirous to dispose of his interest in certain buildings, trade, and stock, in which trade he was engaged with the defendant;

17. In conformity with the rule above stated (p. 14) as to false representations made by the *vendor;* in case of fraud on the part of the vendee, where the purchase was made by an agent, the plaintiff must show, not only that the purchaser was insolvent at the time of the purchase, but that he or his agent, or both, knew of such insolvency. Hence the declarations of the agent to third persons, made while acting for his principal and within the scope of his authority, and going to show such knowledge on the part of both principal and agent, are proper evidence.[1] So, in an action for deceiv-

[1] Hunter *v.* The Hudson, &c. 20 Barb. 493.

---

pending a treaty between them for the purchase by the defendant, the latter falsely and deceitfully represented to the plaintiff, that he was about to enter into partnership in the same trade with other persons whose names he would not disclose, and that those persons would not consent to his giving the plaintiff more than a certain sum for his interest; whereas, in truth, neither A. and B., with whom he was then about to enter into partnership, nor any other intended partners of his, had refused to give more than that sum, but had then agreed with the defendant that he should make the best terms he could with the plaintiff, and would have given him a larger sum, and in fact the defendant charged them with a larger price in account for the purchase of the plaintiff's interest. Held, an action on the case did not lie for this representation, for it was either a mere false representation of another's intention, or at most a *gratis dictum* of the buyer, upon a matter which he was not under any legal obligation to the seller to disclose with accuracy, and on which it was the folly of the seller to rely. But that, at any rate, the count was bad, in not showing that the plaintiff had been damaged by such false representation; inasmuch as it was not alleged that the other intended partners of the defendant would have bid at all without him, or that he would have joined in giving the additional price. Vernon *v.* Keys, 12 East, 632; 4 Taunt. 488. See Cary *v.* Hotailing, 1 Hill, 311.

It is the later and prevailing doctrine, that, where a vendee, who has made a false and fraudulent misrepresentation, obtains by means of it possession of a chattel from a vendor, who intended to transfer both the property and the possession; the property vests in the vendee until the vendor has done some act to disaffirm the transaction; and therefore, if before the disaffirmance the fraudulent vendee has assigned or transferred the chattel to an innocent transferee, the title of such transferee is good against the vendor. See Hilliard on Sales, *Fraud.*

ing and defrauding the plaintiff by obtaining property from him without paying for it, under pretence of a purchase, and upon false representations as to the solvency of the purchasers; it is proper to submit it to the jury to determine, upon the evidence, whether the representations alleged were made; and whether, if made, they were false; and, if false, whether they were made with intent to defraud and deceive the plaintiff. Such a charge is equivalent to a direction that it is necessary there should have been a *scienter*.[1] (*a*)

18. Somewhat analogous to the case of property obtained by *fraud*, is that of property transferred to the lender of money upon *usurious interest*. Upon this subject it is held, that where, in an usurious contract, the delivery of personal property by the borrower to the lender is a part of the transaction,

[1] Armstrong *v.* Tuffts, 6 Barb. 432.

(*a*) An action for a fraudulent representation of the circumstances of one A. was referred to an arbitrator, who found, that the defendant had omitted to state to the plaintiff a certain debt which A. owed him; wherefore the defendant did not give a fair representation of what he knew concerning the credit of A., but in what he said he did not mean to hold out any inducement to the plaintiff to trust A.; and acquitted the defendant of all collusion with A., and of all premeditated fraud, with a view to benefit himself at the plaintiff's expense, and of any intention, at the time of making the representation, of withdrawing his credit from A.; and awarded in favor of the plaintiff. Held, such award was bad; as in substance it acquitted the defendant of any fraud or intention to deceive. Ames *v.* Millward, 2 Moore, 713.

It has been held, that the vendor of goods, which have not been paid for according to agreement, may lawfully regain possession of them, as against the assignee in bankruptcy of the vendee, by a purchase in the name of a third person at a greatly reduced price. Thus the defendant sold goods to A., to be paid for by a bill at two months, and, not being able to obtain it, and doubting A.'s solvency, he employed his broker to repurchase them in his own name, which was done, although at a great loss. A. afterwards became bankrupt, without knowing that the goods had been repurchased by the broker on account of the defendant. Held, an action of trover did not lie by the assignees of A. against the defendant, as there was no fraud on his part. Harris *v.* Lunell, 4 Moore, 10.

the possession of such property by the lender is tortious from the beginning, and trover will immediately lie against him, at the suit of the borrower, without a demand or other evidence of a further act of conversion. It is said, the law regards everything done by a borrower to obtain money upon usurious terms as involuntary, and the result of constraint and compulsion.[1] And, where a usurious loan was connected with the sale of real property by the lender to the borrower, and the latter filed a bill in chancery to rescind the purchase, on the ground of fraudulent representations by the lender, and the bill was dismissed with liberty to bring another suit upon different grounds; held, that the borrower might bring trover for personal property transferred by him as a part of the usurious contract.[2]

19. In further illustration of the connection between contract and tort, it has been said, that one who enters upon land under a contract of purchase, but afterwards fails to make payments according to the contract, and disavows all intent to make them, is as effectually a wrongdoer, as if his original entry had been without color of right.[3] So one entering upon land under an agreement with the husband of the tenant for life, and holding over after her death, is with respect to the remainder-man a mere trespasser.[4]

20. A similar principle has been applied, where a contract relating to *the temporary possession* of property has been violated by the bailee; in which case the sale terminates the bailment, and the bailor may maintain an action of trover for its value. In other words, the contract of *bailment* as well as *sale* may give rise to a claim as for a tort or wrong. (*a*) Thus the owner of cattle leased them with a farm for four years, under an agreement, that, at the expiration of the four years, the lessee might either return the cattle or pay a stipulated price for them; and the lessee sold the cattle before the

[1] Schroeppel *v.* Corning, 5 Denio, 236.
[2] Ibid.
[3] Per Cowen, J., Fuller *v.* Van Geesen, 4 Hill, 171.
[4] Williams *v.* Caston, 1 Strobh. 130.

(*a*) See *Carrier — Innkeeper — Conversion ;* chapters 25, 46.

four years expired. Held, such sale determined the lessee's right of possession, and the owner might maintain trover against both seller and purchaser; and this without a demand, if the purchaser has converted the property to his own use.[1] So the sale of a chattel, by one who has borrowed it for an indefinite period, makes his possession tortious, and the purchaser, on delivery, and taking control of it, and using it as his own, becomes liable to an action of trover without any demand.[2]

21. The same rule is applied, where the bailee deals with the property as his own, beyond the right of so doing given him by the contract. Thus an agreement, by which cattle are to be kept and fed during the winter, and the stock to be liable for the expense of keeping them, with authority to the bailee to sell them to pay such expense, gives to the bailee a right to sell so much of the stock as may be necessary to pay him his debt; but if he sells more, it will be a conversion.[3] So the plaintiffs attached certain sheep belonging to their debtor, and thereby acquired what was supposed by all concerned to be a valid lien. Subsequently the debtor assigned the sheep to the defendant, to be disposed of for the payment of certain debts, the defendant understanding that he was taking his title subject to the lien. The debtor afterwards, with the consent of the plaintiffs and defendant, exchanged the sheep for a less number of other sheep, received a note for the difference, delivered the note to the plaintiffs in part payment, and then a bill of sale of the sheep as security for the balance of their claim. The defendant having disposed of these sheep, held, the plaintiffs were entitled to recover against him in trover, to the extent of their balance.[4] So, where personal property, mortgaged to secure a debt payable on demand, is left in the possession of the mortgagor, an unqualified sale by him of the entire property, for his own benefit, is a wrongful conversion, for which trover will lie.[5] So a taking under

1 Grant *v.* King, 14 Vt. 367.
2 Lovejoy *v.* Jones, 10 Fost. 164.
3 Whitlock *v.* Heard, 13 Ala. 776.
4 Paine *v.* Tilden, 20 Vt. 555.
5 Ashmead *v.* Kellogg, 23 Conn. 70.

color of a contract of purchase from a bailee, made when such bailee was drunk, whether made so for the purpose or not, is tortious, and the owner of the property may maintain replevin therefor.[1] But, in case of bailment for hire for a certain term, the use of the property by the hirer during the term, for a different purpose, or in a different manner from that intended by the parties, will not amount to a conversion for which trover will lie, unless the property be thereby destroyed, or the act show an intent to convert it.[2] (*a*) So one received a yoke of oxen to keep for the owner, and promised to provide food for them for their work, and to return them by a fixed day, or, in case he should pay a certain sum by that day, the owner was to release his right to them. The bailee sold them, and the vendee resold them, before the term expired, and, upon the expiration of the term, the money not having been paid, the owner, after a demand and refusal, brought trover against such vendee. Held, the action would not lie.[3]

22. In conformity with the principles above stated, the plaintiff often has the privilege of *electing*, between the respective remedies prescribed by law for a tort, and for a mere breach of contract. It is said: " Where there is an employment, which employment itself creates a duty, an action on the case will lie for a breach of that duty, although it may consist in doing something contrary to an agreement, (*b*)

[1] Drummond *v.* Hopper, 4 Harring. 327.

[2] Harvey *v.* Epes, 12 Gratt. 153.

[3] Vincent *v.* Cornell, 13 Pick. 294.

(*a*) A bailor may waive his right to treat a misuse of the property bailed as a conversion. But where, pending an action of trover for misuser of a bailment for hire, hire was received; held, the pendency of the suit prevented this from amounting to a waiver. Harvey *v.* Epes, 12 Gratt. 153.

So the delivery of a pledge to the pledger for a temporary purpose, as agent or special bailee for the pledgee, does not impair the title or the possession of the latter, but he may maintain trover for the property. Hays *v.* Riddle, 1 Sandf. 248.

(*b*) Or, where there is a special contract to do or not to do a particular thing, a party is not bound to resort to it, to recover damages for a breach, but may declare in tort, on the ground of neglect of duty. Robinson *v.*

made in the course of such employment, by the party upon whom the duty is cast."[1] And it has been well remarked, with reference to this class of cases, in a case where the election must be made between *trespass* and *assumpsit*: "Neither of these actions would comport exactly with the facts. It is not true that the defendant with force and arms broke and entered the plaintiff's close; nor is it true, that he agreed with the plaintiff to pay him rent for the premises. Yet an action in either of those forms may very well answer to present the question between the parties for legal adjudication."[2] Thus case as well as assumpsit will lie against a bailee for negligence; and a count in trover may be joined with case.[3] So either case or covenant lies against a lessee for waste.[4] So case in the nature of waste will lie against a lessee of a mine, for the removal of a barrier or boundary between it and an adjoining mine, although the act might also be the subject of an action for breach of an express covenant.[5] So the plaintiff, a lessee by deed-poll, assigned his lease to the defendant, subject to payment of the rent and performance of the covenants. The defendant took possession and occupied, and before expiration of the lease

[1] Per Jervis, C. J., Courtenay *v.* Earle, 10 C. B. 83; Ives *v.* Carter, 24 Conn. 392; 2 Sharsw. Bl. Com. 163.

[2] Per Jackson, J., Cummings *v.* Noyes, 10 Mass. 435.

[3] Ferrier *v.* Wood, 4 Eng. 85.

[4] Kinlyside *v.* Thornton, 2 W. Bl. 1111; 2 Saun. 252, *c. n.*

[5] Marker *v.* Kenrick, 13 Com. B. 188.

Threadgill, 13 Ired. 39. The controlling considerations, in favor of one or the other form of action in particular cases, have been thus designated: "Where there is an express promise, and a legal obligation results from it, then the plaintiff's cause of action is most accurately described in *assumpsit*, in which the promise is stated as the gist of the action. But where, from a given state of facts, the law raises a legal obligation to do a particular act, and there is a breach of that obligation, and a consequential damage, there, although *assumpsit* may be maintainable upon a promise implied by law to do the act, still an action on the case founded in tort is the more proper form of action, in which the plaintiff in his declaration states the facts out of which the legal obligation arises, the obligation itself, the breach of it, and the damage resulting from that breach." Per Littledale, J., Burnett *v.* Lynch, 5 Barn. & Cress. 609.

assigned it. The lessor sued the plaintiff and recovered damages, for breaches of covenant committed while the defendant continued assignee. Held, the plaintiff might maintain an action on the case in tort against the defendant, although assumpsit would also lie as upon an implied promise.[1] So a mortgage of a vessel by the defendant to the plaintiffs contained a condition, that the defendant should pay the plaintiffs $3000 with interest, without specifying any time, and also a stipulation that until default the defendant should remain in possession, and in case of default the plaintiffs might take possession and sell, paying said sum from the proceeds, and rendering to the defendant the surplus, if any. The vessel, being in possession of the defendant, was sold by him, as unincumbered, for his own use and benefit, the debt remaining unpaid. The plaintiff brings trover. Held, that the money was not payable immediately, but on request, and therefore there was no breach of the stipulation for the continued possession and use of the property by the defendant, and the resumption of it by the plaintiffs, until after a demand and non-payment thereon or some act equivalent thereto; that such stipulation was not a mere covenant, the only remedy for a violation of which was an action of covenant; nor a mere bailment by the mortgagee of the property, at the will of either of the parties; but was equivalent to a grant or demise of the property to the mortgagor for an indefinite time, defeasible on the non-payment of the money on request; and that the sale was a forfeiture of the right of possession, and vested the same in the mortgagee, so that he might maintain trover.[2] (*a*) So where one granted

[1] Burnett *v.* Lynch, 5 Barn. & Cress. 589.

[2] Ashmead *v.* Kellogg, 23 Conn. 70.

(*a*) Upon grounds analogous to those stated in the text, where there have been fraudulent representations upon a sale as to a material fact, *Courts of Equity* will interfere in favor of a purchaser, even after acceptance of a deed with covenants, and possession taken; but it must appear affirmatively that the representations were known to the vendor to be false, and they must

the right of way to a railroad company through his land by deed, upon condition that the company should fence the road in reasonable time; which they neglected to do; held, they were liable to an action on the case thereby sustained.[1] So, if A. fraudulently represent the circumstances of B. to be good, in order to induce C. to give him credit, and add, "if he does not pay for the goods, I will," an action lies for the misrepresentation, notwithstanding the promise.[2] So it has been held, that a fraudulent purchaser of goods may be charged in assumpsit for the price, or in trespass, at the election of the seller.[3] So trover lies, to recover damages for slaves obtained on the faith of a contract of sale, where the defendant is utterly unable to fulfil the conditions of the contract, if it be the true meaning of the contract that the property shall not vest in the defendant until the conditions be complied with; notwithstanding possession has been delivered, and the plaintiff may have an action of covenant.[4] So an action on the case for deceit lies, for fraudulently selling land which has no real existence, notwithstanding any covenants in the deed, which the plaintiff may treat as a nullity.[5] So for fraudulent representations that the lands are free and clear of all incumbrances, although in the deed there is a covenant against incumbrances.[6] So the plaintiff, the owner of a certificate of deposit in the bank of L., payable to order, caused it to be indorsed, with directions that it

[1] Conger v. Chicago, &c. 15 Ill. 366.

[2] Hamer v. Alexander, 2 New Rep. 241.

[3] Cary v. Hotailing, 1 Hill, 311.

[4] M'Hugh v. Dinkins, 2 Bre. 324.

[5] Wardell v. Fosdick, 13 Johns. 325.

[6] Ward v. Wiman, 18 Wend. 193.

---

be such that the purchaser had no means of discovering their falsity. Tallman v. Green, 3 Sandf. 437.

Where the object of a suit is, to have a contract rescinded and declared void for fraud, equity has jurisdiction, although the same amount of money will be recovered on such rescission, as would be given for damages in an action at law. Mayne v. Griswold, 3 Sandf. 463.

The jurisdiction of the Court of Chancery in matters of fraud is not affected by the fact, that there is a concurrent remedy at law. Ibid.

should be paid to W. & Co., and then transmitted it to them by mail, though without their knowledge or request. It never reached W. & Co., but was stolen on the way, and their names forged upon it; after which it came to the defendants' hands in the ordinary course of business, who collected the money on it, supposing themselves to be the owners of it. Held, the plaintiff had an election, either to sue the defendants in trover, as for a conversion of the certificate, or to recover the amount in an action for the money had and received.[1] So one, whose property has been taken by distress to pay a tax illegally assessed by a religious society, may maintain an action of trespass against the assessors, or for money had and received against the society to which it has been paid.[2] So a deputy sheriff may sue, either in trover or assumpsit, upon a receipt taken in his own name for personal property attached by him.[3] So, in general, the remedy against a public officer, for neglect or misbehavior, may be by an action of the case, alleging his misdemeanor, or by an action of debt, according to the nature of the misfeasance; though never by assumpsit, as on an implied promise to do his duty.[4] So an action on the case lies against the plaintiff in an attachment bill, for the wrongful and malicious suing out of such attachment. The defendant in the bill is not bound to sue in the first instance on the attachment bond.[5] So trespass lies against an officer, who issued a warrant for the collection of militia fines, for which the person assessed was not liable, to recover money paid in order to prevent a levy on his property. Though a bond was given, to secure the repayment of the amount so collected as for fines, provided that the obligee should prosecute the officer and obtain judgment therefor; it is not necessary to sue in assumpsit as for money had and received, but the suit may be in any form of action proper for the purpose.[6]

[1] Talbot v. Bank of Rochester, 1 Hill, 295.

[2] Inglee v. Bosworth, 5 Pick. 498.

[3] West v. Thompson, 1 Williams, 613.

[4] M'Millan v. Eastman, 4 Mass. 378.

[5] Smith v. Story, 4 Humph. 169; Donnell v. Jones, 13 Ala. 490.

[6] Young v. Hyde, 14 N. H. 35.

23. There are however many cases, similar to those already cited, in which the right of election between tort and contract has not been recognized. (*a*) Thus case, and not assumpsit, is the proper remedy, where the purchaser of lands has been defrauded, by the omission of the vendor to inform him of an outstanding incumbrance.[1] So assumpsit will not lie, to recover the price of goods sold and delivered in consideration of a sale of land, which is void by the statute of frauds. The remedy is replevin or trover.[2] (*b*) So the trustees of non-resident debtors claimed, that certain shares of the capital stock of a foreign bank, which were standing upon the books of the agent of the bank in New York in the names of the debtors, which had been assigned with the consent of the trustees to third persons, and by the latter to the trustees, should be transferred to them by the agent. This was refused, and the trustees procured the appointment of referees in pursuance of the statute,[3] to settle the controversy. On the hearing, an objection was made to the jurisdiction of the referees, who reported in favor of the trustees,

[1] Morgan *v.* Patrick, 7 Ala. 185.
[2] Updike *v.* Armstrong, 3 Scam. 564.
[3] 1 R. S. 801, § 20.

(*a*) A very material distinction is, that; if the transaction is exclusively a contract, no action lies without proof of *consideration*. See Lakin *v.* Tibbits, 1 Wis. 500.

If a contract under seal be materially *altered* by parol, so that both cannot be performed, the whole becomes parol, and the remedy for a breach is case, and not covenant. Lawall *v.* Rader, 24 Penn. 283.

After a warranty of a horse as sound, the vendor in a subsequent conversation said, that, if the horse were unsound, (which he denied,) he would take it again and return the money. This is no abandonment of the original contract, which still remains open. And, if the horse be unsound, the vendee must sue upon the warranty. Payne *v.* Whale, 7 E. 274.

(*b*) If, under color of a defective sealed agreement for the lease of land, the land be occupied without the assent of the owner, the remedy is by trespass *quare clausum;* if with his assent, assumpsit for use and occupation may be maintained, the law implying a verbal contract between the parties, of a similar import to the written one. Anderson *v.* Critcher, 11 Gill & Johns. 450.

subject to the opinion of the Court. Held, that the referees had no jurisdiction of the case, the matter in controversy not being *a debt* within the meaning of the statute. And, it seems, neither trespass nor trover will lie, but only assumpsit, or a special action on the case.[1] So, where the foreman of a carriage-maker sold a carriage on his own account to his creditor in payment of the debt; held, the carriage-maker could not maintain an action against the purchaser for the price of the carriage; but he must affirm the sale, in which case he would only be entitled to what the foreman received, or disaffirm it, and bring trover for the carriage.[2] So, where an officer unlawfully refuses to levy an execution upon money in his hands, the remedy is an action on the case, and not assumpsit for money had and received.[3]

23 *a*. On the other hand, a vendee of land, in possession under a contract of sale, remaining open and in force between the parties, is not subject to an action on the case for an injury to the property.[4] So, in case of a covenant between A. and B., by which A. agreed to manage and superintend a farm belonging to B., and "to take charge and care of the stock, &c., on said farm;" an action on the case does not lie against A. for neglecting to take proper care of the stock, but B.'s remedy is upon the covenant.[5] So where, in trover for certain lumber, the plaintiff produced and gave in evidence a note, which had been equitably assigned to him, for money payable in lumber; held, the note gave him no right or title to any lumber in particular, and the only remedy was by an action on the note.[6] So a debtor agreed with his creditor, to let him have a bed and furniture of the value of $28; but no particular articles were pointed out and delivered. Held, on the refusal of the debtor to deliver any bed, &c., the creditor could not maintain trover.[7] So neither case nor assumpsit can be maintained, for breach of duty and con-

[1] Denny and the Manhattan Co. 2 Hill, 220.
[2] Whitlock *v.* Heard, 3 Rich. 88.
[3] Parker *v.* Dennie, 6 Pick. 227.
[4] Stauffer *v.* Eaton, 13 Ohio, 322.
[5] Masters *v.* Stratton, 7 Hill, 101.
[6] Purdy *v.* McCullough, 3 Barr, 466.
[7] Jones *v.* Morris, 7 Ired. 370.

tract in not permitting the plaintiff to cut and carry away timber, when the injury resulted from an injunction in chancery obtained by the defendant. The only remedy is an action on the injunction bond, if broken, or an action on the case, averring malice.[1] So, in Massachusetts, a party, who pays a greater rate of interest than is allowed by law, cannot recover back threefold the amount of the interest paid by an action of trespass on the case, but only by an action of debt or a bill in chancery, as provided by the Rev. Sts. c. 35, § 3.[2] (*a*)

24. The election of remedies sometimes applies as well to the party against whom the action is brought as to the form of action itself. Thus the plaintiff, a consignee of goods from abroad, authorized a factor to indorse the bills of lading for the purposes of sale, and the factor indorsed them to the defendants, (who knew that the latter was a mere agent,) with authority to them, first, to effect sales, and second, to reimburse themselves out of the proceeds for money which they advanced upon the goods; and, before the authority of the factor (who immediately afterwards stopped payment) was countermanded, the defendants sold the goods by auction. Held, they were not liable to the plaintiff in trover;

[1] McLaren *v.* Bradford, 26 Ala. 616. [2] Wiley *v.* Rall, 1 Met. 553.

(*a*) Where one without authority assumes to contract for another, the question, whether the former shall be held liable *upon the contract*, has been much discussed. A late elementary writer thus states the result of the decisions upon this subject: "The question then occurs whether in such a case the agent can be held *on the contract*, and it has been so decided. But we think it the better opinion that the contract is wholly void. It is not the contract of the principal, because he gave no authority to the supposed agent. It is not the contract of the agent, for he professed to act for the principal. So, if one forges a signature to a note, and obtains money on that note, he cannot be held on it as on his promise to pay. But in all such cases the supposed agent may be reached in assumpsit if money be paid to him or work and labor done for him under such supposed contract, or in trespass for special damages for so undertaking to act for another, without authority, or in some other appropriate action; but not on the contract itself." 1 Pars. on Contr. 57.

though it seems they would be liable for money had and received to the use of the rightful owner.[1]

25. The principle of election may be applied, not only to different forms of action, but also as between an action and a defence against an action. It is said, a party who has derived benefit under a contract, and is not in condition to restore what has been received, cannot avoid it on the ground of fraud, but must seek his redress by an action on the case; or, if sued upon the contract, he may *recoupe*. Thus the plaintiff, having taken a lease for three years, afterwards applied to the defendant, the landlord, to be discharged for the last year of the term, which the latter declined, saying, however, that he would try to find a tenant for the plaintiff; but, a few days previous to the commencement of the last year, the parties came to terms, and the plaintiff was discharged, he paying the defendant $100 by way of consideration. Held, though at the time of this arrangement the premises had been re-let by the defendant, and he fraudulently represented the fact to be otherwise, the plaintiff could not maintain assumpsit to recover back the money paid.[2]

26. The question, whether in a doubtful case, or a case partaking or compounded of both tort and contract, the plaintiff has elected the proper form of action, often arises, in connection with the *declaration* and other *pleadings*, and with the point of the *joint or separate liability* of several parties, against whom a claim is set up. As has been already suggested, in actions of tort, the plaintiff is in general bound to prove no more of his declaration than is necessary to constitute a good cause of action; while, in actions of contract, a failure to prove the *whole* declaration may be a fatal variance.[3] So it has been held, that a declaration in case will not be held bad, even on special demurrer, although its conclusion be in debt, if without such conclusion enough

[1] Stiernald *v.* Holden, 6 Dowl. & Ry. 17.

[2] Hogan *v.* Weyer, 5 Hill, 389.

[3] Hutchinson *v.* Granger, 13 Vt. 386.

be stated to make it a good declaration in case. The conclusion will be rejected as surplusage.[1] So it is said, the difference between assumpsit, which is an action directly on the contract, and case, which is collateral to it, is shown by the pleadings; the general issue in the first being *non-assumpsit*, and in the second *not guilty*.[2]

27. In an action on the case against several for a tort, though a conspiracy to commit it be charged in the declaration, one of the defendants may be convicted and the rest acquitted; the foundation of the action being the damage done to the plaintiff, and not the conspiracy.[3] So, in an action on the case, by a passenger in a stage-coach, for an injury caused by its upsetting, he may recover, if he prove the liability of any of the defendants.[4] So, in an action against three, wherein the plaintiff declared that they had the loading of a hogshead of the plaintiff, for a certain reward to be paid to one of them, and a certain other reward to the other two, and that the defendants so negligently conducted themselves in the loading, &c., that the hogshead was damaged; held, the gist of the action was the tort, and not the contract from which it arose; and therefore, on the plea of not guilty, the two being acquitted, judgment might be had against the third, who was found guilty.[5] So a declaration contained two counts in trover, to which a third was added, alleging a conversion of the chattel by selling or otherwise disposing of it, whereby the plaintiff is greatly aggrieved, injured, and prejudiced in his reversionary estate and interest, to wit, to his damage, $1500, and concludes that the defendants, though often requested, have hitherto failed, neglected, and refused, and do still fail, neglect, and refuse to pay the said sum of money, or any part thereof, to the plaintiff's damage, &c. Held, the plaintiff could not recover on this count, as setting forth a cause of action *ex contractu;* but, like the others which preceded it, it must be

[1] Bayard *v.* Smith, 17 Wend. 88.

[2] Henion *v.* Morton, 2 Ashm. 150.

[3] Hutchins *v.* Hutchins, 7 Hill, 104.

[4] M'Call *v.* Forsyth, 4 Watts & Serg. 179.

[5] Govett *v.* Radnidge, 3 E. 62.

considered as *ex delicto*.[1] So, whether an action is, or is not, trespass on the case, within the meaning of the statutes of Connecticut, (tit. 1, ch. xii. § 152,) is determined by the form of the declaration, and not by the subject-matter of the suit. Thus an action, in which the declaration is in form *ex delicto*, and embraces three counts, two upon a false warranty, and the other upon a false representation respecting a horse, is trespass on the case.[2] So a count, which sets out a contract for the sale of a negro, in consideration of a certain sum of money, which is alleged to be less than his real value, and for the further consideration, that the defendant would remove him from the State, and then avers, that the defendant, at the time he made the contract, did not intend to remove said negro, "but falsely and fraudulently represented" that he would, "with intent to deceive and defraud the plaintiff;" is a count in case, and the statement of the contract is mere matter of inducement.[3] So where the plaintiff declares in case, on the defendant's omission of duty, in neglecting to treat a hired slave with proper care and attention during the term; the consideration and terms of the contract of hiring need not be alleged, and, if alleged, they need not be proved as averred.[4] So, where a complaint stated the exchange of two watches, belonging to the plaintiff, for a rifle; that the defendant fraudulently pretended to be the owner of the rifle; that "the defendant, at the time of the sale, &c. did not own the rifle, *and fraudulently sold and traded the same* to the plaintiff, *by reason whereof* the plaintiff was subjected to, and made liable for, a judgment recovered by A. H. C., who had sued for and recovered the rifle," &c.; held, the action was to be regarded as sounding in fraud, and not as a suit on contract, upon the implied warranty of title.[5] So a declaration alleged, that, in consideration of the purchase of a vessel, the sellers affirmed and promised that the vessel was of a certain description, and that the plaintiffs, giving credit

1 Nations *v.* Hawkins, 11 Ala. 859.
2 Humiston *v.* Smith, 22 Conn. 19.
3 Dixon *v.* Barclay, 22 Ala. 370.
4 Mosely *v.* Wilkinson, 24 Ala. 411.
5 Edick *v.* Crim, 10 Barb. 445.

thereto, bought the vessel; but the defendants, not regarding their promise, but contriving to defraud the plaintiffs, deceived them, in that the vessel was not of that description, and, by means of the false affirmation and promise, had injured and defrauded the plaintiffs. The defendants pleaded that they never promised. The plaintiffs produced a bill of sale, which stated the vessel to be as alleged in the declaration, with a warranty of the property; also parol evidence of a similar representation and promise at the time of sale; also evidence that the representation was untrue; but no evidence that the defendants knew it to be so. Judgment for the defendants.[1]

28. And, in general, although in an action on the case in tort, for breach of a warranty of goods, the *scienter* need not be charged, nor, if charged, need it be proved;[2] yet, in an action on the case for deceit in a sale, it is necessary to prove the *scienter*.[3] And where a declaration sets forth, that the defendants, to induce the plaintiff to exchange horses with them, did falsely and fraudulently affirm to him, that their horse was sound, and the plaintiff, giving credit to their affirmation, was induced to exchange, whereas the defendants' horse was not sound, which they well knew, and so the defendants by their false affirmations injured and defrauded the plaintiff; it is case for deceit, and not assumpsit on a warranty.[4]

29. On the other hand, where a complaint alleged, that the plaintiff sold a horse to the defendant, and received in consideration therefor a promissory note made by one W., the defendant warranting that W. was responsible and the note collectable; and that W. was insolvent; and demanded judgment for the amount of the note: held, the action was to be regarded as brought on the contract, and consequently the plaintiff could not recover, on the ground of fraud in the transfer of the note.[5] So, upon a declaration in case, alleg-

[1] Dyer *v.* Lewis, 7 Mass. 284.
[2] Williamson *v.* Allison, 2 E. 446.
[3] Mahurin *v.* Harding, 8 Fost. 128.
[4] Mahurin *v.* Harding, 8 Fost. 128.
[5] Fisher *v.* Fredenhall, 21 Barb. 82.

ing a deceit by means of a warranty made by two defendants, upon a joint sale to him, by both, of sheep, their joint property; the plaintiff cannot recover, upon proof of a contract of sale and warranty by one only, as of his separate property; the action, though laid in tort, being founded on the joint contract alleged.[1] So where the first two counts of a declaration were in *assumpsit*, the third in *case*, charging negligence of the defendants as warehousemen in not safely keeping, &c. goods, and the fourth in trover for the goods; and the plaintiff, having obtained a general verdict of guilty upon proof of the negligence as alleged, entered up judgment and issued a *ca. sa.*, upon which one of the defendants was arrested; held, the imprisonment was unlawful, and the defendant arrested entitled to be discharged.[2] (*a*)

30. No class of cases has given rise to more questions of this nature, than those relating to the duty and liability of *common carriers.* (*b*)

31. It has been held, that, in an action of *assumpsit* against a carrier, evidence to prove negligence is admissible.[3] So it has been held, that, although, in general, tort and contract cannot be joined,[4] yet an action on the case against a common carrier, upon an assumpsit in law, and likewise upon a tort, may be joined.[5] And it is well settled, that an action against a common carrier or innkeeper on the custom of the realm, (*c*) and an action of trover, is founded in tort or mis-

[1] Weal *v.* King, 12 E. 452.
[2] Brown *v.* Treat, 1 Hill, 225.
[3] Smith *v.* Horne, 8 Taunt. 144.
[4] Dalston *v.* Eyenston, 12 Mod. 73.
[5] Boson *v.* Sandford, 3 Mod. 322; Dickson *v.* Clifton, 2 Wils. 329.

(*a*) A demand properly cognizable in a court of equity cannot be united with a claim for damages for a personal tort. Mayo *v.* Madden, 4 Cal. 27.

(*b*) See *Common Carrier.*

(*c*) Declaration, that the plaintiff delivered to defendants, and they accepted and received from him, goods, to be taken care of and carried and conveyed by defendants from L. to B., and there delivered to P. P., for reasonable reward to defendants in that behalf, and thereupon it became the duty of defendants to take due care of such goods, while they so had the charge thereof, for the purpose aforesaid, and to take due and reasonable care in and about the conveyance and delivery thereof as aforesaid; yet

feasance, and therefore such action may be joined, in the same declaration.[1] But it is said, a carrier is liable in respect of his reward, and not of the hundred's being answerable over to him. For the hundred is made liable by statute, but he was so at common law. And the being robbed does not excuse him, because it may be by such combination and consent as cannot be proved.[2] So where, antecedently to the delivery of goods, an order is given to a carrier, who assents to deal with them when delivered in a particular manner; a duty is imposed on him, on receipt of the goods, and the law implies a promise, to deal with them according to the order.[3]

32. The same questions have arisen in reference to other forms of *bailment*. Thus case lies against the keeper of a livery stable, for damaging a horse delivered to him to keep for a reward; without showing that the defendant *agreed* to keep him.[4] So a declaration in case stated, that the plaintiff, an infant, had employed the defendant, a surgeon, to cure her, and then claimed damages for a misfeasance. Plea, that the plaintiff did not employ the defendant. Held, that it was immaterial by whom the defendant was employed; or,

[1] 12 Mod. 73; People *v.* Willett, 26 Barb. 78.

[2] Lane *v.* Cotton, 1 Salk. 143.

[3] Streeter *v.* Horlock, 8 Moore. 283.

[4] Stanian *v.* Davies, 2 Ld. Raym. 795.

---

defendants, not regarding their duty in that behalf, but contriving, &c., did not nor would not take due care, &c., but on the contrary, whilst they had the charge, &c., took such bad care, &c., that the goods were injured, to plaintiff's damage, &c. Pleas, not guilty, and traverse of the delivery and acceptance *modo et forma*. The plaintiff gave no proof of an express contract, but only, without objection, that the defendants were common carriers. The case was proved as to one defendant only, and a verdict was taken against him, and for the other. On motion to enter a nonsuit, on the ground that the action was founded on contract, and therefore a verdict could not pass against one defendant only, held, the declaration might, and therefore must, after verdict, be read, as a declaration against carriers on the custom of the realm, and consequently the verdict was maintainable. It was doubted whether such declaration against carriers on the custom would have been sufficient on special demurrer. Pozzi *v.* Shipton, 8 Ad. & Ell. 963; 1 Per. & Dav. 4.

if material, the plaintiff's submitting to the defendant's treatment was sufficient proof of the allegation of employment by her.[1]

33. A declaration, that the plaintiff retained the defendant, a carpenter, to repair a house before a given day; that the defendant accepted the retainer, but did not perform the work within the time, *per quod* the walls were damaged, is insufficient; for no duty resulted from his situation as a carpenter, and it was not stated that he was to receive any consideration, or that he entered upon his work. But a count is valid, stating that the plaintiff, being possessed of old materials, retained the defendant to perform such work, and to use those materials, but, instead of using those, he used new ones, thereby increasing the expense.[2]

34. Declaration in case, that the defendant was an oil broker, and the plaintiffs, licensed crushers, retained him as such, to sell and deliver for them thirty tuns of linseed oil, according to the contracts of sale, to purchasers, for commission and reward to the defendant in that behalf; which retainer he accepted; that he, as such broker, in pursuance of the retainer, made a contract between the plaintiffs and A., by which the plaintiffs sold to A., and he bought of them, the thirty tuns, at the price, &c., to be delivered by parcels at a certain place and times, each parcel to be paid for in ready money; that the plaintiffs consigned two of the parcels to the defendant, and he delivered them to A. on payment; and that, after the making of the contract, and in pursuance thereof, and of the retainer, the plaintiffs consigned to the defendant, as such broker, the residue of the thirty tuns, to be delivered by him to A. on payment; that the oil arrived, &c., of which the defendant had notice, and took upon himself the delivery according to the contract; and thereupon it became and was the defendant's duty, as such broker as aforesaid, to use all reasonable care that the oil should not be delivered to A. or any other person, without the price

[1] Gladwell *v.* Steggall, 5 Bing. N. R. 733.

[2] Elsee *v.* Gatward, 5 T. R. 143.

being paid to the defendant according to contract; yet the defendant, not regarding such duty, did not use reasonable care, &c., that the oil should not be delivered, &c., without the price being paid, but neglected and refused so to do, and so negligently and carelessly behaved in the premises, that by the defendant's mere carelessness and negligence the last-mentioned oil was delivered to B. and C. without the price being paid by A. or any person to the defendant, by reason whereof, and of A. having become bankrupt and unable to pay, the plaintiffs lost the said oil, and the price thereof, &c. Held, by the Court of Queen's Bench, after verdict for the plaintiffs, that the duty was laid in the declaration, as resulting from the defendant's character of broker; but that the duties of a broker, as defined by statute and common law, did not include those said to have been violated by the defendant. Judgment arrested. But held, by the Court of Exchequer Chamber, on error, that the duty resulted from an express contract described in the declaration, and not simply from the defendant's character of broker; and that for the breach of such duty an action of tort lay. Judgment reversed.[1] (a)

[1] Boorman *v.* Brown, 3 Ad. & Ell. (N. S.) 511; 2 Gale & Dav. 793.

(*a*) Where, after attachment of a boat, a bond was given for its discharge, and the Court afterwards rendered judgment, ordering a sale, and it was accordingly sold on the execution, and the plaintiffs received satisfaction, and the owner of the boat brought trespass against the plaintiff in the execution, who pleaded not guilty; held, the judgment was erroneous, but the judgment and execution would have been a sufficient justification to the plaintiff in the execution, if properly pleaded to the trespass; that the action should have been assumpsit for money had and received; but the justification could not be set up under the plea of not guilty. Judgment for the plaintiff. St. Louis, &c. *v.* Ford, 11 Mis. 295.

A plea of *payment into court* has a different effect, when pleaded to a count in trover and a count for money had and received. In the former case, it admits any evidence, admissible under *not guilty* to reduce the damages; in the other case, it admits of no evidence which, admitting a debt, for a certain cause, goes to reduce its amount by proof of payment or set-off. Therefore, in an action of trover and for money had and received, brought

35. We now proceed to consider the specific subject of *waiver of tort*, which has indeed been often incidentally noticed under the preceding general head of *election of remedies*, but requires to be more particularly explained. Unlike most of the cases already referred to, as illustrating the connection between contract and tort, and which are cases of *express or implied agreement* and a wrongful violation thereof; the technical phrase, *waiver of tort*, refers to a claim for pecuniary compensation under an *implied contract*, *growing out of the wrongful act of the defendant itself.* And it may be stated in general terms, that, where one man wrongfully takes another's property, and turns it into money or money's worth; the latter, although having a clear right to maintain an action as for a tort, may waive the tort, and sue in assumpsit, for money had and received. We shall have occasion also to refer to some other modes, in which a tort may be waived, and a remedy sought as upon a contract. Thus this action (for money had and received) lies, in general, where the defendant tortiously takes and retains the plaintiff's money;[1] or takes his goods and sells them, and receives the produce.[2] So the administrator of one, who had tortiously taken coal from the plaintiff's land, sold and received pay for it, was

[1] Neate *v.* Harding, 6 Exch. 349.

[2] Lamine *v.* Dorrell, 2 Ld. Raym. 1216; Young *v.* Marshall, 8 Bing. 43.

by an administratrix against a party, who, by mistake, had acted as executor *de son tort;* held, under a plea of payment into court, to the whole declaration, the defendant could not prove, in reduction of the amount recoverable under the *indebitatus* count, payments made by the defendant, and which the plaintiff would have been bound to make in the course of rightful administration. Goldy *v.* Goldy, 38 Eng. L. & Eq. 344.

Where the substantial ground of action is contract, the plaintiff cannot, by declaring in tort, render a person liable, who would not have been liable on his promise. Therefore, where the plaintiff declared that, having agreed to exchange mares with the defendant, the defendant, by falsely warranting his mare to be sound, well knowing her to be unsound, falsely and fraudulently deceived the plaintiff, &c.; held, that infancy was a good plea in bar. Green *v.* Greenbank, 2 Marsh. 485. (See *Infant.*)

held liable in assumpsit.[1] So where the plaintiff, a woman, married the defendant, who had another wife, and the defendant leased her land and received rent; held, the plaintiff might maintain assumpsit, notwithstanding the objection that the tenant still remained liable for the rent, the defendant having no legal authority to discharge it.[2] So, the defendant having fraudulently induced the plaintiff to sell goods to A., who could not pay for them; and, on a nominal resale by A., in which the defendant was really concerned, having himself obtained the money; held, the plaintiff might, in an action for money had and received, recover of the defendant the value of the goods unpaid for by A.[3] So, where A. placed in the plaintiff's hand a fund, out of which the plaintiff was directed to satisfy certain acceptances; and the defendant falsely represented to the plaintiff, that he held one such acceptance, and thereby procured from him that amount; held, the plaintiff might maintain an action for money had and received against the defendant; although it seems A. might also have maintained the action.[4] So, in case of goods taken in execution, and sold under a warrant of distress, under a conviction; if the conviction is quashed, the owner may waive the tort, and bring an action for money had and received.[5] So, where goods of one are taken on execution against another, and sold; the former may waive the trespass and bring his action for the amount of the price.[6] (*a*) So the action for money had and received lies against a carrier, who had refused to deliver goods without payment of an exorbitant remuneration, to recover back the surplus, though there had been no tender of any particular amount.[7] So the defend-

[1] Powell *v.* Rees, 7 Ad. & Ell. 426.

[2] Hasser *v.* Wallis, 1 Salk. 28; 11 Mod. 146.

[3] Abbotts *v.* Barry, 2 Brod. & Bing. 369.

[4] Holt *v.* Ely, 1 Ellis & Black. 795.

[5] Feltham *v.* Terry, cited in 1 Cowp. 419.

[6] Ibid.

[7] Ashmole *v.* Wainwright, 2 Q. B. 846.

(*a*) Where goods are taken under process which is illegally executed, the owner may recover the amount paid to release them, and additional damages. Sowell *v.* Champion, 2 Nev. & Per. 627.

ants had required for carriage of the plaintiff's goods more than they were authorized to receive under their charter. The plaintiff, that he might have the goods transported, paid the excess under protest, and brings an action for money had and received to recover it back. Held, as the payments were made in order to induce the company to do what they were bound to do without them, the action was maintainable.[1] So the plaintiff, a Spaniard, was arrested by the defendant for a fictitious debt of £10,000, known to be such by the defendant, upon a writ afterwards set aside. The plaintiff, who was ignorant of the English language, in order to procure a release, agreed in writing to pay £500, and give bail for the balance; and the £500 was accordingly paid. The plaintiff brings this action to recover it back. Held, the action might be maintained.[2] So money paid under protest by a mortgagor, in order to obtain possession of his title-deeds, withheld by the attorney of the mortgagee upon an unfounded claim of lien, may be recovered back as money had and received.[3] So the attorney of a mortgagee with power of sale refused to stop the sale, or deliver up the title-deeds, without payment of an exorbitant demand, which the administratrix of the mortgagors paid, with a protest against the excess. Held, an action might be maintained to recover back such excess.[4]

36. But an action for money had and received does not lie, to recover back money paid for the release of cattle, wrongfully distrained damage feasant.[5] So the plaintiff is let into possession of the refuse spar, produced from a lead mine, situate in land demised to A., a farmer, (as tenant from year to year,) and pays an annual rent for the spar to A.'s landlord, and disposes of it as his property. The defendant from time to time enters upon the land, and carries away portions of the spar, and the plaintiff brings assumpsit for the value. The jury find that A. has an interest in the

[1] Parker v. The Great, &c. 7 M. & Gr. 253.

[2] The Duke de Cadaval v. Collins, 4 Ad. & Ell. 858.

[3] Wakefield v. Newbon, 6 Q. B. 276; acc. Smith v. Sleap, 12 M. & W. 585.

[4] Close v. Phipps, 7 M. & Gr. 586.

[5] Lindon v. Hooper, 1 Cowp. 414.

spar, and has not surrendered it to his landlord. Held, the landlord cannot convey such a title to the plaintiff as will enable the latter (supposing his possession is clearly established) to waive the tortious taking, and bring assumpsit, in the absence of an express contract of sale, though the tenant had never disturbed his possession.[1]

37. While the owner of property, wrongfully appropriated and disposed of, *may* at his election waive the tort and sue in assumpsit; on the other hand, a conversion of property may be treated by the party in fault as waived by a subsequent ratification of the act or transaction by the owner, with full knowledge of all the facts; and the ratification may be either express or implied. Thus if he brings assumpsit against the one who has converted the property, and summons the person to whom it had been transferred as garnishee, it is an implied ratification of the act.[2]

38. It has been questioned, whether any other form of assumpsit can be maintained, upon the ground of waiving a tort, than that for money had and received; and the decisions and dicta, which favor this extended view of the remedy in question, have been closely criticized and seriously doubted. (*a*) There are some cases, however, in the books, of this description; and the principle is laid down by a judge of high authority, that, "with respect to goods, it is a long established rule, that the owner, from whom they have been tortiously taken, may in many cases waive the tort, and state his demand as arising on contract. It is competent for him to treat the party liable to his action as a purchaser, an

[1] Lee *v*. Shore, 2 Dowl. & Ry. 198. [2] Firemen's, &c. *v*. Cochran, 27 Ala. 228.

(*a*) See Jones *v*. Hoar, 5 Pick. 285, n. Assumpsit does not lie for a trespass in cutting and carrying away trees from the plaintiff's land, unless the trees have been sold by the defendant. Jones *v*. Hoar, 5 Pick. 285.

So, if goods are sold upon a condition, and the vendee fails to perform it, but retains the goods and converts them to his own use; the vendor, if he rescinds the sale, cannot waive the tort, and recover the value of the goods in *assumpsit*, but his proper remedy is *trover*. Allen *v*. Ford, 19 Pick. 217.

agent, or a bailee."[1] So Prof. Greenleaf says: "If one commits a tort, by which he gains a pecuniary benefit, as if he wrongfully takes the goods of another and sells them, or otherwise *applies them to his own use*, the owner may waive the tort, and charge him in assumpsit on the common counts, as for *goods sold* or money received, which he will not be permitted to gainsay."[2] So in a late case it is said: "Ordinarily, in the case of torts, it is in the election of the owner of the property wrongfully taken, to bring his action for the tort, or, waiving that, to bring assumpsit, and when he brings the latter, the defendant is estopped to say there was no promise, and that he took the property wrongfully, or to set up his own fraud or wrong in defence of the suit."[3] (*a*)

[1] Per Jackson, J., Cummings *v.* Noyes, 10 Mass. 435-6.

[2] 2 Greenl. Ev. § 108.

[3] Per Thomas, J., Walker *v.* Davis, 1 Gray, 509.

(*a*) The following observations of Prof. Greenleaf, upon the action for money had and received, contain a concise and satisfactory view of the subject under consideration: —

"Where the money was *delivered* to the defendant *for a particular purpose*, to which he refused to apply it, he cannot apply it to any other, but it may be recovered back by the depositor, under the count for money had and received. If it was placed in his hands to be paid over to a third person, which he agreed to do, such person, assenting thereto, may sue for it, as money had and received to his own use. But if the defendant did not consent so to appropriate it, it is otherwise, there being no privity between them; and the action will lie only by him who placed the money in his hands." 2 Greenl. Ev. § 119.

"The count for *money had and received* may also be supported by evidence, that the defendant obtained the plaintiff's money *by fraud*, or false color or pretence. Thus, where one, having a wife living, fraudulently married another, and received the rents of her estate, he was held liable to the latter, in this form of action. And, where the defendant has tortiously taken the plaintiff's property, and sold it, or being lawfully possessed of it, has wrongfully sold it, the owner may, ordinarily, *waive the tort*, and recover the proceeds of the sale under this count. So, if the money of the plaintiff has in any other manner come to the defendant's hands, for which he would be chargeable in tort, the plaintiff may waive the tort, and bring assumpsit upon the common counts. But this rule must be taken with this qualification: that the defendant is not thereby to be deprived of any benefit, which

39. In connection with the general topic now under consideration, may be stated the rule of law as to the effect,

---

he could have derived under the appropriate form of action in tort. Thus, this count cannot be supported for money paid for the release of cattle distrained *damage feasant;* though the distress was wrongful,[1] where the right of common is the subject of dispute; nor for money received for rent, where the title to the premises is in question between the parties; nor in any other case, where the title to real estate is the subject of controversy, that being a question which, ordinarily, cannot be tried in this form of action." 2 Greenl. Ev. § 120.

"Under this count (money had and received) the plaintiff may also recover back money proved to have been obtained from him by *duress, extortion, imposition*, or taking any *undue advantage* of his situation, or otherwise involuntarily and wrongfully paid; as, by demand of illegal fees, tolls, duties, taxes, usury, and the like, where goods or the person were detained until the money has been paid. So, where goods were illegally detained as forfeited; or, where money was unlawfully demanded and paid to a creditor, to induce him to sign a bankrupt's certificate; or, where a pawnbroker refused to deliver up the pledge, until a greater sum than was due was paid to him. So, if the money has been paid under an usurious or other *illegal contract*, where the plaintiff is not *in pari delicto* with the defendant; or, for a *consideration* which has *failed;* or, where the goods of the plaintiff have been seized and sold by the defendant, under an execution to which he was a stranger; or, under a *conviction*, which has since been *quashed;* or, a *judgment*, which has since been *reversed*, the defendant having received the money; or, under *terror of legal process*, which, though regularly issued, did not authorize the collection of the sum demanded and paid. So, where *the person is arrested* for improper purposes without just cause; or, for a just cause, but without lawful authority; or, for a just cause and by lawful authority, but for an improper purpose; and pays money to obtain his discharge, it may be recovered under this count." Ibid. § 121. See Sartwell *v.* Horton, 2 Williams, 370; Marietta *v.* Slocumb, 6 Ohio, N. S. 471; The American, &c. *v.* Mumford, 4 R. I. 478; Gardner *v.* Mayor, &c. 26 Barb. 423; Rick *v.* Kelly, 30 Penn. 527; Bank, &c. *v.* City, &c. 12 La. Ann. 421.

In this connection, we may suitably refer to a leading case upon the general subject of recovering back money wrongfully paid. The case relates immediately to the recovery of money paid under *a judgment*, but involves principles of more general application.

In the case of Moses *v.* McFarlane, 2 Burr. 1009, the defendant had re-

[1] See Skeate *v.* Beale, 11 Ad. & Ell. 983.

upon the relative rights of the parties, of a *judgment* in an action for tort. Such judgment, though in form an *act of*

---

covered against the plaintiff as an indorser, in breach of a written contract, and the plaintiff had paid the amount. The plaintiff then brings this suit for money had and received in the Court of King's Bench. Held, he was entitled to recover. Lord Mansfield said: "This kind of equitable action, to recover back money which ought not in justice to be kept, is very beneficial, and therefore much encouraged. It lies only for money which, *ex æquo et bono*, the defendant ought to refund. It does not lie for money paid by the plaintiff which is claimed of him in point of honor and honesty, although it could not have been recovered from him in any course of law, as in payment of a debt barred by the Statute of Limitations, or contracted during his infancy, or to the extent of principal and legal interest upon an usurious contract, or for money fairly lost at play; because, in all these cases, the defendant may retain it with a safe conscience, though, by positive law, he was barred from recovering; but it lies for money paid by mistake, or upon a consideration which happens to fail, or for money got through imposition, or extortion, or oppression, or an undue advantage taken of the party's situation contrary to laws made for the protection of persons under those circumstances." But it is truly said (2 Smith's Lead. Cas. 337) "the application, however, of the above doctrine to the state of facts in Moses *v.* McFarlane, has frequently been held incorrect; that case was denied to be law by Eyre, C. J., in Phillips *v.* Hunter, 2 H. Bl. 414; by Heath, J., in Brisbane *v.* Dacres, 5 Taunt. 166, and cannot now be considered as of authority." See, also, O'Hara *v.* Hall, 4 Dall. 340; Smith *v.* Lewis, 3 Johns. 157, 169; Cooper *v.* Halbert, 2 M'Mul. 419.

No action lies to recover back money paid under an *erroneous* but unreversed judgment. So held, in an action against a clerk of a court, to whom a fine had been paid, under a judgment alleged to be rendered for more than the amount authorized by law. Wilburn *v.* Sproat, 2 Gray, 431.

A recovery in trover for slaves is a bar to an action of assumpsit for their services. Cook *v.* Cook, 2 Brev. 349. And also to an action of trespass for taking them away. Thompson *v.* Rogers, 2 Brev. 410.

On the other hand, after recovering judgment in assumpsit, the party cannot maintain an action of trespass for the same property, on the ground that the former action could not legally be maintained. Brown *v.* Moran, 42 Maine, 44.

A judgment for the hire of a horse, buggy, and harness, is no bar to another action for injuries done to the buggy and harness while in the hirer's possession. Shaw *v.* Beers, 25 Ala. 449.

So in trover, a plea of a former recovery in assumpsit, for non-performance of the same promises mentioned in the declaration, was held bad.

law, and not a *contract*, operates upon the title like a contract, and may therefore be here properly noticed.

40. It is the prevailing doctrine, that, by a judgment for the plaintiff in trover, (or in trespass *de bon. asporta*,) the property in the goods converted is vested in the defendant, as against the plaintiff. And that, it would seem, from the period of the conversion. Otherwise, by recovery in replevin, or in detinue, unless the plaintiff elects to abandon his property in the goods by issuing execution for the value, instead of resorting to his *distringas ad deliberandum*.[1] And the consequence follows from this rule, that the defendant, having virtually *purchased* the property, may himself dispose of it, and that parties claiming under him may avail themselves of his title. Thus, trover was brought for a bedstead. Plea, a former recovery by the plaintiff, in trover for the same identical bedstead, against A.; averring that the conversion by A., for which that action was brought, was a conversion

[1] Barnett *v.* Brandao, 6 M. & Gr. 640, n. (*a*); Cooper *v.* Shepherd, 3 Com. B. 266; Adams *v.* Broughton, 2 Str. 1078; Andr. 18; Smith *v.* Gibson, Cas. temp. Hard. 303; Brown *v.* Wotton, Cro. Jac. 73; Morrell *v.* Johnson, 1 Hen. & M. 449; Floyd *v.* Brown, 1 Rawle, 121; Marsh *v.* Pier, 4, 273; Rogers *v.* Moore, 1 Rice, 60; Carlisle *v.* Burley, 3 Greenl. 250; Acheson *v.* Miller, 2 Ohio, N. S. 203; Russell *v.* Gray, 11 Barb. 541.

Smith *v.* Scantling, 4 Blackf. 443. See Agnew *v.* M'Elroy, 10 Sm. & M. 552; Young *v.* Black, 1 Cranch, 565; Livermore *v.* Herschell, 3 Pick. 33.

So *an infant*, prevailing on the plea of infancy, in an action on a promissory note, given by him for a chattel which he had obtained by fraud, and refused to deliver on demand; is still liable to an action of tort for the conversion of the chattel, although he had sold it before the demand; more especially where the vendor was intoxicated at the time of the sale. Thomas, J., says: "The fraud or tort was merged in the contract, only when the contract had become complete. The plaintiff, by bringing his action upon the note, declared his willingness to affirm the contract. The defendant, on the other hand, still elected, as he had a right to do, to avoid the contract. This want of assent of the defendant is fatal, and the contract never becomes complete. The title to the cow did not pass. The tort was not waived." The learned Judge proceeds to remark that it would have been otherwise, had the defendant set up a defence which recognized the contract, but sought to *discharge* it, as by insolvency, &c. Walker *v.* Davis, 1 Gray, 506, 509.

not later in point of time than the conversion declared on, and that, before this conversion, A., being possessed of the bedstead, sold it to the defendant, who paid him for the same, and received it under such sale, and that the taking under such sale was the conversion declared on. Held, a good answer.[1] So, after judgment for the plaintiff in trover, the property may be sold under executions against the defendant older than the plaintiff's, although he took no bond in his action of trover for the forthcoming of the property.[2] So the recovery *and satisfaction* of a judgment, in an action of trover, for the conversion of a slave who was drowned while in the possession of the defendant, under a contract of hiring, damages being assessed for her value at the time of the conversion, vest the title in the defendant from the time of the conversion, and hire cannot be recovered for the unexpired part of the term.[3] So, where one commits a trespass by seizing personal property, and then sells it, and the owner recovers judgment against the trespasser for the value of the property and the tortious taking; such judgment changes the property, and the former owner cannot seize or claim it.[4]

41. But in another class of cases it has been held, that mere recovery of judgment in an action of tort *without satisfaction* does not invest the defendant with the title to the property, and is consequently no bar to a subsequent action of the same kind against one who claims under him.[5] So the general rule is inapplicable, if the prior judgment was rendered in a suit between the present defendant and a third person, and not for the entire value of the property. Thus A., being indebted to the plaintiffs, deposited with them, as agent to B., a bill of exchange, as security for a sum advanced by B.; writing as follows: "The bill you will hold,

[1] Cooper *v.* Shepherd, 3 Com. B. 266.

[2] Foremen *v.* Neilson, 2 Rich. Eq. 287; Rogers *v.* Moore, 1 Rice, 60; Robertson *v.* Montgomery, 1 Rice, 87; Chartran *v.* Smith, 1 Rice, 229.

[3] Smith *v.* Hooks, 19 Ala. 101.

[4] Fox *v.* Northern Liberties, 3 Watts & Serg. 102.

[5] Spivey *v.* Morris, 18 Ala. 254; Smith *v.* Alexander, 4 Sneed, 482; Drake *v.* Mitchell, 3 E. 251; Curtis *v.* Groat, 6 John. 168; Osterhout *v.* Roberts, 8 Cow. 43; Sanderson *v.* Caldwell, 2 Aik. 203; Jones *v.* M'Neil, 2 Bai. 466; Jenk. Cent. Cas. 88, p. 189. See 2 Kent, 387, 388, and n.; 2 Sharsw. Bl. 436, n.

subject to B.'s advance; and also for any advances or expenses you have against me." The bill having been, at the instance of the acceptor, surreptitiously taken by the defendant; held, the plaintiffs might recover against him in trover, although B. had previously sued him, and had recovered by the award of an arbitrator the amount of his advance.[1] So the former recovery, to constitute a bar, must be for the same wrong or injury, which is substantially complained of in the second action. Thus trespass lies, for wrongfully continuing a building on the plaintiff's land, for the erection of which he has already recovered compensation: such recovery, with satisfaction, does not operate as a purchase of the right to continue such erection. Therefore, where the trustees of a turnpike road built buttresses to support it on the land of the plaintiff, who thereupon sued them and their workmen in trespass for such erection, and accepted money paid into court in full satisfaction of the trespass; held, after notice to the defendants to remove the buttresses, and a refusal to do so, he might bring another action of trespass.[2]

42. Another point of connection between tort and contract arises from the inquiry, whether, under the circumstances of particular cases, paper securities themselves, which constitute the written evidence of contracts, are the proper subjects of an action for tort. And this question usually depends upon the further question of *title* in the plaintiff or defendant, growing out of the transmission or negotiation of such securities.

42 *a.* Upon this subject it is held, that trover lies against the cashier of a bank, for conversion of bank-notes, delivered to him on a special deposit in bank;[3] or for bank-notes sealed in a letter;[4] (*a*) or for a lost bank-note, which the

[1] Knight *v.* Legh, 4 Bing. 589.

[2] Holmes *v.* Wilson, 10 Ad. & Ell. 503. See, as to the general subject of the effect of a judgment, Gilbert *v.* Thompson, 9 Cush. 348; Norton *v.* Doherty, 3 Gray, 372; M'Dowell *v.* Langdon, 3 Gray, 513; Edwards *v.* Stewart, 15 Barb. 67; King *v.* Chase, 15 N. H. 9; Doty *v.* Brown, 4 Comst. 71; Burt *v.* Sternburgh, 4 Cow. 559; Outram *v.* Morewood, 3 E. 346.

[3] Coffin *v.* Anderson, 4 Blackf. 395.

[4] Moody *v.* Keener, 7 Port. 218.

(*a*) Trover for bank-notes cannot be maintained, for want of property in

defendant has tortiously converted to his own use, though part of the proceeds has been paid by him to the plaintiff. The acceptance of a part does not affirm the taking, so as to waive the tort. But the amount received will go in reduction of damages.[1] (*a*) So trover lies, generally, for the conversion of all negotiable instruments, although drawn by an agent of government, as such.[2] So, where a person deposits notes in the hands of another, to indemnify him against certain liabilities; when these liabilities are discharged, the depositor may claim the notes, or their proceeds, if collected. And, if the bailee has put them beyond his control, it is a conversion, for which he is liable in trover. And the amount of the notes, with interest from their maturity to the time of conversion, and interest on the aggregate from that time to the time of the verdict, is the measure of damages.[3] So the maker of a negotiable note can maintain an action for its conversion against a person, who before it has any legal inception wrongfully negotiates it to a *bonâ fide* holder for value. And he may recover the amount of the note as damages, without averring or proving that he has paid it to the holder. It is sufficient that he is legally liable to pay it.[4] So a bill was drawn by A. and accepted by the plaintiff, for the purpose of being discounted, and having the proceeds applied to other acceptances of the plaintiff; but the other

[1] Burn *v.* Morris, 4 Tyr. 485.
[2] Comparet *v.* Burr, 5 Blackf. 419; Brouwer *v.* Hill, 1 Sandf. 629.
[3] St. John *v.* O'Connell, 7 Port. 466.
[4] Decker *v.* Mathews, 2 Kern. 313.

the plaintiff, if he obtained them by means of a forgery committed by him or with his consent. Coffin *v.* Anderson, 4 Blackf. 395.

But a person who receives notes, obtained by forgery, *bonâ fide* for a valuable consideration, is entitled to hold them, unless he was guilty of gross negligence in receiving them. Coffin *v.* Anderson, 4 Blackf. 395.

(*a*) But, an *exchequer bill*, the blank in which was not filled up, having been placed by the plaintiff for sale in the hands of A., he, instead of selling it, deposited it with the defendants, his bankers, who made him advances to its amount. Held, by three Justices, (Bayley, J., dissentiente,) that trover did not lie; the property in such bill, like bank-notes and bills of exchange indorsed in blank, passing by delivery. Wookey *v.* Pole, 4 Barn. & Ald. 1.

bills, before maturity, were paid by him, he directing A. to hold the first-mentioned bill for his use, and not to part with it without his authority. A. however, for his own purposes, indorsed it to the defendant for a valuable consideration, though with notice that it belonged to the plaintiff, and that he had no authority to part with it. Held, the plaintiff might maintain trover for the bill.[1] So the owner of a note, although he cannot maintain an action thereon in his own name, may maintain trover in his own name for the conversion of it.[2] So the plaintiff may recover, upon proof of his previous possession of the note, notwithstanding the legal title to it, and the right to sue for the money due, are shown to be in another person, unless the defendant shows that he acted under the authority of the real owner.[3] And, in trover for a note, proof that the defendant received it from the plaintiff, and promised to collect it for him, is *primâ facie* evidence of ownership.[4] So where, in a suit upon a note, and upon a plea of accord and satisfaction, it appeared that the maker and payee of the note in suit entered into an agreement, by which a second note and mortgage were deposited with a third person in full satisfaction of the first note, and were to be delivered to the payee on his surrender of the first note; held, the maker had no power afterwards to revoke the agency of the depositary and prevent the delivery of the papers, the property in which, on tender of the first note, passed to the payee, and for which he might maintain trover, and that the plea was sustained.[5] So the unauthorized transfer, by the secretary of an incorporated insurance company, of notes and bills belonging to the company, is a conversion for which trover may be maintained.[6]

43. But, as already suggested, a *legal title* or *right of possession* is necessary, in order to maintain trover for a negotiable instrument. Thus the plaintiff, having possession of a

[1] Evans *v.* Kymer, 1 Barn. & Ad. 528.

[2] Donnell *v.* Thompson, 13 Ala. 440. See Worcester, &c. *v.* Dorchester, &c. 10 Cush. 488.

[3] Lowmore *v.* Berry, 19 Ala. 130.

[4] Ewell *v.* Ellis, 2 Shep. 72.

[5] Creager *v.* Link, 7 Md. 259.

[6] Firemen's, &c. *v.* Cochran, 27 Ala. 228.

note, payable to A. and not indorsed, and claiming the property therein, placed it for collection in the hands of the defendant, who converted the proceeds to his own use. Held, that trover did not lie either for the note or the proceeds, for want of legal title to either.[1] (*a*) So trover will not lie for the conversion of a promissory note, after it has been paid or legally discharged. Though it is otherwise where the word "paid" has been written across the face of it by mistake or without authority.[2]

44. And there are many other cases, in which it has been held that trover does not lie for negotiable securities, upon the ground, generally, that under the circumstances the plaintiff in the action has lost his title to the instrument, or failed to become the legal owner of it. Thus the defendant, to whom the plaintiff was indebted, received a bill from the plaintiff "to get discounted, or return on demand." The defendant sent the bill to A., with directions to place it to his account with A., which A. did, minus the discount. Held, in trover for the bill, that this was substantially a discounting of the bill by the defendant, and he was entitled to a verdict under a plea of not possessed; also, it seems, under the plea of not guilty.[3] So a trader, in contemplation of bankruptcy, delivered bills of exchange to a creditor, who received the money due upon them after the bankruptcy. Held, such receipt was not a conversion, and trover did not lie without proving a demand and refusal before the bills became due.[4] So the assignees of a bankrupt cannot maintain trover for a check, paid by his bankers after the bankruptcy, against the creditor, to whom the check was delivered and the money paid.[5] So, where the defendant, having agreed to lend two persons, who afterwards became bankrupts, £200 to be ap-

[1] Herring *v.* Tilghman, 13 Ired. 392.
[2] Lowmore *v.* Berry, 19 Ala. 130.
[3] Wilkinson *v.* Whalley, 5 M. & Gr. 590.
[4] Jones *v.* Fort, 4 M. & Ry. 547.
[5] Mathew *v.* Sherwell, 2 Taunt. 439.

(*a*) So the equitable owner of a bond, to whom it has not been legally indorsed, cannot bring trover. Killian *v.* Carrol, 13 Ired. 431.

plied to a specific purpose, drew a check on his banker for that sum, and delivered it to them before their bankruptcy; and they, not having used the check, returned it to the lender, after having committed an act of bankruptcy; held, their assignee could not maintain trover for the check.[1] So a person having three bills of exchange applied to a country banker, with whom he had no previous dealings, to give for them a bill on London of the same amount; and the bill given by the banker was afterwards dishonored. Held, this was a complete exchange of securities, and that trover would not lie for the three bills of exchange.[2] So A., B., and C. carried on trade in partnership, and A. was also in partnership with D. A., being indebted to the firm of A., B., and C., before the dissolution of that partnership, unknown to D., indorsed a bill, and paid over money, belonging to A. and D., in discharge of the private debt due from A. to A., B., and C., and immediately afterwards indorsed the same bill to a creditor of the firm A., B., and C. The partnership between A., B., and C. having been dissolved; held, that neither A. and D. nor their assignee in bankruptcy, could maintain trover against B. and C. for the bill, nor assumpsit for the money paid by A.[3] So if a promissory note is given, and other notes are left with the payee as security, and he indorses the former note and transfers the others to the indorsee, who converts them to his own use; the payee is not liable in trover, on tender to him of the amount of the note.[4] So the owner of promissory notes delivered them to the defendant, upon a receipt promising to redeliver them on demand, and the latter collected them when due, and retained the proceeds; after which a receiver of the owner's property was appointed, who demanded the notes of the bailee. Held, the receiver could not maintain trover for the notes against the bailee. His proper remedy was for money had and received.[5] So a party resident abroad drew a bill, and specially indorsed it to the plaintiff,

[1] Moore v. Barthrop, 1 Barn. & Cress. 5.

[2] Hornblower v. Proud, 2 Barn. & Ald. 327.

[3] Jones v. Yates, 9 Barn. & Cress. 532.

[4] Soss v. Emerson, 3 Fost. 38.

[5] Hodges v. Lathrop, 1 Sandf. 46.

a creditor, who transmitted it to the defendant, his agent. The agent procured the acceptance of the drawees, and then gave the plaintiff notice, that he had received instructions to pay him some money on account of his principal. Before any further communication, the agent was instructed by his principal not to pay over the bill to the plaintiff, until his accounts had been investigated. No investigation took place. Held, the bill had not become the property of the plaintiff, and he could not maintain trover for it.[1]

45. The *loss* of negotiable instruments, either casual, or by theft or robbery, has often given rise to questions of this nature. (*a*) Thus, in an action of trover for a Bank of England note, it appeared that the note, dated 12th October, 1820, was lost by the plaintiff in London, in April, 1821, and in June, 1822, was presented for change to the defendant, a money broker in Liverpool, by a person then embarrassed, with whom the defendant was well acquainted, and he changed it by giving bills, which had some time to run, and cash, deducting a commission, without inquiring how the holder became possessed of it. Held, it was for the jury to say, whether the defendant had received the note fairly and *bonâ fide*, in the ordinary course of business, and for full value; and, a verdict being found for the plaintiff, the Court refused to disturb it.[2] So the plaintiff was robbed of a pocket-book, containing, amongst other things, a bill of exchange. In advertising the loss, he merely stated, that "the pocket-book contained papers of no use to any person but the owner." The bill was shortly afterwards presented at the banking-house of the defendants, by a stranger, who stated that he was the son of the indorser. The defendants discounted it. In trover, held, in order to maintain the action, the plaintiff must have done all that his duty required,

[1] Brind *v.* Hampshire, 2 Gale, 33.

[2] Egan *v.* Threlfall, 5 Dowl. & Ry. 326.

(*a*) See Boyle *v.* Roche, 2 E. D. Smith, 335.

in advertising and making known his loss; and the defendants must have failed to act *bonâ fide* and with due caution in receiving the bill. Judgment for the defendants upon the verdict.[1] So a bank-note was stolen from a servant of the plaintiffs. The robbery was advertised in the Hue and Cry Gazette, and in another paper. Some time afterwards the note was received for change, at the banking-house of the defendants in the country, from a stranger, who was not asked how he became possessed of it. In trover, held, the plaintiff must prove due notice of the robbery and want of due caution by the defendants, in taking the note. Judgment for the defendants upon the verdict.[2]

46. But where, in 1830, the plaintiff had his pocket picked of a bank-note, at a public meeting; and the note was paid to the defendant, as he said, upon a bet on the Derby in 1832; but he could not say by whom; held, the plaintiff was entitled to recover in trover.[3] So the plaintiff left, in a hackney coach in London, and lost, her reticule, containing a £100 bank post-bill indorsed in blank; and issued hand-bills proclaiming her loss. The defendant, a banker at Brighton, who had never heard of the loss, cashed the bill for a stranger eight days afterwards. The stranger, on being asked his name, said he was on a journey, and wrote on the bill a fictitious address in an illiterate hand. The defendant did not inquire at what inn he was staying. Held, that the defendant was liable for the amount to the plaintiff.[4] So A., being possessed of a bank-note payable to himself or bearer, sent it in a letter directed to his correspondent. The mail was robbed, and the note came to the hands of the plaintiff, for a valuable consideration. He demanded payment of it of the defendant, (a cashier of the bank,) who refused to pay it, and kept the note. The plaintiff brought trover. Held, that he was entitled to recover.[5]

47. There are various other securities, or written evi-

[1] Beckwith *v.* Corrall, 11 Moore, 335.

[2] Snow *v.* Peacock, 11 Moore, 286.

[3] Easley *v.* Crocford, 10 Bing. 243.

[4] Strange *v.* Wigney, 6 Bing. 677.

[5] Miller *v.* Race, 2 Ken. 189.

dences of debt or of title, the wrongful appropriation of which has been made the ground of an action for tort. Thus one who loses, without culpable negligence, a state certificate indorsed in blank, may bring trover for it against one who has received it of the finder in good faith, and for a valuable consideration.[1] So, where the pledgee of a bond delivers it to the pledger for a particular purpose, as to be exchanged for stock and to return the latter, and the pledger converts the bond to his own use; the pledgee may maintain trover for the bond.[2] So, if an agent, intrusted by a stockholder to receive the yearly dividends, make a fraudulent sale of the stock, by means of a pretended power of attorney, transfer it by personating the proprietor, and abscond; the proprietor may recover the original price paid for the stock, in an action of trover against the vendee.[3] So the bonds or certificates of the corporation of the city of Dublin, certifying that A. B. or the holder or bearer thereof, for the time being, had become entitled to the principal sum of £100 chargeable on the estates of the corporation, with interest, &c.; are not instruments negotiable by delivery only. Trover, therefore, is maintainable by the owner against a transferee by delivery from a third person.[4]

48. But trover will not lie against the *bonâ fide* holder of an annuity ticket, lost by or stolen from a former proprietor, if regularly transferred to the defendant pursuant to the statute by which it was issued.[5] So where the plaintiff, the holder of Prussian bonds, payable to bearer, and issued by the sovereign of that country to secure a national loan, deposited them for a special purpose with an agent, who pledged them to the defendant, without fraud on the part of the latter; held, trover did not lie.[6] So, where a broker had obtained warrants of the West India Dock Company from the defendant by a fraudulent payment, and sent them into the market, where they were purchased by the brokers of the plaintiff for

[1] Biddle *v.* Bayard, 13 Penn. 150.
[2] Hays *v.* Riddle, 1 Sandf 248.
[3] Monk *v.* Graham, 8 Mod. 9.
[4] Gordon *v.* Cuming, 1 Hud. & Br. 54.
[5] Devallar *v.* Herring, 9 Mod. 44.
[6] Gorgier *v.* Mieville, 4 Dowl. & Ry. 641.

cash; held, the plaintiff might maintain trover, the warrants being negotiable and their transfer a constructive delivery of the goods.[1] So A., one of the defendants, having taken shares in a mining company, it became necessary, in order to complete his title, that he should sign a deed of association in London by a certain day. Finding this inconvenient, he desired his son, the other defendant, to sign in his stead, and to let the shares stand in the son's name. The son executed the deed, and received a voucher, certifying him to be proprietor of seventy shares, not transferable without consent of the directors. The son afterwards sold the shares, and paid the proceeds to A., who had become bankrupt; and his assignees bring trover for the voucher and shares. Held, they had a legal title, on which assignees could maintain an action.[2]

49. *Title-deeds* constitute another species of written contract, which is often made the subject of an action for tort. Thus in trover for deeds and stamped pieces of parchment, it appeared that the plaintiff, having contracted to purchase an estate of A., had the deeds prepared at his own expense, and sent them to A. for execution. A. executed, and gave them to a servant to be sent back; the servant delivered them to the defendant, an attorney, who had a demand upon A. for professional business. No directions were given to the defendant, to retain the deeds until the purchase-money should be paid. Some necessary parties refused to execute the deeds, and the plaintiff, having abandoned the contract, demanded them from the defendant, who refused to deliver them up, claiming to have a lien for his demand against A. Held, the plaintiff was entitled to the deeds, at all events cancelled, if not uncancelled.[3] So the plaintiff, wishing to borrow money on a mortgage, delivered the title-deeds to A., the intended mortgagee, for examination, and said that he would pay all expenses. A. handed the deeds to the defendants,

[1] Zwinger v. Samuda, 1 Moore, 12.

[2] Dawson v. Rushworth, 1 Barn. & Ad. 574.

[3] Esdale v. Oxenham, 3 Barn. & Cress. 225.

his own attorneys, to be investigated. The negotiation went off, and the defendants, being requested by the plaintiff to return his deeds, refused to do so, till he paid their bill of costs. On assumpsit to recover back the money so paid, held, the defendants did not act for both parties, and therefore had not a lien against the plaintiff as his attorneys; that, supposing the plaintiff liable to A. for the costs, A. could not communicate a lien to the defendants; that the undertaking of the plaintiff to A., if it amounted to a promise to pay these costs, did not entitle A.'s attorneys to detain the deeds, as it established no privity between them and the plaintiff; and that the plaintiff might have brought trover for the deeds, and was entitled to recover in this action.[1]

50. But a lessor cannot maintain trover against the lessee for the indenture of lease, upon the expiration of the term by forfeiture or otherwise.[2] So the plaintiff delivered to the defendant the title-deeds of the plaintiff's wife's estate. Having afterwards levied a fine of the property to the use of his son; held, the plaintiff could not support *detinue* for the deeds, having lost his title to them by the fine.[3]

51. Other actions for tort or wrong may sometimes be maintained in reference to paper instruments or securities, besides those which are founded upon an unauthorized appropriation of them by the defendant. Thus where a deed is delivered to a man as an *escrow*, to be kept for future identification as evidence, and he puts it on record, an action may be sustained against him by the grantor, to recover compensation for all the trouble and expense necessary to procure and perpetuate testimony, that the deed was never legally delivered.[4] (*a*)

[1] Pratt *v.* Vizard, 5 Barn. & Ad. 808.

[2] Hall *v.* Ball, 3 Scott, N. 577.

[3] Phillips *v.* Robinson, 4 Bing. 106.

[4] Himes *v.* Keighblengher, 14 Ill. 469.

(*a*) With regard to the *course of proceeding* in the class of cases now under consideration; it is held, that, in trover for a note, an omission to allege *its value* can be reached only by special demurrer. Fry *v.* Baxter, 10 Mis. 302.

In trover for any written contract, the plaintiff need not give the date or recite any portion of it in his declaration; but he must allege enough to show who are the parties to the instrument. And, it seems, if the declaration designate the instrument as a *contract*, there ought to be an express averment that it was *in writing*. Pierson *v.* Townsend, 2 Hill, 550.

In trover for a bond or deed, notice to produce it is not necessary, to authorize parol evidence of its contents. Hays *v.* Riddle, 1 Sandf. 248; Oswald *v.* King, 2 Brev. 471.

An entire *want of proof* of unnecessarily particular averments descriptive of the note will not defeat the action; otherwise with a *variance* between the proof and such averments. Ewell *v.* Eillis, 2 Shepl. 72.

In trover for a note, neither payment, set-off, nor fraudulent representations as to its value, can be pleaded in bar. Fry *v.* Baxter, 10 Mis. 302.

With regard to the amount of *damages*, a plaintiff in trover for a note and mortgage is held entitled to recover the full amount due thereon at the time of the conversion. Keaggy *v.* Hite, 12 Ill. 99.

And, in an action of trover by the pledgee of a bond against the pledgor, for wrongfully disposing of the bond, delivered to him for a particular purpose, the measure of damages is the value of the bond, with interest from the time of the conversion; unless such amount exceed the sum due the pledgee, in which case, that sum is the proper measure of damages. Hays *v.* Riddle, 1 Sandf. 248.

In addition to the points of connection between tort and contract, referred to in the text, we may briefly notice the subject of *contracts invalid for illegality*, or in other words *contracts to commit*, or *in consideration of committing, torts;* a copious title in treatises upon contracts, but not requiring to be more than incidentally considered in the present work.

Under this head may be mentioned *immoral* contracts. Thus an agreement in consideration of future illicit cohabitation is void. Walker *v.* Perkins, 3 Burr. 1568. Or even of past illicit cohabitation, if not under seal. Beaumont *v.* Reene, 2 Q. B. 483. Even though the case is one of *seduction.* Ibid. But past cohabitation or seduction will not avoid a specialty founded thereupon. Binnington *v.* Wallis, 4 B. & Ald. 650; Nye *v.* Moseley, 6 B. & C. 133. Unless the parties intend at the time to continue the cohabitation. Friend *v.* Harrison, 2 C. & P. 584. So an action does not lie, for the rent of lodgings let for purposes of prostitution, from the profits of which the landlord expected to be paid. Girardy *v.* Richardson, 1 Esp. 13. See Commonwealth *v.* Harrington, 3 Pick. 29; Jenning *v.* Commonwealth, 17 Ibid. 80; Dyett *v.* Pendleton, 8 Cow. 737. But an action lies for the price of clothes sold to a prostitute. Bowry *v.* Bennet, 1 Camp. 348. Or for washing her clothes. Lloyd *v.* Johnson, 1 B. & P. 340.

So an action does not lie for the price of printing or selling libellous or immoral pictures. Fores *v.* Johnes, 4 Esp. 97; Poplett *v.* Stockdale, R. & M. 337.

Another class of void contracts, are those *against public policy.* Under this head may be mentioned contracts *in restraint of marriage.* Lowe *v.* Peers, 4 Burr. 2225; Baker *v.* White, 2 Vern. 215; Hartley *v.* Rice, 10 E. 52. And on the other hand a *marriage brocage contract*, or a contract to procure a marriage, is also void. Hall *v.* Potter, 3 Lev. 411; Keat *v.* Allen, 2 Vern. 588.

So contracts respecting *the sale or transfer of public offices* are void. Richardson *v.* Mellish, 2 Bing. 236; Duke *v.* Asbee, 11 Ired. 112; Carlton *v.* Whitcher, 5 N. H. 196; Swayse *v.* Hull, 3 Halst. 54; Parsons *v.* Thompson, 1 H. Bl. 322.

So a contract *in general restraint of trade.* But the recent, prevailing doctrine is, that a contract is valid, which only operates in *partial* restraint of trade. Young *v.* Timmins, 1 Tyr. 226; Homer *v.* Ashford, 3 Bing. 322; Alger *v.* Thatcher, 19 Pick. 51; Mott *v.* Mott, 11 Barb. 127; Tallis *v.* Tallis, 18 Eng. L. & Eq. 151.

So a contract, the purpose and effect of which is to *impede public justice*, is void. Bills *v.* Comstock, 12 Met. 468. Such as a contract to compound a criminal prosecution, or suppress evidence. Collins *v.* Blantern, 2 Wils. 347; Jones *v.* Rice, 18 Pick. 440; Burley *v.* Burley, 6 N. H. 200. But see Plumer *v.* Smith, 5 N. H. 553; Price *v.* Summers, 2 South. 578.

But it has been held that such contract is valid, if made merely from motives of kindness, and not for gain. Ward *v.* Allen, 2 Met. 53. So if made to prevent a nuisance. Fallowes *v.* Taylor, 7 T. R. 475.

So a contract in favor of the party injured by a public offence may be valid, if the offender has been previously convicted. Keir *v.* Leeman, 9 Q. B. 371; Sugars *v.* Brinkworth, 4 Campb. 46.

And, on the other hand, all contracts involving *maintenance* or *champerty*, the upholding of suits of third parties, or a division of the proceeds of such suits; are held invalid. Whitaker *v.* Cone, 2 Johns. Cas. 58; Flight *v.* Leman, 4 Q. B. 883; Sweet *v.* Poor, 11 Mass. 549; Harris *v.* Roofs, 10 Barb. 489. The general rule, however, has been much qualified by late decisions and statutes, more particularly in reference to *agents* and *attorneys*, and the sale of *claims* or *titles* to land. See Thurston *v.* Percival, 1 Pick. 415; Spencer *v.* King, 5 Ham. 183; Williams *v.* Protheroe, 3 Y. & J. 129.

Contracts are also avoided by fraud, either as between the parties, or in reference to creditors, or other third persons who are deceived or misled thereby.

So also by illegality, as being in violation of a statute, whether expressly declared void or not, and whether the act be *malum in se* or only *malum prohibitum.* Such are *gaming*, *stock-jobbing*, and *usurious* contracts, where such transactions, as is often the case, are expressly prohibited by law.

CHAPTER II.

TORTS AND CRIMES.

1. What is a crime. The same act may constitute both a tort and a crime. Whether both a civil action and a criminal prosecution may be maintained therefor, concurrently or successively. Whether a civil action lies, without first instituting a criminal prosecution.
10. Private and public *nuisance*.

1. HAVING considered the general subject of torts in connection with *contracts*, we proceed to a brief view of torts as related to *crimes;* which have been defined, as wrongs committed, not against individuals, but against *the public* or *the Commonwealth.*

2. In the first place it is obvious, that the same act may constitute at once an injury to a particular individual, and an offence against the Commonwealth; thereby becoming the subject at the same time of a civil action for damages, and a public prosecution for the purpose of inflicting a penalty or punishment. And the general rule of law is, unquestionably, that although the same questions of fact may be in issue, neither of these proceedings constitutes any bar or defence to the other; (*a*) but that they may be concur-

(*a*) Upon this subject it is remarked by an approved writer: "From the principles announced, it seems to be a general consequence, that a verdict in a civil proceeding will not be evidence either against or for a party in a criminal proceeding. The acquittal in an action ought not to be admitted as evidence in bar of an indictment, because the parties are not the same, and the king or the public ought not to be prejudiced by the default of a private person in seeking his remedy for an injury to himself; especially since upon the trial of the indictment the testimony of the former plaintiff is admissible, which was before excluded by his being a party to the cause. And by such additional evidence the jury may be induced to come to a contrary conclusion. Neither, as it seems, is a verdict for the plaintiff in a civil

rently commenced and proceed *pari passu*, or that one may succeed either the institution or even the final result of the

---

action evidence upon an indictment, for although the defendant has had the opportunity to cross-examine the witnesses and controvert the testimony of his opponent, yet it would be hard that upon a criminal charge, which concerns his liberty or even his life, he should be bound by any default of his in defending his property. In addition to this, there is a want of mutuality, the parties are not the same, and the party would lose the privilege of proceeding against the jury in case of a false verdict by attaint. It is also to be observed, that the adjudication in the civil case would seldom be commensurate with the matter intended to be proved in the criminal case, since evidence sufficient to render a man responsible in damages may be insufficient to prove that he acted with a criminal intention." 1 Stark. on Ev. 197, § 63. And in reference to the *converse* question, the same writer further remarks: "The principles adverted to seem to exclude a verdict in a criminal proceeding from being evidence in one of a civil nature; for, independently of other objections in such cases, the parties are not the same; and therefore there is not such a mutuality as is essential to an estoppel. In an action brought by a private person, the acquittal of the defendant upon an indictment is not evidence, because the plaintiff was no party to the criminal proceeding, and therefore his private remedy ought not to be concluded by the result. In addition to which it may be observed, that an acquittal, however well founded, would seldom, if ever, show conclusively that the defendant had not committed an injury for which he is responsible in damages; for he may be liable in damages without having acted criminally; *è converso*, a conviction upon an indictment is not evidence for the plaintiff in an action for the same wrong; first, because the defendant upon the indictment could not attaint the jury for a false verdict; and secondly, because there is no mutuality; thirdly, because it does not appear that the verdict was not procured by means of the testimony of the interested party. But where, upon an indictment, the defendant confesses his guilt, the confession, it seems, is evidence in a civil proceeding." Ibid. 216, § 71. (The learned writer then proceeds to controvert the authority of Buller's Nisi Prius, as sustaining a different doctrine.) Acc. Betts *v.* New Hartford, 25 Conn. 180.

It has been held, that, in a civil action for assault and battery, the record of an indictment for the same offence, to which the defendant pleaded guilty, is admissible evidence. Corwin *v.* Walton, 18 Mis. 71.

So, where one is indicted for assault and battery, and found guilty, it is not error, on a subsequent civil trial for the same offence, for the Judge to charge, that the finding of the indictment showed that the plaintiff was entitled to some damages. Moses *v.* Bradley, 3 Whart. 272.

other. The reasons of this rule are very obvious. In addition to the consideration already suggested, that an indictment is for punishment, and an action for individual damages; on the one hand a wrongful act may not be criminal, for want of a criminal intent, and, on the other hand, by the testimony of the injured party an indictment may be sustained, while a civil action for the same cause may fail for want of the requisite legal evidence to maintain it.[1]

3. The most prominent and frequent examples of this two-fold liability are the cases of *Assault*, *Libel*, and *Nuisance*. (*a*) And, with regard to the class of private wrongs most nearly associated with the first of these public offences, — that which affects life and limb, or *personal injuries*; — in a late case in Massachusetts,[2] Mr. Justice Metcalf thus refers to an ancient doctrine somewhat in conflict with the rule above stated: "The case of Huggins *v.* Butcher, 1 Brownl. 205, and Yelv. 89, was referred to, where there is a *dictum* of Tanfield, J., in which Fenner and Yelverton, Js., are said to have concurred, that 'if one beat the servant of J. S. so that he die of that beating, the master shall not have an action against the

[1] See Blassingame *v.* Glaves, 6 B. Mon. 38; Thayer *v.* Boyle, 3 Maine, 475.

[2] Carey *v.* Berkshire, &c. 1 Cush. 477.

So, in an action for assault and battery, no evidence implicating one of the defendants was given by the plaintiff, but the defendants, in their cross-examination of a witness, proved that all the defendants had been indicted and convicted for the same offence. Held, sufficient evidence to authorize a verdict against all the defendants. Wolff *v.* Cohen, 8 Rich. 144.

So where, during the pendency of a suit for a perpetual injunction, against a business alleged to be a nuisance, the defendants are tried and convicted on an indictment; the record of their conviction is *primâ facie* evidence in behalf of the plaintiffs, and conclusive, unless the defendants prove that there was a material change in the manner of conducting the business, between the commencement of suit and the finding of the verdict. And the conviction is admissible, without any supplemental bill setting it forth. Peck *v.* Elder, 3 Sandf. 126.

(*a*) See Index. It will be seen, that the question, whether a civil action can be maintained *without* a previous criminal prosecution, has generally arisen in reference to acts which constitute the crime of *larceny*.

other for the battery and loss of service, because the servant dying of the extremity of the beating, it is now become an offence against the Crown, and turned into felony; and this hath drowned the particular offence, and prevails over the wrong done to the master, and his action by that is gone.' This doctrine is also found in most of the digests and abridgments of the English law. (*a*) But whatever may be the meaning or legal effect of the maxim, that a trespass is merged in a felony, it has no application to the cases now before us. In neither of them was the killing felonious, and there is, therefore, no felony, in which a private injury can merge." In conformity with these suggestions, and contrary to the rule of allowing in any case concurrent civil and criminal proceedings, it was formerly held, that a conviction on an indictment of larceny may be pleaded in bar to an action of trespass or trover for taking the same goods.[1] So it has been recently held, that, in trespass *vi et armis* for injuries to the person, the defendant may introduce the record of a prosecution for felony pending against him, and show by parol proof that the indictment and the civil action are founded on the same transaction.[2] So also in South Carolina, under a statute providing for an election be-

[1] Luttrel's case, 6 Mod. 77; *contrà*, 1 Mod. 283. See Rex *v.* Phillips, Cas. temp. Hard. 248; ——— *v.* Mahon, 4 Ad. & El. 575; Jacks *v.* Bell, 3 C. & P. 316; Skuse *v.* Davis, 2 Per. & Dav. 550.

[2] 22 Ala. 613.

(*a*) "Injury to life, in general, cannot be the subject of a civil action, the civil remedy being merged in the offence to the public. In general, all felonies suspend the civil remedies; (Styles, 346, 347;) and before conviction of the offender, there is no remedy against him at law or in equity; (Id. Ibid. 17 Ves. 331;) but after conviction and punishment on an indictment of the party for stealing, the party robbed may support trespass or trover against the offender. Styles, 347. Latch. 144. Sir Wm. Jones, 147. 1 Lev. 247. Bro. Abr. tit. Trespass. And after an acquittal of the defendant upon an indictment for a felonious assault upon a party by stabbing him, the latter may maintain trespass to recover damages for the civil injury, if it be not shown that he colluded in procuring such acquittal. 12 East, 409." 2 Sharsw. Black. 119, note.

tween a civil and a criminal prosecution, where a civil action by the owner and a prosecution by a third person are both pending for the same offence, of harboring a slave, the owner may be required to elect on which case to proceed; and the defendant may require the election to be made when either case is ready for trial.[1] So in an action for assaulting and stabbing the plaintiff, the defendant offered in evidence the record of a trial, on an indictment charging him with stabbing the plaintiff with intent to kill, and also with simple assault and battery. Held, the record was properly admitted in mitigation of damages, the verdict having been not guilty on the counts for murder, and guilty on the count for assault and battery; but not as disproving the fact of stabbing.[2]

4. But it is also held, and this is the prevailing doctrine, as above stated, that the defendant's having been punished *criminaliter* for the same offence cannot be shown even *in mitigation of damages* in a civil action.[3] (*a*)

5. While it has been sometimes doubted whether an action and a prosecution can be maintained for the same act; on the other hand it has been held, that no action would lie, until the defendant had been first criminally prosecuted.

6. With more particular reference to the rights and liabilities of third persons in case of *theft*, and of *criminal proceedings against the thief;* where property feloniously

[1] State *v.* Arnold, 8 Rich. 39.
[2] Porter *v.* Seiler, 23 Penn. 424.
[3] Wolff *v.* Cohen, 8 Rich. 144; Wheatley *v.* Thorn, 23 Miss. 62; Phillips *v.* Kelly, 29 Ala. 628.

(*a*) To trespass, for assault and false imprisonment, the defendants pleaded a commitment of the plaintiff, by them, as justices, for want of sureties, until the next sessions, for a misdemeanor on the Stat. 1 W. & M. c. 18, § 18, giving a penalty of £50 to the Crown; and that, before the sessions, the prosecutor, with the consent of the defendants, agreed to the discharge of the plaintiff; and thereupon, at the sessions, he was discharged by the Court, and accepted such discharge, in satisfaction of the assault and false imprisonment. Held bad on demurrer; for the making up a prosecution for a public misdemeanor is illegal, and no satisfaction; and, if there was any satisfaction, it moved from the prosecutor, and not from the defendants. Edgcumbe *v.* Rod, 1 J. P. Smith, 515.

taken from the plaintiff was sold by the felon to the defendant, who purchased *bonâ fide*, but not in market overt; and the plaintiff gave notice of the felony to the defendant, who afterwards sold the property in market overt; after which *the plaintiff prosecuted the felon to conviction;* held, the plaintiff might recover from the defendant the value of the property in trover.[1] So trover may be brought, where a felon has stolen goods and changed them into notes, if the notes clearly appear to be the product of the specific goods; and the owner of the goods, *who has prosecuted to conviction*, and has omitted to pray restitution, shall recover them in trover, though seized into the hands of the king, by an action against the sheriff.[2] But, in an old case, A. buys plate of the defendant, and gives him a draft, for which he gives receipt as for cash. A. pawns the plate to the plaintiff, a pawnbroker, showing him the receipt as evidence of his title. A. had no money with the banker, was tried for procuring under false pretences, on an indictment preferred by the defendant, and convicted, the plaintiff producing the goods. The defendant upon this took and detained them, and the plaintiff brought trover thereupon. Held, he should recover; for the property was not changed as against the right owner, either at common law, or by the statute of James respecting pawnbrokers.[3] (*a*)

7. In regard to the necessity of prosecuting and convicting an offender in order to maintain an action against him, it is said, "The policy of the law requires, that, before the party injured by any felonious act can seek civil redress for it, the matter should be heard and disposed of before the proper

[1] Peer *v.* Humphrey, 2 Ad. & Ell. 495.

[2] Golightly *v.* Reynolds, Lofft, 89, 90.

[3] Davis *v.* Morrison, Lofft, 185.

(*a*) Whether an auctioneer, who, in the regular course of his business, receives and sells stolen goods, and pays over the proceeds to the thief, without notice that the goods were stolen, is liable to the true owner as for a conversion, is a point upon which there are directly opposite decisions. Rogers *v.* Huie, 2 Cal. 571; Hoffman *v.* Carow, 22 Wend. 285.

criminal tribunal, in order that the justice of the country may be first satisfied in respect of the public offence."[1] (a) So it has been held, that trespass will not lie for taking money, if it appear, either on the evidence or in the pleadings, on the part of the plaintiff, to be felony; except the party has been prosecuted for the crime.[2] So, that trover for the conversion of a stolen slave cannot be maintained against the thief, before the institution of a prosecution against him for the felony.[3]

8. But the more modern and prevailing doctrine is, that the owner of stolen property may maintain an action for converting it against a third person in whose possession he finds it, without first prosecuting the felon.[4] So in the case of involuntary manslaughter in the performance of a lawful act, "where there has not been observed necessary discretion and caution," as the offence does not amount to felony, the private injury is not merged in the public, nor suspended until the public has been avenged. Therefore a father may sue for injuries to his minor son, though they resulted in his death, as for injuries to his servant, if the son is old enough to render service.[5]

9. In a late case,[6] Mr. Justice Bigelow gives the following lucid and comprehensive view of the law upon this subject, as finally established in Massachusetts, and probably the settled American doctrine: —

[1] Crosby v Leng, 12 E. 413. See Stone v. Marsh, 6 B. & C. 551; White v. Spettigue, 13 M. & W. 603.
[2] Lutterell v. Reynell, 1 Mod. 283.
[3] Martin v. Martin, 25 Ala. 201.
[4] Lee v. Bayes, 18 Com. B. 599. Acc. Lee v. Robinson, 37 Eng. L. & Eq. 406; Newkirk v. Dalton, 17 Ill. 413.
[5] Shields v. Yonge, 15 Geo. 349.
[6] Boston, &c. v. Dana, 1 Gray, 83.

(a) "If the thief, by his industry and fresh suit, be not attainted at his suit (Scil. in appeal of the same felony) he shall, for his default, lose all his goods which the thief, at the time of his flight, waived. But if the thief has them not with him when he flies, having perhaps hid them (as it is said), there no default can be in the party; and therefore they shall not be forfeited, for if he makes fresh suit after notice of the felony, it is sufficient." Foxley's case, 5 Co. 109 a. See Gimson v. Woodfull, 2 C. & P. 41; Pease v. M'Aloon, 1 Kerr, 111.

"The doctrine, that all civil remedies in favor of a party injured by a felony are, as it is said in the earlier authorities, merged in the higher offence against society and public justice, or, according to more recent cases, suspended until after the termination of a criminal prosecution against the offender, is the well-settled rule of law in England at this day, and seems to have had its origin there at a period long anterior to the settlement of this country by our English ancestors.[1] But although thus recognized and established as a rule of law in the parent country, it does not appear to have been, in the language of our constitution, 'adopted, used, and approved in the province, colony, or state of Massachusetts Bay, and usually practised on in the courts of law.' The only recorded trace of its recognition in this commonwealth is found in a note to the case of Higgins *v.* Butcher, Yelv. (Amer. ed.) 90 *a*, n. 2, by which it appears to have been adopted in a case at *Nisi Prius* by the late Chief Justice Sewall. The opinion of that learned Judge, thus expressed, would certainly be entitled to very great weight, if it were not for the opinion of this Court in Boardman *v.* Gore, 15 Mass. 338, in which it is strongly intimated, though not distinctly decided, that the rule has never been recognized in this State, and had no solid foundation, under our laws, in wisdom or sound policy. Under these circumstances, we feel at liberty to regard its adoption or rejection as an open question, to be determined, not so much by authority, as by a consideration of the origin of the rule, the reasons on which it is founded, and its adaptation to our system of jurisprudence.

"The source, whence the doctrine took its rise in England, is well known. By the ancient common law, felony was punished by the death of the criminal, and the forfeiture of all his lands and goods to the Crown. Inasmuch as an action at law against a person, whose body could not be taken in

[1] Markham *v.* Cob, Latch, 144, and Noy, 82; Dawkes *v.* Conereigh, Style, 346; Cooper *v.* Witham, 1 Sid. 375, and 1 Lev. 247; Crosby *v.* Leng, 12 E. 413; White *v.* Spettigue, 13 M. & W. 603; 1 Chit. Crim. Law, 5.

execution, and whose property and effects belonged to the king, would be a useless and fruitless remedy, it was held to be merged in the public offence. Besides, no such remedy in favor of the citizen could be allowed without a direct interference with the royal prerogative. Therefore a party injured by a felony could originally obtain no recompense out of the estate of a felon, nor even the restitution of his own property, except after a conviction of the offender, by a proceeding called an appeal of felony, which was long disused, and wholly abolished by Stat. 59, Geo. III. c. 46; or under Stat. 21, Hen. VIII. c. 11, by which the Judges were empowered to grant writs of restitution, if the felon was convicted on the evidence of the party injured or of others by his procurement.[1] But these incidents of felony, if they ever existed in this State, were discontinued at a very early period in our colonial history. Forfeiture of lands or goods, on conviction of crime, was rarely, if ever exacted here; and in many cases, deemed in England to be felonies and punishable with death, a much milder penalty was inflicted by our laws. Consequently the remedies, to which a party injured was entitled in cases of felony, were never introduced into our jurisprudence. No one has ever heard of an appeal of felony, or a writ of restitution under Stat. 21, Hen. VIII. c. 11, in our courts. So far, therefore, as we know the origin of the rule, and the reasons on which it was founded, it would seem very clear that it was never adopted here as part of our common law.

"Without regard, however, to the causes which originated the doctrine, it has been urged with great force and by high authority, that the rule now rests on public policy;[2] that the interests of society require, in order to secure the effectual prosecutions of offenders by persons injured, that they should not be permitted to redress their private wrongs, until public justice has been first satisfied by the conviction of felons; that in this way a strong incentive is furnished to the indi-

[1] 2 Car. & P. 43, *note*.

[2] 12 E. 413, 414.

vidual to discharge a public duty, by bringing his private interest in aid of its performance, which would be wholly lost, if he were allowed to pursue his remedy before the prosecution and termination of a criminal proceeding. This argument is doubtless entitled to great weight in England, where the mode of prosecuting criminal offences is very different from that adopted with us. It is there the especial duty of every one, against whose person or property a crime has been committed, to trace out the offender, and prosecute him to conviction. In the discharge of this duty, he is often compelled to employ counsel; procure an indictment to be drawn and laid before the grand jury, with the evidence in its support; and if a bill is found, to see that the case on the part of the prosecution is properly conducted before the jury of trials. All this is to be done by the prosecutor at his own cost, unless the Court, after the trial, shall deem reimbursement reasonable.[1] The whole system of the administration of criminal justice in England is thus made to depend very much upon the vigilance and efforts of private individuals. There is no public officer, appointed by law in each county as in this Commonwealth, to act in behalf of the government in such cases, and take charge of the prosecution, trial, and conviction of offenders against the laws. It is quite obvious that to render such a system efficacious, it is essential to use means to secure the aid and coöperation of those injured by the commission of crimes, which are not requisite with us. It is to this cause, that the rule in question, as well as many other legal enactments, designed to enforce upon individuals the duty of prosecuting offences, owes its existence in England. But it is hardly possible under our laws, that any grave offence of the class designated as felonies can escape detection and punishment. The officers of the law, whose province it is to prosecute criminals, require no assistance from persons injured, other than that which a sense of duty, unaided by private interest, would naturally prompt.

[1] 1 Chit. Crim. Law, 9, 825.

"On the other hand, in the absence of any reasons founded on public policy, requiring the recognition of the rule, the expediency of its adoption may well be doubted. If a party is compelled to await the determination of a criminal prosecution before he is permitted to seek his private redress, he certainly has a strong motive to stifle the prosecution and compound with the felon. Nor can it contribute to the purity of the administration of justice, or tend to private morality, to suffer a party to set up and maintain in a court of law a defence founded solely upon his own criminal act. The right of every citizen under our constitution, to obtain justice promptly and without delay, requires that no one should be delayed in obtaining a remedy for a private injury, except in a case of the plainest public necessity. There being no such necessity calling for the adoption of the rule under consideration, we are of opinion that it ought not to be engrafted into our jurisprudence.

"We are strengthened in this conclusion by the weight of American authority, and by the fact that in some of the States, where the rule has been established by decisions of the Courts, it has been abrogated by legislative enactments." [1] (*a*)

[1] Pettingill *v.* Rideout, 6 N. H. 454; Cross *v.* Guthery, 2 Root, 90; Piscataqua Bank *v.* Turnley, 1 Miles, 312; Foster *v.* Commonwealth, 8 M. & S. 77; Patton *v.* Freeman, Coxe, 113; Hepburn's case, 3 Bland, 114; Allison *v.* Farmers' Bank of Virginia, 6 Rand. 223; White *v.* Fort, 3 Hawks, 251; Robinson *v.* Culp, 1 Const. Rep. 231; Story *v.* Hammond, 4 Ohio, 376; Ballew *v.* Alexander, 6 Humph. 433; Blassingame *v.* Glaves, 6 B. Monr. 38; Rev. Stats. of N. Y. Part 3, c. 4, § 2; Stat. of Maine of 1844, c. 102.

(*a*) See 1 Bishop on Crim. L. 329; Ib. 333, for a statement of the conflicting law upon this subject in the several states of the Union. The following view of the same subject is in accordance with that stated in the text.

The law is different here from what it is in England respecting the right of the owner to *pursue* or *recover the value of stolen property* which has been sold by the thief. In England the owner cannot bring his action against the thief or against the purchaser from him, until *after conviction* for the larceny, because by the common law the private injury is merged in the public wrong. Nor will an action lie there against a *bonâ fide* purchaser in *market overt* if he has *parted with the property* previous to the conviction. Neither

10. We shall hereafter have occasion to consider the general subject of *nuisance*, as *a tort or wrong to property*. (See *Nuisance*.) In the present connection we may properly remark, that, contrary to the prevailing rule in other cases, no action lies for a public nuisance, unless the party bringing such action has received special and particular damage therefrom;[1] (*a*) and the question has often arisen, whether

[1] Iveson *v.* Moor, 1 Com. 58; Dougherty *v.* Bunting, 1 Sandf. 1; Hatch *v.* Vermont, &c. 2 Williams, 142.

---

of these rules prevail *here*. The doctrine that the private injury is merged in the public wrong is abolished by statute, and the English law of markets overt has not been adopted here. Consequently the owner of goods *feloniously* taken may here bring his action to recover the property or its value, without showing a conviction of the thief, and notwithstanding that the purchaser has parted with the property previous to the conviction. The reason why the owner cannot maintain an action in England, where the purchaser in market overt has parted with the property previous to the conviction of the felon is, that by the purchase in market overt, the owner's right in the property is gone until the conviction of the thief. If, therefore, previous to such conviction the purchaser part with the property, the owner in an action of trover cannot prove that the stolen goods were his property, and that while they were so they came into the defendant's possession, who converted them to his use; for until the conviction the owner has no property in the goods. Thus, it will be perceived, that this doctrine rests upon the law of markets overt, and that law does not prevail here. Hoffman *v.* Carow, 22 Wend. 285, note.

(*a*) The object is, to *avoid multiplicity of suits*. 1 Inst. 56 *a*.

But the right of abating or indicting a public nuisance is not affected by a statute imposing a penalty for the offence, unless negative words are added evincing an intent to exclude common-law remedies. Renwick *v.* Morris, 7 Hill, 575.

Upon this general subject, the case of Henley *v.* The Mayor, &c. 5 Bing. 91, is one of high authority, having been finally settled by the House of Lords, upon the opinion of the Judges; which was, in substance, that, whereever an indictment lies for non-repair, an action on the case will lie in favor of one who suffers any peculiar damage; and that where the Crown, for the benefit of the public, has made a grant imposing certain public duties, which grant has been accepted, the public may enforce performance of the duties by indictment, and individuals peculiarly injured by action. Acc. McKinnon *v.* Penson, 8 Exch. 319.

In an old case it is said: "If men will multiply injuries, actions must be

the facts of the case under consideration were such, as to bring it within the terms of this requisition. Thus no action lies for constantly obstructing a public wharf, thereby preventing the unlading of vessels at the wharf, and the warehousing of merchandise in the neighboring stores.[1] So, in case of a common ferry for the inhabitants to pass toll free, an action lies for taking toll, but not for keeping up the ferry.[2]

11. But it has been held (although this liability is generally created by express statute) that, where a municipal corporation is under legal obligation to repair streets, and an indictment will lie against it for not repairing, and, in consequence of its suffering a street to be out of repair, individuals sustain damages by injuries to person or property, an action will lie against the corporation.[3] So, where the

[1] Dougherty *v.* Bunting, 1 Sandf. 1.
[2] Payne *v.* Partredge, 1 Salk. 12.
[3] Hutson *v.* New York, 5 Sandf. 289.

multiplied too; for every man that is injured ought to have his recompense. Suppose the defendant had beat forty or fifty men, the damage done to each one is peculiar to himself; and he shall have his action. So, if many persons receive a private injury by a public nuisance, every man shall have his action. Indeed, where many men are offended by one particular act, there they must proceed by way of indictment and not of action, for in that case the law will not multiply actions. But it is otherwise when one man only is offended by that act, he shall have his action; as if a man dig a pit in a common, every commoner shall have his action on the case, per quod communiam suam in tam amplo modo habere non potuit, for every commoner has a separate right." Per Ld. Holt, Ashby *v.* White, Ld. Raym. 938. And in a late case in Massachusetts it is said, "where one suffers in common with all the public, although from his proximity to the obstructed way, or otherwise, from his more frequent occasion to use it, he may suffer in a greater degree than others, still he cannot have an action, because it would cause such multiplicity of suits as to be itself an intolerable evil. But when he sustains a special damage differing in kind from that which is common to others, as where he falls into a ditch unlawfully made in a highway, and hurts his horse or sustains a personal damage, then he may bring his action." Prop'rs, &c. *v.* Newcomb, 7 Met. 276. In Louisiana, one injured by a public nuisance, especially if involving a breach of private warranty, may maintain an action. Bruning *v.* New Orleans, &c. 12 La. Ann. 541.

plaintiff was delayed on his journey, and obliged to take a more circuitous route, by the defendant's shutting a gate across a highway; held, he might maintain an action on the case.[1] So, although an action will not lie by an individual for an obstruction in a public highway, unless he sustain a particular damage; yet, if the plaintiff state, that the defendant obstructed, &c., by a ditch and gate across the road, by which the plaintiff was obliged to go a longer and more difficult way, and that the defendant opposed him in attempting to remove the nuisance, this is a sufficient damage to support the action.[2] So an action lies for nuisance, where the plaintiff was obliged, in consequence of an obstruction of a public road, to carry his tithes by a longer and more inconvenient way, the Court remarking that the labor and pains, which the plaintiff had been forced to take with his cattle and servants by reason of the obstruction, might be of more value than the loss of a horse, which was sufficient to support an action.[3]

12. A familiar application of the rule upon this subject, is the case of an injury to *trade or business*, caused by some alteration or obstruction in a highway. In connection with a case of this description it is said: "For an injury which affects all his Majesty's subjects in common, the only mode of proceeding is by indictment; for any special injury which affects an individual beyond his fellows, he may obtain redress by action. The injury to the subjects in general is, that they cannot walk in the same track as before, and for that cause alone an action on the case would not lie; but the injury to the plaintiff is the loss of a trade, which, but for this obstruction to the general right of way, he would have enjoyed; and the law has said, from the Year-Books downwards, that, if a party has sustained any peculiar injury, beyond that which affects the public at large, an action will lie for redress. Is the injury in the present case of that character or not? The plaintiff, in addition to a right of way

1 Greasly *v.* Codling, 9 Moore, 489.
2 Chichester *v.* Lethbridge, Willes, 71.
3 Hart *v.* Bassett, T. Jones, 156.

which he enjoyed in common with others, had a shop on the roadside, the business of which was supported by those who passed — all who passed had the right of way, but all had not shops."[1] So, the defendant having erected a warehouse, projecting several feet into the street, and beyond the plaintiff's warehouse, standing nearly on the line of the street, whereby the latter was obscured from the view of passengers, travel diverted from it, and it was rendered less eligible as a place of business, and the plaintiff was obliged to reduce the rent; held, the plaintiff might maintain an action.[2] So in an action on the case, the declaration stated, that the plaintiff was possessed of a public-house, abutting upon a navigable river; and that the defendant wrongfully and maliciously placed upon the river, and kept there for a long time certain timbers, so as to drift opposite the plaintiff's house, whereby the access thereto was obstructed, and persons who would otherwise have come to the house, and taken refreshments there, were prevented. Plea, not guilty. Held, upon motion for a new trial for misdirection, that it was not a question for the jury whether the plaintiff had sustained any special damage; and, on motion in arrest of judgment, that the declaration did not seem to allege any public nuisance; and, at any rate, it disclosed a private injury to the plaintiff.[3] So in case of an unauthorized city railroad, which is a public nuisance, individuals specially injured, in the access to and from their places of business on the street, may maintain an application for injunction.[4] So under ancient deeds, recognizing a right in the owner of an estate to have a weir across a river for taking fish; if such weir was heretofore made of brushwood, through which the fish might escape into the upper part of the river, he cannot convert it into a stone weir, though in flood times the fish may overleap it; and though the enhancing, straitening, or enlarging of an ancient weir, as well as the new erection

[1] Wilkes v. The Hungerford, &c. 2 Bing. N. C. 281.

[2] Stetson v. Faxon, 19 Pick. 147. See Squier v. Gould, 14 Wend. 159.

[3] Rose v. Groves, 5 M. & Gr. 613; 4 Scott, N. 645.

[4] Wetmore v. Story, 22 Barb. 414. See also, Mayor, &c. v. Marriott, 9 Md. 160; Barnes v. Racine, 4 Wis. 454.

of one, for the purpose of thus stopping fish, is treated as a public nuisance by Magna Charta, c. 23, and 12 Ed. IV. c. 7; and though forty years ago two thirds of the weir in question had been so converted without interruption; an action for the injury may be brought within twenty years.[1] So the keeping of a large quantity of gunpowder in a wooden building, insufficiently secured, and situated near other buildings, thereby endangering the lives of persons residing in the vicinity, is a public nuisance. But, if an explosion occur in consequence of the burning of the building, an individual wounded or injured by it may maintain an action, though the fire was not occasioned by the negligence of the owner.[2] And, upon a somewhat analogous principle, a window frame, erected on a party-wall, was held not to be a common nuisance within the 14th Geo. III. c. 78, so as to deprive the owner of it of his right to the windows, being ancient lights; and, if it were, it would not, without conviction, be an answer to an action for obstructing them.[3]

13. It need hardly be added, that the rule in question is not so strictly construed, as in all cases to preclude a private action, merely because other persons than the plaintiff experience the same annoyance or injury from the act complained of, which is sustained by him. (*a*) Thus, if by means of blasting rocks "all persons on or about the premises of the plaintiff were kept in continual fear and jeopardy of their lives, rendering a proper attention to business full of fear and danger," &c., it would constitute a nuisance, and proper

[1] Weld *v.* Hornby, 7 E. 195.
[2] Myers *v.* Malcolm, 6 Hill, 292.
[3] Titterton *v.* Convers, 1 Marsh. 140.

(*a*) Where a nuisance is a common, although not a joint injury to several persons residing in the neighborhood, they may unite in a bill to restrain it. Brady *v.* Weeks, 3 Barb. 157.

But, if the bill contains a further prayer for their respective damages, it will be *multifarious*. Ibid.

But the objection may be obviated, by striking out this part of the bill. Ibid.

ground for an action on the case.[1] So a *corporation*, although the actual annoyance of which it complains equally affects a large number of persons belonging to or connected with the corporation, may maintain an action therefor. Thus an action on the case lies against a railroad company, for running their cars and engines, ringing bells, blowing off steam, and making other noises in the neighborhood of a church or meeting-house, on the Sabbath, and during public worship, which so annoy and molest the congregation, as greatly to depreciate the value of the house, and render it unfit for a place of worship.[2]

1 Scott *v.* Bay, 3 Md. 431.

2 First Baptist Church in Schenectady *v.* The Schenectady & Troy Railroad Co. 5 Barb. 79.

CHAPTER III.

GENERAL NATURE AND ELEMENTS OF A TORT.

1. HAVING considered *torts* or *wrongs* in their connection with *contracts* and with *crimes*, we now proceed to inquire, for what particular wrongful acts or omissions an action may be maintained, or what are the necessary elements of a *tort.* In the present chapter, we shall not treat in detail of any of those specific wrongs, which will constitute the separate subjects of consideration in the progress of this work; but confine ourselves, as suggested, to those comprehensive views which have a general application to them all. It will be seen, however, that if these principles are more specially applicable to any form of injury than to others; it may be termed the indefinite and somewhat negative injury of *negligence*—the peculiar subject-matter of the action called *trespass on the case.*

2. Upon this subject it is suggested, that the absence of any *precedent* for a particular action, especially where there must have been many occasions for bringing it, is a good, though not conclusive reason for not maintaining such

action.[1] But, on the other hand, it was remarked in an early English case, "It is said this action was never brought before; I wish never to hear this objection again. This action is for a tort; torts are infinitely various, not limited or confined; for there is nothing in nature but may be an instrument of mischief."[2] And the conflicting opinions of different Judges, even in the same case, show that the point in question must be regarded as an unsettled one. Thus it is said by one Judge, "This action is not maintainable for another reason, which I think is a weighty one, now this action is *primæ impressionis;* never the like action was brought before, and therefore as Littleton, s. 108, uses it to prove that no action lay on the statute of Merton, 20 Hen. III. c. 6, *si parentes conquerantur*, for if it had lain, it would have sometimes been put in use; so here. So in the case of Lord Say and Seale *v.* Stephens, Cro. 142, for the law is not apt to catch at actions."[3] While another Judge remarks as follows: "As to the novelty of this action, I think it no argument against the action; for there have been actions on the case brought, that had never been brought before, but had their beginning of late years, and we must judge upon the same reason as other cases have been determined by."[4]

3. The liability to make reparation for an injury is said to rest upon *an original moral duty*, enjoined upon every person, so to conduct himself or exercise his own rights as not to injure another.[5] And it is held that, an injury being shown, the burden of proof is on the defendant to justify the act.[6]

4. Upon this principle, the action of *trespass on the case* lies, in general, where one man sustains an injury by the misconduct or negligence of another, for which the law has provided no other adequate remedy.[7] This action may be

[1] Anthony *v.* Slaid, 11 Met. 291; Carey *v.* Berkshire, &c. 1 Cush. 478; Costigan *v.* The Mohawk, &c. 2 Denio, 609.

[2] Per Pratt, Ch. J., Chapman *v.* Pickersgill, 2 Wils. 145.

[3] Per Powys, J., Ashby *v.* White, 2 Ld. Raym. 944.

[4] Per Powell, J., 946.

[5] Kerwhacker *v.* C. C. &c. R. R. Co. 3 Ohio N. S. 172.

[6] Harvey *v.* Dunlop, Hill & Den. 193.

[7] Griffin *v.* Farwell, 20 Verm. 151; Sheldon *v.* Fairfax, 21, 102.

maintained at common law, where one wrongfully and through fraud and deceit causes damage to another, whether such damage consists in the loss of goods or of money.[1]

5. The distinction, however, is to be observed, that while, on the one hand, one person cannot, in general, maintain an action against another, for doing an illegal or wrongful act, unless he has thereby suffered loss:[2] and further, must show that *he* has been injured, in contradistinction to the injuries of others;[3] so, on the other hand, no action lies for a loss without an injury—*damnum absque injuria.*[4](a) The maxim is, "actio non datur non damnificato."[5] Thus it is necessary to show, in order to maintain an action against an officer for a false return, not only that the return is untrue, but also that the plaintiff has been damaged thereby.[6] So damages for a fraud or false representation cannot be recovered, without some proof that the plaintiff has been injured thereby.[7] So, to maintain an action for aiding a debtor in a fraudulent concealment of his property under the Maine Rev. Stat. c. 148, § 49, the plaintiff must have been a creditor at the time of the concealment, and must continue such without interruption until the commencement of the action. When he ceases to sustain this character, he loses the right of action, and does not acquire it anew by becoming again the owner of the same

[1] Low *v.* Martin, 18 Ill. 290.

[2] Nichols *v.* Valentine, 36 Maine, 322; Winsmore *v.* Greenbank, Willes, 577.

[3] Wright *v.* Defrees, 8 Ind. 298.

[4] Hamilton *v.* Marquis, &c. 3 Ridg. 267; Reed *v.* Conway, 26 Mis. 13. See Brown *v.* Mallett, 5 C. B. 599.

[5] Jenk. Cent. 69.

[6] Nash *v.* Whitney, 39 Maine, 241.

[7] Fuller *v.* Hodgdon, 25 Maine, 243; Ide *v.* Gray, 11 Verm. 615.

(a) Cicero combines all the elements of a tort, as above explained, in the expression, "Damno, dolore, incommodo, calamitate, injuriâ." Cicero, pro Roscio, s. 8.

A late English writer uses the word *injuria* as signifying a *legal wrong,* that is, a wrong cognizable or recognized as such by the law; and *damnum,* as meaning *damage,* not necessarily pecuniary or perceptible, but appreciable, and capable, in legal contemplation, of being estimated by a jury. Broom's Comm. 76.

debt. But it is not necessary that his relation to the debtor should remain absolutely unchanged, if he preserves his character of creditor, whether by an absolute or conditional claim or liability. Thus, if at the time of the concealment he held the debtor's note, and afterwards negotiated the same by indorsement, upon which he remained conditionally liable as indorser until he again became the holder, this would be a sufficient continuity of creditorship.[1] So it has been held, that an action on the case, by one riparian proprietor against another, for erecting a dam on the stream, whereby the water is raised, along the plaintiff's land, above its natural level; cannot be sustained without proof of special damage.[2] (*a*) (See *Watercourse.*)

[1] Thacher *v.* Jones, 31 Maine, 528. [2] Garret *v.* M'Kie, 1 Rich. 444.

(*a*) So the *damage* may sometimes determine the *locality* of the action. Thus an action on the case may be maintained in Ohio, to recover damages for an injury to property in Ohio, occasioned by the diversion of water, though the act which occasioned the diversion may have been committed in Pennsylvania. Thayer *v.* Brooks, 17 Ohio, 489.

In Davies *v.* Jenkins, 1 M. & W. 756, it was held, that an action will not lie against an attorney, who, being retained to sue for a debt a person of the same name as the plaintiff, by mistake and without malice takes all the proceedings, to judgment and execution inclusive, against the plaintiff. The case was treated as one of *damnum absque injuria*, except so far as the injury would be compensated by the costs which the law awards to a defendant prevailing in the suit.

In case against a witness for not obeying a subpœna, it was remarked by the Court, "In such an action, brought for a breach of duty, not arising out of a contract between the plaintiff and the defendant, but for disobeying the order of a competent authority; the existence of actual damage or loss is essential to the action, as the law will not imply a loss to the plaintiff from mere disobedience to the subpœna." Conling *v.* Coxe, 6 C. B. 703.

No action lies, as for a disturbance of a solicitor retained at a public meeting to solicit a bill in parliament, there being no wrongful act by the defendant stated, but only that the defendant, who was the chairman of the meeting, and one of the committee appointed for the dispatch of the business, conspired with others to disturb the plaintiff in his said employment and business, and procured other solicitors to be employed. Thomson *v.* Noel, 15 E. 501.

6. But on the other hand it has been often held, that, in case of wrong or violation of private right, *damage will be presumed.*[1] (*a*) Thus an action on the case lies against an intruder, by one having a right of way, without proof of actual damage.[2] So, on the other hand, one making an unauthorized use of land of another, over which the former has a right of way, is liable to an action without proof of actual damage.[3] So, in an action by a reversioner against a surveyor of highways, for cutting away a small portion of the soil of a bank or fence adjoining a public road; it is no answer that the fence was thereby in fact improved.[4] So, it is held, that, where one constructs a dam, so as to flow back water on the land of another, the law presumes that the act is a damage, and no special damage need be shown in order to sustain a suit.[5] (See *Watercourse.*) So a declaration stated that the defendant, being possessed of a messuage adjoining a garden of the plaintiff, erected a cornice upon his messuage, projecting over the garden, by means whereof rain-water flowed from the cornice into the garden, and damaged the same, and the plaintiff had been incommoded in the possession and enjoyment of his garden. Held, the erection of the cornice was a nuisance, from which the law would infer injury to the plaintiff; and that he was entitled to maintain an action, without proof that rain had fallen between the period of the erection of the cornice and the commencement of the action.[6] So it is held that an action lies for refusing a vote, though the candidate voted for was elected.[7] (*b*) Although it

[1] Laflin *v.* Willard, 16 Pick. 64; Allaire *v.* Whitney, 1 Hill. 484; 3 Bl. Comm. 123; Carter *v.* Wallace, 2 Tex. 200; Parker *v.* Griswold, 17 Conn. 286.

[2] Williams *v.* Esling, 4 Barr, 486.

[3] Appleton *v.* Fullerton, 1 Gray, 186.

[4] Alston *v.* Scales, 2 Moo. & S. 5.

[5] Woodman *v.* Tufts, 9 N. H. 88.

[6] Fay *v.* Prentice, 1 Com. B. 828.

[7] Ashby *v.* White, 2 Ld. Raym. 953.

(*a*) "Every injury imports a damage." Per Ld. Holt, Ashby *v.* White, 1 Salk. 19. "It is the pride of the common law, that, whenever it recognizes or creates a private right, it gives a remedy for the wilful violation of it." Yates *v.* Joyce, 11 Johns. 136.

(*b*) See *Vote.* In Ashby *v.* White, 2 Ld. Raym. 948, 1 Bro. Parl. 45,

has been doubted whether such action lies without proof of *malice*;[1] and expressly decided that it does not.[2] So against a landlord, who distrains for more rent than is due, though the rent due exceeds the value of the goods distrained.[3] So against a banker, having sufficient funds in his hands belonging to a customer, for refusing to honor his check, though no damage ensued.[4] (*a*)

[1] Pryce *v.* Belcher, 3 C. B. 58.
[2] Jenkins *v.* Waldron, 11 Johns. 114.
[3] Taylor *v.* Henniker, 12 Ad. & Ell. 488.
[4] Marzett *v.* Williams, 1 B. & Ad. 415.

---

it was held, by the House of Lords, that to hinder a burgess from voting for a member of the House of Commons was a good ground of action. No one could say, that he had been actually injured or would be; so far from it, the hindrance might have benefited him. But his franchise had been violated. The owner of a horse might be benefited by a skilful rider taking the horse from the pasture and using him; yet the law would give damages, and, under circumstances, very serious damages, for such an act. In the court below, judgment had been rendered, for various reasons on the part of different Judges, in favor of the defendant; one of which reasons was, that the privilege of voting is not a matter of property or profit, so that the hindrance of it is merely *damnum sine injuria*. See Toser *v.* Child, 6 E. & B. 289.

In Massachusetts, an action may be maintained against selectmen, for refusing to receive the vote of a qualified voter, or for omitting to put his name on the list of voters, without proof of malice. But it must be shown, that the plaintiff furnished the defendants with sufficient evidence of being a voter, and requested them to insert his name on the list, before they refused to receive his vote or omitted to insert his name. Blanchard *v.* Stearns, 5 Met. 298.

And a voter, who is challenged at the polls, cannot maintain an action against selectmen for refusing to receive his vote, if they do not act wilfully or maliciously, but under a mistaken belief reasonably caused by his own conduct, that he had abandoned his claim. Humphrey *v.* Kingman, 5 Met. 162.

(*a*) With reference to the question considered in the text, it is quite obvious that one party may often be *injured* or *damaged* by the act of another, without having a right of action for such injury. Such are the familiar cases, of the lawful use of one's own land, seduction, competition in business,[1] and

---

[1] See *Trade-marks.* A declaration stated, that the plaintiff, being the inventor and manufacturer of metallic hones, used certain envelopes for the same, denoting them to be his; and that the defendant wrongfully made other hones,

7. With regard to the *nature* of the act, necessary to constitute a tort or wrong, for which an action may be main-

privileged communications. On the other hand, the instances are still more numerous, as will abundantly appear in the progress of this work, where a party may maintain an action without proving actual damage; as in case of libel, escape, trespass to land, patent or copyright. Judge Story well remarks: "I can very well understand that no action lies in a case where there is *damnum absque injuria.* But I am not able to understand, how it can correctly be said, in a legal sense, that an action will not lie, even in case of a wrong or violation of a right, unless it is followed by some perceptible damage which can be established as a matter of fact; in other words, that *injuria sine damno* is not actionable. On the contrary, from my earliest reading, I have considered it laid up among the very elements of the common law, that, wherever there is a wrong there is a remedy to redress it; that every injury imports damage in the nature of it; and if no other damage is established, the party injured is entitled to a verdict for nominal damages. *A fortiori,* this doctrine applies where there is not only a violation of a right of the plaintiff, but the act of the defendant, if continued, may become the foundation, by lapse of time, of an adverse right in the defendant; for then it assumes the character, not merely of a violation of a right, tending to diminish its value, but it goes to the absolute destruction and extinguishment of it." Webb *v.* Portland, &c. 3 Sumn. 189. And the following illustration has been suggested by an eminent English Judge: "Suppose a trader, with a malicious intent to ruin a rival trader, goes to a banker or other party who owes money to his rival, and begs him not to pay the money which he owes him, and, by that means, ruins or greatly prejudices the party. I am by no means prepared to say, that an action should not be maintained, and that damages, beyond the amount of the debt if the injury were great, or much less than such amount if the injury were less serious, might not be recovered." Per Crompton, J., Lumley *v.* Gye, 2 E. & B. 216.

So it is said, "A greater evil could scarcely befall a country than the rule being frittered away or relaxed in the least, under the idea that, though an exclusive right be violated, the injury is trifling, or indeed nothing at all." Per Cowen, J., The Seneca, &c. *v.* The Auburn, &c. 5 Cow. 176.

So a learned writer remarks, "To warrant an action, some temporal

wrapped them in envelopes resembling the plaintiff's, and sold them as his own, whereby the plaintiff was prevented from selling many of his hones, and they were depreciated in value and reputation, those of the defendant being inferior. Held, the plaintiff was entitled to some damages, though he did not prove that the defendant's hones were inferior, or that he had sustained any specific damage. Blofield *v.* Payne, 4 B. & Ad. 410.

tained, it is held, that any act, by a party who has come rightfully into possession of property, which negatives the right of the owner, or is inconsistent therewith, is *a conversion*, authorizing the action of *trover*.[1] (*a*) So trespass *de bonis asportatis* or replevin is maintained, by proof that the defendant unlawfully intermeddled with, or exercised an authority and dominion over the chattels, against the will, in defiance, or to the exclusion of the owner, more especially if under a claim of right, though there was no manual interference, taking or removal.[2] It is said, "he who interferes

[1] Liptrot *v.* Holmes, 1 Kelly, 381.

[2] Connah *v.* Hale, 23 Wend. 422; Miller *v.* Baker, 1 Met. 27; Neff *v.* Thompson, 8 Barb. 213.

---

damage, be it more or less, must actually have resulted, *or must be likely to ensue.* The degree is wholly immaterial; nor does the law, upon every occasion, require distinct proof that an inconvenience has been sustained. For example, if the hand of A. touch the person of B., who shall declare that pain has or has not ensued? The only mode to render B. secure, is to infer that an inconvenience has actually resulted." Ham. N. P. 39.

Among the old Judges, Lord Holt may be regarded as the strongest advocate of the doctrine in question. He remarks, "If the plaintiff has a right, he must of necessity have a means to vindicate and maintain it, and a remedy if he is injured in the exercise or enjoyment of it; and indeed it is a vain thing to imagine a right without a remedy; for want of right and want of remedy are reciprocal." "Every injury imports a damage, though it does not cost the party one farthing, and it is impossible to prove the contrary; for a damage is not merely pecuniary, but an injury imports a damage, when a man is thereby hindered of his right." As in case of slander. "So if a man gives another a cuff on the ear, though it cost him nothing, no, not so much as a little *diachylon*, yet he shall have his action." So for riding over his ground. So for invasion of a franchise, the remedy merely being different — case instead of trespass. Ashby *v.* White, 2 Ld. Raym. 955.

Upon the theory, that *some* damage is necessary to sustain an action, it is said, the maxim *de minimis non curat lex* is never applied to the positive and wrongful invasion of one's property. Per Cowen, J., Seneca, &c. *v.* Auburn, &c. 5 Hill, 170. See Paul *v.* Slason, 22 Verm. 231.

Thus an action on the case lies for false representations as to the affairs of an insurance company, whereby the plaintiff was induced to effect an insurance, although no actual pecuniary damage has been sustained, beyond the payment of premiums. Pontifex *v.* Bignold, 3 M. & Gr. 63.

(*a*) See *Conversion.*

with my goods, and without delivery by me, and without my consent, undertakes to dispose of them as having the property, general or special, does it at his peril to answer me the value in trespass or trover."[1] Thus one who finds a horse, takes possession of him, and uses him in a way that injures him, is liable to the owner for the injury.[2] So the return of "attached," where the goods are the property of a stranger, subjects the sheriff to an action of trespass. Manual occupation, touching, or removal, is not essential.[3] So, where a sheriff sells, upon an execution, sheep not belonging to the defendant; replevin in the *cepit* will lie by the owner against the sheriff and the purchaser, although at the time of the sale the sheep were at large in a field, and no actual possession has been taken, and no removal made by the purchaser.[4] So a levy upon property, the taking of an inventory, and requiring a receiptor, to prevent its removal, are sufficient evidence of *taking* to sustain replevin.[5] So in case for a wrongful distress, it appeared that the defendant wrongfully seized goods, and placed a man in possession of them for some days. Held, the owner might recover damages, although he had the use of the goods all the time.[6] (*a*)

8. Upon a similar principle, although the facts of a case would justify the party injured in treating the act complained of as a positive and original wrong; he may at his election waive this claim, and sue as for a less direct inter-

[1] Per Sewall, J., Gibbs *v.* Chase, 10 Mass. 128.

[2] Murgoo *v.* Cogswell, 1 E. D. Smith, 359.

[3] Paxton *v.* Steckel, 2 Barr, 93.

[4] Neff *v.* Thompson, 8 Barb. 213.

[5] Fonda *v.* Van Horne, 15 Wend. 631.

[6] Bayliss *v.* Fisher, 7 Bing. 153.

(*a*) But if an officer, having a writ, goes to the debtor, and, finding him in actual possession of goods, informs him that he is directed to make an attachment, and shall do so, but does not in fact interfere with the goods, or take them into his custody; and the debtor informs the officer, that the goods belong to a third person and not to him, but still procures one, other than the owner, to give a receipt therefor; this does not amount to a conversion by the officer. Rant *v.* Sargent, 10 Shep. 326.

ference with his rights. Thus, where the act of taking amounts to a trespass, the plaintiff may waive the trespass and sue for the conversion.[1] So a declaration contained six counts in case, and a seventh count charged that the defendants took and distrained the goods of the plaintiff for rent, of more than sufficient value to satisfy the rent and costs, and then voluntarily abandoned the same; and afterwards wrongfully, injuriously, and vexatiously again took and distrained the same goods for the same rent, and refused to return the same, and converted them to their own use. Held, on motion in arrest of judgment for misjoinder of case and trespass, that, although this second taking of the goods was a trespass, yet the plaintiff might bring case for the conversion, and that the count was an informal one in case, and sufficient after verdict.[2]

9. But it is held, that a person who would recover damages, for an injury occasioned by the conduct of another, must show the relation of *cause and effect* (*a*) between the conduct complained of and the injury;[3] and this relation of cause and effect cannot be made out by including the independent, illegal acts of third persons. Thus a declaration in case against school directors, averring that the plaintiff is a resident of a certain school district, having children which he is desirous of having taught in said school, and that the defendants, contriving to deprive him of this benefit, unlawfully admitted colored children into the school, whereby the plaintiff was deprived of such benefit; is bad on demurrer.[4] So an action does not lie, in favor of one who had agreed with a town, to support, for a specified time and for a fixed

[1] Christopher *v.* Covington, 2 B. Mon. 357; Gilson *v.* Fisk, 8 N. H. 404. See 2 Greenl. Ev. § 226.

[2] Smith *v.* Goodwin, 4 Barn. & Adol. 413. See 2 Greenl. Ev. 210; Vedder *v.* Hildreth, 2 Wisc. 427; Walker *v.* Ellis, 1 Sneed, 515.

[3] Olmstead *v.* Brown, 12 Barb. 657; Butler *v.* Kent, 19 Johns. 223; Barber *v.* Barnes, 2 Brev. 491.

[4] Stewart *v.* Southard, 17 Ohio, 402.

(*a*) It is an ancient maxim of the law, "causa proxima, non remota, spectatur." See Donnell *v.* Jones, 13 Ala. 490.

sum, all the town paupers, in sickness and in health, for assaulting and beating one of the paupers, whereby the plaintiff was put to increased expense for his cure and support.[1] Shaw, C. J., says: "It is not by means of any natural or legal relation between the plaintiff and the party injured, that the plaintiff sustains any loss by the act of the defendant's wife, but by means of the special contract by which he had undertaken to support the town paupers. The damage is too remote and indirect. If such a principle be admitted, we do not see why the consequence would not follow that in a case where an assault is committed, or other injury is done to the person or property of a town pauper, or of an indigent person who becomes a pauper, the town might maintain an action." So an action by the proprietor of a theatre for a libel upon one of his singers, by which she was deterred from performing; was held not maintainable.[2] So, in an action for seduction of the plaintiff's daughter, it appeared that she was deserted, and, through distress of mind caused by the desertion, became ill, whereby a loss of service accrued to the plaintiff. Held, the action could not be maintained, the loss being caused, not by the seduction, but the abandonment.[3] So, by reason of the defendant's failing to repair his fence, the plaintiff's horses escaped into the defendant's close, and were there killed by the falling of a hay-stack. Held, the defendant was not liable.[4] So, where A. assaulted B., and commenced an affray with him, in which B. fired a pistol and injured C., it was held, that, if C. brought an action against B. and recovered damages for the injury, this would not give B. a legal right to recover that amount, as so much to be reimbursed to him, as special damages, in an action against A.[5] So the first count of the declaration alleged, that the plaintiff was the first and true inventor of "improvements in the manufacture of fire-arms, also of cartridges, of priming, and of wads or wadding for

[1] Anthony *v.* Slade, 11 Met. 290.

[2] Astley *v.* Harrison, Peake 194; 1 Esp. 48.

[3] Boyle *v.* Brandon, 13 M. & W. 728.

[4] Powell *v.* Salisbury, 2 Y. & J. 391.

[5] Whatley *v.* Murrell, 1 Strobh. 389.

fire-arms," and petitioned for a patent; that his petition had been referred to the solicitor-general, who had required and allowed the title to be amended, as an invention for "improvements in the manufacture of cartridges and of wads or wadding for fire-arms," and given a certificate of allowance; and that the defendant, well knowing the premises, but maliciously intending to injure the plaintiff, and to prevent him from obtaining letters-patent for his said invention, falsely, fraudulently, maliciously, and wrongfully, and without any reasonable or probable cause, represented to the solicitor-general, that he had an interest in opposing a grant of letters-patent to the plaintiff, and gave notice that he had applied for a patent, and obtained provisional protection, for an invention for "improvements in cartridges," and that, in consequence of the alteration in the title of the plaintiff's patent, he had reason to apprehend, that such alteration in the title might admit of his invention's being embraced in the plaintiff's patent; whereas, in truth, the alleged invention for which the defendant had obtained provisional protection was not his invention, but a fraudulent imitation of the plaintiff's invention, and the defendant had no interest in opposing a grant of letters-patent to the plaintiff. There was a second count, alleging that the defendant's knowledge of the plaintiff's invention was derived from a confidential communication thereof from the plaintiff, and that the defendant was seeking a patent in breach of such confidence; and the declaration concluded with a general allegation of special damage, that by means of the premises the solicitor-general refused to allow the plaintiff's application to proceed, and the plaintiff was thereby prevented from obtaining a patent, and was put to expense in opposing a grant of letters-patent to the defendant, &c. Held, the special damage alleged did not naturally flow from the grievances charged in the first count, and without it the count disclosed no cause of action.[1] So, where the plaintiff had placed a note in the hands of an officer for collection, and the defendant

[1] Haddan *v.* Lott, 15 Com. B. 411.

persuaded the officer not to collect, and the debtor not to pay the debt; it was held, that the plaintiff had no ground for an action on the case.[1] So a creditor cannot maintain an action against a third person, for aiding his debtor to remove, with his property, out of the State.[2] Nor will an action lie, for having fraudulently and wrongfully induced the sheriff to release and discharge from his possession certain negroes, which had been levied on in favor of the plaintiff against a third person, which negroes the defendant removed, so that they could not afterwards be found; the defendant being insolvent.[3] So a creditor cannot maintain an action against his debtor, for perjury committed in the examination of the latter, upon application to take the poor debtor's oath, whereby he obtained a discharge.[4] So no action lies, for representing the plaintiff's ferry not to be as good as another rival ferry, and inducing and persuading travellers to cross at the other, and not at the plaintiff's ferry.[5] Nor against the managers of a public lottery, at the suit of a dealer in lottery tickets, who had purchased a large number of tickets for the purpose of selling them at a profit, on the ground, that, by the negligent and improper conduct of the defendants in managing and conducting the lottery, &c., the public confidence in the fairness of the drawing was wholly lost, and the demand for tickets and the price of them thereby so greatly diminished, that the plaintiff could not sell his tickets, which remained on his hands and were drawn blanks.[6] So an action on the case cannot be maintained by the commissioners' court of a county against the keeper of the poor-house, for debauching and getting with child one of the inmates.[7] So a witness is not liable to a suit, for evidence given by him in a cause, although false.[8] So an action on the case does not lie, for

1 Platt v. Potts, 13 Ired. 455.
2 Matthews v. Pass, 19 Geo. 141.
3 Kelly v. McCaw, 29 Ala. 227.
4 Phelps v. Stearns, 4 Gray, 105.
5 Johnson v. Hitchcock, 15 Johns. 185.
6 Butler v. Kent, 19 Johns. 223.
7 Commissioners, &c. v. McCann, 23 Ala. 599.
8 Grove v. Brandenburg, 7 Blackf. 234; Dunlap v. Glidden, 31 Maine, 435.

that the defendant had taken away his goods, and hidden them in such secret places, that the plaintiff could not come at them to take them in execution.[1] (a)

[1] Browne v. London, 1 Mod. 286.

(a) In various connections, as bearing upon the question considered in the text, of the *right to maintain an action*, for an injury caused *remotely* by the act or neglect of the defendant, without reference to the amount of damages, we shall have occasion to refer to the *measure of damages* for particular torts or wrongs. Some cases may here properly be cited, which more particularly affect the amount of damages.

It has been generally held, in cases of illegal *marine capture*, that mere *profits*, thereby interrupted, could not be included in the damages. The Society, 1 Galli. 314; The Anna Maria, 2 Whea. 327; The Amiable, &c. 3 Ib. 546. So in case of *collision of vessels*. Smith v. Condry, 1 How. 28. See Hunt v. The Hoboken, &c. 3 E. D. Smith, 144; Blanchard v. Ely, 21 Wend. 342; The Spanish, &c. v. Bell, 33 Eng. Law & Eq. 178; Freeman v. Chut, 3 Barb. 424; Horner v. Wood, 16 Barb. 386.

In an action against a railroad company, for the breaking of the plaintiff's leg by a collision; it was held, that he could not recover damages on the ground of a probable second fracture arising from the oblique form of the original one. Lincoln v. Saratoga, &c. 23 Wend. 425.

In an action for seduction, the plaintiff cannot recover the probable expense of supporting the illegitimate child. Haynes v. Sinclair, 23 Verm. 108.

Action against the hundred, under a statute of Geo. I, for injury to buildings of the plaintiff, done by a mob. The plaintiff was a baker; and it appeared that the mob compelled him to sell a quantity of flour for much less than its value; and that they then began to break the windows of the bakehouse and of his dwelling-house. They also broke the lock of a warehouse on the other side of the street, and threw flour into the street. Held, the damage to the warehouse was not consequential to the other, and that he could not recover on account of the sale of the flour. Burrows v. Wright, 1 E. 615. See Greasley v. Higginbottom, 1 E. 636.

Where a prize had been offered for the best plan and model of a machine, to be sent by a certain day; and the plaintiff sent one by railroad, which through the neglect of the company did not arrive seasonably; it was held, that the chance of obtaining the prize could not be estimated in the damages. Watson v. Ambergate, &c. 15 Jur. 448.

In an action for false imprisonment in a ship, the plaintiff cannot recover the expense of leaving the vessel and taking passage in another, unless the imprisonment continued to the moment of trans-shipment, and was the immediate cause of it. Boyce v. Bayliffe, 1 Camp. 58.

10. Upon similar ground it has been held,[1] that, at common law, *the death of a human being*, though clearly involving pecuniary loss, is not the ground of an action for damages; therefore, where the wife of the plaintiff was killed by the overturning of a coach, that he could recover damages for the loss of her society, &c., only up to the time of her death. So no action lies by a husband, whose wife was killed instantaneously by the carelessness of the agents of a railway corporation.[2] (*a*)

[1] Baker *v.* Bolton, 1 Camp. 493; Conn. &c. *v.* New York, &c. 25 Conn. 265.

[2] Eden *v.* Lexington, &c. 14 B. Mon. 204.

(*a*) In the case of Ford *v.* Monroe, 20 Wend. 210, a father was allowed to maintain an action for the killing of his minor son by running over him, and the measure of damages held to be the value of his services till he should have come of age. But see the remarks of Metcalf, J., upon this case, 1 Cush. 478-9. This learned Judge remarks, that by the civil law, and the law of France and Scotland, such action may be maintained.

In application to this specific case, the general principle is laid down, that where one person has *contract relations* with another, an injury to the latter, which affects disastrously those relations, does not constitute a legal injury to the former. Conn. Mutual, &c. *v.* N. Y. &c. 25 Conn. 265. Thus an insurer of the life of a person, whose death is caused by the unlawful act of another, cannot maintain an action against the wrongdoer. As, for example, against a railroad corporation, whose negligence has caused the death of a passenger. The doctrine of *subrogation*, by which the insurer is substituted for the insured, and acquires a right of action in the name of the assured, is held not applicable to this case. *Ib.*

In Ohio, under the act of March 25, 1851, "requiring compensation for causing death by wrongful act, neglect, or default," an action may be sustained by the administrator for the benefit of next of kin, though the deceased leave no widow or children, and the petition allege no special circumstances, showing a pecuniary injury by the death. Lyons *v.* Clev. &c. 7 Ohio, (N. S.) 336.

Under an act of Illinois, enabling the personal representative of a person killed by the act, neglect, or default of another to recover damages, where the person killed might have recovered had not death ensued; the father of a child four years old may recover. Chicago *v.* Major, 18 Ill. 349.

The object of § 2 of this act is to exclude creditors, and prevent the amount being treated as part of the estate of the deceased. The act is not limited to the cases of those leaving widows. *Ib.*

11. It is to be remarked, however, that the liability of a party for the *consequences* of his acts is often found expressed in the books in broad and strong language. It is said, "no wrongdoer can be allowed to apportion or qualify his own wrong."[1] "Every person, who does a wrong, is, at least, responsible for all the mischievous consequences that may reasonably be expected to result under ordinary circumstances from such misconduct."[2] "A man who officiously presumes to interfere with, or make use of, the property of another, without his permission, is liable for all the consequences of such interference, whether he intended any injury to the owner or not."[3] "Where one does an illegal or mischievous act, which is likely to prove injurious to others, and when he does a legal act in such a careless and improper manner that injury to third persons may probably ensue, he is answerable in some form of action for all the consequences which may directly and naturally result from his conduct."[4] Thus, in an action on the case for negligence, where there was conflicting testimony as to the cause of the injury, it is not error for the court to decline to rule, that the cause was too remote to render the defendants liable.[5] So the rule is laid down, that, where the consequences of an unlawful act are immediate, he that does the unlawful act is considered the immediate doer of all that directly follows. He is the *causa causans* and a trespasser.[6] And it is enough to show, that the injury is part of "the chain of effects" resulting from the act complained of.[7] Or that the plaintiff's property has by the wrongful act of the defendant been rendered less valuable for the purposes to which he has devoted it. It need not appear, that its value would be equally depreciated for any other object.[8] So, in an action for obstructing the outlet of a lake, and thereby causing the

[1] Per Tindal, C. J.. Davis *v.* Garrett, 6 Bing. 716.

[2] Per Pollock, C. B., Rigby *v.* Hewitt, 5 Exch. 243.

[3] Wright *v.* Gray, 2 Bay, 464.

[4] Vandenburg *v.* Truax, 4 Denio, 464.

[5] Holmes *v.* Watson, 29 Penn. 457.

[6] Burdick *v.* Worrall, 4 Barb. 596.

[7] Per De Grey, C. J., 2 W. Bl. 892.

[8] First Baptist Church *v.* Sch'y and Troy R. R. Co. 5 Barb. 79.

plaintiff's adjoining lands to overflow, it is no defence, that, from the operation of natural causes, the plaintiff's land would have been overflowed to as great an extent as they had been by the defendant's obstruction.[1] So, where the plaintiff declared in case against the defendant, for not repairing his fences, *per quod* the plaintiff's horses escaped into the defendant's closes, and were there killed by the falling of a hay-stack; held, the damage was not too remote, and the action was maintainable.[2] So where a horse, not properly secured by the owner, is frightened and runs away, he is liable for the consequences, as well as the person causing the fright.[3] So where, in consequence of the wrongful abduction of the plaintiff's slaves, the cattle of his neighbor destroyed his corn, and a flood in the river swept away his wood; it was held, that the plaintiff should recover the value of this property in an action for carrying away the slaves.[4] So, in an action of trespass *qu. cl.*, for removing the roof of the plaintiff's house, he may recover for the loss of an eye directly and immediately caused thereby.[5] So, in an action on the case, the declaration stated, that the plaintiff had bought of C. and son certain goods for a sum mentioned, which the defendant had lent the plaintiff on his personal credit, without agreement for any lien on them in respect thereof, which sum the plaintiff paid to C. and son, who accepted it in payment for the goods; yet the defendant, falsely and wrongfully pretending that he was entitled to such lien, and had a right of preventing delivery to the plaintiff till the said loan should be repaid, wrongfully and maliciously, and without any reasonable or probable cause in that behalf, but under color of the said pretended lien, ordered C. and son not to deliver the said goods to the plaintiff, but to keep them till they received further orders; in consequence whereof C. and son refused to deliver them to him. Plea,

[1] Chapman *v.* Thames Co. 13 Conn. 269.

[2] Powell *v.* Salisbury, 2 Younge & Jer. 391.

[3] McCahill *v.* Kipp, 2 E. D. Smith, 413.

[4] McAfee *v.* Crofford, 13 How. 447.

[5] Hatchell *v.* Kimbrough, 4 Jones, 163.

that the plaintiff never paid C. and son. Held, on demurrer, that the action was maintainable; for, after putting the averment of payment which had been traversed out of consideration, it appeared sufficiently, that the defendant knew that there was no agreement for a lien on the goods, and that there was no obligation on C. and son to deliver the goods to the plaintiff without payment, and that their refusal so to deliver the goods to the plaintiff arose from the defendant's statement, and the damages directly resulted from that act of his.[1] So where the plaintiff, the assignee of a judgment against A., which was a lien on the real property of A., was about to take out an execution and seize a certain lot of land, and the defendant, having notice of the lien and assignment, with intent to defraud the plaintiff of satisfaction of the judgment, pulled down and carried off certain buildings from the land, whereby the lot was made of less value, the plaintiff may have an action on the case against the defendant.[2] (*a*)

[1] Green *v.* Button, Tyr. & Gran. 118. [2] Yates *v.* Joyce, 11 Johns. 136.

(*a*) Although the evidence shows, that the plaintiff was injured by the act or neglect of the defendant; yet, unless the declaration accurately sets forth the cause of injury, the action cannot be sustained.

Thus the declaration, in an action for giving a false character to A., a clerk, alleged, that the defendant fraudulently represented to the plaintiff, that the reason why he had dismissed A. from his employ was the decrease of his business; and that the defendant recommended the plaintiff to try A., and knowingly suppressed and concealed from the plaintiff the fact that A. had been dismissed from his employ on account of dishonesty. It appeared at the trial, that A. had been guilty of dishonesty while in the defendant's employ, but that the defendant had not mentioned that fact to the plaintiff when he recommended him to try A. It further appeared, however, that A. had not been dismissed from the defendant's employ on account of his dishonesty, but really for the reason which the defendant had assigned. Held, this evidence did not support the declaration. Wilkin *v.* Reed, 15 Com. Bench, 192.

In reference to the question, whether *remote damages* may be included in the amount to be recovered, the action itself being sustainable for some

12. And it is further to be observed, that the right to main-tain an action does not in all cases depend upon the inquiry, whether the injury complained of results *immediately* from the defendant's misconduct. On the contrary, an important distinction with reference to the precise *form* of action has been predicated upon this very consideration; implying and taking for granted, that *some* remedy is furnished by the law, though the injury be merely a remote result of the wrongful act complained of. This leads us to a summary statement of the prevailing, though not fully settled rules of law, in relation to the actions of *trespass*, or *trespass vi et armis*, and *case*. (*a*)

---

amount; it is said, a jury is not bound to weigh in *golden scales* the injury done by a trespass. Gillard *v.* Brittan, 8 M. & W. 575.

In an action against a city for injuries to the plaintiff's manufactory, caused by street excavations; he may recover for loss of profits of his business necessarily resulting from the work done by the corporation. Lacour *v.* New York, 2 Duer, 406.

Where a toll-bridge was carried away through the fault of the defendants; it was held, that the amount of tolls, which would be received during the time reasonably required to rebuild, should be included in the damages. Sewall's &c. *v.* Fisk, 3 Fost. 171.

Where the defendant took a horse and wagon of the plaintiffs; held, they might recover for the time and money spent in searching for them. Bennett *v.* Lockwood, 20 Wend. 223.

The defendant undertook to carry the plaintiff's lime in his barge from Medway to London, but deviated from the usual course, and the lime was wet by a tempest and set fire to the barge, which was thus destroyed. Held, the defendant was liable. Davis *v.* Garvett, 6 Bing. 716.

The defendant drove against the plaintiff's carriage, and the plaintiff's friend was thereby thrown from the seat to the dashing-board, which fell on the horse, and he kicked and broke it. Held, the defendant was liable for the damage. Gilbertson *v.* Richardson, 5 Man. Gr. & S. 502.

In an action of trespass for digging into a river-bank near a dam, the plaintiff may recover for the damage of a flood, thereby caused, three week afterwards. Dickinson *v.* Boyle, 17 Pick. 78.

(*a*) It has been held, that, where an injury has been done, partly by an act of trespass, and partly by an act which would be a proper subject for an action on the case, but done at the same time, and causing a common in-

13. In general, the leading distinction between trespass and case is this: — that where the immediate act itself occasions a prejudice, or is an injury to the plaintiff's person, house, land, or other property, trespass is the proper remedy. But where the act in itself is not an injury, but a consequence resulting from it is prejudicial, case is the proper remedy.[1] Thus, where one accidentally drove his carriage against another's, the remedy was held to be trespass, and not case; the injury being immediate; though he were no otherwise blameable, than by driving on the wrong side of the road in a dark night.[2] (a) So, for the working of

[1] Hamilton v. Marquis, &c. 3 Ridg. 267; Day v. Edwards, 5 T. R. 648; 3 E. 593; 1 Mass. 145.

[2] Leame v. Bray, 3 East, 593.

---

jury; either trespass or case may be brought. As in case of a weir or dam, erected partly on the plaintiff's ground, and partly on that of another riparian proprietor. Wells v. Ody, 1 M. & W. 459.

So, where there is an immediate injury attributable to negligence, the party injured has an election, either to treat the negligence of the defendant as a cause of action, and to declare in case, or to consider the act itself as the injury, and to declare in trespass. Blin v. Campbell, 14 Johns. 432.

Thus trespass lies for chasing the plaintiff's horse with dogs, and causing her to run upon a stake, so that she died. James v. Caldwell, 7 Yerg. 38.

The criterion of trespass *vi et armis* is force, directly applied, or *vis proxima*. If the proximate cause of the injury is but a continuation of the original force, or *vis impressa*, the effect is immediate, and the appropriate remedy is trespass *vi et armis*. But if the original force, or *vis impressa*, had ceased to act before the injury commenced, the effect is mediate, and the appropriate remedy is trespass on the case. Thus if a log, thrown over a fence, were to fall on a person in the street, he might sue in trespass; but if, after it had fallen to the ground, it caused him to stumble and fall, the remedy could be only by trespass on the case. 2 Greenl. Ev. § 224; 1 Chit. Pl. 115-120; Smith v. Rutherford, 2 S. & R. 358.

(a) But trespass on the case is a proper form of action for a collision caused by neglect on the part of those having charge of a vessel. Smyrna Steamboat Co. v. Whillden, 4 Harring. 228.

So case, and not trespass, is the proper remedy for injury caused by the negligence of the servants of a corporation. Illinois, &c. v. Reedy, 17 Ill. 580.

Declaration against the defendant for driving his cart against the plain-

quarries and blasting of rocks, whereby large quantities of rocks and stones were thrown upon the dwelling-house and premises of the plaintiff, breaking the doors, windows, &c., trespass *quare clausum fregit* lies, and not case.[1] (*a*) So trespass was held to lie, for originally throwing a squib, which, after having been thrown about in self-defence by other persons, at last put out the plaintiff's eye.[2] So A. took a mare belonging to B., and sold her to C., against whom B. brought replevin and recovered the mare. B. then sues A. in trespass, for damages sustained by the detention of the mare, and for the expense of regaining her. Held, the proper action, if any one would lie, is trespass, and not case.[3] More especially is trespass the proper action, where the act is *wilful* as well as the injury immediate. Thus it was held, that an action on the case, stating that the defendant's servant wilfully drove against the plaintiff's carriage, whereby it was damaged, could not be supported; it should have been trespass.[4] But the law is now well settled, that the master in such case would be liable in neither form, unless the act were done by his express order. (*b*)

14. It will be seen, in the progress of this work, that a *wrongful or malicious intent*, express or implied, is an essential and prominent element, either with reference to the

[1] Scott *v.* Bay, 3 Md. 431.

[2] Scott *v.* Shepherd, 2 W. Black. 893. (This case was said by Lord Ellenborough,—3 E. 596,—to go to the limit of the law.)

[3] Delevan *v.* Bates, 1 Mann. (Mich.) 97.

[4] Savignac *v.* Roome, 6 T. R. 125.

---

tiff's horse with force and violence, alleging it to have been done "by and through the mere negligence, inattention, and want of proper care" of the defendant. On demurrer to this declaration as not being in trespass, held, as a declaration in case it was good. Rogers *v.* Imbleton, 2 New Rep. 117; (in which the leading case of *Leame v. Bray* was questioned, though not distinctly overruled.)

(*a*) But a count, alleging that the defendant, "through his agents, &c. dug the earth from under the plaintiff's house, and from his lot, in such a manner, and so carelessly and negligently, as to cause the plaintiff's house to fall," is not in trespass, but in case. Shrieve *v.* Stokes, 8 B. Mon. 453.

(*b*) See *Master, &c.*

maintaining of the action itself, or the amount of damages to be recovered, in many kinds of tort. (a) In the present connection, we propose to state only the *general* principles of law upon the subject, without reference to these exceptional cases, which rest upon grounds peculiar to themselves.[1]

15. It is held, that one who does an illegal or mischievous act, which is likely to prove injurious to others, is answerable for the consequences which may directly or naturally result from his conduct, though he did not intend to do the particular injury which followed. Therefore where the defendant, having a quarrel with a boy in the street of a city, took up a

[1] See Bird *v.* Line, 1 Com 190.; Rex *v.* Philipps, 6 E. 464; Haycraft *v.* Creasy, 2, 107; Toser *v.* Child, 6 E. & B. 289.

(*a*) See *Slander*, *Malicious Prosecution*, *Assault*, *Damages*.

"In our civil code, it is, in numerous instances, in order to establish a legal right, essential to prove not only a mere external act done, but also to show the mind and intention of the agent. In actions founded, for instance, on malicious injuries, it is necessary to prove that the act was accompanied by a wrongful and malicious intention. The intention of a rational agent corresponds with the means which he employs, and he intends that consequence to which his conduct naturally and immediately tends. This inference is usually one of *fact*, to be made by a jury; but where the inference *necessarily* arises from the facts, it is a conclusion of law.* A man shall be taken to intend that which he does, or which is the immediate and necessary consequence of his act." 2 Stark. Ev. 738.

"There are very many tortious acts which suffice to entitle an aggrieved party to damages, without any reference at all being had to the motive or intent; whilst other cases will as readily suggest themselves in which the animus constitutes an essential element in, if it be not the very gist and substance of, the charge. If a trespass be done to my land, or if my goods are illegally withheld from me, or if I sustain personal injury by reason of the negligence and want of due caution of another, I may maintain against him an action of trespass, trover, or on the case, to support which no evidence will be required of any malicious motive or wrongful intention.

"Whenever the gist of an action is mala fides, fraud or deceit — the motive or intention is a matter peculiarly and especially for investigation before a jury." Broom's Com. 565–6.

---

* It has been said, however, "no question of the intention of parties can be a question of law." Per Williams, J. Blyth *v.* Dennett, 22 L. J. C. P. 79, 80.

pickaxe, and followed him into the plaintiff's store, whither he fled, and, in endeavoring to keep out of the defendant's reach, the boy ran against and knocked out the faucet of a cask of wine, by means of which a quantity of the wine ran out and was wasted; the defendant was held liable to the plaintiff for the damages.[1] So it is held, that although, if one does an injury by *unavoidable accident*, (*a*) an action does not lie; it is otherwise, if any blame attaches to him, though he be innocent of *an intention to injure;* as if he drive a horse too spirited, or pull the wrong rein, or use imperfect harness, and the horse taking fright kill another horse. In such a case the Court refused to grant a new trial, though the Judge, after summing up, instructed the jury that the defendant was liable, even though the accident were unavoidable, and no blame were imputable to him; omitting to direct them to consider, whether the accident was unavoidable, or occasioned by any fault in the defendant.[2] So, where death is occasioned by the wrongful act of another, it is no defence, in an action for damages, that the act was not intentional.[3] So, in trespass *de bonis transportatis*, proof of malice is not necessary to sustain the action.[4] So in replevin, evidence showing *the intention* of the defendant in taking and appropriating property is immaterial evidence. His liability does not depend on his intention.[5] So an action will lie against ministerial officers for any breach of duty, whether intentional and malicious or not.[6] So where one cuts timber, knowing it not to be upon his own land, or

1 Vandenburgh *v.* Truax, 4 Denio, 464; acc. Simmons *v.* Lillystone, 20 Eng. Law & Eq. 445; Tally *v.* Ayres, 3 Sneed, 677; Amick *v.* O'Hara, 6 Blackf. 258.

2 Wakeman *v.* Robinson, 1 Bing. 213.

3 Baker *v.* Bailey, 16 Barb. 54.

4 White Water, &c. *v.* Dow, 1 Smith, 62.

5 Ecker *v.* Moore, 2 Chand. 85.

6 Keith *v.* Howard, 24 Pick. 292; Gates *v.* Neal, 23 ib. 308; Spear *v.* Cummings, ib. 224.

(*a*) It has been sometimes held, that trespass *vi et armis* lies for an injury of which the defendant is the immediate cause, though it happen by accident or misfortune. Loubz *v.* Hafner, 1 Dev. 185; Hodges *v.* Weltberger, 6 Monr. 337. See *Assault*.

upon land which he had a license to cut from, the law presumes that the trespass was wilful.[1] So in trespass *qu. claus.* the defendant pleaded that he had land adjoining the plaintiff's close, and upon it a hedge of thorns; that he cut the thorns, and they *ipso invito* fell upon the plaintiff's land, whereupon the defendant removed them thence as soon as possible. Upon demurrer, judgment for the plaintiff.[2] So, where the plaintiff cut wood on the land of the defendant, with his approbation, and the wood was lying on the defendant's land, and the defendant, for the purpose of clearing up another part of his land, and with no intention to burn the plaintiff's, wood, set fire to the brush in this other part, and the fire escaped from his control, and passed on to the land where the wood was, and consumed it; held, trespass would lie.[3] So, in construing certain statutes, allowing a tender of amends for trespasses committed by negligence or mistake, it was held that those words had reference to *the act of trespass* and not to *the reasons or motives* of the trespasser.[4] So an action for a false representation lies against one who gives a recommendation of character and credit to another, on the strength of which he obtains goods on credit; if the statements were knowingly false, and communicated to the plaintiff, and the credit thereby obtained, although the object was not to defraud the plaintiff in particular; nor the defendant to derive any benefit from the fraud; nor the representations the sole cause of the credit.[5] So one who recommends an agent, by statements knowingly false, is responsible for the misconduct of the agent; without proof of malice, or an intent to injure, or any view to pecuniary interest. The Judge having explained to the jury the distinction between fraud in fact and in law, and the jury having found for the plaintiff, and added, that there was no fraudulent intention in the defendant, but that he had com-

1 Watkins *v.* Gale, 13 Ill. 152.
2 Lambert *v.* Bessey, T. Raym. 422.
3 Jordan *v.* Wyatt, 4 Gratt. 151.
4 Brown *v.* Neal, 36 Maine, 407.
5 Young *v.* Hall, 4 Geo. 95. See M'Cracken *v.* West, 17 Ohio, 16; Boyd *v.* Browne, 6 Barr, 310.

mitted a fraud in the legal acceptation of the term; the Court refused to enter the verdict for the defendant.[1]

16. On the other hand, an act, which does not amount to a legal injury, and violating no legal right, cannot be actionable because it is done with a bad intent.[2] Thus a count in case, for distraining for more rent than was due, is bad, though alleging it to have been done maliciously.[3] (*a*) So insurance companies or their officers are not liable to damages, for having conspired and agreed with each other, from malicious motives, that they would not insure the property of the plaintiff, or any boat in which a particular person should be employed, in order to prevent that person from obtaining employment.[4] And *the motive* of a person's so using his property as to injure his neighbor is held immaterial, if he uses it lawfully.[5] As in case of darkening a neighbor's lights.[6] So, where an officer levied on certain property which was mortgaged, and declared his intention of selling it in disregard and defiance of the mortgage; held, this declaration did not render the taking illegal, so as to sustain an action of replevin brought by the mortgagee.[7]

17. There is, however, a different class of cases, in which the motive and intent of a party have been held material in maintaining or defeating the action. It is said, "damage resulting from fraud, deceit, or malice, always furnishes a good cause of action. But where the injury is not to be traced to any evil motive, the rule is by no means universal that injury is always entitled to redress."[8] Thus where an

[1] Foster *v.* Charles, 6 Bing. 396; 7 Bing. 104.

[2] Stevenson *v.* Newnham, 13 Com. B. 285; Chatfield *v.* Wilson, 2 Williams, 49.

[3] 13 Com. B. 285.

[4] Orr *v.* Home, &c. 12 La. An. 255. Hunt *v.* Simonds, 19 Mis. 583.

[5] Auburn, &c. *v.* Douglass, 5 Seld. 444.

[6] Pickard *v.* Collins, 23 Barb. 444.

[7] Squires *v.* Smith, 10 B. Mon. 33.

[8] Sedgw. on Dam. (3d ed.) 28; Bartholomew *v.* Bentley, 15 Ohio, 659.

(*a*) "If a man sells a book in my library without meddling with it, he does me no harm; but if he takes it away and sells it in market overt, I lose my book." Per Coleridge, J., Cont *v.* The Ambergate, &c. 1 E. & B. 120.

officer, who had an execution against one of two tenants in common, who owned a quantity of salt in a wagon, seized the horses, *in order to effect a levy upon the salt*, he was held not to be liable for trespass.[1] So it is held, that an officer, acting within the scope of his authority, is not responsible in case for an injury, *unless resulting from a corrupt motive*.[2] So trover lies against a sheriff, for taking property covered by deed of trust, and selling it illegally; and, though the suit be instituted before the sale, yet his acts in making the sale are competent to show an original unlawful intention.[3] So, where a sheriff so negligently conducts himself, with reference to personal property levied upon by him, that it is lost, and the execution is satisfied out of the real estate of the defendant, whereby the lien of subsequent mortgage creditors upon the real estate of the defendant in the execution is reduced to the amount of the personal property lost; yet no action lies by such mortgage creditors against the sheriff for malfeasance, unless the conduct of the sheriff be explicitly charged to have been fraudulent, and with intent to diminish the security of the mortgage creditors.[4] So if a person, having the right to enter the dwelling-house of another for a particular purpose, forcibly enter for a different purpose, he is a trespasser.[5] So, whether persons seizing goods exposed for sale, contrary to the provisions of the New Jersey act to prevent the disturbance of meetings for religious worship,[6] are guilty of a trespass or not, depends upon the *quo animo* or intent with which the goods are seized, and not upon their subsequent irregular conduct, although this may be evidence of the intent. The *quo animo* is a question for the jury or the Court below, and cannot be reviewed by the Supreme Court on *certiorari*.[7] And, if there be an intent to injure and an injury, it is immaterial whether the defendant was benefitted. Thus a

[1] Blevins *v.* Baker, 11 Ired. 291.

[2] Stewart *v.* Southard, 17 Ohio, 402; acc. Davies *v.* Jenkins, 11 Mees. & W. 755.

[3] Christopher *v.* Covington, 2 B. Mon. 357.

[4] Bank of Rome *v.* Mott, 17 Wend. 554.

[5] Abbott *v.* Wood, 1 Shep. 115.

[6] Elm. Dig. 458.

[7] Rogers *v.* Brown, 1 Spencer, 119.

false representation, made with intent to injure one, and in relying on which he is injured, is a good cause of action, although no benefit accrues to the party making it from the falsehood.[1] So, in an action founded on deceit, both fraud and damage must be proved. The suggestion of falsehood, and the suppression of truth, though an injury may thence result, will not afford sufficient ground of action, unless such conduct has proceeded from a fraudulent motive, and was intended to produce an injury.[2] So, if A. write a letter to B., desiring him to introduce the bearer to such merchants as he may desire, and describing him as a man of property, and the bearer do not deliver the letter to B., but use it to obtain credit with C.; C. cannot maintain an action for deceit against A., though the representations in the letter are untrue.[3] So, in the absence of all rights acquired by grant or adverse user for twenty years, the owner of land may dig a well on any part thereof, notwithstanding he thereby diminishes the water in his neighbor's well, unless actuated by a mere malicious intent to deprive his neighbor of water.[4]

18. We shall presently have occasion to define *negligence*, as a specific ground of action. In the present connection it may be remarked, that the *intent*, which consists in *the carefulness or negligence* of the defendant, is a material element in an action for tort (*a*). Thus counts in case, for a loss by the falling of a bridge, which merely allege its insufficiency, without charging negligence on the part of the defendants, are insufficient.[5] So an action on the case lies, for *carelessly* carrying fire, whereby the plaintiff's stock-yard was destroyed; but not for an *accidental* or *wilful* burning.[6] So one who sets fire to the stubble on his own field, which, without any fault or negligence on his part, but by inevita-

1 White *v.* Merrit, 3 Seld. 352.
2 Munro *v.* Gairdner, 3 Brev. 31.
3 M'Cracken *v.* West, 17 Ohio, 16.
4 Greenleaf *v.* Francis, 18 Pick. 117.
5 Bridge Co. *v.* Williams, 9 Dana, 403.
6 Maull *v.* Wilson, 2 Harring. 443.

(*a*) See *Negligence.*

ble accident, escapes, and crossing over an open prairie burns the fence of his neighbor, is not liable for the damage.[1]

19. But, on the other hand, it is said, when an injury comes from the exclusive negligence of one party, he cannot shield himself from liability by calling it an *accident.*[2] (*a*) So it is held, that no person can be excused of committing a trespass, unless the act complained of arose entirely without his default. Where, therefore, in trespass for an injury done to the plaintiff's horse, in consequence of the defendant's driving a gig against it; it was proved that the defendant drove a high-spirited horse unskilfully and without a curb-chain; and the defendant pleaded, first, not guilty; and secondly, that his horse took fright and became ungovernable in consequence of a cart being driven furiously against it; which was not supported by evidence; and the Judge was of opinion that the defendant was liable, although he might not have been guilty of an act of negligence, or want of caution; and the jury found a verdict for the plaintiff: the Court refused to grant a new trial, which was moved for on the ground, that it should have been left to the jury to say, whether under all the circumstances the accident was unavoidable, or occasioned by the negligence of the defendant.[3]

20. It has been seen that the consideration, whether an injury is *immediate* or *consequential*, often determines the form of action to be brought on account of it. The same question is sometimes affected by *the intent* of the defendant in doing the act; and these two independent elements may constitute a compound test, which it is somewhat difficult to resolve and accurately apply. Thus it is held, that the distinction between an action of trespass and an action of the

[1] Miller *v.* Martin, 16 Mis. 508.

[2] Beach *v.* Parmenter, 23 Penn. 136. See Winterbottom *v.* Wright, 10 Mees. & W. 109; Howland *v.* Vincent, 10 Met. 371; M'Cahill *v.* Kipp, 2 E. D. Smith, 413.

[3] Wakeman *v.* Robinson, 8 Moore, 63.

(*a*) Liability for accidents is sometimes classed as a liability for *omission*, in distinction from commission. Grant *v.* Mosely, 29 Ala. 302.

case sometimes depends on the degree of caution or carelessness, with which the act complained of was attended, on the part of the defendant.[1] So it is held, that, where an injury is occasioned by the carelessness and negligence of the defendant, an action on the case is maintainable, although the injury is the result of the immediate act of the defendant; provided it be not a wilful act. Where, therefore, the plaintiff, in an action on the case, declared that the defendant carelessly, unskilfully, and improperly drove his gig against the plaintiff's cart and damaged it; held, the action was maintainable.[2]

21. The prevailing doctrine is, however, that, where injury is immediately occasioned by the carelessness and negligence and not the wilful act of the defendant, the plaintiff is merely *at liberty* to bring case, but may maintain trespass at his option.[3] But, where a direct forcible act is done wilfully and intentionally, producing an immediate injury, the only remedy is trespass.[4]

22. Some other cases illustrate the same distinction. Thus case, and not trespass, is the proper form of action, for an injury done to the horse of a customer by the bursting of a steam-boiler at a mill; and it may be maintained by the owner of the horse, though it was at the time in the possession of another.[5] But for driving the plaintiff's beast upon a fence, whereby its death was caused, either trespass or case lies.[6] So the declaration stated, that the defendant took and distrained the growing crops, &c., of the plaintiff, under color and as in the name of distress for rent, which crops, &c., were sufficient to have satisfied the arrears of rent and costs; and that, although the defendant might, under the said distress, have satisfied the said arrears, &c.,

[1] Cole *v.* Fisher, 11 Mass. 137; Claflin *v.* Wilcox, 18 Vt. 605; Schuer *v.* Veeder, 7 Blackf. 342.

[2] Williams *v.* Holland, 3 Moo. & S. 540.

[3] Brennan *v.* Carpenter, 1 R. I. 474; Williams *v.* Holland, 10 Bing. 112; Baldridge *v.* Allen, 2 Ired. 206; Schuer *v.* Veeder, 7 Blackf. 342.

[4] Baldridge *v.* Allen, 2 Ired. 206; Brennan *v.* Carpenter, 1 R. I. 474.

[5] Spencer *v.* Campbell, 9 W. & S. 32.

[6] Waterman *v.* Hall, 17 Verm. 128.

yet he wrongfully and vexatiously made a second distress on the said growing crops, for the same arrears, and wrongfully kept and withheld the said crops, &c., from the plaintiff for a long time, &c. There were other counts in case. Held, although trespass might have lain, the plaintiff was at liberty to sue in case; and that the above count was substantially in case, and therefore not misjoined.[1]

23. The *unlawfulness* of the act complained of is often made the test of the defendant's liability. (*a*) It is held, on the one hand, if a party, *in the exercise of a legal right*, more especially one conferred by express statute, does an injury to another's property, he is not liable for damages, unless they were caused by his want of the care and skill ordinarily exercised in like cases.[2] No action lies for an injury done by a party in the execution of a public trust, acting with due skill and caution, and within the scope of his authority.[3] So, that where the law from a given statement of facts raises an obligation to do a particular act, and there is a breach of that obligation, and consequent damage; an action on the case founded on the tort is a proper action.[4] On the other hand, if an illegal act be done, the party doing or causing the same to be done is responsible for all consequences resulting from the act; and if an act be done from evident necessity, and justified by that necessity, but which, without such necessity, would be illegal, it must appear that such necessity existed at the time, and that every possible diligence and care was taken, in the manner of the execution of the act, to avoid injury being

[1] Lear *v.* Caldecott, 4 Ad. & Ell. N. S. 123.

[2] Thomasson *v.* Agnew, 24 Miss. 93; Morris, &c. *v.* Newark, 2 Stock. 352. See Barnes *v.* Ward, 9 C. B. 392; Coe *v.* Platt, 6 Exch. 752; 7, 460.

[3] Tinsman *v.* Belvidere, &c. 2 Dutch. 148.

[4] Bond *v.* Hilton, Busbee, Law, 308.

(*a*) According to the maxim, "omne quod non jure fit injuriâ fieri dicitur." 1 Inst. 158 *b*. See Donovan *v.* The City, &c. 11 La. Ann. 711; Mahan *v.* Brown, 13 Wend. 261. It is said to be the general rule, that Courts can enforce only *legal* obligations, and redress injuries to *legal* rights. Orr *v.* Home, &c. 12 La. Ann. 255.

done to others or their property.[1] Thus a turnpike corporation, which has failed to comply with the statutory requisition as to width and mode of construction, is liable for damages thereby occasioned, without proof of further neglect.[2] So, in an action of trespass for killing a mare, it is error to refuse an instruction to the jury, "that the plaintiff could not recover, unless proved to their satisfaction that the defendant did kill the plaintiff's mare unlawfully." [3] So, where stones, dirt, &c., are thrown upon the land of another, by persons engaged in doing an unlawful act, as erecting or continuing a nuisance, such persons are liable for all the damage sustained thereby.[4] So the corporation of Pittsburg, having charge of a wharf therein, and receiving tolls for its use, permitted piles of iron to remain thereon for a longer time and nearer the water's edge than was allowed by the city ordinances. A boat anchored at the wharf; soon after, the water rose rapidly and high, carrying the boat farther inland and up the bank. It then fell, and the boat, in order to avoid one of the piles of iron, was necessarily conducted farther into the stream than the line of boats at the wharf above and below. While in this position, in the night it struck on one of the piles of iron, and was struck by some floating body and sunk. Held, that the owners could sustain an action on the case against the city for their loss.[5] So one who constructs a sewer in violation of a city ordinance is answerable for every consequence.[6]

24. But the mere legality of an act does not exempt a party from liability for its injurious consequences. Thus, though the act of sending up a balloon is legal, trespass lies for damage done by its accidentally alighting in the garden of the plaintiff.[7] So in an action for negligent driving, the law or usage of the road is not the criterion of negligence.

[1] Burton *v.* M'Clellan, 2 Scam. 434.

[2] Wilson *v.* Susquehannah, &c. 21 Barb. 68.

[3] Harding *v.* Fahey, 1 Iowa, 377.

[4] Hay *v.* The Cohoes Co. 3 Barb. 42.

[5] Pittsburg *v.* Grier, 22 Penn. 54.

[6] Owings *v.* Jones, 9 Md. 108.

[7] Guille *v.* Swan, 19 Johns. 381; Tally *v.* Ayres, 3 Sneed, 677.

Therefore, where the defendant's carriage was on the wrong side of the road, and, in attempting to pass it on the near instead of the off side, the plaintiff sustained damage; held, it was for the jury to decide the question of negligence, without regard to the law of the road.[1]

25. But the form of action may somewhat depend upon the consideration of lawfulness or unlawfulness. Where an *act* is lawful, as the fixing a spout, and the *consequence* injurious, the remedy is by case, and not trespass.[2] So if in repairing a highway earth is improperly piled against the fence of the adjacent landowner, his remedy is not by an action of trespass upon the freehold, but by a special action on the case.[3]

25 *a*. In reference to the numerous class of cases connected with the institution of former proceedings against the present plaintiff; (*a*) it is held, that case and not trespass is the proper action, for one whose goods have been attached upon a writ, which was abated because another suit was pending for the same cause of action.[4] Or where an injury is occasioned by the regular process of a court of competent jurisdiction, maliciously sued out.[5] So the plaintiff placed in the hands of his attorneys, for collection, a note which he held against the defendant, which was not paid when due. In a few days after the note had been put in suit, the defendant called on the plaintiff and paid his note. The defendant, supposing the case ended, did not enter his appearance, and the plaintiff neglected to inform his attorneys that the note was paid, or, if he did, not until after the declaration was filed. The attorneys were unable to attend court, and the attorney who represented them referred the cause to the Court, who assessed the damages. Execution issued on the judgment, on which the defendant's land

[1] Wayde *v.* Carr, 2 Dowl. & Ry. 255.
[2] Reynolds *v.* Clarke, 1 Strange, 634.
[3] Felch *v.* Gilman, 22 Vt. 38.
[4] Haywood *v.* Shed, 11 Mass. 500.
[5] Warfield *v.* Walter, 11 Gill & Johns. 80; King *v.* Pease, 19 Johns. 375; 13 Geo. 260.

(*a*) See *False Imprisonment; Malicious Prosecution; Sheriff.*

and negroes were levied in execution, and advertised for sale. These were set aside, but after the defendant had commenced a suit against the plaintiff. Held, case and not trespass was the proper remedy.[1]

25 *b.* It is to be further remarked, that, where a party is sued for an act done *under color of process;* if the process be *void*, the action should be trespass *vi et armis;* if *voidable*, trespass on the case.[2] Thus an execution, issued upon a judgment from which an appeal has been taken, and recognizance entered to stay execution, is voidable, and may be superseded, but not absolutely void; and therefore an action, for acts done under color of such execution, should be case and not trespass.[3] While for all acts done under color of legal proceedings, where the Court has no jurisdiction, or where the proceeding is irregular, trespass, and not case, is the proper form of action.[4] So trespass and not case is the proper action against assessors, for assessing one not liable to assessment.[5] So an action against the plaintiff in an execution, for causing an execution against another person to be levied on the plaintiff's goods, is trespass, and not case.[6]

25 *c.* But where selectmen, without right, doom a person who is liable to taxation, and he is compelled by a seizure of his property to pay the tax, he may have a remedy in case or trespass, at his election.[7] So case lies, as well as trespass, for an excessive distress after tender of the rent due.[8] (*a*)

[1] Fripp *v.* Martin, 1 Speers, 236.
[2] Dixon *v.* Watkins, 4 Eng. 139.
[3] Ibid.
[4] Cooper *v.* Halbert, 2 M'Mullan, 419.
[5] Agry *v.* Young, 11 Mass. 220.
[6] Wickliffe *v.* Sanders, 6 Monr. 296.
[7] Walker *v.* Cochran, 8 N. H. 166.
[8] Holland *v.* Bird, 10 Bing. 15.

(*a*) In many of the United States, the distinction between trespass and case has been abolished by express statute. And in construction of such statute it has been held, that, where the plaintiff sets out specially the circumstances of his case, in an action of trespass, it may, under the provisions of the Maine statute of 1835, c. 178, be regarded as an action of trespass or of the case. Leathers *v.* Carr, 11 Shep. 351.

So, according to the Indiana Act of 1843, a writ may be in trespass, and the declaration describe a cause of action in case, or the converse, the

And, if the proceedings complained of are *irregular*, the remedy against the magistrate issuing them is trespass; but the remedy against the person, who procures on insufficient information a process to issue to search the house of another, is case.[1]

26. An unlawful act may be committed *in violation of some express statute*, and this class of torts requires special notice. (*a*) It is said, "Where any law requires one to do any act for the benefit of another, or to forbear the doing of that which may be to the injury of another, though no action be given in express terms by the law for the omission or commission, the general rule of law in all such cases is, that the party so injured shall have an action."[2] (*b*) So, "If the

[1] Riley *v.* Johnston, 13 Geo. 260.

[2] Per Ld. Holt, C. J., Ashby *v.* White, 2 Ld. Raym. 953. See 6 Exch. 752; 7, 460.

statute rendering it immaterial whether the action be named trespass or case in the writ. But the rule as to the *joinder of counts* in trespass and case is not affected by the statute, nor can counts in trespass and trover be joined. Hines *v.* Kennison, 8 Blackf. 119.

The distinction is virtually abolished in Tennessee, Luttrell *v.* Hazen, 3 Sneed, 20; Wisconsin, Schultz *v.* Frank, 1 Wisc. 352; Maine, Massachusetts, and probably some other States.

(*a*) See also, with more particular reference to actions by or against corporations, the title *Corporation*.

(*b*) Case lies against a railway company, for wrongfully omitting their statutory duty in regard to the transfer of shares, and declaring the shares forfeited, and selling them. Catchpole *v.* The Ambergate, &c. 1 E. & B. 111. But, on the other hand, a defendant may set up, under the form of a denial of the charge of causing an injury to the plaintiff's property, that he acted under an authority and in performance of a duty, conferred and imposed by law. Thus, in an action on the case, for injury to a reversionary interest in land, the defendants may prove, under the general issue, that the acts were committed by them in their official capacity, as selectmen, in building a highway, which had been laid out by their predecessors in office across the plaintiff's land. Kidder *v.* Jennison, 21 Vt. 108.

To sustain an action for damages, resulting from the neglect to perform some duty, required either by the common law or by a public statute, it is not necessary to aver, in the declaration, the manner in which that duty is imposed. Therefore, in an action on the case, for an injury resulting from the neglect of a town to keep in sufficient repair a public

law casts any duty upon a person, which he refuses or fails to perform, he is answerable in damages to those whom his refusal or failure injures."[1]

27. For the *abuse* of a privilege given by statute a party is liable to one who sustains injury thereby. Thus one authorized by statute to set fire to a prairie is bound to use every reasonable precaution to prevent injurious results to others; and, in a suit for an injury resulting from the setting of such fire, after the plaintiff has proved the setting of the fire by the defendant, the burden of proof is on the latter to establish an excuse or justification.[2] So, under a city ordinance allowing the extension of vaults under the sidewalk, provided they be kept covered, one who so extends his vault, and leaves it uncovered, is responsible in damages to a passenger injured by falling into it, provided such passenger were using ordinary care.[3]

28. Where a statute furnishes a remedy for a particular injury, without prescribing the precise form of action, such form may be adopted, as is most adapted to the circumstances of the case. Thus an action on the Connecticut statute concerning fences, to recover double the value of repairs made pursuant to the 5th section of that statute, is "an action on the case," within the meaning of the same statute.[4] So it was held, that the treble damages, given by the provincial act of 1 Geo. II. c. 4, were to be sued for in an action of trespass.[5] So, in Massachusetts, trespass was held to be the most suitable action, under the Stat. of 1795, c. 75, § 3, which gives treble damages for cutting down trees, &c., pending an action for the recovery of the land on which such trees are growing.[6]

[1] Per Ld. Brougham, Ferguson *v.* Kinnoull, 9 Cl. & F. 289.
[2] Johnson *v.* Barber, 5 Gilm. 425.
[3] Beardsley *v.* Swann, 4 McLean, 333.
[4] Sharp *v.* Curtiss, 15 Conn. 526.
[5] Prescott *v.* Tufts, 4 Mass. 146.
[6] Peirce *v.* Spring, 15 Mass. 489.

highway, and to erect a railing on the sides of a road and bridge, so raised above the adjoining ground as to endanger the safety of travellers; it was held, that the declaration need not aver that the liability of the defendants was imposed by statute. Griswold *v.* Gallup, 22 Conn. 208.

28 *a*. But where a new right is given by a statute, and a remedy provided for the violation of it, the party is confined to this remedy.[1] So, where a statute authorizes the doing of certain acts, the necessary consequence of which will be to injure the property of another, and at the same time provides a remedy for the recovery of the damages, the party injured is confined to the statute remedy.[2] Thus, where a railroad corporation had the legal right to pass over and destroy a portion of a certain highway, and a general statute of the State provided a specific remedy for this injury; held, that to recover for the acts which were done according to law, the declaration should be specially founded upon the statute, and an action could not be maintained upon a declaration at common law.[3] So, where a surveyor of highways in Maine was required by the selectmen of a town to put a road, then lately laid out, and running through land of A., in a condition to be travelled with safety and convenience; and, in doing it, he and those acting under his direction took for the purpose from the land of A., which lay contiguous to the way, "not planted or enclosed," a quantity of stone necessary for the proper repair of the road; held, A. could not maintain trespass *quare clausum* against the surveyor or those acting under him; such act being authorized by Rev. Stats. c. 25, § 72, and the remedy for compensation being in a different mode.[4] So, where the legislature authorizes the making of a canal, and provides a special mode of redress for those who shall be injured in their property by the natural and necessary effect of making the canal; no action for such injury lies at the common law.[5] So the only remedy for damages to land, necessarily caused in the construction of the aqueduct from Long Pond to Boston, under Stat. 1846, c. 167, is by petition to the Court

[1] Per Walworth, Chancellor, Renwick *v.* Morris. 7 Hill. 575; Butler *v.* State, 6 Ind. 165; Camden *v.* Allen. 2 Dutch. 398; Victory *v.* Fitzpatrick, 8 Ind. 281; M'Cormack *v.* Terre Haute, &c.. 9, 283.

[2] Henniker *v.* Contoocook, &c. 9 Fost. 146.

[3] Ibid.

[4] Keene *v.* Chapman, 25 Maine, 126.

[5] Stevens *v.* Proprietors, &c. 12 Mass. 466.

of Common Pleas under § 6 of that statute, although such injury is to land not finally taken for the location of the aqueduct, but only adjacent thereto.[1] So, where a surveyor of highways, without the written approbation of the selectmen, causes a watercourse to be so conveyed by the side of the road, as to incommode a person's building, or obstruct him in his business, no action lies against the surveyor, but only an appeal to the selectmen under the Rev. Stats. c. 25, § 5.[2] Upon the same ground, an action under the Code in New York, to abate a nuisance, and to recover damages for its erection and continuance, being a substitute for the statute remedy by writ of nuisance; the plaintiff must aver in his complaint all that was before requisite to sustain an action of that nature.[3] So, in Tennessee, the remedy by *motion*, given by the statute against an officer for official delinquency, being merely a substitute for the common-law remedy of an action on the case; whatever would constitute a valid defence in such action is equally available in the proceeding by motion.[4]

29. But the distinction has been taken, that, where a statute does not vest a right in a person, but only prohibits some act under a penalty, the party violating the statute is liable only to the penalty; but, where *a right of property* is vested in consequence of the statute, it may be vindicated by the common law, unless the statute confines the remedy to the penalty. (*a*) Thus a statute vested

[1] Tower *v.* Boston, 10 Cush. 235.
[2] Elder *v.* Bemis, 2 Met. 599.
[3] Ellsworth *v.* Putnam, 16 Barb. 565.
[4] Billingsly *v.* Rankin, 2 Swan, 82.

(*a*) In a late English case it is said, "If indeed the performance of a new duty created by act of Parliament is enforced by a penalty recoverable by the party grieved by the non-performance, there is no other remedy than that given by the act, either for the public or the private wrong; but, by the penalty given in the act now in question (7 & 8 Vict. c. 112), compensation for private special damage seems not to have been contemplated. The penalty is recoverable in case of a breach of the public duty, though no damage may actually have been sustained by anybody; and no authority has been cited to us, nor are we aware of any, in which it has been

in a town the right of disposing of the privilege of taking alewives in a river within the town, and enacted that persons obstructing the passage of the fish should be liable to a certain penalty. Held, the remedy prescribed by the statute was cumulative, and an action on the case might be maintained by a purchaser of the privilege from the town, against any person obstructing the passage of the fish.[1] And various cases are to be found in the books, which seem to conflict with the rule that a remedy provided by statute is to be regarded as exclusive. Thus, although a statute regulating the inspection of beef and pork imposes a penalty upon the inspector for neglect of duty, one moiety thereof to the use of the town wherein the offence shall have been committed, and the other moiety to the use of the person suing for the same; yet a person injured by the inspector's neglect of official duty may recover damages sustained thereby, in an action on the case.[2] So if, in an action under the Kentucky statute, for damage to a beast, by the defendant, within his insufficient enclosures, the plaintiff fail in proving a case within the act; he may yet recover for the trespass at common law.[3] So, where the charter for a canal grants a summary process for injury to lands, such process has been held not to supersede a common-law action.[4] So it has been held that a statute, giving treble damages in case of trespass on land, does not take from the party the common-law remedy.[5] And, more especially, where a statute authorizes a corporation to do certain acts, and provides a remedy for only *a part* of the injury arising therefrom, the injured party may have his action at common law for the residue.[6]

1 Barden *v.* Crocker, 10 Pick. 383.
2 Hayes *v.* Porter, 9 Shep. 371.
3 Stewart *v.* Jewell, 7 Monr. 110.
4 Selden *v.* Delaware, &c. 24 Barb. 362.
5 Tackett *v.* Huesman, 19 Miss. 525.
6 Troy *v.* Cheshire, &c. 3 Fost. 83.

held, that, in such a case as the present, the common-law right to maintain an action in respect of a special damage, resulting from a breach of public duty, (whether such duty exists at common law or is created by statute,) is taken away by reason of a penalty recoverable by a common informer, being annexed as a punishment for the non-performance of the public duty." Per Lord Campbell, Couch *v.* Steel, 3 E. & B. 402, 413.

30. Questions have arisen, as to the effect upon an action of a repeal of the statute under which it was brought. Thus an action was brought under a statute for preventing trespasses on public land. Before the trial the statute was repealed, without any saving of suits instituted. Held, the action was no longer maintainable.[1] But where, pending such action, the law was repealed; but the next year an act was passed, providing that the repealing act should not defeat any action pending at the time of its passage; held, the action was maintainable.[2]

31. We have thus seen that the legality or illegality, in the light of the common or the statute law, of the act complained of, may to a greater or less degree determine, whether it shall constitute an actionable injury. It remains to be more particularly stated, as already suggested, that although a party's original act or conduct may have been right and lawful, there may be such an *abuse* of the powers and privileges which the law confers upon him, as will render him liable to an action, as for a trespass in the first instance. Upon this principle is founded the familiar doctrine of trespass *ab initio*. (*a*) And the rule is well established, that one

[1] Macnahoc, &c. *v.* Thompson, 36 Maine, 365. See chap. 20, s. 19 *a*.

[2] Plantation No. 9 *v.* Bean, 36 Maine, 359.

(*a*) This subject may be regarded as a very obscure one. The decisions are by no means reconcilable, more especially upon the two leading points, whether the authority abused must be *an authority of law*, and whether a mere *omission* is ever sufficient to constitute such trespass. The reader will gather his own conclusions from the cases cited. Mr. Greenleaf says: "If the bailee of a beast kill it, or if a joint tenant or tenant in common of a chattel destroy it, or if a tenant at will cuts down trees, the interest of the wrongdoer is thereby determined, and the possession, by legal intendment, immediately reverts to the owner or cotenant, and proof of the wrongful act will maintain the allegation that the thing injured was in his possession. So if one enters upon land, and cuts timber, under a parol agreement for the purchase of the land, which he afterwards repudiates as void under the Statute of Frauds, his right of possession also is thereby avoided *ab initio*, and is held to have remained in the owner, who may maintain trespass for cutting the trees. And generally, where a right of entry or

who has an authority *by law*, and does not pursue, or abuses it, is a trespasser *ab initio;* otherwise, in general, where the entry, authority, or license is given by *another party.*[1] Thus, where the plaintiff, an attorney, wrote to the defendant, to

[1] Walter *v.* Rumball, 4 Mod. 391; Adams *v.* Rivers, 11 Barb. 390; The Six Carpenters' case, 8 Co. 145 (said to be one of the most celebrated in Lord Coke's Reports, 1 Smith's L. C. 65); Adams *v.* Freeman, 12 Johns. 408; Bradley *v* Davis, 2 Shepl. 44; Garnett *v.* Gwathmey, 5 Blackf. 237; Van Brunt *v.* Schenck, 13 Johns. 414; Hunnewell *v.* Hobart, 42 Maine, 565.

---

other right of possession is given by law, and is afterwards abused by any act of unlawful force, the party is a trespasser *ab initio;* but if the wrong consists merely in the detention of chattels, beyond the time when they ought to have been returned, the remedy is in another form of action." 2 Greenl. on Ev. § 615.

The distinction has been made, that, if a person enters on land, by license of the owner, for a particular purpose, and, after entry, does other acts inconsistent with the authority given him, he does not thereby become a trespasser *ab initio*. *Aliter*, if he enters, by permission, under an agreement with the owner to purchase, and then refuses to carry the agreement into effect. Wendell *v.* Johnson, 8 N. Hamp. 220.

So, that where a person enters *by public license* or authority of law upon the premises of another, and afterwards, in the prosecution of his design, commits any unwarrantable act, the law regards him as a trespasser *ab initio*, and holds him fully answerable for all the injury committed. But, if he enters the premises of a private person by his consent, and afterwards commits an unlawful act, he is liable only for the injury committed subsequent to that act. Ballard *v.* Noaks, 2 Pike, 45.

Blackstone says, "If one comes into a tavern and will not go out in a reasonable time, but tarries there all night, contrary to the inclinations of the owner, this wrongful act shall affect and have relation back even to his first entry, and make the whole a trespass. But a bare nonfeasance, as not paying for the wine he calls for, will not make him a trespasser, for this is only a breach of contract for which the taverner shall have an action of debt or assumpsit against him." 3 Comm. 213.

If a person enter a dwelling-house by permission, and continue there after he has been requested to leave it, he becomes a trespasser *ab initio*. Adams *v.* Freeman, 12 Johns. 408.

Upon the same principle, a person is a trespasser, who, instead of passing along upon the sidewalk of a street, stops on it in front of another's house, and remains there, using towards him abusive and insulting language. Adams *v.* Rivers, 11 Barb. 390. See Lyford *v.* Putnam, 35 N. H. 563 Stone *v.* Knapp, 3 Wms. 501.

call upon him and settle a note left with him for collection; upon which the defendant came to the plaintiff's office, and while there mutilated the note and took it away; held, he could not be made liable as a trespasser for the entry.[1] So, in order to make a man a trespasser *ab initio*, it is held that the acts of abuse must be of such a character as to constitute a trespass if there were no license.[2] A mere *conversion* (*a*) of the property is insufficient.[3] So, *a fortiori*, a mere *non-feasance*;[4] as where, having taken goods under lawful authority, a party refuses to restore them, after his authority to detain them is determined.[5] And where an act is lawfully done, it cannot be made unlawful *ab initio*, unless by some positive act incompatible with the exercise of the legal right to do the first act; the mere intention of doing a subsequent illegal act is not sufficient.[6]

32. The principle in question is often applied (and more rigidly, and it would seem contrary to the prevailing rule, in reference to mere *omissions*, than in any other case,) to *officers*, in reference to the service of civil process. Thus, if a sheriff continue in possession after the return-day of the writ, that irregularity makes him a trespasser *ab initio*, though it will not support the allegation of a new trespass, committed by him after the acts which he justifies under the execution.[7] So, if an officer levy upon property, and advertise it for sale, but neglect to sell it upon the execution, this is a trespass

1 Dumont *v.* Smith, 4 Denio, 319.
2 Adams *v.* Rivers, 11 Barb. 390.
3 Davis *v.* Young, 20 Ala. 151.
4 Gardner *v.* Campbell, 15 Johns. 401.
5 Gardner *v.* Campbell, 15 Johns. 401.
6 Gates *v.* Loundsbury, 20 Johns. 427.
7 Aikenhead *v.* Blades, 5 Taunt. 198.

(*a*) But, as in other cases of trespass, the trespass may be waived, and the plaintiff may proceed as for a mere conversion. Thus A., finding B.'s sheep in his own close, drove them out of the close, and then drove them away to a considerable distance, to the injury of B. Held, that the driving of the sheep away was a wrongful act, which made A. a trespasser *ab initio*, and amounted to a conversion of the property; but that B. might waive the trespass and conversion, and recover for the damage sustained, in a special action on the case. Gilson *v.* Fisk, 8 N. Hamp. 404.

ab initio.[1] Or if a sheriff, or any person in his aid, make replevin after a claim of property notified to him.[2] Or if the bailiff of an inferior court abuses the process of the court.[3] So where a party, whose property was levied on by execution, objected to the sale, on the ground that the property was exempt from execution, but afterwards turned out the property to the sheriff to be sold at a future day; held, this was nothing more than a claim of exemption in order to gain time; that the sheriff, in subsequently selling the property, acted under a claim of authority given by law, and not by the party; (*a*) and that an abuse of his authority made him a trespasser *ab initio*.[4] So, if the distrainer of cattle *damage feasant* impounds them, without having the damages previously ascertained, as provided by statute; he is a trespasser *ab initio*.[5]

33. So trespass lies (and not case) for working an estray, though the original taking be lawful.[6]

34. But, in conformity with the rule already stated, it is held that even public officers cannot be made trespassers *ab initio*, unless by proof of some positive wrongful act, giving character to the original act, and incompatible with the exercise of the legal right to do such original act. Thus, where the plaintiff's vessel was seized under an act of congress, for having contraband freight on board, and the defendant did not make the seizure, but a United States officer, and the

[1] Bond *v.* Wilder, 16 Verm. 393.
[2] Leonard *v.* Stacy, 6 Mod. 140.
[3] Brigs *v.* Collingson, 6 Mod. 71.
[4] Carnrick *v.* Myers, 14 Barb. 9.
[5] Sackrider *v.* McDonald, 10 Johns. 253.
[6] Oxley *v.* Watts, 1 T. R. 12.

(*a*) But where a vessel has been seized by an officer of the customs, who after the seizure commits an abuse of the authority vested in him, and the vessel is then acquitted in the district court, but a certificate of probable cause given; the officer, although liable for the particular act of abuse, is protected by the certificate from being made a trespasser *ab initio*. Van Brunt *v.* Schenck, 13 Johns. 414.

If an officer justify in trespass, under a legal warrant, an act relied on to make him a trespasser *ab initio* should be newly assigned. Jarrett *v.* Gwathmey, 5 Blackf. 238.

defendant, though a deputy collector, assisted in unlading the vessel, but did not have charge of the same, the vessel being in charge of certain soldiers under the officer, and while so in charge, a severe gale arising, the vessel became a wreck; held, the defendant was not a trespasser.[1] And possession of property acquired under legal process, although the proceeding be afterwards dismissed, is not tortious.[2] Nor the taking an unreasonable quantity of goods by attachment.[3] So if an officer, having lawfully seized goods by virtue of a warrant of distress, wantonly removes them to a great distance before the sale, whereby the owner is injured; an action of the case may be maintained against him, but he is not for that cause a trespasser *ab initio*.[4] So a sheriff, having a writ of attachment, entered upon the defendant's land for the purpose of executing the writ, and took and carried away his goods, and deposited them in a place in the open air, but in which they were in no danger of injury, except from malice or wantonness; and a portion of them were afterwards destroyed by a person unknown. Held, the sheriff did not thereby become a trespasser *ab initio*, nor liable as such in trespass for the original entry.[5] And a landlord, (having substantially the rights in this respect of *an officer*,) who has accepted the rent in arrear, and the expenses of the distress, after the impounding, cannot be treated as a trespasser, merely because he retains the goods distrained, although his refusal to deliver them up may amount to a conversion, and render him liable in trover.[6]

35. While, as has been seen, an action lies, in general, for an act in itself unlawful, if also injurious; it is to be further observed, that acts innocent and lawful in themselves may become wrongful and fraudulent, when done without a just regard to the rights of others, and without suitable reference to the time, place, or manner of performing them.[7] Thus it

[1] Stoughton *v.* Mott, 25 Vt. 668.
[2] Smith *v.* Kershaw, 1 Kelly, 259.
[3] Moore *v.* Taylor, 5 Taunt. 69.
[4] Parrington *v.* Loring, 7 Mass. 388.
[5] Ferrin *v.* Symonds, 11 N. H. 363.
[6] West *v.* Nibbs, 4 Com. B. 172.
[7] Van Pelt *v.* McGraw, 4 Comst. 110; First Baptist, &c. *v.* Schenectady, &c. 5 Barb. 79.

is said, "The books of reports abound with decisions, restraining a man's acts upon and with his own property, where the necessary or probable consequence of such acts is to do damage to others."[1] So it is held, that the general rule, that the owner of land may use it according to his pleasure, is subject to this qualification, that he is not at liberty to use it in such a manner as to infringe on the rights of others;[2] unless he has acquired a special right by grant, or as an easement.[3] It is further said, that the maxim, *so use your own that you injure not another's* property, is supported by the soundest wisdom. But the injury intended is a *legal* injury; (*a*) an invasion of some legal right, as erecting a building, or carrying on a business on one's own land, which so obstructs the enjoyment by another of his own property as to be a nuisance; or removing the soil, or placing something on the soil of another. These are violations of absolute legal rights and are strict legal injuries.[4] So an action on the case has been held to lie, for negligently *keeping fire* in the defendant's close, by which the plaintiff

[1] Humphries *v.* Brogden, 12 Q. B. 739.

[2] Pickard *v.* Collins, 23 Barb. 444.

[3] Scott *v.* Bay, 3 Md. 431; Auburn, &c. *v.* Douglass, 5 Seld. 444.

[4] Pickard *v.* Collins, 23 Barb. 444.

(*a*) And a party is not in all cases liable for injury resulting from his use even of the property of another. Thus encamping and hunting upon the public lands in a *wilderness* district is not such an illegal and mischievous act, as to make the party responsible for all injury resulting therefrom; without regard to the amount of care, diligence, and prudence exercised by him to avoid such injury. Bizzell *v.* Booker, 16 Ark. 308.

But, where the defendants put a large quantity of logs upon the ice of a river, and, on the breaking up of the ice, a dam was formed by the logs and ice, and a channel cut through the plaintiff's land, and logs carried upon the land; and the defendants used no care in regard to the logs after they were put upon the ice; held, the defendants were liable. George *v.* Fisk, 32 N. H. 32.

The test of exemption from liability, for injury arising from the use of one's own property, is said in a recent case to be, the legitimate use or appropriation of the property in a reasonable, usual, and proper manner, without any negligence, unskilfulness, or malice. Carbart *v.* Auburn, &c. 22 Barb. 297.

was damaged.[1] (*a*) So one who dug a cellar under the sidewalk of a public street, in front of his estate, and left it in an unfinished state during a storm, whereby the water was turned and flowed into the cellar of an adjoining proprietor, and injured merchandise stowed therein; was held liable for the damage thus occasioned.[2] So, in an action on the case, for placing manure near a well, by which, an extraordinary rain coming on, the water therein was damaged; held, that a person should not place, nor negligently allow a deleterious substance to remain, where the useful waters of another may be corrupted, either by the ordinary or extraordinary, and yet not very uncommon action of the elements.[3] So, although the trade and occupation of carriage-making, or of a blacksmith, is a lawful and useful one; and a building erected for its exercise is not a nuisance *per se;* yet, if such building, though erected on the builder's own land, and occupied in the usual manner, be in an improper place, where its use will probably result in an injury to another; this is of itself a wrongful act, for which the wrong-doer is responsible to one essentially injured thereby.[4] So the fact, that the defendant used proper precautions in the working of his quarries, constitutes no vindication of him for injuries resulting to the plaintiff from blasting.[5] So the

[1] Tuberville *v.* Stamp, 1 Com. 33.
[2] Nelson *v.* Godfrey, 12 Ill. 20.
[3] Woodward *v.* Aborn, 35 Maine, 271.
[4] Whitney *v.* Bartholomew, 21 Conn. 213.
[5] Scott *v.* Bay, 3 Md. 431.

(*a*) But, in a late case, it is held, that, where one sets fire to his fallow wood and timber, and, without misconduct or carelessness on his part, the fire spreads to his neighbor's land and injures his property; no action lies therefor. So, although the weather was unusually dry, if the burning occurred in the month usually selected for that purpose, and though the defendant did nothing to prevent the fire from spreading. Stuart *v.* Hawley, 22 Barb. 619.

And, in general, one using fire for a lawful purpose, and guilty of no negligence, is not responsible for injuries caused thereby. Bizzell *v.* Booker, 16 Ark. 308. See Grannis *v.* Cummings, 25 Conn. 165; Averitt *v.* Murrell, 4 Jones, Law, 322.

owner of land on the shore of a stream or lake, or adjoining the track of a railroad, may lawfully build thereon, though the situation be one of exposure and hazard; and he is nevertheless entitled to protection, against the negligent acts of persons lawfully passing the same, with vessels or carriages propelled by steam-engines, by which such buildings are set on fire; and in such action it is competent for the plaintiff to show, that experienced persons in such employments were accustomed to use precautions which the defendant neglected.[1] So where bricklayers, employed by commissioners to repair a public sewer, performed the work in such a manner as to damage a neighboring house, although the work itself was skilfully executed; held, they were liable to an action.[2] So persons passing a dam, which is rightfully erected on a public stream, must use ordinary care, diligence, and skill; but where these are used, and the dam is such an obstruction to navigation as to occasion loss to those attempting its passage, the party erecting and maintaining the dam must answer in damages, no matter what was the stage of the water at the time of passing it.[3]

36. But, on the other hand, numerous cases recognize the principle, that an action on the case for consequential damages does not lie, for annoyance and hurt received from acts done on land adjoining the plaintiff's, which the proprietor might lawfully do in the exercise of his dominion over his own.[4] Thus, where one properly opens a covered drain upon his own land, which it becomes his duty to close again, in order to prevent the water from setting back and overflowing the adjoining land; he is bound to use ordinary care and prudence in closing such drain, and, if he does so, he is not responsible for any damage to his neighbor's land, caused by the sudden overflow of such drain.[5] So where a person, working in his new ground, within twenty-five

[1] Cook v. The Champlain Trans. Co. 1 Denio, 91.

[2] Jones v. Bird, 1 Dow. & Ry. 497.

[3] Plumer v. Alexander, 12 Penn. 81.

[4] McLauchlin v. Charlotte, &c. 5 Rich. 583.

[5] Rockwood v. Wilson, 11 Cush. 221.

yards of woods, puts fire to log-heaps when the weather is calm, and afterwards the wind, rising, drives the fire with irresistible violence into the woods; he is not liable for damages done by the fire.[1] (a) So ordinary caution and *honest motives* in setting fire to a prairie, and due diligence in preventing it from spreading, are a good defence to an action for injury caused by it;[2] although, if a party, in taking measures to protect his own property from imminent danger of flood, not using ordinary care, injures the property of others, he is not protected from liability by the absence of all *malicious or evil design*, and of all such gross carelessness as would authorize a presumption of bad intention.[3] So, where the owner of a coal mine excavated as far as the boundary (which he was by custom entitled to do), and continued the excavation wrongfully into the neighboring mine, leaving an aperture in the coal of that mine, through which water passed into it and did damage; held, he was liable in trespass for breaking into the neighboring mine, but not in case for omitting to close up the aperture; though a continuing damage resulted from its being unclosed. And therefore that, on the issue of not guilty, the defendant was entitled to the verdict. It was doubted, whether he was under legal obligation to use means on his own land for preventing the flow of water; but held, that, in an action for not using such means, the declaration must allege the duty specifically; and not merely that the defendant wrong-

[1] Averitt *v.* Murrell, 4 Jones, Law, 323.

[2] De France *v.* Spencer, 2 Greene, 462.

[3] Noyes *v.* Shepherd, 30 Maine, 173.

(a) Thomas, J., says (11 Cush. 226): "It is only upon proof of negligence that the action could be maintained. The case is not that of the erection or maintenance of a private nuisance, the doing of an unlawful act; but the doing of a thing lawful in itself, in such careless way as to injure the plaintiffs. The distinction is vital; for nothing can be better settled than that if one do a lawful act upon his own premises, he cannot be held responsible for injurious consequences that may result from it, unless it was so done as to constitute actionable negligence."

fully made the aperture, and omitted for an unreasonable time to close it, whereby, &c. Also, that no such action would lie, if an action on the case has already been brought, for making the aperture and letting in the water, and referred to arbitration, and the plaintiff, being made party to the reference, in respect of any injury to him by any of the matters alleged in the declaration, has had damages awarded and paid to him for such injury; although the damage last complained of is subsequent to the award and payment.[1] So, although one who demises premises, for carrying on a business necessarily injurious to the adjacent proprietors, is liable as the author of the nuisance; where the letting is for a lawful purpose, which can become injurious only under special circumstances, the lessor will not be liable, unless he knew or had reason to believe, that the business would be so conducted as to render it a nuisance.[2] So, where a party entitled to a limited right exercises it to excess, so as himself to cause a nuisance, or create a right of action entire in its nature; (as where a window or a drain is enlarged or applied to other purposes than originally authorized;) as the entire nuisance may be abated, an action for an obstruction of the original right of easement cannot be maintained, until its exercise has been reduced within its original limits; and, if an action is brought for the obstruction, in which the right is declared upon according to its enlarged exercise, and the declaration is not supported by the proof, on a traverse of the right as laid, an amendment will not be allowed, since the effect would be to evade, and not to determine the question really in controversy between the parties. Thus, where the declaration was for obstructing a drain, over which the plaintiff was alleged to have had a right of user, and which he had used for general drainage; and the right proved was only to use the drain, not for foul drainage, but for ordinary refuse water, the

[1] Clegg v. Dearden, 12 Ad. & El. N. S. 576.

[2] Fish v. Dodge, 4 Denio, 311.

plaintiff failed at the trial, and the Court refused an amendment.[1]

37. It will be noticed, that the prominent point of inquiry, in the class of cases which we have been considering, is, whether the defendant has been guilty of *negligence*. But it still remains, without reference to those other incidental points already referred to, which go to prove or disprove legal liability, to speak more directly of the rules of law applicable to *negligence*.

38. Negligence is said to consist in the omitting to do something that a reasonable man would do, or the doing something that a reasonable man would not do; in either case causing, unintentionally, mischief to a third party. A party who takes reasonable care, to guard against accidents arising from ordinary causes, is not liable for accidents arising from extraordinary ones. (*a*) Thus where a company, incorporated for supplying a street with water, constructed their apparatus according to the best known system, and kept it in proper repair for twenty-five years, at the end of which time a frost of unusual severity acted on the apparatus so as to cause injury to the property of another person; held, the company were not liable for negligence.[2] So, on the other hand, when a man erects a building to rent, he is bound to employ reasonable skill and diligence in such erection, regard being had to the uses and purposes for which it was designed; and if, after it was finished, he knew there were defects in it, which unfitted it for the intended purpose, and his lease does not stipulate against its being used for such purpose, and if, thus being used, it suddenly falls and injures

[1] Cawkwell *v.* Russell, 38 Eng. L. & Eq. 351.

[2] Blyth *v.* Birmingham, &c. 36 Eng. L. & Eq. 506.

(*a*) *Ordinary diligence* is said not to be the proper legal phrase to express the degree of care which a party is bound to use. It should be, such diligence as a prudent man in such a situation, and under the circumstances surrounding, would have observed, to prevent accident to others. Bizzell *v.* Booker, 16 Ark. 308.

a laborer employed therein who was guilty of no carelessness, the owner is liable to such laborer for injuries sustained by the fall of the building.[1]

39. But, although the defendant may seem to have exercised ordinary care, and the injury occur in part from natural causes which he could not control, yet a verdict for the plaintiff will not be set aside. Thus the plaintiffs shipped goods on board a steam-vessel, the bill of lading containing the usual exceptions of the act of God, &c. On the evening before she was expected to sail, the boiler was, according to custom, filled with water; but, in consequence of the action of frost, a pipe communicating with it burst, and the water escaped into the hold, and damaged the goods. In an action against the owners, it was left to the jury to say, whether or not, in leaving the boiler filled with water in frosty weather, the owners had been guilty of negligence. They found for the plaintiffs, and the Court refused to disturb the verdict.[2]

40. Negligence is held a mixed question of law and fact; where the facts have been ascertained by the jury, whether they warrant the charge of negligence or not, is a matter of law.[3] But, in some instances, *the Court* may pass upon the question of negligence, and order a verdict for the plaintiff. Thus, in an action in a county court, for negligently driving a horse and cart, the plaintiff having simply proved the fact of a collision, under circumstances which might or might not amount to negligence, the defendant proved, that the accident arose from the horse suddenly beginning to kick, whereby the shafts of the cart were broken and the driver thrown out, when the horse started off, and ran against and injured the plaintiff's horse. The Judge of the county court, upon this evidence, ordered a verdict for the plaintiff, "being of opinion that the breaking of the shafts, even under the cir-

[1] Godly *v.* Hagerty, 20 Penn. 387.

[2] Siordet *v.* Hall, 1 Moo. & P. 561.

[3] Foot *v.* Wiswall, 14 Johns. 304; Moore *v.* Central, &c. 4 Zabr. 268. See United States *v.* Taylor, 5 McL. 242; Curtis *v.* Rochester, &c. 20 Barb. 282; Hayett *v.* Philadelphia, &c. 23 Penn. 373; Oldfield *v.* New York, &c. 3 E. D. Smith, 103.

cumstances stated by the defendant's witnesses, showed a defect in the cart, which raised a presumption of negligence in the owner." An appeal against his decision was dismissed with costs.[1]

41. So, on the other hand, the Court may sometimes properly order a nonsuit, more especially where by his own showing the plaintiff has been guilty of negligence. Thus a gas company, incorporated with the usual powers to take up pavements, &c., for the purpose of laying down and repairing mains, pipes, &c., had for some years supplied gas to a house belonging to the plaintiff; the only means of shutting it off being by a stop-cock within the house, the key of which was kept by the occupier. The last tenant, on quitting, gave notice to the company, that he should not require any further supply; and one of their workmen, at his request, removed a chandelier from one of the rooms, leaving the end of the pipe properly secured. The internal fittings were the property of the plaintiff. Whilst the house remained untenanted, the gas by some unexplained means escaped, and an explosion took place, by which the house was damaged. In case against the company, alleging a breach of duty on their part in not taking proper means to prevent the influx of the gas into the house, the Judge having, upon the above facts, directed a nonsuit, the Court declined to interfere.[2]

42. A much stricter standard than *ordinary care* — testing the word *ordinary* by mere local or limited custom and usage in like cases — has been often applied. Thus the law requires of persons having in their custody *instruments of danger*, that they should keep them *with the utmost care*. Therefore where the defendant, being possessed of a loaded gun, sent a young girl to fetch it, with directions to take the priming out, which was accordingly done, and a damage accrued to the plaintiff's son, in consequence of the girl's presenting the gun at

[1] Templeman *v.* Haydon, 12 Com. B. 507.

[2] Holden *v.* Liverpool, &c. 3 Com. B. 1; Central, &c. *v.* Moore, 4 Zabr. 824.

him and drawing the trigger, when the gun went off; held, the defendant was liable.[1] So in an action by the occupier of the surface of land, for negligently and improperly, and without leaving any sufficient pillars and supports, and *contrary to the custom* of mining in the country where, &c., working the subjacent minerals, *per quod* the surface gave way; upon the plea of not guilty, it appeared that the plaintiff was in occupation of the surface, and the defendant of the subjacent minerals, but there was no evidence how they became so. The surface was not built upon. The jury found, that the defendants had worked the mines carefully and according to custom, but without leaving sufficient support for the surface. Held, the plaintiff was, on this finding, entitled to the verdict; for, of *common right*, the owner of the surface is entitled to support from the subjacent strata; and, if the owner of the minerals removes them, it is his duty to leave sufficient support for the surface in its natural state.[2] So, in an action against mill-owners for not securely fencing a part of the machinery of their mill, whereby injury was occasioned to one of the persons employed there, the Judge left the question to the jury, whether the machinery was fenced *in the ordinary manner*, used and approved as sufficient at the best regulated mills of the district. Held a misdirection; the proper question being, whether the mill was securely fenced, according to the best known method of fencing at the time.[3]

43. And even *the greatest care* has been sometimes held to be no defence. Thus, where the defendants dug a canal on their own lands, and in executing the works blasted the rocks, so as to cast the fragments against the plaintiff's house on contiguous lands; held, that evidence to show the work done in the most careful manner was inadmissible, there being no claim to recover exemplary damages, and the jury having been instructed to render their verdict for actual dam-

1 Dixon *v.* Bell, 5 M. & Sel. 198.

2 Humphries *v.* Brogden, 12 Ad. & Ell. N. S. 739. See Richards *v.* Sperry, 2 Wis. 216.

3 Schofield *v.* Schunck, 30 Eng. L. & Eq. 233.

ages only.[1] So, where a druggist, requested to compound a certain medicine, grinds the different ingredients in a mill used to grind poisonous drugs, without properly cleansing it; the rule, as to the degree of care and diligence necessary to exempt a party from liability, does not apply; but a druggist is *bound to know* the properties of the medicines he vends, and he and his servants are liable to a person, injured by a prescription improperly prepared, even though he used extraordinary care and diligence in compounding the medicine.[2]

44. And in some cases *want of ordinary care* and *gross negligence* have been treated as alike creating a liability for any injury arising therefrom. Thus an action lies against a party, for so negligently constructing a hay-rick on the extremity of his land, that, in consequence of its spontaneous ignition, his neighbor's house is burnt down. And, upon pleas of not guilty, and that there was no negligence; held, that it was properly left to the jury to say, whether the defendant had been guilty of *gross negligence*, viewing his conduct with reference to the caution which *a prudent man* would have observed.[3] So, in an action on the case against the defendant, for carelessly and negligently setting a fire on his own land, whereby the plaintiff's property on adjoining land was consumed; it is not material, whether the proof shows *gross negligence* or only *want of ordinary care*, for in either case the plaintiffs would be entitled to recover only damages to the amount of their actual loss, either vindictive or otherwise.[4]

45. It will be seen hereafter, (*a*) that under some circumstances a loss, affirmatively proved, will be *presumed* to have resulted from the negligence of the defendant, throwing upon him the burden of disproving such negligence. Thus proof

[1] Tremain *v.* The Cohoes, &c. 2 Comst. 163.

[2] Fleet *v.* Hallenkemp, 13 B. Mon. 219.

[3] Vaughan *v.* Menlove, 3 Bing. N. R. 468.

[4] Barnard *v.* Poor, 21 Pick. 378.

(*a*) See *Carrier*, *Railroad*, *Bailment.*

of injury to a passenger on a railroad is held *primâ facie* evidence of negligence.[1] So in an action against a railway company, it is sufficient to show damage resulting from an act of the defendants, which with proper care does not ordinarily produce damage, unless they prove proper care, or some extraordinary accident which renders care useless.[2] (*a*) And the same rule has been sometimes adopted in other cases. Thus it has been recently held, that, in case of alleged careless and unskilful treatment by a surgeon, negligence may be proved by the nature of the act itself; that extrinsic proof is not required.[3]

46. In general, however, a different principle prevails, and the burden of proving negligence is devolved upon the plaintiff. Thus, where the plaintiff was injured by the giving way of the grating over a vault in the sidewalk; it was held, that he must show affirmatively a neglect of duty on the part of the defendant corporation; that it was not sufficient to prove merely that the grate was insufficiently fastened.[4] So, in an action for injury to the plaintiff's land and fences, caused by the negligence of the defendant in setting fire on his own land, and keeping the same; the burden of proof is upon the plaintiff, to show that the injury resulted from such negligence.[5] So where the payee of a written order, requesting the defendant to pay out of the proceeds of a certain judgment, when collected, brings suit, after acceptance, for the defendant's negligence in collecting and failing to pay when collected; the burden of proving negligence is on the plaintiff, and not on the defendant to prove

[1] Zemp *v.* Wilmington, &c. 9 Rich. Law, 84. But see Terry *v.* New York, &c. 22 Barb. 574; Holbrook *v.* Utica, &c. 2 Kern. 236.

[2] Ellis *v.* Railroad Co. 2 Ired. 138.

[3] Leighton *v.* Sargent, 11 Fost. 119.

[4] M'Ginity *v.* Mayor, &c. 5 Duer, 674.

[5] Batchelder *v.* Heagan, 6 Shep. 32.

(*a*) Where the fact of damage from the fire of the railroad was established, and the manner in which the fire was communicated; held, it was immaterial whether the evidence came from the plaintiff or the defendant, and the question of negligence should be left to the jury. McCready *v.* South Carolina, &c. 2 Strobh. 356.

diligence.[1] So in an action against a city by the father of an infant drowned by falling into a water-tank, constructed by the city and not sufficiently protected; the burden of proof is on the plaintiff, to show not only ordinary care on the part of the protectors of the child, but also negligence on the part of the city.[2] So the defendant, having interfered to part his dog and the plaintiff's, which were fighting, in raising his stick for that purpose, accidentally struck the plaintiff and injured him. Held, the parting of the dogs was a lawful and proper act, which the defendant might do by the use of proper and safe means; and if, in so doing, and while using due care, and taking all proper precautions necessary to the exigency of the case, to avoid hurt to others, the injury to the plaintiff occurred, the defendant was not liable therefor; and that the burden of proof was on the plaintiff, to establish the want of due care on the part of the defendant. Held, also, that if, at the time of the injury, both parties were not using ordinary care, the plaintiff could not recover, without showing that the damage was caused wholly by the act of the defendant, and that the plaintiff's own negligence did not contribute as an efficient cause to produce it.[3]

47. In an action for negligence, it is enough that the proof conforms substantially to the declaration. Thus, where the allegation was negligence in the conduct and management of the fires in the furnaces of a steamboat, while such boat was passing the plaintiff's building; it was held competent to prove, that the fires were unusually large when the boat left the dock, shortly before.[4] And the most general statement of the cause of action, if sufficient to put the defendant on his defence, is sufficient, after verdict.[5] Thus a declaration, alleging in substance that the plaintiff's animal, being upon the track of the defendant's railroad, was there negligently and carelessly run over and killed by their train, is sufficient. And such declaration is good after verdict, although the neg-

[1] Gliddon v. McKinstry, 28 Ala. 408.
[2] Chicago v. Mayor. 18 Ill. 349.
[3] Brown v. Kendall, 6 Cush. 292.
[4] Cook v. Champlain, &c. 1 Denio, 91.
[5] Taylor v. Day, 16 Verm. 566.

ligence of the defendants existed in relation to their fences, and not in the management of their train.[1] So a declaration, charging that the defendant wrongfully kept a horse accustomed to bite mankind, and that he knew it, need not allege that the injury occurred through his negligence in keeping the horse.[2] So, where the plaintiff in an action on the case declares, that the defendant, *contriving and maliciously intending* to injure and aggrieve the plaintiff, dug up the soil of a contiguous lot, whereby the foundation wall of the plaintiff's house was injured, &c.; evidence of *negligence* on the part of the defendant will support the declaration; the allegation of malice being immaterial, as it might be struck out as surplusage, and there still be left a good cause of action.[3]

48. The term negligence embraces acts of *omission*, as well as *commission*, and diligence implies action as well as forbearance to act.[4] The torts, which in various points of view we have been considering, consist wholly or chiefly of *misfeasances*. With regard to the right of action for a tort or wrong, which consists in the omission or refusal to do a particular act, or a *nonfeasance;* it is said, if one undertakes to do a thing without hire or reward, no action lies for the nonfeasance. But otherwise where he enters upon the doing it, and any misfeasance be through his neglect or mismanagement. As where one assumes to take up a hogshead of wine in one cellar and lay it down in another, and lays it down so negligently that it is staved, &c.[5] So one, who gratuitously accepts the office of steward of a horse-race, is not responsible for a loss resulting to one who enters a horse for the race, from his mere nonfeasance in omitting to appoint a judge; at all events, unless it appears that he has actually entered upon the duties of his office.[6] So it has been doubted whether, under any circumstances, an action at law lies against a clergyman for refusing to perform the

[1] Smith *v.* Eastern Railroad, 35 N. H. 356.

[2] Popplewell *v.* Pierce, 10 Cush. 509.

[3] Panton *v.* Holland, 17 Johns. 92.

[4] Grant *v.* Moseley, 29 Ala. 302

[5] Coggs *v.* Barnard, 1 Salk. 26, 5 T. R. 143; 1 Saun. 312 c. n. 2; Hyde *v.* Moffatt, 16 Verm. 271.

[6] Balfe *v.* West, 13 Com. B. 466.

marriage ceremony.[1] But it has been held, that an action lies against a farrier for refusing to shoe a horse.[2] This subject, however, will be more appropriately considered in another connection. (*a*)

[1] Davis *v.* Black, 1 Ad. & Ell. N. S. 900.

[2] Lane *v.* Cotton, 1 Com. 106.

(*a*) See *Bailment.*

CHAPTER IV.

ACTIONS BROUGHT BY PLAINTIFFS, WHO HAVE THEMSELVES BEEN GUILTY OF WRONG OR NEGLIGENCE, OR IN PARI DELICTO.

1. HAVING considered the general question, what is necessary, with more particular reference to the wrongdoer himself, to constitute in law a tort or private wrong, we proceed to state and illustrate another comprehensive principle upon the same subject, which applies more especially to the party complaining of such tort, and not to the party charged with committing it.

2. The general rule is, (*a*) that a plaintiff, suing for culpable

---

(*a*) The legal maxims applicable to the subject are "in pari delicto, potior est conditio defendentis," and "volenti non fit injuria." Also, that a plaintiff must come into court *with clean hands.* The plaintiff "must show that he stands on a fair ground, when he calls on a court of justice to administer relief to him." Per Ld. Kenyon, Booth *v.* Hodgson, 6 T. R. 409.

fault or negligence, must himself be without any misconduct or fault, and have used ordinary care; and that, where an injury has resulted from the negligence of both parties, (a) more especially if without any wanton or intentional wrong on the part of either, an action cannot be maintained.[1] So it is the prevailing doctrine, that, to sustain an action on the case for negligence, *the burden of proof* is on the plaintiff to show negligence, wilful or otherwise, on the part of the defendant, and ordinary care on his own part; or, if he did not exercise ordinary care, that this did not contribute to the alleged injury.[2] So there must be affirmative proof of due care *at the very time of the accident*, and it is said neither the urgency of business nor the calls of humanity can be taken into account.[3] And negligence on the part of the

[1] Brown *v.* Maxwell, 6 Hill, 592; Murch *v.* Concord, &c. 9 Fost. 9; Mayor, &c. *v.* Marriott, 9 Md. 160; Brownell *v.* Flagler, 5 Hill, 282; Munger *v.* The Tonawanda, &c. 4 Comst. 349; Birge *v.* Gardiner, 19 Conn. 507; Wynn *v.* Allard, 5 W. & S. 524; Williams *v.* Michigan, &c. 2 Mich. 259; Central, &c. *v.* Moore, 4 Zabr. 824; Brooks *v.* Buffalo, &c. 25 Barb. 600; Dickey *v.* Maine, &c. 43 Maine, 492 Reeves *v,* Delaware, &c. 30 Penn. 454 Jacobs *v.* Duke, 1 E. D. Smith, 271 Timmons *v.* Central, &c. 6 Ohio, N. S 105.

[2] Perkins *v.* Eastern, &c. 29 Maine 307; Dyer *v.* Tolcott, 15 Ill. 300; Galena, &c. *v.* Fay, Ib. 558. But see Moore *v.* Central, &c. 4 Zabr. 268.

[3] Hyde *v.* Jamaica, 1 Williams, 443

As to the effect of wrong or consent on the part of the injured or complaining party upon *criminal* proceedings, see 1 Bish. on Crim. L. 340.

(a) Where land is vacant, and the title is in the State, all occupiers are trespassers, and one cannot maintain trespass against another. Tubbs *v.* Lynch, 4 Harring. 521.

So one trespasser or wrongdoer cannot maintain trover against another Thus persons cutting timber on lands of the United States have not such a property therein as will support trover. Tuley *v.* Tucker, 6 Mis. 58[?]

Contrary to the general rule, that every material fact necessary to be *proved* must also be expressly *alleged;* it is held, that, in case for an injury resulting from the alleged negligence of the defendants, it is not necessary to allege that the plaintiff was without fault. Smith *v.* The Eastern Railroad, 35 N. H. 356.

And, contrary to the general rule stated in the text, in an action against a ferryman, for injuries sustained in crossing the ferry, it is held not incumbent on the plaintiff to prove ordinary care to avoid the injury; but the proof of want of it lies on the defendant. May *v.* Hanson, 5 Cal. 360.

plaintiff is an admissible defence under the plea of not guilty.[1] More especially where damage is done by a party *in the exercise of his lawful rights*, the plaintiff must prove that his loss occurred without fault on his part, and in consequence of the neglect of the defendant.[2] So, although the defendants were guilty of gross negligence, causing damage to the plaintiff, but the plaintiff was also guilty of want of ordinary care, contributing essentially to the injury, he cannot recover.[3]

3. But what is due or ordinary care, must depend upon the circumstances of each case, (see § 17). Thus what would be ordinary care at the crossing of a highway, may be gross negligence at that of a railroad; (*a*) and upon this question the jury are to judge, (see § 18); and, if there are no facts proved from which a deduction can be drawn, the presumption is against the defendant, whose misconduct has rendered the accident possible. (*b*) And, in such a case,

[1] Holden *v.* Liverpool, &c. 3 Com. B. 1.

[2] Waldron *v.* Portland, &c. 35 Maine, 422.

[3] Neal *v.* Gillett, 23 Conn. 437.

(*a*) It is gross negligence in a person to stop on a railroad track, at the usual time for the passage of a train, and allow his attention to be diverted in another direction from the cars, until he is thrown from the track by a collision. Brooks *v.* Buffalo, &c. 25 Barb. 600.

(*b*) In this as in other cases, the question of the liability of one party to another may be affected by the consideration of *notice*. Thus the defendant, owner of a steamboat, agreed to tow a flatboat with cargo, at the risk of the plaintiff, the owner. By gross negligence, in towing too fast, the flatboat was sunk, and the cargo injured. It also appeared, that the flatboat was not skilfully loaded, and the towing thereby made more hazardous, of which, however, the defendant had notice. Held, the defendant was liable. Wright *v.* Gaff, 6 Ind. 416.

But, in case by the executors of a stockholder against the Bank of England, for refusing to transfer stock of the testatrix, and to pay the dividends; it appeared that nearly all the stock had been sold and transferred in her lifetime by her nephew A., who had brought another woman to personate her, and forge her signature. After the sale, the testatrix had repeatedly received the warrants for the reduced dividends in person, and had signed

the burden of proving want of ordinary care on the part of the plaintiff lies on the defendant.[1] Thus in an action for an injury, from being thrown down upon iron instruments placed by the defendant in the highway, contrary to the common law, and to a local act of parliament, the defence set up, under the general issue, was negligence on the part of the plaintiff, of which negligence no distinct evidence was given. The Judge left it to the jury, whether the plaintiff had been so deficient in reasonable and ordinary care, that he had brought the accident upon himself. A verdict having been found for the defendant, it was held, that the instruction was right. But the verdict was set aside as against evidence.[2] So, as further illustrative of the proposition that the whole question is for the jury, in an action against a railway company, for negligence in the management at a station, whereby the plaintiff, a passenger, was injured; the defence was, that the accident arose entirely from the plaintiff's own want of caution. The evidence showed, that the plaintiff arrived at the station about two minutes or less before the time of departure, and, in running along the line, at a place where he ought not to have gone, in order to reach the train, which was some distance ahead on the opposite side of the railway, he fell over a switch-handle, and was considerably hurt. The Judge left it to the jury, whether the injury was occasioned by the negligence of the defendants, or resulted entirely from the plaintiff's careless-

[1] Beatty *v.* Gilmore, 16 Penn. 463; Central, &c. *v.* Moore, 4 Zabr. 824; Johnson *v.* Hudson, &c. 5 Duer, 21.

[2] Mariott *v.* Stanley, 1 M. & Gr. 568.

---

the warrants and the bank-books, being accompanied by A., who mentioned the amount of dividend in her presence. The jury found, that she had the means of knowing of the transfer, but that there was no evidence of actual knowledge; that she had been guilty of gross negligence; and that the defendants had not been guilty of any. Judgment for the defendants. Coles *v.* Bank, &c. 10 Ad. & Ell. 437.

So, in case of injury by an *animal*, no action lies, if the plaintiff knew it to be mischievous, and himself contributed to the injury. Earhart *v.* Youngblood, 27 Penn. 331.

ness. Held, a correct proceeding, although the Judge did not call the jury's attention to the intermediate case of negligence of both parties.[1] (*a*)

4. With regard to the nature or degree of the connection between the plaintiff's own conduct and the injury complained of, it has been held, that, if the *proximate* cause of damage be the plaintiff's unskilfulness, or wilful misconduct, although the *primary* cause be the misfeasance of the defendant, the former cannot recover. (*b*) Thus, although bodily injury be caused to the plaintiff through a breach of duty on the part of the defendant, no action lies, if the plaintiff wilfully, and contrary to the command of the defendant, committed the act which was the direct cause of the injury. Thus an action was brought by the plaintiff, employed in a factory, against the defendants, the occupiers, for not sufficiently fencing a shaft while in motion, as required by Stat. 7 & 8 Vict. c. 15, § 21, whereby the plaintiff got entangled with it and injured. Plea, admitting that the shaft was not sufficiently fenced, but alleging that the plaintiff, contrary to

[1] Martin *v.* Great Northern, &c. 16 Com. B. 179.

(*a*) So an action of trespass cannot be maintained against the master of a vessel, for carrying to sea an officer, who went on board to arrest a person just as the vessel was leaving the wharf; if the plaintiff did not use due diligence to get on shore, after receiving due notice that the vessel's fasts were about to be cast off, and that all persons not belonging on board must leave her. And when the facts are in dispute, the question, whether the plaintiff used due diligence in making the arrest and in attempting to get on shore, is to be decided by the jury. Spoor *v.* Spooner, 12 Met. 281.

So, the pilot having testified that he got the vessel off; that in so doing he acted under the direction of the owner; and that the master had no agency in the matter; it is for the jury to decide, who had the direction and control of the vessel. Ibid.

(*b*) On the other hand, where an injury happens to a party by the proximate wrong of another, the latter shall be liable, even though the remote negligence of the former contributed to produce it. Indianapolis, &c. *v.* Caldwell, 9 Ind. 397, (infra, s. 17.)

Thus the plaintiff's drunkenness is no defence, to an action for damages sustained by him in falling into an uncovered hole, in the sidewalk of a public street. Robinson *v.* Pioche, 5 Cal. 460.

the express command of the defendants, and knowing that it was dangerous to meddle with the shaft, took hold of it and set it in motion, whereby, and not by reason of the negligence of the defendants, the plaintiff was injured. Held, on demurrer, a good plea.[1] More especially does this rule apply, if the mischief be in part occasioned by the misfeasance of a third person. Thus, where the defendant placed lime-rubbish in a highway; and the dust blown from it frightened the horse of the plaintiff, and nearly carried him into contact with a passing wagon; in avoiding which, he unskilfully drove over other rubbish, and was overthrown and hurt: held, he could not recover.[2]

4 *a*. But in an action against a town, for an injury happening through the insufficiency of a road, which it is made their duty by statute to repair; if the road be out of repair, and the injury happen on that account, and the plaintiff or his agents are guilty of no want of care and prudence; the defendants are held liable, notwithstanding *the primary cause* of the injury was the failure of a nut or bolt, which was insufficient or improperly fastened.[3] So, in an action for assault and battery, the defendant cannot show, that the injury was aggravated by the intemperate habits of the plaintiff.[4] And it will be seen hereafter (§ 17) that the rule above stated as to *proximate* and remote causes has been often questioned, and cannot be regarded as settled law.

5. Upon the principle above stated, at common law, if *a collision* happen on land or on water, whether between moving vehicles, or between one such vehicle and a fixed obstruction, (*a*) which is the result of inevitable accident,

[1] Caswell *v.* Worth, 5 Ell. & Bl. 849.

[2] Flower *v.* Adam, 2 Taunt. 314; Grant *v.* Moseley, 29 Ala. 302.

[3] Hunt *v.* Pownal, 9 Verm. 411.

[4] Littlehale *v.* Dix, 11 Cush. 364.

(*a*) It is sometimes held, that, in case of *collision of ships*, where both parties were to blame, or wanting in due diligence or skill; the loss shall be apportioned. Simpson *v.* Hand, 6 Whart. 311. And the maritime law on this subject, founded upon reasons peculiar to itself, doubtless varies from the general rule stated in the text.

or the mutual fault of both parties; each must bear his own loss.[1] And this, whether the negligence is on the part of the plaintiff himself, or of those having the guidance of the carriage or vessel in which he is a passenger; if such injury might have been avoided by reasonable care on his or their part.[2] So one injured by riding against an obstruction in the highway cannot recover damages, if he was riding violently and without ordinary care, and might with due care have seen and avoided the obstruction.[3] In order to support an action for damages received by an obstruction or defect in the highway, two things must concur: 1. an obstruction existing by the fault of the defendant; 2. reasonable or ordinary care on the part of the plaintiff.[4] (a) And, in an action for an injury to the plaintiff, alleged to have been occasioned by the defendant's negligence in driving on the highway, the burden of proof is on the plaintiff, not only to show negligence and misconduct on the part of the defendant, but ordinary care and diligence

[1] Duggins v. Watson, 15 Ark. 118; Brooks v. Buffalo, &c. 25 Barb. 600.

[2] Thorogood v. Bryan, 8 Com. B. 115; Smith v. Smith, 2 Pick. 621; Flower v. Adam, 2 Taunt, 314; Vanderplank v. Miller, 1 M. & M. 169.

[3] Butterfield v. Forrester, 11 E. 60.

[4] Branan v. May, 17 Geo. 136; Griffin v. Mayor, &c. 5 Seld. 456; Garmon v. Bangor, 38 Maine, 443.

(a) With regard to the degree of care required from a traveller upon the highway, it has been held, that, where such traveller, on coming to a bridge, stopped, and ordered his servant to examine its condition, which being reported unsafe, he then ordered him to examine the depth of the stream which was erroneously reported as fordable; these acts showed ordinary care. Branan v. May, 17 Geo. 136. (See *Town.*)

The defendant's gig, in which he was driving at a "brisk trot" through a "narrow street," came in contact with the plaintiff's horse, which was loose in the street, and was walking obliquely across the defendant's course, and killed him. Held, that the accident was owing to the defendant's carelessness, or to his imprudent driving, and that he was liable for the value of the horse. Payne v. Smith, 4 Dana, 497.

Where a traveller, driving with ordinary care, suffers from a collision caused by the carelessness of the driver of another vehicle, either in attempting to pass from behind, or in having an unmanageable horse; he may maintain an action against such driver. Foster v. Goddard, 40 Maine, 64.

on his own part.[1] So it is not sufficient to show that the defendant was on the wrong side of the road.[2] And in an action for damages caused by collision with a locomotive, it is not sufficient to show the negligence of the defendant, provided the plaintiff could with ordinary care have avoided its consequences.[3] So in an action for injury to the plaintiff's steamboat, if the officers and crew were guilty of such negligence, either in respect to the lights required by law or otherwise, as essentially to contribute to the injury, the plaintiff cannot recover.[4] So a plaintiff cannot recover at law for mischief done to his ship, by its being struck by the defendant's ship, in consequence of any degree of improper management of the latter, if the former was improperly managed, and such management *directly* contributed in any degree to the accident. Though, if the negligence of the plaintiff only *remotely* contributed to the accident, the question is, whether the defendant by ordinary care and skill might have avoided it.[5] So, in a collision of boats on the *canals*, if both parties are equally in the wrong, neither of the owners can maintain an action against the other. As where the loss is sustained in the night-time, partly from a want of lights on the boat injured, or from its being out of the proper place on meeting the other boat. In such case, the defendant is answerable only for gross negligence or wanton injury.[6]

6. Upon the same principle, where the plaintiff's property receives injury through the carelessness of the defendant in the construction of a sewer, *no carelessness being imputable to the plaintiff*, he may recover damages for the loss.[7] So one injured by a defect in the covering of a sewer must prove that he could not have escaped by ordinary care.[8] So, in an action for an injury sustained by the plaintiff, from falling

[1] Lane *v.* Crombie, 12 Pick. 177; Adams *v.* Carlisle, 21 Pick. 146.

[2] Parker *v.* Adams, 12 Met. 415.

[3] Moore *v.* Central, &c. 4 Zabr. 268; Runyon *v.* Central, &c. 1 Dutch. 556.

[4] New Haven, &c. *v.* Vanderbilt, 16 Conn. 420.

[5] Dowell *v.* General, &c. 5 Ell. & B. 194.

[6] Rathbun *v.* Paine, 19 Wend. 399.

[7] Reeves *v.* Larkin, 19 Mis. 192.

[8] Owings *v.* Jones, 9 Md. 108.

through a passage into a cellar of the defendant's house, erected on a public street, which was left exposed through the defendant's neglect; the plaintiff cannot recover, if by ordinary or reasonable care he might have avoided the injury.[1] So the owner of certain lots, on the rear of which were houses occupied by his tenants, while improving the front of the lots by putting up buildings there, opened a way for the ingress and egress of the tenants through an adjoining lot. New alley-ways were opened, while the new buildings were enclosed, along the walls of these buildings, which the rear tenants began to use, the way through the adjoining lot still remaining open. The plaintiff, who had two daughters, tenants in the rear, wished to visit them in the night-time, and, finding the alleys by the new houses obstructed, undertook to grope through the basement hall of the new building, fell through, and was injured. Held, he had no right to maintain an action for damages, founded on the negligence of the mechanics engaged on the building.[2] So a trespasser, having knowledge that there are spring-guns in a wood, although he may be ignorant of the particular spots where they are placed, cannot maintain an action for an injury received by accidentally treading on the latent wire communicating with a gun, and thereby letting it off.[3] So, if an action will lie by an administrator against a wrongdoer, for an injury sustained by the acts of the latter, in threatening to prosecute any person who should purchase or remove certain personal property offered for sale by the administrator; it is necessary, to sustain it, to allege special damages, and show that they accrued in consequence of the wrongful acts of the defendant, and not in any degree in consequence of the negligence or omission of the plaintiff. Also, that the property was actually offered for sale, and at a legal sale.[4]

7. Upon the same ground, it is said to be a clear principle

[1] Beatty v. Gilmore, 16 Penn. 463. See Bush v. Johnston, 23 Penn. 209.

[2] Roulston v. Clark, 3 E. D. Smith, 366.

[3] Ilott v. Wilkes, 3 B. & Ald. 304.

[4] Burnap v. Dennis, 3 Scam. 478.

of equity and justice, that no man shall be allowed to *profit by his own fraudulent acts*, or the fraudulent acts of another, in which he knowingly participates.[1] Thus a party cannot maintain trover for the detention of papers, which he had deposited with the defendant in furtherance of a fraudulent purpose.[2] So it has been held, that an action does not lie against an auctioneer, for selling a horse at the highest price bid for him, contrary to the owner's express directions, not to let him go under a larger sum named; though it would be otherwise, if the owner had directed the auctioneer to set the horse up at such a particular price and not lower.[3] So it is held, that one who obtains possession of the property of another surreptitiously, or otherwise wrongfully, cannot support trespass against one who takes it under color of a judgment, although such judgment is fraudulent as to creditors.[4]

8. Upon the same principle, involving also a rule of law connected with the contract of *sale*, a party who *wrongfully violates his own agreement*, in relation to certain property, cannot maintain an action against the other party to the contract for an interference with such property. Thus the defendants sold to the plaintiffs wheat, for which the plaintiffs were to pay by a draft on a London banker. The defendants delivered the wheat to a carrier, and sent the bill of lading to the plaintiffs, but took the wheat again, and sold it before it came to the plaintiffs' possession, because the plaintiffs failed to send such draft. Held, the plaintiffs could not bring trover.[5] So the plaintiff, having a cow at grass in the defendant's field, and being indebted for the agistment, agreed with him that the cow should be a security, that he would not remove her till the debt was paid, and, if he did, the defendant might take her wherever she might be, and keep her till he was paid. The plaintiff removed the cow, not having paid the debt; and the defendant seized her in the high road. In an action of trespass for the tak-

[1] Burtus *v.* Tisdale, 4 Barb. 571.

[2] De Witz *v.* Hendricks, 2 Bing. 314.

[3] Bexwell *v.* Christie, 1 Cowp. 395.

[4] Costenbader *v.* Shuman, 3 W. & S. 504.

[5] Wilmshurst *v.* Bowker, 5 Bing. N. R. 541.

ing; held, the agreement might be set up as a defence, under a plea that the cow was not the plaintiff's.[1] So A. agreed to employ the plaintiff to carry coal in boats which were delivered to him, certain portions of the freight to be retained by A. until they equalled the value of the boats, when the boats were to be delivered to the plaintiff. In an action of trover against the purchaser of A.'s interest, the plaintiff is not entitled to recover to the extent of the payments made, if they are less than the price.[2]

9. So, in order to maintain an action, the plaintiff must himself have complied with the requisitions of the law, connected with the duty of the defendant. Thus, in order to maintain an action against a witness for failing to attend and testify, the plaintiff must prove that he was duly summoned, and his fees duly paid or tendered, according to law. It is not sufficient to prove a waiver on the part of the witness of his right to service and fees.[3] And a party who neglects to avail himself of his legal rights cannot maintain an action, for an act which might have been wrongful, had the former used the privilege given him by law in reference to the transaction. Thus, if a person exempt from militia duty, on being summoned to appear at parade, does not claim his exemption, and offer proof of it, no action will lie against the officer returning him to a court-martial as a delinquent, unless malice, express or implied, be shown.[4] So an action will not lie against a town or its clerk for an omission to index a mortgage, where the plaintiff never examined the records, and was not misled by the omission.[5] Nor for neglect of the clerk to submit his records to the plaintiff for examination, or a representation by him that the premises were free from incumbrance; unless a request to examine the records was made by the plaintiff.[6] So where, on the trial of an action for fraud, the defendant claimed that the plaintiff had been culpably negli-

[1] Richards *v.* Symons, 8 Ad. & Ell. N. S. 90.

[2] Farmers', &c. *v.* McKee, 2 Barr, 318.

[3] Robinson *v.* Trull, 4 Cush. 249; acc. Norris *v.* Lapsley, 5 Cal. 47.

[4] Vanderbill *v.* Downing, 11 Johns. 83.

[5] Lyman *v.* Edgerton, 3 Wms. 305.

[6] Ibid.

gent, in not searching the public records, and therefore was not entitled to recover for any defect of title which might have been discovered on such search, whatever fraudulent representations or concealments the defendant might have made; and the court instructed the jury, substantially, that it was the duty of the plaintiff to exercise ordinary care to ascertain the title to the lands he was about to purchase, and, if he did not, the verdict must be for the defendant; held, the defendant had no cause to complain of the charge, as it was much more favorable than he had a right to require.[1] So, where one beneficially interested in a cause, from ignorance of the law, surrenders his rights, he cannot hold the opposite party to a knowledge of the law, and charge him for the loss occasioned by his own indiscretion.[2] Thus, where a constable levied on and sold property, already bound by executions in the hands of the sheriff, and paid over the money to the plaintiffs in the executions in the sheriff's hands, and the plaintiffs afterwards paid the same back to the constable, under advice that his levy and sale had divested the executions in the sheriff's hands of their lien; held, the plaintiffs could not afterwards charge the sheriff with negligence, although he was advised that the proceedings of the constable had divested the executions in his hands of their lien, and had acted under that advice.[3] So, where fire-arms were taken from a negro, under the South Carolina act of 1819, and the owner, with a knowledge of the proceedings, did not oppose the condemnation by the magistrate, he could not maintain trover against those who seized them and caused them to be condemned. So although, if selectmen, being in session for the purpose of revising the list of voters previous to a town meeting, upon the application of one whom they know to be a legal voter, refuse to place his name upon the list, and inform him that they shall not do so, in consequence of which he omits to offer his vote at the meeting, the selectmen will be liable

1 Watson *v.* Atwood, 25 Conn. 313.
2 Harrison *v.* Marshall, 6 Port. 65.
3 Rice *v.* Parham, Dudley, 373.

notwithstanding he does not offer his vote; it is otherwise, if after such refusal they reconsider their determination and place his name on the list before the opening of the meeting, so that his vote, if offered, would be received at the first voting or balloting.[1] (a) So if one, who has sold on the representation of another concerning the buyer's circumstances, afterwards tells the buyer he will sell him no greater amount without further references, and after that intrusts him to a greater amount; the author of the misrepresentation is not liable beyond the sum due at the date of the plaintiff's declaration.[2]

10. Upon the same principle, a party cannot maintain a suit, for an act which could become injurious to him only by means of some wrongful conduct on his own part. Thus a lessor, during the term, cut down oak pollards growing upon the land, which were unfit for timber. Held, as the tenant for life or years would have been entitled to them, if they had been blown down, and was entitled to their usufruct during the term, the lessor could not, by wrongfully severing, acquire any right to them, and consequently he or his vendee could not maintain trespass against the tenant for taking them.[3]

11. Upon the same principle, no action lies for a single woman, for seducing and getting her with child, under pretence of a design to marry her; unless there were a promise of marriage.[4] So, in an action by the father for such seduction of his daughter, (b) upon the ground of loss of her service, the defendant may prove in bar of the action, that

[1] Bacon *v.* Benchley, 2 Cush. 100.
[2] Hutchinson *v.* Bell, 1 Taunt. 558.
[3] Channon *v.* Patch, 5 B. & C. 897.
[4] Paul *v.* Frazier, 3 Mass. 71.

(a) Upon the same principle, involving also the right gained by long use or prescription, if the grantee of a market under letters-patent from the Crown suffer another to erect a market in his neighborhood, and use it for the space of twenty-three years without interruption, he is by such user barred of his action on the case for disturbance of his market. Holcroft *v.* Heel, 1 Bos. & Pul. 400.

(b) See *Parent*, &c.

the plaintiff permitted the defendant to visit his daughter as a suitor, knowing him to be a married man, and after being cautioned against it; or otherwise connived at her criminal conduct.[1] (*a*) So, although it was treated as only a doubtful point, whether a woman, who cohabits with a man, assumes his name, and represents herself as his wife, can maintain trespass against a sheriff, for taking in execution furniture alleged to be her property, but being in the house in which the parties resided; yet, it having been left to the jury to say, whether, under the circumstances, the property might not have been given up by the woman to the man, during cohabitation, and they having found in the affirmative, the Court refused to disturb the verdict.[2]

12. Upon similar ground, a party who is himself *a trespasser*, in relation to real or personal property, can maintain no action against the rightful owner, for any act done in assertion of his title. (*b*) Thus the proprietor of land, who has the right to immediate possession, may expel a mere

[1] Reddie *v.* Scoot, 1 Peake, 240; Akerley *v.* Haines, 2 Caines, 292; Seagar *v.* Sligerland, Ib. 219.

[2] Edwards *v.* Farebrother, 2 Moo. & P. 293.

(*a*) But, in an action by a father for debauching his daughter, the careless indifference of the father in respect of his daughter in this behalf goes in mitigation of damages only. Zerfing *v.* Mourer, 2 Greene, 520.

For the same purpose, the defendant may offer evidence of the loose principles and conduct, either of the plaintiff or his daughter. Dodd *v.* Norris, 3 Camp. 519.

(*b*) Unless in case of *wilful and intentional* injury by the defendant. Terry *v.* New York, &c. 22 Barb. 574.

It seems that a person is not permitted, for the protection, in his absence, of property against a *mere trespasser*, to use means endangering the life or safety of a human being, whatever he may do where the entry upon his premises is to commit a felony or a breach of the peace; and, where such means are used, the nature and value of the property sought to be protected must be such as to justify the proceeding; full notice of the mischief to be encountered must be given; and the principles of humanity must not be violated; or the owner will be subject to damages for any injury which may ensue. Loomis *v.* Terry, 17 Wend. 496.

intruder by such force as may be necessary, and he will, in any event, acquire a rightful possession of the land; although he will be liable to an action for any breach of the peace, or trespass upon the person of the intruder.[1] (a) So, where A., the owner of cattle, found them in the possession of B., who forbade A. to enter upon his land, and no evidence was given to show how the cattle escaped from A., or how they came into the possession of B.; it was held, that A. might peaceably enter upon B.'s land and take the cattle.[2] (b) So it is said, "If a man takes my goods and carries them into his own land, I may justify my entry into the said land to take my goods again; for they came there by his own act."[3] Though the mere fact, of my goods being placed on another man's land, will not justify my entering thereon, and repossessing myself of the goods, unless they have been feloniously stolen.[4] If, however, they are found in a common, fair, or a public inn, it is said they may be lawfully reseized by the rightful owner.[5] And if fruit drop from the tree of one man upon the land of another, or the tree of one fall upon the land of another, it is said the owner of the fruit or tree may enter upon such land to recover his property, on the ground of *accident*.[6]

13. This particular application of the general rule often comes in question, as has been seen, (§ 12,) with reference to

[1] Beecher *v.* Parmele, 9 Verm. 352.
[2] Richardson *v.* Anthony, 12 Verm. 273.
[3] Vin. Abr. *Trespass*, 1 *a*.
[4] Per Parke, B., Patrick *v.* Colerick, 3 M. & W. 486.
[5] 3 Bl. Comm. 4.
[6] Per Tindal, C. J., Anthony *v.* Haynes, 8 Bing. 192.

(*a*) See *Assault*.

(*b*) Upon similar grounds rests the rule, which however is usually affirmed by express statute, that, if the owner of land find cattle upon his land, he may seize and hold them as a pledge for the payment of damage, where he would be entitled to damages. But, if he seize them where he would not be entitled to damages, the owner of the cattle may maintain trespass against him for damages to the cattle while in his possession; as where the owner of the land has not a sufficient fence against the cattle, (see § 13). Dickson *v.* Parker, 3 How. (Miss.) 219.

injuries done by or to *domestic animals*. (*a*) Thus the plaintiff's sheep were trespassing in the ground of the defendant, who drove them out with a dog. The dog pursued them into the adjoining ground, though the defendant called in his dog as soon as he had driven the sheep off from his own grounds. Held, trespass did not lie.[1] So, when cattle break from the highway into an enclosure, and are there doing damage, and the owner of the land drives them out by means of a dog, using all ordinary care; he is not responsible for injury thereby occasioned to the cattle.[2]

13 *a*. But, on the other hand, the owner of sheep is justified in killing a dog, which had destroyed some of his sheep, and returned upon his premises apparently for the purpose of destroying others, although the dog at the time he is killed be not in the very act of destroying or worrying the sheep; and although it be not shown that the owner of the dog was cognizant of his bad qualities, or that there were means of preventing the injury.[3] So, where the dog of A. is on the land of B. chasing *fowls*, and in the act of destroying one; B. may lawfully shoot the dog in the same manner as if he were chasing and killing sheep, or other reclaimed and useful animals. And it is enough that the fowl is on the land of B., without showing property in the fowl. And the jury are to decide whether the killing of the dog was justified by the necessity of the case, and was requisite to preserve the fowl.[4] So, in trespass for killing the plaintiff's dog, there was evidence tending to show that the dog was vicious, known to be so by the owner, and in the act, at the time, of doing injury to the defendant's property in his garden. Held, it was error to instruct the jury to find for the plaintiff, leaving to them to fix only the amount of damages.[5] So, in an action of trespass for killing a dog, the plaintiff having

1 Beckwith *v.* Shordike, 4 Burr. 2092.
2 Davis *v.* Campbell, 23 Vt. 236.
3 Parrott *v.* Hartsfield, 4 Dev. & Batt. 110.
4 Leonard *v.* Wilkins, 9 Johns. 233.
5 Paff *v.* Slack, 7 Barr, 254.

(*a*) See *Animals*, *Nuisance*, *Property*.

proved the defendant's confession that he killed the plaintiff's dog, who assaulted him in the highway, &c.; it was held, that the confession must be taken all together, and amounted to a justification.[1] So a man is justified in killing an enraged bull, in the necessary defence of himself or of his family.[2]

13 *b*. Upon similar grounds, if the defendant's hogs go into the adjoining land of the plaintiff, by reason of the partition fence, which the plaintiff is bound to keep in repair, being insufficient, he cannot maintain an action of trespass.[3] So laying hold of a horse, and removing him from before the defendant's door, is no trespass, without particular damage.[4] So it is held, that a railroad company is not liable, for negligently running an engine upon and killing the cattle of the plaintiff, which had come from the highway upon the track of the railroad, though there was no physical obstacle to prevent their entry.[5] (*a*)

14. But, on the other hand, it has been held no justification, in trespass for killing a mastiff, "that he ran violently upon defendant's dog and bit him;" but the defendant should state further, that he could not otherwise separate the mastiff from his dog.[6] So it is held no defence for killing a dog, that the dog was trespassing upon another's property, and the defendant, as his servant, when he could not otherwise prevent the dog from doing further injury, killed him.[7] Nor, for shooting the plaintiff's mules, that they had broken into the defendant's enclosure and were injuring his crops.[8] So it is held no answer to an action for injury done by a dog, where the defendant knew the vicious propensity of the animal, to prove that the party injured was himself guilty of some imprudence or negligence in the transaction; as that the plaintiff trod upon the defendant's

[1] Credit *v.* Brown, 10 Johns. 365.
[2] Russell *v.* Barrow, 7 Port. 106.
[3] Shepherd *v.* Hees, 12 Johns. 433.
[4] Slater *v.* Swan, 2 Strange, 872.
[5] The Tonawada, &c. *v.* Munger, 5 Denio, 255.
[6] Wright *v.* Ranscot, 1 Saund. 83.
[7] Tyner *v.* Cory, 5 Ind. 216.
[8] Ford *v.* Taylor, 4 Texas, 492.

(*a*) See *Railroad*.

dog while it lay at his door,[1] or was committing a technical trespass on the defendant's land.[2] So where the defendant, knowing that his dog had been bitten by another dog which was mad, merely fastened the dog, and the child of the plaintiff, approaching the dog, worried him with a stick, upon which the dog flew at and bit him, and the child died of hydrophobia; it was held that the plaintiff might recover the expenses of the apothecary.[3] So, where a party is not bound by prescription, agreement, or assignment of fence-viewers, to maintain a fence between his land and that of an adjoining owner, he may sustain trespass against the adjoining owner, whose cattle escape into his land.[4] (*a*)

[1] Smith *v.* Pelak, 2 Str. 1264.
[2] Sherfey *v.* Bartley, 4 Sneed, 58.
[3] Jones *v.* Perry, 2 Esp. 482.
[4] Thayer *v.* Arnold, 4 Met. 589.

(*a*) Where a man's hogs get on to another's land, and the former lets down a fence to drive them out, instead of driving them through a gap or gate, when there are such; he is guilty of a trespass. Gardner *v.* Rowland, 2 Ired. 247.

Action for the loss of a dog. The defendant was owner and occupier of a wood adjoining a wood of A., and divided therefrom by a low bank and a shallow ditch, not being a sufficient fence to prevent dogs from passing from one wood to the other. There were public foot-paths through the defendant's wood, not fenced off therefrom. The defendant, to preserve hares in his wood, and to prevent them from being killed therein by dogs and foxes, that came in pursuit of hares, kept iron spikes screwed and fastened into several trees, each spike having two sharp ends, and so placed that each end should point along the course of a hare-path, and purposely placed at such a height, as to allow a hare to pass under them without injury but to wound and kill a dog, that might run against one of the sharp ends, and adapted to effect the purpose, none of them being less than fifty yards, and some from 150 to 160 yards, from any foot-path. The defendant kept notices painted on boards at the outside of some parts of the wood, that steel-traps, spring-guns, and dog-spikes were set in that wood for vermin. The plaintiff, with A.'s permission, was sporting in A.'s wood with a valuable pointer; a hare rose in his wood, and was pursued by the dog thereout, over the bank and ditch, into the defendant's wood, though the plaintiff used every effort to prevent it, and in the pursuit ran against one

15. Upon the same ground, a party who has *created a nuisance* can maintain no action for the forcible abatement thereof. (*a*) Thus, if a man in his own soil erect a thing which is a nuisance to another, as by stopping a rivulet, and so diminishing the water used by him for his cattle; the party injured may enter on the soil of the other and abate the nuisance, and justify the trespass; and this right of abatement is not confined merely to nuisances to a house, to a mill, or to land.[1] (*b*) But it is no defence to an action for an assault and battery, that the plaintiff kept a disorderly house, the receptacle of stolen goods, &c., and that the defendants threw down the house as a public nuisance, and in so doing necessarily and unavoidably assaulted the plaintiff, and to some extent, beat, bruised, and wounded him.[2] So, in an action for hooting, yelling, &c., at a theatre, for the purpose of driving the plaintiff, an actor, from the stage, it is no defence, that the plaintiff was on certain specified grounds an unfit person to appear before the public.[3]

[1] Raikes *v.* Townsend, 2 John P. Smith, 9.

[2] Gray *v.* Ayres, 7 Dana, 375.

[3] Gregory *v.* Brunswick, 6 M. & G. 953.

---

of the sharp spikes and was killed. The Court were equally divided in opinion, whether the action was maintainable. Deane *v.* Clayton, 7 Taunt. 489.

(*a*) See *Nuisance*.

(*b*) So even the *prevention* of crime is held sufficient justification for an act otherwise wrongful. (See *Trespass*, *Assault*, *False Imprisonment.*)

Thus a private person may justify breaking and entering the house of another, and imprisoning his person, in order to prevent him from committing murder on his wife. Handcock *v.* Baker, 2 Bos. & Pul. 260.

A somewhat analogous case, is that of the destruction of private property to prevent the spread of *a fire*. Upon this point it is held, that, in an action of trespass for the destruction of goods, by blowing up the building in which they were stored, in good faith and under apparent necessity, to prevent the spread of a conflagration in a city; the common-law plea of necessity is a good justification; and it is not necessary to aver that the defendant was a resident of, or owner of property in, the city, or that his own property was in danger. Hale *v.* Lawrence, 3 Zabr. 590. See Beach *v.* Trudgain, 2 Gratt. 219; Surocco *v.* Geary, 3 Cal. 69.

16. There are some cases, where a party's own agreement, that the defendant might do an act which would otherwise be a tort, may be set up in defence against an action therefor. (*a*) Thus a clause in a lease is valid, which provides, that upon breach of covenant the lessor may enter and expel the lessee and remove his effects by force, if necessary, although a statute requires entry into lands and tenements to be peaceable. By the common law, some degree of force is allowed in expelling an intruder who wrongfully refuses to quit. The owner is not justified in using such force as would tend to a breach of the peace, but may use such force as would sustain the plea *molliter manus;* and to such lawful force the condition in the lease must be considered as referring.[1] And in enforcing an agreement, authorizing the forcible taking possession of premises in case of non-payment of the purchase-money, if more force is used than is necessary, the plaintiff should reply the force, or give evidence of it under the general replication *de injuriâ.*[2]

17. The general principle, however, above stated and illustrated, that one party cannot recover damages from another, where both are in fault or *in pari delicto*, is subject to many qualifications and exceptions, (see § 3). It is said, "Although there may have been negligence on the part of the plaintiff, yet, unless he might, by the exercise of ordinary care and prudence, have avoided the consequences of the defendant's negligence, he is entitled to recover; if by ordinary care and prudence he might have avoided them, he is the author of his own wrong."[3] The doctrine under consideration does not bind him to the utmost possible caution.[4] Thus it is

[1] The Fifty Associates *v.* Howland, 5 Cush. 214. See Dietrich *v.* Berk, 24 Penn. 470.

[2] Ambrose *v.* Root, 11 Ill. 497.

[3] Per Parke, B., Bridge *v.* The Grand Junction, &c. 3 M. & W. 248. Acc. Grant *v.* Moseley, 29 Ala. 302.

[4] Eakin *v.* Brown, 1 E. D. Smith, 36.

(*a*) See *License*, *Estoppel*, *infra*, §§ 26, 30.

held, that the rule of ordinary care to avoid injury does not require a party to *fly* for that purpose, in order to maintain an action for assault and battery.[1] So it has been doubted, whether, in an action for negligence in a transaction based on *a contract* between the plaintiff and the defendant, as for instance by a railway passenger against the corporation, it is a good defence, that the plaintiff's own negligence contributed to the injury.[2] So the fact that a plaintiff is a trespasser, or violator of the law, does not of itself discharge another from the observance of due and proper care towards him; or the duty of so exercising his own rights as not to injure the plaintiff unnecessarily. Neither will it necessarily preclude the plaintiff from a recovery against a party guilty of negligence.[3] (*a*) So it is said, a wrongdoer is responsible for all the consequences which flow immediately from his wrongful or negligent acts; and this rule is the same in civil as in criminal cases, and the responsibility is not relieved by the fact, that the consequences of the injurious act could have been prevented by the care or skill of the injured person.[4] Thus it is no ground for reduction of damages, in an action for injury to hay of the plaintiff by the erection of a dam by the defendant; that the plaintiff might have prevented the injury by expending a sum less than the amount of such injury; the plaintiff being guilty of no negligence.[5] And the general rule, *in pari delicto*, is held subject to the following qualifications: 1. The injured party, although in the fault to some extent, may be entitled to damages for an injury, which could not have been avoided by ordinary care on his part. 2. When the negligence of the defendant is *the proximate cause* of the injury, but that of the plaintiff only *remote*, consisting of some

[1] Heady *v.* Wood, 6 Ind. 82.
[2] Martin *v.* Great Northern, &c. 30 Eng. L. & Eq. 473.
[3] Norris *v.* Litchfield, 35 N. H. 271; Kerwhacker *v.* C. C. R. R. Co. 3 Ohio, N. S. 172.
[4] Phares *v.* Stewart, 9 Port. 336.
[5] Reynolds *v.* Chandler, &c. 43 Maine, 513.

(*a*) See *Railroad*.

act or omission not occurring at the time of the injury. 3. Where a party has in his custody or control dangerous implements or means of injury, and negligently uses them or places them in a situation unsafe to others, and another person, although at the time even in the commission of a trespass, or otherwise somewhat in the wrong, sustains an injury. 4. And where the plaintiff, in the ordinary exercise of his own rights, allows his property to be in an exposed and hazardous position, and it becomes injured by the neglect of ordinary care and caution on the part of the defendant, he is entitled to reparation; for the reason that, although he thus took upon himself the risk of loss or injury by mere accident, he did not thereby discharge the defendant from the duty of observing ordinary care and prudence, or in other words voluntarily incur the risk of injury by the negligence of another.[1]

17 *a.* More especially the general rule *in pari delicto* is held not strictly applicable, where the responsibility of the defendant is by the policy of the law made more rigid than that of the plaintiff; the parties in such case not being considered as *equally* in fault. Thus the principle does not apply to a case, where goods are delivered to a carrier during the peril of a storm. It is for him to decide whether they can be safely received, and if he receives them he is liable from that time.[2] So servants of a railroad, who drive a train, towards a grade-crossing, round a curve, and through a cut, so that it cannot be seen till it is almost at the intersection, at a rate of twenty-five or thirty miles an hour, are guilty of negligence; nor is a traveller who is injured by such action guilty of negligence in not anticipating and providing for such action, nor, in crossing the railroad at such a point, is he bound to give a signal to an approaching train.[3] (*a*) So where, in consequence of unskilful driving, a

[1] Cook *v.* The Champlain, &c. 1 Denio, 91.

[2] New Brunswick Co. *v.* Tiers, 4 Zabr. 697.

[3] Reeves *v.* Delaware, &c. 30 Penn. 454.

(*a*) See *Common Carrier.*

stage-coach was likely to be overturned, and an outside passenger, with a view to his own safety, jumped off, and his leg was broken; it was left to the jury to say, whether he did it rashly and without sufficient cause, or from a reasonable apprehension of danger.[1] So the lessees of a ferry provided steamboats for the conveyance of passengers, goods, and cattle, from A. to B., and also slips for landing and embarking, which were (generally) sufficient for the purpose. Held, that they were liable for an injury sustained by the horse of a passenger, in consequence of the side-rail of the landing-slip (of the dangerous state of which they had been forewarned) giving way, although the horse was at the time under the control and management of its owner.[2]

17 *b*. And it is still another qualification of the general rule, that, in order to sustain an action for the negligence of the defendant, whereby the plaintiff is injured, the plaintiff is only bound to exercise care and prudence *equal to his capacity*. Thus, although a child of tender years may be in the highway through the fault and negligence of his parents, yet, if injured through the negligence of the defendant, he is not precluded from his redress. If the defendant know that such a person is in the highway, he is bound to a proportionate degree of watchfulness,—to the utmost circumspection,—and what would be but ordinary neglect, in regard to what he supposed a person of full age and capacity, would be gross neglect as to a child, or one known to be incapable of escaping danger.[3] And in determining whether the plaintiff has been guilty of such misconduct or want of care as will defeat a recovery by him, the tender age of the plaintiff, in connection with the circumstances of the case, is a material and proper subject of inquiry. Thus where the defendant having set up a gate on his own land, by the side of a lane, through which the plaintiff, a child between six and

[1] Jones *v.* Boyce, 1 Stark. C. 493.

[2] Willoughby *v.* Horridge, 12 Com. B. 742.

[3] Robinson *v.* Cone, 22 Vt. 213.

seven years of age, and other children in the same neighborhood, were accustomed to pass from their places of residence to the highway, and *vice versâ;* the plaintiff, in passing along such lane, without the liberty of any one, put his hands on the gate and shook it, in consequence of which it fell on him and broke his leg; it is a proper instruction to the jury, that, if the defendant was guilty of negligence, he was liable for the injury, unless the plaintiff, in doing what he did, was guilty of negligence, or misbehavior, or of the want of proper care and caution; and, in determining this question, they were to take into consideration the age and condition of the plaintiff, and whether his conduct was not the result of childish instinct and thoughtlessness.[1] So it is not *negligence*, as *matter of law*, that a child between six and seven years of age was permitted to be alone in the streets of New York. It is a question for the jury, under the circumstances of the case.[2] So the defendant negligently left his horse and cart unattended in the street. The plaintiff, a child seven years old, got upon the cart in play; another child incautiously led the horse on, and the plaintiff was thereby thrown down and hurt. Held, that the defendant was liable in an action on the case, though the plaintiff was a trespasser, and contributed to the mischief by his own act; and that it was properly left to the jury, whether the defendant's conduct was negligent, and the negligence caused the injury.[3]

17 *c*. But, in a late case, the plaintiff, a child three years of age, was seriously injured by the breaking of a flag-stone upon which he was standing, in front of a building owned by the defendant, and a part of which was leased by the father of the plaintiff. The jury found that the stone was unsound, but that the defendant had no notice of any facts, which would lead a man of ordinary caution to think it was so. It did not appear that the defendant was bound to erect and main-

[1] Birge *v.* Gardiner, 19 Conn. 507.

[2] Oldfield *v.* New York, &c. 3 E. D. Smith, 103.

[3] Lynch *v.* Nardin, 1 Ad. & Ell. N. S. 29; 4 Per. & Dav. 672.

tain the structure in all events and at his peril; nor that the injury resulted from his negligence, without concurring negligence in the plaintiff. Held, an action did not lie.[1] (a)

[1] Congreve v. Morgan, 4 Duer, 439.

(a) Upon this subject, the following case has been recently decided in Pennsylvania. Pennsylvania Railroad, &c. v. Kelly. (*Legal Intelligencer.*) The case involves other points than those considered in the text, but is still inserted entire.

This was an action on the case, brought by Patrick Kelly against the Pennsylvania Railroad Company, to recover damages for injuries to the plaintiff's son, by negligently breaking his leg, *per quod servitium amisit.*

The plaintiff was at work on the Broad Top Railroad, near Huntingdon, and sent his son James, a boy nine years of age, to town for tobacco. On reaching the turnpike, he attempted to creep under the defendants' cars, which had just arrived and were standing across it. The train started, and his leg was caught by the wheels, and so injured as to render amputation necessary. The jury found, by their verdict, that the defendants were obstructing the crossing, and gave for plaintiff $3,000 damages. On a former trial a verdict had been rendered for $5,000, but a new trial was granted.

The opinion of the Court was delivered by Woodward, J. — This was an action by a father to recover damages for the maiming of his son, a boy of nine years of age, by what is charged as the negligence of the company's agent. The main facts bear a striking analogy to those in the case of Rauch v. Hill & Loyd, decided at the present term. A train of cars was stopped on a road or street that leads into the Borough of Huntingdon, and whilst it stood there, the plaintiff's son, returning from an errand along that road, attempted to pass under the cars. While he was in the act of doing so, they were set in motion, and injured one of his feet so badly that amputation became necessary to save life. Several questions are raised upon the record, by the assignment of errors, which I proceed to notice. 1st. It is said that the Court erred in holding that the Act of Assembly of 20th March, 1845, forbidding the obstructing of the crossings of public roads by locomotives and cars, applied to the Pennsylvania Railroad Company, who were incorporated by a subsequent Act of 13th April, 1846.

If this were so, if the company were not subject to the Act of '45, they would have to show legislative authority to justify their blocking up a street. So far from having any such authority, the 13th section of their charter required them to construct their road in such a manner, as not to impede the passage or transportation of persons or property along any established road. The obstruction which the jury have found in this case, was then

18. Where the plaintiff's own evidence raises a doubt, whether the injury resulted from his own or the defendant's

---

without the authority of law, and therefore illegal. But it was also in plain violation of the Act of 1845, which was a general law, and applicable to the defendants, though subsequently incorporated. On both grounds, or on either, the ruling of the Court can be sustained. Obstructions were certainly defined to consist, not in the transit across the intersecting road, for that is expressly legalized, but in stopping upon it unnecessarily; and, though the Act of '45 imposes a specific penalty, this in nowise affects the question that is presented in this case. This action is for damages arising out of a tort, and the obstruction proved to the satisfaction of the jury, the tort whereon the action rests is established.

2. But it is said in the next place, that the obstruction was the remote, and not the proximate cause of the injury complained of. This position is answered by the observations that were made on a similar point in Rauch's case already referred to. Indeed, the reasoning there applies with more force here, for here the company were engaged in transporting their own cars on their own road, the conductors, and everybody else concerned in the management of the train, confessed to be the company's agents. Now, adjust the acts of stopping and starting ever so nicely to the maxim *causa proxima*, and not a step of advance is taken by the defence, for the company are equally liable for both causes. If you say it was the starting and not the stopping of the cars that did the mischief, the question of the plaintiff's negligence, in suffering his son to be under them, is still in the case, but you have made no progress in the defence, because if they were running in the street the company are as responsible for it as for an injury by the stopping. The nature of the case, however, does not admit of this nice distinction. The conduct of that train of cars was one thing, intrusted as a special duty to one man, and if his mismanagement injured the plaintiff, without fault on the plaintiff's part, the company are liable for it; to split such a single simple individual cause into two causes, and to christen them *proxima* and *remota*, is to embarrass ourselves unnecessarily and to obstruct the cause of justice.

3. We come next to the question of the plaintiff's negligence. There is no dispute about the principle that forbids him to recover damages for an injury which his own negligence or wrongdoing contributed to bring on. What did he do amiss?

He sent his son on a lawful errand, along a lawful highway; was it negligence to permit a boy nine years of age to be abroad on an errand? This is not pretended, but it is said the boy betrayed a want of discretion in going under the cars, and the learned counsel seems to maintain that a boy, nine years of age, is bound to the same rule of care and diligence, in avoid-

negligence; this is wholly a question for the jury,[1] (see § 3). Thus, in an action by the widow of A., a miner, to recover

[1] Beers *v.* Housatonic, &c. 19 Conn. 566; Oldfield *v.* New York, &c. 3 E. D. Smith, 103.

---

ing the consequences of the neglect or unlawful acts of others, which is required of persons of full age and capacity. The case relied on for this startling proposition is Hartfield *v.* Roper, 21 Wend. 617. That case was this: A child of about two years of age was permitted to wander from his father's house, and to be sitting or standing on the beaten track of a public highway, when the defendant, driving a span of horses and sleigh, with two other persons in it, ran over him and injured him.

It appeared that the horses were descending a hill at the foot of which was a bridge, that they were going at a remarkable speed, and that there were no houses along that part of the road, to excite the expectation that people would be found in the road. Under these circumstances the Court held that failure to see the child in time to avert the danger was not culpable negligence, and they reversed the judgment which gave him damages. This case might have been rested on the propriety of the defendant's conduct; he was pursuing his course on the highway in a lawful and appropriate manner, and that distinguishes the case from ours, for here the wrongdoing of the defendants in obstructing the highway is established. But the case is cited for the sake of Judge Cowen's observations on infantile responsibility, and these I dismiss in the language which Chief Justice Redfield employed in concluding his opinion in Robinson *v.* Castle, 22 Verm. 226. The case of Hartfield *v.* Roper, said he, is, so far as it has any application to the present case, altogether at variance with that of Lynch *v.* Nurdin, and far less sound in its principles, and infinitely less satisfactory to the instinctive sense of reason and justice. Lord Drummain's opinion in Lynch *v.* Nurdin, 41 Eng. Com. Law, 422, was subsequent to that of Mr. Justice Cowen, and much worthier, it seems to me, to be followed. If the father is to be held responsible for the discretion of his son, it is only for such discretion as would usually and naturally be expected of a child of his age and intelligence. Was it a violation of that measure of prudence to go under cars standing where they were? We cannot say it was as a legal conclusion, and the jury did not find it as a conclusion of fact. Nay, indeed, it may be well doubted whether most boys, grown familiar with trains of cars by daily observation, would not in like circumstances have acted as this boy acted; to many active and enterprising children risks not absolutely appalling are attractive, especially if others are at hand to witness the daring achievement. Two boys in a neighboring town went under cars, in similar circumstances; and the adjudged cases in the books show that children do frequently incur equal or

compensation for his death, alleged to have been caused by the negligence of the defendants, his employers; it appeared from the plaintiff's evidence, that A. worked in the main road of the pit, taking out coal there; that he had often complained of a large stone in the roof, which was in a dangerous position; that the defendants' manager had said there was no danger, but promised frequently to remove it, yet had not done so; that at last two men had been sent to remove the stone, and, on reaching the spot, they found A. filling his hutch with coals, and waited till he should finish it, but before that had been done the stone fell and killed A. There was conflicting evidence, as to whether the men told A. to fill his hutch first, before they would remove the stone, or whether A. for his own benefit asked the men to wait till he had filled it. Held, reversing the judgment of the Court of Session, in Scotland, that there was evidence to go to the jury; and the two questions for them were — first, was the stone negligently allowed by the defendants to remain in a dangerous position too long; and, secondly, did A. lose his life in consequence of that negligence, and not in consequence of his own rashness.[1]

19. And the question of relative or comparative culpability is so far a question for the jury, that their verdict cannot properly be disturbed, although found for the plaintiff and at the same time recognizing some degree of fault on his part. Thus, if one vessel is damaged by another, and the jury find a verdict for the plaintiff, the Court will not send the case to a new trial, because there may be some ground to believe, that the plaintiff was negligent in navigating his vessel as well as the defendant.[2] So, in an action for improperly navigating a steamboat, whereby the plaintiff's barge was sunk, it appeared that a large steam-

[1] Paterson v. Wallace, 28 Eng. L. & Eq. 48.

[2] Collinson v. Larkins, 3 Taunt. 1.

---

even greater hazards. We cannot therefore account this boy's conduct unnatural or extravagant.

vessel preceded the defendant's steamboat, and partly occasioned the swell, which caused the injury; and also that the plaintiff's barge was improperly trimmed and insufficiently manned. The jury found a verdict for a fourth part of the damage actually sustained, alleging as a ground for so doing, that blame was not attributable to the defendants alone, the barge not being properly trimmed. Held, although this allegation might have been a reason for directing the jury to reconsider their verdict, it furnished no ground for granting a new trial.[1] (a) So, in an action by the owner of a coach and horses against the driver of another coach, for driving the wheels of his coach upon one of the horses attached to the plaintiff's coach; it is a question for the jury, whether the plaintiff's driver was guilty of such misconduct as to prevent the plaintiff's recovery; and the Court cannot properly give peremptory instructions to the jury, that the defendant is entitled to a verdict because of the misconduct of the plaintiff's driver.[2] So, in cases of this nature, it is no ground for a new trial, that the Court omitted to charge the jury upon a supposed or possible state of facts, not proved, or claimed to be proved. Therefore, where the plaintiff, in an action for driving the defendant's carriage against the plaintiff's and oversetting

[1] Smith *v.* Dobson, 3 M. & Gr. 59; 3 Scott, N. 336.

[2] Munroe *v.* Leach, 7 Met. 274.

(a) Upon similar ground, though not involving the question of fault in *the plaintiff*, if persons enter the plaintiff's close adjoining to his paddock, with guns and dogs, not keeping in the footpath; and their dog pulls down and kills one of the plaintiff's deer; and the jury (considering this as an intentional, and not a merely accidental trespass) finds for the plaintiff; the Court will not set aside their verdict; even though the Judge who tried the cause thought it a mere accident. Beckwith *v.* Shordike, 4 Burr. 2092.

But a complaint, not alleging negligence on the part of the defendants as the cause of the damage sued on, with an answer, alleging that the plaintiff's negligence was the cause, entitles the defendant to judgment after a verdict against him. Board, &c. *v.* Mayer, 10 Ind. 400.

it, claimed, that the injury occurred entirely through the negligence of the defendant; and also, that, if the plaintiff was guilty of negligence, the defendant drove his carriage against the plaintiff's by design or gross negligence, and thereby caused the injury; and that, in either of these events, the plaintiff was entitled to recover; and the defendant did not claim to justify himself, on the ground that the plaintiff was guilty of any negligence at the time, but by a course of misconduct pursued by the plaintiff, on the road, previous to the collision, and at some distance from the place where it happened, which misconduct could not possibly concur in directly producing the injury; held, the Court might properly omit to charge the jury as to the effect of negligence on the part of the plaintiff.[1] So, although in an action for damage occasioned by the defendant's negligence a material question is, whether or not the plaintiff might have escaped the damage by ordinary care on his own part; the defendant is not excused, merely because the plaintiff knew that some danger existed through the defendant's neglect, and voluntarily incurred such danger; and the amount of danger, and the circumstances which led the plaintiff to incur it, are for the consideration of the jury. Therefore, where commissioners of sewers had made a dangerous trench in the only outlet from a mews, putting up no fence, and leaving only a narrow passage on which they heaped rubbish; and a cabman, in the exercise of his calling, attempted to lead his horse out over the rubbish, and the horse fell and was killed, for which loss he brought an action: held, that the plaintiff might recover, though he had, at some hazard, created by the defendants, brought his horse out of the stable; and that the case was properly left to the jury, on the question whether or not the plaintiff had persisted, contrary to express warning at the time, (as to which there was contradictory evidence,) in running upon a great and obvious danger.[2] So, in an action against a

[1] Churchill v. Rosebeck, 15 Conn. 359.

[2] Clayards v. Dethick, 12 Ad. & El. N. S. 439.

railway company, for so negligently managing and lighting their station, that the plaintiff, a passenger, was thrown down while on his way to the carriages; upon the plea of not guilty, the defendant's counsel having rested his defence on the ground, that the accident was entirely owing to the want of ordinary care on the part of the plaintiff, and that there was no negligence on the part of the defendants; the Judge left it to the jury to determine this question. Verdict for the plaintiff; and motion for a new trial, on the ground that the Judge ought to have told the jury, that, if the plaintiff contributed by his own negligence to the injury, the defendants were entitled to the verdict, though they might have been guilty of negligence. Held, the defendants were not entitled to a new trial, the issue on which alone they rested their defence having been left to the jury.[1] So, in an action for damages by a collision between carriages, occasioned, as the declaration alleged, by the negligence of the defendant, in so driving his wagon past the horse and wagon of the plaintiff, which were standing on the public highway, that the wheels of his wagon struck against the plaintiff, &c.; the burden of disproving negligence on the part of the plaintiff rests on him, and the defendant has a right to claim an instruction to that effect to the jury; but the question of negligence is exclusively for the jury. And where the plaintiff, in his opening, adduced evidence to disprove negligence on his part, and the defendant met such proof with evidence conducing to show such negligence; the Court rightly charged the jury, that, if the plaintiff did not exercise reasonable care and prudence in leaving his horse unhitched and unattended, he could not recover; and also that with reference to that question, they might consider the character, disposition, and temper of the plaintiff's horse, and the manner in which he had been trained, as well as all the other circumstances of the transaction. Although admitted, that the horse was a spirited animal, the act of the plaintiff, in

[1] Martin *v.* Great Northern, &c. 30 Eng. L. & Eq. 473.

leaving him unfastened and unattended, is not, as matter of law, a want of ordinary care on his part; but the question of negligence is still for the jury.[1]

20. As has been already suggested, the wrong conduct of the plaintiff, relied upon as a defence, must in general be *immediately* connected with the act for which redress is sought. And it may be added in the same connection, that *the parties* concerned in the respective transactions must be *the same*, and so far exclusively the same, as not to occasion any *divided responsibility* on the part of the plaintiff to the defendant. (*a*) Thus it is held no defence to an action of trespass, for entering a dwelling and carrying away goods, that the plaintiff kept a bawdy-house.[2] So the defendant, to prevent the plaintiff's fowls from trespassing on his land, as they had done, spread poisoned food upon the land, having given the plaintiff previous notice that he should do so, and the fowls, coming afterwards upon the land, ate the food, in consequence of which some died. Held, that previous notice, in contradistinction to notice after the fact, was sufficient; but that, notwithstanding such notice, the defendant was not justified in the use of the means he had employed, and was liable in damages.[3] So where geese are trespassing, it is yet unlawful to poison

[1] Park *v.* O'Brien, 23 Conn. 339.
[2] Love *v.* Moynehan, 16 Ill. 277.
[3] Johnson *v.* Patterson, 14 Conn. 1.

(*a*) The distinction is made, that, in an action for the loss of service of the plaintiff's son, caused by an injury received through the negligence of the defendant's servant, in determining whether the negligence of the son concurred in causing the injury, the jury may consider all the circumstances affecting his conduct at the time, including the acts of third persons, and of servants of the defendant, other than the one to whose negligence the injury is attributed in the complaint; although such acts cannot be made a ground of recovery. Gilligan *v.* New York, &c. I E. D. Smith, 453.

In an action for damages sustained by the bite of a dog, the fact that the plaintiff was, at the time of receiving the injury, trespassing on the land of a third person, will not defeat the right to recover, though it may be material on the question of damages. Pierrett *v.* Moller, 3 E. D. Smith, 574.

them, and an action for their value may be maintained.[1] So evidence that the drivers of two coaches, on the same route, mutually attempted several times to intercept each other's progress, by "cutting each other off," is not sufficient to prove, that, in a subsequent collision on the same trip, they were both in fault.[2] So, where the plaintiff, the defendant, and several others were parties to a written contract, by which they were together to engage in the removal of earth, from the land of the defendant to land of all the parties, for the purpose of raising and filling up the same; and, after proceeding in the execution thereof, the plaintiff, with the consent of the others, sold and conveyed his interest to the defendant, subject to the contract; and subsequently the proprietors continued the removal of the earth, and, in so doing, negligently undermined a hill on the plaintiff's land, and thereby caused a *slide* therefrom, which covered and injured *other* lands of the plaintiff; held, the fact of the plaintiff's having originally been a party to the contract did not preclude him from recovering, in case, for such injury.[3] So, in an action of trespass against a sheriff for levying upon property, he must first show that the plaintiffs named in the execution were creditors, before he can defend, by showing that he made the levy in accordance with an execution against other parties, supposed to be the owners of the property, and that the present plaintiff was a fraudulent purchaser.[4] So it has been held that the fact, that one man has personal property within the enclosure of another, does not authorize the former to enter the enclosure, for the purpose of taking such property. He should demand it of the owner of the land, and, if he refuse him permission to take it, such refusal would be evidence of a conversion, for which an action would lie.[5] So, while it has been held, that, in an action for assault and battery, the preceding words, or imputations of the same kind as those which immediately led to the as-

[1] Matthews *v.* Fiestel, 2 E. D. Smith, 90.

[2] Munroe *v.* Leach, 7 Met. 274.

[3] Gardner *v.* Heartt, 1 Denio, 466.

[4] Cook *v.* Miller, 11 Ill 610.

[5] Roach *v.* Damron, 2 Humph. 425.

sault, if previously communicated to the defendant, may be offered in evidence by way of mitigation of damages;—that the inducement to the transaction, and all such particulars, in the conduct of either party, leading to the final act, or forming part of it, as seemed to show in what degree blame attached to them severally, and such acts as would aid the jury in determining the just measure of damages, would be admissible evidence:[1] yet the prevailing and better doctrine is, that matter of provocation cannot be shown in justification of an assault and battery, unless so immediately preceding the assault, as to create a fair presumption, that the violence was committed under the sudden influence of passion excited by it.[2] And the principle more especially applies, where the provocation relates to third persons. Thus evidence of opprobrious languge used by the plaintiff towards the niece and sister-in-law of the defendant, a day or two before the assault, was held inadmissible in mitigation.[3] So in an action for assault and battery, brought against the superintendent of a railroad depot, for expelling the plaintiff from the depot, for a supposed violation of a regulation of the corporation; the defendant cannot give in evidence former violations by the plaintiff of other regulations.[4] (a) So, in trespass for breaking and entering the plaintiff's

[1] Dean v. Horton, 2 M'Mullan, 147.
[2] Coxe v. Whitney, 9 Mis. 531.
[3] Collins v. Todd, 17 Mis. 537; 1 Mass. 12.
[4] Hall v. Power, 12 Met. 482.

(a) But if an innkeeper, who has frequently entered a railroad depot, and annoyed passengers by soliciting them to go to his inn, receives notice from the superintendent of the depot, that he must do so no more; and he nevertheless repeatedly enters the depot for the same purpose, and afterwards obtains a ticket for a passage in the cars, with the *bonâ fide* intention of entering the cars as a passenger, and goes into the depot on his way to the cars; and the superintendent, believing that he had entered the depot to solicit passengers, orders him to go out, and he does not exhibit his ticket nor give notice of his real intention, but presses forward towards the cars; and the superintendent and his assistants thereupon forcibly remove him from the depot, using no more force than is necessary for that purpose;—such removal is justifiable, and not an indictable assault and battery. Commonwealth v. Power, 7 Met. 596.

manor; plea, first, the general issue; second, that from time immemorial there hath been and still is a public port, partly within the said manor, and also in a river, which has been a public navigable river from time immemorial, and that there is in that part of the port which is within the manor an ancient work necessary for the preservation of the port, and for the safety and convenience of the ships resorting to it; that this work was at the several times when, &c. in decay; that the plaintiff would not repair it, but neglected so to do, wherefore the defendants entered and repaired. Replication, *de injuriâ*. Verdict for the plaintiff on the first plea, and for the defendants on the second. Held, that the plaintiff was entitled to judgment *non obstante veredicto*, as the second plea did not state that immediate repairs were necessary, or that any one bound to do so had neglected to repair after notice, or that a reasonable time for repairing had elapsed, or that the defendants had occasion to use the port. And it was doubted whether the plea would have been good, had it contained those allegations.[1] So the defendant's servant, instead of placing his master's truck in the yard provided for it, where he had been directed to leave it on the termination of his day's work, left it standing by the sidewalk in a public street, twenty-six feet in width between the curb-stones, with the shafts shored up or supported in the customary manner by a plank. At the same time, on the other side of the street, and nearly opposite to the defendant's truck, a truck with the horses attached thereto, not belonging to the defendant, had been temporarily left, and was then standing at the distance of from four to six feet from the curb-stone on that side, leaving a sufficient space between the two trucks for a third to pass between them. While the two were thus standing, the driver of a third truck, not belonging to the defendant, attempted to pass between them, and in so doing conducted himself with ordinary prudence and reasonable care, and exercised a sound discretion in determining whether the attempt could be made with safety to persons

[1] Lonsdale *v.* Nelson, 2 B. & C. 302.

lawfully using the street, but, notwithstanding, drove his truck against the defendant's, and, in consequence of the collision, the shafts of the latter were thrown from the plank on which they were supported, and at the same time whirled round on to the sidewalk, on which the plaintiff was then passing, and struck and knocked her down and broke her leg. Held, the defendant was liable in an action on the case for the injury sustained by the plaintiff.[1] So E.'s (charitable) trustees, the plaintiffs, acting under a statute, and provided with a corporate seal, allowed G., their secretary, to keep it in his exclusive custody, but gave him no authority to use it. From time to time during several years, G. forged powers of attorney — procuring two persons to attest, as required by statute, that the corporate seal was duly affixed to such powers — authorizing the defendants, the Bank of Ireland, to transfer certain stock, the property of the trustees. The stock was transferred accordingly, and G. was afterwards prosecuted and convicted of forgery. Action for the value of the stock so transferred; plea, the general issue. The Judge told the jury, that, if the plaintiffs had been negligent in keeping their seal, they should find for the defendants, and they found accordingly. On a bill of exceptions; held, that the negligence proved was not such as would defeat the action, not being in or immediately connected with the transfer itself, but remotely connected with the transfer, which was not the necessary, or ordinary, or likely result of that negligence.[2] (*a*)

[1] Powell *v.* Deveney, 3 Cush. 300.

[2] Bank, &c. *v.* Evans', &c. 22 Eng. L. & Eq. 23.

(*a*) A somewhat analogous principle is recognized in the following case, which however was an action of contract, and not of tort. The defendants, the Westminster Improvement Commissioners, were authorized by acts of Parliament to borrow such sums of money as they should think necessary for the purposes of the act, and to give assignable bonds for the same. In an action by the plaintiff, as transferee of a bond, which recited, that the defendants had in pursuance of the said acts borrowed of one T. P. £5000, for enabling them to carry the said acts into execution; the defendants

21. An analogous, or perhaps another form of the same, exception to the rule *in pari delicto*, may be expressed in the propositions; that one party cannot, upon the ground of wrong or fault on the part of another, justify the violation of a right wholly independent of such wrongful conduct; nor will a mere breach of contract be any justification for forcibly regaining the property to which the contract relates. Thus a defendant, who by violence has regained the possession of property which he had sold and delivered, cannot defend himself against an action of replevin for the property, by proof that he had received nothing.[1] So a declaration in trespass alleged, that the defendant broke and entered, pulled down and demolished, the plaintiff's dwelling-house, in which he and his family were then dwelling and actually present. Plea, that the defendant was entitled to common of pasture on close H. for sheep levant and couchant, &c., as appurtenant to land of which he was the occupier; and that, because the dwelling-house was wrongfully erected on the said close, so that, without breaking, &c., and pulling down, &c., he could not enjoy his said common, the defendant broke and entered, &c., doing no unnecessary damage, &c. Replication, that the dwelling-house at the time when, &c., was the dwelling-house of the plaintiff and

[1] Applewhite *v.* Allen, 8 Humph. 697.

---

pleaded, that at the time, and before the bond was made, C. M. and W. M. were entitled to receive from the defendants certain bonds; that T. P. and others conspired fraudulently to procure for T. P. one of the said bonds to which the said C. M. and W. M. were entitled; and by means of such conspiracy and fraud, they procured C. M. and W. M. to authorize the defendants to give to T. P. one of the bonds; and that the bond sued upon was thereupon given to T. P. by the defendants, and that the defendants had never borrowed any sum of money from the said T. P.; of all which the plaintiff, at the time of the transfer to him of the said bond, had notice. Held bad on general demurrer, because the defendants could not set up as a defence the fraud that had been committed upon C. M. and W. M., by whose directions they had, in pursuance of their contract with them, given the bond to T. P. Horton *v.* The Westminster, &c. 14 Eng. L. & Eq. 378.

his family, who were actually present in, and inhabiting the same, and that the defendant, at the times when, &c., with force and arms and with a strong hand and in a violent manner, broke and entered, &c., and committed the trespasses. Upon demurrer, held, the house being an obstruction to the defendant's common, he might have justified abating so much of it as caused the obstruction, if no person had been therein; but that the justification was not maintainable, since the plaintiff's family were in the house.[1] So, in trover for the conversion of a pledge, delivered by the pledgee to the pledger for a special purpose, it is no defence that the plaintiff wrongfully sold other securities which he had for the same debt.[2] (*a*) So the defendant, in an action of trespass, cannot justify the throwing down of a ladder having a person upon it, although the ladder were unlawfully erected upon the land of the defendant.[3] So, in an action of trespass, for biting and bruising the plaintiff's finger, so that its amputation became necessary, evidence is not admissible, that the plaintiff's habitual intemperance, about and after the time, caused a state of health which resulted in the loss of the finger.[4]

22. The plaintiff's default or want of care is no defence, if brought about by the act of the defendant himself. Thus where A., by the wrongful act of B., loses his presence of mind, and in consequence runs into danger, and receives an injury from the act of B., the latter is not protected by a warning given to A., immediately before the accident.[5] So

[1] Perry *v.* Fitzhowe, 8 Ad. & El. N. S. 757.

[2] Hays *v.* Riddle, 1 Sand. 248.

[3] Collins *v.* Renison, Sayer, 138.

[4] Wheat *v.* Lowe, 7 Ala. 311.

[5] Woolley *v.* Scovell, 3 Man. & Ry. 105.

(*a*) Upon the same principle, in an action against the acceptor of a bill drawn for the balance of purchase-money of articles bought, it is no defence, that, two months after the delivery of the goods, the vendor forcibly retook possession of them; for the vendee cannot treat that as a rescinding of the contract, but must bring trespass. Stephens *v.* Wilkinson, 2 B. & Ad. 320.

the plaintiff manufactured and put into the defendant's steamboat a boiler, engines, and other machinery, under a contract to receive a certain price, a portion of which was to be secured by a mortgage upon the property, when the plaintiff had completed his contract. After the engines and boiler were placed, and partially fastened in the boat, but before the work was completed, or ready to be delivered, the defendant clandestinely went off with the boat to Canada, and on his return refused either to execute the mortgage or to pay for the machinery, or to permit the plaintiff to remove it. In replevin it was held, that the defendant could not show, in mitigation of damages, that the machinery was not constructed and placed in the boat in a workmanlike manner; but was concluded by his election to take the work in its unfinished condition, and must be held to have accepted the job as finished, and to have waived all objections on account of defects; that the presumption was, that the defects would not have existed, had the plaintiff been permitted to finish his work; and the defendant could not be heard to raise the objection of a non-performance, which he himself has occasioned. Also, that the defendant could not show, for the purpose of reducing the damages, what the machinery would be worth, detached from the boat; nor that such machinery, in the boat, as it was when demanded or when placed there, was not worth over a particular sum.[1]

23. In order to maintain the defence *in pari delicto*, upon the ground of injury done by the plaintiff, the defendant must show some *title* to the property which he claims that the plaintiff injured. Thus, as has been stated in another connection, it is generally held that an individual cannot justify damaging the property of another, on the ground that such property is a nuisance to a public right, unless it does him a special injury.[2] (*a*) So one who finds the cattle of another,

[1] Kidd *v.* Belden, 19 Barb. 266.

[2] Dimes *v.* Petley, 15 Ad. & Ell. 276.

(*a*) As to the *abatement* of a nuisance, see *Nuisance*.

depasturing on enclosed land, which he claims as his range, but to which he shows no title, nor right of possession, nor right of pasturage, is liable to the owner for shooting and worrying them.[1] And, unless this proof be offered, the question of gain or loss to the respective parties, resulting from the act complained of, will be immaterial. Thus, in trover for a heifer, the defendant requested the Court to instruct the jury, that, if the plaintiff, at the time of the alleged conversion, suffered his heifer to run at large on the highway, he was guilty of negligence; and that, if the defendant ignorantly took her, without wilfulness or gross negligence, on his part, and was not thereby benefited, the plaintiff, if equally negligent himself, could not recover. The Court did not comply with such request, but did instruct them, that, if the defendant voluntarily took, and so disposed of the heifer, that she was lost to the plaintiff, such taking was a conversion, whether he took her by mistake or otherwise. Held, as it was immaterial whether such taking was or was not profitable to the defendant, and as the plaintiff's loss was none the less real because of his negligence, such course was correct.[2]

24. A special application of the rule *in pari delicto* is found in the case of *illegal* transactions; from which, it is generally held, no claim can arise, that the law will help to enforce.[3] Though a defendant seized property illegally; the plaintiff who held it in violation of law is held not entitled to avail himself of the illegality of such seizure.[4] "A party cannot be heard to allege his own unlawful act; and if such an act be one of a series of facts necessary to support the plaintiff's claim, then that claim must fail. The party who seeks redress in a court of justice must come with clean hands; an action which requires for its support the aid of an illegal act cannot be maintained."[5] Thus, a statute hav-

[1] McCoy *v.* Phillips, 4 Rich. 463.

[2] Platt *v.* Tuttle, 23 Conn. 233.

[3] Foster *v.* Thurston, 11 Cush. 322; Staples *v.* Gould, 5 Seld. 520; Smead *v.* Williamson, 16 B. Mon. 492; Lord *v.* Chadbourne, 42 Maine, 429.

[4] Lord *v.* Chadbourne, 42 Maine, 429.

[5] Per Fletcher, J., 4 Cush. 326.

ing prohibited work, &c., on *the Lord's day*; (a) it is held, that an action cannot be maintained, for a deceit practised in the exchange of horses on that day.[1] So, if the owner of a horse knowingly lets him upon the Lord's day to be driven to a particular place, but not for any purpose of necessity or charity, and the hirer injures the horse by immoderate driving, in consequence of which he afterwards dies; the owner cannot maintain an action against the hirer for such injury, although it is occasioned in going to a different place, and beyond the limits specified in the contract.[2] Nor can a person who travels on the Lord's day, neither from necessity nor charity, maintain an action against a town, for an injury received by him, while so travelling, by reason of a defect in a highway, which the town is by law obliged to repair.[3] Upon the same principle an action will not lie, for goods delivered by the plaintiff to a third person, to sell contrary to law, and by him pledged to the defendant for his own debt.[4] So a declaration in case stated, that the defendant had charged the plaintiff with embezzlement; that it was agreed between A. and the plaintiff, that the defendant should abstain from prosecuting the plaintiff, and that, in consideration thereof, A. should draw, and the plaintiff should accept, a bill of exchange, and that A. should indorse

[1] Robeson *v.* French, 12 Met. 24.
[2] Gregg *v.* Wyman, 4 Cush. 322.
[3] Bosworth *v.* Swansey, 10 Met. 363.
[4] Duffy *v.* Gorman, 10 Cush. 45.

(a) It is said, "By the *common law* of England, it is certain that Sunday is esteemed *dies non juridicus;* and that any order, sentence, decree, or judgment, of any Court, rendered on that day, would be void." Per Parker, C. J., Pearce *v.* Atwood, 13 Mass. 347. In the same case (p. 350) the same learned Judge gives an interesting exposition of the statute relating to the observance of the Lord's day, and of what constitutes *unnecessary* travelling. He considers, as not falling within this description, travelling to visit a sick person, or in consequence of some sudden emergency relating to property; ministerial exchanges; attendance upon marriages or funerals. As to the history of the law relating to the observance of the Sabbath, and more particularly with reference to the holding of Courts on that day, see Lord Mansfield's learned judgment in Swann *v.* Broome, 3 Burr. 1597.

the same to the defendant; that a bill was accordingly drawn, accepted, and indorsed; that the defendant, well knowing the illegal nature of the transaction, and that the plaintiff was not liable to pay the bill, and that there was no reasonable or probable cause for suing him thereon, conspired with B., a pauper, that the bill should be in bond to B., and that B. should sue the plaintiff upon the bill, for the sole benefit of A.; and that an action was accordingly brought, in which the plaintiff prevailed, on the ground of the illegality of the consideration for the acceptance, but was unable to obtain his costs, in consequence of the insolvency of B. Held, inasmuch as the plaintiff could not make out his case, except through the illegal transaction to which he himself was a party, the action would not lie.[1] So, in trespass against a collector of the customs, it is a good justification, that the goods were imported contrary to a non-intercourse act, whereby they became forfeited to the United States. Or that the defendant, suspecting them to have been imported contrary to that act, seized them, and that they were condemned in the district court.[2] So, it being illegal for a person residing in England to raise money by way of loan, to assist subjects of a foreign State to prosecute a war against a friendly government; and the defendant being employed by the plaintiff to negotiate a loan, to assist the Greeks against the Porte; and the plaintiff having lodged with the defendant a fabricated power of attorney, and also certain engraved scrip receipts; and the whole transaction appearing to be founded in fraud: held, in an action of trover for the receipts, it was incumbent on the plaintiff to show that the power of attorney was a genuine document; and, as he had delivered it, as well as the receipts, under a false pretence, he could not recover.[3] And where a large number of pieces of German silver, of the precise size and thickness of Mexican dollars, and made in that form for the purpose of being stamped and milled into

[1] Fivaz v. Nicholls, 2 Com. B. 501.
[2] Sailly v. Smith, 11 Johns. 500.
[3] De Wirtz v. Hendricks, 9 Moore, 586.

counterfeit coin of that description, were taken by the sheriff from a person, who was carrying them at the time to a place of manufacture, for the purpose of having them finished, so that he could put them in circulation as genuine coin, and were detained, under the direction of the prosecuting officer, to be used as evidence against the person from whom they were taken, and also for the purpose of preventing their circulation; held, the owner, in the absence of evidence that they were put in that form without his knowledge, or against his consent, could not sustain trover against the sheriff therefor.[1]

25. And the same principle has been extended to a claim for damages, for an act somewhat more remotely connected with the wrongful conduct of the plaintiff. Thus, where the plaintiff was proprietor of a public building, kept for the purpose of exhibiting the art of pugilism, boxing, or sparring, by persons skilled in that art, for an admission-fee; and brought an action for a libel contained in a newspaper, imputing misconduct to him as such proprietor, and proved that he had sustained damage thereby: held, it was an illegal occupation, as it tended to encourage prize-fighting, and, the jury having found a verdict for the defendant on that ground, the Court refused to disturb it.[2]

26. But the general rule has been held not to interfere with the *right of property*, even in articles the sale of which is forbidden by law; or with the remedy for any violation of such right. Thus *spirituous liquors* are property in New Hampshire; and any person wrongfully dispossessing another thereof is answerable as in the case of other chattels.[3] (*a*) So in Massachusetts the owner of any intoxicating liquors, seized by an officer by virtue of a warrant issued

[1] Spalding *v.* Preston, 21 Vt. 9.
[2] Hunt *v.* Bell, 7 Moore, 212.
[3] Fuller *v.* Bean, 10 Fost. 181.

(*a*) And it has even been held, that a purchaser of spirituous liquors, illegally sold, without license, may maintain an action for deceit and false warranty, if he had no notice of the want of a license. Prescott *v.* Norris, 32 N. H. 101.

under Stat. 1852, c. 322, § 14, may maintain an action against the officer, notwithstanding § 19, which provides that "no action of any kind shall be had or maintained in any Court in this commonwealth, for the recovery or possession of intoxicating liquors or the value thereof, except such as are sold or purchased in accordance with the provisions of this act."[1] Shaw, C. J., says,[2] "The statute does not declare, nor imply that there can be no property in intoxicating liquors; on the contrary, it fully recognizes them as property, and of course entitled to the same security and protection by the law, to which other lawful property and possessions are entitled. The object of the statute is to regulate the purchase and sale of intoxicating liquors, and this prohibition of any action is declared as one of its penal consequences. It prohibits all actions for such liquors, or their value, except such as are sold and purchased in accordance with the act." So the purchaser of intoxicating liquors, sold contrary to this statute, may maintain an action for a wrongful taking of them from his possession, notwithstanding § 19.[3] So, where liquors were purchased of one who had no license, by a person intending to make sale of them without license, who paid for and took possession of them, and also in fact made sale of a portion of them without license; held, the purchaser might maintain trespass against a mere wrongdoer who took them.[4] So the plaintiff purchased wines, for which he paid the duties, and which were removed to his house. He afterwards disposed of a part, and employed the defendant to convey them, who promised to obtain a permit for that purpose; but his servant changed the wine during its transfer. Held, the plaintiff was entitled to recover, although the removal was contrary to the excise laws.[5] (*a*)

[1] Fisher *v.* M'Girr, 1 Gray, 1.
[2] Ibid. p. 47.
[3] Breck *v.* Adams, 3 Gray, 569.
[4] Fuller *v.* Bean, 10 Fost. 181.
[5] Toussaint *v.* Darlam, 3 Moore, 217.

(*a*) It has been very recently held, that, in an action of trespass to recover the value of liquors, the defendant might prove that they were illegally kept

27. And the case of *usury* has been treated as an exception to the general rule upon this subject; the borrower not being regarded as *in pari delicto* with the lender. Thus the defendant lent money at usurious interest to the plaintiff; and, to color the transaction, took a sale and transfer of goods for the amount, with an agreement that they should be resold at a higher price, if a bill drawn by the defendant on the plaintiff for the repurchase-money should be honored. The bill was dishonored, and the defendant retained the goods. Held, the plaintiff might recover in trover for the full value of them, without deducting the money advanced.[1] So, where an agent, intrusted with a negotiable note for the purpose of procuring it to be discounted, pledged it to a stranger, for money loaned to him, for his own use, at usurious interest; held, the transaction being illegal for usury, the lender could not retain the note against the true owner, on the ground that he had received the same in good faith, in the usual course of trade.[2]

27 *a*. The same principle has been applied as between *attorney and client*, although the transaction between them, upon which the action of the latter against the former is founded, was mutually designed to defraud a third person. Thus an attorney, on application of a client, to know whether his equitable interest in certain land could be reached by his creditor, procured from the client an assignment of such interest to himself for an inadequate consideration, promising to reconvey after an arrangement should have been made with the creditor. After the conveyance, the attorney claimed to hold absolutely against the client. Held, although the object of the assignment was to perpetrate a fraud on the creditor, on account of the relations existing between attorney and client, the attorney must be compelled

[1] Hargreaves *v.* Hutchinson, 2 Ad. & Ell. 12.

[2] Kentgen *v.* Parks, 2 Sandf. 60.

---

for sale by the plaintiff, as their *status* was essential to determining their value. Lord *v.* Chadbourne, 42 Maine, 429.

to restore what he had acquired under the assignment, on being repaid what he had disbursed.[1]

28. Another application of the same general principle *in pari delicto*, &c., and which is also more exactly embodied in the other fundamental maxim, that *no man shall take advantage of his own wrong;* is the rule that an action cannot be maintained to recover damages for an act, *which the plaintiff has himself expressly or impliedly authorized or sanctioned.*

29. Prominent among the examples of this rule, is the case of *a license*, given by one man to another to do any act in relation to the property of the former; the doing of which, by virtue of such license, will not in general constitute a tort or wrong. Thus, where one has cut down and pulled trees on another's land, under a valid agreement that he shall have the bark; the bark becomes his property, and he is not liable to an action of trespass for entering upon the land and taking it away.[2] So the plaintiff's father, by oral license, permitted the defendants to lower the bank of a river and make a weir above the plaintiff's mill, whereby less water flowed thereto. Held, the plaintiff could not sue the defendants for continuing the weir.[3] So to trespass for entering a house, the defendant may plead a license to enjoy the premises from such a day, &c.[4] So the plaintiff, being distrained on for rent, gave the defendant, her landlord, the following undertaking, "In consideration of Mr. C. giving me the furniture distrained for rent, I undertake to give him possession of the premises on or before one week from the date hereof." The plaintiff acted on this instrument, by selling some of the furniture for her own use, and at the end of a week the defendant took possession, and the plaintiff sued him in trespass. Held, the plea of *leave and license* was a good defence.[5] So an oral permission to take and use land for a railway is a bar to the recovery of damages for such use,

[1] Ford *v.* Harrington, 16 N. Y. 285.
[2] Nettleton *v.* Sikes, 8 Met. 34.
[3] Liggins *v.* Inge, 7 Bing. 682.
[4] Hall *v.* Seabright, 1 Mod. 15.
[5] Feltham *v.* Cartwright, 5 Bing. N. R. 569.

until the permission is revoked. And such license, when executed, cannot be revoked.[1] So it has been held, that the *revocation* of a license does not justify an action for acts done under it prior to such revocation. Thus a parol license to put a skylight over the defendant's area, (which impeded the light and air from coming to the plaintiff's dwelling-house through a window,) cannot be recalled at pleasure, after it has been executed at the defendant's expense; at least not without tendering the expenses he had been put to; and therefore no action lies, as for a private nuisance, in stopping the light and air, &c., and communicating a stench from the defendant's premises to the plaintiff's house, by means of such skylight.[2] So, where goods upon the plaintiff's land were sold to the defendant, who was to be allowed to enter and take them; held, to an action of trespass, the plea of *leave and license*, and a peaceable entry to take was a good defence, though the plaintiff had, between the sale and the entry, locked the gates, and forbidden the defendant to enter, and the defendant had broken down the gates and entered to take the goods.[3]

30. But the plaintiff may recover for all the trespass not justified by a license which is relied upon in defence.[4] So a license will not constitute a defence for an injury which results from its abuse, and not from a due and proper execution of it. More especially does this rule apply, where the license was not given directly to a party who has been suffered by the defendant to use the property. Thus, to trespass for immoderately riding the plaintiff's mare, the defendant cannot plead, that the plaintiff lent him the mare, and gave him a license to ride her, and that by virtue of this license he and his servant rode the mare by turns.[5] So a verbal license "to dig and carry away ore," given by A. to B., and by B. afterwards transferred to C., will not justify C. in entering by force the enclosure of A., against his express warning. C. in

[1] Miller *v.* Auburn, &c. 6 Hill, 61; Water-Power *v.* Chambers, 1 Stockt. Ch. 471.

[2] Winter *v.* Brockwell, 8 E. 308.

[3] Wood *v.* Manley, 11 Ad. & Ell. 34.

[4] Sawyer *v.* Newland, 3 Verm. 383. See Lyford *v.* Putnam, 35 N. H. 563.

[5] Bringloe *v.* Morrice, 1 Mod. 210.

such a case becomes himself a trespasser, and may be repelled by A. with all necessary force.[1] And a license has been held to be determined by an assignment of the subject to which it relates. Thus, by lease not under seal, A. and B., trustees, on behalf of themselves and the other proprietors of a theatre, of whom the defendant was one, demised it to C. for three years, reserving to themselves and the other proprietors free liberty of admission to the theatre. C., by lease not under seal, let the theatre to the plaintiff for two nights, subject to the terms on which he held it. Held, the license was determined, and an action of trespass might be maintained against the defendant, who entered the theatre during the tenancy of the plaintiff.[2] So the prevailing doctrine is, that a license may be at any time revoked before execution of it, and will then constitute no defence for an act done by virtue of it. Thus the defendant brought trover against A. for a dog, and obtained a verdict for £50 damages, subject to be reduced to 1*s.* on the delivery of the dog to him. By the plaintiff's authority, A. delivered the dog, at the same time demanding it back on behalf of the plaintiff, as his property, at a time named. Afterwards, at this time, the plaintiff having demanded the dog, and the defendant refused to deliver it; the plaintiff brought trover, and the defendant pleaded *leave and license.* Judgment for the plaintiff.[3]

31. Another familiar application of the principle *in pari delicto*, is that of *estoppel*, whereby a party is *estopped* or precluded from complaining of an interference with his property, upon the ground that by his own conduct or declarations he has impliedly authorized such interference. A party will be concluded from denying his own acts or admissions, which were expressly designed to influence the conduct of another, and did so influence it, and when such denial will operate to the injury of the other.[4] Where one by his words or conduct

[1] Riddle *v.* Brown, 20 Ala. 412.

[2] Coleman *v.* Foster, 37 Eng. L. & Eq. 489.

[3] Sandys *v.* Hodgson, 10 Ad. & Ell. 472.

[4] Cummings *v.* Webster, 43 Maine, 192.

wilfully causes another to believe in the existence of a certain state of things, and induces him to act on that belief, so as to alter his own previous position; the former is concluded from averring against the latter a different state of things, as existing at the time.[1]

32. This rule is often applied in case of *sale and purchase.* The general principle is laid down, that the owner of goods, who stands by and voluntarily allows another to treat them as his own, whereby a third person is induced to buy them *bonâ fide*, cannot recover them from the vendee. Thus the plaintiff, the owner of the fittings of a public-house, demised them to A., who thereupon became tenant of the house to B., under an agreement which gave his landlord a lien on the fittings; the plaintiff being present at the execution of such agreement. A. afterwards sold the good-will and fittings, without the plaintiff's knowledge or assent, to the defendant, who, being told by B. that A. was his tenant, bought them *bonâ fide*, in ignorance of the plaintiff's title, and was accepted by B. as tenant in the place of A. Held, on the plea of not possessed, that trover for the fittings did not lie.[2] So, where one of several administrators was present at a levy upon the property of his intestate, and furnished to the officer a list of the slaves, and was present at the sale, and made statements to the bidders; although it did not appear that he acted fraudulently; held, that the administrators were estopped from proceeding against the officer as a trespasser.[3] So the plaintiffs agreed with A., to sell to his firm fifty casks of potashes, for a certain price, cash on delivery. A. thereupon engaged freight for the potashes in a ship, advertised for a voyage to Liverpool. The plaintiffs sent the potashes on board by their carman, who took receipts therefor from the mate. A. then went to the office of the plaintiffs, and stole the receipts from their desk. On the same day he presented them to the owners of the ship, and procured a

[1] Per Ld. Denman, Pickard *v.* Sears, 6 Ad. & Ell. 469; Preston *v.* Mann, 25 Conn. 118. See Francis *v.* Welch, 11 Ired. 215; Downer *v.* Flint, 2 Wms. 527.

[2] Gregg *v.* Wells, 10 Ad. & Ell. 90.

[3] Ponder *v.* Moseley, 2 Florida, 207.

bill of lading in his own name. Drawing a bill of exchange against the shipment, he assigned the bill of lading to B., who, in good faith, made an advance upon the security. C., the master of the ship, refused to deliver the potashes to the plaintiffs, but delivered them to the holders of the bill of lading in Liverpool. The plaintiffs gave no notice of the theft to any one connected with the ship for two or three days. In the mean time they treated with A. and demanded from him pay for the potashes or their return. In an action against C. and A. and his partners to recover the potashes; held, that the conduct of A. in obtaining possession of the property was *fraudulent* rather than *felonious;* and, the plaintiffs having allowed him to assume some of the *indicia* of ownership, so as to justify C. in considering him the lawful owner, and having also neglected to notify C. of the fraud promptly, they could not recover from C.[1]

33. But the question is to be left to the jury, whether the owner of the property sold has by his conduct enabled a third person to dispose of it. Thus the plaintiff, residing in the country, employed A., his agent in London, to import goods. Upon their arrival, A. transmitted the invoice to the plaintiff, but delivered the bill of lading to a warehouse-keeper, in order to get the goods entered and warehoused. In the warehouse-keeper's books they were described as the property of A. By the bill of lading, the goods were to be delivered to the order of the shipper or his assigns, and it was indorsed by the shipper in blank. A. had no authority from the plaintiff to sell the goods, but, after they had been standing in his name in the warehouse-keeper's books nearly five months, sold them to the defendants. Held, in an action of trover, that the jury ought to have been directed that the plaintiff was entitled to recover, inasmuch as A. had no authority to sell; or at least that it ought to have been submitted as a question of fact to the jury, whether the plaintiff had by his conduct enabled A. to hold himself out to the

1 Brower *v.* Peabody, 18 Barb. 599.

world as having the property as well as the possession of the goods.[1] So, where it appeared, in an action of trover brought by A. against B. for a wagon, which had been attached by B., while in the possession of C., as C.'s property, that A. lived four or five miles from C. and had without objection or interference permitted C. to occupy the property; it was held, that proof of these circumstances was admissible to show that A. knew of the conduct of C. in relation to the property, and assented to it; it being the province of the jury to determine their weight.[2] (*a*)

[1] Dyer *v.* Pearson, 3 B. & C. 38. [2] Avery *v.* Clemons, 18 Conn. 306.

(*a*) On the 26th of September, A. sold by contract to B. 100 casks of tallow then lying at a wharf, and on the same day gave him a written order to the defendants, the wharfingers, "to weigh, deliver, transfer, and re-house the same." The next day, B., who had previously entered into a contract with the plaintiffs for the sale of 300 casks of tallow, in part fulfilment of that contract, obtained from the wharfingers, and sent to the plaintiffs the following acknowledgment: "Messrs. C. & Co., we have this day transferred to your account (by virtue of an order from B.) 100 casks tallow, &c., with charges from 10th October." Upon the receipt of this the plaintiffs paid B. the full amount of the tallow. Shortly afterwards the defendants delivered twenty-one of the casks to the order of the plaintiffs. On the 11th of October B. stopped payment, and on the 14th A. sent notice to the defendants not to deliver the remainder of the tallow to B. or his order; and, though the tallow had not been weighed, held, in trover, the defendants were estopped by their acknowledgment, and could not set up in defence a right in A. to stop *in transitu*. Hawes *v.* Watson, 4 Dowl. & Ry. 22; 2 B. & C. 540.

The defendant, a wharfinger, having acknowledged certain timber on his wharf to be the property of the plaintiff; held, that he could not dispute the plaintiff's title in an action of trover. Gosling *v.* Birnie, 7 Bing. 339.

A manufacturer deposited goods with a wharfinger at Stockton, for the purpose of being shipped for the defendant's wharf in London, receiving from him receipts, describing them. The manufacturer indorsed upon these receipts orders upon the defendants to deliver the goods on their arrival to the plaintiffs, the latter having advanced money upon them. The plaintiffs sent the receipts and delivery-orders to the defendants, and demanded the goods. The defendants stated that the goods had not arrived, but promised that when they did arrive they should be forwarded to the plaintiffs. Held, that the defendants, having thus assented to the plaintiff's title to the goods,

34. But a plaintiff will not be held estopped, except by clear and unequivocal acts of admission or acquiescence, and to which the defendant was party or privy. Thus one is liable for cutting timber on another's land, though the latter by mistake led him to believe that the timber was on his own land.[1] So in case for deceit, in the sale of a runaway negro, alleged to be unsound, the defence was, that the plaintiff knew it before purchasing. Held, that evidence was inadmissible, that the plaintiff's wife had carried food to the negro, who was lurking about the plaintiff's farm, before the purchase.[2] So, in trover by one against whom a commission of bankruptcy had issued, against his assignees, to recover goods which they had, as such assignees, sold; it appeared that the bankrupt had assisted the assignees, by giving directions as to the sale; and that, after the issuing of the commission, he gave notice to the lessors of a farm which he held, that he had become bankrupt, and that he was willing to give up the farm; and in consequence the lessors received the lease, and accepted possession of the premises. Held, that the interference of the plaintiff was referable to an intention to take care of the property, and see that the most was made of it, and did not amount to an assent to the sale; and that he was not thereby estopped from bringing an action. Also, that he was not estopped by giving up his lease, the assignees not being parties or privies

[1] 20 Mis. 322.

[2] Hart v. Newland, 3 Hawks, 122.

---

could not afterwards dispute it; and that the plaintiffs might maintain trover upon their refusal to deliver them. Holl v. Griffin, 3 Moo. & S. 732.

Where the plaintiff in trespass *quare clausum* described the *locus in quo* as lot No. 171, and he conveyed lot No. 171, and the evidence showed, that the line, which had by the plaintiff and the owner of No. 172, lying south of No. 171, been acquiesced in for more than fifteen years, was not in fact the true line, but included a part of No. 172, and that the trespass was committed on the strip between that line and the true line, and not on what was originally No. 171; held, the plaintiff was entitled to consider and describe said strip as part of No. 171. Burton v. Larell, 16 Verm. 158.

to that transaction.[1] So the acquiescence in a trespass, of one who has been deceived by a pretence of legal authority, is not such consent as to affect his remedy at law.[2] So the plaintiff, upon the marriage of his daughter, lent to his son-in-law, who was a son of the defendant, certain household furniture. There was evidence tending to prove, that they intended to keep the true nature of the transaction secret from the defendant, and to induce him to suppose that the property was a gift; but there was no evidence of a contract between the plaintiff and the defendant, that any settlement should be made upon the wife, or that the gift of the furniture was an inducement to the marriage. The furniture afterwards came into the possession of the defendant. In an action of trover, held, even if the plaintiff and his son-in-law intended to induce the defendant to believe, that the property was given and not lent, still, if it were lent merely, the defendant, who claimed upon no other ground than that of the alleged deceit upon him, was not entitled to retain it. Also, that, even if the plaintiff had contracted to give the property as an inducement to the marriage, the defendant could not enforce such a contract, nor retain the property if in his possession, as he did not claim through his son.[3] So the plaintiff granted to the defendant by deed a narrow strip of land, "for the purpose of enabling the grantee to erect a mill-dam;" also "the right to build upon the land of the grantor, a mill or factory, somewhere near the northwest corner of S. W.'s land; and also the right to dig a canal or trench from said mill-dam to such mill as may be erected, with the right of passing to and from said mill-dam and mill over the grantor's land." The defendant built a mill-dam on the strip of land, and also a mill near the northwest corner of S. W.'s land, but not on the land of the plaintiff, and dug a canal from the dam, partly through the land of the plaintiff, to the mill, and six years afterwards entered upon the plaintiff's land, through which the canal

[1] Heane v. Rogers, 9 B. & C. 577.
[2] Bagwell v. Jamison, Cheves, 249.
[3] Batchelder v. Lake, 11 N. H. 360.

was dug, to repair and clear out the canal. Held, the deed gave the defendant no right to dig a canal through the plaintiff's land in any other place than that designated, namely, from the dam to a mill on the plaintiff's land; and that the plaintiff might maintain trespass against the defendant, though the plaintiff had acquiesced for six years in the building of the mill and the digging of the canal.[1]

35. Estoppel sometimes consists more directly of a *waiver* on the part of the plaintiff of his right of action for a tort. Thus, where a trespass, at the time it is committed, is left to a referee, the party injured cannot bring an action, though the property be clearly his.[2] So the defendant applied to the bailee of goods for them, saying untruly, that he had authority from the owner, the plaintiff, to sell them, and took the goods, and paid part of the proceeds to the bailee, requesting him to pay it to the plaintiff. The plaintiff received it without objection, and requested the bailee to call on the defendant for the remainder. Held, trespass could not be maintained.[3] So the assignees of a bankrupt, having once affirmed the acts of a person, who wrongfully sold the property of the bankrupt, cannot afterwards treat him as a wrongdoer, and maintain trover.[4] So, when the purchaser of a slave, sold at public auction, pays the purchase-money, after he has been informed of the slave's unsoundness, and of facts which would constitute a fraud in the sale, he cannot afterwards recover damages in an action of deceit, on account of such unsoundness.[5]

36. And the waiver may consist in *an election of remedies.* (*a*) Thus, if a bankrupt, on the eve of his bankruptcy, fraudulently deliver goods to one of his creditors, the assignees may disaffirm the contract, and recover the value of the goods in trover; but, if they bring assumpsit, they affirm the

1 Dickerson *v.* Mixter, 13 Met. 217.
2 Patterson *v.* Pieronnet, 7 Watts, 337.
3 Wellington *v.* Drew, 4 Shep. 51.
4 Brewer *v.* Sparrow, 7 B. & C. 310.
5 Gilmer *v.* Ware, 19 Ala. 252.

(*a*) See *Tort and Contract — Election.*

contract, and then the creditor may set off his debt.[1] So A. assigns goods to B. and C. B. sells to D., who gives a promissory note payable in fourteen days. After this D. assigns to E. all his goods. The note never having been paid, B. refuses to deliver. The possession of the seller, after the agreement and note, is the possession of the buyer, and trover will well lie for the goods; especially as B., being desired by D. to take back the goods, said "I will not; I will have payment," which affirmed the sale.[2]

37. But, in this form of estoppel also, the law requires unequivocal acts of acquiescence to conclude a party's rights. Thus the plaintiff, a provision merchant at Morlaix, sent 314 casks of butter by the defendants' railway, marked A., and addressed "to order at Brewer's Quay." The defendants, concluding, from their habit of carrying butters similarly marked, consigned to Messrs. A. and A., factors, in London, that these were intended for them; and having received directions from A. and A. to send all butters coming to them from Morlaix to Hibernia Wharf; delivered 154 of the casks at that place, the remaining 160 having by accident got to Brewer's Quay. C. and Co., the holders of the bill of lading, had received directions not to let A. and A. have the butters, unless they accepted certain drafts at sight, which they declined to do; and, when C. and Co., applied to the defendants for information as to the 154 casks, they referred them to A. and A. and took no further notice of the transaction. A. and A. afterwards sold the butters at the fair market-price of the day, and rendered an account of sales to the plaintiff; but, before the money was handed over, they suspended payment. Held, that the defendants were liable to the plaintiff for this misdelivery, notwithstanding he had so far adopted the acts of A. and A., as to endeavor to obtain from them the proceeds of the sale; and that the proper measure of damages was the net amount for which the butters had been sold.[3] So one, who has been drawn into

[1] Smith v. Hodson, 4 T. R. 211.
[2] Atkinson v. Barnes, Lofft, 326.
[3] Sanquer v. London, &c. 32 Eng. L. & Eq. 338.

a contract by fraud, may affirm the contract after discovery of the fraud, and sue for the fraud; or may *recoup* the damages in an action by the other party on the agreement.[1] Thus one, who by fraudulent representations is induced to become lessee of an entire lot, of which the lessor only owned a part, may, after discovery of the fraud, enter into possession and occupy during the term, and, in an action for rent, may *recoup* the damages sustained by the fraud.[2] But, after such affirmance, he cannot maintain an action depending upon the rescission of the contract.[3] (*a*)

[1] Whitney *v.* Allaire, 4 Denio, 554. [2] Ibid. [3] Ibid.

(*a*) The subject of *joint torts* will be distinctly considered hereafter. Although the application of the general rule, considered in the present chapter, to *contribution* between parties jointly concerned in the commission of a tort, falls rather under the head of *contracts* than of torts, the following remarks upon the subject may properly be introduced in this connection: —

"If the money appears to have been paid in consequence of the plaintiff's own voluntary breach of legal duty, or, for a tort committed jointly with the defendant, it cannot be recovered. The general rule is, that wrongdoers shall not have contribution one from another. The exception is, that a party may, with respect to innocent acts, give an indemnity to another which shall be effectual; though the act, when it came to be questioned afterwards would not be sustainable in a court of law, against third persons who complained of it. If one person induce another to do an act which cannot be supported, but which he may do without any breach of good faith, or desire to break the law, an action on the indemnity, either express or implied, may be supported. Thus, where the title to property is disputed, an agreement, by persons interested, to indemnify the sheriff for serving, or neglecting to serve, an execution upon the property, if made in good faith, and with intent to bring the title more conveniently to a legal decision, is clearly valid. So, where a sheriff, having arrested the debtor on mesne process, discharged him on payment of the sum sworn to, but was afterwards obliged to pay the original plaintiff his interest, he was permitted to recover the latter sum from the debtor under a count for money paid. So where the sheriff has been obliged to pay the debt, by reason of the negligent escape of the debtor, namely, an escape by the pure act of the prisoner, without the knowledge and against the consent of the officer, it seems he may recover the amount as money paid for the debtor. But if the escape were voluntary on the part of the officer, the money paid could not be recovered of the debtor." 2 Greenl. Ev. § 115; acc. Nelson *v.* Cook, 17 Ill. 443.

It has been recently doubted, whether the doctrine of *contribution* is applicable to a case of tort founded upon contract. Martin *v.* Great Northern, &c. 16 Com. B. 179.

It is held, that the proprietor of a newspaper, convicted and fined for the publication of a libel in the paper, inserted without his knowledge and consent by the editor, cannot recover against the editor the damages sustained by such conviction. Colburn *v.* Patmore, 1 Cromp. Mees. & Rosc. 73.

So, where the plaintiff paid money as indorser on notes discounted by a bank under an arrangement prohibited by statute; and the bank was not allowed to recover the balance due on the notes; held, the plaintiff could not recover from the bank the money paid by him. Mills *v.* Western, &c. 10 Cush. 22.

CHAPTER V.

TORTS TO THE PERSON. — ASSAULT AND BATTERY.

1. HAVING now completed our introductory view of *torts in general*, we proceed to consider them more in detail, as divided into specific wrongs or injuries, committed against the various rights which the law recognizes and protects.

2. The plainest and simplest legal rights are those *of the person*. A man *owns* his body and limbs more unquestionably and unqualifiedly than his stock in trade or his farm. While the latter may be the subjects of mere qualified ownership, and involved in complicated and conflicting claims of title; the former belong absolutely to the individual, and to him alone. Hence *torts to the person* claim our first notice.

3. An injury to the person is termed in law a *trespass*, or more commonly an *assault*, or *assault and battery*.

4. An assault, *insultus*, is defined to be "an unlawful setting upon one's person;"[1] or a threat of violence exhibiting an intention to assault, and a present ability to carry the same into execution.[2] (*a*)

[1] Finch's Law, 202. See Hays *v.* The People, 1 Hill, 351.

[2] Per Jervis, C. J., Read *v.* Coker, 13 C. B. 850; 2 Greenl. Ev. § 82; 1 Steph. N. P. 208.

(*a*) The Cornelian law *de injuriis* prohibited *pulsation* as well as *verberation;* the latter being characterized as accompanied with pain. 3 Bl. Comm. 120; Ff. 47, 10, 5.

The word *percussit* implies an assault. Young *v.* Slaughterford, 11 Mod. 229.

5. Mere *threats* of violence are not sufficient to constitute an assault.[1] (*a*) It is said by an English Judge,[2] "I own I have considerable doubt whether any mere threat, not in the slightest degree executed, that is, a person saying to another, 'if you do not move, I shall use such and such force,' is an assault. My impression is, that it is not. I do not know at what distance it is necessary for the party to be. No doubt, if you direct a weapon, or if you raise your fist within those limits which give you the means of striking, that may be an assault; but if you simply say, at such a distance as that at which you cannot commit an assault, 'I will commit an assault,' I think that is not an assault."

6. The question what constitutes an assault is a question of law, to be determined by the Court. Hence prayers, requiring the jury to decide what is an assault, are erroneous.[3] (*b*)

[1] Stephens *v.* Myers, 4 C. & P. 349; Keyes *v.* Devlin, 3 E. D. Smith, 518.

[2] Pollock, C. B., Cobbett *v.* Grey, 4 Exch. 744.

[3] Handy *v.* Johnson, 5 Md. 450.

It is not essential to constitute an assault, that there should be a direct attempt at violence. Hays *v.* The People, 1 Hill, 351.

(*a*) It is suggested (2 Sharsw. Black. 120 n.) that an action on the case lies for threats, by which consequences of injury are produced.

(*b*) And the same rule applies to an alleged *justification* of an assault. This also is a question of law. But the alleged facts upon which it is based must be left to the jury, and not decided by the Court. Thus, upon an indictment for an assault and battery, by firing a pistol bullet at the prosecutor, evidence having been introduced on the part of the government, tending to prove the offence as charged; the defendant introduced evidence tending to prove that the prosecutor was at the front door of the defendant's house, committing an offensive nuisance; that the defendant ordered him to go away, which he refused to do; that the defendant thereupon beat the prosecutor with the handle of a broom, until the same was broken, when the defendant thrust at him with one of the pieces; and that the defendant then went back into his house, and returned with a pistol, but did not discharge it. The jury having been instructed "that the facts proved were no justification of the assault and battery," held, the instruction was erroneous; and the facts should have been submitted to the jury, with instructions as to what would and what would not amount to a justification. Commonwealth *v.* Goodwin, 3 Cush. 154.

So it is held, that the judge may properly express an opinion as to the evidence tending to prove the alleged assault. Thus the Judge charged the jury, that, if the defendant threatened to whip the plaintiff out of the county, and the plaintiff was afterwards whipped, it would, in the absence of exculpatory evidence, be a strong presumption against him; but if he had only expressed the opinion, that he ought to be whipped out of the county, it would not be so strong a circumstance. Held, there was no error in this charge.[1]

7. Many familiar illustrations are found in the books, of what constitutes an assault. Thus presenting a gun in an angry and excited manner at another has been held an assault, whether loaded or not, if the plaintiff was ignorant upon that point.[2] So it is an assault, if one ride after another, and oblige him to run to a place of safety, in order to avoid injury.[3] Or throw at him a missile capable of doing hurt, with intent to wound, even if it do not hit.[4] Or advance, in a threatening manner, to strike the plaintiff, so that the blow would in a few seconds have reached him, if the defendant had not been stopped.[5] Or take indecent liberties, though not resisted, with a female pupil or patient.[6] (*a*) So a violent attack upon the horse harnessed to a carriage in which the plaintiff was riding, and striking him with a club, is an assault upon the plaintiff.[7] So upsetting a carriage or chair, in which one is sitting.[8] So the defendant ordered the plaintiff

[1] Grigsby *v.* Moffat, 2 Humph. 487.

[2] Beach *v.* Hancock, 7 Fost. 223; Richels *v.* State, 1 Sneed, 606; State *v.* Smith, 2 Humph. 457. Contra, Blake *v.* Barnard, 9 C. & P. 626.

[3] Morton *v.* Shoppee, 3 C. & P. 373.

[4] Ibid.

[5] Stephen *v.* Myers, 4 C. & P. 349.

[6] Rex *v* Nichol, Russ. & Ry. 130; Rex *v.* Rosinski, Ry. & M. 19.

[7] De Marentille *v.* Oliver, 1 Penning. 380.

[8] Hopper *v.* Keene, 7 Taunt. 698.

(*a*) Where one decoyed a female under ten years of age into a building, for the purpose of ravishing her, and was there detected while standing within a few feet of her in a state of indecent exposure; held, though there was no evidence of his having touched her, he was properly convicted of an assault with intent to commit a rape. Hays *v.* The People, 1 Hill, 351.

The consent of a female of that age, or even her aiding the prisoner's attempt, is no defence. Ibid.

to leave his shop, and, on his refusal, sent for some men, who mustered round the plaintiff, tucked up their sleeves and aprons, and threatened to break his neck if he did not go out, and would have put him out, if he had not gone out. Held, an assault upon the plaintiff.[1] But to stand in another's way, and passively obstruct his progress, as any inanimate object would, though by design, is not an assault.[2] Nor, in general, any mere *omission;* as where a man kept an idiot, bedridden brother in a dark room in his house, without sufficient warmth or clothing.[3] Nor to separate persons fighting.[4] So a declaration, which alleges that the defendant broke and entered a house, and committed an assault on the plaintiff therein, is not proved, as to the assault, by evidence, that the defendant, having a right to immediate possession of the house, entered and forcibly took away the windows of the room, in which the plaintiff was sick in bed, without evidence that the defendant knew that the plaintiff was in the house.[5] So *an intent to do harm* is essential, and the *gist* of an assault; and this is a question for the jury, depending on the circumstances of the case. Thus it is no assault, if words are used at the time, showing a purpose not to commit present violence; as where one said, laying his hand on his sword, that if it were not assize-time he would not take such language;[6] or, "Were you not an old man I would knock you down."[7] So, holding a pistol in the hand or hands, pointing in the direction of a man within distance, but not held as if about to fire, and without the immediate intention to fire, is not a presenting, and does not constitute an assault.[8] So, where the defendant, the master of a ship, took a pistol, cocked it, and presented it at the head of the plaintiff, saying, if he was not quiet, he would blow out his brains; and, in an action for assault, the declaration alleged, that the defendant assaulted the plaintiff, and presented a pistol at him loaded with gunpowder, ball,

1 Read *v.* Coker, 24 Eng. L. & Eq. 213; 13 Com. B. 850.

2 Innes *v.* Wylie, 1 Car. & K. 257.

3 Smith's case, 2 C. & P. 449.

4 Griffin *v.* Parsons, 1 Selw. 25, 26.

5 Meader *v.* Stone, 7 Met. 147.

6 Bull. N. P. 15; Richels *v.* State, 1 Sneed, 606.

7 State *v* Crow, 1 Ired. L. 376.

8 Woodruff *v.* Woodruff, 22 Geo. 237.

and shot, and threatened therewith to shoot him and blow out his brains; held, on the plea of not guilty, that the action was not sustained, if the defendant used words showing an intention not to shoot the plaintiff, nor without proof that the pistol was loaded, as alleged.[1] And it has been held, that, although the jury cannot infer a want of intention to do violence or injury merely from the failure to strike, in the absence of any declaration or other circumstances indicating it; yet, if there are any such declarations or circumstances, the jury are bound to take them into consideration in deciding upon the intention.[2]

8. An *assault and battery* is said to be a fighting against the will of the party assailed.[3] And the plaintiff may recover upon a declaration for assault and battery, though the assault only be proved.[4]

9. A *battery* is defined, as the actual infliction of violence on the person.[5] Or an unlawful, that is an angry, rude, insolent, or revengeful touching of the person, either by the defendant or any substance put in motion by him.[6] As by spitting upon a person;[7] pushing another against him;[8] throwing a squib or any missile or water upon him.[9] So striking a horse which a man is riding, whereby he is thrown;[10] or taking hold of his clothes in an angry or insolent manner;[11] or striking the skirt of his coat or a cane in his hand;[12] is a battery: because anything attached to the person partakes its inviolability. So it is a direct trespass, to injure the person of another by driving a carriage against the carriage wherein such person is sitting, although the last-mentioned carriage be not the property nor in the possession of the person injured.[13] Or to cut off the hair of a pauper in the workhouse, with force, and against his consent.[14] Or to

[1] Blake *v.* Barnard, 9 C. & P. 626.

[2] Handy *v.* Johnson, 5 Md. 450.

[3] Duncan *v.* Commonwealth, 6 Dana, 295.

[4] Bro. Abr. Trespass, pl. 40. See Cokely *v.* State, 4 Iowa, 477.

[5] 2 Greenl. Ev. § 84; Bac. Abr. Assault, &c.

[6] 2 Hawk. B. 1, c. 62, § 2.

[7] Regina *v.* Colesworth, 6 Mod. 172.

[8] Cole *v.* Turner, 6 Mod. 149.

[9] Scott *v.* Shepherd, 2 W. Bl. 892; Pursell *v.* Horn, 8 Ad. & Ell. 605.

[10] Dodwell *v.* Burford, 1 Mod. 24.

[11] U. S. *v.* Ortega, 4 Wash. 534.

[12] Respublica *v.* De Longchamps, 1 Dall. 111.

[13] Hopper *v.* Reeve, 7 Taunt. 698.

[14] Forde *v.* Skinner, 4 C. & P. 239.

put a deleterious drug into coffee, in order that another may take it, if it is actually taken.[1] And, in general, it is said, "The least touching of another in anger is a battery. If two or more meet in a narrow passage, and, without any violence or design of harm, the one touches the other gently, it is no battery. If any of them use violence against the other, to force his way in a rude, inordinate manner, it is a battery; or any struggle about the passage, to that degree as may do hurt, is a battery."[2] "The law cannot draw the line between different degrees of violence, and therefore totally prohibits the first and lowest stage of it, every man's person being sacred, and no other having a right to meddle with it in any the slightest manner."[3] (*a*) But an action for

[1] Button's case, 8 C. & P. 660.

[2] Per Lord Holt, Cole *v.* Turner, 6 Mod. 149.

[3] 3 Bl. Com. 120.

(*a*) So an assault and battery is committed, by indecently and fraudulently obtaining possession of the person of a married woman, by one falsely assuming to be her husband; although under such mistake she submits thereto. Rex *v.* Jackson, Russ. & Ry. 487.

A German quack, to whom the parents of a girl took her, to be cured of fits, stripped off all her clothes, and rubbed her with a liquid. She did not resist, but only expressed her dislike to the proceeding. Upon an indictment for assault, the question was left to the jury, whether the defendant believed that the stripping would aid in effecting a cure, and, they having found in the negative, a verdict of guilty was sustained by the Court. Rex *v.* Rosinski, 1 Moo. C. C. 19.

So a medical practitioner had sexual connection with a female patient, fourteen years of age, who was placed under his care by her parents; representing that he was treating her medically, with a view to her cure. Held, if she was ignorant of the nature of the act, and submitted only under the belief of this false representation; the defendant was guilty of an assault. Rex *v.* Case, 1 Eng. L. & Eq. 544.

On the trial of an action by a woman for an assault upon her person, with intention to have illicit intercourse with her, the plaintiff introduced a witness, who testified, that at the time of the alleged trespass he lived with the plaintiff, and one evening, between sundown and early candle-light, the plaintiff was sitting in her bedroom, tending her child; that the defendant came into the keeping-room adjoining the bedroom and asked for a paper; that the plaintiff thereupon directed her daughter to go down into the base-

assault and battery does not lie, unless the defendant was in fault or intended to commit a wrong.[1] As for assisting a drunken man, or preventing him from going without help, though he is thereby hurt;[2] or where a soldier, in discharging his musket by lawful military command, unavoidably hurts another;[3] or a horse by sudden fright runs away with his rider, not being accustomed to do so, and runs against a man;[4] or an injury is done by unavoidable accident, in course of a friendly wrestling match, or other lawful, athletic sport, if not dangerous.[5] (*a*) So it is said to be no assault,

[1] 1 Bing. 213.
[2] Bull. N. P. 16.
[3] Weaver *v.* Ward, Hob. 134.
[4] Gibbons *v.* Pepper, 4 Mod. 404.
[5] 5 Com. Dig. 795, Pleader, 3 M. 18.

---

ment story of the house and get a light; that, while she was gone for that purpose, the defendant went into the bedroom and said something to the child; that soon afterwards the plaintiff exclaimed, "let go of me," "keep your hands off me," "keep your distance;" that, while her daughter was coming in from the basement, with a light, the defendant left the bedroom, and soon afterwards the house; that the position of the witness during the transaction was such, that he could not see either the defendant or the plaintiff, but he knew the voices of both. Held, proper evidence to go to the jury, as an accusation of the trespass, which, though made to the defendant's face, he did not deny. Stratton *v.* Nichols, 20 Conn. 327.

(*a*) It is said, there is a distinction in cases of accident, with regard to the liability of the party, in civil and in criminal proceedings. Thus it is said by Hawkins, that it seems a man shall not forfeit a recognizance of the peace by a hurt done to another merely through negligence or mischance; as where one soldier hurts another by discharging a gun in exercise without sufficient caution; for notwithstanding such person must in a civil action give the other satisfaction for the damage occasioned by his want of care, yet he seems not to have offended against the purport of such a recognizance, unless he be guilty of some wilful breach of the peace. Hawk. P. C. b. 1, c. 60, § 27; Rosc. Cr. Ev. 289.

It has been held, that an action does not lie, for throwing down skins in a yard, being a public place, by which a man's eye was beaten out; it appearing that a wind blew the skin out of the way. Gill's case, 1 Str. 190.

But, where one intoxicated falls against a stove, and spills hot water thereby on another, he is liable in trespass. Sullivan *v.* Murphy, 2 Miles, 298.

if a man punch another with his elbow in *earnest discourse.*[1] But it is a battery, if one of two persons, fighting, unintentionally strikes a third;[2] or if one uncocks a gun without elevating the muzzle, or other due precaution, and it accidently goes off, and hurts a bystander;[3] or negligently discharges a gun;[4] or drives a horse too spirited, or pulls the wrong rein, or uses a defective harness, whereby the horse takes fright and does injury.[5] So, if the injury is done in a boxing match or fight, though by consent, an action lies; the consent only going in mitigation of damages.[6] Upon this point it has been remarked, that it is "a manifest contradiction in terms, to say that the defendant assaulted the plaintiff *by his permission.*"[7] So a plea, that the plaintiff and defendant were soldiers, at exercise, skirmishing with their muskets, and in so doing the defendant *casualiter et per infortunium et contra voluntatem suam*, in discharging his piece, wounded the plaintiff; is bad.[8] But there are cases, as has been seen, in which a somewhat different doctrine has been held, in relation to mutual combats. And the distinction seems to be, between the use of weapons not in themselves dangerous, as cudgels, which may promote activity and courage; and that of dangerous weapons, such as naked swords.[9]

10. With regard to the *defences* to an action for assault and battery, they have been thus concisely and comprehensively enumerated. "Where one who hath authority, a parent or master, gives moderate correction to his child, his scholar, or his apprentice. So also on the principle of self-defence; for if one strikes me first, or even only assaults me, I may strike in my own defence, and if sued for it may plead *son assault demesne*, or that it was the plaintiff's own original assault that occasioned it. So likewise, in defence

[1] Gilb. Evid. 256.

[2] James *v.* Campbell, 5 C. & P. 372.

[3] Underwood *v.* Hewson, Bull. N. P. 16.

[4] Dickerson *v.* Watson, T. Jones, 205.

[5] Wakeman *v.* Robinson, 1 Bing. 213.

[6] Logan *v.* Austin, 1 Stew. 476; Bell *v.* Hausley, 3 Jones, Law, 131.

[7] Christopherson *v.* Bare, 11 Qu. B. 473.

[8] Weaver *v.* Ward, Hob. 134.

[9] Hawk. P. C. b. 1, c. 60, § 26.

of my goods or possession; if a man endeavors to deprive me of them, I may justify laying hands upon him to prevent him, and, in case he persists with violence, proceed to beat him away."[1]

11. With regard to the justification of *self-defence* or *son assault demesne;* it is the general rule, that an assault will justify a blow, unless the battery is excessive.[2] And the following propositions embody the somewhat nice distinctions of the law upon this subject: "If A. strike B., and B. strike again, and they close immediately, and in the scuffle B. maims A., that is *son assault;* but if upon a little blow given by A. to B., B. give him a blow that maims him, that is not *son assault demesne*."[3] "If a person come up to attack me, and I put myself in a fighting attitude, this is not an assault upon my part, and will not make out for that person a plea of *son assault demesne*."[4] (*a*) Before a defendant can *under the general issue* justify beating and wounding the

[1] 3 Bl. Com. 120.

[2] Hazel *v.* Clark, 3 Harring. 22.

[3] Per Lord Holt, Cockcroft *v.* Smith, 2 Salk. 642.

[4] Per Lord Lyndhurst, C. B., Moriarty *v.* Brookes, 6 C. & P. 685.

(*a*) The violence, a resistance of which the defendant seeks to justify, may be committed by others as well as the plaintiff, if there is evidence to connect him with them in the transaction.

Justification, to an action for assault and false imprisonment, under a warrant of the Speaker of the House of Commons; which the plaintiff sought to meet, by evidence of the defendant's using a military force, which was improper, excessive, and unnecessary; and breaking into the plaintiff's house. Held, evidence was admissible, of acts of violence committed by the mob in parts adjacent, though out of sight and hearing of the plaintiff in his house, but who appeared to have the same purposes with those who were near the house. Burdett *v.* Colman, 14 E. 183.

If a justification consist of two facts, each of which would alone be a defence; the defendant will prevail, though he prove but one of them. Thus, where the defendant pleaded that the plaintiff assaulted him while he was attending as high sheriff at an election, and also obstructed him in his duty, wherefore he caused him to be committed; it was held sufficient for the defendant to prove only that he was thus obstructed. Spilsbury *v.* Micklethwaite, 1 Taun. 147.

plaintiff, on the mere ground of misconduct which does not amount to an assault, he must show that he was wholly free from frault.[1] And no *words of provocation* will justify an assault, although they may constitute a ground for the reduction of damages.[2] (*a*) Nor is it any justification, that the plaintiff had "busied herself tattling about the defendant and his wife."[3] Whether the defendant can give in evidence the general bad character of the plaintiff, by way of excuse, especially where such character had no connection with the

[1] Phillips *v.* Kelly, 29 Ala. 628.

[2] Cushman *v.* Ryan, 1 Story, 91; Keyes *v.* Devlin, 3 E. D. Smith, 518.

[3] Suggs *v.* Anderson, 12 Geo. 461.

(*a*) And *previous* provocations are held not admissible for any purpose. The criterion on this point is, whether "the blood had time to cool;" or whether the provocation and assault formed parts of one transaction. Avery *v.* Ray, 1 Mass. 12; acc. Barry *v.* Inglis, 1 Tay, 121; 2 Hayw. 102. Lee *v.* Woolsey, 19 Johns. 319; Willis *v.* Forest, 2 Duer, 310; Collins *v.* Todd, 17 Mis. 537; Burchard *v.* Booth, 4 Wis. 67; Corning *v.* Corning, 1 Seld. 97.

Though former threats or insults will not palliate an assault and battery, yet, if the injury is done in the attempt to prevent the execution of such threats, the fact may be shown in mitigation of damages. Waters *v.* Brown, 3 Marsh. 559. Evidence of declarations of the plaintiff respecting the defendant is not admissible, unless shown to have been communicated to him. Gaither *v.* Blowers, 11 Md. 536.

If made two months before, they are inadmissible, unless communicated to the defendant immediately before the assault. *Ib.*

Evidence, that the plaintiff had said that he did not think the defendant always in his right mind, there being no proof that it was communicated to the defendant, and no pretence that he ever was insane, will not be admissible. *Ib.*

Previous threats of the defendant have been held admissible in aggravation of damages. Sledge *v.* Pope, 2 Hayw. 402. See Ogletree *v.* State, 28 Ala. 693; Morrow *v.* Moses, 8 N. H. 95.

Where the defendant undertakes to disprove malice, the plaintiff may show that the defendant had offered to fight him since the commencement of the action. Mills *v.* Carpenter, 10 Ired. 298.

The defendant may offer in evidence a letter which he had sent to the plaintiff, informing him that he should carry weapons for his defence, solely to show, that he had forewarned the plaintiff that he should arm himself, &c. McMasters *v.* Cohen, 5 Ind. 174.

assault, is very doubtful; though he has sometimes been permitted to prove the conduct or even the character of the plaintiff, as forming the inducement and provocation to the assault.[1] And in an action for assault and battery, where an altercation grew out of a question of veracity between the parties; the defendant was allowed to show that the truth of the matter in dispute was with him, in mitigation of damages.[2] (*a*)

12. Conformably to another part of the rule above stated, (§ 10,) to trespass for an assault and battery the defendant may plead, that the plaintiff, with force and arms and with a strong hand, endeavored forcibly to *break and enter the defendant's close*, whereupon the defendant resisted and opposed such entrance, &c., and, if any damage happened to the plaintiff, it was in defence of the possession of the said close.[3] (*b*) So a battery may be justified by a *molliter manus*

[1] Rhodes *v.* Bunch, 3 M'C. 66; M'Kenzie *v.* Allen, 3 Strobh. 546.

[2] Marker *v.* Miller, 9 Md. 338.

[3] Weaver *v.* Bush, 8 T. R. 78.

(*a*) Evidence, that the person assaulted "was a lazy vagabond, who would not work if he could help it; that money could not be made out of him by legal process; that he had been indebted to the defendant a long time, and would not pay; that the defendant, on the morning of the day on the evening of which the assault was committed, had offered him ten dollars per hour if he would work for him in payment of said indebtedness, and had refused to do it," is not admissible for the defendant, in mitigation or extenuation of the assault. Ward *v.* State, 28 Ala. 53.

(*b*) So, on an indictment for assault and battery, the defendant may show that he owned the premises on which the assault and battery was committed, and that he did the acts complained of in defence of the possession thereof. Harrington *v.* The People, 6 Barb. 607.

And, in New York, if the assault and battery was committed, in resisting persons entering upon the premises to open and work a highway, the defendant may prove, that the highway was laid through his orchard of four years' growth, without his consent. Ibid.

With regard to justification under legal process or authority of law, an attempt to rescue a distress from the plaintiff will justify an assault, but it must be pleaded. Anon. 11 Mod. 64.

A battery cannot be justified by an arrest by legal process; but it should be pleaded, that the defendant laid his hands gently on the plaintiff in

imposuit, because the plaintiff would not go out of the defendant's house when he desired him.[1] So the possessor of a house may assault and use force, in expelling one wrongfully forcing his way in.[2] But the distinction is to be observed, that a *possession in fact* will justify violence, if necessary, to defend it; but a mere *right to the possession* will not justify an assault and battery for the purpose of obtaining possession, whether the plaintiff or a third person be in possession.[3] And where the defence is *son assault demesne* and defence of possession, both parties claiming to have been in possession; the question for the jury is, which party had the actual possession.[4] So the owner of personal property cannot take it from the peaceable, though wrongful, possession of another, by violence on his person.[5] (*a*)

13. The same principle has been applied, in the case of a mere unwarrantable intrusion, without claim of title on either side, and simply upon the ground of impropriety and inconvenience. Thus, in trespass for assaulting and turning the plaintiff out of a police-office; plea, that two of the defendants, being justices of the peace, were assembled in a police-

[1] Tottage *v.* Petty, Rep. t. Hardwicke, 358.

[2] Pitford *v.* Armstrong, Wright, 94.

[3] Parsons *v.* Brown, 15 Barb. 590; Sugg *v.* Anderson, 12 Geo. 461.

[4] Ibid.

[5] Andre *v.* Johnson, 6 Blackf. 375.

---

order to arrest him, and that the plaintiff made resistance in order to rescue himself, and for that reason he beat him. Williams *v.* Jones, Rep. t. Hardwicke, 298.

Under particular circumstances, one man may be justified in laying hands upon another, for the purpose of serving him with process. Harrison *v.* Hodgson, 5 Man. & Ry. 392.

(*a*) In trespass for throwing water over the plaintiff's apartment and herself, it is no plea, that the plaintiff was engaged in obstructing an ancient window of the defendant's house, and that the defendant threw water over her to prevent it. Simpson *v.* Morris, 4 Taunt. 821.

To an action of assault and battery, the defendant may plead, that it was in defence of his possession; but if he says *molliter insultum fecit*, instead of *molliter manus imposuit*, it is bad on demurrer. Jones *v.* Tresilian, 1 Mod. 36.

office to adjudicate upon an information, and were proceeding to hear and determine the same, when the plaintiff (being an attorney) entered with the informer, not as his friend or as a spectator, but for the avowed purpose of acting as his attorney and advocate; and as such, without the leave and against the will of the justices, was taking notes of the evidence of a witness, and acting and taking part in the proceedings, as an attorney or advocate on behalf of the informer; that they stated to the plaintiff, that it was not their practice to suffer any person to appear and take part in any proceedings before them as an attorney or advocate, and requested him to desist from so doing; and, although they were willing to permit the plaintiff to remain in the office as one of the public, yet, that he would not thus desist, but asserted his right to be present, and to take such part; and unlawfully, and against the will of the justices, continued in the office, taking part and acting as aforesaid, in contempt of the justices; whereupon, by order of the above two defendants, the other defendants turned the plaintiff out of the office. Held, on demurrer, a good plea, inasmuch as no person has a right to act as an advocate, on the trial of an information before justices of the peace, without their permission.[1]

14. It is to be observed, however, that the law justifies no more or greater force in defence of one's person or property, than is necessary to effect the object. In technical language, the plea of *molliter manus imposuit* is answered by the replication *de injuriâ suâ propriâ*.[2] (*a*) And a recovery may

[1] Collier *v.* Hicks, 2 B. & Ad. 663.

[2] Scribner *v.* Beach, 4 Denio, 448; Bartlett *v.* Churchill, 24 Vt. 218; Dole *v.* Erskine, 35 N. H. 503; Philbrick *v.* Foster, 4 Ind. 442; Gaither *v.* Blowers, 11 Md. 536.

(*a*) And, if the defendant, having obtained the right to open and close, by filing an admission under a rule of court, justify on the ground of lawful authority; the burden of proof will be on him to show, that he did not use more force than was necessary. Loring *v.* Aborn, 4 Cush. 608.

Action for breaking, &c., imprisonment, and a battery. Plea, a writ, upon which the defendant entered the house and arrested the plaintiff, who after the arrest conducted in a violent and outrageous manner, and could

be had in cross-actions for the same affray, — by the assaulted party, for the first assault and battery; and by the assailant, for the excess of force used, beyond what was necessary for self-defence.[1] It is said, with more particular reference to the plea of *self-defence*, "Though fully justified in retaliating, the party must not carry his resentment such a length as to become the assailant in his turn, as by continuing to beat the

[1] Dole *v.* Erskine, 35 N. H. 503.

---

not otherwise be kept in custody, and therefore the defendant was obliged to push and pull him about. Replication, *de injuriâ*, &c. The arrest and subsequent battery being proved, held, the defendant was bound to prove the outrageous conduct alleged in his plea; and that no new assignment was necessary. Also, that it was a question for the jury, whether the defendant had done more than was necessary to keep the plaintiff safely in custody. Phillips *v.* Howgate, 5 B. & A. 220.

Where the defendant pleaded, that as master of a ship he moderately chastised the plaintiff for disobedience; it was held, that under this replication the plaintiff might show that the beating was excessive. Hannen *v.* Edes, 15 Mass. 347. See Sampson *v.* Smith, Ib. 365.

And the same rule prevails, where the plea is *son assault*, &c. Curtis *v.* Carson, 2 N. H. 539. See King *v.* Phipard, Carth. 280.

Where, in an action for an assault, the plaintiff declared, that the defendant beat, bruised, and wounded him; and the defendant pleaded *son assault demesne;* and the plaintiff replied *de injuriâ suâ propriâ;* and it was proved that the latter, being on horseback, got off, and held up his stick at the defendant, when the latter struck him; held, the plaintiff should have replied specially. Dale *v.* Wood, 7 Moore, 33.

In an action for an assault and battery, if the plea is *son assault demesne*, and the replication *de injuriâ*, the plaintiff has the right to introduce his evidence first; but, if the defendant be permitted to go forward, the plaintiff may still prove the assault and battery charged in the declaration. Young *v.* Highland, 9 Gratt. 16.

Where, in trespass for assault and battery, there is but one count in the declaration, and the plea of *son assault demesne* is supported, the plaintiff cannot afterwards prove another assault and battery. Peyton *v.* Rogers, 4 Mis. 254.

Where a plaintiff replied *de injuriâ* to a plea of *son assault demesne*, it was held to amount to a traverse of the whole plea, and that the plaintiff, without a new assignment or special replication, could prove that the defendant's battery was excessive. Ayers *v.* Kelley, 11 Ill. 17.

aggressor after he has been disabled or has submitted, or by using a lethal or ponderous weapon, as a knife, poker, hatchet, or hammer, against a fist or cane, or, in general, pushing his advantage in point of strength or weapon to the uttermost. In such cases the defence degenerates into aggression."[1] Hence an allegation, that a party gently laid his hands on another, *molliter manus imposuit*, is no justification of *a beating and wounding*.[2] Thus, to an action for an assault and battery and wounding, the defendants pleaded, that they gently laid hands on the plaintiff to arrest him for felony, and did no more injury than was necessary in effecting the arrest. Held, as the plea did not justify the wounding, it was insufficient.[3] So, to a declaration in trespass, charging that the defendant assaulted, seized, violently pulled and dragged about, struck and imprisoned the plaintiff, a plea, justifying the arrest and imprisonment by virtue of legal process, is bad. The plea, in such case, should show that the acts of violence were rendered necessary by the resistance of the plaintiff.[4] So, if the possession of one's property be held by another, the owner may take possession, if he can do so without tumult and riot, or breach of the peace, and may employ his slaves to assist him; but he has no right to use unreasonable violence. And, though a planter has a right to take possession of his property whenever he chooses to demand it of his overseer, and the overseer is bound to surrender it when demanded, and, if he refuse, after reasonable notice to quit, he may be put out with such force as is necessary, and even with the assistance of the planter's slaves; yet the planter has not the right to use more force and violence than the exigency of the case requires.[5] So, where A. lifted the form upon which B. sat, whereby B. fell, it was held no justification for biting off A.'s finger.[6] So it is said, "a civil trespass will not justify the firing a pistol at the trespasser, in sudden resentment or anger. If a person takes

[1] Ali. Princ. 177.

[2] French *v.* Marstin, 4 Fost. 440; 11 Md. 536; 29 Ala. 628.

[3] Boles *v.* Pinkerton, 7 Dana, 453.

[4] Kreger *v.* Osborn, 7 Blackf. 74.

[5] Davis *v.* Whitridge, 2 Strobh. 232.

[6] Bull. N. P. 18.

forcible possession of another's close, so as to be guilty of a breach of the peace, it is more than a trespass; so, if a man with force invades and enters into *the dwelling* of another. But a man is not authorized to fire a pistol on every invasion or intrusion into his house. He ought, if he has a reasonable opportunity, to endeavor to remove the trespasser without having recourse to the last extremity."[1] But one attacked with a knife, and believing and having reason to believe that he is in immediate danger of being wounded, is justified in shooting the assailant.[2] So, in inflicting corporal punishment, a teacher must exercise reasonable judgment and discretion, and be governed, as to the mode and severity of the punishment, by the nature of the offence, the age, size, and apparent powers of endurance of the pupil.[3] The cause must be sufficient, the instrument suitable to the purpose, and he must administer it in moderation.[4] So, when the defendant relies on a prior assault by the plaintiff, an instruction, that, if the plaintiff committed the first assault, and the assault of the defendant was defensive only, there should be a verdict for the defendant; is ground for a new trial, unless it be added, that the assault of the defendant must not be disproportionate to that of the plaintiff.[5] So, in an action of trespass *quare clausum*, and for an assault, battery, and wounding, the defendants pleaded, that the plaintiff had felled a tree across a navigable stream, down which they were conducting a boat, and that to enable them to proceed it was necessary to remove the obstruction; and that the plaintiff stood upon it with an axe, threatening to resist the removal; and they therefore gently laid hands upon him, &c. Held, the plea was insufficient, as it did not justify the wounding.[6] (*a*) So the plaintiff declared for an assault in

[1] Per Holroyd, J., Meade's case, 1 Lewin, C. C. 185.

[2] Rapp *v.* Commonwealth, 14 B. Mon. 614. See Hopkinson *v.* The People, 18 Ill. 264.

[3] Commonwealth *v.* Randall, 4 Gray, 36.

[4] Cooper *v.* McJunkin, 4 Ind. 290.

[5] Brown *v.* Gordon, 1 Gray, 182.

[6] Brubaker *v.* Paul, 7 Dana, 428.

(*a*) The defendants also pleaded, that the public had a prescriptive right to navigate the stream; that the plaintiff obstructed it; that they attempted

seizing and laying hold of him, pulling and dragging him about, striking him, forcing him out of a field into and through a pond, and there imprisoning him. Plea, justifying the assaulting, seizing, and laying hold of the plaintiff, and pulling and dragging him about. Held, no sufficient answer to the entire charge in the declaration.[1] So the defendant, one of the marshals of London, whose duty it was, on the days of public meeting in the Guildhall, to see that a passage was kept for corporators, ordered the plaintiff, who was in front of the crowd, to stand back. The plaintiff said he could not, on account of those behind; whereupon the defendant struck him in the face, saying that he would make him. Held, an unjustifiable assault.[2] So the defendant, a constable, had apprehended a boy fighting, and the plaintiff, a bystander, placed himself before the defendant, to prevent him from committing the boy, and said, "You ought not to handcuff the boy," whereupon the defendant struck him with a stick and took him to the watch-house. Held, if the defendant thought that the plaintiff meant to prevent an arrest, he had a right to commit the plaintiff to the watch-house, but not to beat him; but if the plaintiff merely spoke

[1] Bush *v.* Parker, 1 Bing. N. R. 72. [2] Imason *v.* Cope, 5 C. & P. 193.

---

to remove the obstruction, and, the plaintiff having assaulted them, they, in self-defence, necessarily beat and wounded him "a little," using only such force as was necessary to remove the obstruction. To this plea, the plaintiff demurred. Held, the plea was *primâ facie* a justification of the wounding, the demurrer admitting such an assault on the part of the plaintiff as made it necessary. Also, that, if the wounding was not a necessary consequence of the assault by the plaintiff, there should have been a replication to that effect. Brubaker *v.* Paul, 7 Dana, 428.

While a teamster was standing by his wagon with a heavy whip in his hand, another person took hold of his horse and turned the horse's head, and, being told by the teamster to let go, did so, and struck the horse on the head with his hand, causing the horse to step back three or four feet, but not otherwise doing any damage. Held, these facts did not show a sufficient provocation, to justify the teamster in severely beating the other, and knocking him down with the butt of his whip. Commonwealth *v.* Ford, 5 Gray, 475.

as above mentioned, the whole proceeding was a trespass.[1]

15. Upon the same principle, if one undertakes to possess himself of the lands or goods of another without force, the owner must first request him to depart, and, if he refuse, may then use sufficient force to expel him; but he must not assault him in the first instance.[2] But if the entry, or the attempt to take another's chattels, be made with force and violence, the owner may in the first instance use such force as shall be necessary to subdue the violence of the aggressor. And, where one evidently intends by force or surprise to commit a felony upon a man's person or property, the other party may resist the force by force on his part, and may even kill the assailant, if it be necessary to prevent the injury.[3] (a)

16. With regard to *the pleadings* in an action for assault and battery, the defendant cannot, under the general issue, give in evidence, by way of mitigation of damages, matter of defence, which, if pleaded, would amount to a justifi-

[1] Levy *v.* Edwards, 1 C. & P. 40.

[2] Per Jewett, J., Scribner *v.* Beach, 4 Denio, 448.

[3] Per Jewett, J., Scribner *v.* Beach, 4 Denio, 448.

(*a*) On a trial for an assault and battery, where there was contradictory testimony as to the degree of force used towards the defendant by the complainant, on the defendant's refusal to remove from the complainant's premises, after being requested so to do; the Judge refused the prayer of the defendant to instruct the jury, that, if the complainant committed a battery on the defendant, it was not a proper kind of force to remove the defendant, and that the complainant thereby committed the first assault; but did instruct them, that the complainant had a right, after requesting the defendant to remove, and his refusal, to use proper and reasonable force to remove him, and that the jury must determine, from the testimony, how much and what kind of force the complainant used towards the defendant, and that if in their opinion he used more force than was necessary, or if the force was not appropriate and adapted to effect the purpose of removing the defendant, then they should consider the complainant as having committed the first assault; but if the jury considered the force thus used as necessary and proper, and also appropriate and adapted to effect the purpose of removing the defendant, then the complainant would be justified and would not have committed the first assault. Held, the actual instructions were right. Commonwealth *v.* Clark, 2 Met. 23.

cation.[1] Though it has been held, that he may extract evidence in mitigation of damages on the cross-examination of the plaintiff's witnesses.[2] (a) Thus he cannot, under the general issue, show that the plaintiff was the first aggressor, and that the battery was in defence of his possession.[3] So, in trespass for driving the defendant's cart against the plaintiff, throwing him down, and wounding him, the defendant cannot show, under *Not Guilty*, that there was no negligence on his part, but that the plaintiff accidentally slipped from the pavement, and the defendant unintentionally drove over him; although he might show unintentional accident, arising from a superior agency.[4]

17. As has been already suggested, where the defendant pleads *son assault demesne*, and the plaintiff replies *de injuriâ suâ propriâ;* these pleadings present two questions of fact; first, did the plaintiff commit the first assault; secondly, if so, did the defendant use any more force than was necessary in his defence.[5] And the defendant cannot give evidence in mitigation of damages, nor contradict the averments of aggravated injuries; but only prove an excuse.[6] (b)

[1] Pujolas *v.* Holland, 3 Irish L. R. 533; Meeds *v.* Carver, 7 Ired. 273. See Schneider *v.* Schulty, 4 Sandf. 665.

[2] Moor *v.* Adam, 2 Chitty, 198.

[3] Jewett *v.* Goodall, 19 N. H. 562.

[4] Hall *v.* Fearnley, 3 Adol. & El. (N. S.) 919.

[5] Bartlett *v.* Churchill, 24 Vt. 218.

[6] Frederick *v.* Gilbert, 8 Barr, 454.

(a) So, if the defendant pleads not guilty, with a written notice of special matter, equivalent to a plea of *son assault demesne*, if the evidence sustain such plea, he is entitled to a verdict, although the plaintiff may in the first instance have made out his case. Paige *v.* Smith, 13 Verm. 251.

(b) Where the plea was *son assault demesne*, and the replications, 1st, *de injuriâ;* 2d, excess; and the defendant moved that the second replication be set aside; and the Court gave the plaintiff leave to select which replication he would retain, but he refused to select; and the Court granted the motion: held, there was no error in this proceeding. Reese *v.* Bolton, 6 Blackf. 185.

Where the declaration contains several counts, a plea, which commences and concludes in bar of the action generally, and which obviously and naturally should be understood in a plural and distributive sense, as applying to the different occasions on which the trespasses are charged, must be taken as a plea to the whole declaration, and must answer all that is

18. Where the defendant pleads not guilty and *son assault demesne*, a general verdict of *guilty* necessarily negatives the justification.[1] So a verdict, "We find for the plaintiff, and assess his damages," &c., is responsive to both issues, and good.[2] So, where the defendant pleads a justification, and *molliter manus imposuit*, and the jury find that there was a justification, and also an excessive battery, and assess damages therefor, judgment may be rendered for the damages.[3]

19. In an action for assault and battery, the *venue* is transitory.[4] So, where it was alleged, that the assault and bat-

[1] Pleasants *v.* Heard, 15 Ark. 403.
[2] Rector *v.* Shelhorn, 1 Eng. 178.
[3] Likes *v.* Dike, 17 Ohio, 454.
[4] Hurley *v.* Marsh, 1 Scam. 329; Sturgenegger *v.* Taylor, 3 Brevard, 7.

---

alleged as the direct ground and gist of the action, and must be valid and sufficient in law. Hathaway *v.* Rice, 19 Vt. 102.

Matter of aggravation does not consist in acts of the same kind and description as those constituting the gist of the action, but in something done by the defendant, on the occasion of committing the trespass, which is, to some extent, of a different legal character from the principal act complained of. Ibid.

But a declaration, which charges the defendant with having struck the plaintiff a great many violent blows with a club, and with a raw hide, and with his fist, and with having, with great violence, shaken the plaintiff, and pulled him about, and with having thrown down the plaintiff and then harshly and brutally kicked him, and struck him other violent blows, and with having wounded him, and torn his clothes, exhibits a mere succession of acts of direct trespass, all remediable by an action of the same class, and each requiring some complete justification, or excuse, in the plea. Ibid.

But a plea to such declaration, which professes to answer the "assaulting, beating, and ill-treating," using the explanatory words, "as in the declaration mentioned," will be considered as coëxtensive with the alleged cause of action. Ibid.

But it was held, that a plea to a declaration alleging such acts of trespass, which averred merely that the defendant was a schoolmaster, and the plaintiff was his scholar, and that the plaintiff was insolent, and refused to obey the reasonable commands of the defendant, and thereupon the defendant moderately chastised him, and which set forth no acts on the part of the plaintiff requiring excessive severity on the part of the defendant, such as resistance by the plaintiff; did not disclose a sufficient justification in law for the acts alleged in the declaration. Ibid.

tery were committed "at M., in the county of H., and within the jurisdiction of this Court;" held, not necessary to prove, that they were committed within the town of M.[1]

20. With regard to the *evidence* in an action for assault and battery, the plaintiff is not restricted to the mere act complained of, but is entitled to prove all its immediate, natural, and direct consequences;[2] but not remote consequences.[3] And none but obviously probable effects can be given in evidence, unless stated in the declaration.[4] And, in general, the plaintiff cannot recover for any injury for which a separate action lies, either by himself or another.[5] (*a*)

[1] Hurley *v.* Marsh, 1 Scam. 329.
[2] Hodges *v.* Nance, 1 Swan. 57.
[3] Moor *v.* Adam, 2 Chit. 198.
[4] 1 Mass. 12.
[5] 1 Chit. Pl. 347, 349.

(*a*) The fact, that a blow was given in the presence of a court in session, may be given in evidence in aggravation of damages, though the act might have also been punished by the Court as a contempt. Pendleton *v.* Davis, 1 Jones, Law, 98.

With regard to the damages in this action, see Cochran *v.* Ammon, 16 Ill. 316.

A declaration, in an action of assault and battery by husband and wife, that the defendant, on such a day, drove a coach over the wife and bruised her, by reason whereof the husband laid out divers sums of money for her cure, *et alia enormia*, *&c.*, is good, though entire damages be given; for the *per quod* is only laid in aggravation, and the *alia enormia* too general to suppose damages given for it. Todd *v.* Redford, 11 Mod. 264.

But although, after recovering damages in an action of assault, battery, and wounding, the plaintiff is put to great expense, in consequence of the injury which he received, yet he cannot maintain a second action to recover further compensation for the consequential damage; for it shall be intended that the jury considered all possible consequences on the trial of the first action. Fitter *v.* Veal, 12 Mod. 543.

Thus a recovery, in an action for an assault and battery, is a bar to an action for a subsequent loss, in consequence of the battery, of a part of the skull. Fetter *v.* Beal, 1 Ld. Raym. 339. Holt, C. J., remarked, "if this matter had been given in evidence as that which in probability might have been the consequence of the battery, the plaintiff would have recovered damages for it. The injury, which is the foundation of the action, is the battery, and the greatness or consequence of that is only in aggravation of damages." Acc. Caldwell *v.* Murphy, 1 Duer, 233; 1 Kern. 416.

Evidence is admissible, that the plaintiff complained of the injury, recently after it was received.[1] And the jury may be rightly told to determine, how much injury the plaintiff actually received, or whether he feigned greater suffering than he actually endured.[2]

[1] Yost *v.* Ditch, 5 Blackf. 184.

[2] Porter *v.* Seiler, 23 Penn. 424.

In an action for an aggravated assault and battery, whereby the plaintiff lost a leg, the elements of damage were said to be, 1. Loss of time and labor from the date of the assault till his health was restored; 2. Expenses of medical and surgical attendance; 3. Diminished capacity to work at his trade, arising from the injury; 4. Bodily pain and suffering. Donnell *v.* Sandford, 11 La. Ann. 445.

CHAPTER VI.

FALSE IMPRISONMENT.

1. A VERY frequent and important instance of assault and battery, or, in more general terms, of *injury to the person*, is that technically termed *false imprisonment*.

1 *a*. False imprisonment is *the unlawful restraint of a person contrary to his will*, either with or without process of law.[1] The subject of course involves many nice points connected with the general, constitutional right of *personal liberty*, (*a*)

[1] Bouv. L. D.

(*a*) The prevailing judgment of the Courts in this country is, that the provisions of the United States and of the several State constitutions, relating to personal liberty, have not materially affected the right of arresting, under some circumstances, without a legal warrant. It is said, "It has been sometimes contended, that an arrest of this character, without a warrant, was a violation of the great fundamental principles of our national and state constitutions, forbidding unreasonable searches and arrests, except by warrant founded upon a complaint made under oath. These provisions doubtless had another and different purpose, being in restraint of general warrants to make searches, and requiring warrants to issue only upon a complaint made under oath. They do not conflict with the authority of constables or other peace-officers, or private persons under limitations, to arrest without warrants those who have committed felonies. As to the right appertaining to private individuals to arrest without a warrant, it is a much more restricted authority, and is confined to cases of the actual guilt of the party arrested; and the arrest can only be justified by proving such

as limited and qualified by the liability to arrest and imprisonment, where the rights and safety of other parties require this

---

guilt. But as to constables and other peace-officers, acting officially, the law clothes them with greater authority, and they are held to be justified, if they act, in making the arrest, upon probable and reasonable grounds for believing the party guilty of a felony; and this is all that is necessary for them to show, in order to sustain a justification of an arrest, for the purpose of detaining the party." Per Dewey, J., Rohan *v.* Sawin, 5 Cush. 285.

So it is remarked in Pennsylvania, "The provisions of this section, (of the constitution of Pennsylvania,) so far as concerns warrants, only guard against their abuse by issuing them without good cause, or in so general and vague a form, as may put it in the power of the officers who execute them, to harass innocent persons under pretence of suspicion. But it is nowhere said, that there shall be no arrest without warrant. To have said so would have endangered the safety of society. The felon who is seen to commit murder or robbery must be arrested on the spot or suffered to escape. So although not seen, yet, if known to have committed a felony, and *pursued* with or without warrant, he may be arrested by any person, and even when there is only probable cause of suspicion, a *private person may* without warrant *at his peril* make an arrest. I say at his peril, for nothing short of proving the felony will justify the arrest. These are principles of the common law, essential to the welfare of society, and not intended to be altered or impaired by the constitution. The whole section, indeed, was nothing more than an affirmance of the common law, for general warrants have been decided to be illegal; but as the practice of issuing them had been ancient, the abuses great, and the decisions *against them* only of modern date, the agitation occasioned by the discussion of this important question had scarcely subsided, and it was thought prudent to enter a *solemn veto* against this powerful engine of despotism." Per Tilghman, C. J., Wakely *v.* Hart, 6 Binn. 316.

In this connection, we may refer to some other prominent instances of imprisonment, involving considerations of a public or political nature.

Where a citizen of the United States is arrested as a spy, and detained in custody until that fact can be tried by a court-martial, the person arresting, and the commanding officer by whose orders he is detained, are liable for a false imprisonment; the plaintiff not being subject to the jurisdiction of a court-martial, and the alleged offence not being within the jurisdiction of such Court. Smith *v.* Shaw, 12 Johns. 257.

To an action against the Speaker of the House of Commons, for forcibly and with the assistance of armed soldiers breaking into the messuage of the plaintiff, (the outer door being shut and fastened,) arresting him there,

interference. The subject is also intimately connected with the rights and duties of *judicial and ministerial officers*,

---

taking him to the Tower of London, and imprisoning him there; it is a legal justification, that a parliament was held, which was sitting during the period of the trespasses complained of; that the plaintiff was a member of the House of Commons; and that, the House having resolved, "that a certain letter, &c., in Cobbett's Weekly Register, was a libellous and scandalous paper, reflecting on the just rights and privileges of the House; and that the plaintiff, who had admitted that the said letter, &c. was printed by his authority, had been thereby guilty of a breach of the privileges of that House;" and having ordered that for his said offence he should be committed to the Tower, and that the Speaker should issue his warrant accordingly: — the defendant, as Speaker, in execution of the said order, issued his warrant to the sergeant-at-arms, to whom the execution of such warrant belonged, to arrest the plaintiff, and commit him to the custody of the Lieutenant of the Tower, to receive and detain the plaintiff in custody during the pleasure of the House; by virtue of which first warrant the sergeant-at-arms went to the messuage of the plaintiff, where he then was, to execute it; and, because the outer door was fastened, and he could not enter, after audible notification of his purpose, and demand made of admission, he, by the assistance of the said soldiers, broke and entered the plaintiff's messuage, and arrested and conveyed him to the Tower, where he was received and detained in custody, under the other warrant, by the Lieutenant of the Tower. Burdett *v.* Abbot, 14 E. 1.

So the sergeant-at-arms, charged with the execution of such warrant, is not guilty of any excess of authority, which will make him a trespasser *ab initio*, if, upon the plaintiff's refusing to submit to the arrest, and shutting the outer door against the sergeant, who had demanded admission for the purpose, and declaring that the warrant was illegal, and that he would only submit to superior force; and a large mob having assembled before the plaintiff's house, and in the streets adjoining, so that the sergeant could not arrest and convey the plaintiff to the Tower without danger to himself and his ordinary assistants, if at all, by the mere aid of the civil power; the sergeant thereupon called in aid a large military force; and, after breaking into the plaintiff's house, placed a competent number of the military therein, for the purpose of securing a safe and convenient passage to conduct the plaintiff out of the house into a carriage in waiting, and thence conducted him with a large military escort to the Tower, using at the same time every personal courtesy to his prisoner consistent with the due execution of his duty; which however would not safely admit of delay in the execution of such warrant. Burdett *v.* Colman, 14 East, 163.

In connection with false imprisonment, may properly be stated the general

which will be more fully considered hereafter; (*a*) and with the action for malicious prosecution. (*b*)

2. In general, no actual force, or manual touching of the body, no compulsory seizure, is necessary, to constitute arrest or imprisonment. "It is not necessary, that the person restrained of his liberty should be touched or actually arrested; if he is ordered to do or not to do the thing, to move or

---

principles relating to *habeas corpus*, which is the most summary and effectual remedy for this wrong.

"It is not only a constitutional principle that no person shall be deprived of his liberty without due process of law, but effectual provision is made against the continuance of all unlawful restraint or imprisonment, by the security of the privilege of the writ of *habeas corpus*. Whenever any person is detained with or without due process of law, unless for treason or felony, plainly and specially expressed in the warrant of commitment, or unless such person be a convict, or legally charged in execution, he is entitled to his writ of *habeas corpus*. It is a writ of right, which every person is entitled to, *ex merito justiciæ;* but the benefit of it was, in a great degree, eluded in England, prior to the statute of Charles II., as the judges only awarded it in term time, and they assumed a discretionary power of awarding or refusing it. The explicit and peremptory provisions of the statute of 31 Charles II. c. 2, restored the writ of *habeas corpus* to all the efficacy to which it was entitled at common law, and which was requisite for the due protection of the liberty of the subject. That statute has been reënacted or adopted, if not in terms, yet in substance and effect, in all these United States." 2 Kent, 26.

The Supreme Court of the United States may issue the writ of *habeas corpus*, where one is imprisoned under the warrant or order of any other court. It is in the nature of a writ of error; revising the effect of the process of such inferior court; not an exercise of original jurisdiction. But the Supreme Court has no appellate jurisdiction in criminal cases confided to it by the laws of the United States, and therefore will not issue a *habeas corpus* in case of commitment for contempt adjudged by a court of competent jurisdiction, nor inquire into the sufficiency of the cause of commitment. Kearney, 7 Wheat. 38; Tobias Watkins, 3 Pet. 193; 7 Pet. 568.

No court in the United States, nor any judge thereof, can by *habeas corpus* bring up one committed under a sentence or execution of a state court, except for the purpose of testifying. Dorr, 3 How. 103; Johnson *v.* United States, 3 M'L. 89.

(*a*) See *Officer, Sheriff, Judge, Justice of the Peace;* chapters 19–23.

(*b*) See *Malicious Prosecution;* chap. 8.

not to move against his own free will, if it is not left to his own option to go or stay where he pleases, and force is offered or threatened, and the means of coercion are at hand, ready to be used, or there is reasonable ground to apprehend that coercive means will be used, if he does not yield. A person so threatened need not wait for its actual application. His submission to the threatened, and reasonably to be apprehended, force, is no consent to the arrest, detention, or restraint of the freedom of his motion — he is as much imprisoned as if his person was touched or force actually used; the imprisonment continues, until he is left at his own will to go where he pleases, and must be considered as involuntary till all efforts at coercion or restraint cease, and the means of effecting it are removed."[1] Thus it is held actionable to stop and prevent one by threats from passing along the highway.[2] So if an officer notifies a party that he has come to arrest him under a warrant, the party submits, the officer accompanies him home, remains there all night, and takes him before a magistrate the next day; this is an arrest, although the party is not actually deprived of liberty, nor personally guarded by the officer.[3]

2 *a*. But on the other hand it has been held, that, if a magistrate's warrant be shown by the constable to the person charged with an offence, and he thereupon, without compulsion, attend the constable to the magistrate, and after examination be dismissed; it seems, this is not such an arrest, as will support trespass and false imprisonment.[4] So an action was held not to be maintainable, where the defendant, a schoolmaster, improperly, and under a claim for money due for schooling, refused to allow the mother of an infant scholar to take her son home with her, and the son, though frequently demanded by the mother, was kept at school during a part of the holidays; but there was no proof that he knew of the demand or denial, or that any restraint

[1] Per Baldwin, J., Johnson *v.* Tomkins, 1 Baldw. 601; Pike *v.* Hanson, 9 N. H. 491; Smith *v.* The State, 7 Humph. 43; Homer *v.* Battyn, Bull. N. P. 62.

[2] Blower *v.* State, 3 Sneed, 66.

[3] Courtoy *v.* Dozier. 20 Geo. 369.

[4] Arrowsmith *v.* Le Mesurier, 2 N. R. 211; acc. Berry *v.* Adamson, 6 B. & C. 528.

had been put upon him.[1] So lifting a person in his chair, and carrying him from the room in which he is sitting with others, and excluding him therefrom; is not a false imprisonment.[2]

3. As in other instances of assault, trespass, and not case, is the proper, though not exclusive form of an action for false imprisonment.[3] (*a*) Thus trespass is the proper remedy, for an arrest under process void in itself, or issued by a court without jurisdiction.[4] As, for an arrest under a void warrant.[5] So case will not lie for arresting one without cause of action, unless he be held to excessive bail.[6]

4. To sustain this action, it is sufficient to show such facts as constitute an unlawful imprisonment, without proof of all the collateral circumstances. Thus, in an action for a malicious arrest on a charge of felony, it is not necessary for the plaintiff to give in evidence the whole of the proceedings before the magistrates.[7] So, on the other hand, the defence need prove only enough to constitute a legal justification. Thus in trespass for false imprisonment, and detaining the plaintiff in custody until he had paid eleven shillings, the defendant justified by virtue of an order of a court of conscience to pay ten shillings and fourpence, which not being paid, he took him, &c. Held good, without justifying for the whole eleven shillings.[8]

5. But a justification *by process of law* cannot, in general, be offered under the plea of not guilty. Thus the defendant cannot, under this plea, show a judgment and execution against the plaintiff, under which the arrest and imprisonment took place; even for the avowed purpose of proving that the defendant was not guilty of the trespass.[9]

6. As in other cases of tort, the direct, personal agency of

[1] Herring *v.* Boyle, 1 Cromp. M. & R. 377.

[2] Gardner *v.* Wedd, (cited) 2 Sharsw. Black. 127, n.

[3] Stanton *v.* Seymour, 5 McL. 267.

[4] Allen *v.* Greenlee, 2 Dev. 370.

[5] Price *v.* Graham, 3 Jones, Law, 545.

[6] Neale *v.* Spencer, 12 Mod. 257.

[7] Biggs *v.* Clay, 3 N. & Man. 464.

[8] Swinsted *v.* Lydall, 5 Mod. 295.

[9] Coats *v.* Darby, 3 Comst. 517.

(*a*) See *Case*; and pp. 214, 231, n.

a party is not necessary to give a right of action against him. (*a*) Thus evidence that a bailiff's assistant apprehended a party on false pretence, and that the bailiff, being at hand, took advantage of that apprehension to arrest him on a writ of *ca. sa.*, was held sufficient to establish an issue, that the bailiff illegally seized and imprisoned the party.[1] So trespass lies, for procuring, by awe, fear, and influence, contrary to his own inclination, a sovereign, independent, and absolute foreign prince to imprison the plaintiff.[2]

7. It is a peculiarity of this particular form of trespass to the person — false *imprisonment*, literally so called — that it does not consist in a single act, but in a prolonged or continuous violation of personal liberty. Upon this point it is held, that, every continuation of an illegal imprisonment being a new trespass, a recovery in an action, commenced during the continuance of the imprisonment, is no bar to another action brought after it has ceased, for an assault, battery, and imprisonment; and, if so pleaded, the plaintiff may newly assign for the continuance of the imprisonment.[3] Thus, in an action for assault and false imprisonment, the declaration contained two counts, and the defendant pleaded, first, the general issue; and secondly, that, he and one J. W. having justified as bail for the plaintiff in an action then pending, he arrested the plaintiff, to render him in discharge of the recognizance, and detained him in custody until he had satisfied the demand for which the latter action was brought. The plaintiff replied *de injuriâ;* and it appeared in evidence, that the defendant, in addition to detaining the plaintiff until he had satisfied such demand, caused him to be detained an hour longer, and until he had given a security for the expenses incurred by the defendant's becoming bail. Held, this was one continuing trespass and imprisonment, and therefore that the plaintiff ought either to have newly

[1] Humphery *v.* Mitchell, 2 Bing. N. R. 619.

[2] Rafael *v.* Verelst, 2 W. Black. 1055.

[3] Leland *v.* Marsh, 16 Mass. 389.

(*a*) See *Master*, &c. — *Officer*.

assigned, or to have replied the excess, in order to entitle him to recover for the additional detention or imprisonment, which was unjustifiable or illegal.[1]

8. But, in an action for false imprisonment, where a verdict with £200 damages was given, for one night's confinement in a prison, evidence of a trespass by the defendant on the goods of the plaintiff, arising out of the same transaction, committed on the following day, was held to have been rightly admitted, for the purpose of showing malice.[2]

9. It is to be observed, however, that the very continuance of an imprisonment may itself constitute a wrongful act, although the original arrest was justifiable. (*a*) Thus an action for false imprisonment lies against a superior officer, where the imprisonment at first was legal, but was afterwards aggravated with many circumstances of cruelty, and was continued beyond necessary bounds.[3] So where a captain of a man-of-war imprisoned the defendant three days for a supposed breach of duty, without hearing him, and then released him without bringing him to a court-martial.[4] So a plaintiff is bound to accept, from a defendant in custody under a *ca. sa.*, the debt and costs, when tendered in satisfaction, and to sign an authority to the sheriff to discharge the defendant. And an action on the case will lie for having maliciously refused so to do; and the refusal is sufficient *primâ facie* evidence of malice.[5] So an action on the case lies, for maliciously and without reasonable or probable cause arresting the plaintiff, and detaining him until discharged by a Judge's order, pending a former suit by the defendant for the same cause of action, in which the plaintiff had been arrested and discharged out of custody, by reason of the defendant's delay in declaring; although the

[1] Lambert *v.* Hodgson, 8 Moore, 326.

[2] Edgell *v.* Francis, 1 Man. & Gr. 222.

[3] Wall *v.* Macnamara, cited 1 T. R. 536.

[4] Swinton *v.* Molloy, cited 1 T. R. 537.

[5] Crozer *v.* Pilling, 4 B. & C. 26.

(*a*) See *Trespass ab initio.*

second suit is still pending; and, it seems, although the party arresting had a good cause of action.[1]

10. But where a sheriff, by order of Court, took a convict sentenced to imprisonment into his custody, in order to execute the sentence; and the Court, on the same day, for the purpose of allowing the convict to be called as a witness, without sending to his place of confinement, rescinded the order, and directed the sheriff not to detain him; and on the next day ordered the sheriff to execute the original sentence, which was accordingly done; held, the sheriff was not liable for false imprisonment, unless he detained the party after the first and before the second order.[2] So an officer, having arrested a prisoner at a distance from the jail, must be the judge of the time when he will start for the jail, and the state of the weather in which he will go. He has a right to start at any hour he may choose or his business require, and in such weather as he may find at the time, provided he does not needlessly expose the prisoner's health, or do him a personal injury.[3]

11. Various cases are to be found in the books, in some of which an alleged process of law has been held to be, and in others not to be, a justification for arrest or imprisonment. Sometimes the officer is justified, while the party is held liable; (*a*) and in many cases the question turns upon the form of action, (see pp. 211, 231, n). Thus, in an old case, it is held that trespass for taking and imprisoning the plaintiff cannot be justified, under an order of the Court of Chancery.[4] So it was anciently held, that an action on the case lies, for causing a man to be arrested for a cause in an inferior court, which arose without the jurisdiction of that court; but no action will lie against the officer, it being for a cause of which the Court had jurisdiction.[5] So a capias

[1] Heywood *v.* Collinge, 9 Ad. & Ell. 268.
[2] Coffin *v.* Gardner, 1 Gray, 159.
[3] Butler *v.* Washburne, 5 Fost. 251.
[4] Furlong *v.* Bray, 1 Mod. 272.
[5] Hudson *v.* Cook, Skin. 131.

(*a*) See *Officer — Sheriff.*

is void, where a term intervenes between the teste and the return; and, if executed, an action of false imprisonment lies against the plaintiff.[1] So false imprisonment will lie against the plaintiff, for arresting a person on a judgment set aside for irregularity, but not against the officer, who is justified by the process.[2] So A., being in the custody of the marshal of the King's Bench prison, was brought up to that Court upon an order of the Court, and charged with an attachment for contempt; upon which attachment he was afterwards detained in custody. Held, that trespass was maintainable against the party who caused the order to be served on the marshal.[3] So an arrest cannot be legally made after the return day of the writ.[4]

12. But on the other hand it has been held, that, in an action for maliciously holding to bail, it is not sufficient to prove that the writ was sued out after payment of the debt, if the circumstances afford no inference of malice; but actual malice must be proved.[5] So trespass cannot be maintained, for an injury committed under process of law against the plaintiff, unless the process was void, or had been annulled. Case is the proper remedy. And an attachment for debt, issued by a justice of the peace, stands upon the footing of other process in this respect. Such an attachment, issued by a justice having jurisdiction, the recitals of which, and of the bond taken by him, authorized the emanation of the process, and nothing appearing upon the face of the proceedings or from the proof to invalidate it, is a good justification in an action of trespass against the plaintiff therein, although it appears that he procured it to be issued and executed without cause, and that it was afterwards discontinued and the property restored.[6] So one who sues an action before a justice of the peace, on which the defendant is arrested, is not liable to trespass for a false imprisonment, because from the absence of the justice the action is not entered.[7] So an

1 Parsons *v.* Lloyd, 2 W. Black. 845.

2 Smith *v.* Boucher, Rep. t. Hard. 66, 68.

3 Bryant *v.* Clutton, 1 M. & W. 408.

4 Anonymous, 7 Mod. 52.

5 Gibson *v.* Chaters, 2 B. & Pul. 129.

6 Lovier *v.* Gilpin, 6 Dana, 321.

7 Shaw *v.* Reed, 16 Mass. 450.

officer, who, at the request of a judgment creditor, commits a debtor on execution to the jail farthest from his residence, although requested by the debtor to commit him to a nearer jail in the same county, is not liable to an action by the debtor.[1] So a defendant in an action for false imprisonment, pleading a justification under *mesne process*, may state that the writ issued upon an affidavit to hold to bail, without setting forth the cause of action; for, if a party be arrested maliciously, and without any cause of action, his remedy is by an action for maliciously holding him to bail.[2] So the fact, that a person prefers a criminal charge against another before a justice of the peace, is a witness upon the trial, and employs counsel to conduct it on the part of the people; will not render him liable, in an action for assault and battery and false imprisonment, for the consequences of an erroneous conviction by the justice, where there is nothing to connect him with the unlawful imprisonment of the plaintiff.[3] So, in trespass for an assault and false imprisonment, it appeared that the defendant had given the plaintiff into custody, and had him taken to a police-office, on a charge of felony. The magistrate heard the charge, and remanded the prisoner. On a subsequent examination he was discharged, it being then discovered that the charge had been made under a mistake. The declaration charged the carrying the plaintiff in custody before a magistrate, and the remand, as distinct acts of trespass; and the jury gave damages for both. Held, that damages could not be given for the remand, which was the judicial act of the magistrate.[4] So the plaintiff voluntarily went before a police magistrate, to meet a charge of embezzlement, which was there about to be made against him by the defendant. The magistrate declining to entertain the matter, unless a charge were formally made, the defendant said, "Well, then, I charge him with embezzling 30*s*." The plaintiff was then ordered by a constable into the dock, the

[1] Woodward *v.* Hopkins, 2 Gray, 210.

[2] Belk *v.* Broadbent, 3 T. R. 183.

[3] Peckham *v.* Tomlinson, 6 Barb. 253.

[4] Lock *v.* Ashton, 12 Ad. & Ell. N. S. 871.

charge was gone into, and the plaintiff held to bail. Held, the act of the defendant amounted to no more than calling upon the magistrate to exercise his jurisdiction, and, consequently, that he was not liable to an action of trespass for the imprisonment of the plaintiff.[1] (a)

[1] Brown *v.* Chapman, 6 Com. B. 365.

(*a*) Proof of a warrant to arrest, *on suspicion of high treason*, will not sustain a justification, that the plaintiff was arrested and confined *on a charge of high treason.* Bell *v.* Byrne, 13 E. 554.

Where, in an action for assault and battery and false imprisonment, the defendant pleaded the general issue to all except the false imprisonment, and as to that a special plea, setting out a warrant for felony issued by a justice of the peace, and that by virtue thereof he arrested the plaintiff, &c.; held, a replication, protesting the warrant, and its delivery to the defendant to be executed, and then replying *de injuriâ suâ propriâ absque residuo causæ*, was good. Stickle *v.* Richmond, 1 Hill, 77.

Such a replication is not open to the objection, that it attempts to put in issue several distinct matters, or that the traverse is taken to be a mere conclusion of law. Ibid.

The general replication *de injuriâ*, &c., to such a plea would be bad, whether the justification be under process from a court of record or not of record. Ibid.

In an action of trespass, assault and battery, committed upon an officer by one whom he was attempting to arrest on a warrant, the defendant set up, by way of rejoinder, that the plaintiff at the time, &c., did not acquaint or give notice to the defendant that a warrant had been issued, or that he (the plaintiff) had any warrant or process, &c., nor did the defendant know that a warrant had been issued, or that the plaintiff had any warrant or process; to which the officer surrejoined, that he did acquaint and give notice to the defendant that a warrant, &c., had been issued, concluding to the country. This issue having been found for the defendant, held, not a case for judgment *non obstante veredicto*, and that he was entitled to judgment, though several other issues were found against him. The United States *v.* White, 2 Hill, 59.

In the proceeding under the statute of New York, to prevent the commission of crimes, where the examination of the complainant is reduced to writing, subscribed and sworn to by him, and contains matter sufficient to authorize the issuing of a warrant of arrest; the justice may issue the warrant, although no complaint in writing, separate and distinct from the examination, is made. Bradstreet *v.* Furgeson, 17 Wend. 181.

13. The question often arises, whether and against whom an action can be maintained, for the arrest of a person specially *privileged from arrest.* Upon this subject it is said, an arrest in virtue of a *ca. sa.* issued upon a valid judgment in tort, though made in violation of a personal privilege of the party, will not form the ground of an action for false imprisonment.[1] Certainly not, without proving knowledge of such privilege.[2] Thus an action for false imprisonment does not lie for a person arrested by legal process, but at a time when privileged *redeundo* from the Court.[3] Nor does trespass lie against a plaintiff, for suing out a *capias* and arresting a freeholder for debt.[4] So, the plaintiff being indebted to the defendant, the defendant sued out bailable process, which he delivered to the sheriff to execute, and the

[1] Per Cowen, J., Deyo *v.* Van Valkenburgh, 5 Hill, 242.

[2] Stokes *v.* White, 4 Tyrw. 786.

[3] Cameron *v.* Lightfoot, 2 W. Black. 1190.

[4] Farmers' Bank *v.* McKinney, 7 Watts, 214.

In a warrant of commitment, issued against a person accused for refusing to give security to keep the peace, it is not necessary to allege the offence which he is charged as having threatened to commit; it is enough to state the requirement to give security and the refusal. Ibid.

And it is not necessary that the warrant of arrest should contain a formal adjudication that there is reason to fear the commission of the offence threatened. Ibid.

In an action for false imprisonment, the defendant pleaded in justification, that the act complained of was the arrest of the plaintiff under a warrant issued at the instance of the defendant, who was the city attorney of Utica, for the violation by the plaintiff of an ordinance made by the common council; but the plea did not aver that the plaintiff had in fact violated the ordinance. Held, nevertheless, that the plea was good. Walker *v.* Cruikshank, 2 Hill, 296.

If R. is arrested by virtue of a warrant for the arrest of W., all persons aiding in the arrest are held to be trespassers, even though R. and W. are the same person. Johnston *v.* Wiley, 13 Geo. 97.

In an action for assault, evidence tending to show that the plaintiff had authority to stop the defendant in the road, and take property in the possession of the latter, the execution of such authority being the occasion of the trespass, is both relevant and admissible. Porter *v.* Seiler, 23 Penn. 424.

sheriff arrested the plaintiff whilst attending a trial as a witness under a subpœna. Held, that an action on the case was not maintainable, it not being shown that the defendant had any knowledge of the facts when he delivered the writ to the sheriff to be executed.[1] So, where one sues out a capias, and delivers it to an officer with directions to arrest the defendant immediately, the plaintiff not knowing at the time that the defendant is then privileged from arrest, and the officer arrests him while privileged; the defendant in the capias cannot maintain an action on the case therefor against the plaintiff. The direction to the officer must be understood to order an arrest as soon as the defendant should be subject to arrest.[2]

14. More especially, *an officer* who acts according to his precept in making an arrest is not a trespasser, although the party arrested is privileged from arrest.[3] Thus no action lies against a sheriff or his officer, for arresting a party attending under a summons from a court, though it be alleged that the party was thereby privileged, and that the defendants knew the fact, and made the arrest maliciously. And, if a party be arrested, and the Court order him to be discharged on the ground that he was in attendance under order of that Court, but the officer arresting does not discharge him; the remedy (if any) against the officer is in trespass, not case, though malice be alleged.[4]

15. Similar questions arise, in reference to imprisonment under process, founded upon a paid or discharged judgment. A *ca. sa.* issued on such judgment will protect the officer, but not the party nor the attorney. And an action lies, without obtaining a rule setting aside the process, (*a*) whether the party and attorney were notified of the dis-

[1] Stokes *v.* White, 1 Cromp. M. & R. 223.

[2] Sewell *v.* Lane, 1 Smith, (Indiana,) 167.

[3] Chase *v.* Fish, 4 Shep. 132; 1 Shep. 363.

[4] Magnay *v.* Burt, 5 Ad. & Ell. N. S. 381; 1 Dav. & Mer. 652.

(*a*) In the case of Scheibel *v.* Fairbain, 1 B. & P. 388, an action was

charge or not. But the want of notice is available in mitigation of damages.[1]

16. The most numerous cases of false imprisonment, are those involving the right of peace-officers or private individuals to arrest without warrant or process, in case of actual, supposed, or anticipated crime.

17. It will be seen, that somewhat nice distinctions have been established upon this subject, depending upon the nature and degree of the crime; upon the question whether it is in process of commission, or has been committed just before the arrest, or so long before as to make it a past transaction; and more especially upon the consideration whether the party arresting was an officer or only a private citizen.

18. With regard to the rights of a *constable* in this respect; he has authority, as a conservator of the peace, to arrest a person for a breach of the peace committed within his view, and to detain the offender for a reasonable time, for the purpose of taking him before a magistrate.[2] It is said, "A constable hath great, original and inherent power with regard to arrests. He may, without warrant, arrest any one for a breach of the peace committed in his view, and carry him before a justice of the peace. And in case of felony actually committed, or a dangerous wounding whereby felony is likely to ensue, he may, under probable suspicion, arrest the felon, and for that purpose is authorized (as upon a justice's warrant) to break open doors and even to kill the felon if he cannot otherwise be taken.[3] (*a*) Thus, in case

[1] Deyo *v.* Valkenburgh, 5 Hill, 242.
[2] Vandeveer *v.* Mattocks, 3 Ind. 479.
[3] 4 Bl. Com. 292.

---

held not to lie against a plaintiff in a writ for failing to countermand it after payment of the debt, at least without alleging malice. Heath, J., says, "this action is founded on mere nonfeasance, and no case or precedent has been cited to show that such an action was ever maintained."

(*a*) The following is a recent view of the course of decisions and of what may be considered the existing law upon this point:—

"The authority of a constable to arrest without a warrant, in cases of

of assault and battery, a policeman or constable, who is present and sees the offence committed, is justified in taking the offender at once into custody, without warrant, in order

---

felony, is most fully established. Thus in Hale's Pleas of the Crown, p. 587, it is stated, 'if a felony be committed, and A. acquaint the constable that B. did it, the constable may take him and imprison him, at least till he can bring him before some justice of the peace.' Peace-officers, without warrant, may arrest suspected felons. 5 Dane's Abr. 588. Constables are justified in arresting persons directly charged with felony. The case of Beckwith v. Philbey, 6 B. & C. 605, is a direct authority, that a constable, having reasonable cause to suspect that a felony has been actually committed, is justified in arresting the party suspected, although it afterwards appear that no felony has been committed. Lord Tenterden said, 'a constable, having reasonable grounds to suspect that a felony has been committed, is authorized to detain the party suspected until inquiry can be made by the proper authorities.' In the case of Davis v. Russell, 5 Bingh. 354, the defendant, a constable, being told by A. that the plaintiff had robbed him, and the information being corroborated by a supposed intercepted letter which was shown to him, apprehended the plaintiff and took her to prison. The charge proved unfounded, and the Court directed the jury to consider whether the circumstances stated afforded the defendant reasonable ground to suppose that the plaintiff had committed a felony. This instruction was held to be correct. The case of Wakely v. Hart is to the same effect. The public safety, and the due apprehension of criminals, charged with heinous offences, imperiously require that such arrests should be made without warrants by the officers of the law. As to the right pertaining to private individuals to arrest without a warrant, it is a much more restricted authority, and is confined to cases of the actual guilt of the party arrested; and the arrest can only be justified by proving such guilt. But as to constables and other peace-officers, acting officially, the law clothes them with greater authority, and they are held to be justified, if they act, in making the arrest, upon probable and reasonable grounds for believing the party guilty of a felony; and this is all that is necessary for them to show, in order to sustain a justification of an arrest, for the purpose of detaining the party to await further proceedings under a complaint on oath and a warrant thereon. The probability of an escape or not, if the party is not forthwith arrested, ought to have its proper effect upon the mind of the officer, in deciding whether he will arrest without a warrant; but it is not a matter upon which a jury is to pass, in deciding upon the right of the officer to arrest. The question of reasonable necessity for an immediate arrest, in order to prevent the escape of the party charged with the felony, is one that the officer must act upon, under his official responsibility, and not a

to take him before a magistrate; and he cannot maintain an action against a bystander, for directing the policeman so to take him into custody.[1] (a) And an action will not lie against a peace-officer, for arresting a person *bonâ fide* on a charge of felony, without a warrant, though it turn out that no felony was committed.[2] So, if a constable or other peace-officer has reasonable grounds to suspect one of the crime of receiving or aiding in the concealment of stolen goods, knowing them to be stolen, he may without warrant arrest the supposed offender, and detain him for a reasonable time, for the purpose of securing him to answer a complaint.[3] So a constable is justified in apprehending a person charged on suspicion of felony, if he have reasonable or probable cause to believe him guilty; and, it having been left to the jury to say, whether they thought such reasonable ground existed, and whether they would have acted as he did; held, this direction was right in substance, and that the constable did not exercise an undue degree of coercion, although he apprehended the party a (female) at night, without any warrant, and conveyed her to prison previously to taking her before a magistrate.[4]

[1] Derecourt *v.* Corbishley, 32 Eng. L. & Eq. 186.
[2] Samuel *v.* Payne, 1 Doug. 359.
[3] Rohan *v.* Sawin, 5 Cush. 281.
[4] Davis *v.* Russell, 2 Moore & Payne, 590.

---

question to be reviewed elsewhere." Per Dewey, J., Rohan *v.* Sawin, 5 Cush. 281, 286.

With regard to the rights of other peace-officers, of course substantially the same rule is recognized. Thus *the sheriff* may arrest a person suspected of a capital offence, whose guilt is not certain. 1 Chit. Cr. L. 25; 2 Hale, P. C. 87.

So, without reference to the express statutory provisions usually adopted in this country, it is said, *a justice of the peace* may apprehend or cause to be apprehended, by word only, any person committing a felony or breach of the peace in his presence. 1 Deac. Cr. L. 47.

But it has been held, that a magistrate's mere knowledge of an offence is no sufficient ground for commitment by him, but he should make oath of the fact before another justice. The King *v.* Wilkes, 2 Wils. 158.

(*a*) And in such case the party is liable to indictment for resisting the officer. Reg. *v.* Light, Law Rep. Aug. 1858, p. 243.

19. The power of an officer, however, in this respect, is strictly limited, both as to the acts done, and the time and manner of doing them, by the requirements of the particular case in which he is called upon to interpose, and by the terms of the law relating thereto. Thus, where the parish clerk refused to read in church a notice which was presented to him for that purpose, and the person presenting it read it himself, at a time when no part of the church-service was actually going on; held, although a constable might be justified in removing him from the church, and detaining him until the service was over, yet he could not legally detain him afterwards, in order to take him before a magistrate.[1] So a constable, arresting a man on suspicion of felony, must take him before a justice, to be examined, as soon as he reasonably can. Therefore a plea, justifying a detention for three days, in order that the party whose goods had been stolen might have an opportunity of collecting his witnesses and bringing them to prove the felony, was held bad on demurrer. And it seems that a constable cannot justify handcuffing a prisoner, unless he has attempted to escape, or unless it be necessary in order to prevent him from doing so,[2] (see p. 239). So, where an officer carries a party for trial before a magistrate, before whom the warrant does not authorize a trial, the officer and his assistants, though not the magistrate who issued the warrant, will be liable in trespass to the party arrested;[3] although done without actual force.[4] So, where a statute enacted, that, if an officer "shall detain any offender without warrant longer than such time as was necessary to procure a legal warrant, such officer should be liable to pay," &c.; held, that a town by-law, giving power to an officer to arrest and detain any person without warrant forty-eight hours, was repugnant to this law, and void, and furnished no defence to the officer.[5] (a)

[1] Williams v. Glenister, 2 B. & C. 699.

[2] Wright v. Courst, 4 B. & C. 596; Broughton v. Jackson, 11 Eng. L. & Eq. 386.

[3] Stetson v. Packer, 7 Cush. 562.

[4] Francisco v. State, 4 Zabr. 30.

[5] Burke v. Bell, 36 Maine, 317.

(a) With regard to the rights of an officer in the breaking and entry of

So a clause in the charter of a town, requiring the marshal to suppress all breaches of the peace, and, with or without process, to apprehend all disorderly persons or disturbers of the peace, and convey them before a justice, &c., does not authorize the marshal to make an arrest for a breach of the peace, without process, after the offence has been committed and the disturbance has ceased; and the marshal and his assistants are liable in an action of trespass.[1]

20. As has been stated, the rights and liabilities of private persons, in arresting without warrant, are more restricted than those of peace-officers. But it is held, that, in case of actual felony, an officer *or a private person* may, without malice and upon probable cause, arrest a suspected person, without warrant, in order to bring him before a magistrate.[2] (*a*) Thus, in trespass for false imprisonment, the plaintiff proved that, under a claim of right, he entered a field cultivated and occupied by one of the defendants, and gathered and took away corn there growing, whereupon he was arrested for petit larceny by the defendants, and committed to jail. Held, the defendants might prove in mitigation of damages, that the plaintiff's land had been sold by

[1] Pow *v.* Beckner, 3 Ind. 475.

[2] Brockway *v.* Crawford, 3 Jones, Law, 433.

---

a *dwelling-house*, (see *Dwelling-house*,) it is held that an officer, acting *bonâ fide*, may break and enter a person's dwelling-house to arrest him on a charge of crime, although in the mistaken belief that he is in the house, if he first demand admission, and be guilty of no unnecessary damage or violence. Barnard *v.* Bartlett, 10 Cush. 501.

But a sheriff cannot break the outer and inner doors to enter and search the dwelling-house of another person for a criminal, unless the latter is at the time in the house, and consent is given. And such consent may be withdrawn. Hawkins *v.* Commonwealth, 14 B. Mon. 395. Otherwise, if the criminal dwells in the house, though not the owner. Ibid.

(*a*) "If treason or felony be done, and one hath just cause for suspicion, this is a good cause and warrant in law for him to arrest any man, but he must show in certainty the cause of his suspicion; and whether the suspicion be just or lawful, shall be determined by the justice in an action of false imprisonment brought by the party grieved, or upon a habeas corpus," &c. 2 Inst. 52.

the sheriff, under an execution against the plaintiff himself.[1] So to a declaration in trespass, for assault and false imprisonment, the defendant pleaded, that the plaintiff attempted forcibly to break and enter his messuage or public-house without leave; whereupon he resisted such entrance; and, because the plaintiff behaved himself violently and created a disturbance in the street, by which means a mob was assembled, and the defendant's business interrupted and his customers annoyed, and because the plaintiff threatened to continue such violent conduct, and to renew his attempts and efforts to get into the house; and because no request or entreaty of the defendant to the plaintiff to abstain from and abandon his attempts and efforts was complied with; the defendant, in order to preserve the peace, and to secure himself from a renewal of such attempts and efforts, gave him in charge to a constable, to be carried before a justice of the peace. Held, that the plea was good after verdict.[2] So, in trespass for assault and false imprisonment, the defendant pleaded, that he was possessed of a shop, and carried on the business of a baker therein, and that the plaintiff had been in the shop making a great noise and disturbance, and abused the defendant, and disturbed him in the peaceable possession of his shop, in breach of the king's peace, and thereby obstructed the defendant in the exercise of his business; that the plaintiff went out of the shop into the public street in front of it, and continued there to make a great noise and disturbance, and to abuse the defendant, and thereby caused a great concourse of persons to assemble, and so disturbed the defendant in the possession of his shop, and obstructed his business, in breach of the peace, and thereby caused a great riot and disturbance; that the defendant requested him to desist and depart, but he refused; whereupon the defendant, in order to preserve the peace, sent for certain policemen, and requested them to remove the plaintiff; that they requested the plaintiff to cease making such noise and disturbance, &c., but he refused, and continued making such

[1] Sawyer *v.* Jarvis, 13 Ired. 179.

[2] Ingle *v.* Bell, 1 M. & W. 516.

noise, riot, and disturbance, &c.; whereupon the defendant, in order to preserve the peace, charged them with the plaintiff, and he was taken to a station-house, and thence before a magistrate, who admonished and discharged him. Held, that, even without the allegation of riot, the plea disclosed a sufficient justification. And further, the evidence showing, that the plaintiff, after abusing the defendant in his shop, went into the street outside, and there continued to abuse him; that a crowd of a hundred persons was collected, and the street much obstructed; that the defendant sent for the police, who, on the plaintiff's refusing to go away, took him to the station-house, and before a magistrate, as stated in the plea: held, that these facts amounted to a breach of the peace, and justified the defendant in directing the imprisonment.[1]

20 *a*. There is also an intermediate class of cases, where the party arresting is not strictly a peace-officer, but still acts in a quasi public or official capacity. Thus, in trespass for imprisoning the plaintiff and putting him in irons; the plea was, that the defendant was the commander of a ship-of-war, on the high seas, and that the plaintiff was steward of the ship and servant of the defendant, and had access to the defendant's cabin and charge of the goods there; that money of the defendant had been feloniously stolen out of a desk in the cabin, on two several occasions, just before the said time, when, &c., and that upon each occasion the said desk had been clandestinely opened by means of a key; that the plaintiff had access to and could have obtained the key of the desk, and have opened the same and carried away the said money, and that the defendant then believed, that no other person had or could have obtained access to the key without the knowledge of the plaintiff; wherefore the defendant, suspecting the plaintiff for the causes aforesaid, to be guilty of or concerned in the stealing of the money, did, as such commander, put and detain him in irons, (the same being a reasonable mode of detainer,) until he could examine

[1] Cohen *v*. Huskisson, 2 M. & W. 477.

into and investigate the circumstances of suspicion against the plaintiff according to law; that the defendant did afterwards examine into and investigate the circumstances, and did discharge and release the plaintiff. Held, (after verdict,) that the plea showed a sufficient justification for the imprisonment; also, that the putting in irons must be taken to be a reasonable mode of detainer, and, if there were any excess, the plaintiff should have new assigned,[1] (see p. 236). So the captain of a vessel containing passengers may justify an assault committed for the preservation of due order and discipline on board.[2] So a churchwarden or beadle may lay hands upon another, to turn him out of church and prevent his disturbing the congregation.[3] And to an action of assault and battery, the defendant may plead, that the plaintiff disturbed a congregation while the minister was performing the rites of burial, and that he *manus mollitur imposuit* to prevent such disturbance; and this although he was neither constable, churchwarden, or other officer.[4]

21. But the same limitations and restrictions of the right of arrest, already referred to in the case of officers, are even more rigidly applied to private individuals. It is said, "If people choose to settle private disputes by giving others into custody, they must take the consequences."[5] Hence a plea, justifying an arrest by a private person, on suspicion of felony, must show the circumstances, from which the Court may judge whether the suspicion were reasonable. Using the term *suspicious* is not sufficient.[6] So, where the plaintiff entered a public-house after it had been closed for the night, and refused to tell the defendant, the occupier, how he obtained admission, whereupon he sent for a constable and charged the plaintiff with felony, on which he was detained in custody two days; held, in an action for false imprisonment, the defendant was not justified in making such a

[1] Broughton *v.* Jackson, 11 Eng. L. & Eq. 386. See Wright *v.* Courst, 4 B. & C. 596.

[2] Noden *v.* Johnson, 16 Q. B. 218.

[3] Burton *v.* Henson, 10 M. & W. 105.

[4] Glover *v.* Hynde, 1 Mod. 168.

[5] Per Parke, B., Warwick *v.* Foulkes, 12 M. & W. 509.

[6] Mure *v.* Kaye, 4 Taunt. 34.

charge; his remedy was by turning the plaintiff out of the house.[1] So, in trespass for assaulting the plaintiff, and causing him to be taken to a police-station, and afterwards before a magistrate, upon an unfounded charge of having unlawfully attempted to procure from the banking-house of the defendant a blank cheque-book; the defendant pleaded, that he and certain other persons carried on the business of bankers, and that one T. kept an account with them; that the plaintiff did unlawfully endeavor to obtain from the said bankers a blank cheque-book, by falsely pretending that the said T. was his master, and had sent him for it; that, in pursuance of such unlawful endeavor, the plaintiff induced one A. to go into the banking-house, and to ask for a blank cheque-book, and did falsely pretend to the said A. that the said T. was his master, and did direct the said A. to tell the bankers that the cheque-book was wanted for the said T.; that A. accordingly did so, and stated that he had been so sent by the plaintiff, and that the plaintiff was waiting outside for it; whereupon the defendant accompanied A. to the place where the plaintiff was waiting; and A. stated, in the presence and hearing of the plaintiff, that he had been so sent by the plaintiff: wherefore the defendant, having good and probable cause of suspicion, and vehemently suspecting that the plaintiff had, by such false and fraudulent pretences as aforesaid, unlawfully endeavored to obtain from the said bankers a blank cheque-book for unlawful and unauthorized purposes, committed the trespasses complained of. Held, that the plea was bad, inasmuch as it neither alleged that a felony had been committed, so to make it a good justification at common law, nor that the plaintiff had been "found committing" any offence against the provisions of the 7 & 8 Geo. IV. c. 29, so as to justify his apprehension without warrant, under the 63d section of that statute.[2] So the plaintiff, at night, was making a great noise, affray, disturbance, and

[1] Rose *v.* Wilson, 8 Moore, 362.

[2] Mathews *v.* Biddulph, 3 M. & Gr. 390.

riot in the house of a third person, and the defendant, a lodger, under orders from the owners, attempted to keep the peace and stop the noise. Whereupon the plaintiff assaulted him, and was then taken into custody by him, and kept till the next day, to be carried before a justice. Held, the defendant was liable to an action.[1] So, in an action for an assault and false imprisonment, it is no justification, that the plaintiff, being engaged in an affray, was taken into custody until he could be brought before a justice, without stating that the defendant was an officer or acted under a warrant.[2] So in trespass for assault and false imprisonment, the plea was, that the plaintiff, just before the time when, &c., without leave of the defendant, at an unreasonable hour at night, entered into the defendant's dwelling-house, and, with force and arms, made a great noise and disturbance, and insulted and abused the defendant therein, and disturbed him in the peaceable possession thereof, in breach of the peace; whereupon the defendant requested the plaintiff to cease his noise and disturbance, and depart from out the dwelling-house, which the plaintiff reluctantly did, and threatened the defendant that he would rap at the door till the defendant delivered up a certain book: that the plaintiff did stand at the door, on the defendant's premises, rapping violently, illegally, and wrongfully against it, for two hours, and during that time insulted the defendant, and disturbed him in the possession of his dwelling-house, in further breach of the peace; whereupon the defendant requested the plaintiff to cease his noise and disturbance, and depart off the defendant's premises; which the plaintiff refused to do, and continued knocking, &c., and threatened the defendant to continue the noise and disturbance until he should deliver the book: that the defendant then sent for a constable for the purpose of taking the plaintiff into custody, and thereby preventing him from further disturbing the defendant: that the plaintiff, having ascertained that he was about to be

[1] Phillips v. Trull, 11 Johns. 486.

[2] Ibid.

given into custody, ceased the rapping, which he had violently, &c., continued up to that period, and ran and escaped off and from the defendant's premises; when the defendant immediately pursued the plaintiff, and overtook him near the dwelling-house, and thereupon the defendant, in order to preserve the peace and prevent the plaintiff from continuing to disturb the order and tranquillity of the dwelling-house, and from continuing to make the noise and disturbance at the dwelling-house during the whole night, gave charge of the plaintiff to the constable, and requested the constable to take the plaintiff into custody, carry him before a justice to answer the premises, and to be dealt with according to law; and the constable gently laid hands on the plaintiff for the cause aforesaid, and took him into custody in order to carry him before a justice, to be there dealt with, &c. (justiying the assault, imprisonment, and detention). Verdict for the defendant. Held, on motion for judgment *non obstante veredicto*, that the plea disclosed no defence, it not appearing that the constable had a warrant, and it not being shown that the breach of the peace had been seen by the constable, or was likely, at the time of the apprehension of the plaintiff, to be continued or repeated.[1] So, in trespass for assault and false imprisonment, and taking the plaintiff to a police-station, the plea was, that the defendant was possessed of a dwelling-house, and that the plaintiff entered the dwelling-house, and then and there insulted, abused, and ill-treated the defendant and his servants in the dwelling-house, and greatly disturbed them in the peaceable possession thereof, in breach of the peace; whereupon the defendant requested the plaintiff to cease his disturbance, and to depart from and out of the house; which the plaintiff refused to do, and continued in the house, making the said disturbance and affray therein: that thereupon the defendant, in order to preserve the peace and restore good order in the house, gave charge of the plaintiff to a certain policeman, and requested the policeman to take the plaintiff into his custody, to be dealt

[1] Baynes *v.* Brewster, 2 Ad. & Ell. N. S. 375.

with according to law; and that the policeman, at such request of the defendant, gently laid his hands on the plaintiff, for the cause aforesaid, and took him into custody. It appeared in evidence, that the plaintiff entered the defendant's shop to purchase an article in the shop, when a dispute arose between the plaintiff and the defendant's shopman; that, the plaintiff refusing on request to go out of the shop, the shopman endeavored to turn him out, and an affray ensued between them; that the defendant came into the shop during the affray, which continued for a short time after he came in; that the defendant then requested the plaintiff to leave the shop quietly; but, he refusing to do so, the defendant gave him in charge to a policeman, who took him to a station-house. Held, though the defendant was justified, under the circumstances, in giving the plaintiff in charge to a policeman for the purpose of preventing a renewal of the affray; that the plea was not substantially proved, inasmuch as the alleged assault on the defendant himself was not proved.[1]

22. *False imprisonment*, more especially in civil actions, is sometimes termed in legal language *malicious arrest;* and an action for this precise form of injury requires substantially the same allegation and proof of *malice* and *want of probable cause*, as an action for *malicious prosecution.* (*a*) Hence

[1] Timothy *v.* Simpson, Cromp. M. & R. 757.

(*a*) See *Index*, chap. 8.

Moreover, as has been seen, the same form of action — trespass on the case — is sometimes adopted for false imprisonment, as for malicious prosecution. See pp. 211, 214. "Where the immediate act of imprisonment proceeds from the defendant, the action must be trespass and trespass only; but where the act of imprisonment by one person is in consequence of information from another, there an action upon the case is the proper remedy, because the injury is sustained in consequence of the wrongful act of that other. Per Ashhurst, J., Morgan *v.* Hughes, 2 T. R. 225.

No action lies for malicious arrest, if the plaintiff in the former suit had a probable cause of action for the amount sued for, though not in the particular form of action adopted by him. Thus, where the claim was against two persons separately, and a suit was brought against them jointly, and

the court are bound to give the following instructions to the jury, if asked by the defendant: "The plaintiff must not

---

one arrested, he cannot maintain an action for such arrest. Whalley *v.* Pepper, 7 C. & P. 506.

But an action lies, for causing one to be arrested for too large a sum. Wentworth *v.* Bullen, 9 B. & C. 840; Austin *v.* Debnam, 4 D. & R. 653; 3 B. & C. 139. So, for holding to bail in an inferior Court without jurisdiction. Goslin *v.* Wilcock, 2 Wils. 302. Or when no more than 30*s.* was due. Smith *v.* Cattle, Ib. 376. So, it seems, for maliciously arresting the plaintiff, when the defendant had implied notice of his being discharged under the insolvent act, although done by direction of the plaintiff's attorney, and without his knowledge. Jones *v.* Nicholls, 3 M. & P. 12. One who maliciously, and without probable cause, procures the arrest of another, is liable, notwithstanding the error of the magistrate in ordering the arrest, on an affidavit which charged no punishable act or defence. Barton *v.* Kavanaugh, 12 La. Ann. 332.

In case for maliciously causing the plaintiff to be arrested for £100, the declaration was held bad upon special demurrer, for want of showing what became of the action. Parker *v.* Langley, 10 Mod. 145, 209. But the defect might have been cured by a verdict. Ibid. Or by a plea in bar, admitting the first action to be false and hopeless. Ibid.

It has been held, however, that, in trespass for false imprisonment, the *onus* of justifying rests on the defendant. Therefore, in trespass for causing the plaintiff to be apprehended under an illegal justice's warrant, that the plaintiff might maintain the action without producing the warrant. Holroyd *v.* Doncaster, 11 Moore, 440.

In trespass against a constable for arresting the plaintiff and imprisoning him, the declaration stated that it was done without reasonable or probable cause. Held, that the defendant might, under the general issue, give evidence of the contents of the plaintiff's trunk, for the purpose of showing that he was addicted to burglary. Russell *v.* Shuster, 8 Watts & Serg. 308.

Also, that the character of the plaintiff could not be shown in mitigation of damages. Ibid.

On a question whether there was probable cause for an arrest, evidence of the suspicious behavior of the plaintiff, the day before it was made, is admissible, although there is no proof that the defendant knew of that conduct at the time of the arrest. M'Rae *v.* O'Neal, 2 Dev. 167. See Johnston *v.* Martin, 3 Murph. 248; Bostick *v.* Rutherford, 4 Hawks, 83.

In an action for imprisonment, the defendant may show, in mitigation of damages, that he made inquiry whether it would be safe to permit the plaintiff to be at liberty, and was told by the plaintiff's friends and neighbors

only prove malice, but must also show that there was no probable cause for the prosecution; and the defendant is not bound to prove probable cause until the plaintiff has shown the absence of it; and if the plaintiff show malice, and not the want of probable cause, the defendant cannot be condemned, as it is just as necessary to show the want of probable cause, as it is malice, before a recovery can be had."[1] Upon this ground, in an action for arrest and imprisonment for an alleged infringement of a patent right, it must be shown that the plaintiff was the first inventor, and that the defendant knew it, and that his own patent was void on that account.[2] So the defendant, telling a bail that his principal was likely to abscond, procured from him directions to take his affidavit of justification off the file.

[1] Barton v. Kavanaugh, 12 La. An. 332.

[2] Beach v. Wheeler, 30 Penn. State R. 69.

---

that it would not; and that he seemed desirous to take the best course for the plaintiff and his family. 12 N. H. 521.

But where one, through his own error, mistake, or negligence, causes the arrest and imprisonment of an innocent man, who has given no occasion for suspicion by his own misconduct, the assurance of the complainant, however strong it may be, that the accused was guilty of the crime imputed to him, is not sufficient evidence of probable cause for such arrest. Merriam v. Mitchell, 1 Shep. 439.

In trespass for an assault and imprisonment, B. pleaded that he was a constable, that a felony had been committed, that a reasonable suspicion and belief existed that the plaintiff was guilty of said felony, that one A. and others informed him, the defendant, that the plaintiff was guilty of said felony, and that, for the purpose of carrying the plaintiff before some justice of the peace to be dealt with, he had gently arrested him. Held, on general demurrer, that the plea was bad, for not showing that his informant stated the facts by which he knew or believed the plaintiff to be guilty, and for not setting out those facts. Wasson v. Canfield, 6 Blackf. 406.

In an action for false imprisonment, the defendant pleaded in justification, that the act complained of was an arrest of the plaintiff, under a warrant issued at the instance of the defendant, who was city attorney of Utica, for the violation, by the plaintiff, of an ordinance made by the common council; but the plea did not aver that the plaintiff had in fact violated the ordinance. Held, nevertheless, that the plea was good. Walker v. Cruikshank, 2 Hill, 296.

The directions having been given too late, the defendant obtained, by means of them, an order of a judge for the render of the principal. Held, an action did not lie against him for this proceeding, at the suit of the principal, without alleging and proving express malice.[1] So case was brought by the plaintiffs, as sheriffs of Middlesex, against the defendants, as attorneys of one Power, for falsely representing to the plaintiffs, that one J. W., who was then in their custody as sheriffs, and entitled to his discharge, was another J. W., against whom the defendants, as attorneys for the said Power, had sued out a writ of *ca. sa.*, and delivered the same to the plaintiffs; by reason whereof the plaintiffs wrongfully detained the first-mentioned J. W., and were afterwards obliged to pay £10, and the costs of an action commenced against them by him for the unlawful detainer. The declaration, after stating the delivery of the writ to the plaintiffs, and that the J. W. in their custody was not the same person as the J. W. mentioned in the writ, and that he was entitled to his discharge, went on to aver that the defendants, well knowing the premises, and for the purpose of preventing the plaintiffs from discharging the said J. W., made the false representation. Held, (on error in the Exchequer Chamber, reversing the judgment of the Court of Queen's Bench,) that a plea, that the defendants had reasonable and probable cause to believe, and did believe, their representation to be true, was an answer to the action.[2] So it is a good defence to an action for malicious arrest, that the defendant, when he caused the plaintiff to be arrested, acted *bonâ fide* upon the opinion of a legal adviser of competent skill and ability, and believed that he had a good cause of action against the plaintiff. But, where it appeared that the party was influenced by an indirect motive in making the arrest, it was held to be properly left to the jury, to consider whether he acted *bonâ fide* upon the opinion of his legal adviser, believing that he had a good cause of action.[3]

[1] Porter *v.* Weston, 5 Bing. N. R. 715.

[2] Collins *v.* Evans, 1 Dav. & Mer. 669.

[3] Ravenga *v.* Mackintosh, 2 Barn. & Cress. 693.

23. And, on the other hand, a party will not be deprived of the defence of probable cause once existing, by any mere expression of opinion on the part of a third person. Thus the defendant, having reasonable and probable cause for supposing that the plaintiff made an assault on him with intent to rob him, went for a constable, who, on coming to the place, recognized the plaintiff, and assured the defendant that he was a respectable man, and that he would be answerable for his coming forward to meet the charge. The defendant, nevertheless, persisted in giving the plaintiff into custody, and on the following day preferred the same charge against him before a justice, who dismissed it. In an action for maliciously and without probable cause making such charge before the justice, the Judge stated to the jury, that the plaintiff had reasonable and probable cause for suspicion in the first instance, but that he thought that, on the explanation given by the constable, that ceased; and that, if the jury were of opinion that the defendant was satisfied with such explanation, but persevered in the charge from obstinacy or wounded pride, they should find for the plaintiff. Held, that this direction was wrong; for, as the facts remained unaltered, the representation of the constable could not take away the reasonable and probable cause afforded by those facts.[1]

24. The distinction has been made, that, in trespass for an assault and false imprisonment, the defendants might prove, in mitigation of damages, that, at and shortly before the time of the arrest, there was in the plaintiff's neighborhood an association of persons, engaged in making and passing counterfeit money; and the plaintiff was generally reputed and believed there, to have been one of that association; but that the facts, that the plaintiff was one of that association, and had been engaged in passing counterfeit money, knowingly and with intent to defraud the public, should be specially pleaded.[2]

25. In an action for malicious arrest, the verdict in the

[1] Musgrove *v.* Newell, 1 Mees. & Wels. 582; 2 Gale, 91.

[2] Wasson *v.* Canfield, 6 Blackf. 407.

former case is competent evidence, though very slight in itself, to show want of probable cause. Its weight depends upon the circumstances under which it was rendered, as if given by the jury without leaving their seats, &c.[1]

26. But the discontinuance of the former suit may be very strong evidence to sustain the present action. Thus A. arrested B. on an affidavit of debt for money paid to his use, but did not declare until ruled to do so, and soon afterwards discontinued the action and paid the costs. Held, sufficient *primâ facie* evidence of malice, and the absence of probable cause, to support an action for a malicious arrest.[2]

27. In actions of trespass and false imprisonment, the question of reasonable and probable cause for the apprehension of the plaintiff cannot be left to the jury, although the Judge intimate it as his opinion that the defendants were justified in such apprehension.[3] But the facts must be found by the jury.[4] Thus a plea, justifying the apprehension of the plaintiff on suspicion of felonly, set out various circumstances of suspicion, and, amongst others, a conversation by the plaintiff with one A. At the trial, the whole of the plea was proved, except that the conversation was had with B. In leaving the case to the jury, the Judge told them they must exclude from their consideration the statement as to the conversation with A., and say whether the facts proved, and known to the defendant at the time, were sufficient to cause a reasonable and cautious man, acting *bonâ fide* and without prejudice, to suspect the plaintiff of the offence charged. Held, a misdirection,—inasmuch as it was leaving to the jury what it was the province of the Judge to determine.[5]

28. But, in an action for a malicious arrest, *malice* is a question of fact for the jury, who are at liberty, but not bound, to infer it from the want of probable cause. Thus, where a creditor had caused his debtor to be arrested for

[1] Brant *v.* Higgins, 10 Mis. 728.

[2] Nicholson *v.* Coghill, 4 Barn. & Cress. 21.

[3] Hill *v.* Yates, 8 Taunt. 182; 2 Moore, 80.

[4] Brant *v.* Higgins, 10 Mis. 728.

[5] West *v.* Baxendale, 9 Com. B. 141.

£45, knowing that there was a set-off to the amount of £16 5*s.*, but instructed the bailiff to allow the set-off in case the debtor would settle the debt; and the Judge expressed the opinion, that there was no probable cause for the arrest, and that there was malice in law, and therefore told the jury, that the only question for them was the amount of damages; held, the question of malice should have been left to the jury.[1] (*a*)

29. The question of false imprisonment has sometimes arisen in *military* cases. Thus an action of trespass lies, for an inferior military officer against his superior officer, (both being under martial law,) who imprisons him for disobedience to an order, made under color, but not within the scope, of military authority; although there be a subsequent trial by court-martial.[2] So where a captain imposed a fine upon a private, who was a minor, for neglect of duty, and issued a warrant for the collection of such fine, requiring the

[1] Mitchell *v.* Jenkins, 5 B. & Ad. 588.

[2] Warden *v.* Bailey, 4 Taunt. 67.

(*a*) In case, for maliciously and without reasonable or probable cause causing the plaintiff to be arrested on a capias, under the statute 1 & 2 Vict. c. 110, § 3, the order for which had been obtained upon an affidavit, not fairly disclosing the nature of the contract, for the alleged breach of which the defendants were suing; the Judge, having stated, that, in his opinion, the plaintiff had failed to make out a want of reasonable and probable cause, told the jury, that, to entitle the plaintiff to a verdict, they must be satisfied that there was a total want of reasonable and probable cause, and that the defendants had acted with malice. Held, a misdirection. Gibbons *v.* Alison, 3 Com. B. 181.

Evidence of the value of the services of an attorney, in getting rid of an illegal arrest, is held not admissible in an action for such arrest, unless expressly alleged. Strang *v.* Whitehead, 12 Wend. 64. But see Blythe *v.* Tompkins, 2 App. Prac. R. 468; Foxhall *v.* Barnett, 22 Eng. L. & Eq. 179.

Where, in an action for false imprisonment, the defendant pleads the commission of a felony; the jury may rightly be instructed, in estimating the damages, to regard such plea as a persisting in the charge. Warwick *v.* Foulkes, 12 Mees. & W. 507.

officer to whom it was directed to levy it upon the goods of the delinquent, and for want thereof to take his body, and him commit, &c.; by virtue of which warrant, such minor was imprisoned; in an action of trespass, brought by him against the captain, it was held, 1. That the defendant was not by law empowered to issue such warrant against the plaintiff, and cause him to be imprisoned; 2. That the captain, in issuing a warrant for the collection of a military fine, is not restricted to the form set forth in the statute, but may adapt it to the exigencies of the case; 3. That, in this case, trespass against the captain was the appropriate remedy; 4. That the defendant could not avail himself of the plaintiff's right of appeal from the imposition of the fine, by way of justification or defence in the suit.[1] But where the captain of a military company enrolled in it a member of a fire company, who was exempted from military duty, and he was subsequently fined for non-performance of duty, and imprisoned on a warrant for such fine; held, the remedy was by excuse and appeal, and he could not sustain trespass against the officer.[2]

---

30. In immediate connection with, or more properly, perhaps, as a part of, the subject of injuries to the body or the person, may be considered injuries to *health*. Inasmuch as a large part of the wrongs or neglects, by which the health of individuals is affected, at the same time constitute *nuisances to property*, which are treated at length in other connections; (*a*) it is unnecessary, under the present head,

[1] Mallory *v.* Merritt, 17 Conn. 178. [2] Merriman *v.* Bryant, 14 Conn. 200.

(*a*) See *Action*, *Negligence*, *Nuisance*.

It may be remarked in this connection, that injuries to the body may often be the result of mere negligence, as well as wilful assault. They then become the subjects of an action on the case, and not of trespass. A very prominent and important example of this class of injuries, is found in the

to do more than give a very brief view of the general subject. (*a*) This part of the subject is often regulated by statute.[1]

31. It has been seen, (chap. 1,) that a contract and tort, and the respective rights of action connected therewith, may be *concurrent* or *coincident;* and that the same party may be liable to one person upon contract, and to another for tort, in reference to the same transaction. Upon this ground, if an apothecary administer improper medicines, or a surgeon

[1] See Chit. Gen. Prac. 1, 42; Goodrich *v.* People, 3 Park. (N. Y.) 622.

---

lamentable frequency of railroad disasters, chiefly memorable for their destruction of life and limb.

With reference to the *damages* in this class of injuries, as compared with wilful assaults, it is remarked, "exemplary or punitory damages, or smart-money, as they are often called, are given by way of punishment for intentional wrong, and to operate as an example to others. The law in such cases looks beyond the act and its injurious consequences, to the motive, and metes out its punishment to that also. In such cases the compensation for the actual pecuniary damage is rather subsidiary and incidental. There, the mental suffering, the injured feelings, the sense of injustice, of wrong or insult, on the part of the sufferer, enter largely into the account; and the measure of justice is graduated by that of the offender's turpitude. Here, the damages are strictly compensatory for the actual injury, of which the bodily pain and suffering were an essential part. Sedgw. on Damages, 587, n. See Morse *v.* The Auburn, &c. 10 Barb. 621; Ransom *v.* The New York, &c. 15 N. Y. 415.

(*a*) "Injuries affecting a man's health are where by any unwholesome practices of another a man sustains any apparent damage in his vigor or constitution. As by selling him bad provisions or wine; by the exercise of a noisome trade, which infects the air in his neighborhood; or by the neglect or unskilful management of his physician, surgeon, or apothecary. For it hath been solemnly resolved (Ld. Ray. 214) that *mala praxis* is a great misdemeanor and offence at common law, whether it be for curiosity and experiment, or by neglect; because it breaks the trust which the party had placed in his physician, and tends to the patient's destruction. Thus also, in the civil law, neglect or want of skill in physicians and surgeons, 'culpae adnumeratur; veluti si medicus curationem dereliquerit, male quempiam sumerit, aut perperam ei medicamentum dederit.'" (Inst. 4, 36 & 7) 3 Bl. Com. 122; and Chitty's note. See People *v.* Carmichael, 5 Mich. 10.

unskilfully treat his patient, the law holds them liable, although their contract was with a third person.[1] So a dealer in drugs and medicines, who carelessly labels a deadly poison as a harmless medicine, and sends it to market, is liable to any one who is injured by using it, though he does not purchase directly from such dealer.[2]

32. Under some circumstances, a physician or surgeon will be held very strictly answerable for the consequences of his professional action or neglect. Thus it is held, that, where medicine is administered to a slave without the consent of his owner, the physician is responsible for all the evil consequences which result from his act.[3] (*a*) So an action lies against a surgeon for gross ignorance and want of skill, as well as for negligence and carelessness; though, if the evidence be of negligence only, which was properly left to the jury, and negatived by them, the Court will not grant a new trial, because the jury were directed that want of skill alone would not sustain the action.[4] But in general a physician or surgeon is responsible only for *ordinary* or *reasonable* care and skill, and the exercise of his best judgment in matters of doubt; not for a want of the highest degree of skill.[5] It is the duty of a patient to coöperate with his professional adviser, and to conform to the necessary prescriptions; but, if he will not, or under the pressure of pain cannot, he has no right to hold his surgeon responsible for his own neglect.[6]

[1] Pippin *v.* Sheppard, 11 Price, 40; Gladwell *v.* Steggall, 5 Bing. N. R. 733.

[2] Thomas *v.* Winchester, 2 Seld. 397.

[3] Hord *v.* Grimes, 13 B. Mon. 188.

[4] Sear *v.* Prentice, 8 East, 348.

[5] Leighton *v.* Sargent, 7 Fost. 460; Wood *v.* Clapp, 4 Sneed, 65. See Alden *v.* Buckley, 1 Swan. 69.

[6] Leighton *v.* Sargent, 7 Fost. 460.

(*a*) A physician sued in assumpsit for the value of certain services. He was called to see the defendant, who was ill of typhoid fever. The defendant's wife objected to the plaintiff's visiting the defendant, if he had, and while he had, small-pox patients. This objection was often repeated, and the plaintiff continued to visit such patients, while attending the defendant. Finally, small-pox broke out in the defendant's family. Held, that this evidence was admissible, to reduce the plaintiff's claim for services rendered to the defendant during the fever and small-pox. Piper *v.* Menifee, 12 B. Mon. 465.

The implied contract of a surgeon is not to cure, but to possess and employ, in the treatment of a case, such reasonable skill and diligence as are ordinarily exercised in his profession, by thoroughly educated surgeons; and, in judging of the degree of skill required, regard is to be had to the advanced state of the profession at the time.[1] So the law requires of *a dentist* a reasonable degree of skill and care in his professional operations; and he will not be held answerable for injuries arising from his want of the highest attainments in his profession.[2] So a physician is expected to practise according to his professed and avowed system, where there is no particular system established or favored by law, and no system is prohibited. Hence, in an action for malpractice, evidence to prove that the defendant's treatment of the case was according to the *botanic* system of practice and medicine, which he professed and was known to follow, is admissible.[3]

[1] McCandless *v.* McWha, 22 Penn. 261; Slater *v.* Baker, 2 Wils. 359.

[2] Simonds *v.* Henry, 39 Maine, 155.

[3] Bowman *v.* Woods, 1 Iowa, 441.

CHAPTER VII.

INJURIES TO CHARACTER OR REPUTATION; LIBEL AND SLANDER.

1. THE next class of torts or wrongs, is that of injuries to *character* or *reputation;* which naturally occupies an intermediate place between injuries to the *person*, already treated of, and injuries to *property*, which will occupy a subsequent portion of this work. Character is to some extent a mere *personal* right, like the right to life or limb; and is also, somewhat more appropriately than the rights last named, a subject of *ownership* or *property*. The arrangement of subjects which we have adopted seems therefore the most natural and intelligible one.

2. The first and principal injury to character or reputation, is *slander* or *libel.* (*a*) Although, as will be seen, in some

(*a*) Chancellor Kent says, (2 Comm. 15): "The laws of the ancients, no less than those of modern nations, made private reputation one of the objects of their protection. The Roman law took a just distinction between slander spoken and written." He further remarks: "The law of England, even under the Anglo-Saxon line of princes, took severe and exemplary notice of defamation, as an offence against the public peace; and, in the time of Henry III., Bracton adopted the language of the Institutes of Justinian, and held slander and libellous writings to be actionable injuries. But the first private suit for slanderous words to be met with in the English law, was in the reign of Edward III., for the high offence of charging another with a

respects governed by different rules, these two wrongs are for the most part considered as substantially one and the same; slander being an unwritten or unprinted libel, and libel a written or printed slander. They are so far identical, as to be most properly considered together, with the required references to the points of distinction between them. (*a*)

3. Slander is defined, as the imputation, 1, of some *temporal* offence for which the party might be indicted and punished in the temporal courts; (*b*) 2, of an existing contagious

---

crime which endangered his life. Several Acts of Parliament, known as the statutes *de scandalis magnatum*, were passed to suppress and punish the propagation of false and malicious slander. They are said to have been declaratory of the common law." Ibid. 17.

(*a*) Although slander is not, like libel, *an indictable offence*, yet, it is said, an action for slander is in the nature of *a penal action*, and comes within the general rule, (it seems,) that a tenant is not bound to discover anything which might render him liable to a penalty or forfeiture, or to anything in the nature of a penalty or forfeiture. Per Pratt, J., Baily *v.* Dean, 5 Barb. 297.

It is remarked by a late elementary writer: "The question whether mere words uttered, but not written, are ever indictable, seems not clear on the authorities. Oral blasphemy is a crime; also, an oral challenge to fight a duel; and the public utterance of obscene words has been held, in Tennessee, to be such. There are many cases which recognize the doctrine, that verbal slander, especially against magistrates, corporations, and the like, is indictable. For instance, the words, merely spoken, that 'the last grand jury that presented me are perjured rogues,' have been held sufficient. And an information has been maintained for singing in the streets, songs reflecting on the prosecutor's children, with intent to destroy his domestic happiness. On the other hand, there are cases which decide, that, under the circumstances, the particular words complained of could not lay the foundation of a criminal proceeding; and some of these cases go far to indicate, that no words are indictable as mere slander, but that they must have other foundation on which the crime may rest." 2 Bishop on Cr. L. § 813.

(*b*) In the *ecclesiastical* courts, it has been held that a suit may be entertained, not only for specified defamatory words, but even for general words of detraction or opprobrious language, coupled with or without the charge of defamation, because the latter denote malice and anger, and tend to destroy brotherly charity. Halford *v.* Smith, 4 E. 567; Bartlett *v.* Robins, 1 Wils. 258.

disorder tending to exclude the party from society; 3, an unfitness or inability to perform an office or employment of profit, or want of integrity in an office of honor; 4, words prejudicing a person in his lucrative profession or trade; 5, any untrue words, occasioning actual damage.[1] (*a*)

4. It is held that words are not slanderous unless spoken with *an intent to slander*, and so understood by the hearers.[2] (*b*) Thus words spoken in merriment or jest, (see p. 261,) without malice, or through mere heat and passion. Though, where the speaking of the words, which were actionable *per se*, was fully proved; but the Court charged, that, if the jury believed the defendant spoke them in jest and without malice, (*of which there was no proof*,) they might find for him, which they did; the charge was held erroneous.[3] So, in an old and familiar case, a clergyman, in his sermon, recited as a story out of Fox's Martyrology, that one Greenwood, being a perjured person and a great persecutor, had great plagues inflicted on him, and died by the hand of God; whereas in truth he never was so plagued, and was himself present at that sermon. In an action brought by Greenwood, Wray, J., delivered the law to the jury, that it being delivered but as a story, and not with any malice or intention to slander, the

[1] 1 Chit. Gen. Prac. 43, 44; Brooker *v.* Coffin, 5 Johns. 188; Van Ness *v.* Hamilton, 19 Ib. 367; McEwen *v.* Ludlow, 2 Harr. 12.

[2] Studdard *v.* Linville, 3 Hawks, 474.

[3] Long *v.* Eakle, 4 Md. 454; McKee *v.* Ingalls, 4 Scam. 30; Brown *v.* Brooks, 3 Ind. 518 (holding that *excitement* may be shown *in mitigation*); acc. McClintock *v.* Crick, 4 Iowa, 453.

(*a*) "As far as I can recollect, from determinations in actions for words, there seem to be two general rules whereby courts of justice have governed themselves, in order to determine words spoken of another to be actionable. The first rule is, that the words must contain an express imputation of some crime liable to punishment, some capital offence, or other infamous crime or misdemeanor; and the charge upon the person spoken of must be precise. The second general rule is, that words are actionable when spoken of one in an office of profit, which may probably occasion the loss of his office, or when spoken of persons touching their respective professions, trades, and business, and which do or may probably tend to their damage." Per De Grey, C. J., Onslow *v.* Horne, 3 Wils. 186.

(*b*) See *Malice*, § 105; also, § 51 *et seq.*

defendant was not guilty.[1] So, under the general issue in slander, the defendant may prove either in excuse or mitigation, according to circumstances, that he was *insane* when the words were spoken. But the insanity must be established by direct proof, and not by reputation.[2] And evidence was admitted to prove such insanity, existing at the time of speaking the words, and for several months before and after, but no further.[3] (*a*) So *drunkenness* may be shown in mitigation of damages; but, if the slander be often repeated, when the slanderer is sober and drunk, it is no mitigation.[4] So the defendant may show, to disprove malice and mitigate the damages; that his mind was so besotted by a long course of dissipation, and his character so depraved, that no one who knew him would give any attention or belief to what he might say.[5] So it is held, that an action of slander will not lie, for words spoken under such circumstances, as would not lead persons present to believe that they were spoken as truth.[6] And the defendant may prove the facts and circumstances, in reference to which the words were spoken, for the purpose of showing that he did not intend to impute to the plaintiff the crime, which, standing alone, they would naturally import.[7] (*b*) So, on a plea of not guilty, in an action of slander, the defendant may prove that the plaintiff himself procured the publication of the words charged, with the view to an action.[8] Nor does an action lie for slanderous words, immediately retracted or explained, in the same conversation, and in the hearing of all who heard them spoken.[9]

[1] Cro. Jac. 90.
[2] Yeates *v.* Reed, 4 Blackf. 463.
[3] Dickinson *v.* Barber, 9 Mass. 225.
[4] Howell *v.* Howell, 10 Ired. 84. But see McKee *v.* Ingalls, 4 Scam. 30; Iseley *v.* Lovejoy, 6 Blackf. 412.
[5] Gates *v.* Meredith, 7 Ind. 440.
[6] Haynes *v.* Haynes, 29 Maine, 247.
[7] Williams *v.* Cawley, 18 Ala. 206.
[8] Sutton *v.* Smith, 13 Mis. 120.
[9] Luine *v.* Maton, 13 Tex. 449; Wenchell *v.* Strong, 17 Illin. 597; Brown *v.* Brooks, 3 Ind. 518.

(*a*) A judgment in an action for slander was perpetually enjoined, upon the ground, that, at the time of speaking the words and of rendering the judgment, the defendant was insane or deranged in reference to the subject of the slander. Horner *v.* Marshall, 5 Munf. *466.

(*b*) See *Construction*.

But exculpatory declarations, made subsequently to the speaking of the actionable words, are not admissible in evidence.[1] (*a*) And the jury is bound to presume that a libellous publication has not been explained or retracted, unless the fact is proved by the defendant.[2] (*b*) And it is held that a written statement, made at the trial by the defendant, disclaiming any evil intention towards the plaintiff, cannot be given in evidence on the trial nor sent out with the jury, although allowed by the plaintiff to be given in evidence.[3] So a witness may testify, that he received and understood the defendant's communication as *private and confidential*, although there was no injunction of secrecy from the defendant, or any declaration on his part that it should be so regarded; but, whether the communication was so intended by the defendant, or, if so intended, was nevertheless

[1] Scott *v.* McKinnish, 15 Ala. 662; Kent *v.* Bonscy, 38 Maine, 435. See Darling *v.* Banks, 14 Ill. 46; Duke, &c. *v.* Hasmer, 14 Qu. B. 185.

[2] Matthews *v.* Beach, 5 Sandf. 256.

[3] Hamilton *v.* Glenn, 1 Penn. 340.

(*a*) It seems, a subsequent publication by the defendant, containing a full and unqualified retraction of libellous charges, may be given in evidence in mitigation of damages. Hotchkiss *v.* Oliphant, 2 Hill, 510.

Otherwise of a subsequent publication, in itself libellous, evincing no disposition to recant or disavow the offensive charges in the first article, but attempting merely to construe it in a different sense from that fairly imputable to it. Ibid.

(*b*) Action for slander, and a plea that the defendant, in pursuance of an agreement to that effect, did write and deliver to the plaintiff a certain letter of apology and retraction, which letter the plaintiff accepted in full satisfaction, &c. Replication, that, after the delivery of said letter, the defendant did write a certain other letter of and concerning the first letter, *et sic* the defendant did not give the said letter of apology, &c., in pursuance of said agreement, &c. Held, 1st, that the plea (supposing it to be a good plea by way of accord and satisfaction, which was deemed doubtful,) was no bar to the action, there being evidence of the defendant's intention, that the letter in question was not to be considered as a letter of apology, but merely of retraction. 2d, that the facts stated in the plea might have been given in evidence under the general issue. Eiffe *v.* Jacob, 1 Jebb & Symes, 257.

prompted by malice, is a question for the jury.[1] (*a*) So, the words being spoken while the defendant and witness were alone together, going to a neighbor's house, to get him to read a letter, which the defendant had received relative to his son's death; held, the defendant's declaration to the witness, made in the same conversation, "that his wife was much distressed on account of her son's death," was admissible evidence for him, to show that the words were prompted by grief rather than malice.[2] So, in an old case, the defendant said he had heard that the plaintiff was hanged for stealing a horse; but it appeared that the words were spoken in *sorrow*, and the plaintiff was nonsuited.[3] So, where the words were *themselves* slanderous, but not as explained at the time, and in view of the circumstances of the case; held, they were not actionable, although some persons present did not hear the explanations.[4]

5. But, on the other hand, it has been held that words may be actionable, though spoken *by mistake*. Thus testimony offered by the defendant, to show that the words charged were spoken with reference to a bill in chancery, which he supposed was sworn to by the plaintiff and did contain false allegations, but which he afterwards ascertained was sworn to by another, is inadmissible even in mitigation of damages.[5] So it is no defence, that the words were spoken by the fireside of the defendant, in the presence of but two or three witnesses.[6] So, however honestly the party who publishes a libel believes it to be true, if untrue in fact, the law implies malice, unless the occasion justifies the act, which is a question of law.[7] (*b*) So, in an action of slander, evidence that the defendant was in the habit of talking much about persons and things, and that what he

[1] Stallings *v.* Newman, 26 Ala. 300.
[2] Ibid.
[3] Lev. 82.
[4] Sheout *v.* M'Dowell, 3 Brevard, 38.
[5] Owen *v.* McKean, 14 Ill. 459.
[6] Shaw *v.* Sweeney, 2 Greene, 587.
[7] Darby *v.* Ouseley, 36 Eng. Law & Eq. 518.

(*a*) See *Privileged Communication.*
(*b*) See *Malice;* also, § 116.

said was not regarded by the community as worthy of notice, and seldom occasioned remark, was held not to be admissible, even in mitigation of damages.[1] So it has been held, that it is no defence to an action of slander, that the words were not spoken in earnest, and that the defendant did not expect to be believed,[2] (see p. 257.) So although, where the words are equivocal, or refer to circumstances supposed to be in the minds of the hearers, which materially qualify their import, the circumstances may be inquired into, and the sense in which the hearers understood the words, and in which they supposed the defendant intended them to be received, may be considered by the jury, (see § 51); yet the mere fact, that the defendant charged the plaintiff with theft, in regard to an article which had been either loaned or sold to the plaintiff, but which sale or loan was not known to hearers, will not be a ground of showing, either that the act charged was impossible, or that the charge was not seriously made; nor is it competent to go in mitigation of damages, except as tending to show that the words were spoken in heat and haste.[3] But if a charge of stealing was made in relation to a transaction which would not amount to larceny, the defendant is liable only for special damages.[4]

6. Words may be actionable, though they contain *no direct and positive assertion;*[5] but make the charge upon the plaintiff in ambiguous language or by insinuation. It is sufficient that the words have a criminal signification according to the common understanding of them when used, though in themselves doubtful or even innocent.[6] Though the words said did not in express terms charge the crime, which by innuendo it is stated the defendant meant to impute, and there is no inducement, showing of what the words were spoken; the declaration is held sufficient, if the jury believe that the words will carry the meaning ascribed to them, and were understood, and should have been under-

[1] Howe v. Perry, 15 Pick. 506.
[2] Hatch v. Patten, 2 Gilm. 725.
[3] Smith v. Miles, 15 Verm. 245.
[4] Wright v. Lindsay, 20 Ala. 428.
[5] Anon. 11 Mod. 60; 7 Barb. 260.
[6] Cooper v. Perry, Dudl. (Geo.) 247.

stood by the witness according to that meaning.[1] And if spoken affirmatively as alleged, the declaration is (see ch. 24, § 3,) supported, though the words were spoken in answer to a question put by a third person; unless the plaintiff caused the question to be put, in order to procure a cause of action,[2] (see § 196). Thus, in illustration of these various propositions, in an action for libel, the words, "Is M. H. the gentleman who wrote, &c., the individual who broke jail, while confined on a charge of forgery," are libellous.[3] So *potential* words may be actionable, if they import an act done. Thus, saying a man *could* clip money, when he lived in a particular place.[4] And to say, "I am thoroughly convinced," is a sufficient assertion to be actionable.[5] So it is equally slanderous, to say that a woman is a whore, and that there is a rumor that she is such.[6] So words actionable as slanderous are not the less so, for being preceded by the words "if reports be true," the proof of which, in addition to the words alleged, is not a variance.[7] So to write of a person, that "he is thought no more of than a horse thief and a counterfeiter," is a libel. And a plea of justification, in such case, must allege that the plaintiff had committed the crimes of horse-stealing and counterfeiting. It is not sufficient to aver that he "was thought no more of than a horse thief," &c.[8] (*a*)

[1] Marshall *v.* Gunter, 6 Rich. 419.
[2] Jones *v.* Chapman, 5 Blackf. 88; Yeates *v.* Reed, 4 Ib. 463.
[3] Hotchkiss *v.* Oliphant, 2 Hill, 510.
[4] Speed *v.* Parry, 2 Ld. Raym. 1185.
[5] Oldham *v.* Peake, 2 W. Bl. 959.
[6] Kelly *v.* Dillon, 5 Ind. 426.
[7] Smith *v.* Stewart, 5 Barr, 372.
[8] Nelson *v.* Musgrave, 10 Mis. 648.

(*a*) A declaration alleged, that the defendant published of and concerning a certain court-martial, and of and concerning the plaintiff as a member thereof, a defamatory libel and caricature, consisting of a lithographic picture and representation of the court-martial, and of the plaintiff as a member thereof, in which caricature the court-martial, and the plaintiff as a member thereot, are pointed out by their position and certain grotesque resemblances, and are represented and exhibited in an awkward and ludicrous light, posture, and condition. After verdict, it was held, that it was averred with sufficient certainty, that the plaintiff was specifically and individually libelled. Ellis *v.* Kimball, 16 Pick. 132.

So where the defendant, in speaking of an oath taken by the plaintiff, in a suit before a justice of the peace, and of the defendant's having made a complaint against the plaintiff before the grand jury for perjury, said, "he went to the grand jury and asked them whether they wanted any more witnesses, and they said they had witnesses enough to satisfy them;" held, these words, if laid with proper averments, were actionable, and in such case it is only necessary to aver, that the defendant by means of the words intimated, and meant to be understood by the hearers as charging, that the plaintiff was guilty of the crime imputed; and whether such was his intention, is a question for the jury.[1] So, under a count in an action for slander, alleging generally that the defendant charged the plaintiff with the crime of theft, it is competent for the plaintiff to give in evidence any words, which, although in their ordinary sense doubtful or even innocent, can be shown by the aid of averments and *innuendoes* under the circumstances to be *equivocal* or *ironical*, and to be intended by the defendant and understood by the hearer to impute such crime to the plaintiff.[2] Or for the words, *you will steal*, it being averred in the declaration, that the defendant meant and intended to have it understood and believed, that the plaintiff had been guilty of larceny.[3] Or for the words, *he would venture anything the plaintiff had stolen the book*, if proved to be spoken maliciously.[4] Or for

[1] Randall *v.* Butler, 7 Barb. 260.
[2] Pond *v.* Hartwell, 17 Pick. 269.
[3] Cornelius *v.* Van Slyck, 21 Wend. 70.
[4] Nye *v.* Otis, 8 Mass. 122.

Also, that the libel was set forth with sufficient certainty; for the degree of certainty required in such a case depends on the subject-matter, and where the ridicule consists mainly in ridiculous postures and movements, the use of language somewhat general and indefinite is unavoidable. And, as a caricature picture frequently consists of figures of persons, and of written language attributed to them, by labels apparently issuing out of their lips, it was held, after verdict, that an allegation, that the plaintiff was represented in such a picture as speaking certain words, was a sufficiently certain averment that these words were attributed to him. Ibid.

the assertion that "A. was a whore or she would never ride with B."[1] So a declaration alleged, that the plaintiff was editor of a newspaper called the Massachusetts Cataract, and that the defendant published a false and malicious libel of and concerning the plaintiff, and his violations of the seventh commandment of Scripture, as follows: "To the editor of the Massachusetts Cataract. Can you" (meaning the plaintiff) "break every commandment in the decalogue, and still go unwhipped of justice? Can you" (meaning the plaintiff) "be guilty of breaking the seventh commandment, and cover that noisy and licentious affair? Can you" (meaning the plaintiff) "recollect the tenth commandment, which says thou shalt not covet thy neighbor's wife? If you" (meaning the plaintiff) "recollect this commandment, can you" (meaning the plaintiff) "put your hand upon your heart and say you" (meaning the plaintiff) "have a clear conscience on this subject? Is not conscience a little unquiet? Does it not say hush, be still? It wont do to reveal the things of the prison-house; those things said and done in secret places." Meaning thereby, that the plaintiff had committed the crime of adultery, and that his conscience accused him of this crime. Held, after verdict for the plaintiff, that the declaration was sufficient, although it did not contain a direct averment that the defendant charged the plaintiff with the crime of adultery, nor any colloquium to explain the words.[2] So, in an action for writing and publishing of the plaintiff, that her warmest friends, in giving up their advocacy of her claims, stated that they had realized the fable of the Frozen Snake; if *not guilty* be pleaded, and a verdict of guilty found, the plaintiff is entitled to judgment; since the jury may have understood that the words "Frozen Snake" were meant to charge the plaintiff with ingratitude to friends. And it is no objection, in arrest of judgment, that the words are not explained by innuendo; for the Court will notice that the words are commonly enough understood in this sense to warrant a jury in so

[1] True *v.* Plumley, 36 Maine, 466. [2] Goodrich *v.* Davis, 11 Met. 473.

applying them.[1] So the words, "A report has gone abroad, through the instrumentality of S. W., stating that R. M. had a load or parcel of falsely packed or plated cotton bales; which report is a direct falsehood;" printed and published with malice, were held a libel.[2]

7. But there is also a class of cases, which adopt a more strict rule in regard to the *directness* of the charge complained of. Thus the words, "I never came home and pox'd my wife," were held not actionable, because merely *negative*.[3] Nor does an action lie for the words, "you are as bad as thy wife when she stole my cushion;" without an averment that the felony was committed.[4] Nor for the words, "a man that would do that would steal."[5] Nor for saying in relation to actionable words, a suit for which was barred by the statute of limitations, "I never denied what I have said, and I will stand up to it."[6] Nor for a charge of mere *false swearing*, though intentionally guarded, to prevent its being actionable, as, "He swore to a damned lie, but I am not liable because I have not said in what suit he testified."[7] (*Infra*, ch. 8, § 4.) Nor, "I will take him to Bow Street on a charge of forgery;" because the words do not amount to a charge of felony; nor are they capable of any such unequivocal innuendo.[8] (*Infra*, ch. 8, § 26.) Nor, "P. gave £200 for his warrant to be purser of the Magnanime," (a man-of-war.)[9] (*a*)

[1] Hoare *v.* Silverlock, 12 Ad. & Ell. N. S. 624.
[2] Woodburn *v.* Miller, Cheves, 194.
[3] Clerk *v.* Dyer, 8 Mod. 290.
[4] Upton *v.* Pinfold, 1 Com. 268.
[5] Stees *v.* Kemble, 27 Penn. 112.
[6] Fox *v.* Wilson, 3 Jones, Law, 485.
[7] Muchler *v.* Mulhollen, Hill & Den. 263; Shinloub *v.* Ammerman, 7 Ind. 347; Mehane *v.* Sellars, 3 Jones, Law, 199.
[8] Harrison *v.* King, 4 Price, 46.
[9] Purdy *v.* Stacey, 5 Burr. 2698.

(*a*) A count in slander, alleging that the defendant uttered and published that the plaintiff, who was postmaster at F., "embezzled certain papers," is not supported by proof, that he said "he had no doubt but that the papers were embezzled at F.," or that "he thought the papers were embezzled at the post-office at F." Taylor *v.* Kneeland, 1 Doug. 67.

So a declaration contained the usual inducement, without the averment of any extrinsic facts or circumstances, showing the actionable quality of the words spoken, except that the plaintiff was postmaster at F., and the third

8. If the words charged were spoken *in a foreign language*, they must be so set forth, with an English translation;[1] and, in general, the declaration must aver that the hearers understood them, (*a*) and the plaintiff must prove the speaking of some of the foreign words, and that the translation is correct.[2] So in an action for a libel, written in a foreign language, the plaintiff must set forth the libel in the original; if he only set out a translation of it, the Court will arrest the judgment.[3] But if foreign words were spoken at the same time with the English words, the former may be given in evidence in connection with the latter, to show what charge was really made.[4]

9. The meaning of any word used in an alleged slanderous charge need not be alleged, if it be an English word and well understood, although, from its obscenity, it is not inserted in any dictionary.[5]

10. We proceed now to inquire, what particular charges or accusations are libellous or slanderous.

11. And here it will be seen, that libel and slander are governed by very different rules. (*b*) It is well settled, that

[1] Zeig *v.* Ort, 3 Chandl. 26; Keenholts *v.* Becker, 3 Den. 346.

[2] Hickley *v.* Grosjean, 6 Blackf. 351.

[3] Zenobio *v.* Axtel, 6 T. R. 162.

[4] Keenholts *v.* Becker, 3 Den. 346.

[5] Edgar *v.* McCutchen, 9 Mis. 768.

---

count charged the defendant with having spoken and published, of and concerning the plaintiff, as postmaster, &c., that "he did not think Marlett's resignation, or his petition, had gone to Washington; he had no doubt they were embezzled at F.;" adding, by innuendo, "(at the post-office at F., of which the plaintiff was postmaster,) meaning and intending thereby, that the plaintiff had delayed and prevented the transmission, and resignation, and petition, to the postmaster-general at Washington," &c. Held, the count was fatally defective, the words charged to have been spoken and published not appearing to be actionable. Ibid.

(*a*) But in Ohio, it is held that where words spoken in German, and in a German county, are slanderous, it need not be averred that they were understood. Bechtell *v.* Shatler, Wright, 107.

(*b*) The distinctions between verbal and written slander proceed upon the principle, that words are often spoken in heat upon sudden provocations, and are fleeting and soon forgotten, and therefore less likely to be permanently injurious; while written slander is more deliberate and malicious,

an action may be maintained for words written or printed, for which an action could not be maintained if they were merely spoken.[1]

12. Numerous definitions of *a libel* are to be found in the books, the general result of which, when compared together may be thus expressed.

13. A publication is *a libel*, which tends to injure one's reputation in the common estimation of mankind, to throw contumely or reflect shame and disgrace upon him, or hold him up as an object of hatred, scorn, ridicule, and contempt, although it imputes no crime liable to be punished with infamy.[2] Or to prejudice him in his employment.[3] Especially if calculated to provoke a breach of the peace.[4] So every publication, by writing, printing, or painting, which charges or imputes to any person that which renders him liable to punishment, or which is calculated to make him infamous, odious, or ridiculous, is *primâ facie* a libel, and implies malice in the publisher.[5] So it is a libel, to publish in a newspaper a story of an individual calculated to render him ludicrous, although he may have told the same story of himself.[6] So a letter, written by the defendant to a third person, calling the plaintiff "a villain," is actionable, without special damage.[7] So to write concerning a man, "I look on him as a rascal, and have watched him for many

[1] Thorley *v.* Lord Kerry, 4 Taunt. 355; Bennett *v.* Williams, 4 Sandf. 60; Layton *v.* Harris, 3 Harring. 406; Dudley, 303.

[2] Armentrout *v.* Moranda, 8 Blackf. 426; Villers *v.* Mousley, 2 Wils. 403; Fonville *v.* Nease, Dudley, 303; Miller *v.* Butler, 6 Cush. 71; 4 Pike, 110; Walk. 403; Wright, 47; 4 Mass. 168; Chit. Gen. Prac. 43; 5 Co. 125; The State *v.* Henderson, 1 Rich. 179.

[3] Obaugh *v.* Finn, 4 Pike, 110. See Steele *v.* Southwick, 9 Johns. 211; Cooper *v.* Greeley, 1 Denio, 347.

[4] Tarrance *v.* Hurst, Walk. 403; Newbraugh *v.* Carry, Wright, 47.

[5] White *v.* Nicholls, 3 How. U. S. 266.

[6] Cook *v.* Ward, 6 Bing. 409.

[7] Bell *v.* Stone, 1 B. & P. 331.

more capable of circulation in distant places, and consequently more likely to be permanently injurious. 1 Chit. Gen. Prac. 45. It is also said, though perhaps not with strict accuracy, that the *great distinction* between libel and slander is, "that from a libel damage is always implied by law, whereas some kinds of slander only are actionable without proof of special damage." Broom's Comm. 513, 762.

years," is a libel.[1] So a publication, stating that the plaintiff is about to commence a suit for a libel, but that he will not like to bring it to trial in a particular county, *because he is known there*, is libellous, as it amounts to a charge that the plaintiff is in bad repute in that county.[2] So a written or printed publication, stating that A. "has been guilty of gross misconduct in insulting persons in a barefaced manner," is libellous.[3] Or that "B. would put his name to anything that T. would request him to sign that would prejudice D.'s character."[4] So a writing, in which a party is spoken of in language usually applied to the keeper of *a gaming-house*, is libellous, whether the words are capable of being applied by an innuendo to specific charges of unfair practices or not.[5] So to publish of a person, that "his slanderous reports nearly ruined some of our best merchants."[6] So a charge of *smuggling goods* into the country is libellous.[7] So to write of a person soliciting relief from a charitable society, that she prefers unworthy claims, which it is hoped the members will reject forever, and that she has squandered away money, already obtained by her from the benevolent, in printing circulars abusive of the society's secretary.[8] So to charge an overseer with oppressive conduct towards paupers, in compelling them to receive payment of their weekly parish allowance in orders for flour upon a particular tradesman.[9] So to publish in a newspaper, that the plaintiff requested the holder of a note of which he was the maker, to wait for payment after the same had matured; that the holder accordingly waited, and afterwards, the note being sued, the plaintiff pleaded the statute of limitations and got off scot-free.[10] So a false and malicious publication of *an obituary notice* of one living is a libel.[11] (*a*)

[1] Williams *v.* Carnes, 4 Humph. 9.
[2] Cooper *v.* Greeley, 1 Denio, 347.
[3] Clements *v.* Chives, 9 B. & C. 172; 4 M. & Ry. 127.
[4] Duncan *v.* Brown, 15 B. Mon. 186.
[5] Digby *v.* Thompson, 1 Nev. & M. 485.
[6] Cramer *v.* Noonan, 4 Wis. 231.
[7] Stillwell *v.* Barter, 19 Wend. 487.
[8] Hoare *v.* Silverlock, 12 Ad. & Ell. N. S. 624.
[9] Woodard *v.* Dowsing, 2 M. & Ry. 74.
[10] Bennett *v.* Williamson, 4 Sandf. 60.
[11] McBride *v.* Ellis, 9 Rich. Law, 313.

(*a*) A definition of libel often quoted is as follows. So far as it refers to

14. But it is not libellous, to charge a man with having pleaded the statute of limitations in defence of an action at law, when there is no charge that he made the plea dishonestly. A publication of this kind imports no offence, nor has it a necessary tendency to expose the plaintiff to ridicule, hatred, or contempt.[1] So where the defendant, the editor of a newspaper, owed the plaintiff money upon an award, in speaking of which and of the plaintiff in an article in his paper he said, the money will be forthcoming on the last day allowed by the award, but we are not disposed to allow him to put it into Wall Street for shaving purposes before that period; held, not libellous.[2]

15. It has been already stated, what spoken words are in general actionable. Upon the ground that the most frequent cause of action is the accusation of *crime*, and that most other charges, in order to be actionable, must be made under special circumstances, while this is *of itself* slanderous; the proposition is sometimes laid down, that an action for slander does not lie, except for words which contain an express implication of some punishable offence.[3] (*Infra*, ch. 8, § 1). Or, that words, to be actionable, must either have produced a temporal loss to the plaintiff in special damage sustained, or they must convey a charge of some act criminal in itself and indictable as such, and subjecting the party to an infamous, more especially a corporal, punishment; or some

1 Bennett *v.* Williamson, 4 Sandf. 60.
2 Stone *v.* Cooper, 2 Denio, 293.
3 Bute *v.* Gill, 2 Monr. 65; Wyant *v.* Smith, 5 Blackf. 293; Holt *v.* Schofield, 6 T. R. 691.

---

what may be written *concerning one deceased*, it may be regarded as a *criminal* rather than a *civil* definition. "A malicious publication, expressed either in printing or writing, or by signs or pictures, tending either to injure the memory of one dead, or the reputation of one alive, and expose him to public hatred, contempt, or ridicule." 4 Mass. 168.

Publications defamatory of dead persons are libellous, because they tend to stir up others of the same family, blood, or society to revenge and break the peace by provoking them to vindicate the memory of the deceased, and to wipe off that stain, which the reflections on their ancestors may cast upon them. Rex *v.* Topham, 4 T. R. 127.

indictable offence involving moral turpitude.[1] But words merely abusive and insulting are not actionable, unless special damages are alleged and proved.[2] (*a*) Thus, to charge the plaintiff with having marked a third person's hogs is not actionable.[3] Nor to charge one with the intemperate use of spirituous liquors.[4] As saying of the plaintiff, that "he got drunk on Christmas."[5] (*b*) So the words, "he altered the ear-mark of my hog from mine to his, or procured it to be done," do not, *per se*, import that the mismarking was done for the purpose of fraudulently appropriating the property, and are not actionable without proof of special damage.[6] So an action does not lie for charging one with a *disposition* to commit a crime.[7] Or with *intent* to commit a crime.[8] Though the words, "she put poison in a barrel of drinking-water, to poison me," and other words of the

[1] M'Cuer *v.* Ludlam, 2 Harr. 12; Birch *v.* Benton, 26 Mis. 153; Turner *v.* Ogden, 2 Salk. 696; Young *v.* Miller, 3 Hill, 22; Quinn *v.* O'Gara, 2 E. D. Smith, 388.

[2] Davis *v.* Farrington, Walk. 304.

[3] Johnston *v.* Morrow, 9 Port. 525.

[4] O'Hanlon *v.* Myers, 10 Rich. Law, 128.

[5] Warren *v.* Norman, Walk. 387.

[6] Williams *v.* Karnes, 4 Humph. 9.

[7] Seaton *v.* Cordray, Wright, 101.

[8] M'Kee *v.* Ingalls, 4 Scam. 30.

(*a*) Such words are, however, rendered actionable by statute in Mississippi. Davis *v.* Farrington, Walk. 304.

(*b*) In Massachusetts an action of slander lies, for charging a woman with drunkenness. Brown *v.* Nickerson, 5 Gray, 1.

It is remarked by the Court: "By the law of this Commonwealth (however it may be elsewhere) it is actionable to charge a person falsely and maliciously with an offence that may subject him to a punishment which will bring disgrace upon him, though the punishment be not in itself infamous. (Miller *v.* Parish, 8 Pick. 385.) In that case it was decided that a charge against a woman of an offence that was then punishable by a small fine, was actionable; a punishment for that offence necessarily bringing her into disgrace. And that case is decisive of this. For whether the charge, which this demurrer admits that the defendant falsely and maliciously made against the female plaintiff, be that she was a common drunkard, punishable by confinement in the house of correction, (Rev. Sts. c. 143, § 5,) or only that she was once drunk by the voluntary use of intoxicating liquor, and punishable by a fine of five dollars, (Rev. Sts. c. 130, § 18,) the charge is actionable; for the punishment of a woman for either offence must bring disgrace upon her." Per Metcalf, J. Ib.

same meaning, are actionable.[1] Nor with burning, destroying, and suppressing a will.[2] So words amounting to a charge, that the plaintiff had committed a penitentiary offence, but that he was insane when he committed it, are not actionable.[3] But words, charging that a person has been in the penitentiary of another State, are actionable.[4]

16. Although, in slander for actionable words, actual damage need not be proved; yet words not libellous or slanderous *in themselves* may become actionable by proof of *special damage* resulting from them to the plaintiff. (*a*)

17. But, in order to be thus actionable, they must be of themselves *disparaging;*[5] or, it seems, import either an illegal or an immoral act.[6]

18. And the plaintiff must state in his declaration such special damage, and also prove that it was exclusively and immediately, legally and naturally, the consequence of the words.[7] It is said, "There is no occasion to say anything concerning any future, presumptive, contingent damages, which (the plaintiff) may possibly sustain at some future time (nobody knows when) by reason of (the defendant's) reflections upon him. I know of no case where ever an action for words was grounded upon eventual damages, which may possibly happen to a man in a future situation."[8] Thus

[1] Mills *v.* Wimp. 10 B. Mon. 417.
[2] Ibid.
[3] Abrams *v.* Smith, 8 Blackf. 95.
[4] Smith *v.* Stewart, 5 Barr, 372.
[5] Kelly *v.* Partington, 3 Nev. & M. 116.
[6] Hallock *v.* Miller, 2 Barb. 630.
[7] Ibid.; Vicars *v.* Wilcocks, 8 E. 1; Hastings *v.* Palmer, 20 Wend. 225; Bentley *v.* Reynolds, 1 M'Mull, 16; 2 Hill, 309; Wilson *v.* Runyon, Wright, 651; Haddon *v.* Lott, 29 Eng. L. & Eq. 215; Terwilliger *v.* Wands, 25 Barb. 313; Birch *v.* Benton, 26 Mis. 153; Feray *v.* Foote, 12 La. An. 894.
[8] Per De Grey, C. J., Onslow *v.* Horne, 3 Wils. 187.

(*a*) Where, in slander, the declaration in the same count set forth words which were actionable *per se*, with others which were not so, concluding with an allegation of special damages; to which the defendant pleaded not guilty; held, that, as he had been precluded from demurring, he might, at the trial, raise any question relating to the plaintiff's right to maintain the suit for words not actionable *per se*. Beach *v.* Ranney, 2 Hill, 309.

In such case, the defendant cannot demur to some of the words and take issue upon the others. Dwight *v.* Tanner, 20 Wend. 190.

in case for slanderous words, by reason of which the plaintiff was turned out of her lodging and employment, it appeared that the defendant complained to E. the mistress of the house, who was his tenant, that her lodgers, of whom the plaintiff was one, behaved improperly at the windows; and he added, that no moral person would like to have such people in his house. E. testified, that she dismissed the plaintiff in consequence of the words, not because she believed them, but because she was afraid it would offend her landlord if the plaintiff remained. Held, the action was maintainable, the special damage being the consequence of the slanderous words.[1] But in an action brought by a husband for slander of his wife, the plaintiff proved the uttering of the words to the witnesses, that they had come to the knowledge of his wife, and that her health had been injured by them; but no proof was given of any relation between the words and the effect imputed to them; or that the witnesses were authorized to communicate them to the wife; or that they had the intentions and occasions which would have justified them in communicating the slander; or that they sustained relations from which these could be presumed. Held, the action could not be maintained.[2] And the plaintiff must allege and prove, that by reason of the words he has sustained some damage of a *pecuniary* nature; that his *reputation* has been affected, and thereby the conduct of others towards him; as that he was thereby prevented from receiving something of value — *e. g.* fuel, clothing, provisions, &c. — which else would have been bestowed upon him gratuitously; not mere sickness, bodily or mental suffering, loss of society, or the good opinion of neighbors, &c. Accordingly, in an action by a female for words imputing a want of chastity, an allegation of special damages, showing that the plaintiff had suffered pain of body and mind, — that her neighbors had shunned her, — that she was turned out of the moral reform society, &c., was

[1] Knight *v.* Gibbs, 1 Ad. & Ell. 43.

[2] Omstead *v.* Brown, 12 Barb. 657; 25 Ib. 313.

held not enough to maintain the action.[1] But *loss of marriage* is held sufficient.[2] And it is not sufficient to prove a mere wrongful act of a third person induced by the slander; as that he dismissed the plaintiff from his employment before the end of the term for which they had contracted.[3] In such cases, the plaintiff has a complete remedy against the third person.[4] So where the defendant libelled a performer at a place of public entertainment, provided by the plaintiff, in consequence of which she refused to sing; and the plaintiff alleged that his oratorios had in consequence been more thinly attended; it was held that the injury was too remote, as for aught that appeared such performer might have left from mere caprice or indolence.[5] (*a*)

19. In general, the special damage complained of must be specially set forth. And this rule has been held to apply, whether the special damage is the *gist* of the action, or whether the words are actionable *per se*. Thus in an action for slander, by which the plaintiff lost his customers in trade, he was not allowed to prove, that any persons not named in his declaration left off dealing with him in consequence of the words spoken. And also (it seems) that the customers themselves were the only proper witnesses of the fact; and that their declarations could not be proved.[6] So under an averment, that but for the slander certain persons (naming them) "and divers other persons" would have

[1] Beach *v.* Ranney, 2 Hill, 309; Terwilliger *v.* Wands, 17 N. Y. 54.

[2] Baker *v.* Moody, 5 Cow. 351; Lumey *v.* Maton, 13 Texas, 449.

[3] Vicars *v.* Wilcocks, 8 E. 1.

[4] Beach *v.* Ranney, 2 Hill, 309; Bentley *v.* Reynolds, 1 M'Mull. 16.

[5] Ashley *v.* Harrison, 1 Esp. 48.

[6] Hallock *v.* Miller, 2 Barb. 630; 8 Port. 486.

(*a*) In slander for words not actionable *per se*, in consequence of the speaking of which it is alleged that a third person acted in a particular manner, by which the plaintiff was damnified, it must be shown that the words were spoken in his presence, or caused the injury alleged. Keenholts *v.* Becker, 3 Denio, 346.

As (it seems) that he innocently repeated them to another, who was thereby influenced to withhold from the plaintiff some advantage which he would otherwise have granted him. Per Beardsley, J., Keenholts *v.* Becker, 3 Denio, 346.

employed the plaintiff, proof of non-employment for such cause by any other persons than those named is not admissible.[1] So in an action for words, whereby the plaintiff lost her marriage with J. N., evidence of a loss of marriage with another person is inadmissible.[2] (*a*)

19 *a*. But in a late English case it is held, that, in an action for slander of the plaintiff in his business, with a general allegation of loss of business, also of particular customers, as special damage; the plaintiff may recover for general loss of trade without proving the latter allegation.[3] And, in alleging loss of business, it is not always necessary to name the customers whose business has been thus lost.[4] So the general rule stated above (§ 19,) is subject to reasonable qualification, where under the circumstances it would be difficult or impracticable to allege and prove all the particulars in which the special damage consists. Thus, where an action was brought by a clergyman, for words, in consequence of which, as he alleged, the persons formerly frequenting his chapel had forbidden him longer to preach there; it was held unnecessary to set forth the names of such persons.[5] And it has even been held, that the particulars of damage of this nature cannot be gone into in evidence. Thus, in an action for the loss of the profits of performances at a place of public amusement, it was held, that witnesses might testify to a general diminution of re-

[1] Johnson *v.* Robertson, 8 Port. 486.

[2] Martin *v.* Henrickson, 2 Ld. Raym. 1007.

[3] Evans *v.* Harries, 38 Eng. L. & Eq. 347.

[4] Trenton, &c. *v.* Perrine, 3 Zabr. 402.

[5] Hartley *v.* Herring, 8 T. R. 130.

(*a*) Where words are not actionable in themselves, they cannot be made so by the aid of other words, spoken at a different time and place, which are barred by the statute of limitations. Jones *v.* Jones, 1 Jones, Law, 495.

Nor, in an action for slanderous words not actionable in themselves, can the plaintiff prove that he sustained special damage by means of the repetition of the words by a third person. Stevens *v.* Hartly, 11 Met. 542.

ceipts, but not that particular individuals had given up their boxes.[1]

20. With regard to *the place* of uttering slanderous words, in reference to the action therefor; it is held, that an action for slander will lie in one State, for words spoken in another, actionable at common law.[2] (a) So, under a declaration, which alleged the words to have been spoken at Greece, in the county of Munroe, the plaintiff was allowed to prove that they were spoken at Darlington, in Upper Canada, although it would be otherwise, in certain cases, where the place is a matter of description. And it has been doubted, whether the Courts of New York ought to take cognizance of slanderous words spoken in Canada, if both parties are British subjects. But an action for slanderous words will lie by one citizen of New York against another, though spoken in Canada. And the parties will be presumed citizens, until the contrary appear.[3] So it will be presumed, until the contrary be proved, that the words were spoken in the State where the suit is brought.[4]

21. With regard to the laws of the place, a violation of which is charged by the words complained of; to charge a man with having stolen bank-notes in South Carolina, was held not to be actionable in North Carolina, unless it was shown by proof that, by the laws of South Carolina, such stealing was subject to an infamous punishment. The Court held, also, that they could make no such presumption, as by the common law the stealing of bank-notes was not

1 Ashley v. Harrison, 1 Esp. 48.
2 Offutt v. Earlywine, 4 Blackf. 460; Linville v. Earlywine, 4 Blackf. 469.
3 Lister v. Wright, 2 Hill, 320.
4 Worth v. Butler, 7 Blackf. 251.

(a) An action on the case, for setting up a mark in front of the plaintiff's dwelling-house, in order to defame him as the keeper of a bawdy-house, is not local in its nature; and, if the declaration after describing the house as situate in a certain street called A. Street in the parish of O. A., (there being no such parish,) afterwards state the nuisance to be erected and placed in the parish aforesaid, it will be ascribed to venue, and not to local description; and therefore the place is not material to be proved as laid. Jefferies v. Duncombe, 11 E. 226.

indictable, nor was it indictable in North Carolina, until the passage of the act of 1811.[1] But where, A. and B. being in North Carolina, A. charged B. with having stolen a note from him, "in Halifax, Virginia"; and it appeared that the stealing of notes is larceny in Virginia; these words were held actionable.[2] And in general it is held, as the more recent doctrine, that an action lies for words spoken in the State where such action is brought, charging the commission of a crime in another State.[3] Thus words accusing the plaintiff of stealing in another State are actionable.[4]

[1] Wall *v.* Hoskins, 5 Ired. 177.
[2] Shipp *v.* M'Craw, 3 Murph. 463.
[3] Poe *v.* Grever, 3 Sneed, 664.
[4] Johnson *v.* Dicken, 25 Mis. 580

CHAPTER VIII.

CRIME.

1. We now proceed to consider particularly the various crimes, for an imputation of which an action may be maintained. And it may be stated as a general proposition, that, if the words clearly impute a crime, it is not necessary to allege an intention to charge the plaintiff with such crime.[1] It will be seen that most of the cases relate to accusations of a breach of *honesty* — *crimen falsi* — including more particularly perjury and larceny; and of *chastity.* (*a*) It is however laid down in general terms, though probably somewhat too broadly, that words imputing *an indictable*

[1] Galloway *v.* Courtney, 10 Rich. Law, 414.

(*a*) Occasional examples are found in the books of actions brought for charges of the higher crimes, such as murder and treason. Thus an action lies for saying "G. B. is the man who killed my husband." Button *v.* Heyward, 8 Mod. 24.

So, "You did shut up my sister and murder her, and I will prove it," were held actionable. Rivers *v.* Lite, 2 Strange, 1130.

So the words, "I think the present business ought to have the most rigid inquiry, for he (the plaintiff) murdered his first wife; that is, he administered, improperly, medicines to her for a certain complaint, which was the cause of her death," are actionable; and if doubtful, the doubt is cured by verdict. Ford *v.* Primrose, 5 Dowl. & Ry. 287.

So the words, "F." (the plaintiff) "had the Pretender's picture in his room, and I saw him drink his health, and he said that he" (the Pretender) "had a right to the crown," were held actionable. Fry *v.* Carne, 8 Mod. 283.

offence are actionable *per se.*[1] (*Supra*, § 15.) And on the other hand it is held, that no words are actionable, unless they impute a crime to the plaintiff which *subjects him to punishment.*[2] But the more correct principle seems to be, that, in order to render words actionable of themselves, it is not sufficient that they impute to the plaintiff the violation of a penal or criminal law, but they must charge an offence, indictable or presentable, and which involves *moral turpitude*, or would subject him to an *infamous* punishment.[3] (*a*)

2. In an action for words charging the plaintiff with a crime, it is not necessary to aver or prove that he was physically able to commit the crime.[4] And to utter words imputing a crime is actionable, although the crime could not for other causes be committed by the party charged with it, unless this fact be known or disclosed to the hearer; as to charge a tenant in common of a chattel with stealing it, there being no explanation that he was a tenant in common.[5] So, upon the well-settled principle, that the ground

[1] Kinney *v.* Hosea, 3 Harring. 77.

[2] Ibid.; Dorsey *v.* Whipps, 8 Gill, 457.

[3] Hoag *v.* Hatch, 23 Conn. 585; Burton *v.* Burton, 3 Iowa, 316; 2 Sneed, 473; Gage *v.* Shelton, 3 Rich. 242.

[4] Chambers *v.* White, 2 Jones, Law, 383.

[5] Carter *v.* Andrews, 16 Pick. 1; Kennedy *v.* Gifford, 19 Wend. 241.

(*a*) So, whether a *crime* or *misdemeanor*, as, for instance, that the plaintiff unlawfully sold spirituous liquor to a slave. Smith *v.* Smith, 2 Sneed, 473.

So a charge of poisoning the defendant's cow. Burton *v.* Burton, 3 Iowa, 316.

Or of malicious trespass. Wilcox *v.* Edwards, 5 Blackf. 183.

Or of wilfully burning a school-house (in Kentucky). Wallace *v.* Young, 5 Monr. 153.

Or of maliciously removing the corner-stone of a certain survey of land. Dial *v.* Holter, 6 Ohio, (N. S.) 228.

But not a charge of having cut off the tail of the defendant's horse. Gage *v.* Shelton, 3 Rich. 242.

Nor words charging the defendant with having beaten his wife so that he made her miscarry; as, without an innuendo, they amount to no more than that the plaintiff committed an assault and battery on his wife. Dudley *v.* Horn, 21 Ala. 379.

Or with having whipped his wife. Birch *v.* Benton, 26 Mis. 153.

Or his mother. Speaker *v.* McKenzie, 26 Mis. 255.

of the action of slander is not *jeopardy of punishment*, but *injury to reputation*;[1] it is actionable to accuse of larceny a child under the age of ten years; although not punishable therefor.[2] So a declaration in slander, after averring a colloquium concerning the plaintiff and A., charges the defendant with saying, that A. thinks it a hard matter to commit fornication with "his niece (meaning the plaintiff)." This was held sufficient, without any averment that the plaintiff was A.'s niece.[3] So it is libellous and actionable to write of one, "I did observe J. W. put in a vote for lieutenant-governor very soon after the poll was opened, and when not more than ten or twelve votes had been put in, and a few minutes before the votes were all taken I saw J. W. put in a second vote for lieutenant-governor:" even though J. W. was not present at the election, or though no such election was held.[4] So an action lies for the charge of committing murder in Ireland, without proving murder to be indictable there; it being provided by treaty that persons charged with murder in Great Britain or the United States shall be delivered up by one to the other.[5] (*a*) So in an action for charging the plaintiff with murder, it is not necessary to allege or prove the death of the person said to be murdered. The action may be maintained, though he is still living, if his existence was not known to those in whose presence the words were spoken.[6] And, in an action of slander for a charge of forgery, where the defendant has placed

[1] Poe *v.* Grever, 3 Sneed, 664.
[2] Stewart *v.* Howe, 17 Ill. 71.
[3] Miller *v.* Parish, 8 Pick. 384.
[4] Walker *v.* Winn, 8 Mass. 248.
[5] Montgomery *v.* Deeley, 3 Wis. 709; acc. Poe *v.* Grever, 3 Sneed, 664.
[6] Tenney *v.* Clement, 10 N. H. 52; Stallings *v.* Newman, 26 Ala. 300.

(*a*) A plea, in an action of slander for charging the plaintiff with committing a felony, which admits the speaking of the words charged, but avers other facts in order to show that the words were not actionable, must show, either that it appeared by the whole of the defendant's statements in the same conversation and company, that no felony had been committed and therefore that there was no charge of felony, or that the charge was made known to the defendant by a third person named in the plea before he uttered the words. Parker *v.* McQueen, 8 B. Mon. 16.

his defence upon the ground, that certain papers were the subjects of forgery and had been forged; he has no cause of complaint, that the presiding judge suffers the cause to proceed to trial, and does not instruct the jury that the papers were not the subject of forgery, even if they were not so; for, if the instruction had been that they were not the subjects of forgery, the plaintiff could not have been guilty of that offence, and the instruction must then have been, that the defence had not been made out.[1]

3. Words imputing a crime are actionable, although they describe it in vulgar language, and not in technical terms.[2] And it is not necessary that the words in terms should charge a crime. If such is the necessary inference, taking the words together, and in their popular meaning, they are actionable.[3] (See § 6.) So a count, alleging that the defendant charged the plaintiff with the commission of a crime by its common designation, is good; though the Court may on motion require a specification of the words.[4] So a charge of crime is actionable, though made in indirect terms, if calculated to induce the hearers to suspect that the plaintiff was guilty of the crime alleged. Thus the words, "Some time ago Mr. Norris's stables were burnt, and I lost my horse, and public opinion says you was the author of it, and what public opinion says I believe to be true;" constitute a charge of arson, if the burning was arson; and so also of killing a horse; which is actionable *per se*.[5] So the words, "You have been cropped for felony," are actionable words.[6] Or, "You have committed an act, for which I can transport you."[7] So the words, "That rogue Jo. Tindall that set the house on fire; if anybody will give me charge of him, I will carry him to new-prison;" and another set of words, "Jo. Tindall set the house on fire," were both held actionable.[8] And, in slander, for charging a plaintiff with having burnt his own barn, with intent to defraud an insur-

[1] Sawyer *v.* Hopkins, 9 Shep. 268.
[2] Colman *v.* Godwin, 3 Doug. 90.
[3] Morgan *v.* Livingston, 2 Rich. 573.
[4] True *v.* Plumley, 36 Maine, 466.
[5] Gage *v.* Shelton, 3 Rich. 242; Drummond *v.* Leslie, 5 Blackf. 453.
[6] Wiley *v.* Campbell, 5 Monr. 396.
[7] Curtis *v.* Curtis, 10 Bing. 477.
[8] Tindall *v.* Moore, 2 Wils. 114.

ance company, it is not necessary to aver that the barn was insured, where the natural import of the words is to impute the crime of arson.[1] But the defendant may show, either by evidence or special plea — by the subject and the *colloquium* — that the design was to impute a breach of trust and not a felony.[2]

4. No actions for slander are more frequent than those brought for an accusation of *perjury.*

5. Words charging perjury are *actionable in themselves*, and special damages need not be proved.[3] And an accusation of perjury implies everything necessary to constitute the offence, and, if it refers to extra-judicial testimony, the *onus* lies on the defendant of showing it. It is not necessary, in such a case, to allege a *colloquium*, showing that the charge related to material testimony in a judicial proceeding.[4] So, where the words charged indicate, that, if the plaintiff did testify falsely, his testimony must have been intentionally and corruptly false upon a point material to the issue; it is not necessary that the declaration should allege that the words imputed the crime of perjury.[5]

6. But, inasmuch as perjury consists in taking a false oath, but at the same time all false swearing is not perjury; the distinction often becomes important, in determining whether the particular charge is actionable.

7. The rule seems well settled, that, in an action for accusing another of *false swearing*, the evidence must show that the crime of *perjury* was charged.[6] And in the declaration there must be a *colloquium*, showing that the testimony referred to would, if false, constitute perjury. And it must be proved that the alleged false testimony was given on a trial, and was material to the issue.[7] And it is a defence for the defendant to show that he was not sworn at the trial.[8]

8. As to the comparative accuracy and precision, of

1 Case *v.* Buckley, 15 Wend. 327.
2 Brite *v.* Gill, 2 Monr. 65.
3 Newbit *v.* Statuck, 35 Maine, 315; Holt *v.* Schofield, 6 T. R. 691; Williams *v.* Spears, 11 Ala. 138.
4 Hall *v.* Montgomery, 8 Ala. 510.
5 Williams *v.* Spears, 11 Ala. 138.
6 Butterfield *v.* Baffam, 9 N. H. 156.
7 Harris *v.* Woody, 9 Mis. 113.
8 Snyder *v.* Degant, 4 Ind. 578.

stating the charge of perjury in an action, and the crime itself in an indictment; it has been held, that, in an action for charging the plaintiff with having sworn falsely to a schedule, it is not necessary to state the charge of false swearing in the preliminary part of the declaration, in the terms which would be necessary in an indictment for perjury; but enough ought to appear in words or by legal intendment to show "an oath in a court of justice."[1] But where the defendant *justifies* a charge of perjury, he must prove all the particulars which constitute the crime, viz.: the deliberate deposition, the lawfully administered oath, the judicial proceeding, the absoluteness of the matter testified to, its materiality to the point in question direct or collateral, and its falsity.[2] And, to sustain such plea of justification, the testimony of two witnesses at least, or of one witness, and strong corroborating circumstances, are held to be necessary.[3] (*a*)

[1] Simpson *v.* Vaughan, 2 Strobh. 32.
[2] Hopkins *v.* Smith, 3 Barb. 599.
[3] Bradley *v.* Kennedy, 2 Greene, 231.

(*a*) See *Justification.* A defendant justified a charge of perjury as follows: "The defendant avers that said plaintiff, in swearing to a bill of complaint in the Court at Dresden, against Samuel Steele, executor of John Steele, swore falsely, by stating in said bill that said estate owed nothing, when said plaintiff knew, at the time he swore to said bill, that the estate was indebted," &c. Held, upon this specification proof was not admissible, for it gave the plaintiff no information of the indebtedness to be proved. So though the plaintiff took issue on this plea. Steele *v.* Phillips, 10 Humph. 461.

So, where the defendant pleaded the general issue, and by brief statement alleged that the plaintiff, "after being duly sworn, did falsely and corruptly testify" in a certain manner stated, and that the statements so made by the plaintiff were known by him at the time to have been untrue, "and that the plaintiff committed the offence of perjury on said trial;" if the defendant proves that the plaintiff, upon the former trial, made statements as a witness from the place where witnesses usually stand when testifying, this is not conclusive evidence that the oath was taken, and the plaintiff is not thereby estopped from denying that he was sworn, although such evidence may properly be considered, in determining whether he was sworn, or in mitigation of damages, if the justification is not fully made out; and the brief

9. Upon a published charge against a person, that he is a perjured scoundrel, without an innuendo, an action may be maintained. And if the innuendo gives to such words the significance of a charge of technical felony, it may be treated as surplusage.[1] So the words, "I had a lawsuit with A., and B. swore falsely against me, and I have advertised him as such," were held actionable; the words "I had a lawsuit" necessarily implying a judicial proceeding; and the want of an allegation, that the testimony upon which the charge of perjury was based was material, being cured by verdict.[2] So to say to a witness, whilst giving his testimony, "I believe you swear false," — "It is false what you say," is actionable.[3] Or, to say of his testimony at such trial, "It is false," — "That is false," — "I believe it is false."[4] So to say of a witness, who was giving his testimony upon a material point, in a cause then on trial, "That is a lie," and to repeat this, not only to the witness, but to the counsel of the opposite party, if done maliciously, and with a view to defame the witness, is slander.[5] So the words, "You swore to a lie before the grand jury," are actionable, and need no *colloquium* or inducement.[6] So the words, "You swore false at the trial of your brother John," without an averment that the words were spoken concerning the testimony given by the plaintiff at the trial referred to, were held actionable after verdict.[7] So the words, "He (the plaintiff) has sworn to a lie, and done it meaning to cut my throat," are actionable *per se*.[8] Or the words, "You swore a lie and I can prove it," if used with reference to a judicial proceeding, in which the

[1] Haws *v.* Stanford, 4 Sneed, 520.
[2] Magee *v.* Stork, 1 Humph. 506; Rineheardt *v.* Potts, 7 Ired. 403; Morgan *v.* Livingston, 2 Rich. 573.
[3] Cole *v.* Grant, 3 Harr. 327.
[4] Ibid.
[5] Mower *v.* Watson, 11 Verm. 536.
[6] Persely *v.* Bacon, 20 Mis. 330.
[7] Fowle *v.* Robbins, 12 Mass. 498.
[8] Coons *v.* Robinson, 3 Barb. 625.

statement of the defendant, that "the plaintiff committed the offence of perjury," may be taken into consideration by the jury, with other testimony, as one of the facts, merely, from which they may infer, that the defendant did speak the words as set forth in the declaration. McAllister *v.* Sibley, 25 Maine, 474.

plaintiff had testified as a witness.[1] And it is held, that, under counts charging the speaking of the words, without any *colloquium* concerning the suit in which the perjury was alleged to have been committed, the plaintiff need not prove the suit, or the proceedings therein, or that the words referred to any suit in particular.[2]

10. It is actionable to assert of one, that he committed perjury in taking out a peace-warrant against a party, although the warrant issued was void for want of a seal; for, the oath being before a competent tribunal, and material to the issuing of the warrant, there is no necessity to refer to the warrant as proof of the oath.[3] So, if a justice of the peace issue a state warrant on an insufficient affidavit, and the party accused, on being arrested, proceed to trial before the justice without objection, the insufficiency of the affidavit will not render the proceedings *coram non judice.* And to charge a witness with swearing false on such trial is actionable.[4] And if a witness, on his examination, make a false statement, but afterwards correct it, so that his testimony is ultimately true, he is not guilty of perjury; hence to charge him, without qualification, with swearing false in reference to that statement, is actionable.[5] So it has been held that words are actionable, which imply in the ordinary import that a false oath was taken in a judicial proceeding, though no such proceeding existed.[6]

11. But where a declaration in slander stated a complaint before the grand jury, and that the plaintiff was sworn and gave evidence upon such complaint, and contained a *colloquium* upon the evidence so given, and charged the defendant with having spoken words in themselves imputing perjury to the plaintiff in giving such testimony; held, the action could not be sustained, without proof of such proceedings before the grand jury.[7]

12. An action may be maintained for the charge of false

[1] Lewis *v.* Black, 27 Miss. 425.
[2] Coons *v.* Robinson, 3 Barb. 625.
[3] Bell *v.* Farnsworth, 11 Humph. 608
[4] Henry *v.* Hamilton, 7 Blackf. 506.
[5] Ibid.
[6] Bricker *v.* Potts, 12 Penn, 200.
[7] Emery *v.* Miller, 1 Denio, 208.

swearing, although the oath were not taken in the ordinary course of a judicial trial, if administered according to law. Thus, where the preliminary oath is waived, and by consent the opposite party is sworn as a witness; if he swears falsely, it is perjury; and hence an action lies for saying that he swore falsely upon such trial, without any averment that the preliminary oath was made before he was sworn as a witness.[1] So (in Tennessee, and probably elsewhere,) an arbitration is so far a judicial proceeding, under the laws of the state, that false swearing in such proceeding is perjury; and an action of slander may be maintained, on a charge of swearing falsely in such a proceeding.[2] So the defendant published an account of the proceedings under *a commission of lunacy*, which the plaintiff had attended as a witness, and stated that the plaintiff's testimony, "being unsupported by that of any other person, failed to have any effect on the jury." "The object was to set aside a will." Mr. Jervis commented with cutting severity on the testimony of Mr. O." (the plaintiff). Held, the whole taken together was a libel; and a plea just.fying only the words, "Mr. Jervis commented," &c., was ill.[3] (*a*)

13. But it has been held, that to say of the plaintiff that he had forsworn himself, and that the defendant had three witnesses to prove it, is not actionable, unless the words refer to some judicial proceeding, in which the plaintiff had been sworn; nor can "forsworn" be explained by an innuendo, to mean false swearing in a court of justice.[4] Nor do the words, "she has sworn falsely," import a charge of perjury, unless averred to have been spoken with reference to a *judicial oath*, and to have been meant as a charge of per-

[1] Sandford *v.* Gaddis, 13 Ill. 329.
[2] Moore *v.* Horner, 4 Sneed, 491.
[3] Roberts *v.* Brown, 10 Bing. 519.
[4] Holt *v.* Schofield, 6 T. R. 691.

(*a*) Upon similar ground, it is actionable to charge a person with having wilfully made a false declaration, at a school-district meeting, of his right to vote at such meeting, upon being challenged by a legal voter; as the words impute an indictable misdemeanor, involving moral turpitude. Crawford *v.* Wilson, 4 Barb. 504.

jury.[1] So the words, "You swore falsely on the trial of a case between me and A. before 'Squire J.," are not actionable *per se*.[2] Nor the words, "he (meaning the plaintiff) took a false oath;" and, in a suit for such words, there must not only be in the declaration the requisite inducement and *colloquium*, but also an *innuendo*, explaining the meaning by reference to the previous matter.[3] (*a*) And the *colloquium* and *innuendo* must both be established as true. They are facts, and as such must be submitted to the jury.[4] So it is not actionable, to charge a grand juror with having "forsworn himself by neglecting or refusing to present an offence within his knowledge." This is not an indictable offence.[5] So, where A. swore before a justice, that B. had a certain cow in his possession, belonging to him, and B., in speaking of it, said, that A. had sworn to a lie; in an action of slander brought by A. against B. it was held that the words were not actionable in themselves.[6] So where, in an action for slander, the words as stated in the complaint were, "You have sworn false." — "You have sworn false under oath." — "You have lied under oath;" without any averment that the words were spoken in reference to a judicial proceeding; held, those words are in themselves incapable of a slanderous meaning, and, before they can be made significant of crime, they must be connected with some proceeding in which perjury might have been committed; and that the action would not lie.[7] (*b*)

14. It has been held unnecessary, in an action for a charge of perjury, for the plaintiff to allege what he testified. At all events, the objection is cured by verdict.[8] But a charge

[1] Barger *v.* Barger, 18 Penn. 489.
[2] Dalrymple *v.* Lofton, 2 Speers, 588.
[3] Roella *v.* Follow, 7 Blackf. 377.
[4] Barger *v.* Barger, 18 Penn. 489.
[5] McAnally *v.* Williams, 3 Sneed, 26.
[6] Sluder *v.* Wilson, 10 Ind. 92.
[7] Phincle *v.* Vaughan, 12 Barb. 215.
[8] Whitaker *v.* Carter, 4 Ired. 461.

(*a*) See *Colloquium — Innuendo.*

(*b*) But a charge, that the plaintiff had sworn false under oath, and that, if he had his deserts, he would have been dealt with in the time of it, may naturally be understood to charge the crime of perjury, and, if proved, will sustain an action. Phincle *v.* Vaughan, 12 Barb. 215.

of perjury relates to some matter which would render the plaintiff liable to be indicted.[1] Hence, if one charge another with swearing falsely in relation to a fact which was not *material;* an action cannot be maintained.[2] Thus, in an action for saying, that the plaintiffs had sworn to a lie in giving their testimony in a certain suit, it appeared that the suit was trespass to try titles, and that the witnesses testified, that the defendant in that suit had a field of cotton on the disputed land, which would have made three bales, and which was ungathered at the time of the trial. Held, the testimony was not material to the issue, and the action could not be maintained.[3]

15. But, although the evidence were legally *incompetent,* if objected to, still it may have been *material* within the meaning of this requisition. Thus, as a witness may be convicted of perjury, in falsely swearing to a promise within the statute of frauds, although parol evidence of the promise would not be competent if objected to; such evidence is material, and therefore the action for slander will lie, for imputing perjury in respect thereto.[4] And it has been held, that the plaintiff is not bound to allege or show affirmatively the materiality of his testimony; but the law presumes it material, unless the defendant proves it to have been immaterial.[5] So, where false testimony is charged, as to any particular matter testified to in a suit, and nothing appears at the time or is otherwise known to the hearer, to show that it was immaterial; and it is understood by him as material; the testimony will be so regarded, and the words will show a charge of perjury; nor can such a charge be subsequently avoided in the action for damages, by showing that the evidence was immaterial.[6] At any rate, a *substantial* allegation of materiality is sufficient. Thus a declaration alleged, that the discourse of the defendant was had, concerning a trial between the plaintiff and the defendant before a certain

[1] Wilson *v.* Oliphant, Wright, 153.

[2] Owen *v.* McKean, 14 Ill. 459; Roberts *v.* Champlin, 14 Wend. 120.

[3] Wilson *v.* Cloud, 2 Speers, 1. See McGough *v.* Rhodes, 7 Eng. 625.

[4] Howard *v.* Sexton, 4 Comst. 157.

[5] Coons *v.* Robinson, 3 Barb. 625; Cannon *v.* Phillips, 2 Sneed, 185.

[6] Butterfield *v.* Baffam, 9 N. H. 156.

justice of the peace, and concerning an oath the plaintiff took on said trial before said justice in proving his account. Held, the declaration sufficiently showed the existence of a suit before a competent tribunal, and that the oath taken was as to a matter material to the issue.[1] So the defendant cannot be allowed to show, that his charge of perjury referred to the plaintiff's cross-examination, and that the testimony on cross-examination was immaterial; unless he offers to prove, that his charge was confined to the evidence so given. If the charge was general, such evidence is inadmissible.[2] So, in an action for words uttered without any allusion to facts, the mention of which would have prevented them from amounting to slander, it is not competent to the defendant to give such facts in evidence in explanation of the words. Thus, where the defendant accused the plaintiff of taking a false oath on a judicial trial, without any explanatory words, it was held not competent for him to prove, that he meant to impute falsehood only as to immaterial facts, nor to go into evidence of what was testified at the trial in order to show that they were immaterial.[3]

16. And the question of materiality is for the jury. Thus, in an action for saying that the plaintiff "took a false oath" before referees, the defendant pleaded the general issue, and also in justification that the words were true; and offered evidence in support of the special plea. Held, the jury had a right, under the general issue, to consider whether this evidence showed, that the words had relation to the plaintiff's testimony on immaterial points, and so did not import a charge of perjury.[4]

17. In order to constitute perjury, the Court in which a false oath was taken must have had *jurisdiction* of the cause. Thus, the registers and receivers of the different land-offices being constituted by the acts of Congress a tribunal, to settle controversies relating to claims to preemption rights; an oath administered in such a controversy

[1] Shand *v.* Wilhite, 2 Humph. 434; acc. Dalrymple *v.* Lofton, 2 M'Mul. 112.

[2] Coons *v.* Robinson, 3 Barb. 625.

[3] Stone *v.* Clark, 21 Pick. 51.

[4] Sibley *v.* Marsh, 7 Pick. 38.

before the register alone is extrajudicial, and, as perjury cannot be predicated of such evidence, an action of slander cannot be maintained for a charge of false swearing in such a proceeding.[1] And the declaration in an action of slander for the charge of perjury must allege such jurisdiction. Thus, where a declaration charged the defendant with saying, "you have sworn to a lie, and I can prove it by Joe McClain and his books;" "meaning thereby that the plaintiff was guilty of perjury in the taking of a lawful oath before McClain, clerk of the County Court;" held, the declaration showed no cause of action, because it did not aver that the oath was taken before the clerk, in a matter in which he had authority to administer it.[2] But a *substantial* allegation of jurisdiction has been held sufficient. Thus, in an action of slander, the charge complained of was that of perjury in another action between the present parties before a justice; with an averment, that "the plaintiff was, at the instance of the defendant, examined on oath administered by said justice, according to law, as a witness for the defendant." Held, a sufficient statement of jurisdiction.[3] So it is held, that a declaration for slander, in charging the plaintiff with having "sworn falsely" on the trial of a cause, need not set forth the facts which gave the jurisdiction, nor aver that the justice had authority to administer the oath.[4] So in an action for saying that the plaintiff swore falsely, in a trial before a justice of the peace, as to an account in his favor against the defendant; the plaintiff is not bound to show that the justice was duly commissioned.[5] (*a*)

[1] Hall *v.* Montgomery, 8 Ala. 510.
[2] Jones *v.* Marrs, 11 Humph. 214.
[3] Shellenbarger *v.* Norris, 2 Cart. 285.
[4] Sandford *v.* Gaddis, 13 Ill. 329.
[5] Pugh *v.* Neal, 4 Jones, Law, 367.

(*a*) In an action of slander, for charging the plaintiff with having sworn falsely, and committed perjury, in swearing out an attachment, &c., before a justice of the peace; it was held that, as the statute authorized the justice to issue the attachment on satisfactory proof, it was left to his discretion to decide on the proof, and, where he took the oath of the party, which was not legal evidence, this was an error of judgment and not an excess of jurisdiction, and the proceeding was therefore erroneous only, not void; and

18. We shall have occasion hereafter to consider at length the subject of *privileged communications*, (*a*) as constituting a very important exception to the general law of libel and slander. In relation to the particular charge of perjury, it has been held, that, where a defendant in a judicial proceeding accused one of the witnesses of perjury, the words were not privileged, although used while the cause was pending; and that they were actionable.[1]

19. It will be seen hereafter, that, in an action for slander, the *truth* of the charge is in general a sufficient defence. (*b*) In connection with the particular charge now under consideration, it may here be stated, that, to show the truth of the charge of perjury, the defendant must prove not only that the plaintiff testified to what was *untrue*, but that he did it *corruptly*.[2] The plea is not sustained, if the plaintiff was *honestly mistaken* in what he swore to.[3] But it is also held, that all wilful false swearing is necessarily corrupt. Hence, if the defendant shows that the evidence was *false*, corruption may be inferred.[4] (*c*)

20. *Larceny* or theft is another crime, the charge of which has often been held actionable. Words charging larceny are in themselves actionable; malice is presumed.[5] But it will be seen, that words which merely charge a *taking* of the personal property of another may be slanderous or not,

[1] Eccles *v.* Shannon, 4 Harring. 183.
[2] Chandler *v.* Robinson, 7 Ired. 480.
[3] Jenkins *v.* Cockerham, 1 Ired. 309.
[4] Hopkins *v.* Smith, 3 Barb. 599.
[5] Gaul *v.* Fleming, 10 Ind. 253.

---

perjury may be assigned in an oath erroneously taken, especially while the proceedings remain unreversed. Van Steenburgh *v.* Kortz, 10 Johns. 167.

(*a*) See *Index*.

(*b*) See *Justification*.

(*c*) If the charge be one of having sworn falsely in a judicial proceeding, without the necessary averments to make it an imputation of perjury, a plea of justification, that the plaintiff did swear falsely in the particular proceeding, would be sufficient. Sanford *v.* Gaddis, 13 Ill. 329.

But, if the declaration show that the defendant intended to impute perjury in a particular case, he can only justify by showing perjury in that case. Ibid.

according to circumstances.[1] Thus, "He was put into the round-house for stealing ducks at Crowland," are actionable words.[2] Or, "You stole my box-wood, and I will prove it."[3] Or, "I dealt not so unkindly with you, when you stole my stack of corn."[4] So, he "stole the colonel's cupboard cloth," is actionable, without any precedent *colloquium* either of the colonel or his cloth.[5] So the words, "You get your living by sneaking about when other people are asleep." "What did you do with the sheep you killed?" "Did you eat it?" "It was like the beef you got negroes to bring you at night." "Where did you get the little wild shoats you always have in your pen?" "You are an infernal roguish rascal;" were held to be actionable, as containing a charge of larceny in more instances than one.[6] And an accusation, that one "was whipped for stealing hogs," imports a larceny. It is an accusation of hog-stealing, with the addition that the party had been whipped for it.[7] Or, "he is a thief, he stole my wheat and ground it and sold the flour to the Indians."[8] So the charge of having "stolen boards" necessarily imputes the crime of larceny, without an *innuendo*.[9] So it has been held, though with much doubt, that the words, "He *robbed* J. W." are actionable, as imputing an offence punishable by law. If they were used in any other sense, the defendant must show it.[10] (*a*) So, on motion in arrest of judgment, the words "you robbed White" were held sufficient to sustain the verdict, without a *colloquium*, showing the sense in which the word "robbed" was used.[11] So words charging the plaintiff with having robbed the United States' mail are actionable.[12] So, "He is a thief, and robbed

1 Watson *v.* Nicholas, 6 Humph. 174.
2 Beavor *v.* Hides, 2 Wils. 300.
3 Baker *v.* Pierce, 2 Wils. 695, 696.
4 Cooper *v.* Hawkeswell, 2 Mod. 58.
5 3 Mod. 280.
6 Morgan *v.* Livingston, 2 Rich. 573.
7 Holly *v.* Burgess, 9 Ala. 728.
8 Parker *v.* Lewis, 2 Greene, 311.
9 Burbank *v.* Heard, 39 Maine, 233.
10 Tomlinson *v.* Brittlebank, 4 Barn. & Adol. 630.
11 Tomlinson *v.* Brittlebank, 1 Nev. & Man. 455.
12 Jones *v.* Chapman, 5 Blackf. 88.

(*a*) But the words, "The library has been *plundered*," are not actionable *per se*. Carter *v.* Andrews, 16 Pick. 1.

me of my bricks," is actionable without any introductory averment.[1]

21. It is held, that the word "thief," though capable of a felonious signification, if neither used by the defendant nor understood by bystanders as charging the plaintiff with larceny, is not actionable.[2] The word must be used with the intent to impute crime; which, however, the law will presume, if the contrary intent be not shown.[3] Hence, if one call another "thief," together with many other names of general abuse not imputing crimes, and no other evidence be given to explain the sense in which the word "thief" was used, and the jury find for the plaintiff; the Court will not set the verdict aside, for the action may be maintained for the word "thief."[4] So, to charge one with being a *thieving person*, or to say of him that he stole and ran away, is actionable.[5] So, to say to a person, "You are a thieving puppy," is actionable.[6] So, where the words were, that the plaintiff "will lie, cheat, steal, and swear," it was held, that the Court might, in answer to a broad request of the defendant's counsel to charge that the evidence did not support the declaration, say to the jury, that these words might import that the plaintiff stole.[7] So to say of a person, "I believe he will steal, and I believe he did steal," amounts to a charge of larceny.[8] So to say of a person, "he took my wood, and is guilty of any and everything that is dishonest," connected with the innuendo that the defendant meant that the plaintiff was guilty of larceny, is sufficient, after verdict.[9]

22. But the words, "You are as bad as thy wife when she stole my cushion," are not actionable, without an averment that the felony was committed.[10] Nor the words, "Your father was a horse-stealing rogue, and you are a great

[1] Slowman *v.* Dutton, 10 Bing. 402.

[2] Quinn *v.* O'Gara, 2 E. D. Smith, 388.

[3] M'Kee *v.* Ingalls, 4 Scam. 30; Dudley *v.* Robinson, 2 Ired. 141; Robinson *v.* Keyser, 2 Fost. 323.

[4] Penfold *v.* Westcote, 2 New Rep. 335.

[5] Alley *v.* Neely, 5 Blackf. 200.

[6] Pierson *v.* Stiortz, 1 Morris, 136.

[7] Dottaner *v.* Bushey, 16 Penn. 204.

[8] Ibid.

[9] Ibid.

[10] Upton *v.* Pinfold, 1 Com. 268.

rogue."[1] So where, under the circumstances, the misappropriation of property cannot constitute the offence of larceny; even the direct charge of stealing is not actionable. Thus it is not actionable to charge a weaver with stealing filling, sent to his house to be woven into cloth.[2] So, the property of the bell ropes of a parish church being in the churchwardens, it is not actionable, to say of a churchwarden, that he stole them.[3] (*a*) So, where a party acting as constable arrests a person and takes from him certain personal property, and the latter accuses the former of theft, if the words may be referred to the matter of arrest, they are not actionable.[4] So a declaration, that the defendant said of the plaintiff, in her character of shopwoman, "she secreted 1*s*. 6*d*. under the till, stating these are not times to be robbed," imputes a charge that the plaintiff, when secreting the money, used these words; therefore not an actionable charge.[5] So the words, "J. O. has stole my marle," — "You are a thief; you have stolen my marle," are not actionable.[6] Nor is it actionable, to charge a person with having stolen a "bee-tree," that phrase having reference to the wild, unreclaimed insect, and a standing tree, neither of which is a subject of larceny.[7] So the words, "Thou art one that stole my Lord S.'s deer," imputing a crime punishable, but not infamously, were held not actionable.[8] So the words, spoken of the plaintiff W., "H. R. told me, during the time he was

1 Bellamy *v.* Barker, 1 Strange, 304.
2 Hawn *v.* Smith, 4 B. Monroe, 385.
3 Jackson *v.* Adams, 2 Bing. N. R. 402.
4 Ayres *v.* Grider, 15 Ill. 37.
5 Kelly *v.* Partington, 2 Nev. & M. 460.
6 Ogden *v.* Riley, 2 Greene, 186.
7 Cock *v.* Weatherbey, 5 Sm. & Marsh. 333.
8 Turner *v.* Ogden, 2 Salk. 696.

(*a*) But to charge one who has the care of goods with stealing them, is slander. Gill *v.* Bright, 6 Monr. 130.

So words by a partner, charging his copartner with "pilfering" out of the store, are actionable. Becket *v.* Sterrett, 4 Blackf. 499.

So the taking of articles of dress *animo furandi* from the body of a dead man, drowned and driven ashore from a wreck, is a felony; and consequently words imputing to a person such an act and intent are actionable. Wonson *v.* Sayward, 13 Pick. 402.

managing for Mr. O., that he missed some of the plough-irons from a plough, and went to W. to have others made, and on arriving there, found his clevises in possession of W.; that he claimed the clevises, and W. pretended not to know how they came into his shop, but afterwards acknowledged that he had purchased them from one of the claimant's negroes, and begged him to say nothing about it, as it would ruin him;" are not actionable *per se.*[1] So, in an action by A. against B. for slander, the Court instructed the jury, that "if it had been proved to their satisfaction that B. spoke of A., that A. and B. and one C., had sat down to gamble in a house in D., and while there, C. took out of his pocket-book a five-dollar bill and proposed to bet one dollar at that time; that after the bill was put down on a chance, it was missing, and search was made for it but it could not be found, whereupon the parties agreed to submit to a search, which was accordingly made, but the bill was not found; that after this search, one of the parties proposed to look out of doors for the money, and, accordingly, all the parties went out of the house to search for it, and near the window they found a pocket-book with the clasp unfastened, and in it was the bill belonging to C., which had been missing; that C. took out the bill and handed the pocket-book to A., who took it, and then said, 'Boys, don't tell this on me, for if you do, it will ruin me;' these words were actionable." Held, that these words do not, of themselves, import a charge of larceny.[2] So the words, "Uncle Daniel must settle for some of my logs he has *made away with*," do not of themselves amount to a charge of larceny.[3] Nor the words, accompanied by a *colloquium* of and concerning the plaintiff and his brother, "Those two rascals killed my hogs and converted them to their own use."[4] Nor the words, "You hooked my geese."[5] Nor the words spoken of and concerning the plaintiff, "He is mighty smart after night," "Put

1 Dorsey *v.* Whipps, 8 Gill, 457.
2 Prichard *v.* Lloyd, 2 Cart. 154.
3 Brown *v.* Brown, 2 Shep. 317.
4 Sturgenegger *v.* Taylor, 2 Brev. 480.
5 Hayes *v.* Mitchell, 7 Blackf. 117.

him in the dark and he would get it all," spoken in a conversation with reference to a dispute and difficulty between the plaintiff and defendant, relative to a certain tan-yard, and the division and disposition of the same.[1]

23. And it has been held, that words importing a charge of theft cannot be rendered actionable by proof of collateral facts to which they relate, unless the declaration refer to such facts. Thus, where it was proved that the defendant had said of the plaintiff, that he had stolen "the Spaniard's money," such words being laid without any averment concerning the loss or stealing of the money; held, that the plaintiff was not entitled to prove a report in the neighborhood that a Spaniard's money had been stolen.[2]

24. In general, a verbal charge of mere *fraud* or *dishonesty* is not actionable. And a *cheating*, which does not affect the public, and may be guarded against by common prudence, is not indictable; hence words importing a charge of such cheating are not actionable.[3] Thus, "You are a cheat," spoken of a trader, without laying a *colloquium* of his trade.[4] Nor, "Thou hast nothing but what thou hast got by cheating and cozening," without averring that the plaintiff was of a trade.[5] So saying of a draper, "You are a cheating fellow, and keep a false book, and I will prove it," is not actionable, unless there was some communication concerning the plaintiff's trade, or dealing, by way of buying and selling.[6] So, "He has defrauded his creditors, and has been horsewhipped off the course at Doncaster," though spoken of an attorney, is not actionable, unless spoken of him in his profession.[7] So, "He has defrauded a meal-man of a roan horse," are not actionable words, without special damage.[8] So the words, "He was a rogue, and kept at home a rogue hole and harbored rogues," are not actionable.[9] Nor the words spoken of the defendant, "G—d d—d rogue."[10] So,

[1] Kirksey *v.* Fike, 29 Ala. 206.
[2] Emery *v.* Miller, 1 Denio, 208.
[3] Weirebach *v.* Trone, 2 W. & S. 408.
[4] Savage *v.* Robery, 2 Salk. 694.
[5] Bromefield *v.* Snoke, 12 Mod. 307.
[6] Todd *v.* Hastings, 2 Saund. 307.
[7] Doyley *v.* Roberts, 3 Bing. N. R. 835.
[8] Richardson *v.* Allen, 2 Chit. 657.
[9] Idol *v.* Jones, 2 Dev. 162.
[10] Ford *v.* Johnson, 21 Geo. 399.

where even a declaration for *libel* alleged, without any material introductory averment, that the defendant published, of and concerning the plaintiff, the false, scandalous, and defamatory libel following, viz: "Notice,—any person giving information where any property may be found belonging to H. G. (meaning the plaintiff) a prisoner in the King's Bench prison, but residing within the rules thereof, shall receive 5 per cent. upon the goods recovered, for their trouble, by applying at Mr. L.," &c., (meaning the defendant, and meaning that the plaintiff had been and was guilty of concealing his property with a fraudulent and unlawful intention); held, on general demurrer, that the innuendo, unsupported by any prefatory averment, was too large, and that the words, in themselves, were not actionable.[1] So to charge one with being a *liar* is not actionable.[2] Nor a *swindler*.[3] (*a*)

25. But to *print* of any person that he is a swindler, is a libel, and actionable.[4] So a general charge of *dishonesty*. Thus the defendant wrote concerning the plaintiff, "He is so inflated with £300 made in my service,—God only knows whether honestly or otherwise,—that," &c. Held, without any preliminary averment, to warrant an innuendo, that the plaintiff had conducted himself in a dishonest manner in the defendant's service, and to be actionable.[5] So, though an action will not lie for a libel imputing to a party fraud in his conduct, touching an illegal transaction; if the publication goes farther, and conveys an imputation on the party *dehors* such transaction, it is libellous.[6] So a count in an action for a libel stated, that the defendant, intending to cause it to be believed, that the plaintiff and one J. H. had transferred, or caused to be transferred, a certain amount of bank-stock from the name of one W. T., by means of a power of attorney obtained by them from W. T. by undue influence, at a time

[1] Gompertz *v.* Levy, 9 Ad. & Ell. 282.
[2] Smalley *v.* Anderson, 4 Munr. 367.
[3] Savile *v.* Jardine, 2 H. Black. 531.
[4] Anson *v.* Stuart, 1 T. R. 748.
[5] Clegg *v.* Laffer, 10 Bing. 250.
[6] Yrisarri *v.* Clement, 11 Moore, 308.

(*a*) But it is held, that calling one a *knave* imports that he is dishonest, and is in itself actionable. Harding *v.* Brooks, 5 Pick. 244.

when he was mentally incompetent to do any act requiring reason and understanding, published the following: "There is strong reason for believing that a considerable sum of money was transferred from Mr. T.'s (meaning the said W. T.'s) name, in the books of the Bank of England, by power of attorney obtained from him by undue influence after he became mentally incompetent to perform any act requiring reason and understanding, (thereby meaning that the plaintiff and J. H. had transferred, or caused to be transferred, the said money from the said W. T.'s name in the said books of the said bank, by means of a power of attorney obtained by them from the said W. T. by undue influence exercised by them over the said W. T., and at a time when the said W. T. had become and was mentally incompetent to give a power of attorney, and to perform any act requiring reason and understanding)." The jury having found a general verdict for the plaintiff; held, on motion in arrest of judgment, that the count was good; and that the innuendo did not improperly extend the meaning of the libel.[1]

26. The charge of *forgery* is actionable. Thus the following words: "I never forged any man's hand, but you are a forging rogue," when spoken of an attorney, were held actionable.[2] So the words, "You are a rogue, and I will prove you a rogue, for you forged my name."[3] So words, charging a person with having forged a deposition, are actionable.[4] So, where A. charged B. with having forged a letter in his (A.'s) name, containing these words: "I have to inform you that I have received your money, and want you to come and receive it," an action of slander is maintainable.[5]

27. But where the declaration alleged, that the plaintiff and two others gave a note payable to the defendant or order, and the defendant said of the plaintiff and of the note, "I never put my name on the back of the note, but he must have done it," without an averment explaining the

[1] Turner v. Merryweather, 7 Com. B. 251.

[2] Anon. 1 Com. 262.

[3] Jones v. Herne, 2 Wils. 87.

[4] Atkinson v. Reding, 5 Blackf. 39.

[5] Ricks v. Cooper, 3 Hawks, 587.

sense in which the words were spoken; held, bad, on motion to arrest the judgment.[1] (*a*) So in an action of slander for several sets of words, some of which charged the plaintiff with having sued the defendant on a note he never signed, &c.; the others with having signed the defendant's name to said note, without his permission, &c.; held, the suit would lie for the latter words, but not for the former.[2] (*b*)

28. Saying that the plaintiff *passed counterfeit money* is

[1] Atkinson *v.* Scammon, 2 Fost. 40. [2] Creelman *v.* Morks, 7 Blackf. 281.

(*a*) In case for slander, the first count contains a *colloquium*, that the plaintiff was, at the time when the words were spoken, an agent for a stage-coach company, and that one B. acted as sub-agent, and as such sub-agent received moneys, of which he kept an account in the books of the company, together with way-bills of passengers conveyed in the coaches of the company, and that suggestions had been made that B. had not accounted for all the moneys; it then alleges that the defendant, in a discourse of and concerning the plaintiff's agency, &c., spoke the words, "the plaintiff has altered the way-bills and books, (meaning the way-bills under the care of said B. and the books kept by him as aforesaid,) to make them correspond, for the purpose of screening B. (meaning thereby that the plaintiff, for the purpose of aiding said B. in concealing his frauds upon the said company, has been guilty of the crime of forgery)." The second count, referring to the *colloquium* in the first count, alleges that the defendant uttered the words, "the plaintiff and B. are together in cheating the company, and they will cheat them out of more than the company can make." It was held that the words in these counts were actionable. Gay *v.* Homer, 13 Pick. 535. Held, also, that new general counts, alleging respectively that the defendant charged the plaintiff with forgery, fraud, and a conspiracy to cheat, were for the same causes of action as the original counts above mentioned, and were therefore properly allowed to be filed by way of amendment. Ibid.

(*b*) An action will not lie against one called on for the payment of a note, alleged to have been signed by him as surety, for the speaking of words denying his signature, and that he ever gave authority to another to affix his name to a note; notwithstanding an innuendo that the defendant meant to impute the crime of forgery. Andrews *v.* Woodmansee, 15 Wend. 232.

The mere use of the word "forge" does not render even a libel actionable, where the subject-matter shows that it could not be designed to impute an indictable offence. Thus to write of one "that he had forged words and sentiments for Silas Wright which he never uttered." Cramer *v.* Noonan, 4 Wis. 231.

not actionable, without a *colloquium*, showing that the defendant spoke the words, concerning the commission by the plaintiff of the offence of passing counterfeit money, knowing it to be such.[1] But the words, "In Black-bull yard you could procure broad money for gold, and clip it," were held actionable, because they imported an act.[2]

29. With regard to the charge of *want of chastity*, it is now the prevailing doctrine that words imputing to a female a want of chastity are actionable without proof of special damage; that such words are to be taken in their plain and natural import, and are to be understood by the Court according to the sense in which they appear to have been used, and the ideas which they were adapted to convey to those to whom they were addressed.[3] Thus it is actionable to call a woman a "whore,"[4] without proof of special damage.[5] (*a*)

[1] Church *v.* Bridgman, 6 Mis. 190.
[2] Speed *v.* Perry, 2 Salk. 697.
[3] Truman *v.* Taylor, 4 Iowa, 424.
[4] Pledger *v.* Hatchcock, 1 Kelly, 550. See Smith *v.* Hamilton, 10 Rich. Law, 44; Cook *v.* Bunker, 1 Mon. 269; Rodebaugh *v.* Hollingsworth, 6 Ind. 339.
[5] Smith *v.* Silence, 4 Iowa, 321.

(*a*) This is more especially the case where, as is now generally done, *fornication* is made by statute an indictable offence. It is held in England, that calling a woman a whore is not actionable, except in London and Bristol, where such language is actionable by custom. Steph. N. P. 2557.

Words, charging a woman never married with having had a child, and buried it in the garden, amount to a charge of fornication, and are therefore actionable, in Indiana, by statute. Worth *v.* Butler, 7 Blackf. 251.

So, to publish falsely and maliciously of a woman that she "had a child," with the intention of charging her with fornication, is actionable under the Missouri statute of 1835. Moberly *v.* Preston, 8 Mis. 462.

So in South Carolina, a count charging the defendant with saying the plaintiff is "incontinent," without prefatory matter, and without an innuendo, is good. Watts *v.* Greenlee, 2 Dev. 115.

But the words "which amount to a charge of incontinency," and for which an action of slander is given to a woman by the North Carolina act of 1808, (Rev. Stats. c. 110,) must import, not merely a lascivious disposition, but the criminal fact of adultery or fornication. M'Brayer *v.* Hill, 4 Ired. 136.

To say of a woman, that "she was kept by a man," is actionable as a slander, under that act. Ibid.

A female who is a resident of Alabama, whether a citizen or foreigner, may maintain an action of slander under the act of 1830, which makes "all

So to say, "you are a pimp and a bawd, and fetch young gentlewomen to young gentlemen," is actionable without

---

words spoken and published of any female person of this State, falsely and maliciously imputing to her a want of chastity," actionable in themselves. Sidgreaves *v.* Myatt, 22 Ala. 617.

In an action of slander, brought under the act of Maryland, 1838, c. 114, entitled, "An act to protect the reputation of unmarried women," the declaration charged, that the words were spoken "against the form of the statute in such case made and provided." Held, a sufficient reference to the statute, the charges being an assault on the chastity of a *feme sole*. Terry *v.* Bright, 4 Md. 430.

The purpose of the act was to make all words spoken maliciously, touching the character for chastity of an unmarried woman, slander *per se*, and *primâ facie* actionable. Ibid.

It is actionable, in Kentucky, to charge a woman with adultery. Smalley *v.* Anderson, 2 Monr. 56. So in Ohio. Wilson *v.* Robbins, Wright, 40. But not a man. Ibid.

So, under an Illinois statute, to utter and publish of and concerning a woman words which clearly and unequivocally impute to her adultery, was held actionable. Spencer *v.* McMasters, 16 Ill. 405.

So words in themselves involving a charge of adultery are by the Missouri Revised Code (p. 1011) actionable, without alleging special damage. Stieber *v.* Wensel, 19 Mis. 513.

And it has even been held, that words charging another with *incest*, are not actionable, in North Carolina, under the acts of 1741 and 1805. Eure *v.* Odom, 2 Hawks, 52.

In an action for slander, for charging the crime of incest between the plaintiff and his sister, it must be alleged in the declaration, that both the plaintiff and his sister were at least sixteen years of age when the crime was charged to have been committed, and that the defendant meant to charge that the plaintiff had knowledge of the consanguinity at the time of the illicit intercourse charged. Lumpkins *v.* Justice, 1 Cart. 557; 1 Smith, 322.

In an action of slander by a single woman, (under the act of 1808, Rev. Stats. of North Carolina, c. 110,) where the words charged were, "that she had lost a little one;" "A. B. is a credit to her;" the said A. B. being notoriously an incontinent person; and "she better be listening to the report about herself losing a little one;" it was held sufficient for the defendant to plead and prove that the plaintiff was an incontinent woman. Snow *v.* Witcher, 9 Ired. 346.

The special pleas, in a suit for slander brought by husband and wife, for words alleged to have been spoken against the chastity of the wife, were,

special damage.[1] So the words, "she is a bad character, a loose character," are slanderous, involving a charge of fornication, which may be sufficiently averred by an innuendo, without a *colloquium*.[2] So, in general, an action lies for charging a female, more especially if unmarried, with fornication.[3] More especially for words imputing a want of chastity to an unmarried female, dependent on her labor for support, an action will lie, where the special damages alleged are illness and a consequent inability to labor and earn her living. The loss of the plaintiff's earnings, under such circumstances, is a direct pecuniary loss.[4] So a female, charged with being a prostitute, may maintain an action, provided she can prove special damage, however slight; as, that in consequence of the words, she became dejected in mind and enfeebled in body, so as to be prevented from attending to her ordinary business,[5] or that she sustained a loss of marriage.[6] So it has been held, that words spoken of a female, having a tendency to wound her feelings, bring her into contempt, and prevent her from occupying her rightful position in society, are actionable in themselves. Thus to call a woman "a hermaphrodite" is actionable without alleging special damages.[7] So, to charge a single woman with having two or three little ones by a man, if intended to impute the crime of fornication, followed, as a consequence, by bastard children.[8] So to say of a married woman, that she has the venereal disease, the clap, or the pox.[9]

1 Gavell *v.* Berked, 1 Mod. 32.
2 Vanderlip *v.* Roe, 23 Penn. 82.
3 Miller *v.* Parish, 8 Pick. 384; Kenney *v.* McLaughlin, 5 Gray, 5; Abshire *v.* Cline, 3 Ind. 115.
4 Fuller *v.* Fenner, 16 Barb. 333.
5 Bradt *v.* Towsley, 13 Wend. 253.
6 Baker *v.* Moody, 5 Cow. 351; Lumey *v.* Mator, 13 Tex. 449.
7 Malone *v.* Stewart, 15 Ohio, 319.
8 Symonds *v.* Carter, 32 N. H. 458.
9 Williams *v.* Holdredge, 22 Barb. 396.

1st, that the words were true in the sense ascribed to them in the declaration; 2d, that before the speaking, &c., said wife had been delivered of a bastard child; 3d, that before, &c., she had been guilty of adultery with C. 4th, that before, &c., she had been guilty of adultery with D. Held, that these pleas, except the third, were insufficient. Ricket *v.* Stanley, 6 Blackf. 169. As to the charge of *bestiality* or *the crime against nature*, see Ausman *v.* Veal, 10 Ind. 355; Harper *v.* Delp, 3 Ib. 225.

30. But on the other hand it has been often held, that calling a woman a whore, is not actionable, without showing special damage;[1] as where, in an old case, the words were, "you are a whore, and keep a man to lie with you."[2] Or a charge of fornication.[3] Or, "she is a whore, and had a bastard by her father's apprentice."[4] Or, "she had a bastard;" because it does not appear to be chargeable to the parish.[5] Or saying a woman had a bastard, to hinder her of her marriage with A., which was then in agitation.[6] So a petition of slander, brought by an unmarried female, and alleging that the defendant had charged her with having given birth to a child, without any averments, showing that the hearers understood that the language conveyed a charge of bastardy, or want of chastity, is bad on demurrer.[7] So the words, "You are living by imposture; you used to walk St. Paul's Churchyard for a living," spoken of a woman, with the intention of imputing that she was a swindler and a prostitute; were held not actionable, without special damage.[8]

31. And more especially words have been held not actionable, which make this charge indirectly or by implication. Thus, where the declaration alleged, that the defendant said of the plaintiff, "Mrs. Edwards has raised a family of children by a negro," without any averment of other circumstances; held, the words did not necessarily amount to a charge of fornication and adultery.[9] So to say of a woman, that she "has gone down the river with two whores, to the goose-house," is not actionable, without, or perhaps even with, a *colloquium*, showing what kind of house is meant.[10] So an action of slander was brought by A. and Mary A., his wife, for the following words, charged to have been spoken of the wife, and of and concerning her character for chastity: "Have you heard that B. was hunting up a story in circula-

[1] Linney *v.* Maton, 13 Texas, 449; Boyd *v.* Brent, 3 Brev. 241.
[2] Gascoigne *v.* Ambler, 2 Ld. Raym. 1004.
[3] Byron *v.* Elmes, 2 Salk. 693.
[4] Graves *v.* Blanchet, 2 Salk. 696.
[5] Anon. Ib. 694.
[6] Byron *v.* Emes, 12 Mod. 106.
[7] Wilson *v.* Beighler, 4 Iowa, 427.
[8] Wilby *v.* Elston, 8 Com. B. 142.
[9] Patterson *v.* Edwards, 2 Gilm. 720.
[10] Dyer *v.* Morris, 4 Mis. 214.

tion about C. and Mary A. (meaning, &c.) being seen in the woods together? I saw them in the woods together myself," &c. "If you had seen what I have, you would feel satisfied in your mind. God knows, and I know, that they are intimate;" thereby meaning that said Mary had been guilty of adultery with C. Held, that the words were not actionable, unless they were spoken in a conversation about the wife's character for chastity.[1]

32. With regard to the charge of *disease* as ground of an action for slander or libel, it was held, that writing in a letter, that the plaintiff "stunk of brimstone, and had the itch," is a libel, for which an action lies.[2] So words, charging a person that he has *the gonorrhœa*, are actionable in themselves.[3] But, although it is actionable, without proof of special damage, to charge a person with having a loathsome disorder; a declaration alleging the words in the past tense is bad on demurrer.[4] Thus it is not actionable to say that a person *has had* the pox.[5]

[1] Ricket v. Stanley, 6 Blackf. 169.
[2] Villers v. Monsley, 2 Wils. 403.
[3] Watson v. McCarthy, 2 Kelly, 57.
[4] Nichols v. Guy, 2 Carter, 82.
[5] Taylor v. Hall, 2 Strange, 1189.

CHAPTER IX.

CONSTRUCTION OF LIBEL AND SLANDER; QUESTIONS OF LAW AND FACT; UNDERSTANDING OF HEARERS, ETC.; IN MITIORI SENSU.

1. INASMUCH as libel and slander consist wholly of written or spoken *language*, which is intrinsically and proverbially of doubtful meaning and liable to various interpretation; the question of *construction* becomes a very important one in this branch of the law.

2. The doctrine seems to be well established, that, in all civil suits, the question of libel or no libel, when it arises solely upon the face of the publication, is *a question of law*, upon which the jury must follow the direction of the Court; (*a*) but, if the publication is libellous, it is for the jury, and not for the Court, to say whether it is applicable to the plaintiff.[1] (*b*) Thus, where a libellous article did not

[1] Matthews *v.* Beach, 5 Sandf. 256; Clement *v.* Chives, 4 M. & Ry. 128, b.

(*a*) If the Judge, in an action for a libel, should state to the jury, that there was no evidence of express malice, when there was slight evidence of it, but not sufficient to sustain a verdict, this would not be a sufficient reason for granting a new trial. Remington *v.* Congdon, 2 Pick. 310. (See *Malice.*)

(*b*) It seems, it is the duty of the Judge to rule, upon proper motion or plea, whether the declaration sets out a cause of action, and, if it does, to define a libel, and leave it to the jury whether the publication falls within that definition. Shattuck *v.* Allen, 4 Gray, 540.

It is said in a late case by an eminent Judge: "I have always followed the practice adopted in this case by Lord Abinger, leaving the jury to say whether, under all the circumstances, the publication amounts to libel·

point to any person in particular, but the plaintiff had expressly averred, in his complaint, that it was published of and concerning himself, and proved some facts tending to sustain that averment; held, it should have been submitted to the jury to determine, whether the libel was intended to apply to the plaintiff.[1]

3. And the distinction is sometimes made, that, where the writing complained of as libellous is *plain and unambiguous*, the question, in a civil action, whether it be a libel or not, is a question of law; but when a charge in a written publication is equivocal, the construction of it is a question for the jury.[2] And it has even been held that, upon the trial of an issue of not guilty, it is no misdirection, if the Judge leaves generally to the jury the question, whether the publication be libellous, without stating his own opinion as to the particular publication, or defining what generally constitutes a libel.[3] While, on the other hand, it has been held no misdirection, that the Judge, in addition to leaving the proper questions to the jury, stated his own opinion as to the libellous nature of the publication.[4]

4. In the action for slander, the actual meaning of words in the particular case, and the effective sense in which they were understood, as matter of fact, is a consideration for the jury; but the question what constitutes a crime or

[1] Green *v.* Telfair, 20 Barb. 11.
[2] Snyder *v.* Andrews, 6 Barb. 43.
[3] Baylis *v.* Lawrence, 11 Ad. & Ell. 920; 3 Per. & Dav. 526.
[4] Darby *v.* Ouseley, 36 Eng. L. & Eq. 518.

That practice is analogous to the enactments of Stat. 31 Geo. III. c. 60. The statute, indeed, is applicable only to criminal cases; but it is a declaratory act; and the importance of declaring the law existed only in the case of criminal libels. The act therefore furnishes clear evidence that the Judge is not, in civil cases, bound to state his opinion, whether the application be libellous or not. And this agrees with the late decision of the Court of Exchequer in Parmiter *v.* Coupland. There is, indeed, one case in which a pure question of law may arise. If the Judge and jury think the publication libellous, still if, on the record, it appear not to be so, judgment must be arrested." Per. Ld. Denman, Baylis *v.* Lawrence, 11 Ad. & Ell. 920.

offence, the imputation of which is slanderous, is to be determined by the Court.[1] Thus in slander for the charge of perjury, the materiality of the alleged false testimony is for the Court to determine, and, if left to the jury, it is error.[2] But the meaning of *slang phrases* and *metaphors*, or other expressions of doubtful meaning, may be sufficiently averred in the *innuendo* without a *colloquium*, and the truth of the averment is for the jury to decide.[3] So, where the plaintiff, who had worked for the defendant in making pill boxes, by a machine, owned and kept secret by the defendant, left the defendant, and set up a machine for making similar boxes on his own account; and the defendant, when speaking of the plaintiff's machine, said "the plaintiff stole my patterns to get up his castings by;" held, it was for the jury and not for the Court to decide, whether the defendant intended to charge the plaintiff with larceny.[4] So a declaration in slander, after stating as inducement, that the defendant intended to impute felony to the plaintiff, set out the slanderous words as follows: "I (the defendant) have a suspicion that you (the plaintiff) and B. have robbed my house, (meaning thereby that the plaintiff had feloniously stolen certain goods of the defendant,) and therefore I take you into custody." Held, that the Judge rightly directed the jury, in stating the question to be, whether the defendant meant to impute an absolute charge of felony, or only a suspicion of felony; and that, if the jury believed the latter, the verdict ought to be for the defendant.[5]

5. But on the other hand it is held, that, in an action for slander, it is not erroneous for the Judge to state, under what circumstances words in themselves actionable may be spoken with propriety, and by way of illustration to put

[1] Thompson *v.* Grimes, 5 Ind. 385.

[2] Steinman *v.* McWilliams, 6 Barr, 170.

[3] Vanderlip *v.* Roe, 23 Penn. 82; Smith *v.* Miles, 15 Verm. 245; Usher *v.* Severance, 2 App. 9; Turrill *v.* Dolloway, 26 Wend. 383; Jones *v.* Rivers, 3 Brevard, 95.

[4] Dunnell *v.* Fiske, 11 Met. 551.

[5] Tozer *v.* Mashford, 4 Eng. L. & Eq. 451.

a case, which differs in some respects from the case on trial, and which, as the jury are informed at the time, is not intended to be represented as the one before them.[1]

6. It may be finally added, to the foregoing view of the somewhat contradictory cases on this subject, that, although the Judge is to leave it to the jury, whether under the circumstances a publication is a libel, on the general issue; yet, if they find a verdict for the defendant, where no question is made as to the fact of publication, nor as to its application to the plaintiff; the Court can set aside the verdict. Thus, an article, on the subject of the want of some efficient protection for married women, mentioned two cases, as showing the necessity for legislation; one case being described as that of a husband who acted towards his wife like "a sot and a brute;" and then proceeded: "The other is that of Mrs. H.," (meaning the plaintiff's wife,) "who having been restored to her husband's protection by a decree of the Ecclesiastical Court, found her misery so aggravated by the restitution of her conjugal rights, that she was compelled to resort to the Police Court for the little help the law gives;" adding, that the law did not meet such cases, and that "the condition of woman, when the brute intervenes, is more oppressive than that of the negro." Plea, not guilty. It was not disputed that the passage applied to the plaintiff, but no evidence was given as to the matters referred to. The Court set aside the verdict for the defendant, and granted a new trial.[2]

7. A slander or libel often consists in only *a part* of one and the same verbal statement or written publication. In such case it is held, that a defendant should be tried by all that he has published in the same pamphlet or paper.[3] Thus, where the plaintiff had set out, in his declaration, an article published by the defendant in a newspaper, and on

[1] Taylor *v.* Robinson, 29 Maine, 323.

[2] Hakewell *v.* Ingram, 28 Eng. L. & Eq. 413.

[3] Morehead *v.* Jones, 2 B. Monroe, 210.

the trial the defendant selected a certain portion of the article, which he claimed was proved to be true, and if otherwise was not libellous, and so he prayed the Court to instruct the jury: the Court, after defining a libel, and pointing out what would constitute one, instructed the jury, that they might consider the whole libellous matter in connection with the circumstances proved or admitted, and say what was the meaning of the writing, — what it imputed to the plaintiff as to motives, objects, principles, acts, and character; and, if they were such as to make the writing libellous according to the definition previously given, and it was false and malicious, they would find the matter libellous and sufficient to sustain the action. Held, this direction was unexceptionable.[1] But in an action for libel, a *subsequent* publication cannot be given in evidence for the purpose of determining whether a previous one is libellous. Two articles, to be so used, must appear simultaneously, in the same paper or book.[2]

8. More especially, when the declaration sets forth only a part of the publication alleged to be libellous, and the whole is read to the jury without objection from the defendant; the jury may consider the whole, for the purpose of forming an opinion as to the meaning of that part.[3] So, in judging of the malicious character of an alleged libel, the jury may take into consideration the whole publication; and, if it contains statements concerning other persons, which are malicious, the jury may infer therefrom that what is said of the plaintiff is also malicious.[4]

9. It is the general rule of law in proving a *conversation*, that the words themselves are to be offered in evidence, leaving their construction to the Court or jury. But, upon the ground that the injury caused by slander depends on the *effect* of the words upon the hearers;[5] it has been held, that, where the meaning of words spoken was doubtful, the wit-

[1] Graves *v.* Waller, 19 Conn. 90.
[2] Usher *v.* Severance, 2 App. 9.
[3] Goodrich *v.* Stone, 11 Met. 486.
[4] Miller *v.* Butler, 6 Cush. 71.
[5] Hawks *v.* Patton, 18 Geo. 52.

nesses who heard them may be examined, as to the sense in which they understood them.[1] So, in proving the application of an alleged libel or slander to the plaintiff, witnesses, knowing the parties and circumstances, more especially if the words are addressed to them, may be asked their opinion as to the meaning and intent, and what is their understanding of particular expressions.[2] Thus, on the trial of an action for a libel, in a publication addressed "to the editor of the Massachusetts Cataract," witnesses were permitted to testify, that they understood the publication to apply to the plaintiff. Held, that this testimony was competent, so far as it tended to prove that the plaintiff was such editor, and that for any other purpose it was immaterial; and therefore that its admission was not a cause for granting the defendant a new trial.[3]

10. But it has been held, on the other hand, that, in an action against the editor of a newspaper for a libel, testimony of witnesses is not receivable, that on reading the article they considered the plaintiff as the person intended.[4] So, in an action for slander, witnesses cannot be allowed to state the *impression* the words made upon their minds, but must state positively, or as near as memory will allow, the exact words.[5] And it is clear that words, which are plainly slanderous in the understanding of the bystanders, and from their proper import, cannot be explained by reference to other facts, which were not mentioned by the party at the time he uttered the words.[6] So, although words spoken by the defendant, which are not actionable, may be proved in aggravation or corroboration; the witness cannot be permitted to state whom, or what, he was induced, by current rumor or the conversations of others, to think the defendant meant, when he used the words.[7] So, under the plea of *not guilty*, the defendant cannot prove that the plaintiff acknowledged she knew certain

[1] Morgan *v.* Livingston, 2 Rich. 573. *Contra*, Snell *v.* Snow, 13 Met. 278.

[2] Miller *v.* Butler, 6 Cush. 71; McLaughlin *v.* Russell, 17 Ohio, 475; Tompkins *v.* Wisener, 1 Sneed, 458; Smawley *v.* Stark, 9 Ind. 386.

[3] Goodrich *v.* Stone, 11 Met. 486.

[4] White *v.* Sayward, 33 Maine, 322.

[5] Teague *v.* Williams, 7 Ala. 844.

[6] 6 Humph. 174.

[7] Allensworth *v.* Coleman, 5 Dana, 315.

facts, for the purpose of showing the sense in which the defendant used the expression attributed to him.[1] So evidence of the sense, in which the words were understood, must be of the sense in which they were understood *at the time they were uttered.*[2] And it has been recently held, that a plaintiff has no right to ask a witness, what he considered to be the meaning of the words spoken, except in the cases, 1st, where the words in the ordinary meaning do not import a slanderous charge; in which case, if they are susceptible of such a meaning, and the plaintiff avers a fact, from which it may be inferred that they were used for the purpose of making the charge, he may prove such averment, and then the jury must decide whether the defendant used the words in the sense implied, or not; and 2d, where a charge is made by using a cant phrase, or words having a local meaning, or a nickname, when advantage is taken of a fact, known to the persons spoken to, to convey a meaning, which they understood by connecting the words (of themselves unmeaning) with such facts; in which case the plaintiff must make an averment to that effect, and may prove, not only the truth of the averment, but also that the words were so understood by the person to whom they were addressed; for, otherwise, they are without point, and harmless.[3]

11. The rule once prevailed, of construing doubtful words *most favorably for the defendant*, or *in mitiori sensu.* But this rule applied only where the words were of doubtful import, and might be construed in one of two senses as well as the other.[4] And it is now settled, that, if the words are susceptible of two meanings, one imputing a crime and the other innocent, it is for the jury to decide in what sense the defendant used them.[5] Thus, in an action for these words: "J. B. stole my box-wood;" after verdict for the plaintiff, on motion in arrest of judgment, that the words were not actionable, because they shall be taken to mean wood growing, or the like, whereof only a trespass can be committed; held,

[1] Berger *v.* Berger, 18 Penn. 489.
[2] Briggs *v.* Byrd, 12 Ired. 377.
[3] Sasser *v.* Rouse, 13 Ired. Eq. 142.
[4] Naber *v.* Miecock, Skin. 183.
[5] Cregier *v.* Bunton, 2 Rich. 395; 11 Humph. 507.

the words were actionable.[1] (*a*) And it is also well settled, that, in an action for slanderous words, whether written or spoken, the words are to be taken in their usual, general, popular, and natural sense, and according to the actual or probable apprehension of the bystanders, or their general acceptation; not either *in graviori* or *in mitiori sensu*.[2] (*b*) "It is not sufficient to show by argument, that the words will admit of some other meaning; but the Court must understand them as all mankind would understand them; and we cannot understand them differently in court from what they would do out of court."[3] "It is a general rule of construction in actions of slander, indictments for libel, and other analogous cases, where an offence can be committed by the utterance of language, orally or in writing, that the language shall be construed and understood in the sense in which the writer or speaker intended it. If, therefore,

[1] Baker *v.* Pierce, 2 Ld. Raym. 959.

[2] Gardiner *v.* Atwater, Sayer, 265; Duncan *v.* Brown, 15 B. Mon. 186; Fallenstein *v.* Boothe, 13 Mis. 427; Hancock *v.* Stephens, 11 Humph. 507; Butterfield *v.* Buffum, 9 N. H. 156; M'Gowen *v.* Mainfee, 7 Mon. 314; Naher *v.* Miecock, Skin. 183; Somers *v.* House, Ibid. 364; Watson *v.* Nicholas, 6 Humph. 174; Ogden *v.* Riley, 2 Green, 186.

[3] Woolnoth *v.* Meadows, 5 E. 473.

(*a*) But where, in a sentence of excommunication from a church, read by the pastor on Sunday, in the presence and hearing of the congregation, it was recited, that the defendant had "clearly violated the seventh commandment," and in a subsequent part of the sentence it was declared, "that this church does now as always bear its solemn testimony against the sin of fornication and uncleanness;" it was held that the charge of violating the seventh commandment did not impute the crime of adultery, in its legal and technical sense as an indictable offence. Farnsworth *v.* Storrs, 5 Cush. 412.

Testimony of persons who heard the slanderous words, that they did not believe them, is not admissible in mitigation of damages. Otherwise with declarations of the plaintiff that he was not injured by them. Richardson *v.* Barker, 7 Ind. 567.

An averment of particular facts, showing that the person, in whose hearing the words are alleged to have been spoken, must have known that the defendant meant to impute a crime to the plaintiff, will render ambiguous words slanderous. Dorland *v.* Patterson, 23 Wend. 422.

(*b*) The Court will regard the use of fictitious names and disguises in a libel, in the sense that they are commonly understood by the public. The State *v.* Chace, Walk. 384.

obscure or ambiguous language is used, or language which is figurative or ironical, courts and juries will understand it according to its true meaning and import, and the sense in which it was intended to be gathered from the context, and from all the facts and circumstances under which it was used."[1] Thus to say of the plaintiff that "he was under a charge of a prosecution for perjury; and that G. W. (an attorney of that name) had the attorney-general's directions to prosecute the plaintiff for perjury," justifies a verdict for the plaintiff; as, in the common acceptation of the words, it imputes actual perjury, and not merely a prosecution therefor.[2] So where one said of another that "his character was infamous; that he would be disgraceful to any society; that those who proposed him a member of any society must have intended an insult to it; that he would publish his shame and infamy; that delicacy forbade him from bringing a direct charge, but it was a male child who complained to him;" such words were understood to mean a charge of unnatural practices, and sufficiently certain in themselves to be actionable, without the aid of an innuendo to that purpose.[3] So words charging a party with aiding in procuring an abortion, (a crime created by statute,) when speaking of him as having had illicit intercourse with a woman, are actionable *per se*. If spoken in a sense other than that of imputing the crime, it is incumbent upon the defendant to show it.[4]

[1] Per Shaw, C. J., Commonwealth *v.* Kneeland, 20 Pick. 216.

[2] Roberts *v.* Camden, 9 E. 93.

[3] Woolnoth *v.* Meadows, 5 E. 463.

[4] Bissel *v.* Cornell, 24 Wend. 354.

CHAPTER X.

LIBEL, ETC. — RELATING TO OFFICE, EMPLOYMENT, ETC.

1. We now proceed to consider that class of libellous or slanderous words which consists of imputations made upon a party, not personally, abstractly, or merely as an individual, but in connection with some office held, or employment followed by him, and rendered actionable by their tendency to injure him in that capacity. And there are numerous cases, where words thus become actionable, which in themselves would not be so. (*a*)

2. The general rule on the subject is, that where words are spoken of a person in an office of profit, which have a natural tendency to occasion the loss of such office, or which impute the want of some necessary qualification for, or some misconduct in it, they are actionable.[1] It is said by an eminent Judge: "Every authority which I have been enabled to find, either shows the want of some general requisite, as honesty, capacity, fidelity, &c., or connects the imputa-

[1] Lumby *v.* Allday, 1 Tyr. 217.

(*a*) It is worthy of notice, that, while written or spoken words are often rendered actionable by their application to the party in connection with his office or employment; the same circumstance — that of connection with other individuals or with the community, in such manner as to give them an authorized interest in the communication — often constitutes it a privileged communication, for which no suit can be maintained. (See *Privileged Communication.*)

tion with the plaintiff's office, trade, or business."[1] (a) Thus, as has been seen, it is not actionable to charge a man, generally, with *cheating*. But it is otherwise where he is a *trader*, and the words were spoken of him in his trade.[2] So the terms "cheat" and "swindler" are not actionable, unless spoken of the plaintiff in relation to his business.[3] Thus the words, "you cheated the lawyer of his linen, and stood bawd to your daughter to make it up with him; you cheat everybody; you cheated me of a sheet; you cheated S., and I will let him know it," were held not actionable, without a *colloquium* of the plaintiff's trade or profession.[4] So the words "he has sold the property of the company and pocketed the money," spoken of a person as director and superintendent of a company.[5]

3. Upon the general principle *in pari delicto*, &c., (see chap. 4,) a party who pursues an *illegal* vocation has no remedy by action for a libel regarding his conduct therein.[6] Thus the plaintiff alleged, that he carried on in an honest and lawful manner the trade of a manufacturer of bitters, and that the defendant libelled him in his trade, by publishing that the bitters were made to adulterate porter; *per quod* the plaintiff was ruined. Held, that, under the general issue, the defendant might give in evidence, that the plaintiff's trade was illegal, and that his bitters had been condemned in the Court of Exchequer.[7]

4. To maintain an action for words spoken, on the ground that they were injurious to the plaintiff in his business or occupation, profession or trade, the words must relate to his business character, and must impute to him

[1] Per Bayley, B., Lumby *v.* Allday, 1 C. & J. 301.
[2] Ludwell *v.* Hole, 2 Ld. Raym. 1417.
[3] Odiorne *v.* Bacon, 6 Cush. 185.
[4] Davis *v.* Miller, 2 Strange, 1169.
[5] Johnson *v.* Shields, 1 Dutch. 116.
[6] Hunt *v.* Bell, 1 Bing. 1.
[7] Manning *v.* Clement, 7 Bing. 362. See White *v.* Delavan, 17 Wend. 149.

(a) The distinction has been sometimes made, that, in offices of credit, not of profit, words imputing mere *want of ability* are not actionable; because a man cannot help his want of ability, as he may his want of honesty. How *v.* Prinn, 2 Salk. 695.

misconduct in that character. Imputations on his morality, temper, or conduct, generally, which would be injurious to him, whatever were his pursuit, are not actionable *per se*, even though they tend to injure him in his business. Accordingly, a charge against the keeper of a public house and garden, that he was a dangerous man; that he was a desperate man; that the defendant was afraid to go to such public house alone; and was afraid of his own life; was held not actionable.[1] So the first count in a declaration stated, as inducement, that the plaintiff was a livery-stable keeper, and by that trade and business acquired a profit. The last count stated, that the defendant spoke these words of and concerning the plaintiff, and of and concerning him in his said trade: "You (meaning the said plaintiff) are a regular prover under bankruptcies," (meaning that the said plaintiff was accustomed to prove fictitious debts under commissions of bankrupt.) Verdict for the plaintiff on all the counts. Held, on error, 1st. That the words did not impute a charge against the plaintiff in the way of his trade or business; and 2d. That the innuendo, imputing a crime punishable by law, was badly pleaded, as enlarging the natural meaning of the words used, without resting on any introductory averment of a *colloquium* respecting the proof of fictitious debts; and a *venire de novo* was awarded.[2] So, to charge a clerk to a gas-light company with immoral conduct with women, the imputation having no reference to his office, and the words not being laid to have been spoken of him in his office as clerk, nor proved to have occasioned him any special damage, is not actionable.[3] And an action for libel does not lie, in favor of an individual, for a publication alleged to affect the individual characters of persons, and the trade or business carried on by them, if on its face it does not point to the individuals intended, otherwise than that they pursue a particular trade or business in a specified section of a city; as the publication affects only a class of persons.[4] So the

[1] Ireland *v.* McGarvish, 1 Sandf. 155; Kinney *v.* Nash, 3 Comst. 177; Van Tassel *v.* Capron, 1 Denio, 250.

[2] Alexander *v.* Angle, 1 Tyr. 9.

[3] Lumby *v.* Allday, 1 Tyr. 217.

[4] White *v.* Delavan, 17 Wend. 49.

declaration charged the speaking of the following words of the plaintiff, in his character of justice of the peace: "There is a combined company here to cheat strangers, and Squire Van Tassel has a hand in it. K. A., J. G., and Squire Van Tassel are a set of damned blacklegs;" but it did not show that the imputation was connected with the plaintiff's official conduct. Held, not actionable.[1] So a declaration for slander alleged, that the plaintiff was a salaried superintendent of police at L., and that it was his duty, as such, to conduct himself temperately and with decency and propriety, while on duty, and to hinder and repress indecent and disorderly conduct in the police-office; that the defendant, intending to injure the plaintiff in his office, and cause it to be believed that he had misconducted himself as such superintendent, and cause him to be dismissed from his office, in a discourse which he had concerning the plaintiff, as such superintendent, and concerning the plaintiff's conduct in his office, falsely, &c., spoke and published concerning the plaintiff, and concerning him as such superintendent, and concerning his conduct in his office, the false, &c. words: "I" (meaning the defendant) "saw a letter two or three days since, regarding an officer of the L. police force," (meaning the plaintiff,) "who (meaning the plaintiff) had been guilty of conduct unfit for publication." Judgment arrested, after verdict, on the ground that the declaration did not show how the imputation was connected by the speaker with the plaintiff's office.[2]

5. But, where a publication is libellous in itself, an averment of the plaintiff's official or professional character will not be ground of demurrer, although the libel cannot apply to such character.[3] So a declaration for libel stated that the plaintiff was an attorney, and that the defendant, intending to injure him in his good name, and in his said profession, published a libel of and concerning the plaintiff, and of and concerning him in his said profession; but the plaintiff failed

[1] Van Tassel *v.* Capron, 1 Denio, 250.
[2] James *v.* Brook, 9 Ad. & Ell. N.S. 7.
[3] Gage *v.* Robinson, 12 Ohio, 250.

in proving that he was a certificated and practising attorney. Held, this was not a fatal variance, the words being actionable, although not used with reference to the professional character of the plaintiff.[1]

6. It is held that the law implies damages for slander of officers, only when they are in the office at the time. Thus, where one was twice constable, once in 1843, and again in 1846, and, during the latter period, a person said of him, that while constable in 1843, he had made a false return; held, he could not recover, unless he proved special damage.[2]

7. And it is not enough to show that the plaintiff merely acted in the capacity of a public officer. Thus, in an action for words of and concerning the plaintiff, as "treasurer and collector" of certain tolls and rates, it appeared that the words were spoken of him in his character of collector only. Held, without due proof of his appointment as collector, pursuant to a private act of parliament, the action was not maintainable, even though he had acted as such collector at the time the words were spoken,[3] (see p. 318.) So where a declaration alleged, that the plaintiff had been and was a physician, and exercised that profession in England, and on that account had been and was called Doctor, meaning Doctor of Medicine, and that the defendant slandered the plaintiff in his character of a physician practising in England, and denied his right to be called a Doctor of Medicine; held, the plaintiff must prove that he was entitled to practise as a physician in England, otherwise than by showing the fact of his having so practised, or that he had received the degree of Doctor of Medicine at the University of St. Andrews.[4]

8. Where words derive their actionable quality from extrinsic facts and circumstances connected with an office or employment of the plaintiff, these must be proved.[5] Accordingly, in an action for slanderous words, alleged to have been spoken of the plaintiff as a constable, and imputing to

[1] Lewis v. Walter, 3 B. & C. 138; 4 D. & R. 810.

[2] Edwards v. Howell, 10 Ired. 211.

[3] Sellers v. Killew, 7 D. & Ry. 121.

[4] Collins v. Carnegie, 1 Ad. & Ell. 695.

[5] Kinney v. Nash, 3 Comst. 177.

him misconduct in his proceedings under a bench warrant, placed in his hands for the arrest of an offender who had been indicted, which words were not slanderous except as connected with the indictment and bench warrant; the plaintiff failing to prove the warrant; held, he could not recover.[1] So the declaration must accurately set forth the employment, office, or capacity, to which the slanderous words were applied. Thus an action, for imputing to the plaintiff misconduct as a *constable*, is not sustained, by proving words imputing misconduct to him as agent of the executive of this State for the arrest, in another State, of a fugitive from justice.[2] But in an action for libel, parol evidence is admissible of an averment that the plaintiff was State printer, and President of the Mechanics' and Farmers' Bank; those facts being stated as matter of inducement, and collaterally,[3] (see p. 317.) And, in slander for words spoken respecting the plaintiff's trade, if the words assume that, at the time they were spoken, the plaintiff was engaged in such trade, there is no need of proving that fact.[4]

9. Whether words were spoken of a man in a certain capacity, is a question of fact for the jury.[5] So, whether the words apply to the plaintiff in particular, or to his profession generally. Thus the defendant, having written a letter, blaming the person to whom it was addressed for employing the plaintiff, an attorney, to sue, added, "If you will be misled by an attorney, who only considers his own interest, you will have to repent it. You may think, when you have ordered your attorney to write to Mr. B., he would not do any more without your further orders; but if you once set him about it, he will go to any length without further orders." Held, in an action for defamation, that the jury were properly directed to consider, whether these expressions were meant of the profession in general, or of the plaintiff in particular; and that it was not necessary to leave it to them to con-

[1] Kinney *v.* Nash, 3 Comst. 177.

[2] Kinney *v.* Nash, 3 Comst. 177; Barnes *v.* Trundy, 31 Maine, 321.

[3] Southwick *v.* Stevens, 10 Johns. 443.

[4] Hesler *v.* Degant, 3 Ind. 501.

[5] Skinner *v.* Grant, 12 Verm. 456.

sider, whether this was a confidential communication, or a malicious attack on the plaintiff's character.[1] So the plaintiff in one count alleged, that the defendant charged him with having paid to a certain elector of the town of S. "money to secure the plaintiff's election as a justice of the peace," and, in another count, with "having bought rum and given to some of the electors of that town to secure his election to said office, and with having bought rum and distributed it to secure his said election." Held, the words imported not only an offence punishable by the 17th section of the "act of Connecticut relating to electors and elections," (Stat. 1849, tit. 11, c. 2,) but one involving moral turpitude; but the jury were to find, whether the defendant spoke the words, and, if so, whether he thereby imputed to the plaintiff the crime set forth.[2]

10. With regard to slanderous or libellous charges against *public officers*, it is said, officers and candidates for office may be *canvassed*, but not *calumniated*.[3] (*a*) Thus it is no justification of a slander, published of a town officer relative to his official conduct, and while in the exercise of his office, that the slanderer was a legal voter in the town, and so one of the constituents of such officer.[4] (*b*)

[1] Godson *v.* Home, 1 Brod. & Bing. 7.
[2] Hoag *v.* Hatch, 23 Conn. 585.
[3] Seely *v.* Blair, Wright, 358, 683.
[4] Doods *v.* Henry, 9 Mass. 262.

(*a*) "When any man shall consent to be a candidate for a public office, conferred by the election of the people, he must be considered as putting his character in issue, so far as it may respect his fitness and qualification for the office. And publications of the truth on this subject, with the honest intention of informing the people, are not a libel. For it would be unreasonable to conclude, that the publication of truths, which it is the interest of the people to know, should be an offence against their laws. And every man holding a public elective office may be considered as within this principle; for as a reëlection is the only way his constituents can manifest their approbation of his conduct, it is to be presumed that he is consenting to a reëlection, if he does not disclaim it." Per Parsons, C. J., 4 Mass. 169; acc. Commonwealth *v.* Blanding, 3 Pick. 304; The State *v.* Burnham, 9 N. H. 35.

See *Privileged Communication.*

(*b*) A leading criminal case for libel in Massachusetts was as follows:

11. It is a libel to publish of a *Protestant archbishop*, that he attempts to convert Catholic priests by offers of money and preferment. Thus, in an action for libel, the declaration, without any introductory averment to explain the libel, set it out as follows: "Who do you think was the archbishop who promised M., the priest of the mountains, £1000 in cash, and a living of £800 a year? Why, no less a personage than the Archbishop of Tuam (the plaintiff)!!! The archbishop wrote to a Protestant clergyman, desiring him to make the offer, and to show the letter, but not to surrender it into his possession, unless M. was disposed to accede;" with an innuendo that "the defendant meant by the libel, that the plaintiff had offered the said M. £1000 in cash, and a living of £800 a year, if he would accede to become a Protestant clergyman." On motion in arrest of judgment, on the ground that there was nothing on the face of the libel, as set out in the declaration, to warrant the innuendo, that the offer was made to induce M. to become a

An indictment charged that the defendant, intending to injure the reputation of "one J. K., Esquire, a member of the honorable senate of the General Court of Massachusetts aforesaid, and chairman of the committee of accounts, duly appointed thereto by the legislature of the said Commonwealth, and maliciously intending to deprive the said J. K. of his offices aforesaid, and the confidence of the people of his senatorial district," framed a libel of, concerning, and against J. K., and caused the same to be printed in a public newspaper, under a paragraph headed, "The new nomination in Middlesex," in the following words: "In this committee of accounts (meaning the committee of the legislature aforesaid) which had advertised for sealed proposals for the contract for printing, the honorable chairman, Mr. K., (meaning the said J. K.) proposed, before a seal was broken, that the contract should be given to the Boston Statesman (meaning the proprietors of that paper), provided their proposals were not more than $500 higher than any others. This was no more nor less than a proposal to give $500 from the treasury of Massachusetts to that reprobated Jackson press." It was held, that the publication was not on the face of it libellous, and that the indictment could not be sustained, inasmuch as it did not aver such extrinsic facts as would render the words libellous, with a *colloquium* that the words were published of and concerning such facts. Commonwealth *v.* Child, 13 Pick. 198.

Protestant clergyman; held, the libel imputed immoral conduct to the plaintiff upon the face of it; and, after verdict, the declaration was sufficient.[1] So, to say of *a peer of the realm*, "he is an unworthy man and acts against law and reason," is actionable.[2] But not charging *a member of parliament* with want of sincerity and breaking his word.[3] So, "He is a papist," spoken of *a deputy-lieutenant*, is actionable.[4] Or to say of *a justice and deputy-lieutenant*, a candidate for parliament, "don't vote for him, for he is a Jacobite, and for bringing in the Pretender," &c.[5]

12. To say of *a justice of the peace*, (*a*) that "he makes use of the king's commission to worry men out of their estates," is actionable.[6] Or that "he is forsworn, and not fit to be a justice or to sit upon the bench."[7] Or that a justice of the peace "is a rascal, a villain, and a liar," or "a

[1] Archbishop, &c. *v.* Robeson, 5 Bing. 17; 2 Moo. & P. 32.

[2] Lord Townsend *v.* Hughes, 2 Mod. 152.

[3] Onslow *v.* Horne, 2 W. Black. 750.

[4] Roe *v.* Clarges, 3 Mod. 26.

[5] How *v.* Prinn, 2 Salk. 694; 2 Ld. Raym. 813.

[6] Newton *v.* Stubbs, 3 Mod. 71.

[7] Kirle *v.* Osgood, 1 Mod. 23.

(*a*) In a late criminal case in Massachusetts, the indictment for a libel on W., after averring that he held the office of Judge at the time of its publication, set forth the libel with innuendoes as follows: "We accuse him of disgracing his office, of perverting the law which, bad as it is, is yet worse in such hands; of doing injustice on his seat; of descending from his official dignity; of suffering his personal feeling to interfere with the discharge of his functions. Let W. choke a week or so on this pill, and we have one or two more as hard to swallow in reserve, (meaning *that the defendant had one or two libels on W.* in reserve for future publication). We think we shall do service to God and man by removing this unjust magistrate from the seat he disgraces," (meaning that W. *ought to be impeached of crime and misdemeanors*, and ought to be removed and degraded from his office). There was no express *colloquium* or averment in the indictment, that the libel was of and concerning the removal of W. from office by impeachment. It was held, that the first innuendo did not enlarge the meaning of the words of the libel; and, even if the second innuendo aggravated their meaning, (which it seems it does not,) it might be rejected as surplusage, the words of the libel being sufficient in themselves to sustain the indictment. Commonwealth *v.* Snelling, 13 Pick. 321.

rogue," when speaking of his official conduct.[1] And a publication, charging an officer, authorized to administer oaths, with affixing a jurat to an affidavit, and certifying that the person who signed it was duly sworn, when in fact he was not sworn, accompanied with remarks imputing to the officer a gross violation of duty; is libellous, and is not justified by the mere proof that the jurat was affixed without administering the oath.[2] And a jury are not authorized, in such a case, to say that the publication was intended merely to charge inadvertence, or omission by mistake to administer the oath.[3]

13. But the words, "Sir J. K. is a buffe-headed fellow, and doth not understand law; he is not fit to talk law with me, I have baffled him, and he hath not done my client justice," spoken of a justice of the peace, were held not actionable, without special damage.[4] So words charging a justice of the peace with corrupt conduct, in trying a cause over which he has no jurisdiction, are held not actionable.[5] And words charging the plaintiff, a justice of the peace, with omitting to inform a party who had recovered a judgment before him, of the fact that the constable, who had the execution, had rendered himself liable for not returning the same in time, do not impute official misconduct.[6]

14. It is libellous to publish of one, in his capacity of *a juror*, that he agreed with another juror, to stake the decision of the amount of damages, to be given in a cause then under their consideration, upon a game of draughts.[7]

15. The following words, spoken of *a postmaster*, in reference to his official character: "He would rob the mail for one hundred dollars; yes, he would rob the mail for five dollars," are held actionable.[8] But the mere opening of a letter, whether from curiosity or wantonness, does not involve the

[1] Aston *v.* Blagrave, 2 Ld. Raym. 1369; 1 Str. 618; Kent *v.* Pocock, 2 Str. 1168.

[2] Turril *v.* Dolloway, 17 Wend. 426.

[3] Ibid.

[4] Rex *v.* Darby, 3 Mod. 139. See Prouse *v.* Wilcox, 3 Mod. 163.

[5] Oraam *v.* Franklin, 5 Black. 42.

[6] Van Tassel *v.* Capron, 1 Denio, 250.

[7] Commonwealth *v.* Wright, 1 Cush. 46.

[8] Craig *v.* Brown, 5 Blackf. 44.

idea of moral turpitude, or render a man *infamous*, in the sense which the law imputes to those terms, when settling the doctrine of slander at the common law. Hence the words "he has broken open my letters in the post-office," spoken of the plaintiff, with averments of his being post-master of, &c., do not import, that he unlawfully and in violation of official duty, broke open the defendant's letters; and are not actionable.[1]

16. In Massachusetts, to charge *a minister* with *drunkenness* has been held actionable, without laying a *colloquium* of his office or profession, and without proof of special damage.[2] But, in England, a declaration for slander, by charging a clergyman in holy orders with incontinency, is bad, without showing actual damage, or that he holds some office or employment producing temporal profit.[3] So, in case for a libel, the declaration stated, that the plaintiff was a Roman Catholic priest, and priest of a chapel named, and that the defendant, intending to injure him in his said offices, published of him, in those offices, a libel, which was set out. The alleged libel contained an account of a Roman Catholic having been seen performing a penance, which was suggested to be of a degrading kind, and added, that the party performing the penance said, that his priest would not administer the sacrament to him till he had performed it, and that his priest was the plaintiff. The declaration also set forth certain comments of the defendant accompanying the publication, and in which the Roman Catholic discipline was attacked. But the libel was not otherwise connected with the plaintiff, nor were there any allegations showing how the enjoining of such a penance would affect the character of a Roman Catholic priest. A judgment for the plaintiff was arrested, the Court holding that the publication was not, on the face of it, libellous; and refusing, even upon the assumption that the plaintiff was charged with imposing the penance, to intend that the jury had evidence before

1 M'Cuen *v.* Ladlum, 2 Harr. 12.
2 Chaddock *v.* Briggs, 13 Mass. 248.
3 Gallwey *v.* Marshall, 24 Eng. L. & Eq. 463.

them of any injury to the plaintiff, which the declaration did not show, though some evidence to that purpose was in fact given. But it was also held, that, if the publication had been libellous, it would not have been justifiable, on the ground that it was promulgated at a public meeting, called to petition parliament against making a grant in support of a Roman Catholic college.[1] (*a*)

[1] Hearne *v.* Stowell, 12 Ad. & Ell. 719.

(*a*) A declaration for slander and libel stated, by way of inducement, that the plaintiff was minister of a dissenting congregation at T., deriving emoluments from his said calling; that he had formerly been a draper at S., in partnership with H. P., his brother-in-law; that the partnership had been dissolved, and that there were certain accounts and money transactions between the plaintiff and H. P. in relation thereto; that false and scandalous reports concerning the plaintiff and the said partnership accounts and transactions had been circulated among the congregation at T., and it was proposed that one E. H. should examine into the said accounts and transactions, on the part of the plaintiff; and that a correspondence and discussion afterwards took place between the defendant and one R. A. relating to those accounts and transactions. The first count then proceeded to allege, that the defendant, intending to injure the plaintiff in his office and character of minister of the congregation at T., and to cause him to be deprived of that office, &c., in a discourse of and concerning the plaintiff, and of and concerning him in his said calling and ministry, and of and concerning the said partnership, and the said accounts and money transaction with H. P., spoke these words, — with proper innuendoes, — "I do not go by reports; I go by a knowledge of facts. Mr. H. (the plaintiff) is a rogue; and I can prove him to be so, by the books at S. Mr. H. pretends to say he has been as good as a father to him, (meaning H. P.); but, you see, he has been robbing him. He has cheated Mr. P. of £2000; so you see what sort of a father he has been to him. I will so expose Mr. H. (the plaintiff) that he will not be able to hold up his head in T. pulpit, or any other. I said to Mr. P., I do not wish to see the books, but he desired me to come and see them; and he told me he did not care who saw them. Mr. H. (the plaintiff) has out-generalled him in everything, (meaning that the plaintiff had taken an unfair advantage of the said H. P., and had conducted himself in an improper manner towards him in relation to and in connection with the said partnership and the said accounts). Now, I do not go by what I have heard; but I know it to be true."

In the second count, the words charged were, — "Mr. H. (the plaintiff) has cheated Mr. P., his brother-in-law, of upwards of £2000. Mr. H.

17. To call *an attorney* a cheat is actionable.[1] Or, to say of an attorney, "He is no more a lawyer than the devil."[2]

[1] Rush *v.* Cavenaugh, 2 Barr, 187. [2] Day *v.* Buller, 3 Wils. 59.

(meaning the said E. H.) has been to S., and found all true as I represented to Mr. H. I wonder how any respectable person can countenance such a man by their presence. I have been advising some other persons to go to the Wesleyan chapel; as they would there hear plain, honest men."

The fifth count charged the defendant with having written and published of and concerning the plaintiff, and of and concerning the said partnership transactions and accounts between the plaintiff and H. P., and of and concerning the said false and scandalous reports, "It has all through been admitted, that Mr. H. (the plaintiff) in his dealings with his relatives, kept clear of the meshes of the law. The charges brought against him are not founded on strictly illegal acts, but on overreaching, &c. &c. his late partner."

The sixth count charged the defendant with having, in answer to a letter addressed to him by R. A. (the plaintiff's friend), containing, among other things, the following passage: "You have even said in T., that Mr. H. (the plaintiff) has cheated his relations out of £2000," written and published of and concerning the plaintiff, and of and concerning the said partnership, and of and concerning the said accounts and money transactions between the plaintiff and H. P., and concerning the words referred to in the letter of R. A., as follows: "I beg to tell you that you do not understand the matters at all; that you have been grossly deceived; and that you are advocating a case the most disreputable that has come within my knowledge for many a day; and this you will freely admit, when the facts of it are fully comprehended; and this, my own opinion of the matter, is held in common with all the gentlemen and ministers who have heard both sides of the question," — thereby meaning that the plaintiff had been and was guilty of improper and unbecoming conduct, and had behaved himself in a manner unworthy a preacher and minister as aforesaid.

The declaration then alleged, for special damage, that the plaintiff had been injured in his calling as a minister and preacher, and brought into public scandal, &c., and that divers persons frequenting the said chapel at T. had withdrawn therefrom, and refused to permit the plaintiff to preach there, whereby the plaintiff had been prevented from obtaining profits, &c. It appeared, that the words charged in the first and second counts were intended, and were understood, to convey an imputation that the plaintiff had taken advantage of his brother-in-law in the course of the partnership transactions and accounts, though by what precise means did not appear; and that the libels which were the subject of the fifth and sixth counts were written by the defendant in answer to a letter from the plaintiff's

So, to say of an attorney, "He cannot read a declaration;" without stating a special damage.[1] Or, to say of an attorney in his business, "H. is a rogue, for taking your money, and has done nothing for it; he has not entered an appearance for you; he is no attorney at law; he don't dare to appear before a judge. What signifies going to him? He is only an attorney's clerk and a rogue; he is no attorney."[2]

18. And upon this subject the distinction is made, that to impute to a professional man ignorance or want of skill *in any particular transaction*, is not actionable. The words must be spoken or written of him *generally*.[3] (a) But words imputing to a lawyer a want of integrity, whether used generally of his profession, or particularly as to some one transaction, are actionable. Thus it is actionable to charge an attorney with revealing confidential communications made to him by his client, for the purpose of aiding and abetting another person, with whom he has combined and colluded, and of injuring his client. So it is actionable to impute to an attorney ignorance of his profession.[4]

[1] Jones v. Powell, 1 Mod. 272.
[2] Hardwick v. Chandler, 2 Strange, 1138.
[3] Garr v. Selden, 6 Barb. 416.
[4] Jones v. Powell, 1 Mod. 272.

friend R. A., who had been in correspondence with the defendant on the subject of the charges against the plaintiff, with the sanction and concurrence of the latter. The only evidence of special damage, was that of a witness, who stated that the plaintiff had told him he was to receive £30 a year for preaching in T. chapel; but there was no evidence as to the way in which that sum was to be raised, or who were the parties to pay it; neither was there any evidence that any of the congregation had absented themselves from the chapel in consequence of the reports, or that the plaintiff had sustained any pecuniary damage therefrom.

Held, in the absence of proof of special damage, the words charged in the first and second counts,—not being spoken of the plaintiff in reference to his office of minister,—were not the subject of an action; and the letters declared on in the fifth and sixth counts were in the nature of confidential and privileged communications. Hopwood v. Thorn, 8 Com. B. 293.

(a) Thus to say of an attorney or a counsellor, in a particular suit, "F. knows nothing about the suit, he will lead you on until he has undone you;" is not actionable without alleging and proving special damage. Foot v. Brown, 8 Johns. 64.

19. A declaration averred, that the plaintiff had been legally appointed *administrator*, and had entered upon the performance of his duties, and that the defendant had slanderously said of him, as such administrator, that "he had a room in which were two beds and both beds were full of leather which he had smuggled away at the time of appraisement." Held, the words were actionable without proof of special damage.[1]

20. It is said, the rule may be laid down as a general one, that a charge against *a physician*, as such, of gross ignorance and unskilfulness in his profession, is actionable *per se*. The law presumes damage from the very nature of the charge.[2] (*a*)

[1] Beck *v.* Stitzel, 21 Penn. 522.

[2] Secor *v.* Harris, 18 Barb. 425.

(*a*) In case for a libel, the declaration stated, by way of inducement, that the plaintiff was a barrister, and the editor and proprietor of a weekly publication called "The Medical Times," and also secretary to the committee of "Poor Law Medical Officers," and to the convention of "Poor Law Medical Officers;" that there existed an association called "The National Institute of Medicine;" that certain medical poor-law-union officers were endeavoring to bring about an amelioration of the then-existing system of poor-law medical relief; and that "The National Institute of Medicine" was willing to lend its assistance to the medical poor-law-union officers, and to allow that body the use of certain rooms held by them. The declaration then, in the first count, alleged that the defendant, in a weekly publication called "The Lancet," published, "of and concerning the plaintiff," the following: "In our last, we advised the medical officers of the poor-law-unions to adopt an independent course, to trust to the justice of their cause, and to their own legitimate exertions, for an amendment of the grievances of which they so justly complain;" and, after cautioning those persons not to suffer "The National Institute of Medicine," or "The Committee of Poor-Law Medical Officers," to meddle with their affairs, the libel proceeded: "We would exhort the medical officers to avoid the traps set for them by desperate adventurers, (thereby meaning the plaintiff, among others,) who, participating in their efforts, would inevitably cover them with ridicule and disrepute."

The second count stated, that the defendant further published, "of and concerning the plaintiff," the following: "We need not here dwell upon the impolicy of the connection between the present agitation and 'The National Institute,' — a body which has disgusted the government, — and with other persons not belonging to the profession, (thereby meaning the plaintiff, as

Thus these words, spoken of a physician, though in reference to particular cases, "Doctor S. killed my children. He gave them teaspoonful doses of calomel, and it killed them; they did not live long after they took it. They died right off—the same day," are actionable *per se*.[1] So, saying of a physician "he has killed the child by giving it too much calomel," is actionable in itself.[2] So it has been held, that an action will lie, for words imputing ignorance to *an apothecary* in the practice of his profession.[3]

21. But the distinction is made, that words spoken of a physician, charging him merely with ignorance or misconduct in the treatment of a particular case, are not actionable in themselves, though they become so by proof of special damage. But they are actionable, if, in addition, they convey the charge of general professional ignorance or incompetency, or want of integrity. Thus where a declaration, after alleging that the plaintiff, as a practising physician, had visited and prescribed for Sarah M., averred, that the defendant falsely and maliciously said of the plaintiff, that his treatment of her was *rascally*; it was

[1] Secor *v.* Harris, 18 Barb. 425.
[2] Johnson *v.* Robertson, 8 Port. 486.
[3] Tutty *v.* Alewin, 11 Mod. 221.

---

such barrister as aforesaid,) and whose weekly vocation it is to bring everything belonging to the profession into disrepute and contempt," (thereby meaning that the plaintiff was in the habit, as editor of the said weekly publication called "The Medical Times" as aforesaid, of bringing the medical profession into disrepute and contempt).

The third count described the plaintiff as "a quack lawyer and mountebank, and an impostor;" and the fourth set out matter tending to hold the plaintiff up to ridicule.

After verdict for the plaintiff upon all these counts, with entire damages; held by the Court of Error, that the words charged in the first count were libellous; also, that the words charged in the second count were libellous, without the aid of the innuendo; also, that the count was not objectionable, for want of an averment that the libel was published of and concerning the plaintiff as editor of the weekly publication referred to, that being sufficiently shown by the libel itself. Wakley *v.* Healey, 7 Com. B. 591.

held sufficient.[1] (*a*) But where a declaration for slander alleged, that the defendant used words imputing adultery to the plaintiff, a physician; and the words were laid to have been spoken "of him in profession;" but no special damage was laid: after verdict for the plaintiff, judgment was arrested, because such words, merely laid to be spoken of a physician, are not actionable without special damage; and, if they were so spoken as to convey an imputation upon his conduct in his profession, the declaration ought to show how the speaker connected the imputation with the professional conduct.[2]

[1] Camp *v.* Martin, 23 Conn. 86.

[2] Ayer *v.* Craven, 2 Ad. & Ell. 2.

(*a*) A count in slander, after an indictment that the plaintiff was an apothecary, and had attended the defendant's child, stated the words to be, "He killed my child; it was the saline injection that did it;" innuendo, that the plaintiff had been guilty of feloniously killing the child by improperly and with gross ignorance, and with gross and culpable want of caution, administering the injection. Plea, that the plaintiff had professed to be an apothecary, and the defendant, upon the faith of his being qualified as such, suffered him to attend the child; and the plaintiff did injudiciously, indiscreetly, and improperly, and contrary to his duty in that behalf, administer a saline injection to the child, who thereupon afterwards died; and that the death was caused or accelerated by the injection. Held, that the words contained a charge of manslaughter, and that the plea, which must be taken to confess the words in the sense imputed to them in the count, contained no justification of the words so understood. A second count was upon the following words: "He made up the medicines wrong through jealousy, because I would not allow him to use his own judgment;" innuendo, that the plaintiff had intentionally, and from jealousy and improper motives, made up the medicines which he had administered to the child in a wrong and improper manner; and that such medicines were, to the plaintiff's knowledge, unfit and improper to be administered to the child. Held, that the count was bad; as the words, which were charged to have been spoken of the plaintiff in his profession, did not impute any indictable offence. A third count was upon the following words: "Mr. P. told me that he (the plaintiff) had given my child too much mercury, and poisoned it; otherwise it would have got well." The plea justified so much only of the words as imputed the giving too much mercury. Held bad; inasmuch as the words attempted to be justified were not slanderous. Edsall *v.* Russell, 4 M. & Gr. 1090.

22. Words are also actionable, which are written or spoken falsely of a party in connection with his *trade* or *business*, as well as office or profession. And the principle is, that words spoken of a merchant, trader, or person engaged in business, in which *credit is usual*, making imputations against his credit, are actionable; and it is not confined to merchants and traders exclusively. Thus words imputing insolvency, when spoken of one *engaged in the wooden ware business*, are actionable. And an allegation, that the plaintiff is "engaged in the wooden ware business," is equivalent to an averment, that he is a buyer and seller of wooden ware,[1] (see p. 332). So to say of a merchant, "you keep false books, and I can prove it," is actionable.[2] So the plaintiff declared, that he was a farmer and vendor of corn, and that the defendant said of him, as such, "you are a rogue, and a swindling rascal; you delivered me one hundred bushels of oats, worse by sixpence a bushel than I bargained for." Held, actionable, without proof of special damage.[3] So the words, "he has nothing but rotten goods in his shop," with a *colloquium* of the plaintiff's trade, are actionable.[4] And a publication, charging a maltster with using filthy and disgusting water in the malting of grain for brewing, is libellous *per se*.[5] So to say of a blacksmith, in relation to his trade, "he keeps false books, and I can prove it," is actionable.[6] And to say of a tradesman, "If he does not come and make terms with me, I will make a bankrupt of him, and ruin him," is actionable, without proof of special damage.[7] Or to say to a milliner, "Thou art a beggarly fellow, and not worth a groat."[8] So the declaration stated, that the plaintiff was an auctioneer and appraiser, that the defendant had employed him as an appraiser to value certain goods, and that he spoke of him, and his conduct as to such valuation, "He is a damned rascal; he has cheated me

[1] Carpenter *v.* Dennis, 3 Sandf. 305; 1 Blatch. 588.
[2] Backus *v.* Richardson, 5 Johns. 476.
[3] Thomas *v.* Jackson, 10 Moore, 425.
[4] Bennet *v.* Wells, 12 Mod. 420.
[5] White *v.* Delavan, 17 Wend. 49.
[6] Burtch *v.* Nickerson, 17 Johns. 217.
[7] Brown *v.* Smith, 13 Com. B. 596.
[8] Simpson *v.* Barlow, 12 Mod. 591.

out of £100 on the valuation." Held sufficient, after verdict.[1] So "He is a rogue, a papist dog, and a pitiful fellow, and never a rogue in town has a bonfire before his door but he," spoken of a merchant who made a bonfire at the coronation of King James, was held to be actionable.[2] So to say of a tradesman, "he is a sorry, pitiful fellow, and a rogue; he compounded his debts at 5*s.* in the pound;" although there be no *colloquium* of his trade.[3] So the words "Thou art a broken fellow," spoken of a pawnbroker, with proof of special damage, are actionable.[4] So the following words, alleged to have been spoken of and concerning the plaintiff, and of and concerning his trade and occupation, as clerk for the firm of the defendant and his partner: "Your man (the plaintiff) is plotting to blow me (the defendant) and the concern (the firm) up, and I believe you have a hand in it," are actionable *per se*, when connected by the *colloquium* and innuendo with the plaintiff's occupation as clerk, without an averment of special damage; and that they were spoken in the present time makes no difference.[5]

23. But it has been held, that the plaintiff in an action of slander, who participates in the risks of a mercantile concern, but does not share in the profits, shall not recover for injury to his character as a merchant, without showing special damages.[6] And, in an action for words charging fraud to another as a trader, it must be proved that he was actually in trade at the time the words were spoken.[7] So, an action for saying of a merchant, "he has brought a false bill of lading for half the cargo (meaning the lading of a particular ship) already," whereby he was injured as such merchant, and lost the confidence of several persons, (without naming them); was held not maintainable, and judgment accordingly arrested, because the words did not themselves impute any crime.[8] So, in an action for falsely

[1] Bryant *v.* Loxton, 11 Moore, 344.
[2] Peak *v.* Meker, 3 Mod. 103.
[3] Stanton *v.* Smith, 2 Ld. Raym. 1480.
[4] Anon. 12. Mod. 344.
[5] Ware *v.* Clowney, 24 Ala. 707.
[6] Davis *v.* Ruff, Cheves, 17.
[7] Harris *v.* Burley, 8 N. H. 216.
[8] Feise *v.* Linder, 3 Bos. & P. 372.

and maliciously giving information that the plaintiff was about to offer for sale unwholesome meal, the plaintiff cannot prove an injury to his reputation, without an averment that the defendant stated that the plaintiff knew the meal to be unwholesome.[1]

24. In reference to the *allegations* in actions of this nature, and the proofs offered in support of them, it has been held, that the words spoken of a tradesman, "he is a cheat," are not actionable, without a *colloquium* of his trade;[2] but that words affecting the pecuniary credit of a merchant need not be averred nor proved to have been used in relation to his occupation as a merchant; for in their nature they strike at the root of mercantile character.[3] And where the plaintiff, in an action for a libel, averred, that the libel was published of him as a merchant, and the Court instructed the jury, that the words were actionable without proof of special damage, they having been spoken of the plaintiff as a merchant; and it did not appear upon the bill of exceptions, whether the plaintiff was a merchant in the correct sense of that term, or a mere trader and retail dealer in merchandise; it was held that, if such distinction could in any way be important, the court would intend that the plaintiff was a merchant in the sense requisite for the purposes of the action,[4] (see p. 330). So, in an action for words spoken of a man in the way of his trade, it is not necessary to prove the whole of the words laid in the declaration, unless the words not proved alter the sense of those that are.[5] But a declaration, stating that the defendant published of the plaintiff a false and malicious libel, purporting thereby that the plaintiff's beer was of a bad quality, and deficient in measure, whereby he was injured in his credit and business, was held bad on general demurrer.[6]

25. Some other miscellaneous examples may be cited, of actions brought for imputations upon the plaintiff in connec-

[1] Hemmenway *v.* Woods, 1 Pick. 524.

[2] Bennet *v.* Wells, 12 Mod. 420.

[3] Davis *v.* Ruff, Cheves, 17.

[4] Gates *v.* Bowker, 18 Vt. 23.

[5] Orpwood *v.* Parkes, 12 Moore, 492.

[6] Wood *v.* Brown, 1 Marsh, 522.

tion with his business or occupation. Thus saying of *an innkeeper*, "he is a bankrupt, he will be in the Gazette in a twelvemonth, he is a pauper," is actionable, though he be not liable to the bankrupt laws.[1] Or, "He owes more money than he is worth, he is run away and is broke," spoken of *a husbandman*.[2] So it is actionable to say of *a farmer*, falsely and maliciously, that "the sheriff will sell him out one of these days, and claims against him not sued will be lost."[3] So, "He is broken and run away, and never will return again," spoken of *a carpenter*, is actionable.[4] But not the words, "He has received forty days' wages for work that might have been done in ten days, and is a rogue for his pains."[5] So to say of *a watchmaker*, that "he is a bungler, and cannot make a good piece of work," is not actionable.[6] (*a*)

[1] Whittaker *v.* Bradley, 7 D. & Ry. 649.
[2] Dobson *v.* Thornestone, 3 Mod. 112.
[3] Phillips *v.* Hoeffer, 1 Penn. 62.
[4] Chapman *v.* Lamphire, 3 Mod. 155.
[5] Lancaster *v.* French, 2 Str. 797.
[6] Redman *v.* Pyne, 1 Mod. 19.

(*a*) By the 6 & 7 Vict. c. 86, § 21, the proprietor of a hackney-carriage is required to retain in his possession the license of every driver, &c., employed by him, while such driver, &c., remains in his service. A declaration in case stated, that the plaintiff obtained a driver's license under the act; that he was employed by the defendant, a proprietor of a hackney-carriage, and, under the provisions of the act, delivered the license to him; and that, while the license remained in the defendant's possession, the latter wrongfully and unjustly wrote in ink upon the license certain words, purporting, and then being intended by the defendant, to give a character of the plaintiff as an unfit person to act as a driver of hackney-carriages, that is to say, &c., &c.; by reason whereof the license became defaced and wholly useless to the plaintiff, and the plaintiff was prevented from obtaining employment as a driver, &c. Held, on motion in arrest of judgment, that the action was maintainable; that, without an allegation of malice, the declaration was sufficient; and that case was the proper form. Hurrell *v.* Ellis, 2 Com. B. 295.

A declaration stated, that the plaintiff was a trader, and employed by the board of ordnance to relay the entrance of their office with new asphalte, and the defendant falsely said of him, in his trade, and in reference to the work: "The old materials have been relaid by you in the asphalte work executed in the front of the ordnance office, and I have seen the work done." Innuendo, that the plaintiff had been guilty of dishonesty in the conduct of his said trade, by laying down again the old asphalte, which had been before used at the entrance of the ordnance office, instead of new asphalte, according to his contract. Held, on motion to arrest the judgment, that the declaration was sufficient, and the innuendo not too large, as it put no new sense on the words, but only imputed intention to the speaker. Baboneau *v.* Farrell, 28 Eng. L. & Eq. 339.

CHAPTER XI.

PUBLICATION.

1. PUBLICATION is necessary, to constitute an actionable slander or libel. It is said "publication is nothing more than doing the last act for the accomplishment of the mischief intended by it."[1] "The moment a man delivers a libel from his hands, and ceases to have control over it, there is an end of his *locus penitentiæ;* the *injuria* is complete, and the libeller may be called upon to answer for his act."[2] Publication, however, (as will be seen,) may take place in a variety of ways, and is subject to no technical rules. And, although publication of a libel must be stated in a declaration, it may be collected from the whole of it, and needs not any technical form of words.[3] So, in an action for slander, an allegation that the words were spoken in the presence and hearing of divers persons, or of certain persons named, is a sufficient setting forth of the publication.[4] So in an action, alleging that the words were spoken in the presence of B., it is sufficient to prove the substance of the words alleged, and the sense in which they were spoken, without proving that they were spoken in the presence of B.[5] And where the declaration alleged, that the defendant spoke the words in the presence and hearing of A. and B., and divers other good citizens of the State; held, the declaration need not specify the names of the "other good citizens." Also, that the words might be proved by any person who heard them, though his name was not mentioned in the declara-

[1] Per Best, J., Rex *v.* Burdett, 4 B. & Ald. 126.

[2] Per Holroyd, J., Rex *v.* Burdett, 4 B. & Ald. 143.

[3] Baldwin *v.* Elphinston, 2 W. Black. 1037.

[4] Burbank *v.* Horn, 39 Maine, 233.

[5] Goodrich *v.* Warner, 21 Conn. 432.

tion.[1] So, where a declaration alleged the words to have been spoken in a discourse with A., in the presence and hearing of others; held, it was not necessary to prove that the words were addressed to A.[2] But it has been held, that the word "publish" is insufficient in a declaration for slander, without charging the words to be spoken *in the presence and hearing of others.*[3]

2. With regard to the *proof* of publication, it may be *direct* or *indirect. Direct* publication may be by actual distribution, by speaking or singing of the libel, or painting a sign over another's door, or taking part in a procession, which carried the plaintiff in effigy.[4] Any one who knowingly circulates a libel publishes it.[5] Indirect proof of publication may be by showing the libel to be in the defendant's handwriting or in his possession. Although it has been said[6] that, *until publication*, possession of a libel is no more than the possession of a man's thoughts.[7] (*a*) And the responsibility of the writer even of a private letter, for the publication of a libel contained therein, is not limited to the consequences of a communication of it to the person to whom the letter is addressed, but extends to the probable consequences of thus putting it in circulation.[8]

3. But, to furnish ground of action, a publication must be *malicious*, and the intent is to be gathered from the paper itself and from the circumstances.[9] If the publication is made without the consent of the writer, the offence is not complete as to him.[10] Thus if a libel be *stolen*, that is no publication.[11]

4. In regard to the proof of publication in particular cases, it is held, that, in an action for a libel contained in a

[1] Bradshaw *v.* Pardue, 12 Geo. 510.
[2] Richardson *v.* Hopkins, 7 Blackf. 116.
[3] Watts *v.* Greenlee, 2 Dev. 115. *Contra*, Burton *v.* Burton, 3 Iowa, 316.
[4] 5 Co. 125; 9, 59 *b.*
[5] Layton *v.* Harris, 3 Harring. 406.
[6] Entick *v.* Carrington, 11 St. Tr. 321
[7] Rex *v.* Almon, 5 Burr. 2689; —— *v.* Beere, 1 Ld. Ray. 417; 12 Vin. 229.
[8] Miller *v.* Butler, 6 Cush. 71.
[9] Schenck *v.* Schenck, 3 Harring. 406.
[10] Weir *v.* Hoss, 6 Ala. 881.
[11] Barrow *v.* Lewellin. Hob. 62.

(*a*) See *Parties.*

newspaper, the publication is proved by the production of a newspaper, corresponding in title, &c., with that described in the affidavit lodged at the stamp-office.[1] So a copy of the newspaper in which a libel is published, with proof of the defendant's acknowledgment that he had handed it to the editor for insertion, is proper evidence of publication.[2] (*a*) Or, that the defendant accounted for the stamp-duties of the paper.[3] So, in an action for publishing a libel, evidence sufficient to go to a jury is furnished, by proof that a libel was actually published; that it was a printed paper, since destroyed; that it corresponded with a printed paper produced; and that the defendant printed a paper corresponding with that produced, and sent three hundred to a shop from whence a person actually publishing the libel procured it; and that the libel was on that occasion taken from a parcel apparently containing three hundred.[4] So, where a witness swore that he was a printer, and had been in the office of the defendant, where a paper called the Ontario Messenger was printed, and saw it printed there, and the paper produced by the plaintiff was, he believed, printed with the types used in the defendant's office; this was held to be *primâ facie* evidence of the publication by the defendant.[5]

5. A sealed letter, addressed and delivered to a wife, and containing a libel on her husband, is in law a published libel.[6] So a letter containing a libel was proved to be in the handwriting of the defendant, to have been addressed to a party in Scotland, to have been received at the post-office at C.

1 Mayne *v.* Fletcher, 9 B. & C. 382.
2 Woodburn *v.* Miller, Cheves, 194.
3 Cook *v.* Ward, 6 Bing. 409.
4 Johnson *v.* Hudson, 7 Ad. & Ell. 233.
5 Southwick *v.* Stevens, 10 Johns. 443.
6 Schenck *v.* Schenck, 1 Spenc. 208; Wenman *v.* Ash, 13 Com. B. 836.

(*a*) In a criminal prosecution, it appeared that the libel was published in a newspaper printed in another State, but which usually circulated in a county in the State where the prosecution was instituted, and the number containing the libel was actually received and circulated in such county. Held, competent and conclusive evidence of a publication within such county. Commonwealth *v.* Blanding, 3 Pick. 304.

from the post-office at H., and to have been then forwarded from C. to London to be forwarded to Scotland, and it was produced at the trial with the proper postmarks, and with the seal broken. Held, sufficient *primâ facie* evidence that it reached the person to whom it was addressed, and of a publication to him.[1] And the transmission of a libellous letter by the defendant to his correspondent is a publication.[2] So, if the alleged libel be contained in a letter sent by the defendant to the plaintiff, evidence that the letter was in the handwriting of the defendant, and that he read it aloud in the presence of several persons before it was sent, is sufficient to authorize the reading of the letter to the jury.[3] Or the reading aloud to a stranger of a letter by the writer.[4] So, if a man deliver by mistake a libellous paper out of his study, it is said he would probably be held liable civilly to the parties who suffered by his carelessness; although there is no publication which would maintain an indictment.[5] And it is held that *confidence* between the witness and the defendant, *an injunction of secrecy*, &c., are not inconsistent with publication.[6] But throwing a sealed letter, addressed to the plaintiff or a third person, into the enclosure of another, who delivers it to the plaintiff himself, is not a publication; even though the plaintiff afterwards repeated the contents publicly, and the defendant avowed himself the author. Otherwise, had such third person read the letter, or, on hearing of it, required the plaintiff to do so.[7]

6. If the words have been spoken, or if the libel has been published, *in a foreign language*, or in characters not understood by those who read or see them, there is no publication.[8]

[1] Warren *v.* Warren, 1 Cromp. M. & R. 250.
[2] Ward *v.* Smith, 6 Bing. 749.
[3] M'Coombs *v.* Tuttle, 5 Blackf. 431.
[4] Snyder *v.* Andrews, 6 Barb. 43.
[5] Mayne *v.* Fletcher, 4 M. & Ry. 312 *a*; Rex *v.* Paine, 5 Mod. 167. And see Algernon Sidney's case, 3 St. Tr. 807, and 4 St. Tr. 197.
[6] M'Gowen *v.* Monifee, 7 Monr. 314.
[7] Fonville *v.* Nèice, Dudley, 303.
[8] 2 Stark. Ev. 844; 2 Bouv. Inst. 15.

CHAPTER XII.

PARTIES; INNUENDO AND COLLOQUIUM; JOINT PARTIES; CORPORATIONS AND PARTNERS; HUSBAND AND WIFE; PRINCIPAL AND AGENT.

1. WITH regard to *the parties*, by and against whom an action for libel or slander may be maintained; it is the general rule, that the words must have been spoken *of the plaintiff.*[1] Thus it is held, that courts will not allow two persons to litigate a suit for a libel which consists in an attack upon the chastity of *a third person*, not a party.[2] So the words, "all the bravery you ever showed was in sleeping with your sisters," will not support an action for slander by one of the unmarried sisters of the person to whom they were addressed in presence of others, without proof of extrinsic facts, to show that the speaker meant to charge sexual intercourse with such sisters.[3] So a mother cannot maintain an action for calling her daughter a bastard; although the charge implies her own guilt.[4] But the following written charge: "Charge 4. Refusing to correct George C. in his statement as a witness before Esq. B., when I believe he, J. C., knew his (George's) statement was not true," when shown by proper innuendoes to have been applied to the testimony of George C. on the trial of a certain cause; is a libel on George C.[5] And the evidence to prove the application to the plaintiff will not always be restricted to the time of the libel or slander itself. (*a*) Thus, in an action against the

[1] Harvey *v.* Coffin, 5 Blackf. 566.

[2] Longhead *v.* Bartholomew, Wright, 90.

[3] Millison *v.* Sutton, 1 Cart. 508; 1 Smith, 364.

[4] Maxwell *v.* Allison, 11 S. & R. 343.

[5] Coombs *v.* Rose, 8 Blackf. 155.

(*a*) Where the plaintiff proved that the defendant spoke certain words of her by the name of *Mrs. Edwards*, the defendant was not allowed to

editor of a newspaper for a libel, the plaintiff may show articles in subsequent numbers of the same paper, for the purpose of proving that he was the person intended to be defamed.[1]

2. And the law requires an averment in the declaration, that the plaintiff is the party referred to, more especially where there is any ambiguity in the words. Where the declaration does not attempt by a *colloquium* or innuendo to give a particular application to the language used; and, reading the words in their ordinary sense, it cannot be said with reasonable certainty, that they contain any libellous imputation on the plaintiff; the action cannot be maintained.[2] Thus, where there had been a quarrel between A. and the father of B., who had been accused of stealing a tray of biscuits, and A. said, in the hearing of B., and of other persons, that, if they did not look out, *he would make the tray of biscuits roar;* it was held, in an action of B. against A., that averments should have been laid in the declaration, connecting B. with this language of A., and that evidence of the understanding of those present was admissible in support of those averments.[3] So a declaration stated, that the defendant, contriving, &c., did print and publish of and concerning the plaintiff a libel, containing the false and scandalous matter following; without alleging that that matter was of and concerning the plaintiff; and then set out the libel, which, on the face of it, did not manifestly appear to relate to the plaintiff, and there was no innuendo to connect it with the plaintiff. Held, upon writ of error, that the count was bad.[4]

3. But it has been held, that, if a plaintiff has omitted in his declaration to state that the libel was spoken of himself,

[1] White *v.* Sayward, 33 Maine, 322.
[2] Capel *v.* Jones, 4 Com. B. 259.
[3] Briggs *v.* Byrd, 11 Ired. 353; Harper *v.* Delp, 3 Ind. 225.
[4] Clement *v.* Fisher, 7 B. & C. 459.

---

show, that in other conversations he had used similar words respecting *another Mrs. Edwards.* Patterson *v.* Edwards, 2 Gilm. 720.

he may supply the same by parol evidence.[1] As by the understanding of those who heard it.[2] And a count in slander for words spoken in the third person will be held sufficient after verdict, where the allegation of them is preceded by a *colloquium*, (*a*) and from the whole count it appears with reasonable certainty that they were spoken *of and concerning the plaintiff*, though there be no formal and direct averment of that fact; and, if there be an allegation that the words were spoken *of the plaintiff*, the declaration will be held good after verdict, and it seems even on demurrer, without any *colloquium*.[3] (*a*)

4. But when the words are not in themselves applicable to the plaintiff, no introductory averment or innuendo can give such an application. Thus a declaration, after reciting that the plaintiff was employed in supplying fresh water to ships at H., and had, for that purpose, fitted up a schooner with wooden tanks, and that, the ship M. being at H., the plaintiff conveyed fresh water to the M. in the tanks; complained that the defendant published, of and concerning the plaintiff in his said employment, and concerning the water so supplied to the M., a statement (set forth); that persons on board the M. had become ill soon after leaving H., where they had taken in fresh water, which illness was occasioned by the water; that the water was run into a copper tank, whence the casks were filled alongside; that the poison was imbibed from the tank, and that it behoved the authorities to order its removal, and replace it with an iron one; thereby meaning that the plaintiff had been guilty of supplying bad and unwholesome water to the M.; judgment was arrested.[4]

5. Though defamatory matter may appear to apply only to *a class* of individuals; yet, if the descriptions are capable of being by innuendo shown to be directly applicable to any one individual of that class, an action may be maintained

[1] Newbraugh *v.* Curry, Wright, 511.
[2] Briggs *v.* Byrd, 11 Ired. 353.
[3] Nestle *v.* Van Slyck, 2 Hill, 282.
[4] Solomon *v.* Lawson, 8 Ad. & Ell. N. S. 823.

(*a*) See *Colloquium*.

by him. In such case, the innuendo does not extend the sense of the defamatory matter, but merely points out the particular individual, to whom matter, in itself defamatory, does in fact apply. Therefore, after verdict, a declaration that the plaintiff was owner of a factory in Ireland, and that the defendant published of him and of the said factory a libel, imputing that "in some of the Irish factories (meaning thereby the plaintiff's factory)" cruelties were practised; though there was no allegation, otherwise connecting the libel with the plaintiff; was held good.[1]

6. But where a declaration for libel alleged, that the plaintiff was the editor of a newspaper called the Ogdensburgh Times, and that the defendant published of and concerning him, as editor of said paper, the following words: "We shall from time to time, &c., notwithstanding the denial of the ribald convict and recorded libeller who edits the Times," meaning the plaintiff, the editor of the aforesaid newspaper, called the Ogdensburgh Times, &c.; held, the declaration was bad, as it contained no sufficient averment, showing that the libel referred to and was intended to designate the plaintiff.[2] So the members of a *hose company* cannot maintain a joint action for a charge in a newspaper, that members of a company, not calling names, had committed a theft; the members not being partners, nor in a condition to suffer pecuniary injury from the charge, as a company.[3] So the defendant published in a newspaper the following advertisement: "To bill-brokers and others. — Caution. — Reward. — Whereas information has been given to me that attempts have been made to obtain the discount of a bill of exchange, bearing date, London, May 26th, 1826, and purporting to be drawn by one John Stockley (the plaintiff) upon, and to be accepted by the Dowager Lady P. Turner, for £6,000 with interest, payable twelve months after date, to the order of the said J. Stockley — I do

[1] Le Fann *v.* Malcomson, 1 Clark & Fin. N. S. 637.

[2] Tyler *v.* Tillotson, 2 Hill, 507.

[3] Giraud *v.* Beach, 3 E. D. Smith, 337.

hereby give notice, on behalf of the Dowager Lady P. T., that she has not accepted such bill, and that, if her name should appear on any such instrument, the same has been forged, or her handwriting to the said acceptance of the said bill, if genuine, has been obtained by fraud, in total ignorance on her part of the intended effect of the signature. Any person who will give positive information to me of the party in possession of the said instrument shall be handsomely rewarded. Thomas Binns." Held, that, in the absence of an innuendo, that the plaintiff was the person designed to be charged with the forgery or fraud, the action could not be supported.[1] So in an action of slander for charging the plaintiff with arson, the words laid were, "I next morning saw a track going to and returning from the house. The toes turned in; and I know of but one man who owes me enmity enough to do such a thing, and you know whom I mean. B. D." (the plaintiff). Held, that the words were not of themselves actionable; and, as there was no averment of any matter of fact, tending to identify the plaintiff as the person who made the tracks, the count was demurrable.[2]

7. The usual requirements of the law, in reference to *the party* to whom the libel or slander relates, may be waived or dispensed with by the implied admissions of the parties. Thus where, upon the trial of an action for libel, the counsel on both sides said, that the only question of fact was in regard to the amount of damages, and a verdict was found for the plaintiff; it was held that the defendant could not object, as a ground for a new trial, that the plaintiff had not proved that the libel related to himself, as alleged in the innuendoes.[3]

8. Upon the point, whether a *joint* liability or claim may grow out of slanderous or libellous words; it is held that a joint action cannot be maintained against two or more persons for *slander*, except perhaps in case of *conspiracy*;[4] other-

[1] Stockley *v.* Clement, 12 Moore, 376.

[2] Robinson *v.* Drummond, 24 Ala. 174.

[3] Child *v.* Homer, 13 Pick. 503.

[4] Forsyth *v.* Edmiston, 5 Duer, 653.

wise for a libel.[1] And, where two persons participated in the composition of a libellous letter written by one of them, which was afterwards put into the post-office, and sent by mail to the person to whom it was addressed; such participation is competent and sufficient evidence to prove a publication by both.[2]

9. A *corporation aggregate* may maintain an action for a libel concerning their trade or business, by which they have suffered special damage.[3] So *partners* may join in an action for a libel published of them in the way of their trade.[4] And a publication, purporting to give information as to the credit and standing of a mercantile firm, and charging one member thereof with dishonesty, is libellous *per se*, and an action will lie by the partners for the injury to the business and credit of the firm.[5] But it is held no slander of a firm, to say that one of the partners is broke. The right of action on such words accrues to the individual.[6] (a)

[1] Webb *v.* Cecil, 9 B. Mon. 198.

[2] Miller *v.* Butler, 6 Cush. 71.

[3] Trenton Insurance Co. *v.* Perrine, 3 Zabr. 402.

[4] Forster *v.* Lawson, 11 Moore, 360; Le Fann *v.* Malcomson, 1 Cl. & Finn. N. S. 637.

[5] Taylor *v.* Church, 1 E. D. Smith, 279.

[6] Davis *v.* Ruff, Cheves, 17.

(a) Declaration, that the plaintiff was a banker in partnership with A. and B., and that the defendant falsely and maliciously spoke words of the plaintiff, and of him in his said trade, imputing to him insolvency; by means whereof the plaintiff was injured in his good name, and divers persons believed him to be indigent, and refused to deal with him in his said trade; and one C. withdrew his account from the bank of the plaintiff and his said partners. Plea in abatement, that the plaintiff carried on the said business jointly and undividedly with A. and B., and not otherwise; and that all the damage in the declaration mentioned accrued to A. and B. jointly with the plaintiff, and not to him alone; and that, at the time of the commencement of the suit, A. and B. were living, &c. Held bad, because it was pleaded in terms to the damage, and not to the cause of action; and the special damage to the partnership was not so essentially the cause of action, that without it the action could not have been maintained. And it was doubted, whether the declaration would not have been bad on special demurrer, for blending a cause of action vested in the plaintiff singly with a cause common to the partners. Robinson *v.* Marchant, 7 Ad. & Ell. N. S. 918.

And, where two persons were charged in a bill in equity, as having fraudulently altered certain instruments, without specifying the person who did it; it was held, in an action of slander by one of the parties against the complainants in the bill in equity, that either of the parties charged might sue, but that the charge in the bill was not a libel.[1] (*a*) And on the other hand a charge that A. has committed forgery is supported by proof that A. and B. have committed it.[2]

10. A *wife* may join with her husband, in an action for saying she keeps a bawdy-house.[3] Or for calling the wife a whore, and "the defendant's whore;" and the declaration may conclude *ad damnum ipsorum;* and need not allege special damages.[4] So, in case by husband and wife, for slanderous words spoken of the wife, brought by A., and B. his wife, where the declaration stated, "whereby the said A. lost," &c.; and the plea of justification was, "as to the words complained of being spoken against B., wife of C.;" it was held that there were proper parties to the action.[5]

[1] Forbes *v.* Johnson, 11 B. Mon. 48.
[2] Nichols *v.* Hayes, 13 Conn. 155.
[3] Grove *v.* Hart, Sayer, 33.
[4] Baldwin *v.* Flower, 3 Mod. 120.
[5] Long *v.* Long, 4 Barr, 29.

Where a declaration in slander by J. T. and another averred, that, in a discourse of and concerning the plaintiffs and their business as partners, the defendant said, "J. T. & Co. (meaning the plaintiffs) are down;" held, on special demurrer, that the declaration was bad, for want of a direct allegation that the words charged were spoken of and concerning the plaintiffs, &c., and such defect cannot be supplied by an *innuendo.* But the declaration is clearly sufficient in substance, and would therefore be held good on general demurrer, and, had the declaration averred that the *colloquium* was *with the plaintiffs*, and that the words were spoken in the first person, as "you," &c., it would have been held good even on special demurrer, and without an *innuendo.* Titus *v.* Follet, 2 Hill, 318.

(*a*) Where a publication treats of the manner in which a particular business is conducted, by two individuals carrying on business under the name of a firm, and one of the firm brings an action alleging the publication to be *a libel of and concerning him in his trade and business*, and that its object is to impoverish and ruin *him;* a plea of justification is an admission that the plaintiff is one of the firm. Fidler *v.* Delavan, 20 Wend. 57.

11. A recovery by the husband, for slander of himself and wife, is not a bar to another action by the wife, in which the husband is joined as a nominal plaintiff.[1]

12. Husband and wife cannot, it seems, maintain a joint action for charging them with a crime, which by law a wife cannot commit in company with her husband. But it has been held, that, though the words "A. and his wife stole a thousand dollars in gold" will not support an action of slander by the wife with her husband, as they import a charge of stealing in his presence; yet, if other words, laid in the same count, as spoken at the same time, are actionable, the count is good.[2] (*a*)

13. A party becomes liable to an action for libel or slander — more particularly the former — by any *agency*, direct or indirect, in its publication. In this as in other torts, a liability may grow out of the relation of master and servant, or principal and agent. (*b*) Thus it is held, that the proprie-

[1] Bash *v.* Sommer, 20 Penn. 159. [2] Ibid.

(*a*) In an action of slander by husband and wife, for charging her with having had sexual intercourse with the defendant; it is not necessary to aver that the plaintiffs were husband and wife at the time the words were uttered, if the law punishes both adultery and fornication. Benaway *v.* Conyne, 3 Chand. 214.

And, in general, in an action for slander of a wife, it is not necessary to prove that the plaintiffs were husband and wife at the time of the slander, if it is shown that they were married at the time of bringing the suit. Spencer *v.* M'Masters, 16 Ill. 405.

Where an action is brought *against* husband and wife, for a libel by the wife, no smaller damages are to be assessed, than would be legally recoverable if the libel had been published by her while sole, and the action had been against her alone. Austin *v.* Wilson, 4 Cush. 273.

In a suit against husband and wife, for words spoken by the wife, evidence of the husband's efforts to prevent the circulation of the slander is not admissible in mitigation of damages. Yeates *v.* Reed, 4 Blackf. 463.

And it is not competent for the defendants to prove, that circumstances relating to the plaintiff's conduct were communicated to the husband, before the slanderous words were uttered. Petrie *v.* Rose, 5 Watts & Serg. 364.

(*b*) "When a libel is produced, written in a man's own hand, he is taken

tor or publisher of a newspaper is responsible for whatever appears in its columns. It is not necessary to show, that he knew of the pulication or authorized it.[1] So, although inserted in his absence by persons employed in his office, and without his knowledge or consent.[2] Or even by an agent, to whom he had given express instructions to publish nothing exceptionable, personal, or abusive, which might be brought in by the author of the libel.[3] So notwithstanding the libel is accompanied with the name of the author.[4] But it is held, that an action cannot be maintained against the publisher of a newspaper, if he has no knowledge at the time of publication that the article is libellous. Hence, if he publish an article, which he believes to be a fictitious narrative or mere fancy-sketch, and does not know that it is applicable to any one, he cannot be held responsible, although it was intended, by the writer, to be libellous, and to apply to the plaintiff. In such case, the writer only is answerable.[5] (a) And it is proper to admit evidence of what

[1] Huff v. Bennett, 4 Sandf. 120.
[2] Dunn v. Hall, 1 Smith, 228.
[3] Dunn v. Hall, 1 Cart. 344.
[4] Dole v. Lyon, 10 Johns. 447.
[5] Smith v. Ashley, 11 Met. 367.

---

in the *mainer*, and that throws the proof upon him; and if he cannot produce the composer, the verdict will be against him." Per Holt, C. J., Rex v. Beere, 1 Ld. Raym. 417.

A defendant has been held liable to an action, upon proof of buying a copy of the paper at the regular office, which paper purports on its face to be the property of the defendant. Fry v. Bennett, 4 Duer, 247.

So where a book is purchased from an agent in the usual course of trade, the principal is liable. Bac. Abr. *Libel*, 458. Even though the latter lives at a distance from his shop. Rex v. Dodd, 2 Sess. Cas. 33. And has been long bed-ridden. Rex v. Nutt, Barnard, 308.

By a recent English statute, (6 & 7 Vict. c. 96, § 2,) in an action for a libel contained in any periodical publication, the defendant may plead that it was inserted without actual malice or gross negligence; and that he had publicly apologized or offered to apologize therefor; and he may then pay into Court a sum of money by way of amends. See also 15 & 16 Vict. c. 76, § 70.

(a) The proprietor and publisher of a newspaper, being sued for a libel, filed a specification of defence, stating that he should prove, that the publication complained of was inserted in his paper, during his absence, without

was said by the defendant in directing the printing, in order to disprove actual malice in the publication, and to influence the question of damages.[1] So in an action for a libel contained in a letter; proof that it was written by the defendant's daughter, who was authorized to make out his bills and write his general letters of business, is not sufficient, unless it can be shown that such libel was written with the knowledge, or by the procurement of the defendant.[2]

14. On the other hand, a party may maintain an action for a libel, though it consist of a charge made immediately *against* his agent, but imputing to him some complicity in the agent's conduct. Thus the defendant published of the plaintiffs, coal-merchants, what purported to be a report of an inquiry before a board of guardians respecting the fraudulent conduct of the plaintiffs' agent, who, in performance of a contract for "best coals," had delivered at the workhouse coals of an inferior description, and (by falsifying the weighing-machine by means of a wedge) deficient in weight. The libel commenced, "The way in which Messrs. P. (the plaintiffs) do things at Guildford. Inserting the wedge;"

[1] Taylor *v.* Church, 4 Seld. 452. [2] Harding *v.* Greening, 1 Moore, 477.

---

his consent or knowledge, by accident, and without the knowledge or agency of any person in his employment. On the trial it appeared, that the defendant had employed F. to print the newspaper; that F. employed several workmen under him; and that S., one of F.'s workmen, set up the libellous article in the absence of the defendant, and of the editor of the paper. The defendant proposed to ask a witness "If at or about the time S. printed the article or set it up, he" (the witness) "heard him express ill-will towards the plaintiff, and if so, what he said." Held, the question could not be put. Goodrich *v.* Stone, 11 Met. 486.

In the trial of an action against the proprietor of a newspaper, for a libel published therein by his agent, in his absence, and without his knowledge or consent, the plaintiff may give in evidence an article published in a subsequent number of the same newspaper, with the defendant's knowledge and consent, justifying the publication of the article complained of as libellous, though such article was not published until after the action was commenced. Ibid.

and ended with a recommendation of one of the guardians to "have nothing more to do with Messrs. P.," — innuendo, "the defendant meaning thereby that the plaintiffs were cognizant of and had sanctioned improper and fraudulent conduct by their agent at Guildford, and were accustomed to carry on their said trade there improperly and fraudulently." The defendant pleaded a justification, following the innuendo, and saying that the coals delivered, as mentioned in the libel, were inferior in quality, as the plaintiffs well knew, and deficient in weight. The Judge ruled, that, the defendant having by his plea alleged that the fraud of their agent was sanctioned by the plaintiffs, he must prove it; and he told the jury that they must find for the plaintiffs, unless they were satisfied that the defendant had shown some complicity on their part in the misconduct and fraud imputed to their agent. The jury having found for the plaintiffs; held, that there was no misdirection, and that the libel imputed personal misconduct and fraud to the plaintiffs.[1]

15. While a plaintiff may make a claim for libel or slander upon his agent, the defendant may also seek to justify on the ground of agency. But such plea of justification is required to set forth the facts with precision and accuracy. Thus the declaration stated, that the plaintiff was lawfully possessed of mines and ore gotten and to be gotten from them, and was in treaty for the sale of the ore, and that the defendant published a malicious, injurious, and unlawful advertisement, cautioning persons against purchasing the ore, &c., whereby he was prevented from selling; to which the defendant pleaded in justification, that the adventurers of, or persons having an interest or shares in the mines, thought it their duty to caution persons against purchasing the ore, &c., (pursuing the words of the advertisement). This plea was held ill on special demurrer; 1st, because it did not disclose the names of the adventurers, or who they were; and 2d, because it did not show that the defendant,

[1] Prior *v.* Wilson, 19 Com. B. 95.

in publishing the advertisement, acted under the direction of the adventurers.[1]

16. With regard to the right of action *after the death* of a party, it is held in Massachusetts, that an action on the case for a libel does not survive.[2]

[1] Rowe *v.* Roach, 1 M. & S. 304.

[2] Nettleton *v.* Dinehart, 5 Cush. 544.

CHAPTER XIII.

MALICE, NECESSITY OF, AND EVIDENCE TO PROVE; REPETITION OF SLANDER, ETC.

1. THE very definition of libel or slander, so far as it constitutes a *civil* injury, implies *malicious falsehood*, and the element or ingredient of malice is therefore necessarily involved in all discussions or decisions relating to it. It becomes important, however, in the regular course of our inquiry, to speak more particularly of this special point.

2. With reference to libel and slander it is said, (although the remark is also of general applicability,) that malice does not necessarily mean what must proceed from a spiteful, malignant, or revengeful disposition, but a conduct injurious to another, though proceeding from an ill-regulated mind, not sufficiently cautious before it occasions an injury to another. In vulgar acceptation, malice is a desire of revenge, or a settled anger against a person, but in its legal sense it means *the doing any act without just cause.*[1] "A wrongful act, purposely done, is malicious."[2] But is it also said, in restriction, rather than enlargement of the meaning of this term: "We must go further and see, not merely whether expressions are *angry*, but whether they are *malicious*."[3]

3. With regard to the nature of the malice which must be proved in the action for libel or slander, it is said, in slander there are two sorts of malice, one in law, the other

[1] Jones *v.* Givin, Gilb. Cas. 130. See also Duncan *v.* Thwaites, 3 B. & C. 584; Commonwealth *v.* Bonner, 9 Met. 410; Commonwealth *v.* Snelling, 15 Pick. 337. (See chap. 8, § 24.)

[2] Per Thomas, J., Kenney *v.* McLaughlin, 5 Gray, 5.

[3] Per Tindal, C. J., Shipley *v.* Todhunter, 7 C. & P. 580.

in fact.[1] The distinction between malice *in fact*, in actions for slander, and malice *in law*, is, that the first implies a desire and intention to injure, while the second may exist in connection with an honest and laudable purpose. The second is sufficient to support the action, the first may be further shown in aggravation of the charge and to enhance the damages.[2] Whether matter written or printed by one concerning another is libellous, depends not upon the *intention* of the former to injure the latter, as matter of fact for the jury, but upon the *tendency* of the publication, as matter of law for the Court, to produce the injurious effect.[3] (*a*) The defendant is presumed to intend the natural consequence of his own act.[4] In other words, malice (partly as involved in falsehood) [5] is *conclusively implied* from the deliberate making of a slanderous charge or libellous publication, until explained or justified, excused or extenuated.[6] It is said to be *a conclusion of law*, which the plaintiff is not required to prove, nor the defendant permitted to deny; except in the single case, when the publication would be *privileged*, if not proved by the plaintiff to be in fact malicious. (*b*) In other cases, the denial of malice forms an

[1] Bromage *v.* Prosser, 6 Dow. & R. 296; Jellison *v.* Goodwin, 43 Maine, 287.

[2] Jellison *v.* Goodwin, 43 Maine, 287; 4 B. & C. 246.

[3] Fisher *v.* Clement, 5 Man. & Ry. 730; 10 B. & C. 472.

[4] Haire *v.* Wilson, 9 B. & C. 643; 4 Man. & Ry. 605.

[5] Hudson *v.* Garner, 22 Mis. 423.

[6] Washburn *v.* Cooke, 3 Denio, 110; Yeates *v.* Reed, 4 Blackf. 463; White *v.* Nicholls, 3 How. 266; Bodwell *v.* Osgood, 3 Pick. 379; Usher *v.* Severance, 2 App. 9; Parke *v.* Blackiston, 3 Harring. 373; M'Kee *v.* Ingalls, 4 Scam. 30; Farley *v.* Ranck, 3 W. & S. 554; Byrket *v.* Monohon, 7 Blackf. 83; Parker *v.* Lewis, 2 Greene, 311.

(*a*) It has been remarked upon this subject, perhaps somewhat too unqualifiedly, that "There is no instance of a verdict for a defendant on the ground of want of malice. Numberless occasions must have occurred (particularly in cases where a defendant only repeated what he had before heard, but without naming the author) upon which, if that were a tenable ground, verdicts would have been sought for and obtained; and the absence of any such instance is a proof of what has been the general and universal opinion upon the point." Per Bayley, J., Bromage *v.* Prosser, 4 B. & C. 257.

(*b*) See *Privileged*, &c.

issue, which a jury has no right to determine, and which the Court must therefore reject as immaterial. And allegations in a complaint, relative to the intents and motives of a libellous publication, are not to be deemed material, so as to render it necessary for the defendant to admit or controvert them in his answer.[1]

4. And even in an action for words, constituting *primâ facie* a privileged communication, the defendant's conduct after speaking the words, (as, that he pleaded their truth in justification, and gave no evidence at the trial in support of such plea, and that he refused to admit their falsehood, although the plaintiff offered, if the defendant would so admit, to accept an apology and nominal damages,) may be left to the jury as evidence of express malice. So may the fact, that, after the speaking of the words, the plaintiff, in a judicial proceeding, and in the defendant's presence, gave evidence, imputing fraud to the defendant in a transaction between them antecedent to the speaking of the words.[2] So, if one has reason to believe property is taken under color of claim, the charge of stealing raises a presumption of malice.[3] And a charge of stealing implies malice in the speaker, notwithstanding there is proof that the charge was currently reported and believed in the neighborhood in which the parties resided.[4] So, in an action for words spoken of the plaintiffs in their trade as bankers, it was proved that A. B. met the defendant and said, "I hear that you say that the plaintiffs' bank at M. has stopped. Is it true?" Defendant answered, "Yes, it is; I was told so. It was so reported at C., and nobody would take their bills, and I came to town in consequence of it myself." It was proved that C. D. told the defendant that there was a run upon the plaintiffs' bank at M. Upon this evidence, the Judge, after observing that the defendant did not appear to have been actuated by any ill will against the plaintiffs,

[1] Fry *v.* Bennett, 5 Sandf. 54; Commonwealth *v.* Blanding, 3 Pick. 304; Per Gardiner, J., Howard *v.* Sexton, 4 Comst. 157.

[2] Simpson *v.* Robinson, 12 Ad. & Ell. N. S. 511.

[3] Sexton *v.* Broek, 15 Ark. 345.

[4] Shelton *v.* Simmons, 12 Ala. 466.

directed the jury to find their verdict for the defendant, if they thought the words were not maliciously spoken. Held, upon motion for a new trial, that, although malice was the gist of the action for slander, there were two sorts of malice, malice in fact, and malice in law; the former denoting an act done from ill will towards an individual, the latter a wrongful act intentionally done, without just cause or excuse; and that, in ordinary actions for slander, malice in law was to be inferred from the publishing of the slanderous matter, the act itself being wrongful and intentional, and without just cause or excuse; but, in actions for slander *primâ facie* excusable on account of the cause of publishing the slanderous matter, malice in fact must be proved. Held, therefore, in this case, that the Judge ought first to have left it as a question for the jury, whether the defendant understood A. B. as asking for information, and whether he had uttered the words merely by way of honest advice to A. B. to regulate his conduct; and, if they were of that opinion, then, secondly, whether in so doing he was guilty of any malice in fact.[1]

5. Upon the principle above stated, that malice is *implied;* where the words are actionable, and the plea not guilty, a verdict that "the defendant spoke and published the words in the declaration specified," is a sufficient finding of the malicious intent.[2]

6. A written communication, though not libellous in itself, may become so by extrinsic proof of malice.[3] And testimony, tending to show that the defendant was actuated by a mercenary and selfish purpose, as that he coveted the plaintiff's land, and hoped, by defaming him, to compel him to remove, may be introduced to show actual malice.[4] But, in an action of slander for charging an infant with larceny, evidence of a previous quarrel between the defendant and the plaintiff's father and next friend is inadmissible to prove malice.[5] So, until some of the words have been proved,

[1] Bromage *v.* Prosser, 4 B. & C. 246.
[2] Carlock *v.* Spencer, 2 Eng. 12.
[3] Hart *v.* Reed, 1 B. Mon. 166.
[4] Morgan *v.* Livingston, 2 Rich. 573.
[5] York *v.* Pease, 2 Gray, 282.

evidence of the *quo animo* is inadmissible.[1] (*a*) And the implication of malice may be rebutted, by proof of other parts of the same conversation, explanatory of the alleged slanderous words.[2]

7. It is the prevailing doctrine, that evidence of the defendant's subsequently repeating the slander or libel is inadmissible for the plaintiff *in aggravation of damages*;[3] (*b*) but such evidence, where the defendant's intention is at all equivocal, is clearly admissible *to show malice*.[4] Thus, it is said, "proof of a long practice of libelling the plaintiff

[1] Abrams *v.* Smith, 8 Blackf. 95.

[2] M'Kee *v.* Ingalls, 4 Scam. 30.

[3] Keenhotts *v.* Becker, 3 Denio, 346; Forbes *v.* Myers, 8 Blackf. 74; Goslin *v.* Corry, 7 Man. & Gr. 343.

[4] Lauter *v.* McEwen, 8 Blackf. 435; Bunson *v.* Edwards, 1 Smith, 7. 1 Cart. 164; Root *v.* Lowndes, 6 Hill, 518; Ware *v.* Cartledge, 24 Ala. 622; Schoonover *v.* Rowe, 7 Blackf. 202; True *v.* Plumley, 36 Maine, 466; Vincent *v.* Dixon, 5 Ind. 270; but see Randall *v.* Balter, 7 Barb. 260; Bartom *v.* Brands, 3 Green, 248; Severance *v.* Hilton, 32 N. H. 289; Symonds *v.* Carter, Ibid. 458; Van Derveer *v.* Sutphin, 5 Ohio, N. S. 293.

(*a*) Evidence as to the motives of *the plaintiff* in bringing the suit is immaterial in the issue of a plea of justification. Bradley *v.* Kennedy, 2 Greene, 231.

In an action of slander, the defendant cannot give evidence, in mitigation of damages, that the plaintiff has been hostile to him for a long time, and has proclaimed that he did not wish to live in peace with him. Andrews *v.* Bartholomew, 2 Met. 509; Craig *v.* Catlet, 5 Dana, 323.

(*b*) It has been held, that the plaintiff, after proving the slanderous words, may also prove, *in aggravation of damages*, that the defendant had spoken the same words in other conversations within the statute of limitations, even if *after the commencement of the suit*. Hatch *v.* Potter, 2 Gilman, 725.

The rule stated in the text is held more especially applicable to words actionable in themselves, and spoken or published in relation to other matters than those laid in the declaration. Schenck *v.* Schenck, 1 Spencer, 208.

It is to be observed, however, that the distinction as to the *purpose* of such evidence seems rather verbal than practical, inasmuch as the amount of damages in this action must always materially depend upon the motives of the defendant. And see Symonds *v.* Carter, 32 N. H. 458.

Upon the ground stated in the text, where, in an action for slander, the defendant set up a former recovery for the same cause; held, it was not competent to prove on the trial, that some of the words charged in the declaration, but not contained in the declaration of the former suit, were given in evidence on the trial of such former suit. Campbell *v.* Butts, 3 Comst. 173.

would be evidence to show that the defendant was actuated by malice in the particular publication complained of, and that it did not take place through carelessness or inadvertence; and the more nearly the evidence approaches to proof of a systematic practice of libelling, the more convincing will it be. The circumstance, that the other libels are more or less frequent, more or less remote from the date of the publication of that in question, will affect merely the weight, not the admissibility, of the evidence."[1] Hence, on the trial of an action for a libel published in a newspaper, the plaintiff was allowed to give in evidence a paragraph published subsequently, in which the charge was reasserted, for the purpose of showing the defendant's intention; and, the Judge having instructed the jury to take the two paragraphs with them, and to give the plaintiff such damages as they considered him entitled to under the circumstances, an application for a new trial was refused.[2] And it has been held, that even words barred by the statute of limitations may be considered to determine the malice of others not barred.[3] (*a*) So evidence of words of a similar import to those charged in the declaration, spoken by the defendant afterwards, both before and after the commencement of the

[1] Per Parke, B., Barrett *v.* Long, 3 H. L. Cas. 414.

[2] Barwell *v.* Adkins, 1 Man. & Gr. 807; 2 Scott, N. 11.

[3] Flamingham *v.* Boucher, Wright, 746; Botelar *v.* Bell, 1 Md. 173; Throgmorton *v.* Davis, 4 Blackf. 174; *contra*, Lincoln *v.* Chrisman, 10 Leigh, 338.

(*a*) In an action of slander, for words imputing perjury, an affidavit of the defendant, on which an indictment had been preferred, and which had been made so long before as to be barred by the statute of limitations, charging the plaintiff with the same perjury, is admissible in evidence, as proof of the repetition of the same words in a different form, and with more deliberation, and to show the *quo animo*. Randall *v.* Holsenbake, 3 Hill, S. C. 175. But see 2 Cush. 133. The distinction has been made, that actionable words *different from those laid in the declaration* cannot be given in evidence, unless the statute of limitations has run in respect to them, even if in any case admissible. Root *v.* Lowndes, 6 Hill, 518; disapproving the cases of Thomas *v.* Croswell, 7 Johns. 264, and Inman *v.* Foster, 8 Wend. 602.

action, is admissible for the purpose of showing malice.[1] More especially actionable words, having reference to the slander complained of, may, though spoken after commencement of suit, be proved to show malice.[2] So evidence of other words of *like import* or *imputing the same crime* is admissible, not as showing separate grounds of action, but to prove malice.[3] And other words, besides those charged, may be proved, as evidence of malice, whether actionable or not.[4] So in an action for a libel, the plaintiff, in order to show the *quo animo*, may give in evidence subsequent letters addressed by the defendant to third parties, containing substantially a repetition of the slanderous matter, though the libel declared on is free from ambiguity, and the letters offered were written after the commencement of the action; and without reference to the time intervening between the writing of the respective letters.[5]

8. But it is held that evidence cannot be given, of words spoken on another occasion and *of a different import* from that charged in the declaration. Thus, in an action for saying that the plaintiff had sworn falsely as a witness before arbitrators, evidence that the defendant on a different occasion, in speaking of the arbitration, said, "the way they got the money was no better than a highway robbery," is inadmissible to show "with what mind" the words charged in the declaration were spoken.[6] (*a*) So words spoken after

1 Smith *v.* Wyman, 4 Shep. 13; Kennedy *v.* Gifford, 19 Wend. 256.

2 M'Intire *v.* Young, 6 Blackf. 496; Carter *v.* M'Dowell, Wright, 100; Bodwell *v.* Swan, 3 Pick. 376; Morgan *v.* Livingston, 2 Rich. 573; Hesler *v.* Degant, 3 Ind. 501.

3 Williams *v.* Minor, 18 Conn. 464; Stearns *v.* Cox, 17 Ohio, 590; Thompson *v.* Bowers, 1 Doug. 321.

4 Brittain *v.* Allen, 2 Dev. 120; S. C. 3 Dev. 167; *contra*, 7 Barb. 260.

5 Pearson *v.* Lemaitre, 6 Scott, N. R. 607.

6 Howard *v.* Sexton, 4 Comst 157.

(*a*) So, in an action for charging the plaintiff with *stealing two beds*, it is not competent for the plaintiff, for the purpose of showing malice, to prove that the defendant subsequently entered a complaint against him before a magistrate for stealing *a lot of wood and old iron*; first, because the words used in the complaint do not relate to the charge which is the subject of the action; and secondly, because such using of the words is a proceeding in a

commencement of suit are held not admissible to show malice, unless they expressly refer to those which are the subject-matter of the action, and do not constitute a distinct slander, for which the plaintiff would have a distinct right of action.[1] And it has been held in an action for slander, that, where evidence of other declarations is admitted, the jury should be instructed, that it is admitted for the above purpose alone, and that they are to give damages only for the words charged.[2] But where other actionable words, though objected to, have been given in evidence, it will be presumed, the contrary not appearing, that the evidence was admitted for the above purpose, and the jury properly instructed as to its effect.[3] And it has been lately held, that, in an action for libel, when a subsequent publication is put in evidence to show the *animus* of the defendant, if the judge, in summing up, leaves to the jury whether the proposed publication is libellous, and, if so, to assess the damages, he is not bound to point their attention to the subsequent publication, and tell them not to give damages for it.[4]

9. It will be hereafter seen, that *the truth* is a justification for words otherwise slanderous; but must be specially pleaded, in order to be available. But it is held, that, if the plaintiff prove words not laid in the declaration, tending to show malice, the defendant may, under the general issue, repel the malice, and in mitigation of damages prove those words to be true, even though in themselves actionable.[5]

[1] Taylor *v.* Kneeland, 1 Doug. 67.
[2] Scott *v.* McKinnish, 15 Ala. 662.
[3] Roberts *v.* Ward, 8 Blackf. 333.
[4] Darby *v.* Ouseley, 36 Eng. L. & Eq. 518.
[5] Burke *v.* Miller, 6 Blackf. 155; Wagner *v.* Holbrunner, 7 Gill, 296.

course of justice, before a magistrate having jurisdiction of the supposed offence. Watson *v.* Moore, 2 Cush. 133.

An exception to the admission in evidence, on the trial of an indictment for libel, for the purpose of proving malice, of other libellous publications, previously and subsequently made by the defendant concerning the same person, cannot be sustained, unless the libels offered in evidence appear by the bill of exceptions to have been materially different from the libel set forth in the indictment. Commonwealth *v.* Harmon, 2 Gray, 289.

So the defendant may prove, under the general issue, in mitigation of damages, that the words were spoken on a justifiable occasion, without malice; or circumstances which induced him erroneously to make the charge complained of, believing it to be true, provided the evidence do not necessarily imply the truth of the charge, or tend to prove it true.[1] (a) And a communication will not be presumed to have been made through malice, which was confidential, prudently made, in good faith, and through benevolence to the plaintiff.[2] But the presumption of malice is not rebutted, by proof that the publisher had reason to suspect and believe the charge true.[3]

10. Upon evidence offered to disprove malice, the question of malice is for the jury;[4] to be determined upon all the facts and conversations, in connection with which the words were spoken.[5] Thus, in an action for charging the plaintiff with perjury, it is a question for the jury, whether the words were spoken with a defamatory intention.[6] So the wife of A. before her death requested the wife of B. to advise her daughters. A. married a second wife, and B.'s wife told the daughters of A. by his first wife, that their step-mother was a loose woman, and that they ought on that account to leave their home. In an action of slander by A. against B. and wife, it was held, that the words were *primâ facie* actionable, but that the evidence of the relation between A.'s daughters and B.'s wife ought to have been left to the jury, to find whether there was from the whole evidence any malice.[7]

11. But it has been held, that, if there be a plea of justification, it is error in the court to refer to the jury the question whether the words were spoken in malice.[8] So it has

[1] Abrams *v.* Smith, 8 Blackf. 95; Minesinger *v.* Kerr, 9 Barr, 312; Stees *v.* Kemble, 27 Penn. 112.

[2] Hart *v.* Reed, 1 B. Mon. 166.

[3] Usher *v.* Severance, 2 App. 9.

[4] Abrams *v.* Smith, 8 Blackf. 95.

[5] Nichols *v.* Packard, 16 Verm. 147; White *v.* Nicholls, 3 How. U. S. 266; Erwin *v.* Sumrow, 1 Hawks, 472.

[6] Smith *v.* Youmans, Riley, 88.

[7] Adcock *v.* Marsh, 8 Ired. 360.

[8] Farley *v.* Ranck, 3 W. & S. 554.

(a) See *Privileged*, &c.

been held improper to refer to the jury the question, whether the charge is a malicious attack upon the plaintiff in his calling, or only an imputation of mere general character. Thus the plaintiff, a surgeon, and proprietor of a medical institution, having petitioned the House of Commons against quacks and empirics, the defendant, the proprietor of a periodical publication, in commenting on and criticizing the plaintiff's petition, used expressions charging him with ignorance of his profession generally, and of chemistry in particular. The plaintiff sued the defendant, and declared against him for libelling him in his profession of a surgeon; and the jury were directed, that, if they thought the writing complained of to be no more than a fair comment on the petition, it was no libel; and that they were to consider whether the publication imputed to the plaintiff ignorance in his profession of a surgeon, or merely ignorance of chemistry; and that, if they thought the latter, their verdict must be for the defendant. The jury having, accordingly, found a verdict for the defendant, the Court granted a new trial.[1]

[1] Dunne *v.* Anderson, 10 Moore, 407.

CHAPTER XIV.

PRIVILEGED COMMUNICATIONS.

1. In immediate connection with the subject of *malice*, and as closely associated therewith, we proceed to consider the important topic of *privileged communications*; (*a*) which constitute an exception to the general rules relating to libel and slander, and for the reason that they are not malicious. The rule is well settled, that, if the words were spoken or the publication made *upon a just occasion*, the communication is privileged, and express malice must be shown in order to maintain an action.[1] (*b*) In other words, an action will not

[1] Washburn *v.* Cooke, 3 Denio, 110.

(*a*) In Black *v.* Holmes, 1 Fox & Smith, 35, Bushe, C. J., remarks upon the distinction between communications *privileged from being given in evidence*, and those *privileged from being considered as slanderous.*

(*b*) "The rule is, that, if the occasion be such as repels the presumption of malice, the communication is privileged, and the plaintiff must then, if he can, give evidence of malice. If he gives no such evidence, it is the office of the Judge to say that there is no question for the jury, and to direct a nonsuit or a verdict for the defendant." Per Ld. Campbell, C. J., Taylor *v.* Hawkins, 16 Q. B. 321.

"The occasion on which the communication was made rebuts the inference *primâ facie* arising from a statement prejudicial to the character of the plaintiff, and puts it upon him to prove, that there was malice in fact — that

stood by the witness according to that meaning.[1] And if spoken affirmatively as alleged, the declaration is (see ch. 24, § 3,) supported, though the words were spoken in answer to a question put by a third person; unless the plaintiff caused the question to be put, in order to procure a cause of action,[2] (see § 196). Thus, in illustration of these various propositions, in an action for libel, the words, "Is M. H. the gentleman who wrote, &c., the individual who broke jail, while confined on a charge of forgery," are libellous.[3] So *potential* words may be actionable, if they import an act done. Thus, saying a man *could* clip money, when he lived in a particular place.[4] And to say, "I am thoroughly convinced," is a sufficient assertion to be actionable.[5] So it is equally slanderous, to say that a woman is a whore, and that there is a rumor that she is such.[6] So words actionable as slanderous are not the less so, for being preceded by the words "if reports be true," the proof of which, in addition to the words alleged, is not a variance.[7] So to write of a person, that "he is thought no more of than a horse thief and a counterfeiter," is a libel. And a plea of justification, in such case, must allege that the plaintiff had committed the crimes of horse-stealing and counterfeiting. It is not sufficient to aver that he "was thought no more of than a horse thief," &c.[8] (*a*)

[1] Marshall *v.* Gunter, 6 Rich. 419.
[2] Jones *v.* Chapman, 5 Blackf. 88; Yeates *v.* Reed, 4 Ib. 463.
[3] Hotchkiss *v.* Oliphant, 2 Hill, 510.
[4] Speed *v.* Parry, 2 Ld. Raym. 1185.
[5] Oldham *v.* Peake, 2 W. Bl. 959.
[6] Kelly *v.* Dillon, 5 Ind. 426.
[7] Smith *v.* Stewart, 5 Barr, 372.
[8] Nelson *v.* Musgrave, 10 Mis. 648.

(*a*) A declaration alleged, that the defendant published of and concerning a certain court-martial, and of and concerning the plaintiff as a member thereof, a defamatory libel and caricature, consisting of a lithographic picture and representation of the court-martial, and of the plaintiff as a member thereof, in which caricature the court-martial, and the plaintiff as a member thereot, are pointed out by their position and certain grotesque resemblances, and are represented and exhibited in an awkward and ludicrous light, posture, and condition. After verdict, it was held, that it was averred with sufficient certainty, that the plaintiff was specifically and individually libelled. Ellis *v.* Kimball, 16 Pick. 132.

So where the defendant, in speaking of an oath taken by the plaintiff, in a suit before a justice of the peace, and of the defendant's having made a complaint against the plaintiff before the grand jury for perjury, said, "he went to the grand jury and asked them whether they wanted any more witnesses, and they said they had witnesses enough to satisfy them;" held, these words, if laid with proper averments, were actionable, and in such case it is only necessary to aver, that the defendant by means of the words intimated, and meant to be understood by the hearers as charging, that the plaintiff was guilty of the crime imputed; and whether such was his intention, is a question for the jury.[1] So, under a count in an action for slander, alleging generally that the defendant charged the plaintiff with the crime of theft, it is competent for the plaintiff to give in evidence any words, which, although in their ordinary sense doubtful or even innocent, can be shown by the aid of averments and *innuendoes* under the circumstances to be *equivocal* or *ironical*, and to be intended by the defendant and understood by the hearer to impute such crime to the plaintiff.[2] Or for the words, *you will steal*, it being averred in the declaration, that the defendant meant and intended to have it understood and believed, that the plaintiff had been guilty of larceny.[3] Or for the words, *he would venture anything the plaintiff had stolen the book*, if proved to be spoken maliciously.[4] Or for

[1] Randall *v.* Butler, 7 Barb. 260.
[2] Pond *v.* Hartwell, 17 Pick. 269.
[3] Cornelius *v.* Van Slyck, 21 Wend. 70.
[4] Nye *v.* Otis, 8 Mass. 122.

Also, that the libel was set forth with sufficient certainty; for the degree of certainty required in such a case depends on the subject-matter, and where the ridicule consists mainly in ridiculous postures and movements, the use of language somewhat general and indefinite is unavoidable. And, as a caricature picture frequently consists of figures of persons, and of written language attributed to them, by labels apparently issuing out of their lips, it was held, after verdict, that an allegation, that the plaintiff was represented in such a picture as speaking certain words, was a sufficiently certain averment that these words were attributed to him. Ibid.

spoken or written in a legal proceeding, by a party or counsel, pertinent and material to the controversy, or reasonably deemed necessary to the cause, however defamatory, is *privileged*, and its truth cannot be drawn in question, in an action for slander or libel.[1] No action lies for a statement thus made, whether by affidavit or *vivâ voce*, even though it be alleged to have been made "falsely and maliciously, and without any reasonable or probable cause."[2] Malice cannot be predicated of what is thus said or written.[3] Nor its truth drawn in question, in an action for slander or libel.[4] Nor is it necessary for the defendant, in such action, to deny the allegation of malice.[5] The privilege is as broad as that of a member of a legislative body.[6] Thus words spoken to a magistrate, in the course of a judicial proceeding, though slanderous and malicious, are not actionable.[7] So a *distress warrant*, being the remedy given to the party by law, for the purpose of enforcing a legal right, comes within the reason of this rule.[8] So complaints against an individual for alleged offences, honestly preferred before a judicial officer, will not render the complainant liable for slander; and every such complaint is to be deemed *primâ facie* honest, and to have been made upon good motives. But the question of malice, in such cases, is always an open question, and may be proved, either by express evidence, or attending circumstances.[9] (*a*) And complaints are actionable if made with no *bonâ fide* intention of prosecuting.[10] So libellous charges made before a court not legally competent to investigate them are actionable.[11]

4. Upon the same principle, an action will not lie for

[1] Garr *v.* Selden, 4 Comst. 91.
[2] Revis *v.* Smith, 18 Com. B. 126; Lea *v.* White, 4 Sneed, 111.
[3] Warner *v.* Paine, 2 Sandf. 195.
[4] Garr *v.* Selden, 4 Comst. 91.
[5] Ibid.
[6] Hastings *v.* Lusk, 22 Wend. 410.
[7] Gosslin *v.* Cannon, 1 Harring. 3.
[8] Baily *v.* Dean, 5 Barb. 297.
[9] Briggs *v.* Byrd, 12 Ired. 377.
[10] Marshall *v.* Gunter, 6 Rich. 419.
[11] Milam *v.* Burnsides, 1 Brev. 295.

(*a*) A count in slander, for words spoken, is not sustained by evidence that the defendant signed a written complaint, alleging that the plaintiff had committed a larceny. Hill *v.* Miles, 9 N. H. 9.

libellous words spoken or sworn in a court of justice, in a man's own defence against a charge upon him in that court.[1] So where, in an affidavit to oppose a motion, the defendant alleged that the plaintiff had been guilty of perjury in his affidavit to support the motion; it appearing that the falsity of the statements in the plaintiff's affidavit was a material question; held, that no action would lie against the defendant for a libel.[2] So an action will not lie for defamation, in an affidavit taken in the Court of Chancery, in a cause there depending.[3] So an affidavit made before a magistrate, to enforce the law against a person accused therein of a crime, does not subject the accuser to an action for a libel, though the affidavit be false and insufficient to effect its object.[4] So, in an action for libel, a plea that the publication was part of an affidavit, made and used, on an application to show cause of action, or to mitigate bail, in a former suit between the parties; and that the defendant had reasonable and probable cause for believing, and did in fact believe, that the matter, when so published, was true, and was pertinent and relevant to the suit, in relation to the affidavit to hold to bail, and for the purpose of procuring the relief sought on such application; is a good plea in bar.[5]

5. Nor will an action lie, for words spoken by a person who is managing a prosecution before a justice of the peace, in behalf of the Commonwealth, on a complaint which he has himself preferred.[6] Nor against a barrister, for words spoken by him as counsel in a cause pertinent to the matter in issue.[7] (*a*) Nor against a master, for such words spoken,

[1] Astley *v.* Younge, 2 Burr, 807.
[2] Warner *v.* Paine, 2 Sandf. 195.
[3] Dawling *v.* Venman, 3 Mod. 109.
[4] Hartsock *v.* Reddick, 6 Blackf. 255.
[5] Snydam *v.* Moffatt, 1 Sandf. 459.
[6] Hoar *v.* Wood, 3 Met. 193.
[7] Hodgson *v.* Scarlett, 1 B. & Ald. 232; Jennings *v.* Paine, 4 Wis. 348.

(*a*) An attorney sued his client for professional services. The client pleaded the general issue, and gave notice that he would prove, on the trial, that the attorney conducted the suits and attended to the other business, on account of which compensation was claimed, in "so careless, unskilful, undue, and improper manner," as to render the services of no value. The attorney moved the Court to strike out the notice as false; and the client, in

while acting as counsel for his slave, while he is on trial before a competent tribunal.[1] And even where the plaintiff,

[1] Shelfer *v.* Gooding, 2 Jones, Law, (N. C.) 175.

---

resisting the motion, read and placed upon the files of the Court an affidavit, stating that the plaintiff had revealed confidential communications made to him in his professional capacity by the defendant, and relating to some portion of the business in question, for the purpose of assisting another person who had an interest adverse to the defendant, and that the plaintiff combined and colluded with that person to injure the defendant. The attorney sued his client for libel, reciting these facts in his declaration, and charging the libel to be malicious and impertinent. Held, on demurrer to the declaration, that the matter stated in the affidavit was pertinent to the motion, and therefore privileged, so that the action of libel would not lie. Garr *v.* Selden, 4 Comst. 91.

If an attorney introduce slanderous matter into the pleadings of a cause, without the direction of his client, the latter is not liable. Hardin *v.* Cumstock, 2 Marsh. 481.

Where a party in court said to a witness who had just finished his testimony: "you have sworn to a manifest lie;" the words were held actionable Kean *v.* M'Laughlin, 2 S. & R. 469; acc. M'Claughney *v.* Wetmore, 6 Johns. 82. *Contra*, Badgley *v.* Hedges, 1 Penn. 233.

And, in general, the privilege of parties and attorneys, solicitors and counsel, in respect to words or writings used in the course of a judicial proceeding, does not protect them when they go out of the way to vilify another by words or writing, not material or pertinent to the controversy. Thus where one, acting as counsel for the plaintiff in a justice's court, prepared and presented a declaration in an action of trespass for breaking the plaintiff's close, and for killing and otherwise injuring his sheep, in which, among other provoking expressions concerning the defendant, were inserted allegations that the defendant was "reputed to be fond of sheep, bucks, and ewes, and of wool, mutton, and lambs," and to be in the habit of "biting sheep," and it was added, that "if guilty he ought to be hanged or shot," it was held that an indictment, charging such matter as libellous, and alleging malice, was good on demurrer. Gilbert *v.* The People, 1 Denio, 41.

Nor does the principle of privilege apply, unless the tribunal appealed to has jurisdiction of the application. Thus, upon a requisition to the governor, for the arrest of a fugitive from justice in another State, accompanied by the proper vouchers, according to the act of Congress, it is the duty of the executive to cause the fugitive to be arrested, and delivered to the agent appointed to receive him. And, after having issued a warrant for the apprehension of the fugitive, the governor has no power to entertain an application to recall, revoke, or remodify such warrant. Therefore an affidavit,

who was a minor and a party to a suit in equity, was desirous of changing the solicitor employed; and such solicitor, having notice of his intention, *wrote a letter* to the plaintiff's next friend, who was answerable for the costs of the suit; it was held, that the letter was a privileged communication, though it alleged that the plaintiff, who had been apprenticed to a civil engineer, had had a present made him of his indentures, because he was worse than useless in his office.[1]

6. Nor will an action lie against *a witness*, who, in the due course of a judicial proceeding, and in answer to pertinent questions proposed by the Court or counsel, has uttered false and defamatory statements concerning the plaintiff, even although he did so maliciously, and without reasonable and probable cause, and the plaintiff has suffered damage in consequence.[2]

7. While the proceedings in courts of justice are themselves privileged from the charge of being libellous or slanderous; it is also well settled, as a general rule, that a full, fair, and correct *account of a trial* in a court of justice,

[1] Wright *v.* Woodgate, Tyr. & Gr. 12. 268; Barnes *v.* McCrate, 32 Maine,
[2] Revis *v.* Smith, 36 Eng. L. & Eq. 442.

---

made and used in support of such an application, is not a privileged communication. Hosmer *v.* Loveland, 19 Barb. 111.

If the defendant in an action for a libel justify the publication as being made in the due course of judicial proceedings, it is only necessary to allege, that the publication was made in the due course of judicial administration, and that the form of proceeding was according to the due course of practice in such tribunal. Torrey *v.* Field, 10 Verm. 353.

It is no answer to such plea in this action, that the proceeding was instituted without probable cause and from motives of malice. But if the party went beyond what was warranted by the forms of proceeding in such tribunal, he is liable in this action for the excess, which may be specially replied by way of new assignment; and the question, whether done through malice or from justifiable cause, will then be referred to the jury. Ibid.

Where a verdict is rendered for the plaintiff in an action of slander, the judgment will not be arrested, if the pertinency of the words and the time ot utterance are put in issue and found against the defendant, although from the declaration it appear that the words were spoken in the course of a judicial trial. Hastings *v.* Lusk, 22 Wend. 410.

though not made *verbatim*, and however injurious it may be, is a privileged publication, and not the subject of an action for a libel.[1] And such defence is held to be admissible under the plea of *not guilty*, which puts in issue as well the lawfulness of the occasion of the publication, as the tendency of the alleged libel.[2] Thus in an action for libel, the declaration stated, that the plaintiff and M. had been duly convicted of conspiring to extort money from C., and received judgment; but the defendant published, that the counsel, who moved for judgment, had stated the plaintiff to be the writer of a letter, which was in fact written by M. Plea, not guilty. The plaintiff proved the publication, the indictment, and sentence, the latter being set out in the indictment as an overt act of the conspiracy, and called the counsel as a witness, who deposed that he had in fact made the statement. Held, it was properly left to the jury whether the publication was a libel; and a verdict of not guilty was not contrary to the evidence.[3]

8. And the same rule applies to a report of legal proceedings, not actually entered in Court, more especially if truly made at the request of the party interested therein and for the purpose of effecting the object of such proceedings. Thus a declaration alleged, that the defendant published an advertisement in a newspaper, stating that a *capias* had issued against the plaintiff, and that it had been impracticable to take him, and offering a reward for such information to be given to the sheriff's officer, as would enable him to take the plaintiff; innuendo, that the plaintiff was in indigent circumstances, incapable of paying the debt, and keeping out of the way to avoid being served with process. Plea, that a *capias* had been issued, indorsed for bail, and delivered to the sheriff; that the defendant had kept out of the way to avoid being taken; that the sheriff's officer had been unable to take him; and that the defendant had published the advertisement, at the request of the party

1 Stanley *v.* Webb, 4 Sandf. 21.

2 Hoare *v.* Silverlock, 9 Com. B. 20; Curry *v.* Walter, 1 Bos. & P. 523.

3 Stockdale *v.* Tarte, 4 Ad. & Ell. 1016.

suing out the writ, within four calendar months of the date of the writ, to enable the sheriff and his officer to arrest. Held, a justification.[1] And even a false report of proceedings in court has been held not actionable, without proof of special damage. Thus the plaintiff was possessed of certain shares in a silver mine, touching which shares certain claimants had filed a bill in chancery, to which the plaintiff had demurred. Held, that, without alleging special damage, the plaintiff could not sue the defendant for falsely publishing that the demurrer had been overruled; that the prayer of the petition (for the appointment of a receiver) had been granted; and that persons duly authorized had arrived at the mine.[2]

9. But in general the privilege in question is confined strictly to a correct and simple report of the proceedings referred to.[3] (*a*) It is said, not with exclusive reference to this particular claim of privilege, but with peculiar applicability to it, that conductors of the public press are not privileged in the *circulation of news*;[4] and that "the only case, in which an editor of a newspaper can justify a libel on the ground that it contains an account of a trial, is where he gives a true and accurate report of it; and even in that case it will be for the Court to consider whether it was lawful to publish it."[5] So also, "It must not be taken for granted, that the publication of every matter which passes in a court of justice, however truly represented, is, under all circumstances, and with whatever motive published, justifiable; but that doctrine must be taken with grains of allowance."[6]

[1] Lay *v.* Lawson, 4 Ad. & Ell. 795.
[2] Malachy *v.* Soper, 3 Bing. N. R. 371.
[3] Stanley *v.* Webb, 4 Sandf. 21; Huff *v.* Bennett, 4 Sandf. 120.
[4] Sheckell *v.* Jackson, 10 Cush. 25.
[5] Flint *v.* Pike, 4 B. & C. 484.
[6] Per Ld. Ellenborough, Stiles *v.* Nokes, 7 E. 503.

(*a*) Declaration for a libel published in a newspaper. Plea, that the libel was a true report of the proceedings at a public meeting of commissioners, for putting a local improvement act into execution, and that there was no malice. Held, no answer. Davison *v.* Duncan, 40 Eng. Law and Eq. 215.

So, "It does not follow, that because a counsel is privileged as to what he delivers in a court of justice, a publisher may circulate his expressions all over the kingdom in a printed paper."[1] And, in general, a publication cannot be excused as privileged, upon the ground that its animadversions were a fair and legitimate criticism, unless the truth of the facts upon which these animadversions were founded is established or admitted. The defences of truth and privilege are said to be inseparable; and when that of truth is not pleaded, that of privilege must, of necessity, be rejected. Hence, where the publications set forth are not justified, and assert facts and impute designs, which render them libellous, the defence of privilege cannot be sustained.[2] Thus the publication of *ex parte* preliminary proceedings before a police magistrate is not privileged.[3] So, although the editor of a newspaper has a right to publish the fact that an individual has been arrested, and upon what charge, he has no right, while the charge is in the course of investigation before the magistrate, to assume that the person accused is guilty, or to hold him out to the world as such.[4] So a statement in a newspaper, of the circumstances of a cause tried in a court of justice, given as from the mouth of counsel, instead of being accompanied or corrected by the evidence, is not privileged.[5] Nor can a publication of proceedings in a court of justice be justified, if it contain disparaging observations made by any other than a Judge of the Court.[6] So it is libellous, to publish a highly colored account of judicial proceedings, mixed with the party's own observations and conclusions upon what passed in Court; which contained an insinuation, that the plaintiff had committed perjury, in swearing to an assault upon him, although it did appear, as suggested in the libel, from the testimony of every person in the room, &c., except the plaintiff,

[1] Per Park, J., Roberts *v.* Brown, 10 Bing. 525.

[2] Fry *v.* Bennett, 5 Sandf. 54; Delegal *v.* Highley, 3 Bing. N. R. 950.

[3] Stanley *v.* Webb, 4 Sandf. 21.

[4] Usher *v.* Severance, 2 App. 9.

[5] Saunders *v.* Mills, 6 Bing. 213.

[6] Delegal *v.* Highley, 3 Bing. N. R. 950.

that no violence had been used; for *non constat* thereby, that what the plaintiff swore was false. Neither is it sufficient in a justification to such a libel, where the extraneous matter was so mingled with the judicial account, as to make it uncertain whether it could be separated, to justify the publication by general reference to such parts of the supposed libel as purport to contain an account of the trial, &c., and allege that the said parts contain a just and faithful account of the trial, &c.[1]

10. And the same qualification of the general rule of privilege is to be applied, though the publication is made by a party himself, and concerning a witness in the cause. Thus a public officer, in a report of an official investigation into his conduct, published the testimony of a witness with these comments: "I am extremely loath to impute to C., (the witness,) or S., his partner, improper motives in regard to the false accusations against me; yet I cannot refrain from the remark, that if their motives have not been unworthy of honest men, their conduct in furnishing materials to feed the flame of calumny, &c., has been such as to merit the reprobation of every man having a particle of virtue or honor, &c. They have both much to repent of for the groundless and base insinuations they have propagated against me." Held, a libel.[2] (*a*) So, upon a declaration

[1] Stiles *v.* Nokes, 7 E. 493.

[2] Clark *v.* Binney, 2 Pick. 113.

(*a*) Declaration for a libel, purporting to contain an account of a proceeding before a magistrate, respecting a matter in which he was merely asked for advice, and not called upon to act officially. The libel itself alleged, that A. B. and C. D. stated the matter charged to the magistrate, a great part of which was not actionable when spoken, but became so when written. Plea, that A. B. and C. D. did go before the magistrate and make the statement as set forth, and that the facts charged in it were true. The jury found, that the matters contained in the libel were not true, but that it contained a correct account of the proceedings. Held, first, that, as the matter was not brought before the magistrate judicially, or officially, the defendant could not justify the publication as a correct report of the proceedings; nor on the ground, that the libel mentioned the names of the

for a libel published in a newspaper, which reflected on the plaintiff in his profession as an attorney, the libel was headed

---

parties who stated the matter to the magistrate; because, as to part of the slanderous matter, no action would lie against such parties; but it had become actionable merely from having been published by the defendants, and therefore, by stating the names of the parties, they gave the plaintiff no right of action against them; and further, that, in order to justify the repeating of slander, it was necessary that the party repeating it should, at the time of repeating it, offer himself as a witness to prove the uttering of the slander, and therefore, as the defendants did not state that they themselves heard the slander uttered by A. B. and C. D., but merely what A. B. and C. D. had said, the plea was bad. M'Gregor *v.* Thwaites, 3 B. & C. 24.

Action on the case for libel. The alleged libel stated, that the plaintiff, a tradesman in London, became surety for the petitioner on the Berwick election petition, and falsely stated himself, on oath, to be sufficiently qualified in point of property, when he was not able to pay his debts. It then asked, why the plaintiff, being unconnected with the borough, should take so much trouble, and incur such an exposure of embarrassments, and proceeded: "There can be but one answer to these very natural and reasonable queries: he is hired for the occasion." The defendant justified, stating that the above-mentioned allegations in the libel, (except the hiring, which was not specifically noticed,) were true, and that the publication was a correct report of proceedings in a legal court, "together with a fair and *bonâ fide* commentary thereon." Replication, *de injuriâ*, and issue thereon. Held, that the concluding observation in the libel, not being a mere inference from the previous statement, but introducing a substantive fact, required a distinct justification; and therefore, that, on trial of the above issue, it was properly left to the jury to say, not only whether the evidence made out the facts first alleged, but also whether the imputation that the plaintiff had been hired was a fair comment. Cooper *v.* Lawson, 8 Ad. & Ell. 746.

A declaration for a libel stated, that the plaintiff was taken before a justice to answer a charge of having assaulted A. B., and that the said charge was proceeded upon, and in part heard, and witnesses were examined concerning the same, of which A. B. was one, and the further examination was adjourned to a future day; that at the time of publishing the libel no bill of indictment had been preferred against the plaintiff in respect of the charge, nor any trial had, and the subject-matter of the charge was undetermined, yet that the defendants, intending to hinder and obstruct the course of justice, and to prevent the plaintiff from having a fair trial, maliciously published in a newspaper, on the 10th of July, the following libel: "One A. D., of, &c., underwent a long examination on a charge of having indecently assaulted a female child only thirteen years old. The evidence of the child

with the words "Shameful conduct of an attorney," and then professed to give an account of certain proceedings

---

herself, and her companion, A. D.'s own cousin, displayed such a complication of disgusting indecencies, that we cannot detail it. It is right, however, that we should say that the accused denied the principal facts alleged, and that the children made some slight variation in their evidence." The same count charged the defendants with publishing another libel on the 18th of July, stating that "A. D., who was charged a week ago with attempting to violate the person of a girl of thirteen, was again examined, but no further evidence was heard, and he was ordered to enter into a recognizance for £200, and all the witnesses were bound over to prosecute." There were other counts, setting out the libels, but making no reference to any proceeding before a magistrate. Plea, first, not guilty; secondly, that on, &c., at, &c., before J. H., Justice, the plaintiff did undergo a long examination, &c. (repeating the libel); and that afterwards, to wit, on the 15th day of July, at the public office, Bow Street, the plaintiff was again examined, &c. (repeating the second libel); that the supposed libels contained no other than a true, fair, just, and correct report of the proceedings on the 8th and 15th days of July, and were published with no scandalous, unworthy, or unlawful motive, and that the proceedings took place publicly at the police-office, and the reports thereof were published solely as news of public proceedings. Held, upon demurrer, that this plea was bad, inasmuch as it was no justification of the publication of slanderous matter, that it contained a correct report of a preilminary inquiry before a magistrate. The third plea was, that the several matters and things in the supposed libels contained were true. Held, that this plea was bad, because it was uncertain whether it meant, that the report was a true report of the proceedings, or that the facts mentioned in it were true; and, if the latter were the meaning, then the plea was much too general. The fourth plea, to the whole declaration, stated, that the supposed libel was nothing more than a fair, true, and correct report of proceedings which took place publicly and openly before the justice at the public office. Held, that this plea was bad, because it was no answer to those counts, which did not allege that any proceedings had taken place before a justice. The fifth plea, which was pleaded to the counts containing the libel of the 10th of July, was, that the plaintiff on the 8th of July was before the justice, and underwent a long examination, as in the second plea, and upon that occasion the mother of A. C deposed as follows. The plea then set out the depositions verbatim, and by them it appeared that the libel complained of did not contain a full, fair, and accurate report of what passed at the police-office, and, on that ground, it was held that this plea was clearly bad. The sixth plea, which was pleaded to the libel of the 15th of July, alleged that the plaintiff was examined at the police-office, and

in the Insolvent Debtors' Court, injurious to the plaintiff's professional character. Held, not privileged, as the words "Shameful conduct of an attorney," formed no part of the proceedings in court.[1]

11. The privilege connected with proceedings in courts of justice has also been extended to other *quasi-judicial* tribunals, more especially if their jurisdiction and action are of a *confidential* nature. Thus, as between members of *a Quaker meeting*.[2] So words spoken or written in the regular course of *church discipline*, or before a *tribunal of a religious society*, to or of members of the church or society, are, as among the members themselves, privileged communications, and not actionable without express malice.[3] Though the

[1] Clement v. Lewis, 7 Moore, 200.
[2] Rex v. Hart, 1 W. Bl. 386.
[3] Coombs v. Rose, 8 Blackf. 155; Whitaker v. Carter, 4 Ired. 461.

---

ordered to enter into recognizances, as in the libel mentioned. Held, that this plea was good, inasmuch as the publication of the 15th of July contained no statement of the evidence, nor any comment upon the case, but merely stated the result of what the justice had thought fit to do. Duncan v. Thwaites, 3 B. & C. 556; 5 Dow. & Ry. 447.

Case for a libel in a newspaper; plea, not guilty. The alleged libel purported to be a report of the trial of an action brought by the same plaintiff against other defendants, who had justified; and, after recounting the libel in that action, the proofs in support of the plea, and the summing up of the Judge, closed by stating, that the jury found a verdict for the plaintiff, with £30 damages. It did not appear whether any such trial had in fact taken place, or whether the report was an impartial one. The jury were directed, that if, in their opinion, the report taken altogether indicated a malicious motive, actuating the defendants against the plaintiff, or was injurious to his character by misstatement, or insinuating his being guilty of the matter originally imputed, notwithstanding he was stated to have obtained damages for that imputation; or that the report of such a trial was pure fiction invented by the defendants; their verdict must be for the plaintiff; with the observation, that if they thought that, taking the report altogether, the allegations contained in it to the plaintiff's prejudice were repelled by the verdict which he was stated to have obtained, so as not to be on the face of it injurious to him in the result, they ought to find for the defendants. The jury having found for the defendants, the Court refused to disturb the verdict. Chalmers v. Payne, 5 Tyr. 766; 2 Cr. Mees. & R. 156.

words, "A report raised and circulated by A. B., against Brother C., stating that he made him pay a note twice, and proved by A. B. to be false," written in a church book, are libellous.[1] It is said, (in Massachusetts,) Congregational churches have authority, to which every member by entering into the church covenant submits, to deal with their members for immoral and scandalous conduct; and for that purpose, to hear complaints, to take evidence, to decide, and upon conviction, to administer punishment by way of rebuke, censure, suspension, and excommunication; and all persons who participate in the exercise of this authority, whether by complaining, giving testimony, acting and voting, or pronouncing the result orally, or in writing, provided they act in good faith, and within the scope of the authority of the church, are protected by law.[2] So words spoken in good faith, and within the scope of his defence, by a party on trial before a church meeting, are privileged, and do not render him liable to an action, although they disparage private character.[3] Thus the defendant expressed an opinion founded on the statements of others, that the plaintiff had maliciously killed his horse, and was arraigned therefor by the plaintiff *before the church*. In self-defence, the defendant produced the certificates of the individuals upon whose authority he made the statements; and the plaintiff offered no proof of malice in fact. Held, no action would lie.[4]

12. In general, the principle above stated does not apply to an accusation made by a member of a church, against a person not a member.[5] But, where a member of a church had consented, that the church should investigate any complaint which might be preferred against him in writing by a person not a member; it was held that an action for a libel could not be sustained against such person, making such complaint, without showing express malice. And that evidence, tending to prove the truth of the charges in such

[1] Shelton *v.* Nance, 7 B. Mon. 128.
[2] Farnsworth *v.* Storrs, 5 Cush. 412.
[3] York *v.* Pease, 2 Gray, 282.
[4] Dunn *v.* Winters, 2 Humph. 512.
[5] 8 Blackf. 155.

complaint, might be admitted under the general issue, for the purpose of showing probable cause, and rebutting any presumption of malice.[1] And, as has been stated, the rule does not apply, if the words were spoken *maliciously*, which is a question for the jury.[2] (*a*) And the *decision* of such tribunal, upon the case in connection with which the words were uttered, is incompetent evidence.[3]

13. So it is held, that charges made to a *lodge of Odd Fellows*, by one member against another, for acts in violation of the rules of the order, which charges the lodge has power under those rules to receive and investigate, are *primâ facie* privileged, if made in good faith; and, in an action for slander in making such charges, that, if the defendant had probable cause for presenting them, he is not liable, even though actuated by malice, and so far acting in bad faith. So, that the presenting of charges to a member of the order, for the purpose of procuring his signature, is a privileged communication.[4] But, on the other hand, where A. accused B. of theft, to *certain members* of a lodge of Odd Fellows, of which both were members, and, in an action for slander by A., B. attempted to justify what he said, by showing that it was the duty of Odd Fellows to keep their lodge pure; the justification was held insufficient.[5]

14. Some other miscellaneous cases may be cited, which turn upon the point, whether confidential communications between parties having a common interest in the subject, more especially if of a public nature, are privileged. Thus

[1] Remington *v.* Congdon, 2 Pick. 310.

[2] Smith *v.* Youmans, 3 Hill, S. C. 85; Jarvis *v.* Hathaway, 3 Johns. 180.

[3] Whitaker *v.* Carter, 4 Ired. 461.

[4] Streety *v.* Wood, 15 Barb. 105.

[5] Holmes *v.* Johnson, 11 Ired. 55.

(*a*) In an action for a libel, the defendant pleaded, that the words were used without malice, in a complaint to a church, of which both parties were members, for the purpose of bringing the plaintiff to trial before a committee thereof. The plaintiff replied, that the charge was made wilfully and maliciously; to which replication the defendant demurred. Held, the replication was sufficient, although it contained no averment of want of probable cause. Dial *v.* Holter, 6 Ohio, (N. S.) 228.

the plaintiff, the secretary of the *Brewers' Insurance Company*, being charged with misconduct, was called upon to attend a board of directors, for the purpose of explanation, but declined to do so; whereupon the directors, after hearing the charges, passed a resolution that he had been guilty of gross misconduct, and of dismissal. The defendant, a director of that company, and also of the London Necropolis Company, of which the plaintiff was auditor, communicated the fact of the plaintiff's dismissal "for gross misconduct," at a board meeting of the latter company, and proposed a resolution to dismiss him, and, in answer to an inquiry from the chairman, said that the misconduct consisted in "obtaining money from the solicitors of the company under false pretences, and paying a debt of his own with it;" and, upon the plaintiff's appearing on a subsequent day with his attorney before the board, to meet the charges against him, the defendant refused to go into them. In an action of slander, held, the communication was privileged; and such refusal was no evidence of malice; being consistent with *bona fides*, which was to be presumed until the contrary was proved.[1] So, A. having commenced an action of ejectment to recover possession of a school-house, the district to which it belonged, claiming title to the land on which it stood under a lease from A., appointed B. a committee to procure the lease, have it examined by counsel, and take such steps as might be deemed necessary for the maintenance of their rights. B. accordingly procured the lease, and, having taken legal advice, employed counsel to defend the suit, and then made his report to the district, stating the circumstances under which he obtained the lease — that A. had borrowed it of the person having the custody of it for the district, giving his word and honor that it should be returned promptly, whenever called for; that B. obtained it only after much time and many promises, "owing to the bad faith of A.;" and that the suit commenced by A. could not, in the opinion of counsel, be sustained, "although A., regarding the gratification of per-

[1] Harris *v.* Thompson, 13 Com. B. 333; 26 Eng. L. & Eq. 386.

sonal pique more than the advancement of the interests of the district, and holding light his honor and his duty as a professor of religion, may cause the district much trouble and expense." In an action for a libel, brought by A. against B., it was held, 1st, that the language of the report, if false and malicious, was libellous; 2d, that, in the absence of any justification on the ground of a privileged communication the defendant must be considered as having meant what his language fairly imports; 3d, that it is the exclusive province of the Court to determine the construction of the language used; 4th, that the defendant may show that such language was a communication privileged by the occasion; 5th, that the object and intent of the party in making it, and the fairness and honesty of the transaction, are material subjects of inquiry, proper to be referred to the jury; 6th, that the jury having found in this case that the defendant used the language *bonâ fide*, in the fair exercise of his powers as a committee of the district, the presumption of malice was thereby repelled, and a justification established.[1] So the words, "the Rev. John Robinson, and Mr. James Robinson, inhabitants of this town, not being persons that the proprietors and annual subscribers think it proper to associate with, are excluded this room," published by posting a paper on which they were written, purporting to be a regulation of a particular society, were held not to be a libel.[2] Nor a report made in good faith and with probable cause, by the defendants, as a committee of the College of Pharmacy in New York, to the board of trustees, charging upon the plaintiff acts of incompetency as inspector of drugs for the board of New York, and by the board sent to the Secretary of the Treasury with a view to his removal.[3] Nor a report of the condition of town schools, made and published as required by law, by the superintending committee, and charging the prudential committee of a district with unlawfully employing a teacher and putting her in charge of a school, taking pos-

[1] Haight *v.* Cornell, 15 Conn. 74.
[2] Robinson *v.* Jermyn, 1 Price, 11.
[3] Van Wyck *v.* Guthrie, 4 Duer, 268.

session of the school-house, and forcibly excluding the general committee and the teachers employed by them; but not imputing corrupt motives.[1]

15. But a contrary doctrine has been applied in somewhat analogous cases. Thus the plaintiff was engaged to superintend the works of a railway company, and subsequently, at a general meeting of the proprietors, the engagement was not continued, but a former inspector was reinstated. A vacancy subsequently occurred in the situation of engineer to the commissioners for the improvement of the river Wear, and the plaintiff became a candidate. The defendant wrote to C., introducing D. as a candidate, and, C. having written to the defendant, informing him that another person had succeeded in obtaining the appointment, the defendant wrote an answer to C., reflecting on the conduct of the plaintiff, whilst in the situation of engineer to the railway company. There was a subsequent election, at which the plaintiff was unsuccessful in consequence of this letter having been shown. It appeared that the defendant and C. were both shareholders in the railway company, and that the defendant managed C.'s affairs in the railway. The defendant had not been applied to for his opinion, and the letter, containing the libel, was written after the termination of one election, and before the other was in contemplation. Held, in an action for libel, the letter was not a privileged communication.[2] So in an action for libelling the plaintiff, as a schoolmaster, the evidence was, *inter alia*, that the plaintiff, having been for twenty years schoolmaster at the National School of the adjoining parishes of C. & J., of which the defendant, the rector of C., and another person, the vicar of J., were trustees, was requested by the defendant to undertake the Sunday school of his parish, and declined to do so. The plaintiff was then removed from the mastership of the National School, and set up a school, to gain a livelihood by it, in the defendant's parish, in a school-room used as a dis-

[1] Shattuck *v.* Allen, 4 Gray, 540.

[2] Brooks *v.* Blanchard, 1 Cromp. & Mees. 779.

senting chapel. In a letter addressed to his parishioners, (set out in the bill of exceptions,) the defendant told them, that the plaintiff's attempt betrayed a spirit of opposition to authority, and justified the managers of the National School in removing him; that "no rightly disposed Christian, who received in simple faith the teaching of inspiration, 'obey them who have the rule over you, and submit yourselves,' could expect God's blessing to rest upon such an undertaking," and warned them against countenancing it, either by subscriptions or sending their children to it for instruction; that it would be a schismatical school, and those who aided the plaintiff in any way would be partakers with him in his evil deeds; they were to mark them which cause divisions and offences, and avoid them, &c. Pollock, C. B., directed the jury, that they would not be justified in finding a verdict for the plaintiff, but the paper was privileged, and, there being no evidence of express malice, they were bound to find a verdict for the defendant. Held, that the direction was wrong; that the paper was not privileged; that there was in the circumstances evidence of malice, which ought to have been left to the jury; and that the alleged libel ought to have been submitted to the jury, in order that they might judge whether there was any evidence of malice on the face of it.[1] So words spoken by a subscriber to a charity, in answer to inquiries by another subscriber, respecting the conduct of a medical man in his attendance upon the objects of the charity, are not, merely on account of those circumstances, a privileged communication.[2] And it is no justification of a libel, that the defendant signed the libellous paper, as chairman of a public meeting of citizens, convened for the purpose of deciding on a proper candidate for governor, at an approaching election; and that it was published by order of the meeting.[3]

16. The books abound with other applications of the same doctrine of privileged communications; relating more

[1] Gilpin v. Fowler, 26 Eng. L. & Eq. 386.

[2] Martin v. Strong, 5 Ad. & Ell. 535; 1 Nev. & P. 29.

[3] Lewis v. Few, 5 Johns. 1.

especially to matters of public concern, or in which some object of a public nature, even though more immediately affecting the rights and interests of an individual, is sought to be accomplished by application to the rightful tribunal or authority. As more particularly pertinent to this class of communications, the general rule is laid down, that a communication made *bonâ fide* and without malice, upon any subject-matter in which the party communicating, or the party communicated with, has an interest, or in reference to which the former has a duty, is privileged, if made to a person having a corresponding interest or duty, although it contain criminatory matter which, without this privilege, would be slanderous and actionable. And it has even been held that a communication made *bonâ fide* for the purpose of obtaining redress was privileged, though made to a tribunal, which had no direct authority in respect of the matter complained of.[1] Thus the plaintiff was a justice of the peace for the county, and in the habit of acting at petty sessions held in a borough. The defendant, an elector and inhabitant of the borough, signed a memorial addressed to the Secretary of State for the Home Department, complaining of the conduct of the plaintiff as a justice during an election for a member of parliament, by making inflammatory speeches and inciting to personal violence, and praying that he would cause an inquiry into the conduct of the plaintiff, and, on proof of the allegations, would recommend to her Majesty that the plaintiff be removed from the commission of the peace. The jury having found that the memorial was *bonâ fide*, held, a privileged communication, inasmuch as the plaintiff had both an interest and a duty in the subject-matter; and the Secretary of State had a corresponding duty, a justice of the peace being appointed and removed by the sovereign.[2] So where a selectman, acting officially at a town meeting, during an election, said in good faith, "the plaintiff has put in two votes;" an action of slander cannot

[1] Harrison *v.* Bush, 22 Eng. L. & Eq. 173; 12 Pick. 163.

[2] Harrison *v.* Bush, 22 Eng. L. & Eq. 173; 5 Ell. & Black. 344.

be maintained for these words; more especially if the plaintiff's own conduct was such, as induced the defendant to believe them true.[1] So, where the defendant and twenty-three others, inhabitants of the same county, presented a petition to the council of appointment, stating that the plaintiff, *district attorney*, was actuated by improper motives in his official conduct, and, from malice towards some, and from the emoluments arising from the public prosecutions in other cases, gave rise to many indictments; and praying that he might be removed from office; which petition was read in the council, who removed him from his office; it was held, that an action for a libel would not lie without proof of express malice, or that the petition was actually malicious and groundless, and presented merely to injure the plaintiff's character.[2] So a memorial to the Postmaster-General, in reference to the business of his department, *e. g.* the bidding for contracts which he is authorized to make by law, is a privileged communication. As in case of a memorial by one who had submitted proposals, protesting against the execution of a contract to another, whose proposal had been accepted, and charging upon the latter fraud and collusion with other bidders. Such a memorial, however, is not *absolutely* or *unqualifiedly* privileged, and, if it be proved that there was not probable cause for its statements, the law infers that it was malicious as well as false, and, therefore, a libel. But if the statements are true, they are not libellous, however malicious. So, although untrue, if made in good faith, believing or having probable cause to believe them true. And the burden of proving a want of probable cause is upon the plaintiff, as in an action for malicious prosecution.[3] So an action for libel lies against a party making a communication to the head of a department of the government, charging a subordinate officer, subject to removal by the higher officer, with peculation and fraud; but such action is in the nature of an action for malicious prosecution, and to

[1] Bradley *v.* Heath, 12 Pick. 163.

[2] Thorn *v.* Blanchard, 5 Johns. 508.

[3] Cook *v.* Hill, 3 Sandf. 341; 21 Wend. 329.

be sustained by the same proof of malice and want of probable cause. And where the conduct of such officer has been such, as with the attending circumstances to excite the honest suspicion of a citizen, that he is chargeable with a want of fidelity, or with a fraud as it respects the government, the question of probable cause should be submitted to the jury. And, even after a notice of justification, the proof of which is abandoned on the trial, the defendant may rest his defence on the ground of probable cause; although it would be otherwise, where probable cause is mere matter of mitigation.[1] So an action does not lie for a petition to the legislature for redress, complaining of the attorney-general, if the defendant had reasonable and probable cause of complaint, though the charge was not well founded in fact.[2] So the memorial of a tradesman, addressed to the Secretary at War, complaining of the conduct of a half-pay officer, in not paying his debts, and stating the facts of the case fairly and honestly, according to his opinion and understanding of those facts, is not the subject of an action for a libel; and evidence, showing the occasion of the writing, is admissible under the general issue, though no justification is pleaded.[3] So a representation to a bishop or church judicatory, having power to hear, examine, and redress grievances, in respect to the character or conduct of a minister of the gospel or a member of the church, is *primâ facie* a privileged communication, and, if made in good faith, not actionable. Otherwise, if false or impertinent, made without probable cause or belief in its truth. But the burden of proving its falsehood and malice is on the plaintiff.[4]

17. But, in case for libel, the declaration stated, that the plaintiff was a Roman Catholic priest, and clergyman to a chapel at M., and the defendant, intending to injure him in his offices, falsely and maliciously published concerning the plaintiff in his said offices the alleged libel. The libel was contained in a document, which the defendant read at a

[1] Howard *v.* Thompson, 21 Wend. 319.

[2] Reid *v.* Delarme, 2 Brev. 76.

[3] Fairman *v.* Ives, 1 D. & Ry. 252.

[4] O'Donaghue *v.* M'Govern, 23 Wend. 26.

public meeting, convened to petition parliament against the usual grant to the Roman Catholic college at Maynooth. The defendant introduced the reading of the document by saying, that he would give a specimen of what the Catholic priests, indoctrinated at Maynooth, teach the poor Roman Catholics attending them, in reference to the way of salvation; how they grind them down and debase them almost as low as the beast that perisheth. He then read the document, which purported to have been furnished by a policeman, and to give an account of a man whom the policeman had seen at M. crawling on his hands and knees in a public street, stating that the man had said that he was performing penance, and that the plaintiff, his priest, would not administer the sacrament to him until he had performed such penance. Judgment was arrested, because, even assuming that the libel charged that the plaintiff had refused the sacrament under the circumstances stated, and that it did not merely describe the penitent's apprehension of the plaintiff's displeasure; still the declaration did not inform the Court of the duties of a Roman Catholic priest in imposing penance, and therefore failed in showing that the plaintiff's character would suffer from the imputation. But it was also held, that, if the publication had been libellous, it would not have been privileged by the occasion.[1] So a false complaint, with express malice or without probable cause, contained in a letter from the inhabitant of a school district to the school committee, accusing the schoolmistress of a want of chastity, may be the subject of an action for a libel, and the question of malice is to be determined by the jury.[2] So, though it may be the duty of all persons to give information to his Majesty's proper officers concerning abuses, yet, if one write of another in a letter to such officer, that he is doing something to the prejudice of his Majesty's service, which is not true, this is sufficient evidence of a malicious intention; and, where no excuse

[1] Hearne *v.* Stowell, 4 Per. & Dav. 696.

[2] Bodwell *v.* Osgood, 3 Pick. 379.

is set up by the defendant, the jury may well find him guilty, though there be no other publication, and no further proof of malice. What is a malicious publication, it is for the jury to determine.[1]

18. And the same question of privilege has been raised, in reference to published comments and criticisms upon petitions presented to public authorities. Thus the plaintiff, a surgeon, petitioned parliament against quacks. The defendant, a journalist, commented severely on the contents of the petition, and charged the defendant with ignorance of his profession, pointing out ignorance of chemistry, which, he said, appeared on the face of the petition. The plaintiff sued the defendant for libelling him in his profession of a surgeon. The Judge directed the jury, that if they considered the defendant's attack a fair comment on the plaintiff's petition, — if the charge of ignorance was collected from the petition alone, and was not the spontaneous effusion of malice in the defendant, — the writing in question was no libel; and he also directed them to consider, whether the defendant had imputed to the plaintiff ignorance in his profession of a surgeon, or ignorance of chemistry; for, if they thought the latter, the declaration was not adapted to the plaintiff's case. The jury having found a verdict for the defendant, the Court granted a new trial, costs to abide the event. It was doubted whether a petition to parliament on matters of general importance is such a publication, as renders the petitioner an object of fair criticism and comment.[2]

19. The question of privilege often arises, in reference to *criticisms upon candidates* for political office. It is said, "Every individual has a right to comment on those acts of public men which concern him as a subject of the realm, if he do not make his commentary a cloak for malice and slander. There is, indeed, a material distinction between publications relating to public and to private persons, as regards the question whether they be libellous. That criticism may

1 Robinson *v.* May, 2 J. P. Smith, 3. 2 Dunne *v.* Anderson, 3 Bing. 88.

reasonably be applied to a public man in a public capacity, which might not be applied to a private individual."[1] But it has been held, that defamatory words, actionable in themselves, are not the less so, because spoken of one as *a candidate for parliament.*[2] Nor is a publication privileged, because it relates to one merely known as a politician, and charges him with unfair dealing in reference to the procurement of a public office for another. Thus a publication, alleging that the plaintiff, an influential politician, had been paid $5,000 in cash, for procuring an appointment to office by the governor, and that large sums had also been paid to the plaintiff for other lucrative offices, was held libellous *per se.*[3] And it is no justification of a charge against a town officer of official misconduct, that it was made in open town meeting, by an inhabitant of the town, while animadverting on the conduct of such officer relative to a subject then before the town, in which the defendant was interested as a qualified voter.[4] So a publication concerning a candidate for an elective office is libellous, which charges that he bartered away a public improvement, (*e. g.* a railroad,) in which the constituency for whose suffrages he is a candidate had a deep interest, for the charter of a bank to himself and his associates; and that, if elected, he would be an unfaithful representative and would act counter to the interests of his constituents; that he would by criminal indifference or treachery seriously retard or totally prevent the construction of such railroad; and that he would do all this from motives of personal, political aggrandizement, or to accomplish some sinister and dishonest purpose, or to gratify his private malice.[5] And an action lies for the publication of a libel, imputing to a party corrupt conduct as a member of the legislature, although the libel be published after the expiration of his term of office.[6]

20. The *official transmission of the account or report of*

[1] Per Parke, B., Parmiter *v.* Coupland, 6 M. & W. 108.
[2] Harwood *v.* Astley, 1 New R. 47.
[3] Weed *v.* Foster, 11 Barb. 203.
[4] Dodds *v.* Henry, 9 Mass. 262.
[5] Powers *v.* Dubois, 17 Wend. 63.
[6] Cramer *v.* Riggs, 17 Wend. 209.

the doings of an authorized tribunal, with an accompanying comment or certificate, is privileged, and not actionable. Thus, if *a court-martial*, after stating in their sentence the acquittal of an officer, against whom a charge has been preferred, subjoin thereto a declaration of their opinion that the charge is malicious and groundless, and that the conduct of the prosecutor is highly injurious to the service, the president is not liable to an action for a libel, for having delivered such sentence and declaration to the Judge Advocate.[1] So, where the Commander-in-chief directs a military inquiry into the conduct of a commissioned officer, the report of the president of the Court, transmitted by him to the Commander-in-chief, is privileged.[2] So, in an action against a justice of the peace, for slander in an official certificate by him to the grand jury, the plaintiff must not only prove the words, but express malice in using them; and the occasion of using them will be a *primâ facie* excuse.[3] So the defendants, a committee of the trustees of the College of Pharmacy, in the city of New York, made a report to the board of trustees, which the board adopted, and ordered to be transmitted to the secretary of the treasury of the United States. The plaintiff was at that time inspector of drugs for the port of New York, and the reports contained charges against him tending to show his incompetency for the office, and was transmitted with the view of effecting his removal. Held, that the report so transmitted was a privileged communication, and that the plaintiff would not be entitled to recover, without proof of actual malice, or a want of good faith on the part of the defendants.[4]

21. The same question has arisen, in regard to *the publication of public documents*. Thus, if a petition to parliament be referred to a committee, an action will not lie for printing and distributing a number of copies for the use of the members, although the matter be false and scandalous.[5]

[1] Jekyll *v*. Moore, 2 New R. 341.
[2] Home *v*. Bentinck, 4 Moore, 563.
[3] Sands *v*. Robison, 12 S. & M. 704.
[4] Van Wyck *v*. Guthrie, 4 Duer, 268
——— *v*. Aspinwall, 17 N. Y. 190.
[5] Lake *v*. King, 1 Mod. 58.

So the register of protests of bills and notes, established by acts of parliament, is a public document, to which everybody has a right of access, and the publication of which in a printed paper does not constitute a libel.[1] But it is no defence to an action for libel, that it is part of a document, which was by order of the House of Commons laid before the House, and thereupon became part of the proceedings of the House, and which was afterwards, by orders of the House, printed and published by the defendant; and that the House of Commons heretofore resolved, declared, and adjudged "that the power of publishing such of its reports, votes, and proceedings as it shall deem necessary or conducive to the public interests is an essential incident to the constitutional functions of parliament, more especially to the Commons' House of Parliament as the representative portion of it." And, on demurrer to a plea suggesting such defence, a court of law is competent to determine, whether the House of Commons has such privilege as will support the plea.[2]

22. The same question arises in regard to *public criticism* upon persons or things; (*a*) as in case of a charge of

[1] Fleming *v.* Newton, 1 Clark & Fin. N. S. 363.

[2] Stockdale *v.* Hansard, 9 Ad. & Ell. 1.

(*a*) It is said by an eminent Judge, "We really must not cramp observations upon authors and their works; they should be liable to criticism, to exposure, and even to ridicule, if their compositions be ridiculous; otherwise the first who writes a book upon any subject will maintain a monopoly of sentiment and opinion respecting it. This would tend to the perpetuity of error. Reflecting on personal character is another thing; show me an attack on the moral character of this plaintiff, or any attack upon his character unconnected with his authorship, and I shall be as ready as any Judge who ever sat here to protect him; but I cannot hear of malice on account of turning his works into ridicule." Per Ld. Ellenborough, Carn *v.* Hood, 1 Camp. 355.

"The editor of a public newspaper may fairly and candidly comment on any place or species of public entertainment; but it must be done fairly and without malice, or view to injure or prejudice the proprietor in the eyes of the public. If so done, however severe the censure, the justice of it screens the editor from legal animadversion; but if it can be proved that

publishing immoral and foolish books.[1] Upon this subject the general rule is laid down, that if the plaintiff, in an

[1] Tabart v. Tiffer, 1 Camp. 350.

---

the comment is unjust, is malevolent, or exceeding the bounds of fair opinion, such is a libel, and therefore actionable." Per Ld. Kenyon, Dibdin v. Swan, 1 Esp. C. 28.

It is said, "words, written or oral, which falsely depreciate the value of chattel property, may be made the subject of an action, provided special damage ensue from them. The distinction between a libel or slander on a person in the way of his trade, which is actionable without proof of special damage, and words injuriously reflecting on the quality of his wares and merchandise, is sometimes rather fine." Broom, Com. 514, 764.

But few cases are found in the books, where written or verbal remarks upon *property* — personal or real — have been held actionable under the head of libel or slander.

A statement in a newspaper, that a ship, of which the plaintiff was owner and master, and which he had advertised for a voyage to the East Indies, was not a seaworthy ship, and that Jews had bought her to take out convicts, was held to be a libel on the plaintiff, in his trade and business, for which he might recover damages, without proof of malice or allegation of special damage. Ingram v. Lawson, 6 Bing. N. R. 212.

In an action for slander of title of personal property, in claiming title to such property when offered for sale as the property of another; it was held that the words should be set out; also what title the defendant set up, and that the words were spoken in the hearing of the bidders. Hill v. Ward, 13 Ala. 310.

Also, that, although the title asserted by the defendant was invalid, malice must be proved. Ibid.

And, to rebut malice, the defendant may prove, that he had been advised by a lawyer to forbid the sale, to render his title under a mortgage effectual. Ibid.

In regard to real as well as personal estate it is held, that, to maintain an action for slander of title, there must be malice, express or implied. And the words spoken must go to defeat the plaintiff's title. If they are spoken to protect a person's own property, and prevent others from being cheated, the speaker is excusable. Hargrave v. Le Breton, 4 Burr. 2422; 1 Seld. 14.

And an attorney, delivering such a person's message, is not liable to an action, even though he varies from it, in immaterial circumstances, and without malice. Ibid.

In an action for slander of title, conveyed in a letter to a person about to purchase the estate of the plaintiff, imputing insanity to Y. from whom the

action for publishing disparaging statements concerning his goods, whereby he has sustained special damage, proves

---

plaintiff purchased it, and stating that the title would therefore be disputed, *per quod* the person refused to complete the purchase; held, the defendant, who had married the sister of Y., who was heir-at-law to her brother in the event of his dying without issue, was not to be considered as a mere stranger; and that the question for the jury was, not whether they were satisfied as men of good sense and good understanding that Y. was insane, or that the defendant entertained a persuasion that he was insane, upon such grounds as would have persuaded a man of sound sense and knowledge of business; but whether he acted *bonâ fide* in the communication which he made, believing it to be true, as he judged according to his own understanding, and under such impressions as his situation and character were likely to beget. Pitt *v.* Donovan, 1 M. & S. 639.

A card, published by the defendant, cautioning all persons not to purchase certain land of the plaintiff, and alleging that he obtained the title from him (the defendant) under false pretences, and that he should institute a suit to annul the title; was held under the circumstances not to show malice. McDaniel *v.* Baca, 2 Cal. 326.

The Court below refused to instruct the jury, at the request of the defendant, that, if they believed the receipt specified in the deed was obtained by fraud, they were authorized to find a verdict for the defendant. Held, such refusal was erroneous. Ibid.

It was also held erroneous to instruct the jury, that, where a person injuriously slanders the title of another, malice is presumed. Ibid.

To maintain an action for slander of title, the words must be followed, as a natural and legal consequence, by a pecuniary damage to the plaintiff, which must be specially alleged and proved. Kendall *v.* Stone, 1 Seld. 14.

Thus, where the plaintiff, before the speaking of the words, had entered into a written contract with a third person for the sale of the lands, and, the purchaser, in consequence of the words, having become dissatisfied with the purchase, the contract was at his request cancelled by the plaintiff, and part of the purchase-money, which had been paid, returned to him, (the loss of a sale to that person being the only special damage alleged); held, that the action could not be maintained; that the damages (if any) sustained by the plaintiff were the consequences of his own voluntary act, and not of the words. Ibid.

In Louisiana, the rule, that in an action for slander of title, the defendant, who reconvenes and sets up title, has the burden of proof, does not apply where he is in actual possession. If the defendant's title is not valid, he cannot controvert a confirmation of the plaintiff's title by the government, nor require that the plaintiff's title should be traced from the original

that the publication is false in any material respect, and that he has sustained any special damage therefrom; such proof makes a *primâ facie* case, and malice is to be presumed. If the defendant then proves, that the publication was honestly made by him, believing it to be true; and that there was a reasonable occasion therefor in the conduct of his own affairs, which fairly warranted the publication; such proof renders the publication privileged, and constitutes a good defence, unless the plaintiff can show malice in fact, which is a question for the jury.[1] So a declaration for libel stated, that the plaintiff carried on the business of an engineer, and was the inventor and registered proprietor (under stat. 2 & 3 Vict. c. 17) of an original design for making impressions on articles manufactured in metal, and sold divers articles on which the design was used; that before and at the time, &c., he had sold, and had on sale in the way of his said trade, articles and goods called "self-acting tallow syphons or lubricators;" and that the defendant published a libel of and concerning the plaintiff, and of and concerning the said design, and the plaintiff as the inventor, &c., thereof, and manufacturer of the articles with the said design thereon, and of and concerning the said goods which he had so sold and had on sale, and the plaintiff as the seller, as follows, viz: "This is to caution parties employing steam-power from a person" (meaning the plaintiff) "offering what he calls self-acting tallow syphons or lubricators," (meaning the said design, and meaning the said goods and articles which the plaintiff had so sold and had on sale as aforesaid,) "stating that he is the sole inventor, manufacturer, and patentee, thereby monopolizing high prices at the expense of the public. R. Harlow," (meaning the defendant,) "brass-founder, Stockport, takes this opportunity of saying that such a patent does not exist,

[1] Swan *v.* Tappan, 5 Cush. 104.

---

claimant to the confirmee. Griffon *v.* Blanc, 12 La. An. 5. Moore *v.* Blanc, Ib. 7. Pontalba *v.* Blanc, ib. 8.

and that he has to offer an improved lubricator," &c. "Those who have already adopted the lubricators" (meaning, &c., same innuendo as before) "against which R. H. would caution, will find that the tallow is wasted instead of being effectually employed as professed." There was no direct averment, connecting the tallow syphon with the registered design, mentioned in the first part of the inducement. No special damage was alleged. Held, the words were not a libel on the plaintiff, either generally, or in the way of his trade, but were only a reflection upon the goods sold by him, which was not actionable without special damage.[1] So no action can be maintained by an author, for a publication disparaging his works, in which he has a copyright, without an allegation and proof of special damage.[2]

23. But it is not within the limits of privileged criticism to print of an exhibitor of flowers, in observations touching the exhibition, "The name of G. is to be rendered famous in all sorts of dirty work; the tricks by which he, and a few like him, used to secure prizes, seem to have been broken in upon by some judges, more honest than usual. If G. be the same man who wrote an impudent letter to the Metropolitan Society, he is too worthless to notice; if he be not the same man, it is a pity two such beggarly souls could not be crammed into the same carcass."[3] So, upon demurrer to the declaration, (*a*) a publication commenting upon a printed work is libellous, which imputes to the author a disregard of justice and propriety as a man, represents him as infatuated with vanity, mad with passion, and the apologist from force of sympathy of another stigmatized with ingratitude and perfidy; and which also charges him with publish-

[1] Evans *v.* Harlow, 5 Ad. & Ell. N. S. 624.

[2] Swan *v.* Tappan, 5 Cush. 104.

[3] Green *v.* Chapman, 4 Bing. N. R. 92.

(*a*) In part upon the ground, that the defendant could not on demurrer claim his communication to be privileged; the question of privilege solely appertaining to a jury. Cooper *v.* Stone, 24 Wend. 434.

ing, as true, statements and evidence falsified and encomiums retracted.[1]

24. The question of privilege often arises, in connection with *a charge of crime* made by the party injured, and usually in good faith and without premeditation, against an innocent person. And the general rule is, that a charge of crime, which is a mere expression of suspicion founded upon facts detailed at the time, and made prudently and in confidence to discreet persons, in good faith, with a view to their aid in detecting the offender, and, in case of theft, for example, recovering the property, is not slanderous, but justifiable and proper.[2] Thus where a sheriff, having levied upon certain cattle which were subsequently driven away, employed the defendant, a student-at-law, to ascertain the facts and advise him what to do, who afterwards wrote to the sheriff, that he had ascertained that the plaintiff had been seen driving off the cattle, and that he had no doubt but that the taking was felonious, and advised him to prosecute the plaintiff for larceny; held, a privileged communication for which an action would not lie without proof of actual malice.[3] So a grand jury had an indictment for theft before them, and the defendant, a brother of the man who had lost the money, returning from the court, stated that fact in answer to inquiries made of him, and said that the general opinion was, that if a certain person swore what he had stated, the plaintiff, the accused, would be convicted. The declaration alleged, that the defendant said "he believed he stole the money," but it appeared, that the words, if spoken at all of the plaintiff, were spoken in a private conversation with a brother of the defendant, both being brothers of the man whose money had been stolen, and were overheard by one who had been employed to listen. Held, that the occasion, and the relationship between the parties, afforded a *primâ facie* justification, in the absence of express malice.[4]

[1] Cooper *v.* Stone, 24 Wend. 434.
[2] Grimes *v.* Coyle, 6 B. Mon. 301.
[3] Washburn *v.* Cook, 3 Denio, 110.
[4] Faris *v.* Starke, 9 Dana, 128.

25. But an unlawful attempt by the plaintiff to search the defendant will not justify the latter in charging the former with larceny from his person.[1] And where A. obtains a warrant to search the house of B. for goods suspected to be stolen, and, in accompanying the officer to execute the warrant, tells him that B. has robbed him; this is not a privileged communication.[2] So the defendant, having some cause for suspicion, went to the plaintiff's relations, and charged him with theft. It appearing, however, that his object in making the communication was rather to compromise the felony than to promote inquiry, or to enable the relations to redeem the plaintiff's character; held, that this was not a privileged communication; that malice must be implied; and that the existence of it was not a fact to be left to the jury.[3] So the defendant, who had lodged in the house of the plaintiff, conceiving that he had whilst there lost certain documents, and that the plaintiff had abstracted them from a box in which he had kept them, wrote a letter to the plaintiff's wife, stating his loss, and his suspicions, in language seriously reflecting upon the character of the plaintiff, and intimating that, unless the plaintiff should think proper to return them, he would expose him. Held, not a privileged communication, although made without malice.[4] So, where the defendant had a forged check passed to him by a stranger, and afterwards a relative of the plaintiff, having heard that the defendant had charged the plaintiff with the forgery, of his own accord applied to the defendant (saying however that he came at the plaintiff's request) for information respecting the charge, and to convince the defendant that he was mistaken, and thereupon the defendant told him that the plaintiff was unquestionably guilty, and proposed to arrange the matter by receiving the amount obtained on the check, and on that occasion persisted in the charge after being warned not to do so; held, the conversa-

[1] Kent v. Bonney, 38 Maine, 435.
[2] Dancaster v. Hewson, 2 M. & R. 176.
[3] Hooper v. Truscott, 2 Bing. N. R. 457.
[4] Wenman v. Ash, 13 Com. B. 836.

tion was not privileged, and the plaintiff was entitled to recover without proof of express malice.[1] (*a*)

26. Another class of privileged communications, are those made in connection with some matter of *lawful business*, for the real or professed purpose of imparting information in relation to such business, and usually in confidence and in answer to inquiry. And the general rule has been laid down, that "confidential communications, made in the usual course of business, or of domestic or friendly intercourse, should be liberally viewed."[2] Thus the plaintiff, a trader, being indebted to the defendant upon an unexpired credit, employs A. to sell his goods by auction, and absents himself under circumstances sufficient to induce the defendant to believe that an act of bankruptcy has been com-

[1] Thorn *v.* Moser, 1 Denio, 488. [2] Stallings *v.* Newman, 26 Ala. 300.

(*a*) The defendant, the tenant of a farm, required some repairs to be done at the farm-house, and B., the agent of the landlord, directed the plaintiff to do the work. The plaintiff did it, but in a negligent manner, and during the progress of it got drunk; and some circumstances occurred, which induced the defendant to believe, that the plaintiff had broken open his cellar-door and obtained access to his cider. The defendant, two days afterwards, met the plaintiff in the presence of D., and charged him with having broken his cellar-door, and with having got drunk and spoiled the work. The defendant afterwards told D., in the absence of the plaintiff, that he was confident the plaintiff had broken open the door. On the same day the defendant complained to B., that the plaintiff had been negligent in his work, had got drunk, and he thought he had broken open his cellar-door. Held, that the complaint to B. was a privileged communication, if made *bonâ fide*, and without any malicious intent; that the statement made to the plaintiff in the presence of D. was also privileged, if done honestly and *bonâ fide*, and that the circumstance of its being made in the presence of a third person did not of itself make it unauthorized; and that it was a question to be left to the jury to determine from the circumstances, including the style and character of the language used, whether the defendant acted *bonâ fide*, or was influenced by malicious motives. Held also, that the statement to D., in the absence of the plaintiff, was unauthorized and officious, and therefore not protected, although made in the belief of its truth, if it were in point of fact false. Toogood *v.* Spyring, 1 Cromp. M. & R. 181.

mitted. The defendant gives notice to A. not to pay over the proceeds to the plaintiff, "he having committed an act of bankruptcy." In an action for libel, held, by three Judges against one, a privileged communication.[1] So a banker, remitting the proceeds of a note sent to him for collection, appended to his letter the words, "Confidential. Had to hold over for a few days for the accommodation of L. & H.," who were the makers. Held, that these words have not necessarily an injurious meaning, and that their interpretation was a matter for the jury. Also, that the communication was privileged, and not actionable without actual malice.[2]

27. But it has been doubted, whether a caution *bonâ fide* given to a tradesman, without any inquiry on his part, not to trust another, falls within the exception of privileged communications.[3] So, where C., the mate of a ship, sent to B., a stranger, a letter, charging A., the captain, with gross misconduct; and B. showed the letter to D., the owner, who dismissed A.; it was doubted whether the showing of the letter by B. to D. was a privileged communication.[4] So one who undertakes, for an association of merchants, in a city to ascertain the pecuniary standing of merchants and traders residing in other places, who are customers of some of the members of the association; and who furnishes reports to all members of the association, irrespective of the facts whether they have an interest in the question of the standing of such merchants and traders; is liable for any false reports made by him prejudicial to the credit of the subject of it, although made honestly, and from information upon which he relied.[2]

28. And any facts and circumstances, which indicate a malicious purpose in making such communication, will deprive the party of this defence. And such purpose may be inferred from various circumstances; as from the defend-

[1] Blackham v. Pugh, 2 Com. B 611.
[2] Lewis v. Chapman, 16 N. Y. 369.
[3] Bennett v. Deacon, 2 Com. B. 628.
[4] Coxhead v. Richards, 2 Com. B. 569.
[5] Taylor v. Church, 4 Seld. 452; 1 E. D. Smith, 279.

ant's giving occasion to an inquiry, to which the alleged libel or slander purports to be an answer; or from its being but remotely connected with, or wholly foreign from, the business in which the party communicated with and the plaintiff were connected; or from an obvious rivalry between the plaintiff and defendant in relation to that or other business. And, in such cases, more especially in an action for libel, a verdict rendered for the defendant may sometimes be set aside by the Court, as against law and evidence. Thus the plaintiff inquired of the defendant, if he had accused her of using false weights in her trade. The defendant, in presence of a third person, answered: "To be sure I did. You have done it for years." Held, the latter words were actionable, and not privileged by reason of the plaintiff's inquiry; such inquiry being caused by a former statement of the defendant himself.[1] So where persons are engaged in a business in which credit and a character for punctuality are important, a communication addressed to their creditors, with whom they are in the habit of dealing, in these words, "Confidential. Had to hold over a few days for the accommodation of Q. and H.;" is calculated to injure their business character and credit, and therefore libellous.[2] So, the defendant being a competitor with the plaintiffs for a contract with the Navy Board, for African timber, the plaintiffs obtained the contract. The defendant then agreed to supply the plaintiffs with a portion of the timber, and made no objection to taking their bills in payment. This agreement, however, having been rescinded, on a disagreement as to the terms, the defendant wrote to a merchant at Sierra Leone, who was to supply the timber, and of whom the defendant was a creditor and the sole correspondent in London, a letter, reflecting deeply on the plaintiffs' mercantile character, and putting the merchant on his guard against them; for which, as a libel, the plaintiffs brought an action. The jury having found for the defendant, the Court granted a new

[1] Griffiths v. Lewis, 7 Ad. & Ell. N. S. 61; 16 N. Y. 369.

[2] Lewis v. Chapman, 19 Barb. 252.

trial.[1] So where, in an action for slandering the plaintiffs in their business of bankers, it was proved that W. said to the defendant, "I hear that you say that the plaintiffs' bank at M. has stopped; is it true?" and the defendant answered, "Yes, it is. I was told so. It was so reported at C., and nobody would take their bills, and I came to town in consequence of it myself." Held, it was a question for the jury, first, whether the defendant understood W. as asking for information, and uttered the words merely by way of honest advice to regulate W.'s conduct; and if so, whether, in so doing, he was guilty of any malice in fact.[2] So, in an action for libel, it appeared that the plaintiff was churchwarden, and the defendant clergyman of the same parish, and that, differences having arisen between them in that relation, the plaintiff requested that the defendant's future communications should be by letter to the plaintiff's clerk. The defendant afterwards applied, by letter to the clerk, for money which he conceived to be due to himself from the plaintiff. The clerk answered that the plaintiff denied his liability, and in reply the defendant addressed a letter to the clerk, saying, "This attempt to defraud me is as mean as dishonest." Held, that it was properly left to the jury, whether the above language was justified by the occasion; and that the communication was not in itself privileged, so as to render proof of actual malice necessary to sustain the action.[3]

29. So the circumstance, that a part of a communication is written confidentially and in good faith, and relates to a privileged subject, will not justify another part, relating to another subject. Thus a letter, written for the purpose of obtaining information, to which the writer is properly entitled, yet, if it contain slanderous comments upon an individual, concerning whom no information was expected or desired, and foreign to the avowed object for which it was written; is libellous.[4] So the plaintiff and the defendant were jointly interested in property in Scotland, of which C.

[1] Ward v. Smith, 6 Bing. 749.
[2] Bromage v. Prosser, 6 D. & Ry. 296.
[3] Tuson v. Evans, 3 Per. & Dav. 396.
[4] Cole v. Wilson, 18 B. Mon. 212.

was manager. The defendant wrote to C. a letter, principally about the property, and the conduct of the plaintiff with reference thereto, but containing a charge against the plaintiff with reference to his conduct to his mother and aunt. Held, that though the part of the letter about the defendant's conduct as to the property might be confidential and privileged, such privilege could not extend to the part of the letter about the plaintiff's conduct to his mother and aunt.[1] And where one authorized, by his relation to the party addressed, to make a "privileged communication," in professing to do so, makes a false charge; the inference of malice is against him, and the burden is put on him to show that he acted *bonâ fide*.[2]

30. Under this head of privileged communications, the most numerous class, perhaps, is that of verbal or written statements, made by *masters* or *employers*, in reference to the *character of their servants*. And upon this subject the general rule is, that a servant cannot maintain an action against his former master, for words spoken or a letter written by him in giving a character of the servant, unless the latter prove the malice, as well as falsehood of the charge.[3] It is necessary to show implied malice, by directly negativing the charge, or express malice *aliunde*.[4] And it is no proof of express malice, that the master has communicated to the party inquiring his belief as to misconduct after the plaintiff had quitted his service, nor that he has made a similar communication to persons from whom he received the plaintiff with a good character.[5] And even specific charges of misconduct may be justified.[6] Thus, the defendant having given notice of dismissal to his footman and cook, they separately went to him and asked his reason for discharging them, when he told each (in the absence of the other) that he (or she) was discharged because both had been robbing him; whereupon

[1] Warren *v.* Warren, 1 Cromp. M. & R. 250.

[2] Wakefield *v.* Smithwick, 4 Jones, Law, 327.

[3] Weatherstone *v.* Hawkins, 1 T. R. 110.

[4] Child *v.* Affleck, 4 M. & R. 338.

[5] Ibid.

[6] Weatherstone *v.* Hawkins, 1 T. R. 110.

each brought an action for the words so spoken to the other. Held, a privileged communication.[1] So the defendant, having dismissed the plaintiff from his service on suspicion of theft, upon his coming to his counting-house for his wages, called in two other of his servants, and, addressing them in the presence of the plaintiff, said, "I have dismissed that man for robbing me: do not speak to him any more, in public or in private, or I shall think you as bad as him." Held, a privileged communication; it being both the duty and interest of the defendant, to prevent his servants from associating with a person of such a character as the words imputed to the plaintiff, inasmuch as such association might probably be followed by injurious consequences both to the servants and to the defendant himself.[2] So, in an action for libel, it appeared that the defendant, with whom the plaintiff had lived as servant, in answer to inquiries respecting her character, wrote a letter imputing misconduct to her whilst in that service, and after she left it; and the defendant also made similar verbal statements to two persons who had recommended the plaintiff to her. Held, that neither the letter itself nor the verbal statements proved malice, and that, consequently, the letter was a privileged communication, and the plaintiff not entitled to recover.[3] So the plaintiff, a domestic servant, about to enter the service of B., referred B. for her character to the defendant, in whose service the plaintiff had been. The defendant being then unwell, her husband answered the application, and gave the plaintiff a good character; and B. took the plaintiff into service. The defendant recovered, and, in a letter written to B. on other matters, said that she, the defendant, had lately been much imposed upon in her kitchen. B., in consequence, made further inquiries of the defendant as to the plaintiff's character; and the defendant, in answer, said she suspected the plaintiff of dishonesty. The jury, in answer to the Judge, found that the defendant intended by her

[1] Manby v. Witt; Eastmead v. Witt, 18 Com. B. 544; 37 Eng. L. & Eq. 403.

[2] Somervill v. Hawkins, 10 Com. B. 583; 3 Eng. L. & Eq. 503.

[3] Child v. Affleck, 9 B. & C. 403.

letter to induce inquiries on B.'s part as to the plaintiff; and they found a verdict for the plaintiff, subject to leave to move for a nonsuit. On motion to enter a nonsuit; held, that the defendant was bound to correct any error, as to the plaintiff's character, into which she supposed B. to have been led by the answer to B.'s former application; and that the words were spoken under such circumstances as *primâ facie* to be privileged. Also, that the facts that the defendant alluded to the plaintiff, and induced inquiries about her, were not evidence of malice. Rule absolute for a nonsuit.[1] So the defendant, having a suspicion that the plaintiff, who was his shopman, had in one instance embezzled money, sent for him, and in the presence of a third person charged him with embezzlement, and at the same time discharged him. The plaintiff, being about to enter into a fresh service, referred to the defendant for a character, but, in consequence of what the defendant said, his intended master refused to engage him. Upon this the plaintiff's brother called upon the defendant, and inquired why he had given the plaintiff such a character as prevented him from getting a situation, and in answer to these inquiries the defendant said, "He has robbed me. I believe he has robbed me for years past; I can prove it from the circumstances under which he has been discharged by me." Held, each of these statements was privileged, notwithstanding the first was made in presence of a third party; and that the excess of the defendant's statement on the second occasion did not raise any presumption of express malice.[2]

31. Upon the same ground, words spoken by an employer to his overseer, intended to protect the employer's private interests and property, but not spoken maliciously, are not actionable, although no confidence was expressed at the time of speaking, and although the same words published under other circumstances would be slander.[3]

32. But a statement, made by the late master of a ser-

[1] Gardner v. Slade, 13 Ad. & Ell. N. S. 796.

[2] Taylor v. Hawkins, 5 Eng. L. & Eq. 253.

[3] Easley v. Moss, 9 Ala. 266.

vant to another person, who had thoughts of engaging that servant, is not privileged, where from other evidence, though of a slight description, the jury has inferred actual malice.[1] Thus where a master, *without being applied to*, volunteers to give an unfavorable character of a discarded servant, it is *primâ facie* malicious, and not privileged.[2] And, although a master be not in general bound to prove the truth of a character, given by him to a person applying for it, yet, if he officiously state any trivial misconduct of the servant to a former master, in order to prevent him from giving a second character, and then himself, upon application for a character, give the servant a bad character, the truth of which he is not able to prove, the jury may infer malice.[3] So, in an action for an alleged libel, contained in an answer to inquiries respecting the character of a servant, the plaintiff establishes a case to go to the jury, if there is any evidence, as matter of fact, that the answer was untrue to the defendant's knowledge, or, as to the matters of opinion, that the defendant, in giving the character, did not really act on the opinion which he professes to have entertained. Thus, in answer to an inquiry as to the character of a governess, the defendant wrote a letter in which she said, "I parted with her on account of her incompetency, and not being ladylike nor good-tempered." To this letter there was the following postscript: "May I trouble you, to tell her that, this being the third time I have been referred to, I beg to decline any further applications." In an action by the governess against the defendant, for writing this letter, she gave evidence tending to negative the statement in it of her demerits, and she proved that previously the writer had recommended her as a governess. The Judge directed the jury, that the letter, being an answer to an inquiry, was *primâ facie* privileged; but that the letter itself and the facts proved were some evidence of express malice, to rebut any inference of which, the defendant might have given evidence

[1] Kelly *v.* Partington, 2 Nev. & M. 460.

[2] Pattison *v.* Jones, 3 M. & Ry. 101.

[3] Rogers *v.* Clifton, 3 Bos. & Pul. 587.

that the statement of the character was true, or that she believed or had reason to believe it true. Held, this direction was right.[1] So, A. having discharged his servant, and hearing that he was about to be engaged by B., wrote a letter to B., and informed him that he had discharged him for misconduct. B., in answer, desired further information. A. then wrote a second letter to B., stating the grounds on which he had discharged the servant. In an action by the servant against A., for a libel contained in this letter, it was held, that, assuming the letter to be a privileged communication, it was properly left to the jury to consider whether the second letter was written by A. *bonâ fide*, or with an intention to injure the servant.[2]

33. Whether a publication libellous on its face may be excused as privileged, is a *question of law*, which may properly be raised by a demurrer.[3] And it is not necessary to submit to the jury the question, whether the defendant had made a *fair* and *impartial* statement. For the purpose of determining as to the character of the alleged libel, it is sufficient if the publication be true.[4] So, whether a publication, in itself libellous, is merely a report of the proceedings before a police magistrate, or a positive affirmation of the truth of the facts which it states, is not a question to be submitted to the jury. It is a question of construction, which the Court is bound and is alone competent to determine.[5] And if one authorized to make a privileged communication, state a falsehood, and no evidence is offered of his having heard it, or as to his belief of it; it is erroneous for the Court to leave the question to the jury, whether "in communicating what he had heard and believed to be true," he acted in good faith.[6]

34. But in an action for a libel, in publishing the proceedings of a court of justice, it is proper to submit to the

[1] Fountain *v.* Boodle, 3 Ad. & Ell. N. S. 5; 2 Gal. & Dav. 455.

[2] Pattison *v.* Jones, 8 B. & C. 578.

[3] Fry *v.* Bennett, 5 Sandf. 54.

[4] Huff *v.* Bennett, 4 Sandf. 120.

[5] Matthews *v.* Beach, 5 Sandf. 256.

[6] Wakefield *v.* Smithwick, 4 Jones, Law, 327.

jury, as a question of fact, whether the defendant has made a true publication of such proceedings.[1] So the plaintiffs, printers at M., had been employed by the defendant, the deputy clerk of the peace for the county of K., to print the register of electors for the county, the expense of which is defrayed from the county rate, and allowed by the justice's quarter sessions. In 1854, the defendant employed another printer, who agreed to do the work at a lower rate than that which the plaintiffs required; and he wrote a letter to the "finance committee" appointed to superintend such expenses, in the conclusion of which he imputed improper motives to the plaintiffs in the demand which they made, accusing them of "an attempt to extort a considerable sum of money from the county by misrepresentation." In an action for libel, held, that the occasion of writing the letter *primâ facie* rebutted the presumption of malice; but that it was a question for the jury, whether the sentence complained of as exceeding the privilege was evidence of malice.[2] So, where a libel charged the plaintiff, who had been a minister of France to the United States, with having "traitorously betrayed the secrets of his government," and the proof was, that he had published his instructions; it was held, that a public minister may, if he deems it necessary, publish his instructions; and whether by such publication he has traitorously betrayed the secrets of his government, is a mixed question, on which a jury, in this action, under the advice of the Court, are to decide.[3] So, to publish of a member of congress, "he is a fawning sycophant, a mis-representative in congress, and a grovelling office-seeker; he has abandoned his post in congress in pursuit of an office;" is libellous. But whether the party did leave his post for the purpose imputed to him, or had violated his duty as a representative in congress, are questions for the jury.[4] And, although it is for the Judge to rule whether the occasion creates a

[1] Huff *v.* Bennett, 4 Sandf. 120.

[2] Cook *v.* Wildes, 30 Eng. L. & Eq. 284.

[3] Genet *v.* Mitchell, 7 Johns. 120.

[4] Thomas *v.* Croswell, 7 Johns. 264.

privilege, yet, if it does, but there is evidence of express malice, either from extrinsic circumstances or from the language of the libel itself, the question of malice should be left to the jury.[1] Thus, in an action for slander, it appeared that the defendant, in the presence of a third person, not an officer, charged the plaintiff with having stolen his property, and afterwards repeated the charge to another person, also not an officer, who was called in to search the plaintiff with the consent of the latter. Held, that the charge was privileged, if the defendant believed in its truth, acted *bonâ fide*, and did not make the charge before more persons, or in stronger language, than was necessary; and that it was a question for the jury, and not for the Judge, whether the facts brought the case within this rule.[2]

35. It will be seen hereafter, (*a*) that the plea of *the truth* to an action for slander or libel, if not maintained, is treated as a repetition of the charge, and may enhance the damages.[3] But where, to an action for libel, the defendant pleaded not guilty and a justification, and offered no proof of the justification, but gave evidence that the document was a privileged and private communication with a third party; held, the jury, in forming their opinion (upon the first issue) whether the communication was privileged, ought not to take into consideration the fact, that the justification had been pleaded and abandoned.[4] But, where a plea to an action for libel justifies that the facts charged are true, and the comments *bonâ fide*, it is properly left to the jury to consider, not only whether the facts are proved, but whether the comments also are *bonâ fide*, if they are of themselves actionable, and are not necessary inferences from the facts. Thus, under such a justification of a libel, imputing to the plaintiff, that he had become surety for £500 on an election petition, although he

[1] Cook *v.* Wildes, 5 Ell. & Bl. 328.

[2] Padmore *v.* Lawrence, 11 Ad. & Ell. 380; 3 Per. & Dav. 209.

[3] Gilpin *v.* Fowler, 26 Eng. L. & Eq. 386.

[4] Wilson *v.* Robinson, 7 Ad. & Ell. N. S. 68.

(*a*) See *Justification*.

was at the time in insolvent and insufficient circumstances, and adding that he was hired for the occasion; the observation that he was hired, whether taken as a statement of a distinct fact or a mere comment, is itself actionable, and the jury are to decide whether it is covered by evidence justifying the rest of the libel.[1]

[1] Cooper *v.* Lawson, 1 P. & Dav. 15.

CHAPTER XV.

PLEADING, EVIDENCE, DAMAGES, &c., IN ACTIONS FOR LIBEL AND SLANDER.

1. WITH regard to the rules of *pleading*, in actions for libel and slander; the general rule is, that *the very words* themselves must be given in the declaration, and not merely their *import*, *substance*, *tenor*, or *effect*.[1] (*a*) For the reason,

[1] Attwood *v.* Taylor, 1 M. & Gr. 282 (*n*); Newton *v.* Stubbs, 3 Mod. 71; Forsyth *v.* Edmiston, 5 Duer, 653; Bayley *v.* Johnston, 4 Rich. 22; Zeig *v.* Ort, 3 Chand. 26; Whitaker *v.* Freeman, 1 Dev. 271.

(*a*) This statement is to be received with the qualification, that the common-law rule on the subject has been changed in many, and perhaps most of the States by express statute.

Declaration, that the defendant falsely, wickedly, and deceitfully represented and affirmed to one P. that the plaintiff was a person of a bad character, and had been guilty of immoral conduct, and was not fit to be associated with; and so depraved, and of such a character, that the said P. ought not to permit, or suffer him to reside, or dwell in the house with the said P.'s wife; and that the plaintiff was in other respects disreputable and disgraceful in his conduct. Held, a count for slander; and bad on general demurrer, for not setting out the words verbatim. Sullivan *v.* White, 6 Irish L. R. 40.

It has been held in Massachusetts, that, in an action of slander, the plaintiff may set forth in his declaration either the words spoken or *the substance* of them. Whiting *v.* Smith, 13 Pick. 364. See Lee *v.* Kane, 6 Gray, 495; Baldwin *v.* Soule, Ib. 321.

So a count, setting forth, generally, that the defendant charged the plaintiff with a crime, (naming it,) is good. Allen *v.* Perkins, 17 Pick. 369; Nye *v.* Otis, 8 Mass. 122.

as is said, that this is not an express allegation that they were spoken.[1]

2. And where a declaration for libel sets out a publication which is libellous only by referring to a previous one, such previous publication must appear, in the declaration, to be set out verbatim, and not merely in substance, nor by reference to a previous count in the declaration. (See § 6 et seq.) Therefore judgment was arrested as to the second count of a declaration, which, after reciting that the defendant published a statement "in substance as follows," setting out the publication charged in the first count, charged that the defendant afterwards published, of and concerning the plaintiff, &c., and of and concerning the first publication, a certain statement not in itself libellous.[2] So a declaration for libel stated, by way of inducement, that there were vague reports in circulation, that the plaintiff had done something disreputable and disgraceful in connection with breaking, or causing to be broken, a lock or locks, for the purpose of taking on execution money in the possession of one A. M. B., and then set forth a publication by the defendant in relation to money which he owed the plaintiff, in which it was said, "there will be no locksmith necessary to get at the ready," which, the declaration averred, referred to the reports, and intended to charge the plaintiff with having done something disgraceful. Held, insufficient, and that the substance of the reports should have been stated.[3] (See *infra* § 8, et seq.)

[1] 3 Mod. 71.

[2] Solomon *v.* Lawson, 8 Ad. & Ell. N. S. 823. But see Nestle *v.* Van Slyck, 2 Hill, 282.

[3] Stone *v.* Cooper, 2 Denio, 293.

And under such a count the plaintiff may prove, that the words spoken, though not actionable in themselves, were rendered so by the existence of certain extrinsic facts; a reference to those facts; and the mode in which the words were used; without any averment that they were spoken with reference to any fact whatever. Allen *v.* Perkins, 17 Pick. 369; Nye *v.* Otis, 8 Mass. 122.

But the Court may order a specification or bill of particulars. Clark *v.* Munsell, 6 Met. 373.

As to forms of declaration provided for by statute, see Hawks *v.* Patton, 18 Geo. 52; Holcombe *v.* Roberts, 19 Geo. 588; Gardner *v.* Dyer, 5 Gray, 22.

3. But, in an action for libel, the entire article alleged to be libellous need not be set out; if omitted parts explain those set out, the defendant may avail himself of them on the general issue.[1] Thus a libel charged the plaintiff with being the most artful scoundrel that ever existed, and with being insolvent; but the writer added, that he had never disclosed the matter, nor ever would, except to the person whom he addressed, and his friend. This latter assertion was omitted in the declaration. Held, that the omission was not material.[2] And, in general, it is sufficient to set out the words which are material, and additional words which do not diminish nor alter their sense may be omitted.[3]

4. In case of words actionable *per se*, special damages need not be averred.[4] Nor the name of the person to whom or in whose presence they were spoken.[5] (*a*) So, although malice is the gist of the action, and must be alleged, the word "maliciously" need not be used; it is sufficient if words of equivalent import are used.[6] (See p. 351.)

5. But where words are actionable only in respect of the special damage, that must be set forth with certainty; for it is issuable. Thus, in an action for saying, "you are a whore," by which the plaintiff lost her marriage, the name of the person who refused to marry her must be set forth.[7] (*b*)

[1] Weir *v.* Hoss, 6 Ala. 881.
[2] Rutherford *v.* Evans, 6 Bing. 451.
[3] Spencer *v.* McMasters, 16 Ill. 405; Whiting *v.* Smith, 13 Pick. 364.
[4] Hicks *v.* Walker, 2 Greene, 440.
[5] Ware *v.* Cartledge, 24 Ala. 622.
[6] White *v.* Nicholls, 3 How. U. S. 266.
[7] Wetherell *v.* Clerkson, 12 Mod. 597.

(*a*) See *Publication*, p. 318.

(*b*) See p. 271. In an action for slander, although the words spoken must be set out, *a substantial proof of them*, as alleged, is sufficient. Bassett *v.* Spofford, 11 N. Hamp. 127.

So, though all the actionable words laid in any one count are not proved, yet, if some are, the plaintiff shall have a verdict. Compagnon *v.* Martin, 2 W. Black. 790.

Actions for the charge of *perjury* have perhaps more frequently than any others given rise to questions of pleading. Thus, in a declaration for slander, the plaintiff averred, that the defamatory words were spoken "whilst the plaintiff was giving testimony as a witness under the solemnities of an

6. A declaration for libel or slander may contain *several counts*, either setting forth different words or the same words in different forms. (*a*)

7. The following points are decided with regard to the bearing of different counts upon each other.

8. One count may be aided by reference to *matter of inducement* in a preceding count.[1] (*b*) (See § 129.)

[1] Nestle *v.* Van Slyck, 2 Hill, 282.

---

oath before an acting justice of the peace." Held, the averment was sufficient. Lewis *v.* Black, 27 Miss. (5 Cush.) 425.

So a declaration in slander, for charging the plaintiff with swearing to a lie as a witness in a proceeding before a justice of the peace, in which it is not stated that the justice had jurisdiction or power to administer the oath, or that the testimony was material, although bad on demurrer, is good after verdict. Palmer *v.* Hunter, 8 Mis. 512.

So, in an action of slander, where the charge was, that the plaintiff had sworn to a lie at a certain trial, it was held, that the plaintiff need not set forth in his declaration the whole of his evidence at the trial, unless the defendant had specified the language in which the plaintiff had sworn falsely. Smith *v.* Smith, 8 Ired. 29.

A count in slander, alleging that the defendant maliciously, and without proper cause, made a charge of felony against the plaintiff before a magistrate, is good after verdict. But, if such count sets out the proceedings, it should set forth facts sufficient to show that a complaint or charge of felony was made before a magistrate in his official capacity. Hill *v.* Miles, 9 N. Hamp. 9.

A declaration alleged, that the plaintiff had been appointed as surveyor of a company or society, called "The New England Company," and had been employed by them as such; and that the defendant libelled him in his employment. Held, that it was not necessary to allege with extreme precision the description of the company; or to prove the plaintiff's appointment, the libel being alleged of the plaintiff in his employment. Rutherford *v.* Evans, 6 Bing. 451.

A statute, declaring what words are actionable, is a public law, of which the Court is bound to take notice, and, in declaring for the slander, the statute need not be recited or referred to. Sanford *v.* Gaddis, 13 Ill. 329.

(*a*) It has been held in New York not to be a misjoinder of causes of action, to charge *in the same count* words imputing to the plaintiff that he had counterfeit bills in his possession, with intent to pass the same, *and* that he had in his possession plates in the similitude of bank-bills, with, &c. Dioyt *v.* Tanner, 20 Wend. 190.

(*b*) In an action for a libel, the plaintiff, at the trial, may abandon any

9. Where a declaration contains two or more counts, charging slanderous words at different times, and the words charged in one count are proved to have been spoken on the very day laid in that count; if the defendant justifies them, words contained in a second count, but spoken previously to those alleged and proved in the first, will not support the action.[1]

10. Where the declaration in an action of slander consists of two counts, the one for words charging the plaintiff with perjury, and the other with theft; and the plaintiff introduces evidence in support of both; he may at any time before verdict abandon one count, and the jury be directed to lay out of the case all the testimony applicable to that count.[2]

11. It has been held, that a verdict supported by one count is good, although all the others are bad.[3] But where one of several counts was bad, and some of the words in it were proved, and the jury found a general verdict for the plaintiff; the Court set aside an order of the Judge who tried the cause, to confine the verdict and damages to one of the good counts, and awarded a *venire de novo*.[4]

12. Where, in an action of slander, the declaration contains two counts, alleging the utterance of similar words at different times, and a verdict is returned for the plaintiff on one count, and for the defendant on the other; the counts are not *on several and distinct causes of action*, so as to entitle the defendant to costs, within the true meaning and intention of Rev. Stats. (of Massachusetts) c. 121, § 16.[5]

13. When a plaintiff sets forth in one count the words spoken by the defendant, charging him with a certain offence,

[1] Wright *v.* Bretton, 1 Morris, 286.
[2] Kirkaldie *v.* Paige, 17 Verm. 256.
[3] Marshall *v.* Gunter, 6 Rich. 419.
[4] Empson *v.* Griffin, 11 Ad. & Ell. 186.
[5] Sayle *v.* Briggs, 1 Met. 291.

part of the libellous matter in any one count, and this part may be used, in connection with the remainder, to show the meaning; and he will recover if the part retained be sufficient to maintain an action. Genet *v.* Mitchell, 7 Johns. 120.

and adds a count, which only alleges that the defendant charged him with the same offence; and files a bill of particulars on the second count, in which he gives notice that he shall rely, in support of that count, on the words set forth in the first count; he cannot give notice of any other words besides those set forth.[1]

14. In a count subsequent to the first, alleging that the words were spoken in a discourse, &c., an amendment, by inserting the word *other* before the word *discourse*, is matter of form, and may be allowed after issue joined.[2]

15. Words appearing to be used in one continued discourse constitute only one count. Thus a declaration alleged, that the plaintiff carried on the trade of buying and selling, and was a dealer in an article of fishing tackle called a *winch;* that the defendant used the trade of making and selling winches; that the defendant, contriving to injure the plaintiff in his said trade, and to cause his customers to believe that he was guilty of unlawfully buying goods, well knowing them to have been stolen and dishonestly come by, in a discourse which he had with the plaintiff, of and concerning him with reference to his said trade, and of and concerning the premises, in the presence and hearing of J. F., &c., falsely and maliciously spoke to, and of and concerning the plaintiff, and of and concerning him with reference to his said trade and the premises, the words, &c., "I (meaning the defendant) have been robbed of about three dozen winches (meaning such articles, &c.); a person has been buying things at my shop, and has taken them; you (meaning the plaintiff) have bought two, one at 3*s.* and one at 2*s.*; you (meaning the plaintiff) knew well when you bought them (meaning the said winches) that they cost me (meaning the defendant) three times as much making as you (meaning the plaintiff) gave for them, and that they could not have been come honestly by." The declaration then proceeded: "Whereupon the plaintiff then, in the presence and hearing of the aforesaid persons, said to the defendant," &c., setting

[1] Stevens *v.* Heartly, 11 Met. 542.

[2] Gay *v.* Homer, 13 Pick. 535.

forth further words of the plaintiff respecting winches, and alleging that the defendant, further contriving, &c., thereupon, in the presence and hearing of the said persons, replied, &c., (setting out other words.) Thereby meaning, &c., "that the plaintiff had been and was guilty of buying winches, well knowing the same to have been dishonestly come by, and to have been feloniously stolen by the person of and from whom the said plaintiff had so bought them." After verdict for general damages; held, on motion in arrest of judgment: 1. That the words first set out imputed that the plaintiff had received stolen goods, knowing them to have been stolen. 2. That the words following appeared to be spoken at the same time with the others, and formed with them a continued discourse; that the declaration, therefore, contained only a single count; and, consequently, that the plaintiff was entitled to judgment, even on the assumption that the words last set out gave no cause of action.[1]

16. So, where a declaration of two counts sets out words alleged to have been uttered, some in one discourse, and the remainder in a second discourse, each count containing only the words alleged to have been uttered in one discourse; the declaration will be treated as containing only two counts, though each count contains separate allegations of the uttering of different words in the particular discourse. Therefore, if in each count there be any words set out which are slanderous, judgment for the plaintiff will not be arrested, though the damages be general, and some of the separate allegations recite only words not actionable.[2]

17. We have often had occasion, in various connections, to refer to the *innuendo*, as an important part of the declaration, in actions for libel and slander. Upon this subject it is held, that words, which in themselves do not import a slanderous meaning, must be rendered slanderous by an innuendo, and an averment that they were spoken of the plaintiff. But, if the words are themselves slanderous, the latter aver-

[1] Alfred *v.* Farlow, 8 Ad. & Ell. N. S. 854.

[2] Griffiths *v.* Lewis, 8 Ad. & Ell. N. S. 841.

ment is sufficient.[1] Thus, where the words laid, in their common acceptation, import the charge of a crime, the declaration is sufficient without a colloquium (*Infra*, § 25,) or innuendo. As where the declaration alleged that the defendant said of the plaintiff: "He is a thief and a liar, and I can prove it." Held, that the words, of themselves, in their common acceptation, imported a charge of larceny, and that the declaration was sufficient without a colloquium or innuendo; that if the words were spoken in a different sense, not amounting to the charge which they usually import, and were understood in that sense by those in whose presence they were spoken, the defendant might show this on trial, as a defence to the action.[2]

18. The office of the innuendo is said to be, to explain or apply the words spoken, and annex to them their proper meaning, where there is matter sufficient in the declaration to sustain the action. It cannot extend or enlarge their sense beyond their usual and natural import, unless something is put upon the record by way of introductory matter with which they can be connected. In such case, words, which are equivocal or ambiguous, or fall short in their natural sense of importing any libellous charge, may have fixed to them a meaning, certain and defamatory, extending beyond their ordinary import.[3] (*a*) Its office is, to *point* to the introductory matter in the declaration.[4] Thus, if a publica-

[1] Brittain *v.* Allen, 3 Dev. 167.

[2] Robinson *v.* Keyser, 2 Fost. 323.

[3] Beardsley *v.* Tappan, 1 Blatch. 588; Hays *v.* Mitchell, 7 Blackf. 117; Patterson *v.* Edwards, 2 Gilm. 720; 16 Verm. 83; Joralemon *v.* Pomeroy, 2 N. J. 271; Dorsey *v.* Whipps, 8 Gill, 457; Dottarer *v.* Bushey, 16 Penn. 204; Rex *v.* Alderton, Sayer, 280; Cramer *v.* Noonan, 4 Wis. 231; Tyler *v.* Tillotson, 2 Hill, 507; Wilson *v.* Hamilton, 9 Rich. Law, 382.

[4] 2 Hill, 507; 6 Ala. 881.

(*a*) In other words, the innuendoes in a declaration in slander should be warranted by the previous allegations. Stucker *v.* Davis, 8 Blackf. 414.

And, where the words charged do not amount to slander, they will not be aided by an innuendo. Moseley *v.* Moss, 6 Gratt. 534.

But a declaration, in which the words spoken and the innuendo were first set forth, and then a fact necessary to warrant the innuendo, was held sufficient. Brittain *v.* Allen, 2 Dev. 120; S. C. 3 Dev. 167.

tion be not directly libellous, but only *by allusion*, the fact understood must be stated by introduction, and must be pointed at by explanatory innuendoes.[1]

19. In accordance with these definitions and explanations, it is held that an innuendo is not *an averment of facts*, but *an inference of reasoning*. (*a*) Its sole office is *explanation*, and the only question which it raises is, whether the explanation given is a legitimate deduction from the premises stated; and this question belongs to the Court. When improperly framed, it may in some cases justify a demurrer, but its truth or falsehood is never a question of fact for the jury. Hence, issues taken upon the truth of an innuendo are immaterial.[2]

20. The following examples illustrate the effect of an innuendo.

21. The words, "that you are guilty of the death of A.," may be explained by innuendo to mean the *murder* of A., though the colloquium be only laid of the death.[3] So where the words set forth were, that A. was murdered, and the plaintiff was concerned in it and had a hand in it; innuendo, meaning that the plaintiff aided and assisted in the commission of the murder; it was held sufficient.[4] So a declaration in slander for saying, "A. stole a sheep of his," "innuendo, a sheep of the defendant," is good.[5] And where the term "Filly horse" was explained, by innuendo that the plaintiff's wife was meant, her name being Hoss; it was held good.[6] So an allegation in an action for libel, that the defendant dispersed a paper-writing, accusing the plaintiff of

1 The State *v.* Neese, 2 Tayl. 270.
2 Fry *v.* Bennet, 5 Sandf. 54. See 7 Eng. 625.
3 Oldham *v.* Peake, 2 W. Black. 959, 960.
4 Tenney *v.* Clement, 10 N. H. 52.
5 Muck's case, 8 Mod. 30.
6 Weir *v.* Hoss, 6 Ala. 881.

(*a*) But it is also held, that the subject to which the conversation relates, and the innuendo, which alleges the meaning of it, must both be established as true, before the plaintiff can show a right of action; that they are *facts*, and, as such, must be submitted to the jury. McGough *v.* Rhodes, 7 Eng, 625.

having said, that "the war would not end until the little gentleman, innuendo, the Prince of Wales, was restored," is sufficiently certain.[1] So an averment that the defendant had spoken of and concerning the plaintiff these words: "N. (meaning the plaintiff) burnt it, (meaning the store,) and he (meaning the plaintiff) knew it, and I (meaning the defendant) can prove it;" preceded by a colloquium that the words were spoken of and concerning the burning of a store owned by the defendant, and followed by an averment that the words were intended to charge the plaintiff with a felonious burning, &c.; was held sufficient.[2] So, in a declaration for slander, the first count stated that the plaintiff was a butcher, and that the defendant, contriving to cause it to be believed that the plaintiff had been and was guilty of, in her said trade, fraudulently using two weights to a steelyard (as to which there was no previous direct allegation), by her used in her said trade, and of using improper and fraudulent weights in her said trade, and thereby to injure the plaintiff in her said trade, in a discourse of and concerning the plaintiff in her said trade, and of and concerning M., a son of the plaintiff, and her servant in her said trade, as such servant, and of and concerning the plaintiff having, as supposed by the defendant, by M., as her agent and servant, "used improper and fraudulent weights" in her said trade, and defrauded and cheated in her said trade, and of and concerning her being, as supposed by the defendant, guilty of defrauding and cheating in her said trade, and having, as supposed by the defendant, in her said trade, by M., as her agent and servant, fraudulently used two weights to a steelyard by her used in her said trade, spoke in the presence, &c. of and concerning plaintiff in her said trade, and of and concerning M., as and then being such servant, and of and concerning the plaintiff having, as supposed by the defendant, by M., as her agent and servant, used improper and fraudulent weights in her trade, and being, as supposed by the defendant, guilty of defrauding and cheating in her said

[1] Anon. 11 Mod. 99. [2] Nichols v. Packard, 16 Verm. 83.

trade, and of and concerning the plaintiff having, as supposed by the defendant, in her said trade, by M., as her agent and servant, fraudulently used two weights to a steelyard, by her used in her said trade, these false, &c. words, " M. (meaning the said M., so being such servant) uses two balls to his mother's steelyard," (meaning that the plaintiff, by M. as her agent and servant, used improper and fraudulent weights in her said trade, and defrauded and cheated in her said trade.) On motion to arrest the judgment, held, that the words, being susceptible of both a harmless and an injurious meaning, the innuendo was properly applied to point to the injurious meaning. The second count, with similar preliminary averments and description of the intention of the defendant, and subject of the discourse and of the words, adding that the discourse and words were also of and concerning the defendant himself, alleged that the defendant, in the presence, &c., spoke, in answer to a question put by the plaintiff to the defendant as to whether the defendant had said to G., that the plaintiff's son used two balls to the plaintiff's steelyard, these false, &c. words: " To be sure I (meaning the defendant) did, (meaning that the defendant had said to G. that the plaintiff's son used two balls to the plaintiff's steelyard, and also that the plaintiff, in her said trade, had, by a son of the plaintiff, as her agent and servant, fraudulently used two weights to a steelyard by her used in her said trade;) I (meaning the defendant) will swear to it in any court; you, G., have used them for years (meaning that the plaintiff had in her said trade fraudulently used two weights to a steelyard by her used in her said trade). On motion to arrest judgment; held, that the words, as stated and explained, were actionable.[1]

22. But a declaration for saying " he fired his house," (innuendo, *voluntarily*,) is bad.[2] So the plaintiff averred, that he had in due manner put in his answer on oath to a bill filed against him by the defendant, (but did not pro-

[1] Griffiths *v.* Lewis, 8 Ad. & Ell. N. S. 841.

[2] Anon. 11 Mod. 220.

ceed to aver any colloquium respecting the answer,) and that the defendant said of him that he was forsworn; innuendo, that the plaintiff had perjured himself in what he had sworn in his aforesaid answer to the bill filed against him. Held, this innuendo could not enlarge the sense of the words, by referring them to the answer averred in the prefatory part of the declaration.[1] So a declaration laid the words as follows: "You have robbed me of one shilling tan-money;" innuendo, that the plaintiff had fraudulently taken and applied to his own use one shilling received by him for the defendant, being the produce of a sale of some tan sold by the plaintiff for, and as a servant to, the defendant; but these facts were not otherwise alleged. Held, the innuendo was bad, as introducing new facts; and without it the words were not actionable.[2] So a publication alleged, substantially, that the town commissioners had placed in the hands of the plaintiff, as county treasurer, notes to the amount of $1949.94; that the defendant notified him, that the commissioners, appointed by the judge of the county court to examine his office, were in town, and willing to proceed with the investigation, but the plaintiff said he had not time before the election, and refused; that the plaintiff and his friends had circulated the report, that he had made the proposals to go into the examinations, and that the defendant refused; that the commissioners made a slight examination of the plaintiff's papers, and found among them receipts of one A. for $626.04; that the plaintiff accounted for the receipt of $276.55, and had vouchers for cash paid out, $219.85, and cash on hand, $35; that the defendant "warned" him to have his books and office examined, instead of the few papers which he had exhibited, but he refused; that the plaintiff only reported to the commissioners $276.55, as collected by him, as appears from their certificate; "that there has been $510.45 collected from the claims placed in his hands by the said commissioners," annexing the names of the persons from whom collected. Held, not a libel, and

[1] Hawkes *v.* Hawkey, 8 E. 427. [2] Day *v.* Robinson, 1 Ad. & Ell. 554.

that its meaning could not be enlarged by an innuendo, that the defendant thereby intended to charge the plaintiff with fraud, corruption, embezzlement, or other misconduct in his office of county treasurer.[1] So where a declaration, in an action for slander, alleged, that the defendant falsely and maliciously said of the plaintiff, "she is a bad girl, a very bad girl, and unworthy to be employed by any company in Lowell; meaning thereby, that the plaintiff was a prostitute, and had been guilty of fornication, lewdness, lasciviousness, and wantonness." Held, insufficient, for want of averments and a colloquium, that would warrant the innuendo.[2] So a declaration alleged, that the defendant, in a conversation with one Mrs. R., of and concerning the plaintiff's character for chastity, falsely, &c., spoke, &c., the following words: "Mr. Parvin says that Mrs. Lacey is not a decent woman, and keeps a public-house (meaning a bawdy-house). Mr. Parvin said there was not a decent woman in the house (the plaintiff's house meaning). The church alleges nothing against you (Mrs. R. meaning) except that you live with Mrs. Lacey." It was averred, that by these words, the defendant meant and intended that the plaintiff had been guilty of fornication. The second count charged these words: "There are fifteen members of our church who will be qualified that they believed that Mrs. Lacey is a base woman and keeps a public-house (a bawdy-house meaning). It struck me, when Mr. C. told me so, that that house (meaning plaintiff's) was as bad as any house of ill-fame in the city of New York." It was averred, that by these words the defendant meant that the plaintiff had been and was guilty of fornication. Held, that the innuendoes attached to the words "public-house," namely, "meaning a bawdy-house," were unwarranted; that the words in their ordinary acceptation do not mean a bawdy-house; that the averment that the defendant meant by the words charged, that the plaintiff was guilty of fornication, was not warranted, and that such was not the natural meaning of the words; that in

[1] Henderson v. Hall, 19 Ala. 154.

[2] Snell v. Snow, 13 Met. 278.

this case the words "house of ill-fame" meant nothing more than that the house was one of bad reputation; that if the defendant was in the habit of using the words "house of ill-fame," to convey the idea of "bawdy-house," the declaration, by way of inducement, should have alleged that fact, and that the defect in the declaration was not cured by the verdict.[1] So a declaration for slander stated, that, at the time of the speaking, &c., the plaintiff worked for and was employed by one B. Glass, in his barn, in and about thrashing Glass's corn, and that the defendant, intending to cause it to be believed that the plaintiff had been guilty of felony, falsely and maliciously spoke of and concerning the plaintiff the words, "I saw J. G. coming across Mr. Glass's barton with some barley, and my son said, 'what art going to do with that?' J. G. said he was going to feed pheasants with it, and said, where he had that he could have more, and that he had it at Farmer Glass's barn," (meaning the said barn belonging to the said B. Glass, wherein the plaintiff was so at work and employed as aforesaid, and that the barley so alleged by the defendant to have been in the possession of J. G. was the property of the said B. Glass, and that the plaintiff had stolen the same from the said B. Glass, and given the same the said J. G.) Averment of special damage. Held bad, the innuendo not being borne out by the other parts of the count; and that a demurrer to such count did not imply any admission, by which the defect could be aided.[2]

23. It is to be further observed, that, if the innuendo does enlarge the meaning of the words used, but such words are in themselves actionable, the innuendo may be rejected as surplusage. (*a*) Thus in an action for a libel in a Dublin newspaper, the first count, after the usual prefatory aver-

[1] Dodge *v.* Lacey, 2 Cart. 212.

[2] Wheeler *v.* Haynes, 9 Ad. & Ell. 286, *n.*

(*a*) Haws *v.* Stanford, 4 Sneed, 520. The same has been held in regard to a colloquium. Hudson *v.* Garner, 22 Mis. 423; Rodebaugh *v.* Hollingsworth, 6 Ind. 339.

ments, proceeded thus to set forth the words: "What possessed Lord H., if he knew anything about the country, or was not under the spell of vile and treacherous influence, to make his first visit, and that carefully puffed, to Long's, the coachmaker, the other day? If mere trade was his object, he had several respectable houses open to him;" and accompanied them with the following innuendo: "meaning thereby, that the house of business of the said plaintiff was not a respectable house in the trade, and that the plaintiff himself was of such a character, that he would not be visited in the way of his trade and business, except for some political, or party, or other improper motive." Held, that the words were capable of the meaning thus attributed to them, but if the innuendo was more extensive than the words, it might be rejected as repugnant and void, and the words, being libellous, were actionable without its aid.[1] So an innuendo, that *the Attorney-General* spoken of meant the Attorney-General for *the county-Palatine of Chester*, was rejected.[2] So where the words alleged clearly charge *the killing of a horse*, innuendo, that the defendant intended to charge the plaintiff with *arson;* the innuendo may be stricken out, and the declaration sustained, as alleging the killing of the horse.[3] So, in an action for a libel, the declaration stated, that the defendant falsely, &c., did publish, &c., of and concerning the plaintiff, the false, &c., matter following: "Threatening letters — The Middlesex grand jury have returned a true bill against a gentleman of some property, named French," (meaning the plaintiff,) innuendo, "with this that the said plaintiff will verify, that the said defendant thereby then and there meant to insinuate and have it understood that the said plaintiff had been suspected to have been, and had been guilty of the offence of sending a letter without any name or signature thereby subscribed, directed to one Trotter, threatening to kill and murder the

[1] Barrett *v.* Long, 16 Eng. L. & Eq. 1; Benaway *v.* Conyne, 3 Chand. 214; Hudson *v.* Garner, 22 Mis. 423; Rodebaugh *v.* Hollingsworth, 6 Ind. 339; Nestle *v.* Van Slyck, 2 Hill, 282.

[2] Roberts *v.* Camden, 9 E. 93.

[3] Gage *v.* Shelton, 3 Rich. 242.

said Trotter, a subject of this realm, with a view and intent to extort." Held, that this innuendo was bad, there being no introductory averments to warrant it; but that the publication was libellous *per se*, and therefore that the innuendo might be rejected as surplusage.[1]

24. But if a good innuendo, ascribing a particular meaning to the words, be not supported in evidence, the plaintiff cannot reject it at the trial, and resort to another meaning.[2] So, if the innuendo alleges, that the words were spoken of the plaintiff as a public officer, it must be proved that he held such office. Thus, in an action for slander, the declaration stated, that the plaintiff was treasurer and collector of certain tolls, and that the defendant spoke of and concerning the plaintiff, as such treasurer and collector, certain words, "thereby meaning that the plaintiff, as such treasurer and collector, had been guilty of, &c." Held, the plaintiff was bound by the innuendo to prove that he was treasurer and collector.[3]

25. It remains to be more distinctly explained, as a qualification of the rule above stated, that an innuendo cannot extend the sense of words spoken beyond their natural meaning, *unless something is put upon the record to which the words spoken may be referred*, and by which they may be explained in the innuendo.[4] Or, words not in themselves actionable cannot be rendered so by an innuendo, without *a prefatory averment of extrinsic facts*, which make them slanderous.[5] Where there is no colloquium, the plaintiff is understood to allege that the words were used in their natural and ordinary signification.[6] But, though an innuendo cannot supply the place of a colloquium, yet, if there be a colloquium sufficient to point the application of the words to the plaintiff, if spoken maliciously, he must have judgment.[7]

[1] Harvey *v.* French, 2 Moo. & S. 591.

[2] Williams *v.* Scott, 1 Cr. & Mees. 675.

[3] Sellers *v.* Till, 4 B. & C. 655.

[4] M'Cuen *v.* Ludlum, 2 Harr. 12; Dorsey *v.* Whipps, 8 Gill, 457.

[5] Watts *v.* Greenleaf, 2 Dev. 115. See Brown *v.* Brown, 2 Shep. 317; Harris *v.* Burley, 8 N. H. 256.

[6] Edgerly *v.* Swain, 32 N. H. 478.

[7] Lindsey *v.* Smith, 7 Johns. 359.

And a further point of distinction is, that while, as has been seen, an innuendo cannot be proved, a colloquium introduces extrinsic matter into the pleadings, and is a proper subject of proof.[1] This leads us to speak more distinctly of that part of the declaration for libel or slander, often heretofore referred to, termed the colloquium. The colloquium grows out of the general principle, that, if the words charged to have been spoken are *primâ facie* actionable, no prefatory inducement is required; otherwise, if the words do not naturally and *per se* convey the meaning which the plaintiff would give them, or if a reference to some extrinsic matter or some other words or conversation is necessary in order to explain them.[2] The most familiar illustration of this principle is, that, if the words may be understood in a sense not criminal, there must be a colloquium to show that they were spoken in a criminal sense.[3] (*a*) Thus a count in

[1] Van Vechten *v.* Hopkins, 5 Johns. 211.

[2] Dorsey *v.* Whipps, 8 Gill, 457; Ryan *v.* Madden, 12 Verm. 51; Worth *v.* Butler, 7 Blackf. 251; Galloway *v.* Courtney, 10 Rich. Law, 414; Berwick *v.* Chappel, 8 B. Mon. 486; Linville *v.* Earlywine, 4 Blackf. 470; Wilson *v.* Hamilton, 9 Rich. Law, 382.

[3] Dorsey *v.* Whipps, 8 Gill, 457.

(*a*) In the absence of a colloquium, the question whether the words impute a crime or not, may properly be left to the jury. Thus, in an action of slander, the words charged were "you are a thief," "you are a damned thief." The words proved were, "you are a thief, you stole hoop poles and saw logs from off Delancey's and Judge Myer's land." The Judge left it to the jury to decide, whether the defendant meant to charge the plaintiff with taking timber, or hoop poles already cut down, in which case it would be a charge of felony; or only with cutting down and carrying away timber to make hoop poles; in which case it would amount only to a trespass, and the words would not then be actionable. The jury having found a verdict for the defendant, the Court refused to set it aside. Dexter *v.* Taber, 12 Johns. 239.

We have already (ch. 12) considered the necessity of averring and proving, that the libel or slander *refers to the plaintiff*, and also referred to the case of an accusation against a class or body of individuals of which the plaintiff is an individual member. With reference to this particular point, the bearing of the colloquium sometimes becomes important. Thus, where the declaration states a colloquium with A., of and concerning the children of A., and the plaintiff, one of the children of A., in particular; and that

slander, stating the actionable words to be, that the plaintiff swore to a lie, with an averment that the defendant meant thereby, and was understood, to charge the plaintiff with perjury, is bad, without a colloquium.[1] In such a case, the declaration should aver a count and cause pending, a legal proceeding sanctioned by law in which an oath might be administered, a trial, and testimony given by the plaintiff, and that the defendant spoke the words in a conversation or colloquium had concerning the plaintiff's testimony so given, with an innuendo that he thereby intended to charge the plaintiff with perjury.[2] So, if the proceeding was before arbitrators, the want of an averment, that the plaintiff was legally sworn, is fatal.[3] So the words "thereby accusing the plaintiff of stealing," immediately following words alleged to have been spoken, which do not of themselves amount to a charge of larceny, without any precise colloquium or averment showing such to have been the intention, are not sufficient.[4] So a count, alleging that the defendant used the words, "you moved the corner tree," adding, "the defendant thereby referring to and speaking of a corner tree between said plaintiff and the survey of said chapel," was held insufficient, for want of a distinct averment, showing

[1] Palmer v. Hunter, 8 Mis. 512.

[2] Wood v. Scott, 13 Verm. 42; Sanderson v. Hubbard, 14 Verm. 462.

[3] 14 Verm. 462.

[4] Brown v. Brown, 2 Shep. 317.

---

the defendant said "*your children are thieves and I can prove it;*" the colloquium conclusively points the words, and designates the plaintiff as one of the children intended. Gidney v. Blake, 11 Johns. 54.

But an action does not lie by an officer of a regiment of militia, for a publication reflecting upon the officers of the regiment generally, without averring a special damage. Sumner v. Buel, 12 Johns. 475.

A colloquium may render a charge actionable, merely by reference to some extrinsic fact, not expressed by the charge itself. Thus a colloquium described one A. as a notorious forger, and the declaration then alleged a charge, that the plaintiff was as versatile in circumventing the law of right as A. Held, libellous. Cramer v. Noonan, 4 Wis. 231.

In England, by the *Common-Law Procedure Act* of 1852, (§ 61,) the necessity of a colloquium is dispensed with.

that the words were used in reference to some corner tree of a particular survey.[1] So in an action by husband and wife, for words imputing adultery to the wife, it is necessary to aver that they were husband and wife at the time of speaking the words,[2] (see p. 346, n.). So, inasmuch as simply to burn one's own store is not unlawful; the words *he burnt his own store*, or *there is no doubt in my mind that he burnt his own store; he would not have got his goods insured if he had not meant to burn it*, as a general allegation that the defendant charged the plaintiff with having wilfully and maliciously burnt his own store, will not sustain an action for slander, without a colloquium or averment, setting forth such circumstances as would render such burning unlawful, and that the words were spoken of and concerning such circumstances; and the want of such colloquium or averment will not be cured by an innuendo.[3]

26. In some cases, however, the only colloquium required is, that the words were spoken *of the plaintiff*. Thus in an action of slander the declaration alleged, that the defendant, "in a certain discourse which he then and there had of and concerning the plaintiffs," did falsely speak and publish "of and concerning the said Elizabeth," (one of the plaintiffs,) certain defamatory words set forth. Held, a sufficient statement of a colloquium.[4] So, where the charge itself assumes the existence of a fact, it is itself sufficient proof of such fact.[5] And an averment of the charge is an averment of the fact.[6] So, where the declaration stated that the plaintiff, at the time of the publication of the slanderous words, was, and long before had been a blacksmith, and carried on the business and trade of a blacksmith honestly, and found and provided all such iron as was necessary and required of him in his business, and made correct charges, and always kept honest, true, and faithful accounts with all persons relating to his trade, &c.; yet the defendant, in order to injure the

[1] Berwick v. Chappel, 8 B. Mon. 486.
[2] Ryan v. Madden, 12 Verm. 51.
[3] Bloss v. Tobey, 2 Pick. 320.
[4] Sturtevant v. Root, 7 Fost. 69.
[5] Rodebaugh v. Hollingsworth, 6 Ind. 339.
[6] Ibid.

plaintiff in his business, and cause it to be believed, &c., in a certain discourse of and concerning the plaintiff in his said business, spoke and published the following words, &c. (stating them); this was held sufficient, without a more special averment that there was a discourse of and concerning the plaintiff's *trade*, and that the words were spoken of and concerning his trade.[1] (*a*)

27. And it is to be further observed, that defects in the declaration, relating both to the innuendo and colloquium, may be cured by verdict. Thus, where the declaration, after alleging a colloquium *with* the plaintiff, of and concerning him and a certain note, set out the words as follows: "*you* (meaning *the bearer or holder of the note above described*) may send for V. (meaning the plaintiff) and we will have him punished." Held, sufficient after verdict.[2] So in an action for a charge of false swearing, without the innuendo and colloquium necessary to a charge of perjury; if the defendant plead that the plaintiff did commit perjury, and issue be joined upon this plea, and a verdict given for the plaintiff; this will cure the defect as to the colloquium, and it seems also as to the innuendo, and judgment will be given on the verdict.[3] So, where a declaration for words imputing the forging of a note set out a colloquium concerning the plaintiff, and also concerning a particular note, describing it, and the innuendo, instead of pointing the slanderous matter to that note, referred merely to *a note;* held, that

[1] Burtch *v.* Nickerson, 17 Johns. 217.

[2] Nestle *v.* Van Slyck, 2 Hill, 282. *Contra*, Edgerly *v.* Swain, 32 N. H. 478.

[3] Wood *v.* Scott, 13 Verm. 42; Sanderson *v.* Hubbard, 14 Verm. 462.

(*a*) Where libellous matter is charged against some particular person, who is so ambiguously described, that the person meant cannot be identified without the aid of extrinsic facts; there, by the introduction of proper averments and a colloquium, the words taken in connection with the whole libel may be rendered sufficiently certain to support the action, so as to make it proper to permit the whole to go to the jury, as a question of fact, under the direction of the Judge, who may, however, if the evidence appear to him too vague and inconclusive to warrant a verdict for the plaintiff, order a nonsuit. Van Vechten *v.* Hopkins, 5 Johns. 211.

after verdict the uncertainty in this respect was cured, and the Court must intend that the words proved related to the note described in the colloquium.[1] So a judgment in slander will not be arrested, because an innuendo enlarges the natural meaning of the words.[2] (*a*) But, where the declaration alleges, that the defendant said of the plaintiff, that he had set fire to his own premises; innuendo, that the plaintiff had been guilty of wilfully setting fire to the premises, which, whilst in his occupation, had been destroyed by fire; the Court will not, after verdict, presume, that the jury have found that the defendant meant to impute to the plaintiff that he did the act unlawfully or feloniously as well as wilfully. Nothing more will be presumed after verdict, than was necessary to support the allegations.[3]

28. Defects of this nature are also held to be grounds for *demurrer*, rather than for a motion to *nonsuit*. Thus the words spoken were, "He swore to a lie," and the declaration, treating them as an imputation of perjury, contained a prefatory averment of trial, &c., an innuendo, and between the words and the innuendo, an unskilful averment of the colloquium, or connection between the words and the trial. Testimony was offered to show this connection. Held, although objection might have been taken to the declaration by special demurrer, there was not sufficient ground for ordering a nonsuit on motion.[4] (*b*)

1 Nestle *v.* Van Slyck, 2 Hill, 282.
2 Shultz *v.* Chambers, 8 Watts, 300.
3 Sweetapple *v.* Jesse, 2 Nev. & M. 36.
4 Gale *v.* Hays, 3 Strobh. 452.

(*a*) It may be laid down as the general rule upon this subject, that, after verdict, on a motion in *arrest*, or *on error*, a declaration in slander will be held good, where the words are of doubtful meaning, but capable of a slanderous sense, although there be no averment beyond that of an intent to charge a specific crime. But a stricter rule prevails where a *demurrer* is interposed. Kennedy *v.* Gifford, 19 Wend. 256.

(*b*) It has been held, that the defendant may demur to a *part* of the words laid in a count for slander. Abrams *v.* Smith, 8 Blackf. 95.

But in New York it is held, that, though a count in slander contain some words which are actionable, and others which are not, the defendant cannot

29. In immediate connection with *pleading* in actions for libel and slander, we proceed to the important subject

---

plead as to the former and demur as to the residue, but must either plead or demur as to the whole count. Root *v.* Woodruff, 6 Hill, 418.

If the declaration does not contain any cause of action, the proper way of taking advantage of it is to demur. But where a nonsuit had been ordered, the court refused to set it aside, on grounds of convenience, as it was clear that the plaintiff could not recover. Boyd *v.* Brent, 3 Brev. 241. See Wilson *v.* Hamilton, 9 Rich. Law, 382.

In Missouri, in actions of slander and libel, an objection to a plea of justification, as insufficient, cannot be taken on trial, or after the verdict. Evans *v.* Franklin, 26 Mis. 252.

A few miscellaneous points of pleading, in actions for libel and slander, remain to be mentioned.

It has been held, that indecent words, tending only to aggravate damages, need not be repeated in a declaration for slander. Stevens *v.* Handly, Wright, 121, 123; acc. Commonwealth *v.* Holmes, 17 Mass. 336.

Publication of a libel must be stated in the declaration, but may be collected from the whole of it, and requires no technical form of words. (See p. 335.) Baldwyn *v.* Elphinstone, 2 W. Black. 1037.

Where the defendant in an action for a libel, in his plea, set forth *in hæc verba* two declarations by the plaintiff, in two other actions for libels, by the same plaintiffs; the Court ordered them to be struck out, as being an oppressive incumbrance on the record. Spencer *v.* Tabele, 9 Johns. 130.

In actions of slander, the time may be stated with a *continuando*, and the place may be alleged with a *videlicet*. Burbank *v.* Horn, 39 Maine, 233.

In case for words not actionable *per se*, averring special damage, "not guilty," puts in issue, not only the speaking of the words, but also the special damage alleged. Willey *v.* Elston, 8 Com. B. 142.

Where the defendant, in a suit for slander, brought by husband and wife, pleads the general issue and several pleas in justification, the marriage of the plaintiff is admitted by the pleas. Ricket *v.* Stanley, 6 Blackf. 169.

Where the declaration, in an action of slander, for the charge of false swearing, does not show that the words spoken were material, yet, if a plea of justification shows that fact, the defect in the declaration is cured. Witcher *v.* Richmond, 8 Humph. 473.

So where, in an action for slander, the defendant justifies, and in so doing supplies the omission of a material fact in the complaint, that will cure the defect. But where the plaintiff demurs to one plea or answer, and the omission or averment is found in another, such admission or averment will not avail the plaintiff as supplying the deficiencies in his com-

of *justification*, which the law in general requires to be set up by a special plea in bar, and does not allow under the defence of *the general issue* or *not guilty*.

---

plaint; the plea or answer containing the admission not being before the court on the demurrer. Ayers *v*. Covill, 18 Barb. 260.

After judgment by default in slander, entire damages assessed by the jury, and final judgment accordingly, it is too late to object to the sufficiency of the pleas or the venue. Wickham *v*. Baker, 4 Blackf. 517.

To say of a person "he has sworn false;" or "he has taken a false oath," is not actionable; and the meaning of these words cannot be enlarged by innuendo; yet these words may be aided so as to support the declaration, if the defendant, in his plea of justification, allege or confess that he spoke the words by reason of a false oath taken by the plaintiff in a court of competent jurisdiction. But if the defendant plead the general issue, and give notice of his justification, the notice will not help the declaration, for it is not considered a special plea, nor does it form any part of the record. Vaughan *v*. Havens, 8 Johns. 109.

The defendants in an action of slander pleaded not guilty, and at a subsequent term offered a plea of the statute of limitations, which was rejected by the court. Allensworth *v*. Coleman, 5 Dana, 315.

It is held, in Massachusetts, that the statute of 1793, c. 75, § 2, which enables a party whose action has failed through unavoidable accident, informality, &c., to commence a new action, which, but for this statute, would have been barred by the statute of limitations, does not apply to actions of slander or other actions arising *ex delicto*. Cook *v*. Darling, 2 Pick. 605.

To an action of slander, the defendant pleaded not guilty within six months, and that the words charged were true, and the jury found the truth of all the pleas. Held, that under the act of 1794, c. 1, in Tennessee, authorizing the defendant to plead as many pleas as may be necessary for his defence, there was nothing irregular in this finding, and the judgment thereupon. Kelly *v*. Craig, 9 Humph. 215.

If to a plea of the statute of limitations, the plaintiff reply, that the words were spoken within the prescribed time, he must prove the speaking of some of the actionable words within that time. Huston *v*. McPherson, 8 Blackf. 562.

If no notice is given of a defence under the statute of limitations, the plaintiff may give in evidence words spoken more than two years before the commencement of the action. But where the declaration alleged the words to have been spoken on a particular day, within two years; and the plaintiff produced evidence of words spoken more than two years before the commencement of the action; the defendant was allowed, without terms, to file a plea of the statute of limitations. Brickett *v*. Davis, 21 Pick. 404.

30. The usual if not the only defence of justification consists in an allegation of *the truth* of the charge complained of. This to a civil action, either for libel or slander, is a sufficient answer. In other words, to write or speak the truth is not in law libellous or slanderous. But it is equally well settled,

---

In New York, *the code* has made an important change in the rules of pleading in actions for libel and slander, in not requiring extrinsic facts, showing the application of the words to the plaintiff, to be stated in the complaint. But extrinsic facts, when the proof is necessary to determine the meaning of the words, as libellous or slanderous, must still be stated. Fry *v.* Bennett, 5 Sandf. 54.

Under the same code, an *answer* in an action of slander, denying the speaking of the words, cannot also set up matter in mitigation of damages. This is allowed only where the defendant justifies the slanderous words. Where there is no justification, the rule is the same as under the old system. Evidence in mitigation may be given on the trial of the issue made as to the speaking of the words. Myer *v.* Schultz, 4 Sandf. 664.

Facts pleaded in mitigation of damages, in an action for a libel, are not *material* in the sense of section 168 of the code. Nor are such facts a defence to which the plaintiff can demur or reply. But he may, upon the trial, contest their truth or their admissibility in evidence. Newman *v.* Otto, 4 Sandf. 668.

In an action for slander, matter in mitigation can be pleaded, only when the defendant alleges the truth of the matter charged as defamatory. Ayers *v.* Covill, 18 Barb. 260.

Where, in an action for slander, the plaintiff is fully informed by the notice given by the defendant of the facts the latter proposes to prove on the trial, such evidence, if otherwise proper, will not be excluded, merely because the notice states that such facts will be proved "in mitigation of damages," instead of saying *in justification*. Baker *v.* Wilkins, 3 Barb. 220.

The effect of the evidence to be given by a defendant, on the trial of an action for slander, is a matter of law and not of fact, and need not be stated in the defendant's notice of special matter, accompanying a plea of the general issue. Ibid.

It is held in Maine, that the rule of practice seems to be, that the plaintiff shall have the opening and closing of his cause, whenever the damages are in dispute, unliquidated, and to be ascertained by a jury. Therefore, in actions of slander, where the defendant in pleading admits the speaking of the words, and avers that they were true, and does not plead the general issue, the plaintiff is entitled to open and close. Sawyer *v.* Hopkins, 9 Shep. 268.

that *under the general issue* the defendant cannot, either in bar of the action or mitigation of damages,[1] give evidence of the truth of the charge, (*a*) or of facts *tending* to prove the truth.[2] (*b*) Or, in general, (in order to disprove malice,)

[1] Douge *v.* Pearce, 13 Ala. 127; Kelly *v.* Dillon, 5 Ind. 426; Underwood *v.* Parks, 2 Str. 1200; Taylor *v.* Robinson, 29 Maine, 323; Thompson *v.* Bowers, 1 Doug. 321; Shepard *v.* Merrill, 13 Johns. 475; Bisby *v.* Shaw, 2 Kern. 67; Van Ankin *v.* Westfall, 14 Johns. 234; Haws *v.* Stanford, 4 Sneed, 520; Abshire *v.* Cline, 3 Ind. 115; Darling *v.* Banks, 14 Ill. 46; Stees *v.* Kemble, 27 Penn 112. See Galloway *v.* Courtney, 10 Rich. Law, 414.

[2] Petrie *v.* Rose, 5 W. & S. 364; 15 Ala. 662; Updegrove *v.* Zimmerman, 13 Penn. 619; Teagle *v.* Deboy, 8 Blackf. 134; Burke *v.* Miller, 6 Blackf. 155.

(*a*) "No rule can be more firmly established than that the defendant cannot give in evidence the truth of the imputation, without pleading such truth as a justification. Since the case of *Underwood* v. *Parks*, there has never existed a doubt on the subject." Per Tindal, C. J., Manning *v.* Clement, 7 Bing. 367.

In an action of slander, the defendant offered a notice, proposing to give in evidence under the general issue facts proving, or tending to prove, the truth of the words spoken, and proposing to apply those facts either in justification or in mitigation of damages, and stating the facts relied on, which, though they might be properly submitted to the jury in connection with other evidence in support of a justification, did not, alone, prove the truth of the words. Held, the notice was insufficient, and that the facts stated were not admissible in evidence under the general issue, with such notice or without any notice, either in justification or in mitigation of damages. Brickett *v.* Davis, 21 Pick. 404.

As an illustration of the strictness of the rule in reference to the plea of truth, it is held, that, in an action for slander in charging the plaintiff with incest; a plea, that the plaintiff told the defendant that her brothers had had sexual and illicit intercourse with her, is bad. Abshire *v.* Cline, 3 Ind. 115.

(*b*) Where a party is sued for republishing a libellous article in a newspaper, and the republication is accompanied by remarks tending to a justification, but not amounting to it, the defendant is not permitted to prove the truth of the remarks in mitigation of damages, because the evidence would tend to prove the charge well founded. Evidence in mitigation must be such as admits the charge to be false. Cooper *v.* Barber, 24 Wend. 105.

It is said by an approved writer, "If the plaintiff, in proof of malice, relies upon the falsity of the charge, the defendant may rebut the inference by evidence of the truth of the charge, even under the general issue." 2 Greenl. Ev. § 421. The same writer, however, subsequently remarks, in

of circumstances which excited suspicion, and furnished reasonable cause for belief on his part, that the words spoken were true.[1] (a) Or of facts and circumstances which

[1] Watson v. Moore, 2 Cush. 133; Gilmer v. Ewbank, 13 Ill. 271.

---

nearer conformity with what has been stated as the settled rule of law, "It is perfectly well settled, that, under the general issue, the defendant cannot be admitted to prove the truth of the words, either in bar of the action, or in mitigation of damages. Ibid, § 424.

The fact that the same matter, which is specially pleaded, might be given in evidence under the general issue, is not in slander always a sufficient ground for rejecting the special plea; but, if the speaking of the words be admitted by the plea, and the other facts relied upon show that the plaintiff is not entitled to the action, the plea is proper. Parker v. M'Queen, 8 B. Mon. 16.

In New York, under the code, the defendant may allege in his answer the truth, and also facts tending to prove the truth, in mitigation of damages; and, although the evidence fails to prove the justification, it may be submitted to the jury in mitigation of damages. Bisby v. Shaw, 2 Kern. 67.

So under the code the defendant may prove, in mitigation of damages, facts and circumstances which disprove malice, although they tend to establish the truth, and without alleging the truth. Bush v. Prosser, 2 Kern. 347; 13 Barb. 221; acc. West v. Walker, 2 Swan, 32; Wagner v. Holbrunner, 6 Gill, 296.

Accordingly, where, in an action for charging the plaintiff with keeping a house of ill-fame, the answer denied the complaint, and as a partial defence alleged lewd and lascivious conduct by the plaintiff's family, not amounting to a justification; evidence of such conduct is competent, to reduce the amount of damages. Bush v. Prosser, 2 Kern. 347.

But where, in an action for a libel, the defendant pleaded not guilty, and gave notice of certain facts to be proved at the trial, and afterwards applied for leave to strike out the notice; the Court refused to grant the motion, unless he would make affidavit of the falsehood of the matters stated in the notice. Clinton v. Mitchell, 3 Johns. 144.

(a) Where the libellous words charged in the declaration were, "But this is not the first time that the idea of falsehood and M. B. (meaning the plaintiff) have been associated together in the minds of many honest men," (meaning, &c.); held, evidence that "sundry honest men, to wit A. B. (naming seven persons) and others, believed and considered the plaintiff not to be a man of truth, but addicted to falsehood," was not admissible in justification; and that the defendant could only justify the charge by proving the fact. Brooks v. Bemiss, 8 Johns. 455.

form a link in the evidence to make out a justification.[1] (*a*) So, in an action for libel, a plea that the words are true, and therefore that the defendant is not guilty, concluding to the country, is bad.[2] And, where *express notice* of the defence is by law substituted for a special plea, *the truth* must be set up as a defence in that form.[3] So, in Pennsylvania, evidence of the truth is not admissible under the plea of not guilty, with leave, &c.[4] So the plaintiff does not, by proving *a repetition* of the words after commencement of suit, give the defendant a right to prove them true, under the general issue, in mitigation of damages.[5]

31. *Not guilty* and *the truth* may be pleaded together.[6] The Court will not order that one of the pleas be struck out; and the same evidence may be offered under the former plea, as if pleaded alone.[7] Thus, in an action for charging the plaintiff with *perjury*, the defendant, in mitigation of damages, may show the general bad character of the plaintiff for veracity when on oath.[8] So, although he has also given evidence in support of the plea of justification.[9] Or after the plaintiff has introduced testimony, to rebut the evidence given by the defendant in support of his justification.[10] And where there are distinct charges in the same libel, the general issue may be pleaded to some, and a justification to others.[11] (*b*)

[1] Scott *v.* M'Kinnish, 15 Ala. 662.
[2] Lawton *v.* Hunt, 4 Rich. 458.
[3] Snyder *v.* Andrews, 6 Barb. 43.
[4] Kay *v.* Fredrigal, 3 Barr, 221.
[5] Teagle *v.* Deboy, 8 Blackf. 134.
[6] Miller *v.* Graham, 1 Brev. 283; Buhler *v.* Wentworth, 17 Barb. 649.
[7] Ormsby *v.* Douglas, 5 Duer, 665.
[8] M'Nutt *v.* Young, 8 Leigh, 542; Pope *v.* Welsh, 18 Ala. 631.
[9] Hamer *v.* McFarlin, 4 Denio, 509.
[10] Stone *v.* Varney, 7 Met. 86.
[11] Van Derveer *v.* Sutphin, 5 Ohio, N. S. 293; 4 Comst. 162; Torrey *v.* Field, 10 Verm. 353.

(*a*) But it is held, more especially where matter charged to be libellous is not so *primâ facie*, that the defendant may, to repel the inference of malice, prove facts showing grounds for suspicion, under the plea of not guilty, and may, in such case, prove the truth of the matter published. Hart *v.* Reed, 1 B. Mon. 166; Wagner *v.* Holbrunner, 7 Gill, 296.

So, that under the general issue any matter may be given in evidence in mitigation, which does not tend to and falls short of a justification. Snyder *v.* Andrews, 6 Barb. 43.

(*b*) In an action for libel, where the answer contained, 1st, a denial of

32. It has been sometimes held, that, where the defendant in an action for slander pleads the general issue, and also in justification, that the words spoken were true, the plaintiff need not prove the speaking of the words upon the trial of the general issue.[1] So, where the defendant pleaded the general issue and also a special plea in justification, which was adjudged bad upon demurrer, in which he admitted the speaking of the words; held, the special plea might be used upon the trial of the general issue, as evidence to prove the speaking.[2] But the prevailing doctrine is, that, where the general issue, as well as pleas admitting the speaking of the words, are pleaded, the plaintiff must prove the cause of action in the same manner as if the special pleas had not been filed.[3] And the latter pleas do not amount to an admission of record of the speaking of the words charged.[4]

33. It has been held in New York, that, in an action for libel, mitigating circumstances can only be pleaded, when the libel is justified.[5] So, in New Hampshire, in an action of slander, if the brief statement purports to justify the speaking of the words charged, the speaking of them must be fully and distinctly admitted and justified, or the statement will be held defective.[6] But it has been held that a plea, that the libellous matter complained of "is true in substance and effect," means that it is true in every material particular.[7]

34. Upon the same principle, if the defendant plead the

[1] Jackson *v.* Stetson, 15 Mass. 48.
[2] Alderman *v.* French, 1 Pick. 1.
[3] Ricket *v.* Stanley, 6 Blackf. 169.
[4] Wright *v.* Lindsay, 20 Ala. 428.
[5] Matthews *v.* Beach, 5 Sandf. 256.
[6] Folsom *v.* Brown, 5 Fost. 114.
[7] Weaver *v.* Lloyd, 4 D. & R. 230.

---

the publication, and, 2d, matter in justification and excuse, and the plaintiff demurred to the answer for insufficiency, specifying as grounds of demurrer objections only to the matter of justification and excuse, and judgment was given for the plaintiff on the demurrer; held, that the demurrer had reference only to the portion of the answer objected to, and that by the judgment the denial of the publication was not struck out of the answer. Matthews *v.* Beach, 4 Seld. 173.

truth in justification, to support the plea, he must prove the crime charged to the satisfaction of the jury,[1] and beyond a reasonable doubt.[2] Where the evidence does not satisfy the jury of the truth of the slanderous words, the plaintiff is entitled to damages.[3] And this even though the truth is a mere *negative*. Thus the plaintiff made an affidavit, that the defendant had engaged to pay certain taxes; the defendant said that the affidavit was false, and that he would have the plaintiff indicted for perjury. The plaintiff thereupon brought an action against the defendant for those words, to which the defendant pleaded a justification. Held, the burden of proof was on the defendant, to show that the plaintiff's affidavit was false, though the proof involved a negative.[4] So, in an action of slander, if the defendant plead the general issue, and give notice that he shall justify the words by proving them to be true, and on the trial give evidence tending to prove the truth; it is a correct instruction to the jury, that, if they are satisfied that the defendant made the charge, they should find a verdict for the plaintiff, unless upon the whole evidence they are satisfied that the charge was true; that the burden of proof is on the defendant to establish that fact; and that, if the jury doubt as to that fact, they should find for the plaintiff.[5] (*a*)

[1] Offutt *v.* Earlywine, 4 Blackf. 460.
[2] Shortley *v.* Miller, 1 Smith, 395.
[3] Kincade *v.* Bradshaw, 3 Hawks, 63.
[4] Hinchman *v.* Lawson, 5 Leigh, 695.
[5] Sperry *v.* Wilcox, 1 Met. 267.

(*a*) Under a statute which permits a defendant indicted for a libel to give the truth in evidence, but providing that this evidence shall not be a justification, unless it be made to appear that such matter was published with good motives and for justifiable ends; the burden is on the defendant, not only to prove the truth, but also that it was published with good motives and for justifiable ends. Commonwealth *v.* Bonner, 9 Met. 410.

With regard to the *order* in which proofs of a justification may be offered, where, in an action for slander, in charging the plaintiff with altering and forging the records of a religious society, the defendant specified the truth and set forth in his specification the entries alleged to be forged; it was held that he might prove the forgery, by first introducing the book of records of

35. It is a further extension of the same general principle as to the *strictness* of a justification, that although, where several distinct things are charged, the defendant may justify as to one, even if he may fail as to the others; (*a*) as to that one, the justification must be full. (*b*) And the rule applies alike to the plea itself and the evidence offered in support of it. The plea of justification must aver the truth of the material charge or charges, in language as broad as the charge in its full and legal sense; it must answer the whole ground of action relied on. Thus, if the charge is perjury, it will avail nothing to prove that the plaintiff swore falsely through an innocent mistake.[1] The proof must be of wilful and corrupt falsehood.[2] And a plea of justification, in an action of slander for false swearing, must not only state the circumstances under which the false swearing occurred, but also that the matter sworn to was material to the cause

[1] Fero v. Ruscoe, 4 Comst. 162; The State v. Burnham, 9 N. H. 34; Torrey v. Field, 10 Verm. 353; Van Derveer v. Sutphin, 5 Ohio, N. S. 293.

[2] M'Kinly v. Rob, 20 Johns. 351.

---

the society, showing therein the entries alleged to be forged, and then proving by the testimony of the person who acted as chairman, and who also made minutes of the proceedings, what actually took place at the meeting. Waters v. Gilbert, 2 Cush. 27.

(*a*) So, in a suit for libel, the defendant may plead in justification to part of the declaration or parcel of the supposed libel; but, if he attempt to designate the portion, by setting it forth *in hæc verba*, the omission or substitution of a single word will be a fatal variance. Torrey v. Field, 10 Verm. 353.

(*b*) In an action for words imputing one crime, the defendant, *under the general issue*, will not be allowed to prove that the plaintiff had been guilty of another crime even of the same nature. Randall v. Holsenbake, 3 Hill, S. C. 175; Ridley v. Perry, 4 Shepl. 21.

Evidence of the facts contained in a special plea, tending to show that the words spoken were true, or of other facts of the same tendency, or of a general report that the plaintiff was guilty of the crime imputed to him, cannot be received in mitigation of damages. Alderman v. French, 1 Pick. 1.

But it has been held, that, in an action for a charge of false swearing, evidence of what the plaintiff did swear may be given in mitigation of damages. Arrington v. Jones, 9 Port. 139.

of action.[1] Thus to a declaration in slander, alleging that the defendant had charged the plaintiff with having sworn falsely, the defendant pleaded the general issue, and gave notice that he would prove on the trial, "that the plaintiff was guilty of the fact charged upon and imputed to him by the defendant, in the several conversations in the declaration mentioned, and that, if the words were uttered and published as charged in the declaration, the defendant had good reason for uttering and publishing, and did it from good motives, and for justifiable ends." Held, that this notice was fatally defective; especially in omitting any averment that the plaintiff wilfully and deliberately swore falsely; and that the defendant could not, upon the trial, introduce any evidence under it.[2] So, where a slanderous charge of forgery is justified, the defendant will be held to a strict proof.[3] So in an action of slander for making a positive charge of theft against the plaintiff, the defendant cannot justify the charge, by proving that the defendant had just ground for believing the plaintiff to be a very dishonest man.[4] So, in case of libel, the justification, in order to be sufficient, must be as broad as the libel. Therefore it is no answer to a libel, charging a party with having been actively and profitably engaged in smuggling during the late war, that he had violated the revenue laws in a single instance and in a time of peace.[5] (*a*) So, the plaintiff's ship being advertised for freight and passengers, the defendant published that she was unseaworthy, and had been bought by Jews to take out convicts. Justification as to the whole,

[1] M'Gough *v.* Rhodes, 7 Eng. 625.
[2] Thompson *v.* Bowers, 1 Doug. 321.
[3] Steely *v.* Blair, Wright, 683.
[4] Woodruff *v.* Richardson, 20 Conn. 238.
[5] Stilwell *v.* Barter, 19 Wend. 487.

(*a*) So a libel, containing general charges against an individual, "of hardness towards the poor," of "dissoluteness of morals," &c., purporting to be conclusions from instances of bad conduct previously narrated in the publication, cannot be justified by proof of other instances not mentioned by the writer. Bartholemy *v.* The People, 2 Hill, 248.

that the allegation of unseaworthiness was true. Held insufficient.[1]

36. But where the defendants justified, and proved the truth of a libel, charging the plaintiff with having acted in a grand swindling concern at Manchester; but omitted any justification of a portion of the publication, which would not, by itself, form a substantive ground of action for libel; and the jury found for the defendants on the part of the libel which was justified; the Court refused to enter a verdict for the plaintiff on the passage not justified.[2] And where, to a declaration for libel, imputing to the plaintiff barbarous cruelty to his horse, the defendant pleaded: first, that the libel was true in all its particulars; and second, that it was true in substance and effect; and the jury found that the first plea was true, with the exception of two statements, containing particulars of aggravated cruelty to the horse; and that the second was true in substance and effect; and gave a shilling damages, subject to the opinion of the Court as to the propriety of their verdict: held, that the verdict was right.[3]

37. And where a libel imputes a dishonest, corrupt, or criminal *intent*, a plea of justification must show not only the facts, but also the intent.[4] So, in an action for a libel, imputing to the plaintiff the commission of a crime under aggravated circumstances, it is necessary to justify the aggravating portion, as well as the substantial charge of crime. Thus, where the declaration set out a libel, in which it was alleged that the plaintiff was tried for murder, and that "it was understood that the counsel for the prosecution were in possession of a damning piece of evidence, viz: that he had spent nearly the whole of the night preceding the duel in practising pistol-firing;" and the plea stated that the plaintiff had committed murder, but did not show that he had practised pistol-firing the night before; held, the justification was insufficient.[5]

[1] Ingram v. Lawson, 5 Bing. N. 66.
[2] Clarke v. Taylor, 2 Bing. N. 654.
[3] Weaver v. Lloyd, 4 Dowl. & Ry. 230.
[4] Gage v. Robinson, 12 Ohio, 250.
[5] Helsham v. Blackwood, 5 Eng. L. & Eq. 409.

38. So a justification must plead and prove *the very charge;* not one of a similar character, although of the same or even greater enormity.[1] (*a*) Thus the defendant imputed to the plaintiff, a clergyman, these words: "Mr. S. said the blood of Christ had nothing to do with our salvation, more than the blood of a hog." Held, that testimony, tending to prove that the plaintiff denied the divinity of Christ and the doctrine of his atonement, and said he was a created being, a good man and perfect, his death that of a martyr, but that there was no more virtue in his blood than that of any creature; was not admissible, either in justification or mitigation.[2] So, in an action for charging that the plaintiff had criminal intercourse with one A. at a particular time and place, the defendant cannot justify, by showing such intercourse with A. at another time and place.[3] And the charge of criminal intercourse with A. cannot be justified by proving intercourse with B.[4] Nor the charge of stealing a dollar from A., by proving that the plaintiff had stolen a dollar from B.[5] So a libel containing general charges against an individual, of hardness towards the poor, dissoluteness of morals, &c., purporting to be conclusions from instances of bad conduct previously narrated in the publication, cannot be justified by proof of other instances.[6] And in an action for charging the plaintiff with perjury, it is not competent for the defendant to give evidence of any other perjury than that laid in the declaration,

[1] Torrey *v.* Field, 10 Verm. 353; Andrews *v.* Vanduzer, 11 Johns. 38; M'Clintock *v.* Crick, 4 Iowa, 453.

[2] Skinner *v.* Grant, 12 Verm. 456.

[3] Sharpe *v.* Stephenson, 12 Ired. 348.

[4] Watters *v.* Smoot, 11 Ired. 315.

[5] Self *v.* Gardner, 15 Mis. 480.

[6] Bartholemy *v.* The People, 2 Hill, 248.

(*a*) And, when any circumstance is stated which is descriptive of, and identifies, the offence, it must be averred and proved, for the purpose of showing that it is the same offence. But, though the plea is not favored, yet, when other descriptive circumstances are proved, so as to show clearly that it is the offence charged, a slight variation in some of the other circumstances, which may be ascribed to mistake, will not be fatal; as if it was on Saturday, instead of Sunday, and the like. Sharpe *v.* Stephenson, 12 Ired. 348.

and affirmed to be true by a plea of justification.[1] Thus, in an action for charging the plaintiff with perjury in making a certain statement, set out in the declaration, as a witness in a certain case, the defendent pleaded, that the plaintiff did commit perjury by making that statement, and that on the same trial he committed perjury by another statement made by him on the same trial, and not set out in the declaration. On demurrer to both pleas, the first was held good, and the second bad.[2] So, in an action for charging the plaintiff with having stolen the defendant's shingles, a justification, stating that the plaintiff had sold the defendant's shingles without his authority, and afterwards denied that he knew anything respecting them, without alleging that the plaintiff took them privately or feloniously; is bad as a justification, nor can those facts be given in mitigation of damages.[3] And the justification must apply to the charge upon which the plaintiff relies. Thus, in slander, the defendant having offered a deposition, tending to sustain a plea in justification of a part of the words laid in the declaration; the plaintiff objected to the deposition, stating that he did not rely upon the words to which the plea related. The Court sustained the objection, directing the jury to disregard those words, and held, the rejection of the deposition did not injure the defendant.[4]

39. But any evidence *tending* to prove the truth of the charge is admissible. Thus the defendant, in an action of slander for having charged the plaintiff and his partner with a fraudulent sale of their property, with intent to cheat their creditors, in pursuance of a conspiracy between them and the purchaser, having pleaded the truth; held, evidence of the purchaser's insolvency at the time of the purchase was admissible, to prove the sale fraudulent. And, evidence of the conspiracy having been introduced, the defendant may then prove, that, before the partnership was entered into, the purchaser recommended the plaintiff's partner to the

[1] Whitaker *v.* Carter, 4 Ired. 461.
[2] Starr *v.* Harrington, 1 Smith, 360; 1 Cart. 515.
[3] Shepard *v.* Merrill, 13 Johns. 475.
[4] Hesler *v.* Degant, 3 Ind. 501.

witness as "a safe and suitable person to sell goods to on credit," and that the witness sold goods to the firm, on that recommendation, for which he had not been paid.[1]

40. In actions for libel, the plea, answer, or notice in justification must contain all the substantial averments of other special pleas. Though the libel is long, general averments are not admissible, in order to avoid prolixity, but the plea must specifically point out the acts of which the plaintiff was guilty, in order that the Court may see whether the defendant was justified in what he published.[2] (*a*) A justification generally in the words of the libel, where the libel is general, is not sufficient.[3] Thus a justification of a charge of swindling must state the particular instances of fraud, by which the defendant means to support it.[4]

41. A plea of justification must justify the libel according to the sense given to it by the plaintiff; not merely repeat the charges and aver them to be true, though amplified by the addition of time, places, and circumstances. So the charges must be *directly* met, and not *argumentatively* or *by inference*.[5] And the plea admits the truth of the innuendoes in the declaration.[6] So, when the charge is made directly, the plea of justification should aver the truth of the charge, as laid in the declaration; but when the charge is made by insinuation and circumlocution, so as to render it necessary to use introductory matter to show the meaning of the words, the plea should aver the truth of the

[1] Odiorne *v.* Bacon, 6 Cush. 185.

[2] Johnson *v* Stebbins, 5 Ind. 364; Van Derveer *v.* Sutphin, 5 Ohio, N. S. 293.

[3] Anson *v.* Stuart, 1 T. R. 748.

[4] Ibid

[5] Fidler *v.* Delavan, 20 Wend. 57.

[6] Ibid.

(*a*) So, in a justification of slander, that the defendant named the original author of it at the time, it is not sufficient to allege, that the original slanderer used such and such words, or to that effect; although, in the libel declared on, the defendant stated that another had spoken the same slanderous words of the plaintiff, or words to that effect; but the defendant must give the very words used, though it be only necessary to prove some material part of them. Maitland *v.* Goldney, 2 E. 426.

charge which the declaration alleges was meant to be made.[1]

42. The foregoing requisitions, however, relating to the defence of justification, are not so strictly enforced, as to interfere with the real merits, or operate with unreasonable harshness upon the defendant. Thus it is enough, if the proof *substantially* support a plea of justification.[2] And where a libel consists of specific charges, a general answer, averring their truth, is sufficient.[3] So to the words that the plaintiff signed the defendant's name to a note, without his permission, a plea, that the plaintiff did sign the defendant's name to said note without his permission, was held to be good.[4] So the plaintiff, a dissenting minister, charged the defendants, the proprietors of a newspaper, with publishing therein the following libel against him, viz: "A serious misunderstanding has recently taken place amongst the independent dissenters of Great Marlow and their pastor, in consequence of some personal invectives publicly thrown out from the pulpit by the latter, against a young lady of distinguished merit and spotless reputation. We understand, however, that the matter is to be taken up seriously." The defendants, in justification, pleaded, that the plaintiff, just before his preaching and delivering a certain discourse or sermon, addressed by him as such pastor or minister to a certain congregation of dissenters in a certain chapel, and whilst he was officiating in the said chapel as pastor or minister, spoke and published from a certain part or station of the said chapel, assigned to him as pastor and minister for the preaching and delivery of the discourse or sermon, to and in the presence of the congregation, of and concerning one M. F., these scandalous words following: "I have something to say, which I have thought of saying for some time, namely, the improper conduct of one of the female teachers; her name is Miss F.; her conduct is a bad example and disgrace to the schools, and if any of the children dare ask her to go home, she shall be turned out of the

[1] Snow v. Witcher, 9 Ired. 346.
[2] Wilson v. Nations, 5 Yerg. 211.
[3] Van Wyck v. Guthrie, 4 Duer, 268.
[4] Creebnan v. Morley, 7 Blackf. 281.

school and never enter it again; Miss F. does more harm than good;" and thereby gave great offence to divers of the dissenters, to wit, one A. B., one C. D., and one E. F., and occasioned a serious misunderstanding amongst the dissenters in the declaration mentioned. The jury having found a verdict for the defendants on this plea; held, on a motion in arrest of judgment, that it was a sufficient answer to the libel as charged in the declaration.[1]

43. But where the defendant, in a case of slander, admitted in his answer, that while he was conducting his own cause before a justice, and examining the plaintiff as a witness, he interrogated him, "Do you say I put you on William's land?" that the witness answered, "I do," and that the defendant replied, "That's a lie;" and the answer further alleged, that the plaintiff's answer to the defendant's question, and his statement that the defendant put the witness on William's land, were untrue; held, the answer was not good as a justification.[2]

44. The effect of a *conviction* of the plaintiff of the crime charged has sometimes been brought in question under the plea of justification. Thus, to an action for libelling the plaintiffs in their business of sellers of medicines, by publishing that the defendants had crushed the hygeist system of wholesale poisoning, pursued by the scamps and rascals; the defendants pleaded and proved the conviction of two of the vendors of the plaintiffs' pills, for manslaughter. Held, that the plea was sufficient, and sufficiently proved, though it did not justify the words scamps and rascals; and though one of the victims died, notwithstanding he had taken fewer pills than the vendor recommended; it appearing that a larger number would only have accelerated his death. Held also, that it was not necessary for the defendants to show that they had completely crushed the system.[3]

45. And the effect of a *pardon* has sometimes been brought in question. Thus, in an action for accusing the plaintiff of

[1] Edwards *v.* Bell, 8 Moore, 467.
[2] Lewis *v.* Black, 27 Miss. 425.
[3] Morrison *v.* Harmer, 3 Bing. N. 759.

having stolen an axe several years before from one L.; it was held, that the defendant might defeat the action by proving the truth of the words, notwithstanding the plaintiff, after having been convicted of the offence, was regularly pardoned. Otherwise, it seems, if the words be "You *are* a thief," or, "He *is* a thief."[1] (*a*)

46. It has been held, that a plea of justification in slander should be as specific and certain, as an indictment for the offence charged by the slander.[2] So it is the prevailing doctrine, that, to sustain the plea, the evidence of the offence must be such, as would be sufficient to prove the offence beyond a reasonable doubt, and to convict the plaintiff, in an indictment.[3] Thus, in an action for charging the plaintiff with perjury, and a plea of justification, the Court should instruct the jury, that, to support the plea, there must be two concurring witnesses to the falsity of every material fact of the testimony of the plaintiff, alleged to be false, or one witness, and corroborating circumstances equivalent to one witness.[4] So, in an action of slander for a charge of perjury, the defendant asked the Court to instruct the jury, that "one witness, corroborated by other witnesses, to admissions, or other circumstances equivalent, in the opinion of the jury, to another witness, is, if believed, sufficient to make out a justification of the charge of false swearing." Held, that the instruction ought to have been given, it being pertinent to the issue and evidence.[5] (*b*) And the same rule

[1] Baum *v.* Clause, 5 Hill, 196. See Cuddington *v.* Wilkins, Hob. 81.

[2] Steele *v.* Phillips, 10 Humph. 461; Snyder *v.* Andrews, 6 Barb. 43.

[3] Gants *v.* Vinard, 1 Smith, 287; 6 Barr, 170; 8 Blackf. 495; 35 Maine, 315; Hopkins *v.* Smith, 3 Barb. 599; Landis *v.* Shanklin, 1 Cart. 92; Shoulty *v.* Miller, Ibid. 544; Swails *v.* Butcher, 2 Cart. 84.

[4] Steinman *v.* McWilliams, 6 Barr, 170.

[5] Crandall *v.* Dawson, 1 Gilm. 556.

(*a*) In this connection it may be stated, that, while an action lies for charging a crime, the prosecution of which has been barred by the statute of limitations; the defendant may justify and prove the truth, notwithstanding the criminal prosecution may be barred. Van Ankin *v.* Westfall, 14 Johns. 234.

(*b*) It has been held, that the testimony which the plaintiff gave on the

with regard to pleading and proof has been applied, in an action of slander for charging the plaintiff with *larceny;*[1] though in such case it has been held not necessary to set forth the charge with the precision which would be required in an indictment for that crime.[2]

47. But on the other hand it has been held, that the defendant is not bound, in justifying, to produce such evidence as would convict the plaintiff if he were on trial for the offence;[3] but the ordinary rule of evidence in civil cases applies.[4] (*a*) Thus the distinction is made, that although, in an action for charging the plaintiff with perjury, it is necessary for the defendant, if he pleads a justification, to support his plea with such proof as would be required to convict the plaintiff on an indictment for that offence; yet it is not necessary, as in a criminal prosecution, that it should be of that degree of certainty requisite to remove all reasonable doubt from the minds of the jury. A mere preponderance is sufficient.[5]

48. It is the prevailing doctrine, that a plea of justification, if untrue, and not maintained by the evidence, is an aggravation of the charge, evinces continued and express malice, and may properly be considered by the jury to increase the damages.[6] And, where both the general issue and justification are pleaded, the special plea may be considered by the jury in estimating damages, as evidence tending to show malice, although not evidence for the plaintiff to support the

[1] Wonderly *v.* Nokes, 8 Blackf. 589.

[2] Thompson *v.* Barkley, 27 Penn. 263.

[3] Kincade *v.* Bradshaw, 3 Hawks, 63.

[4] Barfield *v.* Brett, 2 Jones, Law, 41; Folsom *v.* Brown, 5 Fost. 114.

[5] Spruil *v.* Cooper, 16 Ala. 791.

[6] Robinson *v.* Drummond, 24 Ala. 174; Fero *v.* Ruscoe, 4 Comst. 162; Wilson *v.* Nations, 5 Yerg. 211; Updegrove *v.* Zimmerman, 13 Penn. 610; Smith *v.* Wyman, 4 Shep. 13.

---

trial, when the alleged perjury was committed, may be received as evidence, to be considered by the jury. Newbit *v.* Statuck, 35 Maine, 315.

(*a*) With more particular reference to the *pleadings* or *allegations* in civil and criminal cases, it is suggested by an approved elementary writer, that *greater* precision may be necessary in a plea than an indictment; and that variances as to sums or magnitudes, which would not be fatal in the latter, would be so in the former. 2 Stark. Ev. 878.

general issue.[1] But the contrary doctrine has been sometimes held, that a plea of justification, though no evidence is given in support of it, is not to be considered in determining the question of damages;[2] more especially, if interposed in good faith, with probable cause to believe, and the honest belief, that it will be sustained; or at most that the defendant is liable only for the actual additional damage thereby caused.[3] But it is for the jury to consider, whether such plea was interposed upon proper motives.[4]

49. Where the defendant pleaded not guilty, and at the same time filed a notice of justification, which was read to the jury, but withdrawn by consent of the Court, after the plaintiff's case was closed; it was held that this fact might be taken into consideration by the jury in estimating damages.[5] But it has also been held, that, where pleas of justification are withdrawn, they are no longer a part of the proceedings, and therefore not legal evidence to the jury.[6] And, in an action for a libel, evidence of the defendant's procuring depositions, &c., to prove the truth of his charges, and afterwards declining to plead a justification, may be properly referred to the jury on the question of malice, but not on the question of damages.[7] So an invalid and insufficient plea of justification in an action of slander, upon which no judgment could have been rendered, is entitled to no weight in aggravation of damages, under the plea of not guilty.[8]

50. With regard to the mode of meeting a plea of justification, it has been held, that, in an action of slander against one who charged the plaintiff with perjury, in saying that he knew the character of A., and would believe him under oath; the plaintiff may prove, in reply to a plea of justification, that A. was entitled to belief under oath, on the goodness of

[1] Doss v. Jones, 5 How. (Miss.) 158.

[2] Shortley v. Miller, 1 Smith, 395; Murphy v. Stout, Ib. 256; Shank v. Case, 1 Cart. 170.

[3] Fulkerson v. George, 3 Abb. Pr. R. 75.

[4] Sloan v. Petrie, 15 Ill. 425.

[5] Beasley v. Meigs, 16 Ill. 139; Spencer v. McMasters, Ib. 405.

[6] Gilmore v. Bordens, 2 How. (Miss.) 824.

[7] Bodwell v. Osgood, 3 Pick. 379.

[8] Braden v. Walker, 8 Humph. 34.

his character.[1] And where a defendant, in an action for libel, had charged the plaintiff with having falsely accused him of a crime; and the defendant gave proof, in mitigation, of the falsehood of the accusation; held, the plaintiff was entitled to reply, with evidence of its truth.[2] So, if a justification is pleaded, the plaintiff may introduce evidence of former good character in aggravation of damages, although it has not been impeached by evidence.[3] (*a*)

1 Howell *v.* Howell, 10 Ired. 82.

2 Woodburn *v.* Miller, Cheves, 194.

3 Scott *v.* Peebles, 2 Sm. & M. 546.

(*a*) In slander for calling the plaintiff a whore, the words were laid to have been spoken in 1842. The plea was, that the plaintiff, while sole and unmarried, on the 1st of January, 1834, had carnal connection with one A. The replication was, that the plaintiff, before and at the time mentioned in the plea, was betrothed to the said A; that afterwards, on the 6th of June, 1834, she was lawfully married to him; that she lived with him a virtuous life until the 1st of August, 1836, when he died; and that she had ever since continued to live in innocent and virtuous widowhood. Held, on general demurrer, that the replication was insufficient. Alcorn *v.* Hooker, 7 Blackf. 58.

In slander, for charging the plaintiff, in the presence of "sundry persons," with larceny, the defendant pleaded, that he spoke the words in giving testimony as a witness in a certain cause. Held, that the defendant might prove what his testimony was, and that the plaintiff, if he meant to proceed for speaking the words on some other occasion than that named in the plea, should have newly assigned. Nelson *v.* Robe, 6 Blackf. 204.

In an action for libel, in publishing that the plaintiff was a defaulter, a mortgage executed by the plaintiff to the United States, and a foreclosure thereon, is competent evidence in justification; but evidence of any acts of the government respecting the plaintiff's indebtedness, after the publication of the alleged libel, is not admissible in rebuttal. Roberts *v.* Miller, 2 Greene, 122.

It has been held, that, where the defendant has pleaded both the general issue and a justification, evidence offered in support of the plea of justification may be considered by the jury *in mitigation of damages.* Duncan *v.* Brown, 15 B. Mon. 186; Landis *v.* Sharklin, 1 Smith, 78.

So that a defendant, justifying, and failing in his proof, may offer evidence in mitigation of damages. Morehead *v.* Jones, 2 B. Mon. 210.

But on the other hand it is held, that, where the defendant pleads a justification alone, but his evidence under that plea fails to make out a full justification, he is not entitled to *any benefit* from such evidence. Fero *v.* Ruscoe, 4 Comst. 162.

51. In addition to the justification of *the truth*, which applies alike to slander and libel; it has been sometimes held a good defence, in an action of slander, to show that the words spoken were but the *repetition* of what was uttered by some other person, whose name was given at the time; unless it be proved that the repetition was malicious. But the burden of proof is on the defendant, to show that he only repeated the words of another, and that he named the author at the time; whether the defence be presented under the general issue or by a special plea.[1] Upon this ground, the plaintiff need not, in his declaration, negative such matter of defence. Thus an action lies for the words, "thou art a sheep-stealing rogue, and Farmer Parker told me so," without averring in the declaration that Farmer Parker did not tell the defendant so.[2] So it is no justification, to plead merely that A. B. told the slander to the defendant;[3] without further averring that such person had in fact made the statement.[4] Nor that the defendant was informed by a third person of the charge set forth, without giving the name of such person. This could only be good evidence in mitigation.[5] Nor that the defendant, *after speaking the words, and before action*, disclosed to the plaintiff the author of the words.[6] (*a*)

[1] Haynes *v.* Leland, 29 Maine, 233; Easterwood *v.* Quin, 2 Brev. 64; Buirs *v.* M'Corkle, 2 Browne, 90; Kelly *v.* Dillon 5 Ind. 426; Church *v.* Bridgeman, 6 Mis. 190; 9 T. R. 17.

[2] Gardiner *v.* Atwater, Sayer, 265.

[3] Davis *v.* Lewis, 7 T. R. 17.

[4] Robinson *v.* Harvey, 5 Mon. 519.

[5] Parker *v.* McQueen, 8 B. Mon. 16.

[6] Skinner *v.* Grant, 12 Verm. 456.

And in Massachusetts it has been held, that, where the defendant pleads a justification alone, the case does not come within Stat. 1826, c. 107, § 2; so that, if he fails to establish his plea, malice is to be inferred, and evidence, that he spoke the words believing them to be true, cannot be received in mitigation of damages. Hix *v.* Drury, 5 Pick. 296.

(*a*) Upon the subject considered in the text, we may cite the following remarks of eminent Judges and commentators, tending strongly to the conclusion, that the defence in question can be set up, if at all, only in mitigation of damages: —

"The public may be ignorant of the worthlessness of the original author, and may be led to attach credit to his name and slander, when both are mentioned by a person of undoubted reputation." Per Kent, C. J., Dole *v.* Lyon, 10 Johns. 449.

But it has been held, that declarations of the husband, pending an action for the slander of his wife, that he believed the

---

"A man must not go about repeating slander, and saying of whom he heard it. It is no justification for him, that he at the time he repeats the slander gives up the name of the person from whom he heard it. If the defendant had said, at the time he spoke the words, that he heard the slanderous matter from another person, and named that person, and now at the trial had proved that he in fact did hear the slander from that person, it would be matter of mitigation." Per Alderson, B., Bennett *v.* Bennett, 6 C. & P. 588. On the other hand it is said, —

"If a person say, that such a particular man (naming him) told him certain slander, and that man did in fact tell him so, it is a good defence to an action to be brought by the person of whom the slander was spoken; but if he assert the slander generally, without adding who told it to him, it is actionable. Then it is said, that it is sufficient to repel such action to disclose by the defendant's plea the person who told him the slander; but that is clearly no justification, after putting the plaintiff to the expense of bringing the action. The plaintiff can only impute the slander to the man who utters it, if the latter do not mention the person from whom he heard it. The justice of the case also falls in with the decisions on this subject. It is just, that when a person repeats any slander against another, he should at the same time declare from whom he heard it, in order that the party injured may sue the author of the slander." Per Ld. Kenyon, Davis *v.* Lewis, 7 T. R. 19.

A writer of high authority remarks, that "this doctrine (of justifying the has of late been repudiated in England." 2 Greenl. Ev. § 424, n.

And Messrs. Hare & Wallace present the following clear and concise his-repetition of a slander) has been solemnly denied in the United States, and tory of the course of decisions upon the subject: "In the Earl of Northampton's case, 12 Coke, 132, 134, it was resolved, that if one publish that he heard another, naming him, say that the plaintiff was a traitor or a thief, in an action on the case, if the truth be such, he may justify. Later decisions, in admitting the authority of this resolution, have always construed it very strictly, by holding that such a plea, to be good, must show that the defendant, at the time, disclosed a certain cause of action against another, by naming him at the time of speaking, and by stating the precise words used by him; and that such person was amenable to the plaintiff's action; and it was further held in several cases that such a defence is not to be considered as amounting to a justification, but only as raising a presumption, *primâ facie*, that the defendant did not circulate the slander maliciously, which presumption may be rebutted by testimony showing positive malice, and if the repetition is found to have been malicious, the defence altogether

defendant had not originated the slander, but had only repeated it, is admissible in mitigation of damages;[1] and that, in mitigation, the defendant may show that some statements of another person had been communicated to him.[2] And damages cannot be recovered for the repetition of words repeated *at the request* of the plaintiff.[3]

52. But, as has been suggested, where slanderous words are spoken, and the author given, a defendant may still be guilty of slander.[4] A defendant cannot justify the repetition of slanderous words, by merely proving that, when he repeated them, he stated that he had heard them from another whom he named; but he must also prove, that he repeated them upon a justifiable occasion and with justifiable intentions, and believed them to be true.[5] And a *plea* of repetition must show, that the defendant at the time disclosed a certain cause of action against another person, by naming him at the time and giving the precise words used; that such person was liable to the action; that the defendant believed the charge to be true; and that he repeated it on a justifiable occasion.[6] It is said, when the repetition of slander is unlawful, for want of these palliating circumstances, it is not an ordinary or necessary legitimate consequence of the original act of uttering the slander, and cannot be used to make out the relation of cause and effect between the original slander and the effect attributed to it; which injury might

[1] Evans *v.* Smith, 5 Mon. 363.

[2] Galloway *v.* Courtney, 10 Rich. 414.

[3] Haynes *v.* Leland, 29 Maine, 233.

[4] Sexton *v.* Todd, Wright, 317; Evans *v.* Smith, 5 Mon. 363; Miller *v.* Kerr, 2 McCord, 285; Austin *v.* Hanchet, 2 Root, 148.

[5] M'Pherson *v.* Daniels, 5 M. & Ry. 251; 12 Barb. 657; Cates *v.* Kellogg, 9 Ind. 506.

[6] Larkins *v.* Tarter, 3 Sneed, 681.

---

fails. But the late English cases go yet further, and decide that the plea must show that the defendant believed the matter to be true, and that he repeated it on a justifiable occasion, which, in effect, completely overrules the resolution in Northampton's case; and these decisions have been generally recognized and approved in this country; but not in Maine, where the older English practice is adhered to." Gilman *v.* Lowell, 1 Amer. Lead. Cas. 202, n.

not have happened but for the unjustifiable and illegal interference of another.[1] Hence it is well settled, that an oral slander, repeated by one naming his informant, is justifiable or not, *according to the intention and motives* of the person repeating it.[2] Unless it appears that a party acted *without malice*, or if he did not believe the charge to be true, he is not justified in repeating a slanderous charge, although he names the author at the time. The *quo animo* with which the charge is repeated is the controlling consideration.[3] (*a*)

[1] Olmstead *v.* Brown, 12 Barb. 657.

[2] Johnston *v.* Lance, 7 Ired. 448; Dole *v.* Lyon, 10 Johns. 447.

[3] Cummerford *v.* McAvoy, 15 Ill. 311; Jones *v.* Chapman, 5 Blackf. 88.

(*a*) But the following instruction, asked for by the plaintiff, was rightly refused, as the report might not have been slanderous: "If the defendant gave circulation to a report maliciously against the plaintiff, it will not justify him, even if he gave his author at the time." Abrams *v.* Smith, 8 Blackf. 95.

So the following instruction, asked for by the plaintiff, was also refused: "A person, who gives currency to a slanderous report, does it at his peril; and if in this case the defendant, by repeating the words, gave currency to the report conveyed by the words in the declaration, (not covered by the demurrer,) he was bound to justify and prove them true, or else he cannot justify the speaking of them; and malice is inferred in the speaking." Held, that the repeating or first speaking of slanderous words may be often justified, without proving them to be true. Also, that malice is not always inferred from the speaking of words, which, unexplained, are actionable. Also that the Supreme Court, not being informed of the circumstances under which the words mentioned in this instruction were spoken, must presume the circumstances to have been such as justified the refusal of the instruction. Ibid.

As has been already suggested, one ground of the general rule, that repetition of a slander, under certain circumstances, is not actionable, is, that the plaintiff has his more direct and appropriate remedy against the originator of the slander. And the consideration, whether in a particular case such remedy exists, may sometimes determine the validity of the defence; more especially if connected with the other grounds already referred to. Thus, in an action for words spoken of the plaintiff in his trade, importing a direct assertion made by the defendant, that the plaintiff was insolvent, the defendant pleaded, that one T. W. spoke and published to the defendant the same words, and that the defendant, at the time of speaking and publishing them, declared that he had heard and been told the same from

53. It has already been suggested, that, in reference to the particular ground of defence or justification which we are now considering, even supposing it to be still recognized, *libel* and *slander* do not, as in most other respects, stand on the same footing. The doctrine is well settled, that, in an action for *libel*, it is no justification, that the libellous matter was previously published by a third person, and that the defendant, at the time of his publication, disclosed the name of that person, and believed all the statements contained in the libel to be true.[1] (*a*) Thus it is no defence to an action

[1] Fidman *v.* Ainslie, 28 Eng. L. & Eq. 567; Clarkson *v.* M'Carty, 5 Blackf. 574; Larkins *v.* Tarter, 3 Sneed, 681; Crespigny *v.* Wellesley, 5 Bing. 392; 2 Moo. & P. 695. See Brooks *v.* Bryan, Wright, 760.

---

and by the said T. W. Held, upon demurrer, that this plea was bad; first, because it did not confess and avoid the charge mentioned in the declaration, the words in the declaration importing an unqualified assertion made by the defendant in those words, and the words used in the plea importing that the defendant mentioned the fact on the authority of T. W. Secondly, because it did not give the plaintiff any cause of action against T. W., inasmuch as it did not allege that T. W. spoke the words falsely and maliciously. Thirdly, because it is not an answer to an action for oral slander, for a defendant to show that he heard it from another, and named the person at the time, without showing that the defendant believed it to be true, and that he spoke the words on a justifiable occasion. M'Pherson *v.* Daniels, 10 B. & C. 263.

So it has been held to be no defence, that the defendant only uttered the words of other persons, naming them, if such other persons are citizens of another State, so that they cannot be sued. Scott *v.* Peebles, 2 Sm. & M. 546.

(*a*) It was long since doubted, whether a defendant can, by naming the original author, justify the publishing in writing of slanderous words, especially after knowing that they were unfounded. Maitland *v.* Goldney, 2 E. 426.

It was said, "If one repeats, and another writes a libel, and a third approves what is writ, they are all makers of such libel; for all persons who concur, and show their assent or approbation to do an unlawful act, are guilty." Regina *v.* Drake, Holt, 425.

To a declaration for a libel in a newspaper, the defendants pleaded, first, that the libellous matter was a true and correct account of a statement made by A. and B. before a magistrate; and second, that the facts therein stated

against the editor of a newspaper for publishing a libel, though no express malice be shown, that he avowedly copied the article from another specified paper, expressing his disbelief in some of the allegations contained in it, but saying nothing in affirmance or denial of the libellous charges.[1]

54. Upon the general subject now under consideration it is said, that *the repetition of a slanderous report* is actionable, and the defendant cannot justify by proving the existence of the report, without also proving it to be true.[2] (*a*)

[1] Hotchkiss *v.* Oliphant, 2 Hill, 510.

[2] Hampton *v.* Wilson, 4 Dev. 468; Smalley *v.* Anderson, 4 B. Mon. 367; Hancock *v.* Stephens, 11 Humph. 507; Kennedy *v.* Gifford, 19 Wend. 256; Mayer *v.* Pine, 4 Mich. 409; Dame *v.* Kenney, 5 Fost. 318.

---

were true; and the jury found for the defendants on the first plea, and for the plaintiff on the second. Held, that the plaintiff was entitled to judgment *non obstante veredicto* on the first plea, on the following grounds: 1. The statement, though correct, did not relate to a matter of which the magistrate had cognizance. 2. The defendants had printed and published that which would not have been actionable as oral slander, and consequently were not protected by giving the names of the authors at the time of the publication. 3. Supposing the matter actionable as oral slander, the defendants had not by their plea offered themselves as witnesses to prove the words against the authors. M'Gregor *v.* Thwaites, 4 Dowl. & Ry. 695.

Where, in an action for a libel, the declaration alleged, that the defendant had composed, written, and published the libellous matter, and it appeared from the libel itself, that the defendant had given references to another work, whence the matter was taken, but which were omitted in the declaration; held, the variance was fatal, inasmuch as the sense of the libel declared upon was different from that produced in evidence. Cartwright *v.* Wright, 1 Dowl. & Ry. 230.

In mitigation of damages, the defendant was allowed under the general issue to show, that he copied the statement from another newspaper; but not that it had appeared concurrently in several other newspapers. Saunders *v.* Mills, 6 Bing. 213.

(*a*) Upon the point whether such evidence is admissible *in mitigation of damages*, the authorities are somewhat contradictory. It has been held, that the defendant may prove a general report of the truth of the words spoken, to disprove malice, and in mitigation of damages, but not in justification. Nelson *v.* Evans, 1 Dev. 9; Morris *v.* Barker, 4 Harring. 520; Van Derveer *v.* Sutphin, 5 Ohio, N. S. 293.

Also, that, if words are spoken as current report, or as expressing regret,

That a man may slander or libel another as effectually by circulating rumors or reports, or by putting his communica-

---

that fact may be given in evidence to mitigate damages. Young *v.* Slemons, Wright, 124.

Thus, in an action for charging the plaintiff, an unmarried woman, with fornication, evidence is admissible in mitigation of damages, that it had become a matter of common and general report that the plaintiff had committed fornication. Case *v.* Marks, 20 Conn. 248.

But where the plaintiff in such case, after objecting to the testimony offered by the defendant, and after it was excluded by the Court, withdrew her objection, and the defendant notwithstanding neglected to examine the witness on that point, and the plaintiff had a verdict; it was held, that the error of the Court in excluding the testimony was, under these circumstances, no ground for a new trial. Ibid.

In an action brought in Alabama, for calling the plaintiff *a hog-thief*, evidence of a common report that the plaintiff had been accused of that crime in Mississippi, and had run away, is not admissible in mitigation of damages, without showing previously that the plaintiff's general character is bad, and that such report was believed by his neighbors. Bradley *v.* Gibson, 9 Ala. 406.

Nor is evidence of such report admissible, in connection with a knowledge and belief of the report by the defendant, to rebut the presumption of malice and in mitigation of damages, unless accompanied by a distinct admission that the charge is false. Ibid.

So, in an action involving falsity, it is not sufficient to authorize a verdict for the defendants on the ground of *their belief*, that, from the plaintiff's character and particular instances of bad conduct, they believed that he would state a falsehood for the purpose of injuring one he hated or disliked. There should, at least, have been reasonable ground for their belief, in facts proved before the jury and believed by them. Duncan *v.* Brown, 15 B. Mon. 186.

And it is the prevailing doctrine, that, in an action of slander, common report of the truth of the fact, which the slanderous words assert, is not admissible in mitigation of damages. Scott *v.* McKinnish, 15 Ala. 662; Bodwell *v.* Swan, 3 Pick. 376; Fisher *v.* Patterson, 14 Ohio, 418; Dame *v.* Kenney, 5 Fost. 318.

Nor the reputation of having committed particular wrongful acts or crimes, and having been convicted of such crimes. Fisher *v.* Patterson, 14 Ohio, 418.

Thus, in slander, for charging the plaintiff with stealing, the defendant cannot prove under the general issue, in mitigation of damages, that there was a report, in the neighborhood of the plaintiff, that he had been guilty of stealing. Young *v.* Bennett, 4 Scam. 43.

tions, spoken or written, in the shape of hearsays, as by making distinct assertions of the slanderous matters, and asserting them as truths of his own knowledge,[1] (see p. 261). In a late case it is well remarked, " It is no answer, in any forum, to say, that she only repeated the story as she heard it. If the story was false and slanderous, she must repeat it at her peril. There is safety in no other rule. Often the origin of the slander cannot be traced. If it were, possibly it might be harmless. He who gives it circulation gives it its power of mischief. It is the successive repetitions that do the work. A falsehood often repeated gets to be believed." [2] Hence a repetition of a slander already in circulation, without expressing any disbelief of it, or any purpose of inquiring as to its truth, though made without any design to extend its circulation or credit, or to cause the person to whom it is addressed to believe or suspect it to be true, is actionable.[3] And where the only evidence was, that the

[1] Schenck v. Schenck, 1 Spencer, 208.

[2] Per Thomas, J., Kenney v. McLaughlin, 5 Gray, 5.

[3] Ib.

So, in a case of slander for charging the plaintiff with perjury, the existence of prior reports, charging the plaintiff with the crime imputed to him by the defendant, without any offer to explain their extent or effect upon the character of the plaintiff, is not, under a plea of justification, legal evidence in mitigation of damages. Sanders v. Johnson, 6 Blackf. 50.

And the defendant cannot introduce evidence of what two or three persons had said in relation to the character of the plaintiff. Regnier v. Cabot, 2 Gilm. 34.

Nor evidence calculated to excite a suspicion of the offence charged upon the plaintiff, but falling short of proof. Ibid.

So it is no mitigation of slanderous words, for the speaker to aver that he can prove the truth of the words by a third person. James v. Clarke, 1 Ired. 397.

In an action for the publication of a libel, the defendant asked a news collector, who wrote a part of the article complained of, " what inquiries and examinations he made, and what sources of information he applied to before making the communications," which tended to charge the plaintiff with dishonesty and bad faith ? Held, the question was incompetent, and the defendant, as a foundation for such question, could not prove that there was a general anxiety, in the community, in regard to the facts stated in the publication. Sheckell v. Jackson, 10 Cush. 25.

defendant repeated a slander, already in circulation, to one person, who testified that she did not believe it, or think any worse of the plaintiff for having heard it; and the jury were instructed, that, if the defendant repeated the slander, conveying to any extent the idea that it was true, or that the defendant believed it to be true, this action would lie; but that it would be otherwise, if the defendant repeated the slander without any design to extend its circulation or credit, or to cause the person to whom it was addressed to believe or suspect it to be true; and returned a verdict of a trifling amount for the plaintiff; held, the plaintiff was entitled to a new trial.[1] So it is no justification of a slander, that the defendant, at the time he spoke the slanderous words, accompanied them with an explanation that such was the common report, and that he spoke the words as merely giving the report.[2] So a justification of a libel, that there was a reason for thinking the imputation was true from what had been said, is bad on demurrer, more especially if it is not stated what had been said, and by whom.[3] And it is not competent for the defendant to prove by a witness present, that another person had imputed to the plaintiff the offence alleged, in the words which were the cause of the action.[4] So, where a witness testifies, in an action of slander, that the defendant charged the plaintiff with a certain offence, the defendant cannot prove by the witness, that he (the witness) had before told the defendant, that the plaintiff was guilty of that offence.[5] (*a*) So, in an action of slander for

[1] Kenney *v.* McLaughlin, 5 Gray, 3.
[2] Wheeler *v.* Shields, 2 Scam. 348; Moberly *v.* Preston, 8 Mis. 462.
[3] Lane *v.* Howman, 1 Price, 76.
[4] Poppenheim *v.* Wilkes, 1 Strobh. 275.
[5] Clark *v.* Munsell, 6 Met. 373.

(*a*) But where the plaintiff waived objection to the admission of the declarations of a third person, offered by the defendant in mitigation of damages, to show that he did not originate the slander, and that the plaintiff's character was not above suspicion; it was held, that other declarations of the same person, upon the same subject, made before and after the commencement of the action, were properly admissible for the plaintiff. Jeter *v.* Askew, 2 Speers, 633.

charging the plaintiff with the murder of A., what A. said, though near death, and under the full impression that he would not recover, is not admissible under the plea of justification.[1] And, in general, the defendant cannot, in order to support his plea of justification, give evidence of transactions or conversations between himself and others, to which the plaintiff was not privy.[2] (*a*)

55. The *evidence* or *proofs*, in an action for libel or slander, have, of course, been constantly referred to, through all the preceding inquiries upon the subject. Without repeating what has been already said in various connections, we proceed to state a few rules of law relating more exclusively to this particular point.

56. It has been already stated (p. 407) that, as a general rule, the *words* of a libel or slander must be set forth in the declaration. Another rule, relating more especially to the *proof* of the allegations in the declaration, is, that the words alleged and the words proved must precisely correspond. In case of libel, slight *variances* between the words charged and the words contained in the libel are fatal to the action.[3] So in slander, it is not sufficient, in order to support the action, to prove words *equivalent* to those alleged.[4] Nor the *substance* of them,[5] though explained in the same sense by the defendant himself.[6] Thus, in an old case, the declaration was, "she is as very a thief as any which robbeth by the highway side;" but the words proved were, "she is a *worse* thief," &c. Wray, C. J., was of opinion that these words were *all one*, but Gawdy and Fenner, Justices,

[1] Barfield *v.* Brett, 2 Jones, Law, 41.
[2] Jenkins *v.* Cockerham, 1 Ired. 309.
[3] Winter *v.* Donovan, 8 Gill, 370; Street *v.* Bushnell, 24 Mis. 328; Birch *v.* Benton, 26 Mis. 153.
[4] Moore *v.* Bond, 4 Blackf. 458; Sanford *v.* Gaddis, 15 Ill. 228; Slocumb *v.* Kuykendall, 1 Scam. 187.
[5] Eisely *v.* Moss, 9 Ala. 266.
[6] Armitage *v.* Dunster, 4 Doug. 291.

(*a*) But it has been held that, in an action for slander in charging the defendant with having sworn falsely as to the residence of an individual, declarations made by that individual, as to his residence, not in the presence of the plaintiff, are admissible as evidence against him. Cherry *v.* Slade, 2 Hawks, 400.

ruled otherwise.[1] So a declaration, "you would steal, and you will steal," is not sustained by evidence of the words, "a man that would do that would steal."[2] So there is a variance, though words alleged are proved, if others actually used are not set forth, which affect the sense of the former. As where a part of the words import a charge of crime, but the whole, taken together, do not.[3] And slanderous words, charged as addressed to the plaintiff in the second person, are not supported by evidence of words spoken of him in the third person, though so spoken in his presence.[4] Nor *vice versâ*.[5] So a count, charging that words were spoken *affirmatively*, is not supported by proof of the same words spoken *by way of interrogation*.[6] And it is a fatal variance, in an action for libel, if the characters of the libels alleged and proved are essentially different, though the slander imputed may be the same. Thus an action for a libel, charging in one count that the defendant published it as purporting to be a letter from A. to B.; and in another, generally, that the defendant published the libellous matter; is not sustained by proof of a publication, wherein the defendant stated, that, in a debate in the Irish House of Commons several years before, the Attorney-General of Ireland had read such a letter, and then stating the libellous matter as said by him in commenting upon that letter.[7] So, in an action for defamation of the plaintiff's wife, the words alleged in the declaration were, "the plaintiff's wife is a great thief, and ought to have been transported seven years ago." The words proved were, "she is a bad one, and ought to have been transported seven years ago." Held, that the words proved did not support the declaration.[8] So the averment, "L. is pregnant and gone with child seven months," is not supported by proof of words, "Have you heard anything about L.'s being pregnant

[1] Lady Ratcliffe *v.* Shubley, Cro. Eliz. 224.

[2] Stees *v.* Kemble, 27 Penn. 112.

[3] Edgerly *v.* Swain, 32 N. H. 478.

[4] Stannard *v.* Harper, 5 M. & Ry. 295; Culbertson *v.* Stanley, 6 Blackf. 67.

[5] Cock *v.* Weatherby, 5 Sm. & M. 333; 15 Ill. 228.

[6] Sanford *v.* Gaddis, 15 Ill. 228.

[7] Bell *v.* Byrne, 14 E. 554.

[8] Hancock *v.* Winter, 2 Marsh. 502.

by Dr. P.?"[1] Nor a declaration, charging one with saying, "Dr. F. is not a physician, but a two-penny bleeder;" by proof of the words, "If Dr. F. is a two-penny physician I am none, I am a regular graduate and no quack."[2] Nor a count, charging the defendant with speaking slanderous words, by proof that he maliciously procured another to speak them.[3] Nor the allegation, that the defendant called the plaintiff a whore, by proof that he called her a strumpet.[4] So, where the declaration alleges, "You swore false," and the proof is, "you have sworn false," there is a variance.[5] So a declaration, that the words spoken were in reference to an oath taken by the plaintiff before the register and receiver of a land-office, touching the entry of land, is not sustained by proof of an oath taken before a notary-public, concerning the same subject-matter.[6] So an allegation, that the plaintiff "had sworn a lie, and that it was in him, for he had sworn what he (the defendant) could prove to be a point-blank lie;" is not sustained by the words, "the plaintiff had sworn off a just account, and that he (the defendant) would or could prove it."[7]

57. But on the other hand it is held, that, in an action of slander, it is not necessary to prove the identical words charged, but proof of words substantially the same is sufficient. Thus, where a declaration charges the words, "McK.'s wife is a whore," it is supported by proof of the words, "she (McK.'s wife) is a whorish bitch."[8] So a slight variance in the names of the defendants in an indictment referred to, as set forth in the declaration, and contained in the record, may be cured by parol proof of the identity of the persons.[9] So where, in an action of slander, the plaintiff alleged that the words were spoken relative to testimony of the plaintiff, in a suit in which S. was plaintiff and H. defendant; held, evidence *aliunde* was admissible, to show that

[1] Long *v.* Fleming, 2 Miles, 104.
[2] Foster *v.* Small, 3 Whart. 138.
[3] Watts *v.* Greenlee, 1 Dev. 210.
[4] Williams *v.* Bryant, 4 Ala. 44.
[5] Sanford *v.* Gaddis, 15 Ill. 228.
[6] Phillips *v.* Beene, 16 Ala. 720.
[7] Berry *v.* Dryden, 7 Mis. 324.
[8] Scott *v.* McKinnish, 15 Ala. 662; Miller *v.* Miller, 8 Johns. 74; acc. M'Clintock *v.* Crick, 4 Iowa, 453.
[9] Mamilton *v.* Langley, 1 M'Mul. 498.

the record of an action by S. and W. against H. was the action referred to in the declaration; and that there was no variance.[1] (*a*) And the transposition of the names of the parties to the suit, as a witness in which the plaintiff was charged with having sworn falsely, is not a fatal variance.[2] So, on an allegation that the defendant charged the plaintiff with perjury in a suit of A. and B. *v.* C. and D., the variance is not fatal, if it be shown that the charge was made in reference to the case of a cross-bill, by one of the defendants in such case, against the complainant and co-defendants.[3]

58. And it is no variance, more especially in an action for slander, that the proof does not sustain *all* the allegations in the declaration.[4] It is necessary for the plaintiff to prove some of the words precisely as charged, but not all of them, if those proved are in themselves slanderous,[5] and enough to sustain the cause of action, and do not differ in sense from those alleged.[6] So, although a libel read in evidence con-

[1] Hibler *v.* Servoss, 6 Mis. 24.
[2] Teague *v.* Williams, 7 Ala. 844.
[3] Wiley *v.* Campbell, 5 Monr. 560.
[4] Skinner *v.* Grant, 12 Verm. 456; Purple *v.* Hooton, 13 Wend. 9.
[5] Eisely *v.* Moss, 9 Ala. 266; Nestle *v.* Van Slyck, 2 Hill, 282.
[6] Nichols *v.* Hayes, 13 Conn. 155; M'Kee *v.* Ingalls, 4 Scam. 30; Scott *v.* Renforth Wright, 55; Hancock *v.* Stephens, 11 N. H. 507; Iseley *v.* Lovejoy, 8 Blackf. 462.

(*a*) But if the defendant justify by plea, and allege a suit by S. and S. against H., in which the plaintiff committed perjury, and offer in evidence the record of an action by S. and W. against H., the variance is fatal. 6 Mis. 24.

So the words charged were, "that Poppenheim was a very bad man; he was a calf-thief, and the records of the court would prove it." All the words were proved; but the words, "he has been indicted for calf-stealing," were proved to have been uttered between the words "he was a calf-thief," and the words "the records of the court would prove it." It was held that this did not constitute a variance in the substance of the charge. Poppenheim *v.* Wilkes, 1 Strobh. 271.

But where the declaration alleged, that the words were spoken of and concerning the evidence given by the plaintiff, on a complaint made by him before a justice of the peace, on the 20th of March, 1820, and the proof was that the complaint was made on the 8th of March, 1820. Held, the variance was not material. McKinly *v.* Rob, 20 Johns. 351.

tain matter in addition to that set out in the declaration, there is no variance, if the additional part do not alter the sense.[1] Thus upon a declaration for the words, "he is a maintainer of thieves, and a strong thief;" the jury found that these words were spoken, except the word "strong;" and judgment was given for the plaintiff.[2] So, in an action for the words, "If Sir John Sydenham might have his will, he would kill all the true subjects of England, and the King too; and he is a maintainer of papistry and rebellious persons;" the jury found that all these words were spoken, but with the prefix, "I think in my conscience." After long discussion and a divided opinion among the Judges, both in the court below and upon writ of error, judgment was finally rendered for the plaintiff.[3] So an averment, "he stole my staves and rails," is proved by evidence of the defendant's saying this, with the prefix "he is a damned rogue," and the addition, "I can prove it."[4] So a declaration, that the libel was published in a newspaper called The Ontario Messenger, is sustained by a paper headed Ontario Messenger, the article *the* being no part of the description of the title of the paper, but only introductory to it.[5] So, in an action for slander, in charging the plaintiff with perjury, the colloquium - set forth the trial of an indictment for a *riot*, and the record produced was for a *riot and assault*. Held, the variance was immaterial.[6] So a declaration alleged, that the plaintiff was an attorney, and had been employed as vestry clerk in the parish of A.; and that while he was such vestry clerk, certain prosecutions were carried on against B. for certain misdemeanors, and in furtherance of such proceedings, and to bring the same to a successful issue, certain sums of money, belonging to the parishioners, were appropriated and applied to the discharge of the expenses incurred on account of the said proceedings; yet the defendant, intending, &c., to injure the plaintiff in his

[1] M'Coombs *v.* Tuttle, 5 Blackf. 431.
[2] Bargis's case, Dyer, 75.
[3] Sydenham's case, Cro. Jac. 407.
[4] Pasley *v.* Kemp, 22 Mis. 409.
[5] Southwick *v.* Stevens, 10 Johns. 443.
[6] Mamilten *v.* Langley, 1 M'Mul. 498; 15 Ill. 228.

profession of an attorney, and to cause him to be esteemed a fraudulent practiser in his said profession, and in his office as vestry clerk, and to cause it to be suspected that the plaintiff had fraudulently applied money belonging to the parishioners, on, &c., at, &c., falsely and maliciously published of and concerning the plaintiff, and of and concerning his conduct in his office as vestry clerk, and of and concerning the matters aforesaid, the libel, &c. It appeared on the production of the libel at the trial, that the imputation was, that the plaintiff had applied the parish money in payment of the expenses of the prosecution after it had terminated. Held, that this was no variance, because it did not alter the character of the libel, the fraud imputed to the plaintiff being the same, whether the money was misapplied before or after the proceedings had terminated; and that the allegation, that the libel was published of and concerning the matters aforesaid, did not make it necessary to prove precisely that the libel did relate to every part of the matter previously stated.[1]

59. We have already considered the important subjects of *publication*, and of *the party liable* to an action for libel or slander. (ch. xi. xii.) It remains, in connection with the present topic of *evidence*, to refer more particularly to *the proof* upon these respective points.

60. A libellous paper, in the handwriting of the defendant, found in the house of the editor of a newspaper in which the libel complained of appeared, is admissible evidence against the defendant, notwithstanding several parts of it have been erased, and are omitted in the newspaper, provided the passages erased do not qualify the libel.[2] So, where a witness swears that he is a subscriber for a specified newspaper, and, being shown several papers of the same name and date, containing the alleged libels, testifies that the papers are in all respects similar to those left at his office, and that the articles contained in the papers produced are the same that he read in the copies left at his office; this

[1] May *v.* Crown, 3 B & C. 113.

[2] Tarpley *v.* Blabey, 2 Bing. N. 437.

is a sufficient proof of publication, without proving a loss of the papers originally left with the witness.[1] So, where a person has admitted that he was the author of a libel in a certain newspaper, any other newspaper of the same impression may be read to the jury, and is not secondary evidence.[2] But, if the defendant alleges, in mitigation, that a libellous book was published against him by the plaintiff, and, in support of such case, a bookseller produces, from his own possession, a printed book, stating his belief that it is one of a number of copies published at his shop; this is not evidence for the jury, that another book with the same contents was actually published.[3]

61. In an action for libel, evidence of the loss of the libellous paper declared upon may be given, and the plaintiff may then prove by secondary evidence the making, contents, and publication of the paper.[4] But, if the defendant, after publication of the libel, takes and retains possession of it, he must have notice to produce it and refuse, before parol evidence can be given of its contents.[5] And where, to sustain an action of slander, the proof sought to be made was, that the slander was uttered and published by an affidavit made by the defendant before a magistrate, imputing to the plaintiff the offence of hog-stealing; and the only evidence of the existence of the affidavit was an imperfect memorandum of it in the handwriting of the magistrate, who was alive and out of the State; and there was no sufficient proof of its being in whole or in part a copy; it was held that the evidence was not sufficient to sustain the action.[6]

62. The question has often arisen, whether, and under what circumstances, and by which of the parties, evidence in relation to *general character* may be introduced.

63. In analogy with the general rule, that, where the ground of action is an injury to something belonging to the plaintiff, the value of the thing injured may, and in-

[1] Huff v. Bennett, 4 Sandf. 120.
[2] M'Laughlin v. Russell, 17 Ohio, 475.
[3] Watts v. Frazer, 7 Ad. & El. 223.
[4] Gates v. Bowker, 18 Verm. 23.
[5] Winter v. Donovan, 8 Gill, 370.
[6] Sanders v. Rollinson, 2 Strobh. 447.

deed must be shown, as the basis of the amount of damages; it has been held, that the plaintiff in an action of slander is entitled to give in evidence in chief his general character,[1] although not attacked by evidence on the part of the defendant.[2] But it is also held, and this is the prevailing doctrine, upon the general ground that the character of the plaintiff is *presumed* to be good, until proved bad, that evidence of the good character of the plaintiff is inadmissible, except to repel an attack upon it, by plea of justification or by evidence.[3] The allegation of the plaintiff's character and good repute is held to be mere *inducement*, which can only be put in issue by an appropriate plea. The general issue would not traverse it, except so far as to allow the defendant to introduce evidence against the plaintiff's character in mitigation of damages.[4] Thus, where the publisher of a remonstrance against giving a tavern license, on the ground that the applicant wishes to make his tavern a resort for the idle and dissipated, is sued for libel; the plaintiff cannot give evidence of his good character.[5] So the plaintiff cannot offer evidence given by the defendant, in support of the plea of justification, of his general good character, to disprove the truth of the words, nor to support his own character, until it is attacked by the defendant.[6] (*a*)

[1] Sample *v.* Wynn, Busb. 319. See Harding *v.* Brooks, 5 Pick. 244.

[2] Williams *v.* Haig, 3 Rich. 362.

[3] Dame *v.* Kenney, 5 Fost. 318; 2 Comst. 548; M'Cabe *v.* Platter, 6 Blackf. 405; Rhodes *v.* James, 7 Ala. 574; Scott *v.* Peebles, 2 Sm. & M. 546.

[4] Sidgreaves *v.* Myatt, 22 Ala. 617.

[5] Flitcraft *v.* Jenks, 3 Whart. 158.

[6] Wright *v.* Schroeder, 2 Curt. 548.

(*a*) Where a declaration for a libel, after stating the plaintiff's good name, &c., alleged that the defendant, well knowing the premises, and maliciously intending to injure the plaintiff, &c., and to bring him into great scandal and disgrace, and to cause it to be believed that the plaintiff had been guilty of the crime of treason, and of the publication of treasonable sentiments, &c., published the libel, &c.; it was held, that these were not averments necessary to be proved, but mere suggestions, by way of inducement to the libel. Coleman *v.* Southwick, 9 Johns. 45.

Upon a declaration, that the plaintiff was never guilty *nor suspected* of the crime imputed to him, it has been held that the defendant may offer

64. But, although the point has sometimes been considered doubtful,[1] it is now well settled, that evidence of the plaintiff's *general bad character* is admissible under the general issue, in mitigation of damages;[2] though not, either for that purpose or to defeat the suit, evidence of particular facts tending to show the truth.[3] (*a*) More especially the defendant may attack the general character of the plaintiff *in respect to the subject-matter of the charge.*[4] And evidence of the bad character of the plaintiff is admissible, although the defendant has justified that the imputation was true; for, if the justification should fail, the question of damages would remain.[5] As where, in an action for charging the plaintiff with perjury, the pleas were not guilty and justification. In such case, the defendant may show the general bad character of the plaintiff for veracity when on oath.[6] So, upon a charge of unchastity, the character of the plaintiff for chastity.[7] And such evidence, it seems, is admissible, where the statute of limitations and a justification are pleaded.[8] Although, it seems, under the plea of justification alone, the general character of the plaintiff cannot be given in evidence.[9]

65. It has been held, that evidence of bad character must

[1] Fort *v.* Tracy, 1 Johns. 46.
[2] Sayre *v.* Sayre, 1 Dutch. 235; Smith *v.* Smith, 8 Ired, 29. See Leonard *v.* Allen, 11 Cush. 241.
[3] Burke *v.* Miller, 6 Blackf. 155.
[4] Wright *v.* Schroeder, 2 Curtis, 548.
[5] Young *v.* Bennett, 4 Scam. 43.
[6] M'Nutt *v.* Young, 8 Leigh, 542.
[7] McCabe *v.* Platter, 6 Blackf. 405; 6 Barr, 170.
[8] Sanders *v.* Johnson, 6 Blackf. 50.
[9] Steinman *v.* M'Williams, 6 Barr, 170.

evidence to show that he had been suspected. Leicester *v.* Walter, 2 Camp. 251.

But, where a libel was actionable only in respect to an office of the plaintiff, and the declaration alleged a due discharge of its duties; held, the defendant could not offer evidence to contradict this allegation. Dance *v.* Robson, 1 M. & M. 294.

(*a*) More especially, the defendant cannot rely upon particular facts, not connected with the charge for which the suit is brought. Thus, in an action for a libel upon the plaintiff's character as an attorney of the Superior Court of the city of New York, evidence, that his application for admission to practice as an attorney of the Supreme Court had been denied, is not admissible for any purpose. Huff *v.* Bennett, 2 Seld. 337.

be confined to that particular trait or quality, to which the imputation relates. Thus, in an action of slander founded on a charge of perjury, no evidence as to the character of the plaintiff can be given, in mitigation of damages, except for *veracity.*[1] Under special circumstances, however, this restriction may be dispensed with. Thus, in an action for charging the plaintiff with perjury, if the plaintiff prove the words, and then ask the witness, what is the plaintiff's general character when on oath, and when not on oath, as a man of truth; and the witness answer the question favorably; the defendant, in cross-examining the witness, may ask him what is the plaintiff's general moral character.[2] So, on the other hand, where, in an action of slander, the defendant's evidence casts an imputation on the character of the plaintiff for honesty, it may be rebutted by testimony as to his general character.[3] So, in slander for the charge of perjury, where the plaintiff is permitted to give evidence of his character to protect himself, it is error to confine him to evidence of his general character for truth and veracity.[4] (*a*)

66. As already suggested, it has been sometimes held, that, where the evidence given by the defendant, in support of a plea of justification, though insufficient to prove such plea, tends to affect the general character of the plaintiff on the subject of the charge, he may reply by evidence of general good character in that particular.[5] Thus it is held, that, in an action for charging the plaintiff with perjury, if the defendant set up the truth in defence, the plaintiff may prove

[1] Bell *v.* Farnsworth, 11 Humph. 608.

[2] Lincoln *v.* Chrisman, 10 Leigh, 338.

[3] Petrie *v.* Rose, 5 M. & S. 364; Dame *v.* Kenney, 5 Fost. 318.

[4] Steinman *v.* M'Williams, 6 Barr, 170.

[5] Wright *v.* Schroeder, 2 Curt. 548.

(*a*) And it is laid down, generally, that, where the general character of the plaintiff may be inquired of, it is his general character *taken as a whole*, and not in respect to one particular. Hence, in an action for charging the plaintiff with perjury, it is error to admit evidence of the general character of the plaintiff for *truth and veracity.* 6 Barr, 170.

his general good character for truth.[1] The weight of authority is, however, that such evidence is not admissible. The conflicting cases may possibly be reconciled by the doctrine laid down in a late decision, that, where the defendant has not attacked the plaintiff's general character *in evidence*, the plaintiff cannot introduce proof of his good character to rebut a justification.[2]

67. In an action for slander, the plaintiff may give in evidence *his own rank and condition* of life, to aggravate the damages; and the defendant may avail himself of such evidence, when it will legally tend to mitigate the damages.[3]

68. It has been held, that evidence of *the pecuniary condition of the defendant* and his standing in the community may be given, wherever the plaintiff is entitled to vindictive damages, and as showing the amount of injury, if for no other purpose.[4] But the weight of authority is the other way.[5] So it is held, that the defendant cannot prove his own property in mitigation of damages.[6]

69. We have already had occasion, in various connections, to refer to the introduction of evidence, *in mitigation of damages*, which is insufficient to establish a legal defence to the action. It remains to speak briefly of the prominent cases of this description referred to in the books.

70. It has been held that, in an action of slander, the defendant may show in mitigation of damages, that he was incited and provoked to the utterance of the words, by some act or declaration of the plaintiff, contemporaneous, or nearly so, with them, if shown to have been the immediate and proximate cause or provocation. It is not sufficient, although it is necessary, to show, that it occurred and was

[1] Byrket *v.* Monohon, 7 Blackf. 83; acc. Harding *v.* Brooks, 5 Pick. 244; Ruan *v.* Perry, 3 Caines, 120; Townsend *v.* Graves, 3 Paige, 435. But see *contra*, Houghtailing *v.* Hilderhouse, 1 Comst. 522; 2 Barb. 149; Matthews *v.* Hantly, 9 N. H. 146; Her *v.* Cromer, Wright, 441.

[2] Severance *v.* Hilton, 4 Fost. 147. See Bartholemy *v.* The People, 2 Hill, 248.

[3] Bennett *v.* Hyde, 6 Conn. 24; Beehler *v.* Steever, 2 Whart. 314; Larned *v* Buffington, 3 Mass. 546.

[4] Adcock *v.* Marsh, 8 Ired. 360; Fry *v.* Bennett, 4 Duer, 247. See Case *v.* Marks, 20 Conn. 248; Lewis *v.* Chapman, 19 Barb. 252.

[5] Morris *v.* Berker, 4 Harring. 520; Ware *v.* Cartledge, 24 Ala. 622.

[6] Case *v.* Marks, 20 Conn. 248.

communicated to the defendant before the speaking of the words.[1] But this may be proved by the defendant's own declaration, and the jury is to determine, whether the language which the defendant used was used because of such provocation received from the plaintiff.[2] So, in an action for libel, though the defendant cannot give in evidence, in mitigation of damages, a distinct and independent libel on himself, published by the plaintiff; yet, where the publication is so recent, as to afford a reasonable presumption that the libel by the defendant was published under the influence of the passions excited by it; or where it is explanatory of the meaning of, or the occasion of writing, the libel complained of, such evidence is admissible; although the libel complained of does not expressly refer and profess to be a reply to the former publication, if such reference appears on comparing the two.[3] So, in an action for a libel, the defendant may give in evidence a former publication of the plaintiff, to which the libel was an answer, in order to explain the subject-matter, occasion, and intent of the defendant's publication, and in mitigation of damages. But such prior publication by the plaintiff, though a libel on the defendant, does not amount to a justification of the defendant's libel, nor will it be received in evidence as such.[4] And it must be shown with precision that such libel by the plaintiff relates to the libel by the defendant.[5] And it is not competent for the defendant to read in evidence an article published in another newspaper, with which the plaintiff had no apparent or real connection, even though the commentaries of the editor upon the libel in question profess to be an answer to it.[6] So, in an action for slander, the defendant cannot be allowed to prove the existence of *former controversies* between him and the plaintiff in mitigation of damages.[7] Nor irritating and taunting language

[1] Moore *v.* Clay, 24 Ala. 235; Watts *v.* Frazer, 7 Ad & Ell. 223; 1 Md. 173; *contra*, Boarland *v.* Edson, 8 Gratt. 27.

[2] Botelar *v.* Bell, 1 Md. 173.

[3] Child *v.* Homer, 13 Pick. 503.

[4] Hotchkiss *v.* Lothrop, 1 Johns. 286.

[5] Tarpley *v.* Blabey, 2 Bing. N. 437.

[6] Hotchkiss *v.* Oliphant, 2 Hill, 510; Haws *v.* Stanford, 4 Sneed, 520.

[7] Lister *v.* Wright, 2 Hill, 320.

addressed to him *by the father of the plaintiff*, immediately previous to the uttering of the slanderous words.[1] (*a*)

71. As has been already suggested, (*b*) under the general issue, in an action for libel, the defendant may prove anything in mitigation, which does not tend to a justification, but which falls short of or disproves it. (*c*) Therefore, in an action for a libel, in charging the plaintiff with extorting money, for the purpose of hushing up a complaint of a criminal nature, preferred by him; proof that the person accused did in fact make a complaint before a magistrate, alleging that the plaintiff and another person had combined together to extort money from him by means of said criminal charge, and that the material facts alleged in the libel were on that

[1] Underhill *v.* Taylor, 2 Barb. 210.

(*a*) While a defendant may rely upon former charges made *by the plaintiff*, it has been held, in reference to former charges against the plaintiff, made by himself, that the defendant, in an action for a libel, is not allowed to give in evidence, in mitigation of damages, a former recovery of damages against him, in favor of the same plaintiff, in another action for a libel, which formed one of a series of numbers published in the same Gazette, and contained the libellous words charged in the declaration in the second suit. Tillotson *v.* Cheetham, 3 Johns. 56.

(*b*) See *Justification.*

(*c*) It is held not competent to a defendant, in mitigation of damages in an action of slander, to give evidence of facts and circumstances which induced him to suppose the charges true at the time they were made, if such facts and circumstances tend to prove the charges, or form a link in the chain of evidence to establish a justification; although he expressly disavows a justification, and fully admits the falsity of the charges. Purple *v.* Horton, 13 Wend. 9. *Contra*, Van Derveer *v.* Sutphin, 5 Ohio, N. S. 293, as to *reports;* for the purpose of disproving malice, Ibid. See Mayer *v.* Pine, 4 Mich. 409. In an action of slander for accusing a wife of want of chastity, the defendant may prove, in mitigation of damages, that, with the knowledge of the defendant, she and an unmarried man had lived alone together in one house. Reynolds *v.* Tucker, 6 Ohio, N. S. 516.

But in an action for accusing the plaintiff of burning the defendant's mill, and adding that he could prove it; the defendant cannot, under the general issue, show a threat by the plaintiff, of which the defendant had notice, that he would ruin him and drive him out of town. Mayer *v.* Pine, 4 Mich. 409.

occasion sworn to by the accused, in an affidavit made by him, is admissible, for the purpose of showing that the defendant's publication was not a falsehood wickedly and wantonly coined for the occasion, but that it had what seemed to be truth for a basis. And, though the jury regards such evidence as a justification, that is not a subject of review upon a bill of exceptions.[1] So it has been held, in an action for slander, that the defendant may give in evidence under the general issue facts tending to mitigate the damages, which he will not be permitted to do, when he has pleaded the truth in justification. And if, through the fault of the plaintiff, he, at the time of speaking the words, and when he pleaded the justification, had good cause to believe they were true, he may show this in mitigation of damages.[2] (*a*)

72. In regard to evidence of the defendant's subsequent admissions or declarations, it is held that his statements, subsequent to the bringing of the action, are admissible against him, to show that he spoke the words charged, or explain his meaning in speaking them.[3] But, where the defendant, in an action of slander, for charging the plaintiff with adultery with C., after pleading the general issue, with notice that he should justify the charge by proving its truth, introduced first some direct evidence of the crime charged, and then circumstantial proof tending to show grossly familiar, indecent, and wanton conduct between the plaintiff and

[1] Stanley *v.* Webb, 21 Barb. 148; Bourland *v.* Eidson, 8 Gratt. 27.

[2] Larned *v.* Buffington, 3 Mass. 546.

[3] Witcber *v.* Richmond, 8 Humph. 473.

(*a*) Under a plea of justification to an action for slander and malicious prosecution, evidence tending to show that the defendant had reason to believe, from the plaintiff's conduct, that the charge was true, may be considered in mitigation of damages, although it does not support the plea. Shoulty *v.* Miller, 1 Cart. 544.

So, on the general issue, the defendant may give in evidence, in mitigation of damages, any circumstances tending to show, that he spoke the words under a mistaken construction placed upon conduct, which was in fact no justification. Haywood *v.* Foster, 16 Ohio, 88.

C.; after which he offered a witness to prove, that the plaintiff, during such conduct, declared to the witness that he preferred married women, because, if any consequences followed from his connection with them, their husbands would be responsible; held, that proof of such declaration was not admissible, either in support of the justification or in mitigation of damages.[1] (*a*)

73. In relation to *rebutting* evidence, where a defendant in an action of libel had charged the plaintiff with having falsely accused him of a crime, and, on the trial, the defendant gave proof, in mitigation, of the falsehood of the accusation; held, the plaintiff was entitled to reply with evidence of its truth.[2] So in an action of slander, for charging the plaintiff with stealing a deed, made to him by the defendant, of a certain farm, the defendant, in order to prove the truth of the charge, gave evidence (*inter alia*) that the plaintiff, on being charged by the defendant with stealing the deed, took the deed from the register's office, and reconveyed the farm to the defendant. Held, the plaintiff was rightly permitted to prove, by way of rebutting the inference which might be drawn from this evidence, that one of his friends advised him to make the deed of reconveyance, for the purpose of avoiding the expense of a lawsuit.[3]

74. In reference to the damages in actions of this nature; it is held, in general, that *exemplary* or *punitory* damages may be recovered, in case of express, wanton, or unmitigated malice.[4]

[1] Gillis *v.* Peck, 20 Conn. 228.

[2] Woodburn *v.* Miller, Cheves, 194.

[3] Sperry *v.* Wilcox, 1 Met. 267.

[4] Gilreath *v.* Allen, 10 Ired. 67; Kinney *v.* Hosea; 3 Harring. 397; Fry *v.* Bennett, 4 Duer, 247; Cramer *v.* Noonan, 4 Wis. 231.

(*a*) Where A. published a libel taken from a paper published by B., as an extract from a paper published by C.; in an action by C. against A., for a libel, it was held, that the testimony of D., that he had heard A., before he published the libel, ask E. whether he had not seen it in the paper of C., and that E. answered "he had," was inadmissible, in mitigation of damages, but that E. himself should be produced, if his declarations were proper evidence. Coleman *v.* Southwick, 9 Johns. 45.

75. With regard to the elements or ingredients of the damages, the jury are to determine from all the circumstances of the case what damages ought to be given, and are not confined to mere pecuniary loss or injury, and, unless the damages are flagrantly outrageous and excessive, or such as to satisfy the Court that the jury acted from prejudice, partiality, or corruption, the verdict should not be disturbed.[1] So damages may be given for mental suffering, circumstances of indignity, public disgrace, and other actual discomfort, even though the defendant believed the charges to be true.[2] So the jury, in assessing damages, should consider the probable future as well as the actual past;[3] and the expenses to which the plaintiff has been put, by being compelled to come into court to vindicate his character.[4] And the jury are to determine the amount of damages *from the facts proved*, and not *from the opinions of witnesses*.[5]

76. The damages, as in other cases of tort, are to be predicated upon the value of the thing injured, which in this case is character or reputation. Thus, in an action for words imputing unchastity, the jury are to give damages commensurate with the injury sustained. If the plaintiff is an innocent and virtuous female, and her character has been destroyed by the slanders of the defendant and others, they should give liberal damages; but, if the plaintiff has so destroyed her character by her own lewd and dissolute conduct, as to have sustained no injury from the words, they may give only nominal damages.[6]

77. Although the amount of damages is a question for the jury, yet the Court are bound to give them correct and sufficient instructions as to the rule of law upon the subject.[7] Thus, where an action for libel is connected with and grows out of a controversy in the Methodist Episcopal Church, a refusal to instruct the jury, that the damages should not be estimated upon consideration of any injury to the church, its

[1] Spencer *v.* McMasters, 16 Ill. 405; Southwick *v.* Stevens, 10 Johns. 443.
[2] Fry *v.* Bennett, 4 Duer, 247.
[3] True *v.* Plumley, 36 Maine, 466.
[4] Hicks *v.* Foster, 13 Barb. 663.
[5] Alley *v.* Neely, 5 Blackf. 200.
[6] Flint *v.* Clark, 13 Conn. 361.
[7] True *v.* Plumley, 36 Maine, 466.

ministers, or members, is wrong; and a general instruction, to find such damages as under all the circumstances they thought right and proper for the injury to the plaintiff's feelings and reputation, is insufficient.[1] So it is no ground of exception, that the Judge advised the jury, that, under the circumstances proved, the damages ought to be more than nominal.[2]

78. As already stated, a verdict will not be set aside for excessive damages, unless they are so flagrantly outrageous, as manifestly to show that the jury were actuated by passion, partiality, prejudice, or corruption.[3] Thus in an action for slander, in charging the plaintiff with adultery, where the plaintiff was superintendent of an almshouse, and the defendant a man of property, and the words were spoken at a town meeting, on a debate relative to the appointment of a new superintendent; a verdict for $707 was sustained.[4] So in an action by an unmarried female, an assistant in an almshouse, for the same charge, a verdict of $591.[5] So in an action brought by a schoolmistress, against a man of wealth and influence, for accusing her of want of chastity, a verdict for $1400.[6] So a verdict, for charging the plaintiff with stealing a horse, for $500.[7] For perjury, $2736.[8] For a charge of adultery in a female, made in gross and indecent language, there being no proof of the pecuniary condition of the defendant, $334.[9]

79. With regard to *the form of the verdict;* where a declaration in slander contains several counts, and two of them charge the speaking of the words at different times, and there is a general verdict for the plaintiff; the judgment will not on this account be reversed.[10] So where the jury found "the defendant guilty of wilful and malicious slander," and assessed the plaintiff's damages; held, by fair intendment, the

[1] Duncan *v.* Brown, 15 B. Mon. 186.
[2] Matthews *v.* Beach, 5 Sandf. 256.
[3] Coleman *v.* Southwick, 9 Johns. 45; Clark *v.* Binney, 2 Pick. 113; Shute *v.* Barrett, 7 Ib. 82; 16 Ill. 405.
[4] Shute *v.* Barrett, 7 Pick. 82.
[5] Oakes *v.* Barrett, 7 Pick. 82.
[6] Bodwell *v.* Osgood, 3 Pick. 379.
[7] Teagle *v.* Deboy, 8 Blackf. 134.
[8] Sanders *v.* Johnson, 6 Blackf. 51.
[9] Ross *v.* Ross, 5 B. Mon. 20.
[10] Bradley *v.* Kennedy, 2 Greene, 231.

slander found by the verdict must mean that complained of in the declaration.[1] So, where the defendant filed several pleas, alleging the truth in justification, to all of which the plaintiff put in a general replication, that the defendant *de injuriâ sua*, &c., spoke the words, and the verdict, which was for the plaintiff, followed the issue, without affirming or denying the truth of the allegations in the several pleas; held, the verdict was correct in form.[2] But where some counts in a declaration of slander are good and some bad, a verdict taken generally will be reversed, though taken on counts supposed to be good.[3] So, where a declaration in slander contains five counts, a general verdict assessing the plaintiff's damages at a certain sum is not responsive to any count in the declaration.[4]

80. Questions have sometimes arisen, as to the effect of an assessment of damages, upon *default* or *demurrer*. Thus on a motion to set aside the assessment of damages, on a judgment by default in an action for a libel, it was held, that, by the interlocutory judgment, the publication of the libel and the truth of the innuendoes were admitted; and that the defendant, before the jury of inquiry, is not to be permitted to call their attention to the other paragraphs contained in the same publication, in order to show a different meaning of the words complained of, from that set up by the plaintiff.[5] But, in an action of slander, it was held, that, after a judgment on demurrer to a declaration, containing several counts, and an assessment of damages, the plaintiff cannot enter a *nolle prosequi* as to one of the counts and take judgment on the others, but should obtain leave of the Court for that purpose, before awarding the writ of inquiry; and, one of the counts being held bad, and the assignment of damages considered as applying to all the counts, the judgment below was reversed.[6]

[1] Benaway *v.* Conyne, 3 Chand. 214.

[2] Harding *v.* Brooks, 5 Pick. 244.

[3] Harker *v.* Orr, 10 Watts, 245.

[4] Cock *v.* Weatherby, 5 Sm. & M. 333.

[5] Tillotson *v.* Cheetham, 4 Johns. 56.

[6] Backus *v.* Richardson, 5 Johns. 476.

CHAPTER XVI.

MALICIOUS PROSECUTION.

1. Somewhat analogous to the action for libel and slander, is that for *malicious prosecution;* which, though involving an injury to the person, as connected with false imprisonment, and also to property, on account of the necessary cost and expense of defending against unfounded demands or accusations; is primarily, more especially in case of a criminal prosecution, a wrong to *character* or *reputation.* (*a*)

(*a*) No action lies for malicious prosecution of an alleged *assault*, which is not a crime involving moral turpitude, without proof of actual damage. Therefore, if the complaint was ignored by the grand jury, the plaintiff, in order to maintain this action, must prove the necessary expenditure of money to obtain an acquittal. Freeman *v.* Arkell, 3 D. & R. 671. See Byne *v.* Moore, 5 Taun. 191. It is remarked by late learned writers upon this subject: "It is, certainly, only in the case of a *crime*, or, at least, an indictable offence involving moral turpitude, the verbal imputation of which would be slander, that the mere preferring of an indictment, or issuing of a warrant, or other instituting of a criminal proceeding, without arrest or special damage, is actionable." Indeed it was said by Patteson, J., in *Gregory* v. *Derby*, 8 Carr. & P. 749, in the case of a charge of stealing, on which a

2. The general principle is laid down, that an action lies for maliciously causing one to be indicted, whereby he is

---

warrant was issued, that if the party was never apprehended, no action would lie; and by the Court, in *O'Driscoll* v. *McBurney*, 2 Nott & M'Cord, 54, 55, that there can be no prosecution without an arrest. But probably these remarks should be confined to cases where the charge is not slanderous, or, at least, where arrest is specially made the *gravamen* in the declaration; for, if a slanderous charge be made before a magistrate and a warrant demanded, and a warrant thereupon issue, it is believed, that this form of action is the appropriate remedy; but if no warrant issue, the remedy is slander, in the form of "imposing the crime of felony." Munns *v.* Dupont, 1 Am. Lead. Cas. 216, 217, n.

The same learned annotators cite with approval the following observations, respecting the nature of the crime for the charge of which this action may be maintained. "To sustain the action of malicious prosecution, technically so called, the indictment must charge a *crime;* and then the action is sustainable *per se*, on showing a want of probable cause. There is another class of cases, which are popularly called actions for malicious prosecution, but they are misnamed; they are actions on the case, in which both a *scienter* and a *per quod* must be laid and proved. I allude now, first, to actions for false and malicious prosecutions for a mere misdemeanor, involving no moral turpitude; secondly, to an abuse of judicial process, by procuring a man to be indicted, as for a crime, when it is a mere trespass; third, malicious search-warrants. In all these cases, it will be perceived that they cannot be governed by the ordinary rules applicable to actions for malicious prosecutions. It is said by most of our law-writers, that, in such cases, you must not only prove want of probable cause, but also express malice and actual injury or loss, as deprivation of liberty, and money paid in defence. The express malice necessary to sustain such actions, ought to be laid and proved, and this is what I understand by the *scienter.* As in an action for a false and malicious prosecution for a misdemeanor, it must be laid and proved, that the party knowing the defendant's innocence, still of his mere malice preferred the charge. So, in the second class of cases, it will not do to say, that you indicted me, as for a crime, for a trespass, without any probable cause, for in such a case no injury is done to the plaintiff, and no fault is established against the defendant, for which he can be punished. But when to this statement we superadd the facts, that the defendant, knowing that the trespass complained of was no crime, yet procured the plaintiff to be indicted as for a crime, malice is clearly made out; and, if the plaintiff has sustained any injury, the action will lie." Per O'Neall, J., Frierson *v.* Hewitt, 2 Hill, 499. It will be seen, however, by the following examples of the action for malicious prosecution, that the dis-

damnified either in person, reputation, or property.[1] Or for advising and procuring a third person to institute a mali-

[1] Savile v. Roberts, 1 Salk. 14; 1 Ld. Raym. 374.

---

tinctions above stated, in regard to the nature or magnitude of the offence charged in the former proceeding, have not been uniformly recognized.

Thus the action has been maintained, for procuring the plaintiff to be indicted, for conspiring to lay a bastard child to the defendant; such conspiracy being punishable at common law. Pedro v. Barrett, 1 Ld. Raym. 81.

So one, who falsely and maliciously charges another with *perjury* before the grand jury, on which he is arrested and held to bail, is liable to an action for malicious prosecution. Setton v. Farr, 1 Rice, 303.

So an action in the nature of conspiracy lies, after acquittal, for causing a person to be falsely and maliciously indicted for *trespass*. Norris v. Palmer, 2 Mod. 51.

And an acquittal on an indictment for a common trespass shows the prosecution to have been malicious, because the prosecutor might have brought a civil action, in which the defendant, on being found not guilty, would have been allowed costs; and therefore an action on the case will lie, on account of the expenses to which he was put by the indictment. 2 Mod. 306.

And, in general, a charge, falsely and maliciously preferred, that will authorize a justice to issue his warrant, and have the accused brought before him for examination, touching a matter that will subject him to a criminal prosecution, is sufficient to sustain an action on the case for a malicious prosecution, without regard to the grade of the offence, or the technical form in which the charge is preferred. Long v. Rogers, 17 Ala. 540.

So an action on the case lies, for maliciously obtaining or executing *a warrant to search a house*, for smuggled goods, where none such are found. Cooper v. Boot, 1 T. R. 535.

But it has been held, that an action on the case will not lie, for a malicious prosecution before a naval court-martial, for an offence cognizable therein. Johnstone v. Sutton, 1 T. R. 493; 1 Brown, P. C. 76.

Nor for delaying to bring an officer under arrest to a naval court-martial; it being a military offence, and the defendant not having been tried for it. Ibid. 548.

An averment, that the defendant maliciously and without probable cause preferred an indictment, setting it forth, is proved, if only a part of the charges were malicious and without probable cause. Reed v. Taylor, 4 Taunt. 616.

A declaration, for maliciously indicting and procuring the plaintiff to be indicted, is sustained, although the defendant preferred the indictment

cious prosecution.[1] "Whenever there is an injury done to a man's property by a false and malicious prosecution, it is most reasonable that he should have an action to repair himself."[2] So, if it *puts him to expense*, though it neither scandalizes him nor affects his personal security,[3] or causes *any special damage*.[4] Hence, in an action for malicious prosecution, it was held not to be error, to refuse to strike from the declaration an averment, that the prosecution injuriously affected *the interests and credit* of the plaintiff; such injuries forming a legitimate ground for recovering damages.[5] And the plaintiff may recover, not only for the unlawful arrest and imprisonment, and the expenses of his defence, but also for the injury to his fame and reputation.[6] Such recovery is therefore a bar to a subsequent action of *slander*, for the accusation uttered for the purpose of procuring the arrest at the time when it was made.[7] The elements of the action are said to be, "Damage to a man's fame, as if the matter whereof he is accused be scandalous; 2, where a man is put in danger to lose his life, or limb, or liberty; 3, damage to a man's property, as where he is forced to expend money in necessary charges to acquit himself of the crime of which he is accused."[8] But, in an action for maliciously suing out an attachment against *a partnership*, the jury, in estimating the damages, can consider only the injury to the partnership trade or business, and not to the private feelings of the partners, nor can special damage, by loss of reputation, credit, business, or customers, be proved, unless specifically alleged.[9]

3. But a distinction is to be noticed between this action

[1] Mowry *v.* Miller, 3 Leigh, 561; Pardu *v.* Connerly, 1 Rice, 49; 1 Ld. Raym. 374.

[2] Per Pratt, C. J., Chapman *v.* Pickersgill, 2 Wils. 145.

[3] 1 Ld. Raym. 374.

[4] Ibid.

[5] Goldsmith *v.* Picard, 27 Ala. 142.

[6] Sheldon *v.* Carpenter, 4 Comst. 578.

[7] Ibid.

[8] Per Holt, C. J., Savile *v.* Roberts, 1 Ld. Raym. 374.

[9] Donnell *v.* Jones, 13 Ala. 490.

unwillingly, and solely because he was bound over to do so, if he was himself the cause of his being so bound over, by originally making a malicious charge before the magistrate. Dubois *v.* Keats, 3 Per. & Dav. 306.

and that already considered, (ch. 6,) for *false imprisonment.* Thus a count which avers, "that the defendant falsely, maliciously, and without probable cause, charged the said plaintiff with the crime of felony, and, upon said charge, falsely, maliciously, and without probable cause, caused the said plaintiff to be arrested by his body, and to be imprisoned and kept and detained in prison for a long time, namely, for the space of one day then next following, at the expiration of which said time he, the said defendant, caused the said plaintiff to be released and set at liberty, and wholly abandoned his said prosecution;" is not a good count in case for malicious prosecution, but is a good count in trespass for false imprisonment.[1] And, with regard to the precise nature of this action, as distinguished from others somewhat analogous, it is said: "There is no similitude or analogy between an action of trespass, or false imprisonment, and this kind of action. An action of trespass is for the defendant's having done that, which, upon the stating of it, is manifestly illegal. This kind of action is for a prosecution, which, upon the stating of it, is manifestly legal."[2] (*a*) So, also, it is said, "There is a wide distinction between an action against the prosecutor for a malicious prosecution, and an action against a magistrate for a malicious conviction. In the former case, proof that there was in reality no ground for imputing the crime to the plaintiff, shows that the prosecution was instituted without probable cause, and malice may be inferred from thence. What passed at the trial is, in this case, immaterial. The prosecutor may have sworn to the truth of the charge, but that will not show that he had a probable cause for it. In an action against the magistrate for a malicious conviction, the question is, not whether there was any actual ground for imputing the crime to the plaintiff, but whether, upon the hearing, there appeared to

[1] Ragsdale *v.* Bowles, 16 Ala. 62. [2] Johnstone *v.* Sutton, 1 T. R. 544.

(*a*) An arrest is not necessary to be proved, to support an action for a malicious prosecution. Stapp *v.* Partlow, Dudley, (Geo.) 176.

be none. The plaintiff must prove a want of probable cause for the conviction, which he can only do, by proving what passed at the hearing before the magistrate, when the conviction took place. The magistrate has nothing to do with the guilt or innocence of the offender, except as they appear from the evidence laid before him. The conviction must be founded upon that evidence alone, and it is impossible to show, that there was no probable cause for the conviction, without showing what that evidence was."[1] (*a*)

4. With regard to the requisite facts to be proved for the purpose of maintaining this action, the plaintiff must allege and prove that he *has been prosecuted by the defendant*, either criminally or in a civil suit, and that *the prosecution is at an end;* that it was instituted *maliciously, and without probable cause;* and that he has *sustained damage* thereby.[2] (*b*) Proof of express malice is not enough, without showing also the want of probable cause. (*c*) Nor want of

[1] Per Gibbs, C. J., Burley *v.* Bethune, 5 Taun. 583.

[2] Carman *v.* Truman, 1 Brown, P. C. 101; Griffin *v.* Chubb, 7 Tex. 603; Hall *v.* Suydam, 6 Barb. 83; Johnstone *v.* Sutton, 1 T. R. 493; Jacks *v.* Stimpson, 13 Ill. 701; Kendrick *v.* Cypert, 10 Humph. 291; Vanderbilt *v.* Mathis, 5 Duer, 304; Davis *v.* Cook, 3 Iowa, 539; Greenwade *v.* Mills, 31 Miss. 464.

(*a*) See *Judge, Justice, Officer.*

(*b*) "This action ought not to be maintained without rank and express malice and iniquity." Per Holt, C. J., Savill *v.* Roberts, 12 Mod. 208.

The grounds of it are, "Upon the plaintiff's side, innocence; upon the defendant's, malice." Per Parker, C. J., Jones *v.* Gwynn, 10 Mod. 217.

(*c*) In an action for maliciously indicting the plaintiff for stealing cattle, it appeared that the plaintiff, who was driving his cattle to market, had, on passing the defendant's farm, received into his drove two of the defendant's cattle, and had proceeded on his journey with them seventy miles, when he was overtaken by the defendant, who charged him with the theft, and the plaintiff paid him a large sum to settle the affair. The defendant was likewise informed, that the plaintiff had on his route driven off cattle belonging to another person. Held, the action would not lie, though it was shown that the defendant had instituted the prosecution from malicious motives, and the plaintiff had been acquitted. Fosbay *v.* Ferguson, 2 Denio, 617.

It has been held, that the want of an averment, that the prosecution was carried on without probable cause, is cured by verdict. Weinberger *v.* Shelly, 6 W. & S. 336.

probable cause, without malice.[1] It is said, "A person actuated by the plainest malice may nevertheless have a justifiable reason for the prosecution. On the other hand, he may have good reason to make the charge, and yet be compelled to abandon the prosecution by the death or absence of witnesses, or the difficulty of producing adequate legal proof."[2] And the burden of proof of these elements of the action is strictly upon the plaintiff; and it is erroneous to shift the burden of proof from the plaintiff to the defendants, by instructing the jury, that, if the defendants acted upon information, the jury must be satisfied that they believed in its truth. They should be instructed, that they are bound to presume that the defendants believed in the truth of the information upon which they acted, unless it clearly appears from the evidence that the evidence was false, and that they knew it to be so.[3]

5. With regard to *the parties*, by and against whom this action may be maintained; (*a*) it is held that a principal is liable for the acts of his agent.[4] And a person who, without

[1] Riney *v.* Vanlandingham, 9 Mis. 816; Frissell *v.* Relfe, 9 Mis. 859; McNeese *v.* Herring, 8 Tex. 151; Vanderbilt *v.* Mathis, 5 Duer, 304; Davis *v.* Cook, 3 Iowa, 539; Cummings *v.* Parks, 2 Cart. 148; Wells *v.* Parsons, 3 Harring. 505; Hardin *v.* Borders, 1 Ired. 143; Feazle *v.* Simpson, 1 Scam. 30; Payson *v.* Caswell, 9 Shep. 212; Dodge *v.* Brittain, 1 Meigs, 84; Hall *v.* Hawkins, 5 Humph. 357; Wood *v.* Weir, 5 B. Mon. 544; Leidig *v.* Rawson, 1 Scam. 272; Ewing *v.* Sandford, 21 Ala. 157; Anderson *v.* Buchanan, Wright, 725; Arbuckle *v.* Taylor, 3 Dow. 160; Foshay *v.* Ferguson, 2 Denio, 617; Morgan *v.* Hughes, 2 T. R. 231; Wiggin *v.* Coffin, 3 Story, 1; Byne *v.* Moore, 1 Marsh. 12.

[2] Per Tindal, C. J., Williams *v.* Taylor, 6 Bing. 186.

[3] Carpenter *v.* Shelden, 5 Sandf. 77.

[4] Michell *v.* Williams, 11 M. & W. 213.

But on the other hand it is held, that the words "falsely and maliciously" will not support a declaration for malicious prosecution; an averment to the effect that there was no probable cause is indispensable, and the defect is not cured by a verdict. Maddox *v.* M'Gainnis, 7 Monr. 371.

(*a*) An action on the case for a malicious prosecution does not by law *survive* in Massachusetts. Nettleton *v.* Dinehart, 5 Cush. 543.

An action will lie by a master for the malicious prosecution of his slave. Locke *v.* Gibbs, 4 Ired. 42.

As to an action for malicious prosecution against an *administrator*, see Pierce *v.* Thompson, 6 Pick. 193.

authority, prosecutes a groundless action *in the name of another*, is liable to the defendant in such action, for the expenses and damages to which he has thereby been subjected, beyond the amount of the taxed costs; although the latter did not call in court for the authority to commence such suit.[1] (See p. 486.) And, contrary to the general rule on the subject, where one prosecutes a suit against another in the name of a third person, without authority, he is liable to the person so sued, though he was not actuated by malice; nor will the amount of damages be diminished by the fact, that such third person had a good cause of action.[2] But an action on the case, for causing a writ of *habeas corpus* to be issued, and served upon the party therein alleged to be restrained, without his authority, and against his consent, cannot be maintained, if the complaint was made by authority from the plaintiff, and at his request, expressed either directly to the defendant, or indirectly through some other person.[3] And where a declaration alleged, that the defendant unlawfully and maliciously did advise, procure, instigate, and stir up T. to commence and prosecute an action on the case against the plaintiff; wherein certain issues were joined, as to which the plaintiff was acquitted; it was held, that no cause of action appeared, the declaration not showing *maintenance*, (inasmuch as the action appeared not to have been commenced when the defendant interfered) and not alleging want of reasonable and probable cause for the action.[4]

6. If *an attorney*, from malicious motives, procure from justices of the peace an unauthorized order of attachment, operating injuriously upon the defendant's rights, he is liable as well as his client.[5] So an attorney is liable for an unlawful and malicious arrest, upon a claim which he knows to be unfounded.[6] (*a*) But it has been held, that an action for a

[1] Moulton *v.* Lowe, 32 Maine, 466.

[2] Bond *v.* Chapin, 8 Met. 31; Foster *v.* Dow, 29 Maine, 442.

[3] Linda *v.* Hudson, 1 Cush. 385.

[4] Flight *v.* Leman, 4 Ad. & Ell. N. S. 883; acc. Fivaz *v.* Nicholls, 2 Com. B. 501; Savile *v.* Roberts, 1 Salk. 14; Grove *v.* Brandenberg, 7 Blackf. 234.

[5] Wood *v.* Weir, 5 B. Mon. 544.

[6] Stockley *v.* Hornidge, 8 C. & P. 16.

(*a*) See *Attorney*.

malicious prosecution will not lie against one attorney for suing another in an inferior court, or for suing on the retainer of a client, although he knew there was no cause of action.[1] And the later doctrine is, that an action cannot be maintained against an attorney at law for bringing a civil action, unless he commenced it without the authority of the party in whose name it was sued, or unless there was a conspiracy between them to bring a groundless suit, the attorney knowing it to be groundless, and commenced without any intention or expectation of maintaining it.[2]

7. We shall hereafter consider the general subject of *joint* claims and liabilities in actions of tort. (*a*) With regard to joint liabilities in connection with this action, the action for *conspiracy* is sustained, by proof of damage arising from a prosecution instituted maliciously and without probable cause.[3] But an action cannot be sustained against *a firm*, and those individual partners of it who had no concern in the prosecution, merely because one of the partners may have so prosecuted, for an alleged theft of property belonging to the firm.[4] So, if an action is commenced by two persons in the name of one of them, upon reasonable and probable cause, and the defendant is arrested and imprisoned, the action entered, and depositions are taken, which show manifestly that the defendant has a good defence, and that the plaintiff has no reasonable cause of action, and still the action is not discontinued, nor the defendant discharged from imprisonment; these facts do not furnish the defendant with a ground of action against the two persons for a malicious suit, for the omission to discontinue the action and discharge the defendant is the neglect of the plaintiff alone.[5] (*b*)

[1] Anon. 1 Mod. 209, 210.
[2] Bicknell *v.* Dorion, 16 Pick. 478.
[3] Page *v.* Cushing, 38 Maine, 523.
[4] Arbuckle *v.* Taylor, 3 Dow, 160.
[5] Bicknell *v.* Dorion, 16 Pick. 478.

(*a*) See *Joinder*.

(*b*) In reference to an action for malicious prosecution, brought *by* one of joint party defendants in the former proceeding; where A. and B. are maliciously prosecuted for conspiracy, and A. employs and pays an attorney,

8. Cases have arisen where *public officers*, who have been called upon to act officially in connection with the proceedings complained of, are joined as defendants in the suit for malicious prosecution. Thus, if a declaration for a malicious prosecution charge three persons, one of whom was the justice of the peace, with a conspiracy illegally to arrest and imprison the plaintiff, the conspiracy may be collected by the jury from the circumstances of the case; but, if it appear that the justice of the peace was persuaded by the others that it was not a bailable offence, and that from ignorance of the law, and not from malice of the heart, he committed the plaintiff, he ought to be found not guilty.[1] And it seems that an action against a district attorney and another person, for maliciously contriving to have the plaintiff indicted, and by false representations obtaining an indictment against him for perjury, they knowing that he had not committed it, and by their false testimony obtaining a verdict of guilty against him, which was afterwards set aside and a *nolle prosequi* entered; cannot be maintained.[2] But, where the plaintiff claimed that the defendant maliciously, and for the purpose of getting up the prosecution complained of, procured a complaint to be drawn and laid before a grand juror, and the prosecution was without reasonable or probable cause; it was held, that, if these facts were made out, the defendant was liable, although the prosecution was afterwards carried on by the grand juror; but if, on the contrary, the defendant, knowing the facts, and having good cause for believing the plaintiff's guilt, only went to the grand juror, and fairly and

[1] Muriel *v.* Tracy, 6 Mod. 170. [2] Parker *v.* Huntington, 2 Gray, 124.

---

and both are acquitted; in an action by A. for malicious prosecution, he may recover the amount so paid, unless they had distinct defences, the cost of which was severable. Rowlands *v.* Samuel, 11 Qu. B. 41.

A. and B. jointly recognized to prosecute and testify in a proceeding against C., but A. only employed the attorney, at whose request B. attended before the magistrate and the grand jury. Held, a joint action against A. and B. could not be maintained against B. Eagar *v.* Dyott, 5 C. & P. 4.

honestly, and without any sinister motive, laid before him the facts and the grounds of his belief, and then left him to decide for himself, according to his judgment, as to what was proper to be done, and the defendant had no particular connection with the prosecution, more than any other citizen, except that, having more knowledge and proof, he was called by the grand juror to testify; he was not liable.[1]

9. In an action against several defendants for malicious prosecution, the separate acts and declarations of some ought not to be admitted in evidence to charge others not then present, in the absence of any proof of conspiracy. Nor can the jury, upon the question of malice, and in determining the amount of damages, take into consideration facts, establishing against some of the defendants a case of *false imprisonment;* that constituting a distinct cause of action, for which those defendants may be rendered liable in another suit.[2]

10. Although want of probable cause and malice must both *exist* in order to sustain this action; yet, in reference to the *mode of proving* these respective facts, there is a material and well-established difference. The want of probable cause cannot be inferred from any degree of express malice, but malice may be implied from the want of probable cause;[3] (*a*)

[1] Goodrich *v.* Warner, 21 Conn. 432.

[2] Carpenter *v.* Shelden, 5 Sandf. 77.

[3] Hall *v.* Suydam, 6 Barb. 83; Horn *v.* Boon, 3 Strobh. 307; Jacks *v.* Stimpson, 13 Ill. 701; Stone *v.* Crocker, 24 Pick. 81; Kendrick *v.* Cypert, 10 Humph. 291; Johnstone *v.* Sutton, 6 Mod. 73, n.; Johnston *v.* Browning, Ib. 216; M'Cormick *v.* Conway, 12 La. An. 53.

(*a*) The mere termination of the former suit or prosecution in favor of the present plaintiff does not raise a presumption of malice. Johnson *v.* Chambers, 10 Ired. 287.

The want of probable cause "must be substantially and expressly proved, and cannot be implied. From the want of probable cause, malice may be, and most commonly is implied; the knowledge of the defendant is also implied. From the most express malice, the want of probable cause cannot be implied. A man from a malicious motive may take up a prosecution for real guilt, or he may from circumstances, which he really believes, proceed upon apparent guilt; and in neither case is he liable to this kind of action."

without proof of any angry feeling or vindictive motive.[1] (*a*) The distinction, however, is laid down, that, where there are no circumstances to rebut the presumption, that malice alone could have suggested the prosecution, malice may be inferred from the want of probable cause. Also, where the defendant's conduct will admit of no other interpretation, except by presuming gross ignorance. Malice, however, is in no case *a legal presumption* from the want of probable cause; it being for the jury to find from the facts proved, where there was no probable cause, whether there was malice or not.[2] And it is further held, upon the same subject, that although, where one who has reasonable ground for belief of guilt institutes criminal proceedings against another, he is not liable in an action for malicious prosecution, whatever may have been his motives; yet, if he acts *rashly*, *wantonly*, or *wickedly*, the presumption of malice is conclusive, and he is responsible.[3] "The facts ought to satisfy any reasonable mind, that the accuser had no ground for the proceeding but his desire to injure the accused."[4] And, in an action for *abuse of legal process*, it is not necessary to aver or prove that the process is at an end, or that it was sued out maliciously or without probable cause.[5] (See p. 482). So there can be no probable cause for a prosecution, to accomplish a purpose *known to be unlawful*.[6] Thus, where a prosecution is instituted, and the defendant arrested, for the purpose of extorting money from

[1] Burhans *v.* Sandford, 19 Wend. 419.

[2] Griffin *v.* Chubb, 7 Tex. 603; Merriam *v.* Mitchell, 1 Shep. 439; Hall *v.* Hawkins, 5 Humph. 357; Wood *v.* Weir, 5 B. Mon. 544.

[3] Travis *v.* Smith, 1 Penn. 234.

[4] Per Tindal, C. J., Williams *v.* Taylor, 6 Bing. 186.

[5] Page *v.* Cushing, 38 Maine, 523.

[6] Ibid.

Johnstone *v.* Sutton, 1 T. R. 544, 545. See also the remarks of Mr. Justice Parke, in Mitchell *v.* Jenkins, 5 B. & Ad. 594; and of Tindal, Ch. J., in Williams *v.* Taylor, 6 Bing. 186.

As will more fully appear hereafter, the question of probable cause is for the Court; that of malice, for the jury. Page *v.* Cushing, 38 Maine, 523.

(*a*) "The term *malice*, in this form of action, is not to be considered in the sense of spite or hatred against an individual, but of *malus animus*, and as denoting that the party is actuated by improper and indirect motives." Per Parke, J., Mitchell *v.* Jenkins, 5 B. & Ad. 594.

him; in an action for malicious prosecution, he need not prove malice or want of probable cause, as in such case the law implies both.[1] So it is evidence of malice, that the defendant said, "I indict him to stop his mouth."[2]

11. It has been sometimes held, that an action for a malicious prosecution will not lie for bringing *a civil suit*, although it were groundless.[3] Thus for holding a defendant to bail, upon an unfounded claim, a civil action being *a claim of right*, to be pursued only at the peril of *costs*, if not sustained.[4] And although an action is held to lie for suing in the name of a third person;[5] yet a distinction is made between suing in the name of a *solvent* and an *insolvent* person.[6] The explanation of this difference between criminal prosecutions and civil actions is found in part in the fact, that the common law, in order to hinder malicious, frivolous, and vexatious suits, provided that every plaintiff should find *pledges*, which were amerced if the claim was false. And after this practice ceased, statutes provided costs for a prevailing defendant. But the qualified doctrine is now well settled, in relation to civil actions, (corresponding with the rule as to criminal prosecutions,) that no action lies to recover damages sustained by being sued in a civil action, *unless it was malicious and without probable cause.*[7] (a) It is said, "There are no cases in the old books, of actions for

[1] Prough *v.* Entriken, 11 Penn. 81.

[2] Per Maule, J., Heslop *v.* Chapman, 23 Law T., Qu. B. 49.

[3] Beauchamp *v.* Croft, Keilw. 26; Savile *v.* Roberts, 6 Mod. 73, n.; Bird *v.* Line, 1 Com. 190; Vanduzen *v.* Linderman, 10 Johns. 106.

[4] Thomas *v.* Rouse, 2 Brev. 75; 12 La. An. 785; Roret *v.* Lewis, 5 D. & L. 373. See Magnay *v.* Burt, 5 Qu. B. 394.

[5] Cotterell *v.* James, 11 C. B. 728.

[6] Waterer *v.* Freeman, Hob. 266; Rechell *v.* Watson, 8 M. & W. 691.

[7] Baugh *v.* Killingworth, 4 Mod. 14; White *v.* Dingley, 4 Mass. 433; Cox *v.* Taylor, 10 B. Mon. 17. See Wengart *v.* Beashove, 1 Penn. 232; Herman *v.* Brookerhoof, 8 Watts, 240; Jamison *v.* Duncan, 12 La. An. 785.

(a) No action lies for *irregularly* suing out an attachment, but for suing it out *maliciously*. Williams *v.* Hunter, 3 Hawks, 545.

In an action on the case for wrongfully suing out an attachment, it is sufficient to show a want of probable cause. It is not necessary to show that the defendant was actuated by malice. Kirkham *v.* Coe, 1 Jones, Law, 423.

suing where the plaintiff had no cause of action; but of late years, when a man is maliciously held to bail, where nothing is owing, or when he is maliciously arrested for a great deal more than is due, this action has been held to lie, because the costs in the cause are not a sufficient satisfaction for imprisoning a man unjustly, and putting him to the difficulty of getting bail for a larger sum than is due." [1] Thus an action lies for suing the plaintiff in an inferior court, maliciously, and arresting him, when that court had no jurisdiction of the cause.[2] (a) Or for suing in a proper court, but proceeding there vexatiously.[3] Also for alleging excessive damages, so that the defendant could not procure bail.[4] Or for holding one to bail in an inferior court, without probable cause, when no more than thirty shillings was due.[5] So for holding one to bail merely for purposes of vexation.[6] So a declaration alleged, that the defendant sued out a *fi. fa.* upon a judgment against the plaintiff in an action of trespass, under which the sheriff took goods of the plaintiff to the amount of the damage, and returned that the goods remained in his hands for want of purchasers; and that the defendant, well knowing this, to the intent to vex the plaintiff, sued out another *fi. fa.*, under which the sheriff levied the money on other goods of the plaintiff, and paid it over to the defendant. Held, on motion in arrest of judgment, that the action was maintainable. Hobart, C. J., says: "The plaintiff was twice vexed and grieved, and that wil-

[1] Per Ld. Camden, Goslin *v.* Wilcock, 2 Wils. 302.
[2] Goslin *v.* Wilcock, 2 Wils. 302.
[3] Bird *v.* Line, 1 Com. 190.
[4] Ibid.
[5] Smith *v.* Cattel, 2 Wils. 359.
[6] Thomas *v.* Rouse, 2 Brev. 75.

(a) While an action lies *upon the ground* that the court in which a civil action is brought has no jurisdiction; it is also held, that want of jurisdiction, in the court before which a criminal prosecution was instituted, constitutes no defence to an action for malicious prosecution. Hence, it is not necessary to aver or prove jurisdiction, provided the malice and falsehood of the charge be put forward as the *gravamen*, and the arrest or other act of trespass alleged merely as a consequence. Morris *v.* Scott, 21 Wend. 281; *Infra*, § 14.

fully, by the defendant, who had first one execution inchoate, which he ought to have followed, knowing it, and not to have taken another, for else he might take twenty executions.

12. Another ground of action for malicious prosecution has been the institution of proceedings in *bankruptcy*. Thus an action on the case lies for maliciously suing out a commission of bankruptcy, notwithstanding the specific remedy given in the statutes of bankruptcy.[2] (*a*) So the declaration alleged, that the defendant falsely and maliciously caused and procured the plaintiff to be adjudged a bankrupt. It appeared, that the defendant presented a petition to the Court of Bankruptcy, and made an affidavit that the plaintiff had upon summons admitted part of the debt, but swore that he had a good defence as to the residue, and that the plaintiff had not within seven days after filing the admission paid or tendered to him the sum admitted to be due; and thereupon the plaintiff was adjudged a bankrupt. Held, that the declaration was proved, and the defendant liable to an action, though the affidavit did not show that an act of bankruptcy had been committed under § 82 of Stat. 12 & 13 Vict. 106, and though the commissioner made a mistake, in point of law, in adjudging the plaintiff to be a bankrupt. Crompton,

[1] Waterer *v.* Freeman, Hob. 205, 266; 1 Browl. 12.

[2] Brown *v.* Chapman, 1 W. Black. 427.

(*a*) So, where the common law gives a remedy for maliciously suing out an *injunction*, without probable cause therefor, such remedy is not merged into the one acquired by the giving of an injunction bond, but both exist together. Cox *v.* Taylor, 10 B. Mon. 17.

But the injunction must be charged in the declaration as an abuse of the process of court, through malice and without probable cause. Otherwise, the remedy is on the bond. Robinson *v.* Kellum, 6 Cal. 399.

Damages were refused to a builder, against whom an injunction had been sued out, where the whole foundation of his claim was a supposed hindrance thrown in his way in executing a building contract, which confessedly required for its execution the use of a side wall erected by the plaintiff in the injunction, and for which he had not been compensated. Jamison *v.* Duncan, 12 La. An. 785.

J., said: "There is not the less wrong in causing the act to be done, because the act would be illegal at any rate. In a popular sense, a person who puts the law in motion causes the thing to be done. All that is necessary is, that the defendant should falsely and maliciously cause the act; and he does that when he swears falsely, and the act would not be done without his so swearing."[1] So, in an action for maliciously suing out a commission against the plaintiff, under which he was adjudged a bankrupt, and his goods were seized, but which was afterwards superseded; the plaintiff proved, in addition to these facts, an action of trespass brought by him against the defendant for the seizure; a plea, alleging the bankruptcy; issue joined on that fact, and a verdict for the plaintiff. Also, that shortly before the commission was taken out, he had removed some goods, under circumstances which did not make the removal an act of bankruptcy, but were probably relied on by the defendant as having that effect. It was not shown that this was the fact upon which the commissioners made their adjudication, or by which the defendant supported his plea in the former action. Held, this was sufficient evidence to throw on the defendant the *onus* of proving probable cause.[2]

13. The question sometimes arises, whether an action will lie for the malicious *continuance* of a prosecution, which was lawfully commenced. (See p. 499.) It is held, that an action on the case will not lie against a party suing out a writ, if he neglect to countermand it after payment of the debt. At least, unless malice be averred.[3] So no action will lie, for not preventing, but permitting and suffering the plaintiff to be arrested, after payment of debt and costs, owing to the defendant, upon a writ sued out before such payment; malice being the gist of all actions for injuries of that nature.[4] Nor against an execution creditor or his attorney, for issuing a *fi. fa.* indorsed to levy the whole sum recovered by a judgment, which, to the knowledge of both, has been partly satis-

[1] Farlie *v.* Danks, 30 Eng. L. & Eq. 112; 4 E. & B. 493.

[2] Cotton *v.* James, 1 B. & Ad. 128.

[3] Shiebel *v.* Fairbain, 1 B. & Pul. 388.

[4] Page *v.* Wiple, 3 E. 314.

fied by payments, unless malice and want of probable cause be alleged and proved.[1] So, if a defendant, before execution, pay the debt and damages, and the plaintiff sign a release; and afterwards, within the year, take the defendant in execution; yet it is held that an action will not lie for this vexation.[2] So, although one may be liable for the continuance of a prosecution, after notice of it, though not commenced by him; yet mere attendance at the hearing does not necessarily render a party liable, though the proceeding were commenced by his agent.[3] But where a plaintiff sues out a writ, and causes it to be served, and then neglects at the return day to appear and prosecute his suit, and the magistrate is not present at the time and place of return, with the writ, whereby the defendant incurs expense and loss; the defendant may have a remedy against the plaintiff therefor by an action on the case.[4] So, upon an allegation that the defendant, upon a writ of *ca. sa.*, properly issued at his instance, for a large amount, but a great part of which had been afterwards satisfied, had falsely and maliciously, and without any reasonable or probable cause, procured the sheriff to issue a warrant, to take and keep the plaintiff, &c., and had falsely and maliciously, and without any reasonable or probable cause, procured the warrant to be indorsed to levy the larger amount, whereupon the plaintiff had been taken and detained for four weeks, and whereby he had suffered in his business and credit; held, upon demurrer, to disclose a sufficient cause of action; for it was alleged that the act was malicious, &c., and such an act might injure the plaintiff, as by rendering it more difficult for him to raise means to satisfy the debt really due; and it was alleged, in effect, that it had conduced to some part, at least, of his detention in prison.[5]

14. The principle has been sometimes laid down, that,

[1] De Medina *v.* Grove, 11 Ad. & Ell. N. S. 152.

[2] Baugh *v.* Killingworth, 4 Mod. 14.

[3] Weston *v.* Beeman, 27 Law T. Exch. 57.

[4] Mann *v.* Holbrook, 20 Verm. 523. See Stevens *v.* Wilkins, 8 Verm. 230.

[5] Churchill *v.* Siggers, 26 Eng. L. & Eq. 200; 3 Ell. & Bl. 929.

where a prosecution against a party *never legally existed*, he cannot maintain an action for a malicious prosecution.[1] Thus it is held, that a record of a prosecution and acquittal, before a justice of the peace who had no jurisdiction of the case, is not sufficient to sustain such action.[2] So a declaration, for wrongfully and vexatiously suing out an attachment before a justice of the peace in Mississippi, which does not show that such justice had authority by the laws of that State to issue attachments, and which contains no averment connecting the defendant with the levy thereof, discloses no ground of action, and is bad on demurrer.[3] But the contrary rule is sometimes laid down, and is supported by the weight of authority.[4] More especially, if the act be done *knowingly*.[5] And in an action on the case for maliciously suing out an attachment against the plaintiff, the defendant cannot raise the objection, that the affidavit, which he made to procure the attachment, and on which the writ was issued, was insufficient to authorize the issuance of an attachment.[6] So a count, alleging that the defendant falsely charged the plaintiff with, &c., before a justice, and procured the justice to make his warrant, &c., is not objectionable, because the alleged charge does not authorize the issuing of a warrant.[7] And an action will lie for a malicious indictment, although the plaintiff could not have been punished on the indictment.[8] Or for the malicious prosecution of a bad indictment.[9] So an action for malicious prosecution may be maintained, although the warrant for the party's arrest does not describe the offence with which he was charged, and the affidavit warrant for commitment and recognizance misdescribes it.[10] So it is no defence, that the warrant, on which the plaintiff was arrested, was not sealed.[11] And one who prosecutes another for perjury, in swearing to what could

[1] Braneboy *v.* Cockfield, 2 M'Mul. 270.

[2] Bixby *v.* Brandige, 2 Gray, 129.

[3] Marshall *v.* Betner, 17 Ala. 832.

[4] Atwood *v.* Monger, 6 Mod. 73. See Hays *v.* Younglove, 7 B. Mon. 545; Goslin *v.* Wilcock, 2 Wils. 302.

[5] Bird *v.* Line, 1 Com. 190.

[6] Forrest *v.* Collier, 20 Ala. 175.

[7] Collins *v.* Love, 7 Blackf. 416.

[8] Pedro *v.* Barrett, 1 Ld. Raym. 81.

[9] Pippett *v.* Hearn, 5 B. & Ald. 634; Chambers *v.* Robinson, 2 Strange, 691; Wicks *v.* Fentham, 4 T. R. 247.

[10] Ewing *v.* Sanford, 19 Ala. 605.

[11] Kline *v.* Shuler, 8 Ired. 484.

not amount to perjury, it being immaterial, cannot be protected, in a subsequent suit against him for a malicious prosecution, by proving the truth of his charge.[1]

15. As has been already intimated, it is held to be a full answer to an action for malicious prosecution, that the plaintiff was really guilty of the offence charged, or apparently guilty, and therefore that the defendant had probable cause for the prosecution.[2] Hence it is competent for the plaintiff, to disprove the charge preferred against him by the defendant, for the purpose of showing the want of probable cause, and to raise the presumption of malice.[3]

16. As we have seen, the want of probable cause must be proved by some affirmative evidence; (*a*) unless the defendant, by pleading singly the truth of the facts involved in the prosecution, dispenses with this proof. And, where the prosecutor was a witness at the trial, and the jury acquitted the defendant; in an action against the prosecutor for malicious prosecution, the acquittal does not raise a presumption of the want of probable cause.[4] Thus, where the plaintiff was indicted for a conspiracy and acquitted; in an action by him for malicious prosecution, it was held that the record of the verdict did not support the averment of a want of probable cause.[5]

17. It has been sometimes held, that the necessary allegation, that the prosecution was without probable cause, relates to *the fact*, not to *the defendant's knowledge of it*.[6] (*b*) That

[1] Smith *v.* Deaver, 4 Jones, Law, 513.

[2] Whitehurst *v.* Ward, 12 Ala. 264; Plummer *v.* Gheen, 3 Hawks, 66.

[3] Long *v.* Rogers, 17 Ala. 540; Katterman *v.* Stitzer, 7 Watts, 189.

[4] Griffin *v.* Chubb, 7 Tex. 603.

[5] Bell *v.* Pearcy, 11 Ired. 233.

[6] Mowry *v.* Miller, 3 Leigh, 561.

(*a*) An averment that the prosecution was without probable cause is indispensable, and its omission fatal. Lohrfink *v.* Still, 10 Md. 530. In regard to *damages*, if the plaintiff was imprisoned, special damages need not be proved; the law will presume damage. Garrison *v.* Pearce, 3 E. D. Smith, 255.

(*b*) See p. 499. In Massachusetts, since the abolition of special pleadings, the defendant may give evidence of facts tending to prove the plaintiff

the real point of inquiry for the jury is, whether there *was* probable cause for the prosecution, and not whether the defendant had probable cause to believe the plaintiff guilty, or whether he had probable cause to institute the suit.[1] So, that the want of probable cause does not necessarily imply malice; but the defendant may prove matters showing probable cause, though he did not know them at the time he instituted the prosecution.[2] And that the right to recover in such action depends upon *the entire innocence* of the plaintiff, and malice in the defendant.[3] And that the defendant is only to be fixed with want of probable cause, by what he knows when he commences the prosecution, but he may protect himself by proving any facts which tend to show the plaintiff guilty.[4]

17 *a*. But on the other hand it is held, that, although the defendant may not be able to show probable cause, or the plaintiff may prove a state of facts from which the want of it

[1] Hickman *v*. Griffin, 6 Mis. 37.

[2] Bell *v*. Pearcy, 5 Ired. 83; Hall *v*. Hawkins, 5 Humph. 357; Wood *v*. Weir, 5 B. Mon. 544.

[3] Bell *v*. Pearcy, 5 Ired. 83.

[4] Johnson *v*. Chambers, 10 Ired. 287.

---

guilty, both in proof of probable cause, and in mitigation of damages; although he does not show that these facts were known to him at the time of the complaint. Bacon *v*. Towne, 4 Cush. 217.

As will be hereafter more distinctly explained, in an action for malicious prosecution, the facts material to the question of probable cause must be found by the jury; and the Judge is then to decide, as a point of law, whether the facts so found establish probable cause or want of it. Among these facts, are the defendant's knowledge of the alleged grounds of accusation at the time when he prosecuted; and his belief, at that time, that the conduct forming such ground of accusation amounted to the offence charged. If the defendant did not so believe, the want of reasonable and probable cause is established, though the imputed offence appear, *primâ facie*, to have been committed by the plaintiff, and the fact to have been known to the defendant before the charge was made. The absence of belief must be proved by the plaintiff. And, if it be not proved, the defect is not supplied (for the purpose of showing want of probable cause) by evidence that the defendant made use of the charge as a means of obtaining an unfair advantage over the plaintiff. Turner *v*. Ambler, 11 Ad. & Ell. N. S. 252.

may be inferred; yet, if the defendant acted under an honest belief that the plaintiff was guilty of the offence for which he was charged, no recovery can be had against him.[1] That "reasonable and probable cause must be that which exists in the mind of the party at the time of the act in question."[2] That those facts and circumstances which were known to the prosecutor at the time he instituted the prosecution are to be alone considered, in determining the question of probable cause.[3] Thus, in an action for a malicious prosecution for perjury, the question of probable cause should not be submitted to the jury, upon the fact of the guilt or innocence of the plaintiff, but upon that of the belief of the defendant that the plaintiff testified to a fact admitted to be untrue.[4] And, in fine, that the question of probable cause does not turn on the actual guilt or innocence of the accused, but upon the belief of the prosecutor concerning such guilt or innocence.[5] (*a*)

18. In affirmance of the views last stated, probable cause for instituting a prosecution is held to be such a state of facts known to and influencing the prosecutor, as would lead a man of ordinary caution and prudence, acting impartially, reasonably, and without prejudice, to believe, or entertain an honest and strong suspicion, that the person accused is guilty.[6] (*b*)

[1] Chandler *v.* McPherson, 11 Ala. 916; Greenwade *v.* Mills, 31 Miss. 464.

[2] Delegal *v.* Highley, 3 Bing. N. 950; James *v.* Phelps, 11 Ad. & Ell. 489.

[3] Swaim *v.* Stafford, 3 Ired. 289.

[4] Seibert *v.* Price, 5 W. & S. 438.

[5] Hall *v.* Suydam, 6 Barb. 83; Raulston *v.* Jackson, 1 Sneed, 128; Barton *v.* Kavanaugh, 12 La. An. 332.

[6] Bacon *v.* Towne, 4 Cush. 217; Rice *v.* Ponder, 7 Ired. 390; Rickey *v.* McBean, 17 Ill. 63; Jacks *v.* Stimpson, 13 Ib. 701; Foshay *v.* Ferguson, 2 Denio, 617; Ash *v.* Marlow, 20 Ohio, 119; Fitzgibbon *v.* Brown, 43 Maine, 169.

(*a*) It is said, "That which is founded on the accuser's own knowledge will require proof to that extent to warrant such a charge, whereas that which rests on suspicion only will be satisfied by circumstances sufficient to induce suspicion on the mind of a cautious person." Per Bayley, J., Davis *v.* Noake, 6 M. & S. 32.

(*b*) The defendant may prove, that A. communicated to B., with a request that B. would make it known to the defendant, the fact that A. saw the plaintiff do the criminal act complained of, and that this information was

And it has been held not sufficient to establish the want of probable cause, that the defendant might, by the use of proper deliberation, care, and inquiry, have ascertained that the crime alleged had not been committed.[1] (a)

18 *a*. But mere *good faith*, in making an accusation, is not a sufficient defence.[2] Nor the mere belief of a prosecutor, that he had good cause for commencing criminal proceedings; if all the facts and circumstances under which he acted clearly show that there was no probable cause for his acts, and that his belief was groundless, and could not have been formed without the grossest ignorance and negligence. And, if no probable cause in fact existed, and the defendant failed to use such precaution as a prudent man would use to ascertain that fact, although he acted entirely without malice; yet, in such case, malice will be inferred from the want of probable cause.[3] It is said, "If a case is trumped up out of very weak and flimsy materials, for purposes of annoyance or of frightening other people, and deterring them from committing depredations upon private property; there is a want of probable cause."[4] As where one is assaulted in consequence of his own acts of provocation, and knowing

1 M'Gann *v.* Brackett, 33 Maine, 331.

2 Hall *v.* Suydam, 6 Barb. 83; Lawrence *v.* Lanning, 4 Ind. 194; Barton *v.* Kavanaugh, 12 La. An. 332. See Bacon *v.* Towne, 4 Cush. 217.

3 13 Ill. 701. See Long *v.* Rogers, 19 Ala. 321.

4 Stevens *v.* Mid. Rail. Co. 10 Exch. 356.

---

communicated to the defendant before the complaint was made. Bacon *v.* Towne, 4 Cush. 217.

(*a*) So, in an action for maliciously suing out *a domestic attachment*, it is not necessary for the defence to show a fraudulent intention in the debtor, to authorize the attachment, but only that the conduct of the debtor was such, as to render the suit a measure of *reasonable precaution*. M'Cullough *v.* Grishobber, 4 W. & S. 201. See Bacon *v.* Towne, 4 Cush. 217.

But it is not allowable for the plaintiff to prove, that, by common reputation in the neighborhood in which the defendant resided, it was supposed that he had gone to an adjacent State on a visit of business or pleasure. Though what he said previous to leaving home is admissible evidence in his favor, as a part of the *res gestæ*. Pitts *v.* Burroughs, 6 Ala. 733.

this fact procures an indictment against the assailant, who is acquitted.[1] So prosecuting, without legal cause, in order to obtain payment of a debt, or restitution of goods unlawfully detained; is a malicious prosecution.[2] So where the prosecutor believed, that the person whom he causes to be indicted for theft took the goods under the erroneous belief that he had a lien upon them, or other right to take and detain them.[3] So mere *ignorance of law* cannot be set up, to support the defence of probable cause. Thus, in an action against one claiming to be part-owner of a ship, for maliciously bringing an action of replevin against the owner of the other part, the jury were instructed, on the subject of probable cause, that the legal presumption, that every one knows the law, was applicable to the case, and that the defendant must be presumed to have known that an action of replevin would not lie, unless he could show the contrary. Held, the instruction was correct.[4] So a belief, that a given state of facts would constitute the crime charged, when it did not, would not furnish probable cause.[5] The distinction, however, is made, that, if one complains to a magistrate of the loss of his property, and that another has taken or appropriated it, and the magistrate erroneously treats the case as a felony, and issues his warrant accordingly; the complainant is not responsible.[6] Otherwise, if he charge a felony, though by the magistrate's advice.[7]

19. The same general propositions may be illustrated by adding, that the belief and grounds of belief of a prosecutor, in determining the question of probable cause, are to be referred to the time, nature, and circumstances of the prosecution itself, not to a remote period or a different transaction, in connection with which probable cause may have existed. Thus evidence of the declaration of the plaintiff, that he had some years before inflicted a beating on his

[1] Hinton v. Heather, 14 M. & W. 131.

[2] Brooks v. Warwick, 2 Stark. 393; M'Donald v. Rooke, 2 Bing. N. C. 219.

[3] Huntley v. Simson, 2 H. & N. 600.

[4] Wills v. Noyes, 12 Pick. 324. See Baldwin v. Weed, 17 Wend. 224.

[5] Hall v. Hawkins, 5 Humph. 357; Faris v. Starke, 3 B. Mon. 4.

[6] Leigh v. Webb, 3 Esp. 165; Clarke v. Postan, 6 C. & P. 423.

[7] Huntley v. Simson, 27 Law, J., Exch. 137.

wife, is not admissible, to show probable cause for procuring an indictment against him, for inflicting a beating upon her, of which, it was alleged, she had died.[1] So in an action for a malicious prosecution for perjury, before a justice of the peace, the defendant cannot prove that the grand jury, at a previous term of the court, directed the solicitor to bring in a bill of indictment against the plaintiff for perjury.[2] So, in an action for a malicious prosecution of the plaintiff, for maliciously removing a fence between his land and land of the defendant, the dividing line between which had been settled by arbitration; evidence of prior wrongful removals of the fence by the plaintiff, before the submission to arbitration, is inadmissible to prove probable cause.[3] So, in an action against the defendant, for giving the plaintiff into custody on a charge of stealing oysters from an oyster-bed; the defendant cannot, for the purpose of proving *bona fides* on his part, give evidence of a prior conviction of a third party for stealing oysters from the same bed; such conviction not having come to the defendant's knowledge at the time of his giving the plaintiff into custody.[4] So, in an action for maliciously suing out an attachment, evidence that another attachment against the plaintiff was in the hands of the sheriff, and was levied on the same property at the same time that the defendant's was levied, is inadmissible for the defendant.[5] (*a*) So a plea to an action for a malicious charge

[1] Tims *v.* M'Lendon, 3 Strobh. 557.
[2] Butler *v.* Johnson, 10 Ala. 459.
[3] Tillotson *v.* Warner, 3 Gray, 574.
[4] Thomas *v.* Russell, 25 Eng. L. & Eq. 550.
[5] Yarbrough *v* Hudson, 19 Ala. 653.

(*a*) But the defendant may prove the issuance of another attachment, and notice thereof to himself, previous to the issuance of his own attachment, as tending to rebut the presumption of malice. 19 Ala. 653.

And a deed of trust, executed by the plaintiff prior to the issuance of the attachment, is admissible evidence for the defendant in such an action; and also any proof tending to show that it was fraudulent, or that it was part of a plan to enable the plaintiff to dispose of his property fraudulently; or that he was in embarrassed circumstances at the time of its execution; or that the property conveyed by it was subsequently run off by the beneficiary to another State. Ibid.

before a magistrate, justifying the charge on the ground that the plaintiff had committed the offence imputed to him, is not sufficient, unless it allege that *at the time of the charge* the defendant had been informed of, or knew, the facts on which the charge was made.[1] (See p. 493.) So, where there were circumstances of a suspicious character against the plaintiff, which would amount to probable cause, if unexplained, yet, if these were denied and satisfactorily explained to the prosecutor, before he commenced his prosecution, he cannot avail himself of the defence of probable cause.[2] (*a*)

[1] Delegal *v.* Highley, 3 Bing. N. 950. [2] Honeycut *v.* Freeman, 13 Ired. 320.

So, in an action for vexatiously suing out an attachment, it is competent for the defendant to prove, in mitigation of damages, that the plaintiff was indebted to him in Georgia, and that he ran away from that State with his property to avoid the payment of his debts. Melton *v.* Troutman, 15 Ala. 535.

In an action by A., for the malicious prosecution by C. of an indictment against A. and B., evidence of the misconduct of C. towards B., after his apprehension, tending to show the bad motives of C., is admissible. Caddy *v.* Barlow, 1 M. & Ry. 275.

(*a*) In an action on the case for malicious prosecution, in causing the plaintiff to be arrested on a charge for feloniously taking property, it is sufficient evidence of want of probable cause, that the party making the complaint knew that the other party claimed and had at least a *primâ facie* right to the property. Weaver *v.* Townsend, 14 Wend. 192.

But, in an action for causing the plaintiff to be indicted for obtaining goods by false pretences, evidence that he had been guilty of conduct which, to men unskilled in technical rules of the law, would excite a well-grounded suspicion that a crime had been committed, is sufficient to warrant a verdict for the defendant. Baldwin *v.* Weed, 17 Wend. 224.

Thus, where a party, who had been a member of a firm, obtained goods from another after the dissolution of the firm, and, without making any representation whatever, gave for the goods the accountable receipt of the firm, the vendor parting with the goods upon his previous knowledge of the existence of the firm and his ignorance of its dissolution, and not upon the assumption by the purchaser of a character which did not belong to him; it was held, that, although an indictment for obtaining goods on false pretences did not lie, the conduct of the party afforded probable cause for the prosecution, and entitled the defendant to a verdict. And a verdict for the plaintiff was set aside. Ibid.

19 *a*. Nor is it evidence of probable cause, that the accused were *generally suspected*, or were *generally believed to be guilty*, of the crime charged.[1] So the character, habits, and appearance of a man, and the public opinion about him, though coupled with the fact that the crime was committed where he, with others, was present, will not amount to probable cause.[2]

19 *b*. Upon similar ground, on the other hand, if a prosecutor on a charge of larceny has reasonable cause, at the time he institutes the prosecution, to believe that his goods have been stolen, he is not liable to an action for malicious prosecution, though he may have afterwards discovered that his goods had not in fact been taken out of his possession, but had been accidently mislaid.[3] (*a*) And a declaration, alleging

[1] Brainard *v*. Brackett, 33 Maine, 580.
[2] Holburn *v*. Neal, 4 Dana, 120.
[3] Swain *v*. Stafford, 4 Ired. 392.

The charge against the plaintiff was, that, upon the trial of a cause in which he was examined as a witness, and was a material witness, he had sworn falsely, that he had no interest in the event of the suit. If such was his testimony, it was clearly shown that there was no probable cause for believing it to be false; but the main controversy upon the trial was, whether he had in fact sworn, as the defendants in making the charge had alleged. Held, that, in order to justify the defendants, it was not necessary for them to prove, that the plaintiff had thus sworn in terms, but only in substance, although not in words, that he had no interest which could disqualify him as a witness. Bulkley *v*. Smith, 2 Duer, 261.

It has been held that probable cause for a criminal prosecution will not be proved, by a trifling and merely formal violation of law. Thus, where a witness swore, that a magistrate had said, upon the return of a warrant, "that he would commit the defendant unless," &c., and the magistrate in fact said, "he would bind the defendant over unless," &c.; the variance was held not to constitute probable cause for a prosecution for perjury. Cabiness *v*. Martin, 3 Dev. 454.

Nor will the plaintiff be required to prove any fact, not necessarily involved in his innocence of the crime charged upon him. Thus, in an action for malicious prosecution for stealing a horse, it is not necessary for the plaintiff, in order to show a want of probable cause, to prove a good title to the property, or that the defendant actually knew it. Sexton *v*. Brock, 15 Ark. 345.

(*a*) It is not incumbent on the Judge, however, in such a case, to call the

that the defendant maliciously commenced a suit against the plaintiff and attached his property, is not supported by evidence that the defendant, having made the attachment under a belief that he had a good cause of action, maliciously detained the property after he had learned that his suit was groundless.[1] (See p. 490.)

20. In regard to a suit for malicious prosecution of *a civil action*, and the question of probable cause therefor, it is held, that, if what the defendant says or does is in pursuance of *a claim of title*, he is not responsible.[2] But an action has been held to lie, for enforcing a debt by an unreasonable and excessive seizure of property, even though the creditor had no other convenient mode of doing it. Thus a creditor in Maine, whose demand against a debtor in Massachusetts amounted to the sum of $124, attached under a writ, claiming $1500, a vessel belonging to the debtor, which was in Maine ready for sea, to the amount of $2000, the vessel being worth a much larger sum; but the debtor had no other property in Maine subject to attachment. Held, an action would lie for malicious prosecution.[3] So an action will lie, for falsely and maliciously suing out a writ of attachment against the plaintiffs' effects, to their injury, though they were indebted to the defendant.[4] And where there are mutual dealings between two parties, and items known to be due on each side of the account, an arrest for the amount of one side, without deducting what is due on the other, is malicious and without probable cause.[5] So although, where there are mutual dealings, if one party has not an opportunity of knowing both sides of the account, he may, to effect an adjustment, sue on the debit side, without regard to the credits; yet, in the case of a partner, who may examine the books,

[1] Stone *v.* Swift, 4 Pick. 389.
[2] Baily *v.* Dean, 5 Barb. 297.
[3] Savage *v.* Brewer, 16 Pick. 453.
[4] Tomlinson *v.* Warner, 9 Ham. 103.
[5] Austin *v.* Debnam, 3 B. & C. 139.

attention of the jury specifically to the circumstance, that the injury alleged in the declaration is the preferring a charge which is *then* maliciously made. Dubois *v.* Keats, 11 Ad. & Ell. 329.

such a proceeding, accompanied with an attachment of property, may be evidence that the suit was malicious.[1] (*a*)

21. Questions have often occurred, in relation to the probable cause necessary to justify an *attachment*, where this remedy is provided only in certain special contingencies. It is held no answer to an action for a malicious suing out of an attachment, that the defendant had good reason to believe, and did believe, that the plaintiffs were about to make a disposition of their property, so as to hinder and delay their creditors.[2] (*b*) So in an action, for wrongfully and vexatiously suing out an ancillary attachment, a fraudulent assignment, made by the debtor three days afterwards, cannot justify the defendant, unless the fraudulent intent on the part of the debtor existed at the time the attachment issued.[3] So in an action against the defendant, for maliciously suing out an attachment against the plaintiff's estate, it is not allowable for the latter to prove, that, by common reputation in the neighborhood in which the former resided, it was supposed that he had gone or was about to go to an adjacent State on a visit of business or pleasure.[4] (*c*) Nor a declaration by the plaintiff, made about a week before the attachment issued, that he was intending to leave the State temporarily; but not in the hearing of the defendant. Nor

[1] Pierce *v.* Thompson, 6 Pick. 193.

[2] Donnell *v.* Jones, 13 Ala. 490.

[3] Ibid. 17 Ala. 689.

[4] Pitts *v.* Burroughs, 6 Ala. 733.

(*a*) Upon this point it is remarked by an eminent Judge: "I can conceive a case, where there are mutual accounts between parties, and where an arrest for the whole sum claimed by the plaintiff would not be malicious; for example, the plaintiff might know that the set-off was open to dispute, and that there was reasonable ground for disputing it. In that case, though it might afterwards appear that the set-off did exist, the arrest would not be malicious." Per Parke, J., Mitchell *v.* Jenkins, 5 B. & Ad. 594.

(*b*) But the fact, that the defendant in the attachment was insolvent, is evidence going to the damages, though not to the action. 13 Ala. 498.

(*c*) But what he said previous to leaving home is admissible evidence in his favor, as a part of the *res gestæ*. 6 Ala. 733.

the plaintiff's declarations to that effect, made after the attachment issued.[1]

22. Conformably to the general principles above stated, in an action for a malicious prosecution, the defendant, to show probable cause and negative malice, may give in evidence, that he proceeded in the case *in good faith*, upon *the advice of counsel* learned in the law, given upon a full representation of the facts.[2] (*a*) Thus, in an action for procuring the plaintiff to be indicted, &c., the defendant may repel the imputation of having prompted the prosecution, by proof that the persons who appeared as prosecutors before the grand jury first took the advice of a lawyer upon the facts, and were informed by him that the indictment could be sustained.[3] So, where a party acts *bonâ fide* in consulting counsel, and pursuant to his advice commences a suit, believing that he has a good cause of action, he will not be answerable in an action for a malicious suit.[4]

22 *a*. But it has been doubted whether this defence can be set up, where the party omits to state to his counsel a fact well known to him, but which he honestly supposed was not material; or omits, through ignorance, to state a material fact which actually existed.[5] And it is well settled that he must show, that he communicated to such counsel all the facts bearing upon the guilt or innocence of the accused, which he knew, or by reasonable diligence could have ascertained.[6] So it has been held, that the opinion must have been honestly sought and understandingly given, the state-

[1] Havis *v.* Taylor, 13 Ala. 324.

[2] Williams *v.* Vanmeter, 8 Mis. 339; Leaird *v.* Davis, 17 Ala. 27; 27 Maine, 266; *contra*, Collard *v.* Gay, 1 Tex. 494.

[3] Chandler *v.* McPherson, 11 Ala. 916.

[4] Stone *v.* Swift, 4 Pick. 389.

[5] Griffin *v.* Chubb, 7 Tex. 603.

[6] Ash *v.* Marlow, 20 Ohio, 119.

(*a*) Upon somewhat analogous ground, although one is liable for procuring a search-warrant maliciously and without probable cause; he is not liable merely for going before a magistrate and laying before him fair grounds of suspicion, truly stated, so far as the complainant knows or has the means of knowing, whereupon the magistrate in the exercise of his judgment issues the warrant. Cooper *v.* Booth, 3 Esp. 144; 1 T. R. 535. . . . .

ment of facts correct, and the opinion well founded.[1] (a) Nor will this defence be available, if the defendant was influenced by passion, or a desire to injure the plaintiff; or if he received from other counsel learned in the law, whose counsel he sought, advice of a contrary character.[2] And it is a question for the jury, whether he acted *bonâ fide* on the opinion given him by his professional adviser, believing that the plaintiff was guilty of the crime of which he was accused, or that he had a good cause of action against the plaintiff.[3]

22 *b.* We now proceed to a more particular consideration of that peculiar element in the action for malicious prosecution which has been already repeatedly referred to — *the want of probable cause.* It will be seen that the distinctions upon this subject are numerous and somewhat metaphysical, and all the cases by no means entirely reconcilable.

23. The question of probable cause, in an action for malicious prosecution, is *a mixed question of law and fact.* Where the facts are uncontested, it is the duty of the Judge to apply the law and determine the issue. If there are contested facts, he should charge the jury hypothetically, upon the state of facts claimed by each party.[4] It is said, " In some cases the reasonableness and probability of the ground for the prosecution has depended, not merely upon the proof of

[1] Kendrick *v.* Cypert, 10 Humph. 291; Hewlett *v.* Cruchley, 5 Taunt. 277.

[2] Stevens *v.* Fassett, 27 Maine, 266.

[3] Hall *v.* Suydam, 6 Barb. 83.

[4] Bulkeley *v.* Ketletas, 4 Sandf. 450; Garrison *v.* Pearce, 3 E. D. Smith, 255; Graff *v.* Barrett, 29 Penn. 477.

(*a*) But the contrary and more reasonable doctrine has been held, that, if a prosecutor has fairly submitted to his counsel all the facts that he knows are capable of proof, and has acted in good faith on the advice given, he is not liable to an action for malicious prosecution, even if the facts did not warrant the advice and prosecution. Walter *v.* Sample, 25 Penn. 275; Hall *v.* Suydam, 6 Barb. 83.

In case of a criminal prosecution for obtaining goods on false pretences, the omission of the defendant, in consulting with the district attorney, previous to submitting the case to the grand jury, to state the circumstances under which the vendor parted with his goods, does not destroy the defence of probable cause. Baldwin *v.* Weed, 17 Wend. 224.

certain facts, but upon the question whether other facts which furnished an answer to the prosecution were known to the defendant at the time it was instituted. In other cases the question has turned upon the inquiry, whether the facts stated to the defendant at the time, and which formed the ground of the prosecution, were believed by him or not. In other cases the inquiry has been whether, from the conduct of the defendant himself, the jury will infer that he was conscious he had no reasonable and probable cause. But in these, and many other cases which might be suggested, it is obvious that the knowledge, the belief, and the conduct of the defendant, are so many additional facts for the consideration of the jury, so that in effect nothing is left to the jury but the truth of the facts proved, and the justice of the inferences to be drawn from such facts, the judge determining as matter of law, according as the jury find the facts proved or not proved, and the inferences warranted or not, whether there was reasonable and probable ground for the prosecution, or the reverse."[1] In other words, whether the circumstances alleged, to show probable cause, or the contrary, are true, and existed, is a matter of fact; but whether, supposing them true, they amount to a probable cause, is a question of law.[2] A party has a right to the opinion of the Court distinctly on the law, on the supposition that he has established, to the satisfaction of the jury, certain facts.[3] Thus, where the facts had not been found by the jury, it was held erroneous to instruct them "that admitting all the testimony in favor of the plaintiff to be. true, yet he had not shown a want of probable cause."[4] So, in an action for malicious prosecution upon the charge of obtain-

[1] Per Tindal, C. J. Panton *v.* Williams, 2 Qu. B. 194.

[2] Hall *v.* Suydam, 6 Barb. 83; Stone *v.* Crocker, 24 Pick. 81; Travis *v.* Smith, 1 Penn. 234; Leggett *v.* Blount, 2 Tayl. 123; Wells *v.* Parsons, 3 Haring. 505; Weinberger *v.* Shelly, 6 Watts & Serg. 336; Plummer *v.* Gheen, 3 Hawks, 66; Nash *v.* Orr, 3 Brev. 94; Paris *v.* Waddell, 1 M'Mull. 358; Pomeroy *v.* Golly, Geo. Decis. Part I. 26; Dodge *v.* Brittain, 1 Meigs, 84; Horn *v.* Boon, 3 Strobh. 307; Ash *v.* Marlow, 20 Ohio, 119.

[3] Plummer *v.* Gheen, 3 Hawks, 66; Greenwade *v.* Mills, 31 Miss. 464; 29 Penn. 477.

[4] Furness *v.* Porter, Walk. 442.

ing the goods by false pretences, the presiding Judge inquired of the jury, first, whether they thought the plaintiff obtained the property by falsely pretending that it was for a third person. This question being answered affirmatively, the inquiry was then made, whether the jury thought that the defendant, at the time of instituting the prosecution, believed that the plaintiff intended to defraud him of the price. This being answered in the negative, the Judge ruled that there was a want of probable cause.[1]

23 *a.* But it is said to be "difficult to lay down any general rule as to the cases where the opinion of a jury should or should not be taken." [2] And it is sometimes held, that a mixed question of law and fact may be properly left to the jury.[3] So, that it is the duty of the Court to instruct the jury, that, if they find certain facts from the evidence, *or draw from them certain other inferences of facts*, there is, or is not, probable cause; thus leaving the questions of fact to the jury, and keeping their effect, in point of reason, for the decision of the Court as a matter of law.[4] And that the jury, on the question of probable cause, are not to be confined entirely to the evidence offered by the defendant, but are to consider the whole evidence.[5] So, that where there is a conflict of evidence, and *the credibility of testimony* is to be passed upon, it is proper for the Judge to submit to the jury, whether the facts relied on as evidence of probable cause, or of the want of probable cause, are true, and, if requested by the defendant's counsel, it is the duty of the Judge to state to the jury his opinion, distinctly, whether probable cause is or is not established, if they find the truth of the facts relied on by the defendant as evidence of probable cause.[6] Thus, in an action for maliciously indicting the plaintiff for perjury, it appeared that the evidence on which perjury was assigned was given against the defendant, B., in an action in which he was the defendant, and in which the evidence for him

[1] Williams *v.* Banks, 1 F. & F. 557.

[2] Per Ld. Tenterden, Blackford *v.* Dod, 2 B. & Ad. 184.

[3] Stevens *v.* Lacour, 10 Barb. 63.

[4] Beale *v.* Roberson, 7 Ired. 280.

[5] Sims *v.* M'Lendon, 3 Strobh. 557.

[6] Hall *v.* Suydam, 6 Barb. 83.

contradicted that of the plaintiff, A. The defendant, on being told of the plaintiff's evidence, said he would indict him for perjury. The defendant's informant said, he thought there was no ground for such indictment; but the defendant replied, that he should move for a new trial, and the indictment would stop the mouths of the plaintiff and the opposite party for a time. Held, that the jury were properly asked, whether the defendant believed there was reasonable and probable cause for the prosecution; and, they having found that he did not, that the Judge was right in ruling that there was no such cause.[1] So, where the second of a set of bills of exchange was presented and protested, owing to the absence of the drawee, and the first of exchange arrived nine days after, and was paid, together with costs of protest of the second; and, two months after, suit was commenced on the protested bill: held, in an action for malicious prosecution, the question, whether the former plaintiffs knew that the bill was in fact paid when they commenced suit, was a question for the jury.[2] So, where A. arrested B., upon the advice of his special pleader that he had a good cause of action, but afterwards, upon being ruled to declare, discontinued proceedings; and B. brought an action for a malicious arrest without any reasonable or probable cause; held, that the reasonableness or probability of the cause was a mixed question of law and fact for the jury; and that they were rightly told by the Judge, that, if they believed the defendant to have acted *bonâ fide*, upon the advice he had received, he was entitled to a verdict; otherwise, they ought to find for the plaintiff.[3] So, in an action for a malicious prosecution for sheep-stealing, it appeared that the plaintiff was possessed of a sheep, which the defendant claimed as one of several stolen from him; and, the plaintiff having appealed to a neighbor, as to its being one of a pen of sheep which he had bought at a fair, he said it was not one

[1] Haddrick *v.* Heslop, 12 Ad. & Ell. N. 267.

[2] Weaver *v.* Page, 6 Cal. 681.

[3] Ravenga *v.* Mackintosh, 4 D. & Ry. 187.

of that breed. The defendant then took away the sheep. The plaintiff sued him in the County Court; and the defendant indicted the plaintiff, but he was acquitted. The sheep was not the defendant's; but the jury found that the defendant believed that it was, and that he had reasonable ground for so believing. The Judge thereupon ruled, that there was reasonable and probable cause for the prosecution. Held, by Coleridge, J., and Crampton J., (Erle, J., dissenting,) that, under the circumstances, the fact of the defendant's belief, and the finding of the jury that he had reasonable ground for that belief, were sufficient to justify the ruling of the Judge.[1]

23 *b*. It is to be further remarked, however, as has been already suggested, with more special reference to the respective provinces of the Court and the jury; that the question of probable cause, *upon established facts*, is *a question of law*.[2] Thus, in an action for a criminal prosecution, whether there was probable cause, no contradictory testimony being given, is a question for the Court to decide. If no inculpating testimony was given, the law itself declares that there was no probable cause.[3] So, if all the facts which the evidence *tends to prove* do not amount to probable cause, the question of probable cause is to be decided by the Judge, and not to be submitted to the jury.[4] It is therefore erroneous for the Judge to submit it to the jury to determine, whether the facts and circumstances in evidence afforded the defendants ground for believing, that the plaintiff was guilty of the offences which they laid to his charge.[5] (*a*) So, where there

[1] Douglass *v.* Corbett, 37 Eng. L. & Eq. 153.

[2] Stevens *v.* Fassett, 27 Maine, 266; Marks *v.* Gray, 42 Ib. 86.

[3] Taylor *v.* Godfrey, 36 Maine, 525. See Greenwade *v.* Mills, 31 Miss. 464.

[4] Stone *v.* Crocker, 24 Pick. 81.

[5] Carpenter *v.* Shelden, 5 Sandf. 77.

(*a*) Upon the respective provinces of Court and jury with reference to the combined questions of malice and want of probable cause, it is held, that, to maintain an action, the plaintiff is bound to prove the entire want of probable cause, and probable malice; that is, malice in fact, as distinguished from malice in law.

is evidence *tending to establish* the conclusion, that there was an agreement or understanding between the parties, authorizing the plaintiff to do the act for which the alleged malicious prosecution was commenced, it is proper for the Judge to charge the jury, that if, from the evidence, they should be of the opinion that there was such an agreement or understanding, then there was want of probable cause for instituting the prosecution.[1] So, in an action by an attorney, for maliciously and without probable cause indicting him for sending a threatening letter, it appeared, that, his clients having inquired of the defendants, as to the truth of a repre-

[1] Stevens v. Lacour, 10 Barb. 63.

Malice, therefore, when the case turns upon its proof, is a question of fact for the jury. But probable cause is in all cases a question of law, in relation to which the Judge is bound to express a positive opinion, as upon every other question of law, which a Judge is required to determine.

If the Judge is of the opinion, that the facts admitted or clearly established are not sufficient to prove a want of probable cause, he must either nonsuit the plaintiff, or direct the jury to find a verdict for the defendant.

But if the facts, upon which, in his judgment, the case depends, upon the evidence are doubtful, he must instruct the jury, that, if they shall be found by them in a certain manner, they do or do not amount to a want of probable cause.

If, instead of such a direction, he leaves it to the jury to determine, not only whether the facts alleged by the plaintiff are true, but whether, if true, they prove a want of probable cause; he commits a fatal error.

Hence, the Judge having instructed the jury to consider and determine, whether the facts and circumstances known to the defendants were reasonable grounds for their believing that the charge which they had made against the plaintiff was true; held, erroneous, as necessarily involving a submission to the jury of the question of probable cause; the existence of reasonable grounds for believing the charge preferred to be true, and of a probable cause for making it, being only different forms of expressing the same truth.

Also, that, when the existence of facts constituting a probable cause is admitted or established, the presumption of law is, that the defendant entertained and acted upon the belief which these facts justified.

Hence, unless this presumption is repelled by proof on the part of the plaintiff, the question of the actual belief of the defendant ought not to be submitted to the jury. Bulkley v. Smith, 2 Duer, 261.

sentation, made by a person who had offered to buy goods of them, the defendants replied, that they would not be responsible for the debt, but believed the person had the employment he represented. The goods were then supplied to him. His representation turned out to be false, and the plaintiff, by direction of his clients, wrote a letter to the defendants, demanding payment of them of the price of the goods obtained from his clients through the defendants' representation, and stating that the circumstances made it incumbent on his clients to bring the matter under the notice of the public, if the defendants did not immediately discharge the amount; that he had instructions to adopt proceedings, if the matter were not arranged in the course of the morrow; and that, as those measures would be of serious consequence to the defendants, he hoped they would prevent them by attention to his letter. The defendants were then summoned before a magistrate, to answer a charge of obtaining goods under false pretences. The plaintiff served the summons and attended with his clients, and the complaint was dismissed. The defendants afterwards indicted the plaintiff for sending a threatening letter contrary to the 7 & 8 Geo. IV. c. 29, § 8, and he was acquitted. On the trial in this action, the Judge, without leaving any question to the jury, decided that there was reasonable and probable cause for preferring the indictment. Held, that the decision was correct, and that the evidence did not raise a question of fact for the jury, whether the defendants *bonâ fide* believed that they had a reasonable cause for indicting, but a pure question of law for the Judge, whether the defendants had such reasonable cause.[1] So, upon the trial of an action, for maliciously indicting the plaintiff without reasonable or probable cause, the plaintiff proved a case which, in the opinion of the Judge, showed, that there was no reasonable or probable cause for preferring the indictment. The defendant then called a witness, to prove an additional fact, and, that being proved, the Judge was of opinion, that there was reasonable or probable

[1] Blackford *v.* Dod, 2 B. & Ad. 179.

cause for preferring the indictment. Held, there being no contradictory testimony as to that fact, and there being nothing in the demeanor of the witness who proved it to impeach his credit, the Judge was not bound to leave it to the jury to find the fact, but that he might act upon it as a fact proved, and nonsuit the plaintiff.[1]

23 *c.* But, on the other hand, where the prosecution was under stat. 7 & 8 Geo. IV. c. 30, § 6, for maliciously and feloniously obstructing a mine, and the plaintiff was acquitted, on the ground that he committed the obstruction under a claim of right by his employer, and by such employer's direction; and in this action, for malicious prosecution, it was proved that there had been disputes between the employer and the defendant on the subject, before the obstruction, and that the defendant knew from the plaintiff, that the obstruction was effected in assertion of his employer's alleged right; held, that the Judge was not justified in nonsuiting, or in directing a verdict for the defendant, on the ground of there being reasonable and probable cause; but that the question was for the jury.[2] So, in an action for charging the plaintiff with a felony, maliciously, and without reasonable or probable cause; held, that the Judge was warranted in leaving to the jury, instead of deciding himself, the existence of probable cause, upon the following state of facts: The plaintiff, a servant, being discharged from service on a Friday, took away with her from her master's house a trunk and bag, the property of her master. The master wrote to her the next day, demanding his property, and threatening to proceed criminally on the Monday following, if it were not restored. The plaintiff being absent from home when the letter was delivered, no answer was returned; whereupon the master, the same day, Saturday, had her taken into custody, but, when she was brought before the magistrates on Monday, declined to make any charge.[3]

23 *d.* So the question of *motive* or *purpose*, on the part of

[1] Davis *v.* Hardy, 6 B. & C. 225.
[2] James *v.* Phelps, 11 Ad. & Ell. 483.
[3] M'Donald *v.* Rooke, 2 Bing. N. 217.

the defendant, in connection with the prosecution, is a proper question for the jury. Thus, in an action for maliciously indicting A. for perjury, it appeared that the defendant B., in 1824, preferred the indictment, and gave evidence before the grand jury; that the bill was found, removed into the King's Bench, and tried in 1827, and that B., who was then in custody, was brought into court under a *habeas corpus* obtained by his attorney, on the ground that he was a material witness; but he did not give evidence, and A. was acquitted. The Judge, in his direction, told the jury, that, if the defendant did not appear at the trial as a witness, from a consciousness that he had no evidence to give which would support the indictment, then there was a want of probable cause, and they should find for the plaintiff; but, if his non-appearance did not proceed from that cause, then there was no proof of want of probable cause, and they should find for the defendant. The defendant offered no evidence; and the jury found for the plaintiff. Held, a correct instruction.[1] So the question of the defendant's *belief* of the facts, relied upon to prove probable cause, has been held peculiarly proper for the jury. Thus, in an action against the defendant for taking the plaintiff to a police-office, and causing him to be imprisoned without reasonable or probable cause, on a charge that he had uttered menaces against the defendant's life; held, that it was not for the Judge to determine whether the menaces justified the charge, until the jury had found whether the defendant believed the menaces.[2]

23 *e*. But the number and complication of the facts proved, and the inferences to be drawn from them, are held not to change the general rule, that the question of probable cause *upon the facts* is a question of law for the Court; and it is still the duty of the Judge to inform the jury, if they find the facts to be proved, and the inferences to be warranted by such facts, that the same do or do not amount to reasonable or probable cause, so as thereby to leave the question of

[1] Taylor *v.* Williams, 2 B. & Ad. 845.

[2] Venafra *v.* Johnson, 10 Bing. 301.

fact to the jury, and the abstract question of law to the Judge.[1] (*a*)

24. As has been already stated, in order to sustain this action, malice, as well as want of probable cause, must be proved. Of this malice various definitions are found in the books. (*b*)

24 *a*. In a legal sense, any unlawful act, which is done wilfully and purposely, to the injury of another, is, as against that person, malicious.[2] And an averment, that an attachment was sued out "wrongfully, fraudulently, and in order to oppress and injure said plaintiff," is equivalent to an averment that it was sued out "maliciously."[3] So the jury may rightly be told, that if, upon the evidence, they believe that the defendant *acted from an improper motive*, they might infer malice.[4] And malice, in the sense of the law, does not presuppose personal hatred or revenge, but may be implied, under certain circumstances, from a total want of probable cause, or from gross and culpable omission to make

1 Panton *v.* Williams, 1 Gale & Dav. 504.

2 Griffin *v.* Chubb, 7 Tex. 603; 3 Story, 1.

3 Forrest *v.* Collier, 20 Ala. 175.

4 Haddrick *v.* Heslop, 12 Ad. & Ell. N. S. 267.

(*a*) In an action for the malicious prosecution of the plaintiff, on a charge of burning his own building for the purpose of defrauding the insurers, the Judge instructed the jury, in reference to the question of probable cause, that the evidence tended to prove three propositions: 1, an intent or motive in the plaintiff to commit the crime; 2, guilty conduct or acts, or knowledge of the plaintiff; 3, that the fire was the act of an incendiary; and that any two of these propositions, if proved, would constitute probable cause, but that neither alone would be sufficient. Held, this instruction was not correct; but the evidence to prove the prominent facts should have been distinctly laid before the jury, with specific instructions as to what leading facts or classes of facts, in evidence, if proved, would or would not constitute reasonable or probable cause; leaving the facts and the inferences to be drawn from them to be found by the jury. Bacon *v.* Towne, 4 Cush. 217.

(*b*) It is said (3 Steph. N. P. 2275), "*Malitia* is an abstract of *malus*, which imports what is wicked. Among the Romans it signified a mixture of hatred and fraud." (See chap. 13, § 2.)

suitable and reasonable inquiries.[1] So, to do a wrong or unlawful act, as by the institution of an unlawful suit, knowing it to be such, constitutes malice, although done to obtain a lawful end.[2] And, on the other hand, where the defendant instituted a criminal prosecution against the plaintiff for illegally and violently taking possession of a schoolhouse, with the purpose of getting possession of it himself; it was held, in an action for malicious prosecution, that such prosecution was founded on an indirect and malicious motive.[3] But it is held, that the want of due care, and a reckless design to accomplish an object, regardless of the rights of others, do not necessarily constitute malice.[4] So also, that the plaintiff must show a particular malice in the defendant towards himself; although this may be done by proof of threats and expressed ill-will, or may be inferred from the total want of probable cause.[5] And, to sustain the averment of malice, the charge must be *wilfully false.* Thus where a person, having lost a bill of exchange which he supposes to have been stolen, goes before a magistrate, and relates the circumstances of the loss; and the magistrate grants his warrant to apprehend A. B. on a charge of having "feloniously stolen, taken, and carried away" the bill of exchange, (language which the complainant did not use when he laid his information;) and upon subsequent investigation of the case it turns out to be no felony: case does not lie for maliciously procuring the magistrate to grant his warrant.[6]

24 *b.* Malice is *a question of fact* for the jury, who *may* infer it from want of probable cause, though not bound to do so.[7] (*a*) Thus, in an action for a malicious suit and im-

[1] Wiggin *v.* Coffin, 3 Story, 1.
[2] Wills *v.* Noyes, 12 Pick. 324.
[3] Kendrick *v.* Cypert, 10 Humph. 291.
[4] McGunn *v.* Brackett, 33 Maine, 331.
[5] Brooks *v.* Jones, 11 Ired. 260.
[6] Cohen *v.* Morgan, 6 D. & Ry. 8.
[7] Newell *v.* Downs, 8 Blackf. 523; 19 Ala. 327; Garrison *v.* Pearce, 3 E. D. Smith, 255.

(*a*) In an action for commencing a suit against the plaintiff without authority, evidence of express malice on the part of the defendant towards the plaintiff, although not necessary, is still competent. Smith *v.* Hyndman, 10 Cush. 554.

prisonment, the suit having been for infringement of a patent; if there was no infringement, and no reasonable cause for the plaintiff in that suit to believe that there had been, malice may be inferred by the jury, unless disproved by other evidence in the cause.[1] But a charge is erroneous, that, if the facts establish a want of probable cause, malice is a necessary implication, independent of the circumstances in proof.[2] And if the defendant cannot justify by proof of probable cause, he may still rebut the presumption of malice, by showing facts and circumstances calculated to produce, at the time, on the mind of a prudent and reasonable man, a well-grounded belief or suspicion of the party's guilt.[3] (*a*)

25. With regard to the *form of action* for malicious prosecution; it is held, that either trespass or case will lie for such prosecution, although instituted before a court having no jurisdiction.[4] (*b*) Case is the proper remedy, for the *malicious*

[1] Beach *v.* Wheeler, 24 Penn. 212.
[2] Ewing *v.* Sandford, 19 Ala. 605.
[3] Ewing *v.* Sandford, 21 Ala. 157.
[4] Hays *v.* Younglove, 7 B. Mon. 545.

(*a*) Evidence of malice towards third persons is inadmissible. Barton *v.* Kavanaugh, 12 La. & An. 332.

A question may arise, as to the admissibility of evidence, to meet the proof of want of malice on the part of the defendant. Thus A. and B. were arrested under a warrant issued by a justice of the peace, charging them with having unlawfully taken the prosecutor's daughter from his premises, and detaining her against her will and consent, with intent to carry her out of the State. After the termination of the prosecution, A. brought an action against the prosecutor for a malicious prosecution. To rebut the presumption of malice, the defendant proved his own declarations, made after the abduction of his daughter, but before the issuing of the warrant, expressing his willingness that B. might marry his daughter. It was held, 1. That the plaintiff might prove that these declarations were communicated to B., although the defendant was not present when the communication was made. 2. That B. did not detain the young lady against her will and consent. 3. That, at the time of the institution of the prosecution, the defendant entertained unfriendly feelings towards the family of which the plaintiff was a member. Long *v.* Rogers, 19 Ala. 321.

(*b*) See p. 224. A count for malicious arrest, after stating the suing out of the writ, &c., alleged that the defendant, while the plaintiff was confined in jail, obtained possession of a sealed letter of the plaintiffs, containing

use of process regularly issued from a court of competent jurisdiction; but when the proceeding complained of is

---

money, opened, concealed, and detained the same for several days, &c. Held, that the averment concerning the letter was not stated as a distinct and substantive cause of action, but merely as aggravation. Ford *v.* Kelsey, 4 Rich. 365.

A count, alleging that the defendant falsely and maliciously, and without probable cause, charged the plaintiff with perjury, and procured him to be arrested thereon, and imprisoned twelve hours, and carried before a justice, who, after a hearing, discharged the plaintiff, was held not to be so defective as to authorize the jury to disregard it. Collins *v.* Love, 7 Blackf. 416.

In an action on the case, the declaration complained, that the defendant caused an execution to be issued and levied upon his lands and goods, and the same to be sold by the sheriff, and the money arising from the sale applied to the satisfaction of the said execution; and that afterwards the judgment upon which the execution was issued "was set aside and rendered of no effect, &c., and afterwards a verdict rendered in the same case for the defendant (now the plaintiff), whereby it was established that the said defendant (now the plaintiff) was not in arrears or in anywise indebted to the said plaintiff (now the defendant)," by means whereof the said plaintiff was greatly injured, &c. Held, that the declaration did not contain such a cause of action, as that the defect could be cured by the verdict of the jury. Cooper *v.* Halbert, 2 M'Mul. 419.

In an action for malicious prosecution, damages for an abuse of the process of the law, by cruel and oppressive conduct, are not recoverable, unless a count charging such abuse is inserted in the declaration; and such count, it seems, may be joined with a count for malicious prosecution. Baldwin *v.* Weed, 17 Wend. 224.

In Alabama it is held, that a count in case for malicious prosecution must aver the issuance of process, properly describing it, and the plaintiff's arrest and imprisonment by virtue thereof. Sheppard *v.* Furniss, 19 Ala. 760.

It is not necessary in a declaration to describe by name the offence with which the plaintiff was charged, nor to draw the legal conclusion resulting from the act of the prosecutor. Long *v.* Rogers, 17 Ala. 540.

So an allegation, that the defendant "falsely and maliciously, and without any reasonable or probable cause, charged the plaintiff with having feloniously stolen a certain horse of the defendant's," is sufficient to show that the crime of larceny was imputed to the plaintiff, and that the justice before whom the charge was made was authorized to issue a warrant against him. Cox *v.* Kirkpatrick, 8 Blackf. 37.

So a declaration, that the defendant falsely, &c., before a certain justice of the peace, charged the plaintiff with having wilfully and maliciously set on

merely *irregular*, trespass is the remedy. But the form of action does not always determine the character of the count; it may be adjudged a count in trespass or in case, according to the facts stated in it, and the conclusions which the law draws from those facts.[1] (*a*) One arrested on criminal pro-

[1] Sheppard *v.* Furniss, 19 Ala. 760.

fire and burned a certain district school-house, (naming the district, township, and county,) contains a legal description of arson. Bartlett *v.* Jennison, 6 Blackf. 295.

A declaration in case, for wrongfully suing out an attachment, is bad on demurrer, if it does not specially deny the ground set forth in the affidavit for suing out the attachment. Tiller *v.* Shearer, 20 Ala. 527.

A plea to such an action, which avers that the attachment "was not sued out wrongfully, maliciously, or vexatiously, or without reasonable or probable cause," presents a substantial defence to the action, and is not demurrable. Marshal *v.* Betner, 17 Ala. 832.

In New York, an affidavit to obtain an order for the arrest of the defendant, in an action for malicious prosecution, must set forth the facts relied on as presumptive evidence of the want of probable cause. It is not sufficient to state in general terms the existence of malice and the want of probable cause. Vanderpool *v.* Kissam, 4 Sandf. 715.

But a defendant may not, in his answer to a complaint for falsely, without probable cause, &c., causing the plaintiff to be arrested, set forth minute facts and incidents to show probable cause. An answer, denying the allegations in the complaint, and setting up no new matter, is sufficient. Radde *v.* Ruckgaber, 3 Duer, 684.

But it has been held, that a plea of probable cause must set out the facts on which the defendant prosecuted, Legrand *v.* Page, 7 Monr. 401; and that a plea, stating in general terms that the defendant has a probable cause for the prosecution, is insufficient, Brown *v.* Connelly, 5 Blackf. 390.

Whether probable cause is admissible in evidence under the general issue, is a point variously decided. Faut *v.* M'Daniel, 1 Brev. 173; Horton *v.* Smelser, 5 Blackf. 428; Ibid. 390.

It is held in a late case, that, in an action for maliciously and without reasonable cause refusing to accept a tender of debt and costs, for which the plaintiff was in execution at the defendant's suit, the defendant may give evidence of probable cause under the plea of not guilty. Hounsfield *v.* Drury, 11 Ad. & Ell. 98.

(*a*) With regard to the form of action in case of *arrest* or *imprisonment*, case is a proper remedy, for maliciously arresting and causing to be committed to jail the plaintiff's slave, as a runaway, when the defendant knew that he was not a runaway. Hamilton *v.* Feemster, 4 Rich. 573.

cess, charging an act which is not a crime, has his remedy in trespass, and case will not lie.[1] So falsely, maliciously, and without any probable cause, procuring the warrant of a justice, to search the premises, and apprehend the person of A., on suspicion of felony, and thereby causing his premises to be searched, and his person imprisoned, is properly the subject of an action on the case, and not trespass.[2] (*a*) But a declaration, that the defendant falsely and maliciously made an affidavit, and upon said affidavit falsely and maliciously caused and procured the plaintiff to be arrested, and imprisoned for ten days, at the expiration of which, the plaintiff, in order to procure his release and discharge, was forced to and did pay to said defendant a large sum of money, to wit, &c., and was thereupon discharged and released, &c.; is a good cause in trespass.[3]

26. The legal *termination* of the suit or prosecution complained of is necessary, in order to maintain an action for malicious prosecution. And if there is no evidence of the fact, it is not error in the Court to refuse to leave it to the jury, to find whether or not the prosecution was determined.[4] Thus case will not lie for a malicious indictment or other

[1] Maher *v.* Ashmead, 30 Penn. 344.
[2] Elsee *v.* Smith, 1 D. & Ry. 97.
[3] Sheppard *v.* Furniss, 19 Ala. 760.
[4] Hardin *v.* Borders, 1 Ired. 143; M'Bean *v.* Ritchie, 18 Ill. 114.

The distinction between case and trespass is said to be this: where the immediate act of imprisonment proceeds from the defendant, the action can only be trespass; but where the act of imprisonment by one person is in consequence of information from another, there an action on the case is the proper remedy. Morgan *v.* Hughes, 2 T. R. 225.

(*a*) A positive oath, that a felony is actually committed, is not necessary, to justify a magistrate in granting his warrant to search the premises, and apprehend the person, of a party suspected; and though it may be trespass in the magistrate, to grant an illegal warrant, yet it is ground for case, in the person who causes and procures such warrant to issue, if done maliciously, and without reasonable or probable cause. 1 D. & Ry. 97.

Trespass will not lie, in Missouri, against a party, for suing out an attachment, in a suit on a debt not payable until after the commencement of the suit; the issuing of the attachment being a judicial act of the justice of the peace issuing it. Ivy *v.* Barnhartt, 10 Mis. 151. (See *Judge*.)

prosecution, without showing what became of that indictment, or how the proceedings were terminated;[1] unless, as is said, the prosecution was in a foreign country.[2] So an action for malicious prosecution of a civil suit will not lie, until the final termination of the suit; and the complaint must allege a want of probable cause, by averring that the suit was finally determined in favor of the defendant therein.[3] Thus where an action is discontinued by withdrawing an appeal, this must be done before the action has a legal end.[4] So an action does not lie for the malicious suing out of an injunction against the plaintiff, until the injunction is finally disposed of, or the suit in which it was sued out is terminated.[5] Nor for a commission of bankruptcy, upon a mere order to supersede it.[6] Nor, in general, after a mere order to stay proceedings.[7] Nor upon suffering a judgment of *nol. pros.*, as in case of nonsuit, to be entered by the defendant; this being a mere *omission to prosecute.*[8]

26 *a.* But where the former suit was a proceeding by attachment against the plaintiff, as having departed the county with intent to defraud his creditors, it is not necessary that he should prove the determination of the former suit in his favor; such proof is required, only where he had an opportunity to make a defence in the former action.[9] (*a*)

[1] Parker *v.* Langley, 10 Mod. 145, 210; Lewis *v.* Farrel, 1 Str. 114; Sayer, 162; Cole *v.* Hawks, 3 Monr. 208.

[2] Young *v.* Gregory, 3 Call, 446.

[3] Bird *v.* Lime, 1 Com. 190; Fisher *v.* Bristow, 1 Doug. 215; Pantsune *v.* Marshall, Sayer, 162.

[4] Howell *v.* Edwards, 8 Ired. 516.

[5] Tatum *v.* Morris, 18 Ala. 302.

[6] Poynton *v.* Forster, 3 Camp. 60; Whitworth *v.* Hall, 2 B. & Ad. 698.

[7] Wilkinson *v.* Howell, 1 M. & M. 495.

[8] Burhans *v.* Sandford, 19 Wend. 417.

[9] Bump *v.* Betts, 19 Wend. 421.

(*a*) But where, on an attachment against a non-resident debtor, a bond was given for its discharge under the statute; and, in a suit on the bond, there was a judgment of *nol. pros.* against the plaintiff for not declaring; it was held, that such judgment was not *primâ facie* evidence of the want of probable cause in suing out the attachment. Roberts *v.* Bayles, 1 Sandf. 47.

A judgment for the defendant in attachment does not estop the plaintiff, when sued for wrongfully and vexatiously suing it out, from proving that the debt, upon which the attachment issued, was actually due. Such evidence is admissible to show probable cause, and repel the presumption of malice. Marshall *v.* Betner, 17 Ala. 832.

So an action lies, for using process for a private purpose, not warranted by the requirement of the writ or the order of court; even though there was a good cause of action, and though the former suit is not terminated. As where the defendant, having issued a writ against the plaintiff, caused the officer to use the writ for the purpose of compelling the plaintiff by arrest to give up a certain paper in his possession.[1] So an action has been held to be *primâ facie* sustained, by proof that the suit complained of was voluntarily discontinued, throwing upon the defendant the *onus* of showing probable cause.[2] (*a*) So by proof of a rule to discon-

[1] Grainger *v.* Hill, 5 Sc. 580. See Heywood *v.* Collinge, 9 Ad. & Ell. 274.

[2] Burhans *v.* Sandford, 19 Wend. 417. *Contra*, Ford *v.* Kelsey, 4 Rich. 365.

(*a*) A. arrested B. for money paid to his use on the 10th of December, was ruled to declare on the 17th, filed a declaration on the 24th, and discontinued the action, upon payment of costs, on the 31st. Held, in case for a malicious arrest, that this was sufficient *primâ facie* evidence of malice and want of probable cause. Nicholson *v.* Coghill, 6 D. & Ry. 12.

In the following case, the effect of a previous *award* between the parties was brought in question, in an action for malicious prosecution. The defendant having been a partner in trade with the plaintiff, and the firm having occupied a store, belonging to the heirs of one on whose estate the defendant was administrator; the defendant brought an action for money had and received against the plaintiff, to recover a general balance, and likewise actions in the names of the heirs, but without their knowledge, against the plaintiff and himself, for rent. All these suits were submitted to arbitrators, with an agreement that they should consider the rent as having been paid by the defendant, and they awarded that a certain sum was due to him. In an action by the plaintiff against the defendant, for bringing these suits, alleged to be malicious, it was held that the plaintiff, in order to prove malice, might show that nothing was due from him in the first suit as the partner of the defendant. Also, that the submission and award were not conclusive evidence of probable cause for bringing the several suits, nor of a waiver of the plaintiff's right to sue for damages on the ground of their being malicious. Pierce *v.* Thompson, 6 Pick. 193.

The rule, that the suit must be terminated before an action will lie for a malicious prosecution, is to be qualified by the exception, that such action may sometimes be brought after, and on account of, some particular proceeding in such suit, though the latter be still pending. Thus case lies, as has been seen, (p. 519,) to recover the damages actually sustained by the wrongful suing out of *an attachment;* and, if malice also is shown, vindictive dam-

tinue on payment of costs, and that the costs were taxed and paid, though obtained only on the oath of the plaintiff.[1]

[1] Bristow v. Heywood, 4 Camp. 213; Brook v. Carpenter, 3 Bing. 297; 11 Moo. 59.

---

ages may be recovered, without, in either case, waiting for the determination of the attachment suit. And, in general, the costs and reasonable fees paid in the attachment suit are also recoverable as damages. Seay v. Greenwood, 21 Ala. 491.

Several suits were commenced against A., and judgments rendered against him, which, on appeal, were reversed. Before the mandate of the appellate court had been obeyed, A. sued the former plaintiffs for malicious prosecution. Held, that, as the suits against him were not ended when he brought this suit, it could not be maintained that the judgments of the court below, in favor of the plaintiffs, as the parties had appeared and been heard on the merits of the cases, were proof of probable cause, unless they had been obtained by fraud; and that this should be averred in the declaration, and be proved. Spring v. Besore, 12 B. Mon. 551.

A declaration in case charged that the defendant, falsely and maliciously, and without probable cause, made affidavit in the Court of Exchequer that the plaintiff was indebted to the Queen in a sum named, and was in embarrassed circumstances, and that the debt was in danger; by means whereof the defendant, maliciously and without probable cause, caused a commission to issue and an inquisition thereon to be taken, whereby it was found that the plaintiff was indebted to the Queen in the sum named; and the defendant afterwards, falsely, maliciously, and without probable cause, procured a writ of extent to be issued and delivered to the sheriff, under which the plaintiff's goods were seized, which writ of extent was afterwards superseded in the Court of Exchequer, "and the said writ of extent was then and is ended;" whereas the plaintiff was indebted only in a small portion of the sum named, and was not in embarrassed circumstances, and the debt was not in danger, as the defendant knew, and special damage was alleged, from loss of credit, by a creditor's selling the plaintiff's property under a power of sale given as a security, and another creditor's making an affidavit and giving notice to make the plaintiff a bankrupt. Held, on demurrer to the plea, that the declaration was good, without showing that the proceedings in the Exchequer were at an end, otherwise than by the averment that the writ was at an end, the issuing of the writ being the grievance. Plea, that the writ was superseded, at the request of the plaintiff, and by the grace and favor of the Queen, on terms of the plaintiff's paying costs of the execution of the writ of extent; and was not otherwise superseded or ended. On special demurrer, for that the plea did not avoid any allegation of the declaration, or was an argumentative denial of the supersedeas and termination

27. With regard to the *mode* in which a criminal prosecution must have been terminated, in order to lay the foundation of an action for malicious prosecution, the authorities are not perfectly reconcilable. In reference to the preliminary steps of a criminal accusation, it is held, that, to support an action for taking out a warrant against the plaintiff, he must show a discharge from arrest or recognizance.[1] But the action may be maintained, where a criminal warrant is sued out from a justice of the peace, although it is not placed in an officer's hands, nor further proceeded on.[2] And an averment of an examination of the plaintiff before a justice of the peace, touching the alleged offence, and a discharge by him therefrom, is a sufficient averment that the prosecution is ended.[3] Another rule is, that an action will not lie, for maliciously causing the plaintiff to be arrested on a criminal charge before a magistrate, unless the proceeding be so far ended, that nothing more can be done by the prosecutor without commencing anew.[4] Thus the plaintiff was arrested in Courtland county, by virtue of an indorsed warrant issued in the county of Seneca, upon a charge of having obtained money by false pretences, and was released from custody, on his entering into a recognizance in Courtland county, for his appearance at the next Seneca general sessions. He appeared accordingly, but the complainant did not appear, nor were any subsequent steps taken under the warrant. Held, the recognizance was a nullity, and, as the plaintiff still remained liable to be arrested under the warrant, he could not maintain an action against the complainant for a malicious prosecution.[5]

27 *a*. In relation to the *final* proceedings in a criminal

[1] Murray *v*. Lackey, 2 Murph. 368.
[2] Holmes *v*. Johnson, Busb. Law, 44.
[3] Long *v*. Rogers, 17 Ala. 540; Secor *v*. Babcock, 2 Johns. 203.
[4] Clark *v*. Cleveland, 6 Hill, 344.
[5] Ibid.

---

of the suit; held, that the plea was ill, being consistent with the facts in the declaration, and not justifying the act complained of. Craig *v*. Hasell, 4 Ad. & Ell. N. S. 481.

prosecution, the general rule is laid down, that "it must appear that the plaintiff was *acquitted* of the charge; it is not enough, that the indictment was ended by the entry of a *nolle prosequi;* though if the party pleaded not guilty, and the Attorney-General confessed the plea, this would suffice:"[1] and it has been held, that if a *nolle prosequi* was entered, and a judgment thereupon rendered that the defendant "go hence, thereof acquit, without day," the acquittal is sufficient to warrant the suit.[2] So, in order to maintain this action, it is said not to be necessary to show an acquittal which will bar a second prosecution for the same offence; nor any judicial decision upon the merits.[3]

27 *b*. But, in an action for preferring a criminal complaint against the plaintiff, evidence that a recognizance had been taken from him, and an indorsement subsequently made upon the affidavits taken by the police magistrate, in these words: "Bail discharged, April 20th, 1843," and an entry to the same effect made in the book of minutes kept by the clerk of the criminal court; is not sufficient proof that there was an end of the criminal prosecution, before commencement of suit.[4] So, although failure to apply for the continuance of a peace recognizance, temporarily granted, is evidence that the prosecution is at an end; it is not such an acquittal, as will raise any presumption of want of probable cause.[5] So it has been held, that the fact of the grand jury returning "no bill" against the plaintiff is not, *primâ facie*, sufficient evidence of the want of probable cause, to save the plaintiff from a nonsuit.[6] (*a*) More especially in an

[1] 2 Greenl. Ev. § 452; Parker *v.* Farley, 10 Cush. 279.

[2] Chapman *v.* Woods, 6 Blackf. 504.

[3] Per Cowen, J., Clark *v.* Cleveland, 6 Hill, 344.

[4] Bacon *v.* Townsend, 6 Barb. 426.

[5] Pharis *v.* Lambert, 1 Sneed, 228.

[6] Fulmer *v.* Harmon, 3 Strobh. 576.

(*a*) But, *contra*, even without a discharge by the Court. Woodruff *v.* Woodruff, 22 Geo. 237.

An action lies for a malicious prosecution, though the plaintiff be acquitted on a defect in the indictment. Wicks *v.* Fentham, 4 T. R. 247.

The record of a judgment of *nol. pros.* is held not of itself *primâ facie* evi-

action for a malicious indictment, *unde legitimo modo fuit acquietatus;* evidence of a *nol. pros.* is not sufficient to maintain this declaration. *Nolle prosequi* is no discharge of the *crime*, but of the *indictment*.[1] (*a*) So if, in an action for instituting proceedings before a magistrate, upon which the plaintiff was bound over and subsequently indicted, it appears that the indictment has been withdrawn by a *nolle prosequi*, on account of a formal defect therein, and that a second indictment has been returned, upon the same evidence, for the same, or a substantive part of the same charge; the original complaint and the proceedings thereon must be considered as the actual cause of the second indictment.[2] So, where the plaintiff relies upon a judgment of *nol. pros.*, or of discontinuance, the defendant may show that such judgment was entered through mistake or inadvertence, or otherwise explain it.[3] So, where the defendant has caused the plaintiff to be twice indicted, and the attorney of the Commonwealth has entered a *nolle prosequi* on the second indictment, "it appearing that the accused has been formerly acquitted of the offence charged against him in this indictment," the defendant may show that the

[1] Goddard *v.* Smith, 1 Salk. 21.
[2] Bacon *v.* Towne, 4 Cush. 217.
[3] Roberts *v.* Bayles, 1 Sandf. 47.

---

dence of want of probable cause. Roberts *v.* Bayles, 1 Sandf. 47; Parker *v.* Farley, 10 Cush. 279.

(*a*) The declaration in the action for malicious prosecution must precisely conform to the mode in which the proceedings were terminated. Thus a declaration, alleging that the plaintiff was arrested, entered into recognizance, and was afterwards therefrom discharged, and that the prosecution was wholly ended and determined, is not sustained by proof of acquittal before a petit jury. The word "discharged" is not equivalent in pleading to "acquitted," which term alone expresses a discharge upon trial *per pais*. Law *v.* Franks, Cheves, 9.

So, on the other hand, upon similar ground, an averment that the plaintiff "had been discharged out of custody, fully acquitted, and discharged of the said felony," is not sustained by proof, that the plaintiff was discharged on a return of *ignoramus* by the grand jury on the indictment. Hester *v.* Hagood, 3 Hill, 195.

second indictment was for a different offence from the one first charged, and that so there was probable cause for the second accusation.[1] Thus there is a material variance, between an indictment "for drawing and depositing in and across a highway a quantity of stones," and one "for building a stone wall in and upon the same highway." Hence, in an action for a malicious prosecution brought against the prosecutor of the last-mentiond indictment, it being proved that the plaintiff was guilty of the offence therein charged, and it not appearing upon proper averments, that the two indictments were for the same offence; held, the defendant had shown probable cause for the prosecution.[2]

28. It has been held, that if the jury in the former trial entertained sufficient doubts upon the evidence, to induce them to pause before returning a verdict of acquittal, this is sufficient evidence of probable cause.[3] The principle, however, is usually stated with great qualification.[4] And in a late case it has been distinctly decided, that, although an action cannot be maintained unless the plaintiff has been fully acquitted; and a *nolle prosequi* is not sufficient; the plaintiff is not bound to prove that he was acquitted by the jury, promptly, without hesitation, delay, or deliberation.[5]

29. On the other hand, the question, of course, arises, as to the effect upon the action for malicious prosecution, of any judgment or decision in the course of the former proceedings, *unfavorable* to the present plaintiff. A *final* termination, adverse to him, as already explained, is fatal to the action. (*a*) And it has been held, upon this point, that if the

[1] White *v.* Ray, 8 Pick. 467.
[2] Ibid.
[3] Smith *v.* McDonald, 3 Esp. Cas. 7; Grant *v* Dend, 3 Rob. (Lou.) 17; 2 Greenl. Ev. § 457.
[4] 2 Stark. Ev. 916.
[5] Bacon *v.* Towne, 4 Cush. 217.

(*a*) In an action for maliciously suing out an attachment process, it is not competent for the plaintiff to show, that most of the debt was due for usurious interest, when the judgment in the attachment suit is for the whole sum claimed. Jones *v.* Kirksey, 10 Ala. 839.

Where the original action has been settled by the defendant's paying a

plaintiff was convicted of the offence charged, before a court or magistrate having jurisdiction of the subject-matter, and without undue means of the prosecutor, as, for instance, chiefly or wholly by his false testimony; this will be conclusive evidence of probable cause, although the plaintiff was afterwards acquitted by a jury.[1] (*a*) But proof, that the examining magistrate bound the accused over to appear at court is not conclusive evidence of probable cause;[2] even if at all admissible;[3] the proceeding of the justice being sometimes held an *ex parte* examination, to inquire whether the plaintiff should be put on his trial, and not a final judgment on the facts.[4] But a judgment of a court of competent jurisdiction, in favor of the former plaintiff, although afterwards reversed, is held conclusive evidence that he had probable cause for instituting the suit.[5] And the qualified rule has been recently adopted, that a verdict of guilty, *founded upon correct legal instructions*, is conclusive evidence of probable cause, although set aside for newly-discovered evidence, and although a *nolle prosequi* was finally entered.[6] (*b*) And conviction before a magistrate, appealed from and reversed, has been held not

[1] Payson *v.* Caswell, 9 Shep. 212; Witham *v.* Gowen, 2 Shep. 362; Griffis *v.* Sellars, 4 Dev. & Batt. 176; Herman *v.* Brookerhoff, 8 Watts, 240; Whitney *v.* Peckham, 15 Mass. 243. See Mellor *v.* Baddeley, 2 Cr. & M. 678.

[2] Ash *v.* Marlow, 20 Ohio, 119; Ewing *v.* Sandford, 19 Ala. 605.

[3] Bacon *v.* Towne, 4 Cush. 217.

[4] Kendrick *v.* Cypert, 10 Humph. 291.

[5] Kaye *v.* Kean, 18 B. Mon. 839.

[6] Parker *v.* Farley, 10 Cush. 279.

---

sum of money, he cannot contend that there was not probable cause. Marks *v.* Gray, 42 Maine, 86.

(*a*) If the condemnation of goods, for not entering and paying duty, by sub-commissioners, be reversed by the commissioners of appeal, an action for a malicious prosecution does not lie against the informer. Reynolds *v.* Kennedy, 1 Wils. 232.

(*b*) Upon the same principle, if an indictment has been found a true bill, express malice must be proved, in an action for maliciously prosecuting the indictment. Golding *v.* Crowle, Sayer, 1.

So a "true bill" found constitutes a presumption of probable cause, and a plaintiff in an action for a malicious prosecution, who had proved his general good character, and the defendant's malice, was nonsuited, for want of express evidence to rebut this presumption. Brown *v.* Griffin, Cheves, 32.

conclusive evidence of probable cause, although, if the trial was fair and full, entitled to great consideration.[1]

30. While an action for malicious prosecution cannot be maintained, without proof that the former prosecution or action has terminated in favor of the present plaintiff, it is somewhat questionable, upon the authorities, whether the record of such termination is of itself even *primâ facie* evidence of the want of probable cause. The weight of authority seems to be that it is not.[2]

31. With regard to *the evidence* in actions for malicious prosecution; it is held that a copy of the indictment, duly certified, is admissible in evidence, and the original need not be produced.[3] (*a*) So the information made by the defend-

[1] Goodrich *v.* Warner, 21 Conn. 432.

[2] Johnston *v.* Martin, 3 Murph. 248; Bostick *v.* Rutherforth, 4 Hawks, 83, that it is *contra*, Scott *v.* Simpson, 1 Sandf. 601; McBean *v.* Ritchie, 18 Ill. 114; Hay *v.* Weakley, 5 C. & P. 361; Cotton *v.* James, 1 B. & Ad. 134.

[3] Faut *v.* M'Daniel, 1 Brev. 173.

(*a*) But it is sometimes held, that a copy of the record and acquittal on an indictment for felony shall not be admitted in evidence, without producing an order of the Court which tried the indictment, to authorize it. Kelley *v.* Rickett, 2 Brev. 144; R. M. Charl. 228. See Caddy *v.* Barlow, 1 M. & Ry. 275.

The origin of this practice, which, however, cannot be considered to prevail in the United States, has been thus explained: "It has been considered, that if, in the event of every acquittal, the prosecutor were liable to an action, the apprehension of that consequence would deter persons from becoming prosecutors, and crimes would go unpunished; and with regard to actions, it has also been considered that the trial of a private claim in a public court of justice is matter of right, and if the party do not succeed, his payment of the defendant's costs is a sufficient compensation. The presumption, therefore, is in general in favor of the prosecutor and of the plaintiff, that they properly instituted the proceeding; and with respect to prosecutions for felony, the Judges at the Old Bailey, 6 Car. 2, resolved, 'That no copy of any indictment for felony be given without special order, upon motion made in open court, at the general gaol delivery; for that the late frequency of actions against prosecutors, which cannot be without copies of the indictment, deterreth people from prosecuting for the king upon just occasions.' But it has been well observed, that the power of the Judges to make such resolution and order was, to say the least, questionable; and the better opinion is, that an acquitted defendant is entitled, as a matter of right, to a copy of the record of his acquittal, as well in felo-

ant, upon which the plaintiff was arrested, may be sent out with the jury.[1] And the record of the Police Court in which the complaint was tried may be used by the plaintiff in evidence.[2] So, in an action for malicious prosecution against the prosecutor, and the justice before whom the proceedings were instituted, the affidavit and warrant issued thereon are competent evidence.[3] So, in a suit against A. for malicious prosecution, an affidavit charging the plaintiff, &c., proved to have been made by A., and agreeing with that described in the declaration, is admissible evidence for the plaintiff.[4] So a memorandum made by a justice of the peace, at the time of the trial of a prosecution before him, showing the judgment which he rendered, is admissible

[1] Seibert *v.* Price, 5 Watts & Serg. 438.

[2] Brainard *v.* Brackett, 33 Maine, 580.

[3] Cooper *v.* Turrentine, 17 Ala. 13.

[4] Collins *v.* Love, 7 Blackf. 416.

---

nies as misdemeanors." 1 Chit. Gen. Prac. 49; Brown *v.* Cumming, 10 B. & C. 70.

In Legatt *v.* Tollemey, 14 E. 306, Lord Ellenborough said: "It is the duty of the officer charged with the custody of the records of the Court, not to produce a record but upon competent authority, which at the Old Bailey is obtained upon application to the Court, pursuant to the order which has long prevailed there, and with respect to the general records of the realm, upon application to the Attorney-General. But if the officer shall, even without authority, have given a copy of a record, or produce the original, and that is properly proved in evidence, I cannot say, that such evidence shall not be received. The order at the Old Bailey does not state that actions against prosecutors cannot be maintained without an order first obtained for a copy of the indictment, but only that they cannot be maintained without copies."

In Rex *v.* Branger, 1 Leach, C. C. 32, Willes, C. J., said: "Every prisoner, upon his acquittal, has an undoubted right and title to a copy of the record of such acquittal, for any use he may think fit to make of it." By St. 14 and 15 Vict. c. 99, § 13, production of the record is dispensed with.

Where a sheriff is prosecuted for false imprisonment, and justifies the imprisonment by virtue of a State's warrant against the plaintiff, a copy of the bill of indictment found against the plaintiff on the charge for which he was arrested is not admissible; nor is the fact that an indictment was found against him admissible, if at all, without offering the whole of the proceedings. McCully *v.* Malcom, 9 Humph. 187.

evidence, to show the termination of the prosecution.[1] So it is sufficient evidence of the termination of the prosecution, that the defendant therein was bound to appear to answer at court to a criminal charge, and that he did appear, and was not re-bound; especially if a minute appear on the State solicitor's docket, that he does not think the evidence sufficient to convict.[2]

32. With regard to *parol* evidence of the proceedings, offered to explain, control, or contradict the record; it is held that the judgment of the magistrate, by whom the plaintiff was bound over, if relied upon as evidence of probable cause, cannot be controlled or impeached by evidence that he acted unfairly and improperly in the examination.[3] But where a record shows a prosecution by —— Stone, the plaintiff may show by parol that —— Stone and the defendant are the same person.[4]

33. It is not incumbent on the plaintiff, in proof of want of probable cause, to give in evidence all the testimony introduced before the magistrate.[5] But the evidence introduced on the trial of the prosecution is admissible, for the purpose of showing reasonable and probable cause, and may be proved by any competent witness.[6] And where, upon a complaint for larceny, the justice recorded the testimony of the prosecutor, the plaintiff may give such parol evidence of this testimony, as is consistent with the written statement, and tends to a more exact specification of the thing stolen.[7] So, where A. was arrested for larceny at the instance of B., and, on being discharged, brought an action for malicious prosecution against him; A. may prove that B. was present, when two witnesses swore before a magistrate to facts showing that the larceny was not committed by A.; and the record of proceedings before the magistrate need not be produced.[8] (*a*)

[1] Long *v.* Rodgers, 18 Ala. 321.
[2] Rice *v.* Pindar, 7 Ired. 390.
[3] Bacon *v.* Towne, 4 Cush. 217.
[4] Stone *v.* Powell, 9 Mis. 435.
[5] Bacon *v.* Towne, 4 Cush. 217.
[6] Goodrich *v.* Warner, 21 Conn. 432.
[7] Watt *v.* Greenlee, 3 Murph. 246.
[8] Watt *v.* Greenlee, 2 Hawks, 186.

(*a*) In an action for malicious prosecution, the plaintiff counted on three

34. It is no defence, in an action for malicious prosecution of an indictment, that the warrant on which the plaintiff was arrested was not sealed, or that the name of the defendant did not appear on the indictment as prosecutor. Evidence that the defendant procured the warrant, and wagered that he would convict the plaintiff, sufficiently proves his connection with the prosecution.[1]

35. The magistrate, by whom the warrant was issued, is a competent witness, to prove that it was issued upon the oath of the prosecutor; and the contents of the oath, when it was not reduced to writing.[2] So the defendant may prove by the magistrate, what the testimony before him was on the part of the government, in order to show probable cause and disprove malice; and it is not necessary, for this purpose, that the witnesses or their depositions should be produced; but, if produced, and if the witnesses or deponents are unable to recollect what their testimony was, it may nevertheless be proved by the magistrate. (*a*)

36. In a suit for causing an indictment and trial for perjury, where the plaintiff introduces affidavits made by the defendants, and laid before the grand jury, the statements thereof in favor of the defendants are made evidence, subject to being explained and rebutted like other testimony.[3]

[1] Kline *v.* Shuler, 8 Ired. 484.

[2] Spears *v.* Cross, 7 Port. 437.

[3] Scott *v.* Simpson, 1 Sandf. 601.

---

distinct prosecutions, on the same day, before a justice of the peace, and three acquittals; but the justice's record showed an arraignment and discharge of the plaintiff in one case only. Held, that parol evidence was not admissible, to show that the plaintiff was prosecuted, arraigned, and discharged on three complaints, although the justice was no longer in office, and had declined to make up any further record of the proceedings. Sayles *v.* Briggs, 4 Met. 421.

(*a*) The plaintiff having introduced the magistrate as a witness, while he was under examination, the defendant's counsel called upon the counsel for the plaintiff, to produce the affidavits upon which the warrant was issued. Held, the Judge properly allowed the plaintiff to proceed in the examination of the witnesses, without producing the affidavits. Stevens *v.* Lacour, 10 Barb. 63.

But where the defendant in an attachment suit brings an action against the plaintiff, for maliciously suing out the attachment, and offers in evidence, in connection with the answers of the plaintiff to interrogatories filed in that suit, under the statute, the interrogatories, and his own affidavit therein, for the purpose of explaining the answers, without pointing out the necessity of any explanation, or the particular part relied upon for the purpose; the Court may properly reject the whole.[1] (*a*)

37. With regard to proof of the testimony or declarations of the parties to the action for malicious prosecution, in connection with the former proceedings; it has been sometimes held, that the testimony of the defendant, given before the magistrate, is not admissible to show probable cause, unless he alone had knowledge of the facts testified to.[2] On the other hand it has been held, that the defendant may prove what he swore before the committing magistrate, whether the facts were peculiarly within his knowledge or not. And, as the wife is not a competent witness for her husband, that the same rule will apply to testimony given by her.[3] (*b*)

[1] Melton *v.* Troutman, 15 Ala. 535.

[2] Riney *v.* Vanlandingham, 9 Mis. 816.

[3] Gardner *v.* Randolph, 18 Ala. 685; Johnson *v.* Chambers, 10 Ired. 287.

(*a*) Certain beer-pumps in the custody of H. were attached as the property of W., and delivered by the officer to H. for safe-keeping. In the absence of H., they were taken away by W., and a person who claimed them as his property. H. thereupon made a complaint against W., charging him with stealing the pumps. In an action brought by W. against H. for a malicious prosecution, H. gave in evidence a card which had been posted up at his place of business, and had been seen there by W., if not put up by him; advertising that W. made and sold beer-pumps. Held, this card, though inadmissible as evidence of the pumps attached, was evidence of probable cause for making the complaint, it having some tendency, though very slight, to induce the defendant to believe that the plaintiff was the owner. Wilder *v.* Holden, 24 Pick. 8.

(*b*) In an action of contract by the defendant against the plaintiff, both parties having testified, the defendant caused the plaintiff to be arrested for perjury, and he was discharged. The plaintiff then brings this action for

38. In a suit for malicious prosecution, instituted by the defendant against the plaintiff and two others, the declarations of one of the two others, not made in the presence of the plaintiff, cannot be introduced by the defendant, for the purpose of showing probable cause.[1] But, where the charge upon which an action for a malicious prosecution is founded, is that of unlawfully taking away and detaining the defendant's daughter without her consent, the declarations of the daughter, made about the time of the alleged abduction, conducing to show her willingness to go, are admissible as part of the *res gestæ*.[2] So the defendant may show, that, in relation to the prosecution complained of, he said, when called upon to give his deposition, he was reluctant to prosecute the plaintiff, because he feared him; that the plaintiff had struck him, and he did not wish to incur his additional displeasure by a prosecution; this being part of the *res gestæ*, and material on the questions of malice and probable cause.[3]

39. With regard to evidence of *character* in this action; unless the plaintiff in his declaration claims damages for injury to his reputation, evidence of character is inadmissible.[4] And if the plaintiff disclaims any special damages for injury to his character, the defendant cannot attack such character, either to rebut the evidence of malice, or in mitigation of damages.[5] (*a*) But, in general, it seems, evidence of

[1] Brainard *v.* Brackett, 33 Maine, 580.

[2] Long *v.* Rogers, 17 Ala. 540.

[3] Goodrich *v.* Warner, 21 Conn. 432.

[4] Downing *v.* Butcher, 2 M. & R. 374.

[5] Smith *v.* Hyndman, 10 Cush. 554.

malicious prosecution. Held, the defendant might offer in evidence his own testimony in the former action. Richey *v.* M'Bean, 17 Ill. 63.

(*a*) Where the fact of the defendant's sobriety was in issue, persons long and intimately acquainted with him were admitted to testify as to his habits of temperance. Beal *v.* Robeson, 8 Ired. 276.

And evidence of character given on the former trial may be shown in the present action. Thus, if evidence touching the present defendant's character constituted part of the evidence given on the prosecution, such evidence is admissible in an action for malicious prosecution. Goodrich *v.* Warner, 21 Conn. 432.

the general bad reputation of the plaintiff is admissible, to rebut the proof of want of probable cause, and also in mitigation of damages.[1] Thus, in an action for a malicious prosecution for larceny, the defendant may show that the plaintiff's only occupation was horse-racing and gambling.[2] Or that he was of notoriously bad character.[3] So the defendant may show, in mitigation of damages, that after the prosecution the plaintiff's character was bad on subjects unconnected with the felony.[4]

40. In reference to the measure and amount of damages for this injury; it is held that the plaintiff cannot recover for a loss in the sale of goods, caused by an assignment, which he was driven to make by such prosecution.[5]

41. Where the former suit on a bill which had been paid was accompanied by an attachment, under which the property of the drawer was held for four months, when it was released by giving bond; and the jury gave $15,000 damages; and no misconduct was shown on the part of the jury; and it was not charged that the verdict was given under the influence of passion or prejudice: held, the Court could not disturb the verdict, unless it clearly appeared that injustice had been done.[6] So in a case where the jury gave £10,000 damages, the Court refused to interfere.[7]

[1] Bacon *v.* Towne, 4 Cush. 217. *Contra*, Fitzgibbon *v.* Brown, 43 Maine, 169.

But evidence of the defendant's character for truth, at the time of the present or former trial, is not admissible, before the defendant has testified; and then only for the purpose of testing his credibility. Ibid.

[2] Martin *v.* Hardesty, 27 Ala. 458.

[3] Rodriguez *v.* Tadmine, 2 Esp. 721. See Newsam *v.* Carr, 2 Stark. R. 69.

[4] Bostick *v.* Rutherforth, 4 Hawks, 83.

[5] Donnell *v.* Jones, 13 Ala. 490.

[6] Weaver *v.* Page, 6 Cal. 681.

[7] Leith *v.* Pope, 2 W. Bl. 1326.

CHAPTER XVII.

INJURIES TO PROPERTY. NATURE AND DIVISION OF PROPERTY.

1. Having treated of injuries to the *person* or *body*, and to *character* or *reputation*, we now proceed to the remaining class of private wrongs — wrongs to *property.* These are not only in point of fact more numerous and frequent than the others, but in nature they are far more various and complicated. For this difference the reasons are very obvious. A bodily injury partakes of the simplicity or *unity* of the subject which it affects. So character or reputation is in nature *one*, and libel or slander (including the kindred wrong of malicious prosecution) is accordingly the only form of injury to which it is liable. But property is of various kinds; such as *real and personal, absolute and qualified, perpetual and temporary;* and for this cause alone the wrongs committed against property must be correspondingly various. (*a*) But,

---

(*a*) In reference to the fact, that injuries to the person and to real and personal property frequently grow out of one and the same occurrence, it is said, "injuries arising from keeping mischievous animals, and from public nuisances, also frequently affect personal property; and on the other hand, many of the wrongs affecting personal property may also affect persons, as negligence in riding horses, and driving carriages," &c. 1 Chit. Pl. 137, n.

in addition, injuries to property are in themselves of great variety; being committed with or without force, immediately or consequentially, by misfeasance or nonfeasance, by direct invasion of another's possession, or by an unauthorized use of one's own property, causing damage to another. With reference to the injuries themselves, they include disseisin, (a) trespass, nuisance, conversion, waste, fraud, and negligence; and, with reference to the remedies by which such injuries are redressed, the *actions* of ejectment, (a) trespass, trover, case, and waste. The former of these modes of classification is the one adopted in the present work. (See Preface.) The injury is treated as the principal — the action as only the accessory or incident. Thus we treat, not of the *action of trespass*, and therein of the wrongs for which such action may be brought, but of the *injury of trespass*, and therein, incidentally, of the action which may be brought for such injury. So we treat of *conversion* as another injury to property, involving a consideration of *trover*, the appropriate remedy therefor; and not of *trover*, as including the wrong for which it is made by law the peculiar remedy.

2. As already suggested, injuries to property are of various kinds, and, in treating of them as injuries and not merely as the subjects of special actions or remedies, it is somewhat difficult to decide upon the most natural and intelligible arrangement and classification. It will be seen that a twofold system has been adopted; depending, in part, upon the comprehensiveness of the injury, as a component part of the general subject of torts or wrongs, and therefore a natural sequel to the second chapter of this work, which treated of wrongs and remedies, generally; and in part upon the consideration, whether the injury in question may be done to property of any kind, or whether it is restricted to a particular description of property, the former being considered before the latter. Upon these grounds, it will be seen that,

---

(a) For obvious, technical reasons, the wrong of disseisin and the remedy of ejectment are not included in the plan of the present work.

first in order among specific injuries to property, we treat of *nuisance*, the very name of which imports the generality of its application, being in fact but another term for wrong or injury. And for the other reason suggested, we treat of *trespass*, which is a wrong alike to real and personal property, before *conversion*, which applies to personal property alone.

3. But, in advance of the whole subject of this class of injuries, it is necessary to state some general principles in relation to property itself, and the elements or incidents involved in those wrongs committed against it which the law will notice or redress. Our plan does not involve any minute or extended discrimination between the different kinds of property, although those distinctions often determine the legal character of particular injuries, and more especially of the various remedies therefor. In other words, throughout the whole course of the work, it is assumed and taken for granted, that real estate and personal estate, for example, are entirely different subjects of ownership; and that an incorporeal right or privilege connected with land is in nature different from the land itself; and these differences are no further formally defined or explained, than is necessary in stating the principles of law which govern wrongs and remedies. (*a*) Upon the general subject of property, therefore, it is sufficient for our purpose to say, that property is *the right and interest which one man has in things*, to the exclusion of others; including, not only the right to possess and use, but also to dispose of them. And, with reference to the great divisions of property into *real* and *personal*, that "things real are such as are permanent, fixed, and immovable, which cannot be carried out of their place; as lands and tenements; things personal are goods, money, and all other movables; which may attend the owner's person

(*a*) It will be seen, with some few exceptions, founded on technical grounds, which affect the remedy rather than the right, that the law of torts is substantially the same in reference to all kinds of property.

wherever he thinks proper to go. *Land* comprehends all things of a permanent, substantial nature. *Tenement* is a word of still greater extent; and though in its vulgar acceptation it is only applied to houses and other buildings, yet in its original, proper, and legal sense, it signifies everything that may be *holden*, provided it be of a permanent nature, whether it be of a substantial and sensible, or of an unsubstantial, ideal kind. Thus *liberum tenementum*, frank-tenement, or freehold, is applicable not only to lands and other solid objects, but also to offices, rents, commons, and the like. But an *hereditament* includes not only lands and tenements, but whatsoever may be *inherited*, (*a*) be it corporeal or incorporeal, real, personal, or mixed."[1] And it may be added, with respect to the great, subordinate classification of real property itself, that *corporeal* property consists of "houses, lands, and every other visible, tangible, and immovable property." *Incorporeal* property is "a property which cannot in general be touched, and has no *corpus;* such as rights of common, or rights of way, and other easements, and rights which, though they may be enjoyed in, upon, over, or relating to land or other corporeal property, yet in consideration of law constitute no right to the land itself."[2]

4. There is, however, in addition to property distinctly real or distinctly personal, an intermediate kind, partaking somewhat of both, which demands a brief preliminary notice, with reference to the injuries of which it may be the subject.

5. Under this head may be classed, in the first place, *fixtures*. Fixture is said to be a term in general denoting the very reverse of the name. It is something not originally constructed as part of a building, but formerly a movable chattel, and afterwards annexed to the building or land for

[1] 2 Bl. Com. 16. [2] 1 Chit. Gen. Prac. 5.

(*a*) Meaning, whatever descends to the heir, instead of passing to the executor or administrator.

the more convenient enjoyment thereof, and which, at the will of the owner, is at all times readily capable of being removed, though at the time annexed.[1] So fixtures are defined, as "things fixed in a greater or less degree to the realty."[2] Or (rather with reference to the privilege connected with them than the things themselves) "the right of severance of chattels attached to the soil, and not part of the freehold."[3] Conformably with either of these definitions, until actually removed, a fixture is a part of the freehold;[4] though, when lawfully severed, it becomes personal property, and may be sued for in replevin.[5] And, in general, to constitute a fixture, there must be a complete annexation to the soil.[6] This rule, however, does not apply to the constituent and subordinate parts of a dwelling-house, such as doors, blinds, and shutters, which, though even temporarily detached, are held to be parts of the realty.[7]

6. The question of fixtures is commonly said to arise in three cases. 1. Between heir and executor. That is, when the owner of real estate dies, the question is, whether things attached to the land shall pass with, or as a part of it, to the heir, or as personal property to the executor. 2. Upon the death of a tenant for life, by whom erections have been made, between his executor and the remainder-man or reversioner. 3. Between landlord and tenant; which relation has given rise to most of the cases decided upon the subject; the privilege of removal being more liberally construed in favor of a tenant than in any other instance. (a) And, with reference to the relative rights of landlord and tenant upon this subject, it may be stated, in general, that a tenant may remove *implements of trade*, such as furnaces, kettles, or boilers; *machinery*, as a steam-engine, pump, or post-windmill; *buildings for trade*, if this is the primary

[1] 1 Chit. Gen. Prac. 161.
[2] 2 Kent, 344, n.
[3] Horsfall v. Key, 17 L. J. Exch. 266.
[4] 1 Hill. Real Prop. 19.
[5] Heaton v. Findlay, 12 Penn. 304.
[6] Amos on Fixt. 5. 274, and *seq.*
[7] Winslow v. Merchants', &c. 4 Met. 314.

(a) See *Landlord*.

object; and articles of *ornament or domestic use*, such as glasses, chimney-pieces, bookcases, and, in general, things necessary to *domestic comfort*, which may be easily severed, and will be equally useful in another dwelling.[1]

7. To this very brief preliminary statement it is sufficient to add, that the nature of the title or ownership, which appertains to fixtures, in the various relations above mentioned, must of course determine both the right and the form of action for any injury of which they may be the subject. (*a*)

8. While the rules of law relating to fixtures for the most part apply to personal chattels affixed to a building, somewhat analogous questions have occurred, in relation to an entire building itself, and the respective ownership of the building and the land on which it stands. In general, a building is presumed to belong to the owner of the land. And this presumption cannot be controlled even by the wrongful act of the party who erects it. Thus, if one man take another's timber wrongfully, and use it in erecting or repairing buildings upon his own land, it becomes his property.[2] And the same rule applies, where the timber consists of the materials of a building, taken down by one man and

[1] 1 Hill. Real Prop. 22.

[2] Amos on Fixt. 9, n. a.

(*a*) See *Waste, Conversion, Trespass, Replevin, Landlord.*

It is held that trover will not lie against a *bonâ fide* purchaser without notice of a fixture wrongfully severed from the freehold. Cope *v.* Romeyne, 4 McLean, 384.

The owner of a house, in which there were fixtures, sold it by auction, nothing being said about the fixtures; and a conveyance of the house was executed, and possession given to the purchaser, the fixtures still remaining in the house. Held, they passed by the conveyance; and, even if they did not, the vendor, after giving up the possession, could not maintain trover for them. A few articles, which were not fixtures, were also left in the house; and the demand described them, together with the other articles, as fixtures, and the refusal was of the fixtures demanded. Held, upon this evidence, the plaintiff could not recover them in this action. Colegrave *v.* Dias Santos, 2 Barn. & Cress. 76.

In trespass, upon a declaration for taking *goods, chattels, and effects*, the plaintiff may recover the value of fixtures. Pitt *v.* Shaw, 4 Barn. & Ald. 206.

belonging to another. Thus, if a mortgagor of land with a house upon it take down the house, and use the materials in erecting another upon other land, and then convey the latter land with the house to the defendant; the mortgagee cannot maintain trover for such materials.[1] (*a*)

8 *a*. So, in general, a building is treated in law as an integral or inseparable part of the land. Thus where, in an action of trespass *quare clausum*, the plaintiff complains not only of injury done to his land, but that his dwelling-house was also destroyed, and the cause is tried upon a plea of title, and there is a verdict against the defendants; the plaintiff cannot, on a writ of error, insist that the dwelling-house was personal property, and that trespass would lie against the defendants for its destruction. The gist of the action necessary to maintain it, is the injury to the land; the additional allegation being merely aggravation.[2] So where A., owning a house and land, sold the house to B., and the land to C., and subsequently they were both sold on execution upon a prior judgment against A., and bought in by C.; it was held, that the sheriff's deed gave a paramount title to C., and that B. could not bring trover for the house.[3] So a house built by one person upon the land, and partly with the materials of another, with an agreement, that, upon payment of a specified sum by the builder, for the land and materials, the owner should convey the house and land to him; is not the personal estate of the builder, but the real estate of the owner of the land.[4] And, *a fortiori*, the con-

[1] Peirce *v*. Goddard, 22 Pick. 559.

[2] Houghtaling *v*. Houghtaling, 5 Barb. 379.

[3] Goff *v*. O'Conner, 16 Ill. 421.

[4] Hutchins *v*. Shaw, 6 Cush. 58.

(*a*) So where the hirer of personal property wrongfully annexes it to his real estate, which he then sells to one without notice, the lender cannot reclaim his property from the purchaser, but his only remedy is by action against the hirer. Fryatt *v*. The Sullivan Co. 7 Hill, 529. See § 17 and *seq*.

If a building be blown down by a tempest, its fragments are not by that act converted into personalty, but pass with the realty to a purchaser at sheriff's sale. Rogers *v*. Gilinger, 30 Penn. R. 185.

verse of the rule above stated is true, that if one man erect buildings upon the land of another, voluntarily and without any contract, they become a part of the land, and the former has no right to remove them.[1] (a)

9. But, on the other hand, one man may own, as personal property, a building erected upon the land of another; as where the former erects it by agreement with the latter.[2] So, if personal property is attached by a person to a building of which he is the owner, and is used as part of the furniture of the building, for the convenience of the business of its occupants, but is attached in such a manner that it can be removed without injury to the building and the property; it does not thereby become a part of the freehold, so as to pass by deed thereof. And, though the owner of the chattel may have had knowledge of its being so placed, and may have omitted to reclaim it for five years and until after the conveyance, yet he may maintain trover for it against the purchaser.[3] And the general rule, as to the presumption of concurrent ownership of land and building, may be controlled by the nature of the land and building, and the uses to which the latter is applied. Thus where, in an action of trespass for taking and carrying away the plaintiff's "small fish-house or camp," and burning up or destroying his "wooden camp or small house," upon an island in another State, it appeared that the structure was a building without a cellar, about nineteen feet square, used by the plaintiff and his men in the Spring, while catching salmon; held, neither the declaration nor evidence showed the property to be real estate.[4] (b)

[1] 1 Hill, Real Pr. 5.

[2] Wells v. Bannister, 4 Mass. 514; Ashmun v. Williams, 8 Pick. 402; Curtiss v. Hoyt, 19 Conn. 154.

[3] Cross v. Marston, 17 Verm. 533.

[4] Rogers v. Woodbury, 15 Pick. 156.

(a) So, where the defendant built a rail fence on the land of the plaintiff, who moved and kept the rails without breach of the peace; it was held that trover did not lie. Wentz v. Fincher, 12 Ired. 297.

(b) An action for pulling down bath-houses on a beach must be trespass, not case. Harwood v. Tompkins, 4 Zabr. 425.

10. Similar questions have arisen in reference to *growing trees*. These are presumed to belong to the owner of the soil, and a declaration in trespass, for cutting down and carrying away the plaintiff's trees, is good, without an averment that the land where the trees were growing belonged to the plaintiff.[1] (*a*) But trees, though standing upon and rooted in the soil, may be the subject of a distinct ownership. If the limbs of a tree overhang another man's ground, they still belong to the owner of the root.[2] And it is held, that, although both the roots and branches of a tree extend to land of an adjoining owner, the whole tree, with all its fruit, belongs to the owner of the land on which it stands.[3] But it is said, if a tree grows in a hedge, which divides the land of A. and B., and by the roots takes nourishment in the land of A. and also of B., they are tenants in common of the tree."[4] And a tree, standing directly upon the line between adjoining owners, belongs to both alike; and either may maintain trespass against the other for cutting and destroying it.[5]

11. Whether *trees* or *wood*, owned apart from the land, constitute real or personal property, is somewhat doubtful. It has been held that trees reserved from a conveyance for life will pass with a subsequent transfer of the reversion.[6] But a grant of trees is said to pass them as chattels, for an injury to which the grantee may maintain trespass.[7] So, if the grantee of land cuts and removes from it the trees, belonging to another, the owner of the trees may bring re-

[1] Gronour *v.* Daniels, 7 Blackf. 108.
[2] 1 Hill, Real Pr. 10.
[3] 1 Swift, 104; Addi. on Wrongs, 154.
[4] 2 Rolle, Rep. 255.
[5] Griffin *v.* Bixby, 12 N. H. 454.
[6] Liford's case, 11 Co. 47.
[7] Stukely *v.* Butler, Hob. 10. See Wright *v.* Barrett, 13 Pick. 44; Clap *v.* Draper, 4 Mass. 266; Sawyer *v.* Hammott, 3 Shepl. 40; Putney *v.* Day, 6 N. H. 430.

(*a*) Under the Revised Statutes of Illinois, giving the owner a certain penalty for each tree of a particular description cut on his land without his permission, to be recovered by an action of debt, he must aver and prove that he is the owner in fee-simple of the land. Edwards *v.* Hill, 11 Ill. 22.

plevin in the *cepit* against him.[1] (*a*) And, whether a sale of growing wood is a sale of real estate, may depend on the

[1] Warren *v.* Leland, 2 Barb. 613.

(*a*) In an action of trespass for cutting down timber-trees, the rule of damages is the value of the timber when it is first cut down and becomes a chattel. This rule, however, it seems, is not applicable to cases of cutting down ornamental trees, or where the trespass is attended with circumstances of aggravation. Bennett *v.* Thompson, 13 Ired. 146.

And it is held in Maine, that the damages should include not only the value of the trees, but the injury occasioned by cutting them prematurely, and the injury done to the land, with damages at the rate of six per cent. Longfellow *v.* Quimby, 33 Maine, 457.

Under the third section of the Pennsylvania Act of March 29, 1824, either trespass or trover may be maintained for entering upon a person's land, without his consent, and cutting and removing timber-trees. If there is a trespass merely, double damages may be given; if, in addition, the trees felled have been converted to the use of the wrongdoer, treble damages may be recovered in trespass, and also in trover. By the words, "as the case may be," is meant, that, if the trespass be waived, and trover brought, treble damages for the injury done may be recovered in that form of action. Either the jury or the Court may assess the double or treble damages. Welsh *v.* Anthony, 16 Penn. 254.

All vegetable productions, as well as trees, *primâ facie* belong to the soil. A different ownership must be established by "contract, custom, or special rules of law." Calhoun *v.* Curtis, 4 Met. 415.

But any product of the soil, raised annually by labor and cultivation, when ripe, is, for most purposes, personal estate. Planters', &c. *v.* Walker, 3 Sm. & M. 409; Coombs *v.* Jordan, 3 Bland, 312.

Trover lies for trees planted in boxes in a garden. Olive *v.* Vernon, 6 Mod. 170.

The plaintiff, claiming a right to cut *rushes* on a common, cuts five or six loads, which the defendants carry away. Trover lies. Rackham *v.* Jesup, 3 Wils. 332.

In replevin for carrying away grain, the defendant may show that the title is in himself. By the entry of the owner, claiming right, and the severance of the grain, it becomes his chattel, and replevin will not lie by a former occupant. Otherwise, if the grain was sown by the plaintiff, who was in actual possession at the time of such severance. Elliott *v.* Powell, 10 Watts, 453.

Trespass lies upon an exclusive right to dig turf in a certain moss in a waste; or a right to a sole and separate pasture for a time. But not a right in common with others. Wilson *v.* Mackreth, 3 Burr. 1824.

terms of sale; as whether the wood is to stand any time, to be sustained and nourished by the soil.[1] (*a*) But *trees cut*

[1] 1 Hill, Real Pr. 11.

Where A. conveyed to B. a tract of land, with the horses, cattle, and all the crops on the ground, in trust to pay A.'s debts; and, at the date of the deed, there was a corn-crop on the land, which was destroyed by frost, and A., who remained in possession, planted another which was converted by C.; held, that B. could maintain trover, either under the deed or because the crop belonged to him as having been raised upon his land. Black *v.* Eason, 10 Ired. 308.

But the demandant in ejectment, after he has been put in possession, cannot maintain trover for the crops previously severed: his remedy is an action for *mesne profits*. Brothers *v.* Hurdle, 10 Ired. 490.

(*a*) C. conveyed to W. by deed all the timber on C.'s land, "said W. to have five years to get off said timber, and to have no right to the wood which may arise from cutting the timber." C. afterwards conveyed the land to R. "excepting a lease of all the timber thereon given by said C. to W.," and R. conveyed the same land to R., Jr. Held, this conveyance to W. was not a grant of any such interest in the land, as to give him exclusive possession thereof; that W.'s right of entry to cut and carry away the timber was terminated at the end of five years; and that R. Jr., without previous entry, might maintain trespass against W.'s assigns, for cutting and carrying away, timber after the expiration of five years. Reed *v.* Merrifield, 10 Met. 155.

The grantor of land reserved to himself and his heirs "all the saw-mill timber on the land standing or being, or which may hereafter stand or be, on the said land or any part thereof." Held, the grantor and his assignees had only a right to the saw-mill timber then on the land, or to such trees as might thereafter become fit for saw-mill timber, when they became fit, but that they had no right to prevent the grantee of the land from cutting down pine saplings, though these might, if left undisturbed, have become saw-mill timber at some future time. Robinson *v.* Gee, 4 Iredell, 186.

Held, also, that, if the person claiming under such reservation of saw-mill timber had been injured by the grantee's cutting down such timber, his proper remedy was by an action of trespass *quare clausum*. Ibid.

Where a son, at the suggestion and by the agency of his father, who was insolvent, purchased and gave his notes for a lot of land, with timber growing theron; and, by an agreement between the father and son, the father was to cut off and sell the timber, to pay for the labor and other charges out of the proceeds, and to appropriate the balance towards payment of the notes given for the purchase-money, and to pay any remaining surplus to the son; it was held, that trees cut, and lumber sawed, under this agreement, were the property of the son, who might maintain trespass against

down become personal property, and do not pass by a deed of the land; neither has the purchaser constructive possession of them as bailee, or agent for the owner, or any special property in them, which will maintain trespass against a party who unlawfully removes them.[1] So timber-trees, cut for sale by the tenant for life of the land, become the personal property of the remainder-man, and he may maintain replevin for them.[2]

12. Similar questions arise, in relation to movable property casually found upon land. Thus sea-weed, thrown upon the sea-shore, belongs to the owner of the shore.[3] So wreck, as against all the world but the former owner.[4] And where wood and timber floats in the water covering a man's land, he has the exclusive right to seize it, and retain it till reclaimed by the owner in reasonable time.[5] So trover lies to recover *flotsam* wrongfully taken after it comes to land.[6] But it is held that the owner of land upon which property is stranded cannot appropriate it to his own use, though he may cast it back into the stream, after the owner has been notified and neglected to remove it.[7] And the lessor of a farm, lying on the bank of a river, cannot bring replevin for drift-wood taken from the river and piled up on the farm by the lessee; having no property therein.[8]

13. *Mines* constitute another species of property of peculiar character. And the same general presumption of ownership applies to them, as to buildings, trees, and other property *above* the surface of the ground. In trespass for digging and carrying away lead ore from the lands of the United States, they are not entitled to recover as damages

[1] Brock *v.* Smith, 14 Ark. 431.
[2] Richardson *v.* York, 2 Shep. 216.
[3] Phillips *v.* Rhodes, 7 Met. 323. See Hill *v.* Lord, Law Rep. Sept. 1860, p. 287; Maine.
[4] Barker *v.* Bates, 13 Pick. 255.
[5] Rogers *v.* Judel, 5 Verm. 223.
[6] Lady Wyndham's case, 2 Mod. 294.
[7] Foster *v.* Juniata, &c. 16 Penn. 393.
[8] Dyer *v.* Haley, 29 Maine, 277.

---

an officer for attaching the same as the property of the father, and recover damages to the full value of the property at the time of the trespass. Mitchell *v.* Stetson, 7 Cush. 435.

the value of the ore after it is dug; the injury done the soil is the gist of the action, and ore extracted must be considered in aggravation of damages.[1] But an action may be maintained for an injury to the mine alone. Thus, in *copyhold* lands, although the *property* in mines be in the lord, the *possession* of them is in the tenant. The latter, therefore, may maintain trespass against the owner of an adjoining colliery, for breaking and entering the subsoil and taking coal therein, although no trespass be committed on the surface.[2] So, in case of a mortgage of leasehold coal mines and barges, &c.; if the mortgagor afterwards demises the mines, and assigns the barges, the mortgagee may bring trover against one who tortiously seizes and sells the barges and part of the produce of the mines.[3] So trespass (and not case) will lie, for encroaching on a lead-mine, though the plaintiff has no property in the soil above the mine, but only a liberty of digging.[4] (*a*)

[1] United States *v.* Magoon, 3 McLean, 171.

[2] Lewis *v.* Branthwaite, 2 B. & Ad. 437.

[3] Fraser *v.* Swanzea, &c. 3 Nev. & M. 391.

[4] Harker *v.* Birkbeck, 1 W. Bl. 482; 3 Burr. 1556.

(*a*) The question of title, depending upon use or abandonment, has sometimes been applied to a mine. Thus in trespass for breaking and entering a close and digging coals; the plea was, that the close was part of fee-farm lands of R., that the mines under those lands were granted, &c., and the defendant derived title under that grant. Replication, that no right of entry accrued within twenty years of the trespass, and issue thereon. It appeared that the grantees had dug, within twenty years, under other fee-farm lands in R., but not under the plaintiff's; and that the plaintiff or his predecessors had not dug. Held, the defendants were not barred. Hodgkinson *v.* Fletcher, 3 Doug. 31.

A., being seised of the manor of F., and of the demesne lands thereof, and of all coal mines therein in fee, grants to B. part of the lands in fee, excepting and reserving to himself, his heirs and assigns, all tithes of corn arising therefrom, and also excepting and always reserving, out of the said grant, to himself and his heirs, all the coals in the lands so granted, together with free liberty for himself, his heirs, and his and their assigns and servants, from time to time and all times thereafter during the time that he and his heirs should continue owners of the demesne lands of F., to sink and dig pits, or otherwise to sough and get coals in the said lands, and to sell and

14. When the surface of land belongs to one man and the minerals to another, no evidence appearing to regulate or qualify their rights, the latter cannot remove the minerals, without leaving support sufficient to maintain the surface in its natural state. The owner of the surface close, while unincumbered by buildings and in its natural state, is entitled to have it supported by the subjacent mineral strata; and, if the surface subsides and is injured by their removal, though conducted without negligence and according to custom, he may maintain an action.[1] Thus a lease of alum mines gave the lessee the right to obtain alum from certain coal wastes. A subsequent lease of the coal mines provided, that nothing thereby granted shall injure the rights of the parties holding the alum mines. The alum

[1] Humphries v. Brogden, 1 Eng. L. & Eq. 241.

---

carry away the same with carts and carriages, or otherwise to dispose of the same coals at his and their will and pleasure, he and his heirs from time to time giving and paying to the grantee, his heirs and assigns, such satisfaction for damage, which the grantee and his heirs should sustain by reason of getting and carrying away the said coals in the said lands, as two gentlemen, neighbors, indifferently chosen by the grantor and grantee, their heirs and assigns, should from time to time award. An heir of the grantor having aliened the manor and demesne lands of F. and the coals therein, in fee, to C., the latter entered the lands granted to B., and dug pits and carried away coals therefrom; and, trespass being brought against him and his servants, held, on demurrer, 1. That under the general exception and reservation contained in the grant to B., the coals remained in A. and his heirs, and would pass to his or their assigns under the word "heirs;" and 2d. That the special liberty as to the manner of taking the coals was not restrictive, but in furtherance of the previous exception of the coals out of the grant, and would enure for the benefit of C., as owner by purchase of the manor and demesne lands of F. Lord Cardigan v. Armitage, 3 Dowl. & Ry. 414.

If the owner of land grants the subsoil, reserving the surface, the grantee may maintain an action against him for digging holes in the subsoil to a greater extent than is necessary for the use and cultivation of the surface; and, on the other hand, is liable to the owner of the surface for so carrying on his mining or subterraneous operations as to interfere with the fair use of the surface. Cox v. Glue, 12 Jur. 185; 5 C. B. 551; Wilkinson v. Proud, 11 M. & W. 33; Rowbotham v. Wilson, 8 Ell. & Bl. 142.

existed in the coal wastes. The lessees of the coal could not thoroughly work it, without removing the pillars which supported the roof; but this would render it impossible to reach the alum. Held, the coal pillars could not be removed.[1] But a grantee of land, not granted expressly for building purposes, has no right, except by express grant or prescription, to a necessary support for buildings; and can maintain no action against the owner of the subsoil, by whose mining operations, in connection with the weight of such buildings, the land is made to sink.[2] Otherwise, if the land would have fallen without the buildings. In such case, the party may recover for the injury to both buildings and land.[3]

15. *Pews* constitute another subject of peculiar ownership. It is held in England, that an action at common law will not lie for disturbing another in the possession of a pew, unless annexed to a house in the parish;[4] because the plaintiff has not the exclusive possession, the possession of the church being in the parson.[5] So possession alone for above sixty years is not a sufficient title to maintain an action upon the case, even against a wrongdoer; but the plaintiff must prove a prescriptive right, or a *faculty*, and should claim it in his declaration as appurtenant to a messuage in the parish.[6] This rule, however, proceeds upon the ground, that a pew, in England, is a *franchise*, depending either on a grant from the ordinary or on prescription: but a pew in a church or meeting-house is, in the United States, generally, though not uniformly, deemed real estate.[7] Hence trespass *quare clausum* lies for violation of the right of possession of pews.[8] So a tenant in common of a meeting-house may maintain trespass for an injury to a pew, against one having no title either in the pew or house.[9] So, where a meeting-house was conveyed to trustees *to be used*

[1] Earl, &c. *v.* Hurlet, 8 Eng. L. & Eq. 13.
[2] Bonomi *v.* Backhouse, 33 Law T. R. 333.
[3] Brown *v.* Robins, 4 H. & N. 191.
[4] Mainwaring *v.* Giles, 5 B. & Ald. 356.
[5] Stocks *v.* Booth, 1 T. R. 430.
[6] Ibid. 428.
[7] 1 Hill, Real Pr. 4. See Voorhees *v.* The Presbyterian, &c. 11 Barb. 103; The Minister, &c. 16 Ib. 237.
[8] Jackson *v.* Rounseville, 5 Met. 127.
[9] Murray *v.* Cargill, 32 Maine, 517.

for public worship only, and the deeds of pews referred to this conveyance; it was held that a pew-owner had the exclusive right to his pew at all times, and might use any means to shut out others, which would not annoy other pew-owners.[1]

16. As has been already suggested, the separation of erections or structures, from the land of which they have made a part, presents peculiar questions of ownership. Thus the severance of a part of the freehold changes that part from realty to personalty, but does not divest the owner of his property or right to immediate possession; which will sustain an action of trover or detinue, and, if the taking be wrongful, of replevin.[2] So grass severed from the freehold becomes personal property, and, in an action on the case for its destruction by a fire set upon the prairie, the plaintiff is not required to show title to the land on which it was cut.[3] So one who has built *a bridge*, for public use, on the soil of, and under license from another, may maintain trespass *de bonis asportatis* against a wrong-doer who pulls down part of it, and takes away the materials. For, when severed from the bridge, the property in the materials reverts to the original owner.[4] So, where the defendant distrained fixtures, and some days afterwards severed and removed them for sale; held, in trover, that, though for the purposes of that action the plaintiff necessarily treated the fixtures as goods and chattels, the defendant, by whose wrongful act they had been brought into a chattel state, could not say that as goods and chattels he had a right to distrain them.[5]

17. In the same connection, we may refer very briefly to the title by *accession;* being, in general terms, the right to all which is produced by, or becomes either naturally or artificially united with, one's real or personal property; as, for instance, fruits, the young of animals, and new articles

[1] Jackson *v.* Rounseville, 5 Met. 127.
[2] Hail *v.* Reed, 15 B. Mon. 479.
[3] Johnson *v.* Barber, 5 Gilm. 425.
[4] Harrison *v.* Parker, 2 J. P. Smith, 262.
[5] Dalton *v.* Whitten, 3 Gale & Dav. 260.

manufactured from old materials. As already explained in reference to erections upon land, one man may sometimes gain a title to the property of another upon the principle of accession, even if he took it wilfully, as a trespasser, and not through mere ignorance or mistake. But, with this and perhaps some analogous exceptions, the general rule undoubtedly is, that whatever alteration of form property may have undergone, the owner may claim it, if he can prove the identity of the materials; at all events, if such materials are susceptible of being restored to their original form. And somewhat similar to the title by *accession*, is the case of *confusion* or intermixing of goods belonging to different owners. Upon this subject the general rule is, that, if done by consent, such owners become tenants in common; if otherwise, the whole belongs to the innocent owner; unless the goods can be easily distinguished and separated, like distinct articles of furniture, for example; in which case no change of ownership takes place. So it is held, that if corn or flour, mixed together, be of equal value, the owners share equally.[1] And, on the other hand, the *fraudulent* mixing by one person of his own goods with the goods of another, in such a manner that the property of each can no longer be distinguished, constitutes a confusion of goods, if the goods mixed are of unequal value; but the innocent party is entitled to the whole, and may maintain trover for them even against a *bonâ fide* purchaser.[2] Thus, in illustration of these various principles, a party may maintain a replevin for boards, made from trees wrongfully cut on his land.[3] So, where a workman agreed to make the plaintiff a desk out of boards furnished by him, and, while it was in the process of manufacture, with some materials wrought into it which were found by the workman, it was attached as his property; held, the plaintiff might maintain tres-

[1] Bro. Abr. *Property*, pl. 23; Poph. 38, pl. 2; Ward *v.* Eyre, 2 Bulst. 323; Colwill *v.* Reeves, 2 Camp. 575; Hart *v.* Ten Eyck, 2 Johns. Ch. 108; Betts *v.* Church, 5 Johns. 348; Brackenridge *v.* Holland, 2 Blackf. 377; Huff *v.* Earl, 3 Ind. 306.

[2] Hesseltine *v.* Stockwell, 30 Maine, 237; Bryant *v.* Ware, Ib. 295.

[3] Davis *v.* Easley, 13 Ill. 192.

pass against the officer.[1] So a person, who without license enters on land of the United States, cuts down timber, and converts it into cord wood, acquires no title to the wood by the doctrine of *accession*.[2] (*a*) So, where the wheat of the plaintiff was mixed with that of the defendant, by being put into a common bin with the consent of both parties, and the defendant afterwards sold the whole; held, that the intermixture created a tenancy in common between them, and that the sale by the defendant rendered him liable to the plaintiff in trover.[3] So the mere taking by one man of the mill logs of another, and mixing them with his own, will not constitute *confusion* of goods; but, if he fraudulently takes the logs, and manufactures them into boards, and intermixes these boards with a pile of his own, so that they cannot be distinguished, with the fraudulent intent of thereby depriving the plaintiff of his property; the owner of the logs thus taken may maintain replevin for the whole pile of boards.[4] (*b*)

[1] Stevens *v.* Briggs, 5 Pick. 177.
[2] Brock *v.* Smith, 14 Ark. 431.
[3] Nowlen *v.* Colt, 6 Hill, 461.
[4] Wingate *v.* Smith, 7 Shep. 287.

(*a*) But where the defendant, without license, felled trees on land belonging to the United States, and cut them up into cord wood; and subsequently the land was sold by the United States to the plaintiff, who forbid the defendant's removing the wood; and the defendant entered upon the land and removed the wood, and the plaintiff brought an action of trespass against him; held, this action could not be sustained to the extent of recovering damages for the wood, but the plaintiff was entitled to nominal damages for breaking and entering his close. 14 Ark. 431.

(*b*) With regard to the rights of *creditors* in case of confusion of goods, if the goods of a stranger are in the possession of a debtor, and so mixed with those of the debtor that the officer, on due inquiry, cannot distinguish them, the owner can maintain no action against the officer for taking them, until notice and a demand of his goods, and a refusal or delay of the officer to redeliver them. Bond *v.* Wood, 7 Mass. 123.

If the hirer of chattels for an indefinite time put them with his own, for the purpose of using them to greater advantage, they being of such a nature as to be easily distinguished and separated at any time; and, while thus in his possession, the whole are attached, taken away, and sold as his property; the general owner may maintain trespass against the officer for them. Sib-

18. Another article of property of a peculiar description consists of *animals*. We shall hereafter (*a*) have occasion to consider the liability of the owner or keeper of animals for any injuries committed *by* them. The nature of *property in animals*, involving the right of action for injuries done *to* them, has never been better explained, than by the great English commentator, who upon this, as upon many other subjects, states the principles derived from the codes of the natural, the civil, and the common law, with a conciseness and perspicuity rarely equalled by any other elementary writer. "With regard to *animals*, which have in themselves a principle and power of motion, and (unless particularly confined) can convey themselves from one part of the world to another, there is a great difference made with respect to their several classes. — They are distinguished into such as are *domitæ*, and such as are *feræ naturæ;* some being of a *tame*, and others of a *wild* disposition. In such as are of a nature tame and domestic, (as horses, kine, sheep, poultry, and the like,) a man may have as absolute a property as in any inanimate beings; because these continue perpetually in his occupation, and will not stray from his house or person, unless by accident or fraudulent enticement, in either of which cases the owner does not lose his property. — The stealing, or forcible abduction, of such property as this, is also felony; for these are things of intrinsic value, serving for the food of man, or else for the uses of husbandry. But in animals *feræ naturæ* a man can have no absolute property. (*b*) — Other animals, that are not of a

---

ley *v.* Brown, 3 Shep. 185. Upon the general subject of *accession* and *confusion*, more particularly with reference to the measure and amount of damages in *trover*, see Betts *v.* Lee, 5 Johns. 348; Curtis *v.* Groat, 6 Ib. 468; Babcock *v.* Gill, 10 Ib. 287; Brown *v.* Sax, 7 Cow. 95; Baker *v.* Wheeler, 8 Wend. 505; Pierce *v.* Schenk, 3 Hill, 28; Green *v.* Farmer, 4 Burr. 2214; Dresser, &c. Co. *v.* Waterston, 3 Met. 9; Wingate *v.* Smith, 20 Maine, 287; Benjamin *v.* Benjamin, 15 Conn. 347; Martin *v.* Porter, 5 M. & W. 302; Wood *v.* Morewood, 3 Qu. B. 440, n.; Riddle *v.* Driver, 12 Ala. 591.

(*a*) See *Nuisance*, chap. 19.

(*b*) "A man may have property in some things which are of so base a

tame and domestic nature, are either not the objects of property at all, or else fall under another division, namely, that of *qualified*, *limited*, or *special* property." — "A qualified property may subsist in animals *feræ naturæ per industriam hominis*, by a man's *reclaiming* and making them tame by art, industry, and education; or by so confining them within his own immediate power, that they cannot escape and use their natural liberty. Our law apprehends the most obvious distinctions to be, between such animals as we generally see tame, and such as are therefore seldom, if ever, found wandering at large, which it calls *domitæ naturæ*, and such creatures as are usually found at liberty. Such are deer in a park, doves in a dove-house, and fish in a private pond or in tanks. These are no longer the property of a man, than while they continue in his keeping or actual possession; unless they have *animum revertendi*, which is only to be known by their usual custom of returning." — "But if a deer, or any wild animal reclaimed, hath a collar or other mark put upon him, and goes and returns at his pleasure; or if a wild swan is taken, and marked, and turned loose in the river, the owner's property in him still continues, but otherwise, if the deer has been long absent without returning, or the swan leaves the neighborhood." "A qualified property may also subsist with relation to animals *feræ naturæ, ratione impotentiæ*. As when hawks, herons, or other birds build in my trees, and have young ones there, I have a qualified property in those young ones, till such time as they can fly, or run away, and then my property expires."[1]

19. In conformity with these principles, for an injury to a *dog* an action may be maintained, even without showing that he had pecuniary value.[2] And trover lies for a dog, which was lost, and which the defendant refuses to deliver,

[1] 2 Bl. Comm. 389-394.

[2] Parker *v.* Mise, 27 Ala. 480. See State *v.* M'Duffie, 34 N. H. 523; Wheatly *v.* Harris, 4 Sneed, 468; M'Cowis *v.* Singleton, 2 Rep. Con. Ct. 244.

nature that no felony can be committed of them, as of a blood-hound or mastiff." 12 H. 8, 3; 18 H. 8, 2; 7 Co. 18 a.

unless paid for his keeping.[1] So a statutory provision, that any person may kill any dog being without a collar, is no defence to an action for converting such dog to the defendant's own use.[2] Upon the same principle, trespass lies for breaking a man's close, and there hunting and carrying away his *conies;* for, although conies are *feræ naturæ*, yet, while they are on a man's soil, he has a property in them *ratione loci.*[3] And firing at wild fowl, to kill and make profit of them, by one who was at the time in a boat on a public river or open creek, where the tide ebbs and flows, so near to an ancient decoy, or preserve and resort for the taking of wild fowl, on the shore (about two hundred yards) as to make the birds there take flight, the defendant having before fired at a greater distance from the decoy, which brought out some of the birds from thence; though he did not fire into the decoy-pond;—is evidence of a wilful disturbance of and damage to the decoy, for which an action on the case is maintainable by the owner.[4] And trover lies for *wild geese*, which have been tamed, and have strayed away, but without regaining their natural liberty.[5] But where a declaration stated, that the plaintiff was possessed of a close of land with trees growing thereon, to which *rooks* had been used to resort and settle, and build nests and rear their young in the trees, by reason whereof the plaintiff had been used to kill and take the rooks and the young thereof, and great profit, &c., had accrued to him; yet that the defendant, wrongfully and maliciously intending to injure the plaintiff, and alarm and drive away the rooks, and to cause them to forsake the trees, caused guns to be discharged near the plaintiff's close, and thereby disturbed and drove away the rooks, whereby the plaintiff was prevented from killing the rooks and taking the young; held, on motion in arrest of judgment, that this action was not maintainable, inasmuch as rooks were a species of birds *feræ naturæ*, destructive in their habits, not

[1] Binstead *v.* Buck, 2 W. Black. 1117.

[2] Cummings *v.* Perham, 1 Met. 555.

[3] Sutton *v.* Moody, 5 Mod. 375.

[4] Carrington *v.* Taylor, 11 E. 571; Chit. Gen. Prac. 188; Keeble *v.* Hickeringhall, 3 Salk. 10.

[5] Amory *v.* Flynn, 10 Johns. 102.

known as an article of food, or alleged so to be, and not protected by any act of parliament, and the plaintiff could not therefore have any property in them, or show any right to have them resort to his trees.[1]

19 *a*. But one may acquire title to a wild animal, even as against another party on whose land it is taken. Thus, the plaintiff's dogs having hunted and caught, on the defendant's land, a hare, started on the land of another, the property is thereby vested in the plaintiff, who may maintain trespass against the defendant for afterwards taking away the hare. And so it would be, though the hare, being quite spent, had been caught up by a laborer of the defendant for the benefit of the hunters.[2] Bees, which take up their abode in a tree, belong to the owner of the soil, if unreclaimed; but, if reclaimed and identified, to their former owner.[3] And merely finding a tree on another's land, which contains a swarm of bees, and marking it, does not give the finder a title to the bees.[4]

20. It will be seen hereafter, (*a*) that the form of action for injuries done by animals depends upon the nature of the injury; case being the form for the mere keeping of an injurious animal, and trespass for directly inciting it to do mischief, or in some instances for its direct invasion of property. A similar distinction applies, where an animal is itself injured. (*b*) Thus, where a dog is set upon horses, one of which is killed in jumping out of the field; trespass is the appropriate remedy.[5] So for killing cattle by shooting and chasing them from their range, trespass is the proper remedy.

[1] Hannam *v*. Mockett, 2 B. & C. 934.
[2] Churchward *v*. Studdy, 14 E. 249.
[3] Goff *v*. Kitts, 15 Wend. 550.
[4] Gillet *v*. Mason, 7 Johns. 16.
[5] Painter *v*. Baker, 16 Ill. 103.

(*a*) See *Nuisance*.

(*b*) With regard to the pleadings in actions of this nature, it is held that a declaration for an injury to *cattle* is not supported by evidence of injury to *mules*. Brown *v*. Bailey, 4 Ala. 413.

A declaration in trespass, for shooting and killing a mare, should use the words *wilful and malicious*, or others equivalent. Ridge *v*. Featherstone, 15 Ark. 159.

If they die of starvation in consequence of being driven from their range, case.[1] So trespass is the proper remedy, where a dog is killed by a direct administration of poison, as where the poison is thrown down to the dog mixed up with food; but, when the defendant puts the poisoned food where he knows the dog will pass along and get it, case.[2] So, if a man place dangerous traps, baited with flesh, in his own ground, so near to a highway, or to the premises of another, that dogs passing along the highway, or kept in his neighbor's premises, must probably be attracted by their instinct into the traps; and in consequence of such act his neighbor's dogs be so attracted, and thereby injured; an action on the case lies.[3]

21. Questions in relation to animals, — as well for injuries done *by*, as *to* them, which may therefore be considered together, — often arise from their being *at large*, (*a*) and thereby committing trespasses, for which they are *distrained*, *impounded*, or otherwise interfered with, by private individuals or public officers. The rights and liabilities, however, connected with this part of the subject, depend very much upon local law and express statutes, relating to fences, field-drivers, public pounds, and replevin. (*b*) In general, it

[1] M'Coy *v.* Phillips, 4 Rich. 463.
[2] Dodson *v.* Mock, 4 Dev. & Batt. 146.
[3] Townsend *v.* Wathen, 9 E. 277.

(*a*) In construction of the familiar phrases in reference to this subject, *at large*, and *keeper*; it is held that cattle are liable to be impounded, as "going at large in the highways, and not under the care of a keeper," if not under the efficient control of such keeper; although they are intrusted to a servant, with other cattle, to be driven to pasture, and have only left the drove a mile before reaching it, and turned into a different road, which also leads to the pasture, over which they have sometimes been driven; and there remain feeding; and the servant returns in less than an hour to the place where they escaped. Bruce *v.* White, 4 Gray, 345.

One who finds cattle at large, without a keeper, and drives them along the highway till he finds a field-driver, is not himself a keeper. Ibid.

A turnpike is a public highway, within the meaning of a statute, which requires field-drivers to take up and impound cattle going at large in the public highway. Pickard *v.* Howe, 12 Met. 198.

(*b*) See *Replevin*.

is held, that the owner of animals, in allowing them to be at large, takes all the risk of their loss, or of injury to them by unavoidable accidents.[1] So, independently of express statutory requirement, it is not the duty of a landowner to fence against animals *feræ naturæ*, but the owner of such animals must keep them at his peril, and is liable for damage done by them on another's land, whether fenced or not.[2] Thus, it is held, that, at common law, the owner of a close is not obliged to fence against the cattle of the occupant of an adjoining close; and that a statute, imposing the duty on adjoining proprietors of land to erect and maintain fences, recognizes the same principle; for the object and design of fencing is not to keep the cattle of others off the premises, but to keep at home the cattle of the occupant. And the principle is held to have equal application to the owners of land adjoining public highways. So, where no obligation is imposed by statute, covenant, or prescription, a railroad company are held not bound to fence their land.[3] (*a*) So, where

[1] Kerwhacker *v.* C. C. & C. R. R. Co. 3 Ohio, (N. S.) 172; Wright *v.* Wright, 21 Conn. 329.

[2] Canefox *v.* Crenshaw, 24 Mis. 199.

[3] Hurd *v.* Rutland, &c. 25 Verm. 116.

(*a*) But in New York the qualified doctrine is held, that, at common law, where the cattle of one of two adjoining proprietors are found trespassing upon the land of the other, the owner of the cattle, to excuse himself, must show not only that the portion of the fence which the other proprietor was bound to repair was out of repair, but also that the cattle passed over such defective portion; and that the act of 1838, (Stat. p. 253,) in New York, has not changed the rule. Accordingly, in a case where it appeared that both portions of a boundary fence, which had been divided, were out of repair, and it was not shown over what part the cattle passed; it was held, that the party suffering damage by the cattle of the other was entitled to recover. Deyo *v.* Stewart, 4 Denio, 101.

Sect. 44 of the article of the Rev. Sts., relating to "division and other fences," constitutes a statutory bar to every action brought to recover damages for injuries done by cattle entering through a defective fence, which the party complaining is bound to maintain, in any town where the electors have prescribed what shall be a sufficient fence. Hardenburgh *v.* Lockwood, 25 Barb. 9.

In Maryland, in a county where there is no act of the legislature regulating partition fences, the principles of the common law will prevail; that

cattle enter upon a railroad from the highway, at a place where the railroad crosses the highway, such entry is a trespass, notwithstanding the provisions of the Revised Statutes of New York respecting fences and cattle, and the regulations of the town, under the statutes, requiring fences of a particular kind, and allowing cattle to run at large on the highways, and notwithstanding there is no obstacle to prevent the entry of cattle from the highway upon the railroad.[1] So cattle are not *lawfully* upon an adjoining close, within the meaning of a statute using this term, unless they are there by the consent of the owner of the land, or of some one having an interest in it, although the land may have been unfenced, and they may have passed upon it directly from the highway, where they were permitted to go at large by a vote of the town. And, in such case, although the owner of the land adjoining the highway could not maintain trespass on account of the cattle coming upon his premises, yet he could remove them, and guard against their ingress, and the owner would have no cause of complaint. And where cattle, allowed to go at large upon the highway, pass from it over the unfenced lands of two other persons, and from thence upon the land of the plaintiff, which was likewise unfenced; he can maintain trespass therefor against their owner, as he was not bound by law to fence against them.[2] So the owner of improved land may use all lawful means to enforce his right to exclusive possession, although

[1] Tonawanda Railroad Co. *v.* Munger, 5 Denio, 255.

[2] Lord *v.* Wormwood, 29 Maine, 282.

---

the tenant of a close is not obliged to fence against an adjoining close, unless by force of prescription, but he is bound at his peril to keep his cattle on his own close. Richardson *v.* Milburn, 11 Md. 340.

So, in a late English case, trespass was brought for driving the plaintiff's sheep, and leaving them in a highway, by which they were injured. Plea, that they were wrongfully in the defendant's close, depasturing, wherefore the defendant drove them into an adjoining highway. Replication, that they escaped into the close from an adjoining close of the plaintiff, through a defect in the fence, which the defendant was bound to repair. Held, the replication answered the plea. Carruthers *v.* Hollis, 8 Ad. & Ell. 113.

the land may not be surrounded by a legal fence. Thus, if cattle trespass upon such land, he may drive them off by setting a dog upon them with ordinary care and prudence, in reference to the size and character of the dog, or the manner of setting him upon the cattle and afterwards pursuing them.[1] And it is not indispensable to the right of a land-owner to impound cattle, which are doing damage in his enclosure, that the fence adjoining the highway, over which the cattle entered, should have been legally sufficient for a fence between enclosures not upon the highway.[2] And even an act, providing that "no person shall recover for damages done upon lands by beasts, unless in cases where, by the by-laws of the township, such beasts are prohibited from running at large, except where such lands are inclosed by a fence," &c., does not change the common law, nor require individuals to fence their lands, but only precludes recovery of damages in case they are not fenced; nor does this statute apply to such lands as are not usually fenced, such as rail-road tracks, which cannot be entirely fenced.[3] (*a*)

22. The *distraining* or *impounding* of animals, either going at large on the highway or trespassing upon private lands, as

[1] Clark *v.* Adams, 18 Verm. 425.
[2] Davis *v.* Campbell, 23 Verm. 236.
[3] Williams *v.* Michigan, &c. 2 Mich. 259.

(*a*) But, in Connecticut, the owner or occupier of land is obliged to fence it against cattle, at his own risk, and, if his land is not fenced, he can neither recover damages, nor impound, for a trespass by cattle. Wright *v.* Wright, 21 Conn. 329.

So, by the Revised Statutes of Maine, sheep escaping from the land of their owner, into contiguous land of another owner, cannot be impounded for doing damage, if no division had been made of the partition fence. Webber *v.* Closson, 35 Maine, 26.

So in Massachusetts, in an action on the case, for rescuing sheep distrained for going at large, not under the care of a keeper, on the common and undivided lands of the island of Nantucket, it is no defence, that the place where the sheep were taken, and the place where they were rescued, were uninclosed lands, held in severalty; that, between the taking and the rescue, the sheep were continuously on the lands; and that the defendants were the proprietors of such lands, and the owners of the sheep rescued. Field *v.* Coleman, 5 Cush. 267.

already suggested, is for the most part regulated by statutes, which, in the different States, with a general resemblance, vary in their specific provisions. It is the general rule of the common law, that property *in actual use* cannot be distrained. But the following case was held not to fall within this principle. Trespass for taking the plaintiff's dog. Plea, distress damage feasant in a close. Replication, that the dog, when taken, was in the actual possession of the plaintiff's son and servant, B., and then under the personal care of, and being used by B. Held, the replication did not show such user of the dog as exempted it from seizure.[1]

23. Cattle cannot be impounded for a mere nominal trespass. Hence, if the appraisers find that no damage was done, replevin lies.[2] So a party impounding cattle must show a full and entire compliance with the requisitions of the statute, or he becomes a trespasser *ab initio*.[3] And the action of replevin, usually given by the statute to one whose beasts are unlawfully distrained or impounded, does not exclude all other remedies at common law; but trespass will still lie.[4] (*a*) But trespass does not lie against a *pound-keeper*, merely for receiving cattle tortiously taken; for he is bound to keep whatever is brought to him. Otherwise, if

[1] Bunch *v.* Kennington, 1 Ad. & Ell. N. S. 679.

[2] Osgood *v.* Green, 33 N. H. 318.

[3] Fitzwater *v.* Stout, 16 Penn. 22; orse *v.* Reed, 28 Maine, 481.

[4] Coffin *v.* Field, 7 Cush. 355.

(*a*) There is no relation of *debtor and creditor* created by law between the impounder of animals and the pound-keeper, in relation to the expense of keeping and feeding the animals; and, in the absence of any express contract that the impounder will pay such expense, the pound-keeper has no remedy against him therefor. Williams *v.* Willard, 23 Verm. 369.

And, if the animals be impounded without authority of law, so that the impounder committed a trespass, it will not enable the pound-keeper to recover of the impounder such expense, in an action upon book account. Ibid.

Where a person takes an estray to keep for the owner, but neglects to pursue the course prescribed by law, he is not liable in trover, unless he uses the estray, or refuses to deliver it upon demand. Nelson *v.* Merriam, 4 Pick. 249.

he goes beyond his duty and assents to the trespass.[1] So a pound-keeper, who receives and impounds beasts for going at large, and refuses to deliver them to the owner, on demand, unless his fees and those of the field-driver are paid, is not liable therefor in an action of replevin.[2] Nor does replevin lie, merely upon the ground that the cattle were not suitably provided for, or were ill-treated, in the pound.[3] So an action on the case cannot be maintained, for detaining cattle distrained damage feasant, where a tender of amends was made after they had been impounded.[4] But the owner of beasts impounded does not waive the right to maintain trespass against the field-drivers for irregularities or omissions, by paying the fees of the field-drivers and pound-keeper; nor by declaring to a third person after the commencement of the action, that he should require the defendants to prove, that the place where they took the beasts was a public highway.[5]

24. A town *pound*, *ex vi termini*, is an enclosed piece of land, secured by a firm structure of stone, or of posts and timber placed in the ground.[6] And pound-keepers, under statutes relative to impounding, have no authority to confine cattle taken *damage feasant* in any other place, as, for instance, in the pound-keeper's own yard, there being no public pound.[7] So a pound-keeper, by taking beasts from the pound and driving them elsewhere to feed, for his own convenience, loses his custody of them, and the owner may take them away and maintain replevin for them if retaken.[8] But where the defendant, a field-driver, took up the plaintiff's horse going at large, and seasonably drove him to the pound-keeper's house, and there left him in the barn, directing the keeper's wife to tell him, on his return, to put the horse in the pound, which he did, but the next day put the

[1] Badkin *v.* Powell, 2 Cowp. 476; Mellen *v.* Moody, 23 Verm. 674.
[2] Folger *v.* Hinckley, 5 Cush. 263.
[3] Pickard *v.* Howe, 12 Met. 198.
[4] Sheriff *v.* James, 8 Moore, 334; 1 Bing. 341.
[5] Coffin *v.* Field, 7 Cush. 355.
Wooley *v.* Groton, 2 Ib. 305.
Collins *v.* Larkin, 1 R. I. 219.
[8] Bills *v.* Kinson, 1 Fost. 448.

horse back in the barn, without the knowledge of the defendant; held, replevin did not lie.[1]

25. In regard to *the time* within which an owner of cattle must assert his claim for an unlawful impounding, a statute, which requires that the owner of beasts impounded shall replevy or redeem them within forty-eight hours after he shall receive notice of the impounding, must be construed as determining that limit, if the damages can be so soon ascertained; if not then, as soon as they are ascertained. And, if they are not ascertained within the forty-eight hours, but subsequently, and a certificate of their amount is furnished to the pound-keeper, the owner of the beasts cannot sustain replevin against the pound-keeper, until he has first paid the damages and all fees and costs.[2] But where a statute provided, that, where appraisers are appointed to determine the amount due from the owner of an impounded beast for damages, &c., which is not forthwith paid, the person impounding may cause the beast to be sold by auction, first posting up a notice of the sale twenty-four hours beforehand; and a beast impounded was sold twenty minutes before the expiration of twenty-four hours from the time when the appraisement was completed, although more than twenty-four hours from the time of posting up the advertisement; held, the sale was invalid, and the field-driver a trespasser *ab initio*, whether any actual injury had been sustained by the owner or not.[3]

26. In regard to the *notice* required by law in case of impounding, it is held that actual knowledge, by the owner of beasts impounded, of the impounding thereof, is not equivalent to the written notice required by the statute.[4] So, if the statute requires, that the notice contain "a description of the beasts, and a statement of the time, place, and cause of impounding;" a notice, given by a field-driver to the owner of beasts impounded for going at large in the highway, which states that the beasts "were running at large, and were

[1] Byron v. Crippen, 4 Gray, 312.
[2] Mellen v. Moody, 23 Verm. 674.
[3] Smith v. Gates, 21 Pick. 55.
[4] Coffin v. Field, 7 Cush. 355.

trespassing upon the premises of other individuals," does not state a sufficient cause of impounding.[1] But the field-driver's name may be signed by another person, if done at the field-driver's request.[2] So the notice need not state the hour of the day when the beasts were impounded. And proof that notice was left in the hands of one of the owner's family, at his dwelling-house, is sufficient to authorize a jury to find that it was left at his place of abode.[3] And a notice given by a field-driver to the owner of cattle, that they are impounded for going at large on the public highway, is *primâ facie* evidence that they were so at large, and puts on the owner the burden of proving the contrary.[4] So the field-driver may show, not only that he gave the plaintiff the personal notice required by law, but also that he *posted* notices, according to the provisions of the statute, applicable where there is no party entitled to personal notice.[5] Where the owner of cattle impounded commences an action of replevin against the field-driver, within twenty-four hours after they are impounded, he waives the statutory notice. And, if a writ to replevy the cattle is filled up within twenty-four hours after they are impounded, with the intent of the plaintiff at all events to have it served, whether the defendant shall give notice within twenty-four hours or not; the action is commenced when the writ is so filled up, although it is not served, nor given to an officer for service, and no replevin bond is executed, until after the expiration of twenty-four hours from the time of the impounding.[6] (*a*)

[1] Sanderson *v.* Lawrence, 2 Gray, 178.
[2] Pickard *v.* Howe, 12 Met. 198.
[3] Ib.
[4] Pickard *v.* Howe, 12 Met. 198; Bruce *v.* Holden, 21 Pick. 187.
[5] Pickard *v.* Howe, 12 Met. 198.
[6] Field *v.* Jacobs, 12 Met. 118.

(*a*) In Massachusetts it was formerly held, that, where a field-driver impounds beasts for being at large, it is his duty to leave with the pound-keeper a memorandum or certificate of the cause of impounding, and of his fees and expenses. Bruce *v.* Holden, 21 Pick. 187.

But it is otherwise under the Revised Statutes. Pickard *v.* Howe, 12 Met. 198.

The former rule, however, still prevails, in reference to the impounding of cattle trespassing upon private lands. Thus the defendant took up beasts doing damage on his land, and impounded them in his own enclosure for several hours, and then drove them towards the town-pound, and delivered them, in the highway near the pound, to the pound-keeper, (who was also a field-driver,) as cattle taken doing damage, but did not leave with the pound-keeper a written memorandum, as required by Massachusetts Rev. Sts. ch. 113, § 6, stating the cause of impounding and the sum that he demanded for the damage done. The pound-keeper put the beasts into the pound, and gave the owner the notice, required to be given by field-drivers when they impound beasts taken up for going at large contrary to law. Held, that the defendant was a trespasser *ab initio.* Sherman *v.* Braman, 13 Met. 407.

In Maine, the certificate left with the pound-keeper must state the town in which the impounder resides, and also the town in which the enclosure, wherein the damage was alleged to have been done, was situated; and the advertisements should state the time of impounding. Morse *v.* Reed, 28 Maine, 481.

CHAPTER XVIII.

TORTS TO PROPERTY.—POSSESSION.

1. UNDERLYING the entire superstructure of property in general, which was considered in the last chapter, and indeed constituting the original foundation of all property, and therefore for the most part an essential incident to the class of wrongs which we are about to consider, is the elementary fact of *possession;* which therefore, in its connection with torts, requires to be very distinctly explained.

2. That possession, so far as wrongs are concerned, is vitally involved in the idea of property, appears from the very classification of wrongs, already referred to, (p. 2,) into wrongs to things in *possession* and to things in action. Thus it is said,[1] "Property in chattels personal, may be either in *possession;* which is where a man hath not only the right to enjoy, but hath the actual enjoyment of, the thing: or else it is in *action;* where a man hath only a bare right, without any occupation or enjoyment. And

[1] 2 Bl. Com. 389.

of these the former or property in *possession*, is divided into two sorts, an absolute and a qualified property." The same writer remarks:[1] "Actual possession is, *primâ facie*, evidence of a legal title in the possessor; and it may, by length of time, and negligence of him who hath the right, by degrees ripen into a perfect and indefeasible title. And, at all events, without such actual possession no title can be completely good."

3. It will be seen, of course, that *the nature* of possession depends much upon the nature of the subject of it; as in case of real and personal property, generally; and, more especially, that possession of an easement, for example, does not require possession of the corporeal property to which such easement appertains, but only a present right of enjoying the easement. So it will be seen, that possession involves very different rights and liabilities as between the possessor and a mere stranger or wrongdoer, and as between such possessor and one having the right of property, present or future, in the same subject-matter. (*a*)

4. With these preliminary explanations, we proceed to consider the subject of *possession*, as affecting torts or wrongs to property.

5. It is the general rule — applicable alike to real and personal property (*b*) — that possession is both sufficient and necessary to maintain an action for a tort or wrong; more especially that "bare possession gives a right as

[1] 2 Bl. Com. 196.

(*a*) See *Reversion*, *Landlord*, *Action on the Case*, *Waste*, *Nuisance*.

(*b*) The only distinction between real and personal property in reference to this particular point is thus expressed: "The immediate right to real property must be vested in one person only; whereas a special property, in the case of personalty, may be in one, as in the instance of carriers, while the absolute right to it may exist in another. When a competition arises between those two persons, the right of the latter must prevail; but, as against all other persons, a special property is sufficient." Per Ld. Kenyon, Webb *v.* Fox, 7 T. R. 396.

against a wrongdoer, for the invasion whereof an action of *trespass* will lie."[1] (a)

6. Thus it is held, that he who is in actual possession of land, whether he have a title or not, may maintain trespass against any other person except the real owner or him who has the right of possession.[2] More especially if the plaintiff's possession is *peaceable and exclusive.*[3] So one in possession of land at the time of an injury to it may maintain trespass for the injury, though out of possession at the time of suit brought.[4] So it is held that a prior possession of land, accompanied with acts of ownership, *by one through whom the plaintiff deduces title*, will authorize a recovery against a defendant, who is afterwards found in possession, without title or claim to the premises.[5] And resumption of possession, by the rightful owner, will not defeat the prior wrongful possessor's action of trespass against a stran-

[1] Per Ashurst, J., Smith *v.* Milles, 1 T. R. 475; Outcalt *v.* Durling, 1 Dutch. 443; Crawford *v.* Waterson, 5 Florida, 472; Todd *v.* Jackson, 2 Dutch. 525; Gourdier *v.* Cormack, 2 E. D. Smith, 200; Chambers *v.* Donaldson, 11 E. 66; Branch *v.* Doane, 18 Conn. 233.

[2] Brown *v.* Manter, 2 Fost. 468; Inhabitants, &c. *v.* Thacher, 3 Met. 239; Johnson *v.* McIvain, 1 Rice, 368; Hamilton *v.* Marquis, &c. 3 Ridg. 267. See Murldrow *v.* Jones, 1 Rice, 64; 1 Pike, 448.

[3] Palmer *v.* Aldridge, 16 Barb. 131.

[4] Smith *v.* Ingram, 7 Ired. 175.

[5] Cox *v.* Davis, 17 Ala. 714.

(a) The general rule is sometimes expressed in the qualified form, that, to maintain *trespass*, either in case of real or personal property, the plainiff must show in himself either actual or constructive possession, or the immediate right of possession, at the time of the tortious entry or taking. Otherwise the remedy of the owner is *case* or *trover*. Davis *v.* Young, 20 Ala. 151; Brown *v.* Thomas, 26 Mis. 335; Heath *v.* West, 8 Fost. 101; Halligan *v.* Chicago, &c. 15 Ill. 558; Hoyt *v.* Gelston, 13 Johns. 141, 561; Dunham *v.* Stuyvesant, 11 Johns. 569.

In New York a declaration in *replevin* must allege that the goods and chattels replevied were *the property* of the plaintiff. It is not sufficient for the plaintiff to say that they were taken by the defendant out of his *possession*, and that he was entitled to the possession of them. Bond *v.* Mitchell, 3 Barb. 304. (See *Replevin.*)

An action upon the case cannot be maintained by one who has the legal title and right of possession to land, against a person who enters upon such land, cuts timber, and commits other trespasses. Robertson *v.* Rodes, 13 B. Mon. 325.

ger.[1] And the identity of the close and possession may be established, by any person who knows the lines and corners, or who can prove the plaintiff's possession.[2] So, where both parties rely merely on a possessory title, a contract by one to purchase the land of the owner is admissible in evidence, for the purpose of showing the character of the possession.[3] (*a*)

[1] Cutts *v.* Spring, 15 Mass. 235.
[2] Leadbetter *v.* Fitzgerald, 1 Pike, 448.
[3] Moore *v.* Moore, 8 Shep. 350.

(*a*) In an action of trespass *qu. cl.*, the plaintiff must make out affirmatively, the burden of proof being upon him, where a monument named in his title-deed stands, and that it includes the place which defendant entered upon. Robinson *v.* White, 42 Maine, 209.

An acknowledgment in writing of the demandant's title, made by the tenant in a writ of entry, is sufficient evidence of such title to be submitted to the jury, in a subsequent action of trespass brought by the demandant against the tenant for an entry on the land. Kellenberger *v.* Sturtevant, 7 Cush. 465.

So where the defendant entered under the plaintiff's title, as a purchaser in fee, he is not compelled to go beyond the source from which both the plaintiff and himself derive title, but he may produce evidence of any independent title, if he can do so. Hill *v.* Robertson, 1 Strobh. 1.

So the verdict in one action of trespass is evidence, in another between the same parties, of the plaintiff's possession at that time; and his possession will be presumed to continue, unless the contrary appear. Stean *v.* Anderson, 4 Harr. 309.

A lease, including part of the premises in dispute, from the plaintiff's devisor to the defendant, which had expired several years before the suit was commenced, was held to be such an admission of the plaintiff's title, as at least to throw upon the defendant the burden of showing a paramount title. Gourdin *v.* Davis, 2 Rich. 481.

In an action of tort for breaking and entering a close, under an answer setting up the defendant's possession for more than twenty years previously, and also soil and freehold in the defendant, the defendant may give in evidence admissions of his title by the plaintiff and those under whom the plaintiff claims. Gilbert *v.* Felton, 5 Gray, 406.

Where, in an action of trespass for cutting trees, the plaintiff, without introducing any paper title, proved, by the oral testimony of two witnesses, that the land on which the trespass was committed belonged to him, and the testimony was not objected to at the time; it was held, that the defendant had no right afterwards to ask the Court to instruct the jury, that the title

6 *a*. Upon the same principle, possession of personal property under a general bailment is sufficient to maintain trover against a stranger. Where, therefore, the owner of furniture let it in writing to the plaintiff on hire, and he placed it in a house occupied by the wife of a person who had become bankrupt, and it was seized by order of the assignees; held, the plaintiff might recover in trover, without producing the agreement.[1]

6 *b*. And, in case of actual possession, the right of property is held immaterial. (*a*) Or an allegation of property is

[1] Burton *v*. Hughes, 9 Moore, 334.

---

to the land was not sufficiently proved, on account of the want of documentary evidence. Clay *v*. Boyer, 5 Gilm. 506.

The relative bearing of possession and property upon the rights of the parties may be modified by the *pleadings*. Thus, to a declaration in trespass, charging that the defendant broke and entered the plaintiff's workshop while the plaintiff was inhabiting and present in it, and, while the plaintiff was so inhabiting and present, pulled it down; the defendant pleaded, that the workshop was the defendant's, and not the plaintiff's. Held, that, on issues joined upon these averments, it was immaterial whether the plaintiff was or was not inhabiting and present at the time of the alleged trespass; and that the defendant was entitled to the verdict, upon proof that he had a right to the soil. Burling *v*. Read, 11 Ad. & Ell. N. S. 904.

So, on the trial of the issue of property in the plaintiff, it is not necessary for him to prove that the defendant took the property out of his possession. Kerley *v*. Hume, 3 Monr. 181.

Where the evidence shows conclusively that the title to the property claimed is in the plaintiff, it is error to submit the question of title to the jury. Fullam *v*. Cummings, 16 Verm. 697.

(*a*) The ancient legal maxims upon the subject still maintain their original authority:—"*In pari causa possessor potior haberi debet.*" "*Pro rei possessore in dubio est pronuntiandum.*"

It has been sometimes held, that *trover* is founded exclusively on the right of *property*. Hastler *v*. Skull, 1 Tayl. 152.

Or, at least, cannot be maintained without a property in the plaintiff, either general or special. Hotchkiss *v*. M'Vickar, 12 Johns. 403; Sheldon *v*. Soper, 14 Ib. 352; Glaze *v*. M'Million, 7 Port. 279; Taylor *v*. Howall, 4 Blackf. 317; Barton *v*. Dunning, 6 Ib. 209; Grady *v*. Newby, Ib. 442.

Or a right of property and of possession. Redman *v*. Gould, 7 Blackf.

proved by possession, more especially if coupled with a qualified interest.[1] Hence, where, to a declaration for

[1] Outcalt *v.* Darling, 1 Dutch. 443.

361; Danley *v.* Rector, 5 Eng. 211; Kemp *v.* Thompson, 17 Ala. 9; Purdy *v.* M'Cullough, 3 Barr, 466.

And the distinction has been made, that, though in trespass the defendant cannot show property or a paramount title in a stranger, it is otherwise in trover. Cook *v.* Howard, 13 Johns. 276.

And that he might prove it even by the admission of the plaintiff. Glenn *v.* Garrison, 2 Harr. 1.

The rule, however, may now be considered as well settled, that, in both these forms of action alike, possession is in general sufficient and necessary as against a stranger or wrongdoer. In other words, possession constitutes or proves property, until a better title is shown. See 2 Greenl. Ev. § 637; Mount *v.* Cubberly, 4 Harr. 124; Barwick *v.* Barwick, 11 Ired. 80; Knapp *v.* Winchester, 11 Verm. 351; Fairbanks *v.* Phelps, 22 Pick. 535; Allen *v.* Smith, 10 Mass. 308; Ames *v.* Palmer, 42 Maine, 197.

Thus a declaration in trover, not alleging possession by the plaintiff as of his own property, is held bad even after verdict. Sevier *v.* Holliday, 1 Hemp. 160.

Whether a mere *servant* can maintain any action for injury to property in his possession, will be considered hereafter. See *Master*, &c. See also Story on Bailm. § 93, g. h. i.; King *v.* Dunn, 21 Wend. 253.

But a consignee, receiving goods merely for transshipment, has a sufficient interest to maintain trover. Fitzhugh *v.* Weiman, 5 Seld. 559.

And a general *bailee*, without hire, may maintain trover for property taken from his possession, against all persons but the rightful owner. Faulkner *v.* Brown, 13 Wend. 63; White *v.* Bascom, 2 Wms. 268.

And, on the other hand, such action does not lie in favor of the bailor. Thus, where a horse, hired for a given time, is levied on, before the expiration of the time, and sold under an execution against the bailee; the general owner cannot maintain trover against the sheriff, either before or after the determination of the bailment. Caldwell *v.* Cowan, 9 Yerg. 262.

It is held, however, that, to maintain trover by virtue of a special property, one must have an absolute vested interest. Tuthill *v.* Wheeler, 6 Barb. 362.

Case may be maintained where trover might not lie, for want of possession. Thus the plaintiff, the owner of a factory and the machinery in it, gave a bond to S., conditioned to convey them to S., when certain negotiable notes, given as the consideration, should be paid; and that S. should have possession so long as he continued to pay the notes as they became due, and no longer. Possession was delivered immediately, pursuant to the

breaking and entering the plaintiff's close, the defendant pleaded, 1st, not guilty; 2d, that the close was not the close

---

bond. Before the first note became due, the machinery was attached as S.'s property, and removed from the factory by the officer, who before the removal had full notice of the plaintiff's title, and the machinery was afterwards sold on execution. The plaintiff then brought an action against the officer, in which the declaration contained counts in trover and case. Held, case might be maintained, and the measure of damages was the value of the machinery as it stood in the factory before its removal. It was doubted whether trover could be supported, although it *seems* that, if S. himself had removed and sold the machinery, trover would lie against the vendee. Ayer *v.* Bartlett, 9 Pick. 156.

In an action on the case by a bailor, against one who commits a trespass on the property; the plaintiff is entitled to at least nominal damages, though no actual injury is done. White *v.* Griffin, 4 Jones, Law, 139.

The general owner has a constructive possession, as against his bailee or tenant, who, having a special property, has violated his trust by destroying that which was confided to him. 2 Greenl. Ev. § 615.

And it has been recently held, that, if the bailee of a chattel, who has no authority, as against the bailor, to retain or dispose of it, mortgage it as a security for his own debt, and the mortgagee take possession under the mortgage; the bailor may maintain an action of trespass therefor against him. Stanly *v.* Gaylord, 1 Cush. 536.

Either in trover or trespass against a stranger, one having a special property may recover the whole value, holding the balance beyond his own interest in trust for the general owner; but, if the suit be against the latter, he is entitled to a deduction of the value of his interest. King *v.* Dunn, 21 Wend. 253.

With regard to the relative nature of the two actions, trespass and trover, it may be further remarked, that, where damages are given in trespass for the value of goods destroyed or lost, the verdict and recovery may be pleaded in bar to an action of trover for the same trespass or conversion. Sanders *v.* Egerton, 2 Brev. 45.

As already explained, the term *possession* may bear a peculiar meaning, when applied to mere incorporeal rights or qualified privileges. A few examples, however, may illustrate the application of the general principle stated in the text to this kind of property.

In a possessory action for an injury to an *easement*, the plaintiff need not set out his title, unless the defendant appears to be tenant of the land. But, if he offers to do it, and sets out an insufficient title, it will be bad. Dorney *v.* Cashford, 1 Ld. Raym. 266.

Where A. grants liberty, license, power, and authority to B. and his

of the plaintiff; 3d, that the close was the soil and freehold of the defendant; held, that evidence of possession was

---

heirs to build a bridge on his land, and B. covenants to build the bridge, for public use, and to repair it, and not to demand toll; the property in the materials of the bridge, when built and dedicated to the public, still continues in B., subject to the right of passage by the public; and, when severed and taken away by a wrongdoer, he may maintain trespass for the asportation. Harrison *v.* Parker, 6 E. 154.

So the contractors for making a navigable canal, having, with the permission of the owner of the soil, erected a dam of earth and wood upon his close, across a stream there, for the purpose of completing their work, have a possession sufficient to entitle them to maintain trespass against a wrongdoer. Dyson *v.* Collick, 5 B. & Ald. 600.

So one who has contracted with the owner of a close for the purchase of a growing crop of grass there, for the purpose of being mown and made into hay by the vendee, has such an exclusive possession of the close, though for a limited purpose, that he may maintain trespass *quare clausum* against any person entering the close and taking the grass, even with the assent of the owner. Crosby *v.* Wadsworth, 6 E. 602.

So it is not necessary, in order to maintain an action for the destruction of stacks of grain and hay by reason of a fire set by the defendant, that the plaintiff should be the owner of the freehold where such stacks were standing. Armstrong *v.* Cooley, 5 Gilm. 509.

So, where the owner of land rented it to another to raise a crop of corn thereon; and, before the crop was gathered, the owner sold it, and the purchaser turned a number of hogs into the field; held, this was a trespass on his part. Rodgers *v.* Lathrop, 1 Smith, 347.

But it is held, that, though an action of trespass *quare clausum* may be sustained upon a *temporary* interest in the plaintiff, it must be an *entire* or *exclusive* interest. Thus a right of ingress and egress in an outgoing tenant, after the determination of his lease, for the purpose of gathering and taking away the growing crops, will not enable him to maintain trespass against the succeeding tenant; who has a right to seed down the field on which such crop stands before it comes to maturity. Dorsey *v.* Eagle, 7 Gill & John. 321.

And, on the other hand, in the case of carrying on a farm *at the halves*, the owner of the farm is not so far divested of the possession, that he may not maintain trespass in his own name for any injury to the inheritance. As to the growing crops, in which the parties have a joint interest, they should join in the action. But, where the tenant in such case disclaimed all occupancy of a portion of the land, in reference to which a controversy existed between the owner of the land and a third person, and refused to

sufficient to entitle the plaintiff to a verdict on the second plea.[1] So, where the declaration, in an action of trespass, or

[1] Heath v. Milward, 2 Bing. N. R. 98.

---

take possession of it, it was held, that the owner of the land might sue in his own name for an injury to the crops upon such portion. Cutting v. Cox, 19 Verm. 517.

So the lessor of a farm, who stipulates that the crops, &c. shall be consumed on the farm, and remain his property till the performance of certain acts, may maintain trespass, if they are removed in violation of the stipulation. Gray v. Stevens, 2 Wms. 1. See Blake v. Dow, 18 Ill. 261.

In trover for ore brought by lessees of a *mine*, it is sufficient, under a plea of "not possessed," to show occupation of the mine, without proving title in their lessor. Taylor v. Parry, 1 Man. & Gran. 604.

So, in an action on the case for disturbance of *common*, it is not necessary for the declaration to state title to the common; but only that the plaintiff was possessed of a tenement, &c., and had a right of common in the place where, &c. Strode v. Byrt, 4 Mod. 418.

But where one is seized in fee of a close, upon which certain burgesses have a right, during a portion of the year, to depasture their cattle, and have, during that period, exclusive possession of the close; he may maintain an action of trespass against a party who, during that period, commits a trespass in the subsoil by digging holes; though not against one who merely rides over the close. Cox v. Glue, 5 Com. B. 533.

A party claiming ownership in a field granted to the plaintiff a parol license to search therein for minerals. The plaintiff, acting under this license, dug pits in the field and threw up sand and gravel, mixed with ore, which the defendant took away, professing to act under the authority of a third party. Before the defendant took away the sand, gravel, and ore, the party who gave the plaintiff the parol license granted him a similar license by deed. Held, the plaintiff was entitled to maintain trover for the sand, &c. Northam v. Bowden, 32 Eng. L. & Eq. 559.

It will be seen hereafter, — see *Watercourse, Mill*, chap. 20, — that one of the most important incorporeal rights known to the law is that of a *watercourse*. But, notwithstanding the peculiar nature of this privilege, which ordinarily makes an injury done to it a proper subject of an *action on the case*, which is not a possessory action; the general rule stated in the text is still held to be applicable.

Actual possession, under claim of title, is sufficient to sustain an action on the case for diverting water from a mill, or for overflowing land; and therefore evidence, showing that the plaintiff had no title to the land on which the mill was situated, is inadmissible. Bromer v. Merrill, 2 Chandl. 46. Kimbrall v. Walker, 7 Rich. 422.

trespass on the case, for an injury to land, alleges that the plaintiff was well seized and possessed of the land, as a good indefeasible estate in fee-simple; it is sufficient on the trial for the plaintiff to show a lawful possession at the time

---

So the right of a person to the enjoyment of a water privilege, of which he is in the quiet use or possession, cannot be questioned, by one who shows no adverse claim. Howard *v.* Ingersoll, 17 Ala. 780.

So, where one has acquired a right to flow the water from his mill through the land of another, temporarily, by his mere license or permission, and entered upon the exercise of the right; he may maintain an action against another for obstructing his right. Case *v.* Weber, 2 Cart. 108.

So an action to recover damages for diverting water from land must be brought by the person in possession. Rathbone *v.* McConnell, 20 Barb. 311.

So, though a statute authorize the building of dams in navigable streams by the "owners" of adjoining lands; in an action for an injury to the plaintiff's mill, by the backing of the water, by means of a dam of an inferior proprietor, the declaration need not aver that the plaintiff was an "owner of adjoining lands;" but an averment that he was "lawfully possessed of the mill and water-power" is sufficient, and even more than sufficient, as possession is all that can be required. Bigler *v.* Antes, 21 Penn. 288.

But although, in an action for flowing land by a party in possession, his title cannot be disputed for the purpose of defeating the action; for the purpose of ascertaining the amount of injury, the nature and character of the plaintiff's interest may be inquired into. Bassett *v.* Salisbury, &c. 8 Fost. 438.

In accordance with another distinct branch of the general rule upon this subject, (§ 12,) in an action on the case for diverting water from a mill, it is not sufficient for the defendant to show an outstanding right in some third person, to take the water for the use of the premises occupied by the defendant, paramount to the plaintiff's right to the water, without showing title from such third person to himself. Rogers *v.* Bancroft, 20 Verm. 250.

But it is held, that a plaintiff cannot recover for injury done his land by the erection of a milldam, where paramount title is shown in another by his own evidence. Morris *v.* M'Carney, 9 Geo. 160.

And, in an action on the case for diverting a watercourse from the lands of the plaintiff, his possession is sufficiently alleged by an averment, that at the time of the commission of the wrongs he was "seized in his demesne as of fee;" seizin in law being sufficient, and the diversion being an injury both to the freehold and the possession. Hart *v.* Evans, 8 Barr, 13.

when the injury complained of was committed. And a judgment for the plaintiff in such a case, upon the general issue, is conclusive evidence between the parties and their privies, only of such title as the plaintiff was bound to prove.[1] And a mere possessory right to personal property, though the title be in another, has been held sufficient to maintain even *an action on the case.* Therefore, if the general issue be pleaded to an action on the case for taking the plaintiff's goods, it will not be sufficient for the defendant to show that the plaintiff had no property in them, if he had possession.[2] And in an action on the case for an injury relating to real estate, against a stranger, the plaintiff need not show title in himself; though it is otherwise where an owner of the soil is the defendant.[3] (*a*) So a tenant at will, in actual possession of the land, may maintain trespass *quare clausum* against a stranger, for cutting and carrying away trees.[4] And mere prior occupancy of land, however recent, and without property, gives a good title to the occupant, whereon he may maintain trespass against all the world, except such as can prove an older and better title in themselves.[5] So, in an action on the case against a wrongdoer, the plaintiff, if in possession, need not set forth whether he has a title by grant or prescription; for that goes to *the right.*[6]

7. The same principle is still further illustrated or extended by the rule, that actual possession, *whether rightfully or wrongfully obtained*, is a sufficient title against a mere stran-

[1] Parker v. Hotchkiss, 25 Conn. 321.
[2] Templeman v. Case, 10 Mod. 25.
[3] Stroud v. Birt, 1 Com. 7.
[4] Hayward v. Sedgley, 2 Shep. 439.
[5] Catteris v. Cowper, 4 Taunt. 547; Walter v. Rumball, 4 Mod. 392.
[6] Hebblethwaite v. Palmes, 3 Mod. 51, 52; S. P. Langford v. Webber, 3 Mod. 132.

(*a*) Although possession, without proof of title, is sufficient to maintain an action, yet, in an action of trespass *quare clausum*, under the general issue of not guilty, the plaintiff is not bound to rely upon the mere fact of possession, but may also prove the legality thereof, and his title to the premises, and so entitle himself to greater damages. Hunter v. Hatton, 4 Gill, 115.

ger or wrongdoer.[1] (a) Thus a possession of lands, as open or exclusive as the nature of the land will admit, operating a disseizin of the true owner, will enable the disseizor to maintain trespass against a mere wrongdoer, even though such possession has continued less than twenty years.[2] So one in possession of glebe land, under a lease void by Stat. 13 Eliz. c. 20, by reason of the rector's non-residence, may yet maintain trespass upon his possession against a wrongdoer.[3] So, in trespass by one claiming title under proprietors of common land, the defendant, who shows no title, cannot defend, on the ground that the plaintiff took no title, by reason of informality in the proceedings of the proprietors in making the grant.[4] So the finder of a jewel, though he does not acquire an absolute property or ownership, may maintain trover therefor against any person, not the rightful owner.[5] And on the other hand it has been held, that, if goods are lost, there can be no possession, upon which there can be a trespass.[6] So, where an execution creditor purchases the goods levied on, though such purchase may be of questionable validity, yet he has, by virtue of the levy and the possession, such a special property in the goods, that he may maintain trover for them.[7] So, where a sheriff, by virtue of an attachment, seized goods, and delivered them to the plaintiff to be taken out of the district and sold; held, though the delivery to the plaintiff was irregular, yet he might maintain trover against a wrongdoer, who took the goods out of his possession.[8] So the title of a deputy sheriff, in personal property seized by him on execution, is sufficient to maintain trespass against a stranger for a tortious dis-

[1] Carter v. Bennett, 4 Florida, 283; Linnard v. Crossland, 10 Tex. 462; Knapp v. Winchester, 11 Verm. 351.

[2] Clancey v. Houdlette, 39 Maine, 451; Moore v. Moore, 8 Shep. 350; Myrick v. Bishop, 1 Hawks, 485; Richardson v. Merrill, 7 Mis. 333; Webb v. Sturtevant, 1 Scam. 181.

[3] Graham v. Peat, 1 E. 244.

[4] Dolloff v. Hardy, 26 Maine, 545.

[5] Armory v. Delamirie, 1 Strange, 505; Clark v. Malory, 3 Harring. 68. See Wyman v. Hurlburt, 12 Ohio, 81.

[6] Wright v. The State, 5 Yerg. 154.

[7] Schermerhorn v. Van Volkenburgh, 11 Johns. 529.

[8] Bank of Kentucky v. Shier, 4 Rich. 233.

(a) See chap. 4.

turbance in his possession of it; notwithstanding his failure to sell the property at the time advertised.[1] So a statute provided, that all pressed hay offered for sale should be branded in a prescribed way, and imposed a penalty upon any person who should offer for sale any bundle not so branded. The plaintiff agreed with the town, which owned certain hay, while it was stored, and before it was pressed, to purchase it, delivered in pressed bundles, at a certain price, the weight to be ascertained after it was pressed; and the town agreed to deliver it when pressed. It was pressed and delivered accordingly, and the price paid by the plaintiff; but the brands were not upon the bundles. Held, the plaintiff's possession was sufficient to enable him to maintain trover for the hay against a wrong-doer.[2] So a suit lies for injuring a mill by obstructing a stream, though the mill-dam is a public nuisance.[3] So, where the plaintiff bought and paid for a ship stranded on the English coast, but the transfer was not regular; and he tried to save her, but she went to pieces; and the defendant possessed himself of parts of the wreck, which drifted on his farm; held, the plaintiff's possession enabled him to recover for them in trover.[4] (*a*)

[1] Gibbs *v.* Chase, 16 Mass. 125.
[2] Bartlett *v.* Hoyt, 9 Fost. 317.
[3] Haller *v.* Pine, 8 Blackf. 175; Simpson *v.* Searey, 8 Greenl. 138.
[4] Sutton *v.* Buck, 2 Taunt. 302.

(*a*) See chapter 4. The same principle applies to a defence as to an action. Thus, if a slave be given to the donee verbally, and possession pass with the gift, though the gift be void by statute, the donor cannot maintain trover therefor against the donee without a previous demand and refusal. Duckworth *v.* Overton, 1 Swan. 381.

So, if the plaintiff in trespass *quare clausum* shows no title, he cannot object that a deed under which the defendant claims title and holds possession is invalid. Brown *v.* Pinkham, 18 Pick. 172.

And this principle more especially applies, where the defendant's interference with the property was in its nature official, and occurred during an interruption of the plaintiff's title.

The vessel of the plaintiff was seized by A., an officer of the customs, under the revenue laws, and was directed by the collector to be detained; and,

8. While possession is *sufficient*, it is also in general *necessary*, to maintain an action for tort. (*a*) Thus, to maintain trespass *quare clausum*, the plaintiff must have either a title or exclusive possession, and there must be no adverse possession in any other person.[1] So, in trespass *de bon. asport.*, the plaintiff must have had, at the time of the trespass, the actual or constructive possession of the goods, or at least a general or special property in them and a right to the immediate possession.[2] And the general owner of goods cannot sustain either trespass or trover, when there is an outstanding possession in another, accompanied with a special property.[3] And one who has never had actual possession of personal property, and is not the general owner, though he may have a special property, cannot maintain replevin or trover against another in the actual custody of the property.[4] So an officer, in whom a right to the custody of chattels is vested by act

[1] Cong. Society *v.* Baker, 15 Verm. 119; Payne *v.* Clark, 20 Conn. 30; Richardson *v.* Milburn, 11 Md. 340; Bedingfield *v.* Onslow, 3 Lev. 209.

[2] Hume *v.* Tufts, 6 Blackf. 136; Cannon *v.* Kinney, 3 Scam. 9; M'Farland *v.* Smith, Walk. 172; Bell *v.* Monahan, Dudley, 38; Dallam *v.* Fitler, 6 W. & S. 323; Edwards *v.* Edwards, 11 Verm. 587; Lunt *v.* Brown, 1 Shep. 236; Freeman *v.* Rankins, 8 Ib. 446; Barron *v.* Cobliegh, 11 N. H. 557; Potter *v.* Washburn, 13 Verm. 558; Hoyt *v.* Van Alstyne, 15 Barb. 568.

[3] Bourne *v.* Merritt, 22 Verm. 429.

[4] Holiday *v.* Lewis, 15 Mis. 403.

---

during the detention, the defendant, another officer interested in the seizure and conusant of the facts, used the vessel with the consent of the plaintiff, for his private purposes, and afterwards restored her to the plaintiff. The vessel was afterwards acquitted in the District Court, and a certificate of probable cause of seizure granted by the Judge, but the plaintiff refused to receive the proceeds of the vessel, which had previously been sold under an order of the Court. In an action of trespass, held that the defendant, not being implicated in the first taking, either as an actor, or standing in such relation to the plaintiff as would make him a party to the seizure, could not be made a trespasser *ab initio;* and that the plaintiff had not, after the seizure, and when the defendant made use of the vessel, the possession of her or a right to reduce her to his actual possession, which was essential to maintain an action of trespass. Van Brunt *v.* Schenck, 11 Johns. 377.

(*a*) The remarks elsewhere made, in various connections, with respect to the action of *trespass on the case*, supply the requisite limitation to this general proposition.

of parliament, has not, in respect of such right merely, such a property in them, as will enable him to maintain an action for the wrongful detention of them. Thus parish officers, or other persons, by whom parish books, &c., are appointed by the inhabitants in vestry assembled to be kept, cannot bring trover against an ex-warden for the books of accounts, assessments, &c., kept by him during the period in which he was in office, and with the possession of which he has never parted.[1] So, where a colonel had purchased horses for government, and, being approved of by the proper inspecting officer, they were sent under the care of a sergeant to the receiving depot for his Majesty's use; held, the colonel had not such a special property, as to maintain trover for one of them, which was taken out of the possession of the sergeant as a distress for a turnpike toll.[2] (*a*) So a party, who let his house ready furnished, cannot maintain trespass against the sheriff for taking the furniture under an execution against the lessee, though notice were given that the goods belonged to the plaintiff; because trespass is founded on a tort done to *the possession*.[3] So in trover by a guardian, if the declaration allege that the property claimed, being in the possession of his ward, was lost, &c., it is bad on demurrer, in not showing that the guardian was entitled to the possession.[4] So the plaintiff, a sheriff, made a levy on personal property of the defendant, and left it in possession of two other per-

[1] Addison *v.* Round, 6 Nev. & M. 422.
[2] Hopkinson *v.* Gibson, 2 J. P. Smith, 202.
[3] Ward *v.* Macauley, 4 T. R. 489.
[4] Dearman *v.* Dearman, 5 Ala. 202.

(*a*) A. B. owed the sum of £4 11*s.* 1½*d.* to the prosecutor, and, the latter having demanded payment, the prisoner said he would settle with him on behalf of A. B. He took out of his pocket a piece of paper, stamped with a sixpenny stamp, and put it on the table, and then took out some silver in his hand. The prosecutor wrote a receipt for the sum mentioned on the stamped paper, and the prisoner took it up and went out of the room. On being asked for the money, he said "it is all right," but never paid it. Held, that this was not a case of larceny, the prosecutor never having had such a possession of the stamped paper as would enable him to maintain trespass. Regina *v.* Smith, 9 Eng. L. & Eq. 532.

sons, taking from them a paper under seal, by which they acknowledged the receipt of the property, agreed to deliver it at a specified time and place, and, on failure thereof, authorized a confession of judgment against them for the amount of the debt and costs in the suit and the cost of the writ. Held, that trespass would not lie for taking away the property before the time for delivery had expired, because until that time the plaintiff was not entitled to possession.[1]

9. But it is to be further distinctly stated, as already suggested, that a person having the title to real estate, without actual possession, but with *a right of immediate possession*, and there being no adverse possession, can maintain trespass.[2] Thus a declaration in trespass for entering and cutting timber on the plaintiff's close need not aver that he was in possession.[3] So trespass lies on behalf of the United States against one cutting and carrying away timber from the public lands.[4] So there can be no adverse possession as against the United States. And, on the sale of lands by the United States, the patent transfers to the purchaser the entire legal estate and seizin, to as full an extent as the government held them.[5]

10. The question sometimes arises, as to the rights and liabilities growing out of a *joint* possession, either in reference to joint owners themselves, or as between a portion of them and third persons. (*a*) Where two parties have a concurrent or mixed possession of land, neither having any other title, nor any exclusive priority of possession, one of them cannot maintain trespass against the other. Thus a town took possession of a tract of uninclosed land to which it had no title, and forbade all persons to take cranberries therefrom, except on terms which were prescribed by the town, and

[1] Lewis *v.* Carsaw, 15 Penn. 31.

[2] Smith *v.* Yell, 3 Eng. 470; Mason *v.* Lewis, 1 Iowa, 494; Davis *v.* Bourg, 20 Ala. 151; Brown *v.* Ware, 25 Maine, 411; 2 Gilm. 652; Payne *v.* Clark, 20 Conn. 30; Dejarnett *v.* Haynes, 23 Miss. 600; Clark *v.* Draper, 19 N. H. 419.

[3] Gray *v.* Cooper, Wright, 500.

[4] Cotton *v.* The United States, 11 How. 229.

[5] Cook *v.* Foster, 2 Gilm. 652.

(*a*) See *Joint Owners, Tenants in Common.*

with which most persons complied for several years. Before the town took possession, H. had claimed a right in the land, although he could not show any title, and had taken cranberries growing thereon, and continued to take them afterwards under a claim of right. Held, that the possession of H. and of the town was mixed or concurrent, and that the town could not maintain trespass against persons who took cranberries from the land under a license from H.[1] So where a precinct, owning a meeting-house, became upon their own application incorporated into a town, after which for thirty-five years the meeting-house and all parochial affairs were under the sole management of the town, but, from some proceedings of the town, such as exempting certain inhabitants from taxes for the support of public worship, it could be inferred that the town acted with reference to the continued existence of the precinct, and as their agent: it was held that the precinct might reorganize themselves; that the meeting-house continued to be their property; and that, while they had the control of it, and the occupation of it for the purposes for which it was built, the use of it for municipal purposes did not give such an exclusive possession, as would enable the town to maintain an action of trespass against any person for pulling down the meeting-house by the authority of the precinct.[2] So, where two persons cultivated a crop of corn, in a field to which each claimed, but neither had a title, and of which neither had the actual possession; and one of them afterwards gathered the corn, piled it in heaps, and left it for a week; held, he did not thereby acquire such an exclusive possession of the corn, as to enable him to maintain an action against the other for removing it.[3]

10 *a*. But it is said, "If there are two persons in a field, each asserting that the field is his, and each doing some act in the assertion of the right of possession, and if the question is, which of those two is in actual possession? I

[1] Inhabitants, &c. *v.* Thacher, 3 Met. 239.

[2] Milford *v.* Godfrey, 1 Pick. 91.

[3] McGahey *v.* Moore, 3 Ired. 35.

answer, the person who has the title is in actual possession, and the other person is a trespasser. They differ in no other respects."[1] And where one is part-owner of personal property, and has the possession and control over it, with power to sell, he may maintain trover in his own name against a wrongdoer who converts it.[2] (*a*)

[1] Per Maule, J., Jones *v.* Chapman, 2 Exch. 821.

[2] Hyde *v.* Noble, 13 N. H. 494.

(*a*) In case against the owners of a steamer for negligence, whereby buildings were fired, the declaration contained three counts; in one of which the plaintiff counted on his own seizin; in the second, on his seizin and possession; and in the third on his possession. The plaintiff having shown title in himself to seven eighths of the property injured, and actual possession of the whole, it was held, that, for the purpose of showing to what damages he was entitled under the third count, he might show that he held the remaining eighth under a valid contract to purchase, and therefore that the admission, as evidence, of a deed of such eighth part, bearing date subsequent to the injury complained of, as it could not prejudice the defendant, was no ground for reversal of the judgment. Schenck *v.* Cuttrell, 1 New Jersey, 5.

Trespass for assault. Plea, that the plaintiff was wrongfully and unlawfully in a certain close of the defendant, Bagge, without, &c., whereupon the said defendant, and the other defendant, as his servant, and by his command, requested the plaintiff to depart, and because, &c., (justifying the assault). Plea, also, that before, &c., eleven members of a certain cricket club, called the Lynn Club, to wit, &c., and eleven members of a certain other cricket club, called the Litcham Club, to wit, &c., were lawfully possessed of a certain close, and were lawfully playing a game of cricket in and upon the said close; that the plaintiff was wrongfully and unlawfully in and upon the said close, and interrupted, &c., the playing, &c., whereupon the defendant, Bagge, in his own right, and by the command and authority of the ten other members of the Lynn Club, and the said eleven members of the Litcham Club, requested the plaintiff to depart out of the said close, and to desist from interrupting the playing of the said game, which the plaintiff refused to do; whereupon the defendant, Bagge, in his own right, and by the command, &c., and the other defendant, as the servant, &c., removed the plaintiff from and out of the said close, &c. Replication, to the first of the above pleas, that the same close was the close and soil of the plaintiff together and along with the said Bagge and the other members of the Lynn Club, as joint tenants thereof, and that the plaintiff was then as such joint tenant possessed, &c., and that the defendant, Bagge,

11. Questions also arise as to the effect of possession of only *a part of the property* upon the title to the whole. And upon this subject the rules are; that proof of an entry into part in the name of the whole is sufficient; as where one, having half entered at the window, was forcibly dragged out:[1] although possession by the owner of part of a tract of land is the possession of the whole tract, only so long as no other person is in the actual adverse possession of any part; and, as soon as another takes possession of any part, either with or without title, the former possessor loses the possession of that part, and cannot maintain trespass for any act done on such part, while he is thus out of possession of it.[2] (*a*) Thus where, in a possessory action, the plaintiff

[1] 3 Stark. Ev. 1193; Bro. Seisin, 20, 23.

[2] Ring *v.* Ring, 4 Dev. & Batt. 164.

had nothing in the said close except as joint tenant with the plaintiff, &c. And as to the other plea, *de injuria.* It appeared at the trial, that, whilst the game was being played between eleven members of the Lynn Club, (the defendant being one,) and eleven members of the Litcham Club, the plaintiff, who was a member of the Lynn Club, but not one of the eleven players, took the place of one of the players, and thereupon a misunderstanding arose, which led to the assault complained of, in the forcible removal of the plaintiff from off the space of ground upon which the match was played, and which was tabooed off for the purposes of the game, and within which only the players were properly at liberty to go. The close in question was occupied, at an annual rent, under an agreement between the owner of the soil and the Lynn Cricket Club, of which the defendant, Bagge, was the president. A verdict was found for the plaintiff. Held, that the agreement established the issue on the first plea, as to the plaintiff's joint possession. Also, that the issue on the other plea was properly found for the plaintiff, the ground of justification being, that the twenty-two members of the Lynn and the Litcham Clubs were possessed of the close, and that the trespass had been committed in the exercise of such right. Holmes *v.* Bagge, 18 Eng. L. & Eq. 406.

(*a*) Upon a similar principle, in trespass *quare clausum*, although it is necessary to prove all the abuttals of the close as laid in the declaration, it is not necessary to show a title to, or possession of, the whole close, but only such part as includes the trespass. Wheeler *v.* Rowell, 7 N. H. 515; Tyson *v.* Shurry, 5 Md. 540.

claimed several parcels of land by purchase at a sale on execution, and the sheriff's deed; held, if the defendant was in possession of any one parcel, the plaintiff might recover all the parcels described in his declaration and the sheriff's deed.[1] And possession of part of a lot of land, with definite boundaries, under a written contract of purchase, not recorded, from one who has no title to the lot, is sufficient to extend, by construction, to the whole lot, so as to enable the occupier to sustain trespass against a stranger to all title, who cuts timber thereon; notwithstanding a provision in the contract, that the purchaser shall not cut timber until he has complied with the conditions of purchase.[2] So, to an action of trespass for cutting down and converting trees, which the defendant justified, upon the ground that they grew upon his soil and freehold, the plaintiff replied, that the trees were his freehold, and not the freehold of the defendant. Held, the replication was proved, by showing that they grew on a certain woody belt, fifteen feet wide, which surrounded the plaintiff's land, but was undivided by any fences from the several closes adjoining, of which it formed a part, belonging to different owners; that from time to time the plaintiff and his ancestors, at their pleasure, cut down for their own use

[1] Corwill *v.* House, 6 Ala. 710. [2] Hunt *v.* Taylor, 22 Verm. 566.

So, where the declaration alleges, that a trespass was committed upon a close described as "Greyhound Forest," the plaintiff need not prove the boundary lines of the whole tract, if he shows himself in possession of a part. Tyson *v.* Shurry, 5 Md. 540.

So if a party at the same time enter upon two or more closes, he may be treated as guilty of but one trespass, and a recovery may be had for the whole injury upon one count. Halligan *v.* Chicago, &c. 15 Ill. 558.

But where the plaintiffs in an action of trespass against B., claiming title to a larger tract of land, which included the *locus in quo*, offered in evidence the record of a judgment in their favor against C. in an action of ejectment for such larger tract, for the purpose of showing an act of ownership by the plaintiffs in relation to the *locus in quo*; it was held that such judgment, being between different parties, and in relation to a different subject-matter, was inadmissible. Southington, &c. *v.* Gridley, 20 Conn. 200.

the trees growing within the belt; that the several owners of the different closes enclosing the belt never felled trees there, though they felled them in other parts of the same closes; and that, when they made sale of their estates, the trees in the belt were never valued by their agents, because they were reputed and considered to belong to the plaintiff and his ancestors, in which the several owners acquiesced.[1] So by his induction a parson is put in possession of a part for the whole, and may maintain an action for a trespass on the glebe land, although he has not taken actual possession of it.[2] So, if a vendor sell goods by sample, to be delivered to the vendee within a month, and take earnest, and within a month send them by his servant to the vendee's premises, and, when part are unloaded, the rest are distrained for toll; the delivery is complete, so that the vendee may bring trespass for the seizure.[3]

12. Possession and the right of possession are of course no less available as a ground of *defence* than as a cause of *action*. Thus, in a plea of justification or excuse for an entry to abate a nuisance, caused by the flowing of certain land by the plaintiff's dam, it is sufficient, if the defendant allege that he was *possessed* of an undivided moiety of such land, without stating his title. The possession thus alleged must be taken to be lawful, and it seems he would have the right to abate, although his possession was only for a term.[4] So in trespass for taking cattle damage feasant, if the defendant justify under a lease, it is sufficient for him to say that he was possessed of the place where, &c., without stating a particular title.[5] So a sale was made of a wagon, upon condition that the vendee should take it and use it, and, whenever he paid the purchase-money, it should become his property, but, if he did not pay for it, he should pay for the use of it; and it was accordingly delivered to him. Held, he became a lessee, with the right of possession until the wagon

[1] Stanley v. White, 14 E. 332.

[2] Bulwer v. Bulwer, 2 B. & Ald. 470.

[3] Blakey v. Dimsdale, 6 Mod. 162, n.

[4] Great Falls Co. v. Worster, 15 N. H. 412.

[5] Searl v. Bunnien, 2 Mod. 70.

or the purchase-money should be demanded; and consequently the owner could not, before such demand, maintain trover against an officer, who had attached and sold the wagon on execution as the property of the vendee.[1] (*a*) So, in an action of trespass *quare clausum*, a plea that the close was the close and soil of the defendant is not a plea of *liberum tenementum;* and the defendant has only to prove right of possession.[2]

12 *a*. And any title, whether freehold or possessory, in the defendant, may be given in evidence, if such title shows that the right of possession was in the defendant, or not in the plaintiff.[3] Thus it is a general rule, in actions of trespass to try title, that the plaintiff must recover on the strength of his own title, and not on the insufficiency of the defendant's.[4] So the defendant may, under the plea of the general issue, give in evidence *liberum tenementum*, or the right of possession in himself or those under whom he claims; if the right be general, and exclusive of any superior claim of the plaintiff as to the whole, or the same part, of the premises; and not confined to a particular purpose, such as the enjoyment of an incorporeal hereditament.[5] (*b*) So a tenant of land, claiming title, and having a possession which gives him a lawful right to "betterments," is not liable as a trespasser *quare clausum*, for acts done by him on and to the

[1] Fairbank *v.* Phelps, 22 Pick. 535.

[2] Millison *v.* Holmes, 1 Cart. 45; 1 Smith, 55.

[3] Floyd *v.* Ricks, 14 Ark. 286.

[4] Hughes *v.* Lane, 6 Tex. 289.

[5] Ferris *v.* Brown, 3 Barb. 105; Sage *v.* Keezecker, 1 Morris, 338; Millison *v.* Holmes, 1 Smith, 55.

(*a*) The vendor having subsequently to the sale demanded payment, but accepted a part-payment; held, he thereby impliedly waived any further payment at the time, and confirmed the sale subject to the condition. 22 Pick. 535.

(*b*) Thus the defence, that the *locus* is a public highway, raises a question of title, which cannot be tried before a justice. Randall *v.* Crandall, 6 Hill, 342.

But the question of actual possession is not one of *title*, within the meaning of a statute using that term; and a justice of the peace may therefore determine it. Ehle *v.* Quackenboss, 6 Hill, 537.

land, during the time of the possession by which his right to betterments became matured.[1] So, in a leading case relating to *fixtures*, (see chap. 17,) to trespass for breaking and entering, &c., and pulling down and taking away certain buildings, &c.; the defendant, as to the breaking and entering, suffered judgment by default, and pleaded *not guilty* as to the rest. Held, such plea was sustained, by showing that the building taken away, which was of wood, was erected by him, as tenant of the premises, on a foundation of brick, for the purpose of carrying on his trade, and that he still continued in possession of the premises at the time when, &c., though the term was then expired.[2]

12 *b*. Upon the same principle, where to an action of trespass the defendant pleaded, that the *locus in quo* belonged to the United States, and that one of the defendants had, long before the commission of the supposed trespasses, and at the time thereof, a "claim title" to said land, and had built a dwelling-house thereon, and was then and there the owner thereof, and, as such, he and the other defendants, as his servants, entered said land as they lawfully might, and removed said dwelling-house, &c.; the plea was held insufficient, as it did not allege possession in the defendant at the time of the plaintiff's entry.[3] (*a*)

[1] Paine *v.* Morr, 35 Maine, 181.
[2] Penton *v.* Robart, 2 E. 88.
[3] Ross *v.* Nesbit, 2 Gilm. 252.

(*a*) Trespass for an assault. The defendants justified, in defence of the possession of the dwelling-house of one W., and by his command. New assignment, that the trespass was committed out of the dwelling-house, "to wit, in and upon a certain bridge in a certain farm, called 'Bengrove Farm,' and in divers, to wit, two gardens, two fields, and two folds of and in the same farm, and for another and different purpose." Plea to the new assignment, that W. was possessed of the dwelling-house, and also of the yards, fields, and folds which belonged to the dwelling-house, and were adjacent thereto; and that the trespasses newly assigned were committed in defence of the said possession, by removing the plaintiff; and that the defendants "did then take the plaintiff by the nearest and most direct way to a certain public highway near to the said dwelling-house, &c., as they lawfully might for the

12 *c*. In general, in an action of trespass to land, the defendant can justify, on the ground that he entered as *the servant* of one in whom are the title and right of possession.[1] (*a*)

[1] Everett *v*. Smith, Busb. 303.

---

cause aforesaid." Upon demurrer to the replication, it was objected that this plea did not justify taking the plaintiff to the highway, as it did not show that it was necessary to do so, or that the highway adjoined the dwelling-house, &c. Held, that the plea was good, as it intended to confess trespasses committed on the bridge, yards, fields, and folds, and to justify them as committed in defence of the possession; that with these the removal to the highway had no necessary connection, and might be treated as surplusage. To the above plea the plaintiff replied, stating the seizin of W. in Bengrove Farm, and a demise of it to one J. as tenant from year to year; that J. thereupon became possessed, and, being indebted to one B., by indenture granted to him all the growing and other crops then or thereafter on the farm, as security for the principal and interest, and gave B. a power, (on default in payment,) peaceably to take them into his possession; that default was made; that the fields, &c. were parcel of the farm demised to J.; that at the same time, &c., W. was possessed thereof, and there were growing crops therein, belonging at the time of the execution of the indenture and afterwards to J.; that during the continuance of the term, and while J. was in possession, and before W. became possessed, the plaintiff, as B.'s servant, entered and took possession, and continued in possession of the said growing crops until W. became possessed of the farm, &c., the same being a reasonable time; and that he was removed before the lapse of a reasonable time, and although he produced the indenture, and gave the defendants notice of the purpose for which he remained in possession. Held, that, as the replication stood upon the right of a person, claiming under a tenant from year to year, to remain on the premises, and retain possession of the crops after the landlord had resumed possession, it should have stated how the tenancy came to an end; that there was no presumption as to a determination by the landlord rather than by the tenant; nor, supposing that B. was entitled to the crops after his interest as tenant in the premises had determined, that they were ripe or fit for harvesting, or that they needed any cultivation, for which the plaintiff's continuing in possession was necessary. Hayling *v*. Oakey, 18 Eng. L. & Eq. 532.

And the general principle was laid down, that a party who insists upon remaining on the land of another against his will, and therefore *primâ facie* against right, ought to show all the circumstances which makes such possession lawful, and abridge the general rights of property. Ibid.

(*a*) The owner of a sleigh conveyed it in mortgage to A., and afterwards

But a plea of *license* will not be sustained by proof of a lease.[1] So in trespass by the United States, a permit to enter upon the lands, which contained lead ore, may be admitted in evidence to show the nature and object of the entry.[2] (*a*) So possession may be *by* or *through*, as well as *under*, another trespass *quare clausum*. Thus, upon a plea that the defendant was seized in his demesne as a fee of a messuage, &c., in the parish, and that he and all those whose estate, &c., have a right of way for himself, his and their farmers and tenants, occupiers of the messuage, &c., over the *locus in quo*, to and from the messuage, &c., as appertaining thereto; and a replication, that the defendant, &c., have not the said way as appertaining, &c.; held, that the defendant's showing that he was seized in fee of an ancient messuage in the parish, to which a right of way, as pleaded, over the *locus in quo* belonged, was sufficient to support his plea, although the messuage was let to, and in the occupation of a tenant, and the defendant only occupied a newly-built house in the parish at the time of the trespass. Also, that a plea that the defendant was seized in his demesne as of fee, &c., was good, without alleging that the defendant was occupier.[3]

13. On the other hand, *the want or absence of possession* may sometimes be set up as a defence; possession being the foundation of the alleged liability upon which the action is founded. Thus the defendant resided with his father upon

[1] Johnson *v.* Carter, 16 Mass. 443.
[2] U. S. *v.* Geer, 3 McLean, 571.
[3] Stott *v.* Stott, 16 E. 343.

---

delivered it in pledge to the plaintiff. The defendant, by authority and direction of A., took possession of the sleigh; and the plaintiff brings an action of trespass against him. Held, such mortgage and authority were admissible, under the general issue, as an answer to the action. Fuller *v.* Rounceville, 9 Fost. 554.

(*a*) A final receipt, by an officer of the government authorized to act in the premises, for rent, is a full discharge, being subsequent to the trespass alleged, although the officer may never have accounted for the money received. United States *v.* Geer, 3 McL. 571.

a farm; of which the defendant had a deed and his father a life lease. Action for damages done to the plaintiff's close by the defendant's cattle. It appeared, that the cows kept upon the farm had trespassed upon the plaintiff's farm, but that the defendant owned but one cow, which was also kept upon the farm. Held, evidence competent for the jury, and from which they might find for the plaintiff.[1] (*a*) So in an action for nuisance, it is sufficient to state the defendant's possession of the property, by means of which the nuisance is caused.[2] And for either misfeasance or nonfeasance, as for leaving open a door, or not repairing fences, ways, or watercourses, the action should be, in general, either against the party doing the act, *or the occupier*, not the owner.[3] So the occupier of a house is bound to rail or fence in the area; and, if an accident happen, it is no defence, that the premises had been in the same situation for many years before the defendant came in possession.[4] So the occupant of a house, having a cellar opening upon the highway, is bound, in using it, to take reasonable care that the *flap* be so placed and secured, as not, under ordinary circumstances, to fall in or occasion injury. But, if he have so placed and secured it, and a wrongdoer throw it over, the occupant is not liable.[5] So in an action for an injury from falling down an unprotected area, the declaration stated, that the defendant was possessed of the premises, and that they were adjoining "a certain common and public street and highway." It appeared, that the defendant had agreed with the owner of the premises, (two carcasses of houses,) to finish one of them, for doing which he was to have the other, and that

[1] Cram *v.* Dudley, 8 Fost. 537.
[2] Stancliffe *v.* Hardwick, 3 Dow. P. C. 766.
[3] Mathews *v.* West, &c. 3 Camp. 403; Cheetham *v.* Hampson, 4 T. R. 318; Rider *v.* Smith, 3 Ib. 766; Sutton *v.* Clarke, 6 Taunt. 44.
[4] Coupland *v.* Hardingham, 3 Camp. 398.
[5] Daniels *v.* Potter, 4 C. & P. 262.

(*a*) It has been held, that, at common law, a party, into whose land agisted cattle escape, and there do damage, may maintain trespass against the general owner of the cattle or against the agister at his election. Sheridan *v.* Bean, 8 Met. 284.

workmen employed by him were then actually at work upon them; but not that any conveyance had been made to him. The street, which had been forming for six years, and led from a public street to a new road across fields, over which the way had been publicly used for five or six years, was unfinished, one half only being lighted, the other neither lighted nor paved; but the inhabitants had paid the highway and paving rates. Held, this was sufficient evidence to go to a jury, of a possession in the defendant and a dedication of the street to the public.[1] So the defendant was administrator of one of two mortgagees of real estate, on which was a mill and a reservoir dam. While the premises were in possession of certain persons under license from the other mortgagee, who had subsequently quitclaimed all his interest therein to the defendant, the dam broke away, as the plaintiffs alleged, because of its original insufficiency and subsequent want of repair, and carried away the plaintiff's bridges. Held that, if so, the defendant was not liable for the loss, not being in possession by himself nor by his tenants.[2] So, in an action by the owners of a mill, for damages occasioned by the diversion of water for the use of another mill, in the absence of evidence that the defendants are in the occupation or ownership of the latter, the plaintiff will be nonsuited.[3] So an action on the case for flowing lands will not lie against a former owner of land, who erected a dam and built a mill, by means of which the injury is done, where other persons are in possession, and there is no evidence that they hold as his tenants. The action must be against the persons in possession.[4] Though a mortgagee of a mill-dam, &c., who has taken possession for breach of condition, is liable for the unpaid annual damages for flowing land, awarded against the mortgagor.[5] So the occupant, not the owner, of land, is bound to repair drains and sewers. Hence, in a suit by

[1] Jarvis v. Dean, 11 Moore, 354.
[2] 11 Cush. 299.
[3] Sidelinger v. Hagar, 41 Maine, 415.
[4] Blunt v. Aikin, 15 Wend. 522.
[5] Fuller v. French, 10 Met. 359.

an adjoining owner for non-repair thereof, the declaration must allege occupation.[1]

13 *a*. And although the owner of property may, under some circumstances, as occupier, be responsible for injuries, arising from acts done upon that property by persons who are there by his permission, though not strictly his agents or servants; in general, such liability does not attach to him, as owner, even for the use of a thing which he himself erected. Therefore, an action does not lie against the owner of premises, for a nuisance arising from smoke out of a chimney, to the prejudice of the plaintiff in his occupation of an adjoining messuage; on the ground that, having erected the chimney, and let the premises with the chimney so erected, he had impliedly authorized the lighting of a fire therein. And, the premises having been in the occupation of a tenant, at the time the fires were lighted, the defendant is entitled to a verdict on a plea of "not possessed;" which refers to the time when the nuisance was committed, and not when the chimney was erected.[2]

13 *b*. And, even if title or ownership alone in the defendant would furnish a ground of action; yet possession, if alleged, must be proved. Thus in an action of trespass, upon a statute, which provides, that every owner or keeper of any dog shall forfeit to any person injured by such dog double the amount of damages sustained by him; if the declaration allege that the defendants were the owners and keepers of the dog, the plaintiff must prove that they were both.[3]

14. Upon the same principle is founded the well-established rule, that, if the defendant in an action of trover has no possession, actual or constructive, at the time of demand and refusal, and there has previously been no tortious taking or withholding; he is not liable, though he may have forcibly interposed obstacles to the owner's obtaining posses-

[1] Russell *v*. Shenton, 3 Ad. & Ell. N. S. 449. See Bell *v*. Twentyman, 1 Ib. 766.

[2] Rich *v*. Basterfield, 4 Com. B. 783.

[3] Buddington *v*. Shearer, 20 Pick. 477.

sion.[1] (a) So, where a person, lawfully coming into possession of the property of another, has parted with it previous to a demand; the remedy is not trover, but case or assumpsit.[2] So trover cannot be maintained against one who has never had possession of the property, and has had nothing to do with it, except that he has taken a mortgage on it to secure a debt, from a person claiming to be the owner.[3] (b) And, if *actual possession* be not in all cases necessary, still there can be no conversion, without either such possession, or the exercise of such a claim of right or dominion as assumes that the party is entitled to possession, and to deprive the opposite party of it. Thus, where an officer counted certain logs, frozen in the ice, declared them to be attached, took a receipt for them, and made a return upon his writ to that effect, of which he lodged a copy with the town clerk, and, in ten days, the action was settled and the attachment dissolved; held, not a conversion.[4]

15. It has been held, that an action cannot be maintained on the ground of possession of a chattel or of real estate, where the legal title is in another, and the plaintiff has only *a trust*.[5] Thus, where a slave is conveyed in trust for the use of a married woman, who is entitled to possession; an action for conversion must be brought by the trustee.[6] And,

[1] Boobier *v.* Boobier, 39 Maine, 406; Kelsey *v.* Griswold, 6 Barb. 436. See Zachery *v.* Race, 4 Eng. 212; Brockway *v.* Burnap, 16 Barb. 309.

[2] Kelsey *v.* Griswold, 6 Barb. 436.

[3] The Matteawan, &c. *v.* Bentley, 13 Barb. 641.

[4] Fernald *v.* Chase, 37 Maine, 289.

[5] Lespeyne *v.* M'Farland, 2 Tayl. 187; Jones *v.* Taylor, 1 Dev. 435.

[6] Richardson *v.* Means, 22 Mis. 495.

(a) See *Trover, Conversion.*

(b) Upon the same principle, the owner of goods stolen, prosecuting the felon to conviction, cannot recover the value of them in trover from the person who purchased them in market overt, and sold them again before conviction, notwithstanding the owner gave him notice of the robbery while they were in his possession. For, in order to maintain trover, the plaintiff must prove that the goods were his property, and that while they were so they came into the defendant's possession, who converted them to his use. But he has a right to restitution of the goods in specie. Horwood *v.* Smith, 2 T. R. 750, 755.

on the other hand, a trustee, though having a mere naked trust, may bring trover for trust property.[1] So, where a slave was given to A. in trust for B., a married woman; who, by the terms of the trust, had possession of the slave; held, the right of action for an injury to the slave, which caused his death, was in the trustee.[2] So a secret resulting trust, arising from the fact that property was paid for with the defendant's money, the possession never being surrendered to him, is no defence to an action of trover, brought by the party having the legal title.[3] But in trover by a guardian, if the declaration allege that the property claimed, being in the possession of his ward, was lost, &c., it is bad on demurrer, in not showing that the guardian was entitled to the possession.[4] (a) But, on the other hand, where a

[1] Coleson v. Blanton, 3 Hayw. 152; Thompson v. Ford, 7 Ired. 418; Burnett v. Roberts, 4 Dev. 81.

[2] McRaeny v. Johnson, 2 Florida, 520.

[3] Guphill v. Isbell, 8 Rich. 463.

[4] Dearman v. Dearman, 5 Ala. 202.

(a) Property in remainder was devised to a *feme sole*. After her marriage, the intervening life-estate was conveyed to her sole use, &c. Upon a bill filed by her on the insolvency of her husband before entering upon the land, an interlocutory decree was made, declaring that her right, &c. ought to be vested in a trustee, &c., followed by a final decree appointing a trustee "to take charge of complainant's property," without formally vesting him with the legal title. The wife then entered into possession. Held, that her possession was that of her trustee, and that he had sufficient title to maintain trespass, that being necessary to maintain the "charge" given him. Rogers v. White, 1 Sneed, 68.

The plaintiff, residing abroad, shipped sugars under a bill of lading, addressed to A. in London, directing him to sell the sugars on the plaintiff's account, and place the net proceeds to the credit of B., to whom the plaintiff was indebted for advances made previously to the shipment. The invoice stated the plaintiff to be the shipper. A., on the arrival of the sugars, pledged them to the defendants for advance made by them to him; and, having become bankrupt, the plaintiff authorized an agent to demand the sugars of the defendants; but they sold them, and the proceeds were demanded after the sale by the agent, with the authority of the plaintiff. Held, that the latter had a sufficient title in the sugars to sue the defendants in trover, as the right of possession was in him, and B. had only an equitable interest; and that the defendants, by selling the sugars after the

vendee of land goes into possession, the legal title remaining in the vendor, the vendor cannot maintain an action on the

---

demand by the plaintiff's agent, were guilty of a conversion. Sellick *v.* Smith, 11 Moore, 469.

Deed of land, naming no grantee, one third thereof "for the use of a school-house thereon, if the neighboring inhabitants see cause to build a school-house thereon." A school-house was built thereon by a school district, and afterwards the defendant, as agent of a school district *de facto*, acting as successor of the former district, leased a part of the tract to the plaintiff for ten years. The plaintiff held over after the expiration of the ten years; and a school district, which had been duly constituted after the lease was made, authorized the defendant to enter on the tract and take possession thereof for the district. He entered accordingly, and the plaintiff brought an action of trespass against him. Held, that, though no legal estate passed by the deed, yet a trust was thereby created, which the Court would be authorized and bound as a Court of Equity to protect, and would appoint a trustee to take the legal estate from the grantor's heirs, who would be bound to convey it to him; that the lease was admissible in evidence against the plaintiff; and that he was estopped to deny that A. was duly appointed agent of the school district *de facto*, or that the district had a good title to the tract. Bailey *v.* Kilburn, 10 Met. 176.

In 1785, W. conveyed to A., B., and C. a tract of land formerly belonging to the town of S., bounded westerly on the Connecticut River, "in trust for the use of the inhabitants of the first parish in S. for a burying-ground forever," with words of inheritance in the *habendum* clause, and with a covenant of warranty. Long before this conveyance, a part of the tract had been set apart and appropriated by the town as a burying-ground; and had been used as such, while the town and parish were identical, and after the separate organization of the parish. About the time of the conveyance, the parish made provision for fencing the burying-ground, and erected, about the year 1800, a fence on the top of the bank of the river. That part of the tract which constituted the shore and bank of the river was unsuitable for a burial-place, and was never used as such; and in 1842 the parish conveyed it to the plaintiff, who brought an action of trespass against the defendant, who defended under a license from the town. Held, the deed conveyed a fee-simple estate; that, if the parish had not the legal estate, but only the equitable estate, (which was not decided,) yet, as they were in possession, they could hold against all persons not claiming under the original grantees; and, as they entered and claimed title under the deed, they acquired a seisin of all the land therein described; and the plaintiff, their grantee, could well maintain his action. Stearns *v.* Palmer, 10 Met. 32.

case against a wrongdoer, for an injury to the inheritance during such possession, although it does not appear that the vendee has entitled himself to a conveyance; nor can he recover damages arising out of the rescission of the sale by reason of such injury.[1]

16. The question of possession sometimes arises, in reference to an authority conferred upon *public officers* relating to the property which is alleged to have been injured. Thus the commissioners of sewers cannot maintain trespass against the commissioners of a harbor, for breaking down a wall or dam, erected by the former, as such commissioners, across a navigable river; the authority, to be exercised by them on behalf of the public, not vesting in them a sufficient property or possessory interest.[2] So upon the ground, that, in order to bring trespass, a party must, at the time of the trespass, either have actual possession, or else a constructive possession, in respect of the right being actually vested in him; trespass will not lie, by the assignees of a bankrupt against a sheriff, for taking the goods of the bankrupt in execution, after an act of bankruptcy, and before the issuing of the commission; notwithstanding he sells them after the issuing of the commission, and after a provisional assignment and notice from the provisional assignee not to sell. But the assignees may bring trover.[3] (a)

[1] Ives *v.* Cress, 5 Barr, 118. See Rood *v.* The New York, &c. 18 Barb. 80.

[2] Duke of Newcastle *v.* Clark, 2 Moore, 666.

[3] Smith *v.* Milles, 1 T. R. 475.

(*a*) It has been held, in Maine, that the minister of a parish, settled for life or for years, being seised of the freehold in the ministerial land, upon condition, and answerable for waste, may maintain trespass against a stranger for an injury done to the freehold, and that the suit is not abated by the termination of the estate pending the suit. Cargill *v.* Sewall, 1 App. 288.

But it has been since decided, that the minister of a religious society cannot, as such, maintain trespass *quare clausum* for the use of the society. Cox *v.* Walker, 26 Maine, 504.

A city authorized a gas company to set up and establish lamp-posts along

17. As has been already intimated, possession is good ground of action against a party having himself no title, although a third person may have a better title than the plaintiff. Thus, in trespass or trover for seizing goods in the possession and apparent ownership of the plaintiff, it is the well-established rule, although occasional decisions have been made to the contrary, that the defendant cannot set up the title of a third person, to defeat the action;[1] at least without specially pleading, that the possession of the plaintiff was fraudulent;[2] or proof of some title or interest derived from such third person.[3] So, in an action of trespass *quare clausum*, the defendant cannot avail himself of the title of a third person, without showing both the title and the command or permission of that person.[4] Thus a plea of freehold in a third party is bad.[5] So A., who owned a slave, died intestate, and no administration was ever granted on his estate; but his next of kin took possession of the slave and kept him for seven years. They then sold him to B., who kept him for ten years, and then died, when his executor sold him to C., who had possession of him for four years. The slave then ran away, was caught and imprisoned, and taken out of jail by D., who, upon demand, refused to deliver him to C. Held, that C.'s possession was good as against every one but the administrator of A., should any exist, and that he was entitled to an action of trover against D., who was a mere wrongdoer, and set up no title in himself.[6] So in trover, and a plea of *not guilty*, and *not the plaintiff's property*, it appeared that the plaintiff was in possession of goods

[1] Nelson *v.* Cherrill, 1 Moo. & S. 452; Fiske *v.* Small, 25 Maine, 453. See Grover *v.* Hawley, 5 Cal. 485; Rotan *v.* Fletcher, 15 Johns. 207; Duncan *v.* Specr, 11 Wend. 54; Hurst *v.* Cook, 19 Wend. 463; Stonard *v.* Dunkin, 2 Camp. 341; King *v.* Richards, 6 Whart. 418; Lae *v.* Towle, 3 Esp. 114.

[2] Huddleston *v.* Spear, 3 Eng. 406.

[3] Harker *v.* Dement, 9 Gill, 7.

[4] Merrill *v.* Burbank, 10 Shep. 538.

[5] Richardson *v.* Merrill, 7 Mis. 333.

[6] Craig *v.* Miller, 12 Ired. 375.

---

the streets of the city; and the company erected, managed them, &c. Held, they had sufficient title and possession to maintain trespass for an injury to them. Roche *v.* Milwaukee, &c. 5 Wis. 55.

which he claimed as his own property, under an assignment to him from O. The defendants seized the goods in the plaintiff's possession, claiming them under an assignment from O. to them, made whilst O. was in apparent ownership of the goods, but of a later date than the assignment to the plaintiff. This was the conversion. The defence was, that the assignment by O. to the plaintiff was fraudulent as against the defendants. This was left to the jury, who found for the plaintiff. The defendants also offered as a defence to prove, that O. had become bankrupt before the plaintiff took possession, and that the goods were in his order and disposition, and therefore vested in the assignees before the conversion. Held, this defence was not admissible, but, the plaintiff being in possession, and the defendants being wrongdoers, not claiming in any way under the assignees, the defendants could not set up the *jus tertii* as a defence in trover.[1] So in trespass, for taking goods in possession of the plaintiff, where both parties claim under the same person, neither can deny the title of such person, or set up an outstanding paramount title in a stranger, unless he can connect himself with the true owner.[2] And it is no defence, that the plaintiff had given a mortgage of the property, which had become forfeited, without showing a connection between the defendant and the mortgagee.[3] So, where a horse, belonging to the United States, was taken by the enemy, and shortly after retaken by the plaintiff, who continued in the possession, until it was taken from him by the defendant, an officer in the army of the United States, acting under the orders of a superior officer, but not the authority of the United States; it was held that the plaintiff could maintain trespass, the law presuming until the contrary be proved, that the United States never intended to interpose any claim to the property.[4] And, in trespass against an officer, for taking goods from the plaintiff's possession, on execution against a third person; it

[1] Jeffries *v.* Great Western, &c. 5 Ell. & Black. 802; 34 Eng. L. & Eq. 122.

[2] Barwick *v.* Wood, 3 Jones, Law, 306. See King *v.* Orser, 4 Duer, 431; Whitney *v.* Brunette, 3 Wis. 621.

[3] Hanmer *v.* Wilsey, 17 Wend. 91.

[4] Cook *v.* Howard, 13 Johns. 276.

is even held that an authority to do so from the owner of the goods does not constitute a justification to the officer; but the plaintiff is entitled to nominal damage for the injury to his possession. And the measure of damages is the actual value of the goods, and any further reasonable sum, for injury and vexation by delay caused by the act of the defendant.[1] So, where the defendant in an action of trespass offered to prove the right of property in a third person, but was not permitted to, and the bill of exceptions did not set out the evidence, or a possessory right in the plaintiff; it was held that the evidence offered was irrelevant, and that a new trial would not be granted.[2]

17 *a*. And, as has been already suggested, the same rule prevails, even where the plaintiff came wrongfully into possession of the property. Thus a party having a legal title to, and having had possession of a slave, though acquired fraudulently, may maintain an action against any third person who aids the slave to escape.[3] So, where A. caught up a mare and colt, which were straying, and kept them for a year and more, and worked the mare, and the mare was shot dead by the defendant; it was held that A.'s possession was sufficient to maintain trespass.[4] So a reversioner, who has by wrong regained possession of land which was under a lease, may maintain trespass against a mere stranger who has invaded his possession.[5] So where the owner of goods assigns and delivers them to another person, as security for a debt, and the assignee assigns and delivers them to the plaintiff, by an instrument void as against the provisions of a statute, with the assent of the original owner; an action of trespass can be maintained therefor, against one who takes them without right and as a mere wrongdoer.[6] So a plaintiff in trespass, having the sole and exclusive possession, may recover against a wrongdoer the whole damage done by the defendant, though the conveyance from some of those under whom he claimed title was defective.[7]

[1] Rogers *v.* Fales, 5 Barr. 154.
[2] Crawford *v.* Bynum, 7 Yerg. 381.
[3] Law *v.* Law, 2 Gratt. 366.
[4] Boston *v.* Neat, 12 Mis. 125.
[5] Rollins *v* Clay, 33 Maine, 132.
[6] Barker *v.* Chase, 11 Shep. 230.
[7] Curtis *v.* Hoyt, 19 Conn. 154.

18. But, as has been already suggested, possession furnishes only *presumptive* evidence of title. Thus it is held, that, in trover for a note, possession of the note by the plaintiff is *primâ facie* evidence of ownership, *against one who shows no title to it.*[1] So, in replevin for certain hogs taken by the defendant, as deputy sheriff, on an execution against A., it is a correct charge to the jury, that, if A. was found in the possession of the hogs, he would be presumed to be the owner; but that this presumption would yield to proof, and that any proof would be sufficient, if it produced belief in the minds of the jury that the title was in another.[2] And hence, *a title in the defendant himself*, or one under whom he claims or with whom he is in privity, is a good defence to an action founded on possession.[3] (*a*) Thus, where the defendant in trespass has proved title to the goods, the plaintiff cannot recover upon his possession without proof of a better title.[4] So where a tenement is in the possession of a wrongdoer, the person entitled to possession may enter peaceably, in the absence of the wrongdoer, and retain the possession.[5] And a person cannot be made liable in trespass, for entering upon his own land in the wrongful possession of another, and exerting a right of ownership; nor can any unlawful acts committed in the execution of this right, be so connected with it, as to make him liable in damages as a trespasser *ab initio*.[6] (*b*) Thus the person entitled to possession of a house may enter peaceably, in the absence of a wrongdoer in possession, and lock the doors thereof.[7] So a dis-

[1] Donnell *v.* Thompson, 13 Ala. 440.
[2] Park *v.* Harrison, 8 Humph. 412.
[3] Hutchinson *v.* Lord, 1 Miss. 286; Jones *v.* Water-lot Co. 18 Geo. 539.
[4] Champion *v.* Smith, 1 Brev. 243.
[5] Culver *v.* Smart, 1 Smith, 50.
[6] Johnson *v.* Hannahan, 1 Strobh. 313; Inskeep *v.* Shields, 4 Harringt. 345.
[7] Culver *v.* Smart, 1 Cart. 65.

(*a*) Proved, in case of real property, either by deed or other documentary evidence, or by an actual adverse and exclusive possession for twenty years. Brest *v.* Lever, 7 M. & W. 593.

(*b*) In Ohio, where the owner of a stray raft (within thirty days after it was taken up) regained possession thereof by force, without offering to prove his right or pay reasonable charges, it was held that the taker had no right under the statute to replevy it. Coverlee *v.* Warner, 19 Ohio, 29.

seizee, having a right of entry, and entering peaceably on land, no one being thereon, and taking possession under his title, thereby acquires the right to maintain an action of trespass against the disseizor and others for a subsequent breach and entry.[1] So, in trespass *quare clausum fregit*, the defendant may show, *in mitigation of damages*, that the plaintiff was in possession of the premises at the time of the alleged trespass, by disseizin of, and trespass on, the defendant.[2] And where a defendant in trespass wishes to defend as having the right of possession, he may plead the general issue; he is not bound, even if permitted, to plead such right specially.[3]

18 *a*. But a right to the possession of real estate will not justify an assault and battery to obtain possession; though possession in fact justifies the use of violence, if necessary to defend it.[4] So, in order to maintain this defence, the defendant must have not only title, but the right of possession. Thus where, in trespass, the defendant pleads title, and the plaintiff replies facts, which show that he was in possession at the time, and that the right of possession was out of the defendant, or those under whom he entered, though the title set up is not legally vested in the plaintiff; the replication is good.[5] And replication of possession in virtue of a parol purchase is good to the plea of *liberum tenementum*.[6] And mere ownership of the soil is not in all cases a justification of an alleged trespass committed thereupon. (*a*) Thus a grant, to one and his heirs and assigns forever, of all the trees and timber standing and growing in a close, with free liberty to cut and carry them away at pleasure, conveys an estate of

[1] Tyler *v.* Smith, 8 Met. 599.

[2] McDonald *v.* Lightfoot, 1 Morris, 450.

[3] Sage *v.* Keesecker, 1 Morris, 338.

[4] Parsons *v.* Brown, 15 Barb. 590.

[5] Phillips *v.* Kent, 3 Zabr. 155.

[6] Hope *v.* Casom, 3 B. Monr. 544; Castro *v.* Gill, 5 Cal. 40. See Hicks *v.* Bell, 3 Cal. 219; Larve *v.* Gaskins, 5, 164.

(*a*) In trespass *quare clausum*, where neither party had actual possession, it is erroneous to instruct the jury, that the defendant would not be liable for the act, if he did it "in the *bonâ fide* assertion of a claim of title, which he thought to be good." Shipman *v.* Baxter, 21 Ala. 456.

inheritance in the trees and timber; and the grantee may maintain trespass *quare clausum* against the owner of the soil for cutting down the trees.[1]

19. The general doctrine, of the sufficiency and necessity of possession, as the foundation of a legal claim or defence, is further illustrated by the well-established principle, that possession may be *constructive*, as well as actual. (*a*) The rule is well settled, that the general owner of property holds constructive possession, and may maintain trespass, though the actual possession (more especially if without claim of title) be in another.[2] Thus, to maintain trespass *quare clausum*, the plaintiff must have *actual or constructive possession.* Where no one has the actual possession, the person having title has the constructive possession. But he cannot bring trespass against one having actual possession.[3]

19 *a*. But *actual* possession is sometimes held to consist in mere constructive acts of ownership. Thus the *actual* possession of crown land, under a parol license from the crown, is held to entitle a party to maintain trespass against a wrongdoer. And payment of a nominal rent to the crown, the occasional occupation of the land by sporting over it, and taking the grass by a servant, constitute sufficient evi-

[1] Clap *v*. Draper, 4 Mass. 266.

[2] Cary *v*. Hotailing, 1 Hill, 312; Crenshaw *v*. Moore, 10 Geo. 384.

[3] Vance *v*. Beatty, 4 Rich. 104; Stean *v*. Anderson, 4 Harring. 209; Dobbs *v*. Gallidge, 4 Dev. & Bat. 68; Cohoon *v*. Simmons, 7 Ired. 189. See Webb *v*. Sturtevant, 1 Scam. 181; Graham *v*. Houston, 4 Dev. 232; Van Rensselaer *v*. Radcliffe, 10 Wend. 639; Miller *v*. Fuller, 4 Ham. 433; Foster *v*. Fletcher, 7 Mon. 536; Owings *v*. Gibson, 2 A. K. Mar. 515; Cabrine *v*. Westerfield, 3 Ib. 331; Mason *v*. Lewis, 1 Iowa, 494; Poole *v*. Mitchell, 1 Hill, 404.

(*a*) Possession once proved is presumed to continue. Thus, in trespass to try titles, an allegation that the plaintiff was in possession on the 1st of January, and that the defendant entered with force and arms on the 2d, was held to be a sufficient possession at the time of ouster. Parker *v*. Haggerty, 1 Ala. 632.

So, when the defendant in trover fails to give any account of the manner in which he acquired possession, he will be presumed to hold from or under the person, who is shown to have had the possession for several years next before the defendant acquired it. Barnes *v*. Mobley, 21 Ala. 232.

dence of such actual possession.[1] So the plaintiff's possession by enclosures need not be proved, in an action of trespass against one neither proving nor claiming title to the land; if the land has been used by the plaintiff, it is sufficient.[2] It is said, "Every man's land is in the eye of the law enclosed and set apart from his neighbor's, and that, either by a visible and material fence, as one field is divided from another by a hedge, or by an ideal invisible boundary existing only in the contemplation of law, as when one man's land adjoins to another's in the same field."[3] So cutting wood upon a wood-lot, up to a well-known and determinate line, although there is no fence upon the line, during a period of thirteen years, constitutes such actual possession, as will support trespass against any who do not show better title in themselves.[4] More especially an entry upon land under a deed, claiming title; cutting and selling timber from time to time; and exercising general acts of ownership; are sufficient to maintain an action of trespass against a stranger.[5] So a deep navigable watercourse, surrounding a party's land, is a sufficient enclosure, to render an entrance thereon by other persons, for purposes of hunting, a breach of his close, and to entitle him to damages, as for a trespass.[6] And one who shows title in himself may maintain trespass *quare clausum*, for a trespass upon vacant and wild lands, although he has never had actual possession, either by formal entry or occasional occupancy.[7] Thus a purchaser of lands from the United States may maintain trespass for an injury to the freehold, after the purchase, by a person entering and keeping possession, without claim or title, even before the purchase.[8] (*a*) And where the plaintiff claims title

[1] Harper *v.* Charlesworth, 6 Dowl. & Ry. 572; 4 B. & C. 574; 14 Pick. 297, acc.

[2] Tyson *v.* Shurry, 5 Md. 540.

[3] 3 Bl. Comm. 209. See Gleason *v.* Edmands, 2 Scam. 448; M'Gregor *v.* Comstock, 17 N. Y. 162.

[4] Chandler *v.* Walker, 1 Fost. 282; Machin *v.* Gearner, 14 Wend. 239.

[5] Sawyer *v.* Newland, 3 Verm. 383.

[6] Fripp *v.* Hasell, 1 Strobh. 173.

[7] McGraw *v.* Bookman, 3 Hill, S. C. 265.

[8] Gale *v.* Davis, 7 Mis. 544; Blevins *v.* Cole, 1 Ala. 210.

(*a*) But the actual occupancy of one half quarter section of land does

by adverse possession, and shows acts of dominion over the *locus in quo*, which was part of a highway, and especially cutting wood thereon for his fires; the defendant cannot prove, for the purpose of showing that these acts did not constitute adverse possession, that, when the plaintiff so cut wood, it was, and long had been, customary for any person who chose, although not owning the fee of the highway or of the adjacent land, to cut wood for his fires from such highway; without proving or claiming that any such acts were done in the *locus in quo*.[1] So, by a vote of the proprietors of a township, a lot of land was appropriated for a meeting-house. In 1727, after the erection of the meeting-house, the town was incorporated, and assumed the charge of its parochial affairs. The land around the meeting-house was called the "common" or "the meeting-house land," was always open, and was intersected by several highways and other ways. It was also used as a site for horse-sheds, and for all the ordinary purposes incident to a place of worship, and as a training-field. The town meetings had been held at the meeting-house. In 1754 and 1763, the proprietors voted to sell portions of the "meeting-house land," and they had also at different times exercised other acts of ownership over portions of this land. It was held, that the first parish, which was the successor of the town in its parochial capacity, might maintain trespass against a stranger, who had ploughed up a portion of the land, which was used for purposes incidental to a place of worship.[2] (*a*)

[1] Evans *v.* Bidwell, 20 Conn. 209.

[2] First Parish in Shrewsbury *v.* Smith, 14 Pick. 297.

not draw after it the possession of an adjoining unoccupied quarter section, upon which the occupant had exercised acts of ownership by cutting logs for his saw-mill, so that he can maintain trespass *quare clausum* against one who had also cut logs thereon, and was in the actual occupation of adjoining land. Blackburn *v.* Baker, 7 Port. 284.

(*a*) Constructive possession may be set up for a defence, as well as a ground of action; and this both *positively* for the defendant and *negatively* against the plaintiff. Thus, while the possession of part of a tract of land, by the owner of the whole, is the possession of the whole; it is otherwise with

19 *b*. But it has been held, that making pole bridges, over a ditch on the side of a public road, for driving cattle into a

---

a trespasser, whose possession extends only to actual occupancy. Kincaid *v*. Logue, 7 Mis. 167; Sloane *v*. Moore, Ibid. 170.

Thus a purchaser of land, adjoining that of which he is in actual possession, is constructively in possession to the extent of the boundary of both tracts; and one who enters on that possession, and builds a cabin and locks it up, is not in possession beyond the actual close, and cannot maintain trespass against the former for cutting timber on the land. Fish *v*. Branamon, 2 B. Mon. 379.

Upon the same principle, if the party having the legal title to land enter thereon (as by going thereon, and beginning to plough, &c.) with intent to take possession, although he does not declare such intent; he may maintain trespass against one wrongfully in possession at the time of entry, and who, without quitting possession, desires the owner to go away, and in fact continues his wrongful possession afterwards. Butcher *v*. Butcher, 7 B. & C. 390.

The effect of constructive possession will be limited by the purpose of the parties in the act which constitutes it. Thus where A. delivered to B. the key of his house, for the purpose of putting B. in the possession of goods therein, but not of the house itself; held, B. had not such a possession of the house, as would support trespass for breaking and entering it. Davis *v*. Wood, 7 Mis. 162.

Possession being available as *evidence of title*, an instruction to the jury, in an action of trespass for taking and carrying away goods, that, in order to entitle the plaintiff to a verdict, he must show a *title* to the property, or to some part of it, at the time of the alleged trespass, is not erroneous. Roberts *v*. Wentworth, 5 Cush. 192.

It is to be observed, that there is a distinction between constructive possession and a mere *right of entry;* which, in case of real property, is not sufficient to maintain trespass. Hollis *v*. Goldfinch, 1 B. & C. 205.

And it is said (3 Steph. N. P. 2632), (although, as appears in the text, the remark is of very limited application,) "a distinction exists between personal and real property respecting the rights of the owner. In the first case the general property draws to it a sufficient possession to enable the owner to support trespass, though he has never been in possession; but in the case of land and other real property, there is no such constructive possession; and unless the plaintiff had the actual possession by himself or his servant at the time when the injury was committed, he cannot maintain this action."

The following may be mentioned as examples of this rule: Before entry and actual possession, a *parson* cannot maintain trespass, though he may have the freehold in law. (9 Vin. Abr. *Entry*, 449 C.) Or an heir.

tract of swamp land, and the ranging of cattle on the same, and occasionally cutting a few timber trees, is not such a possession, as will maintain the action of trespass.[1] So it has been held, that where a person owns two tracts of land by different titles, but adjoining each other, the possession of one is not the possession of the other.[2]

20. A *deed*, (*a*) conveying the land to the plaintiff in fee, without entry, is *primâ facie* sufficient evidence of ownership, as against a person making no claim either to the title or to the right of possession.[3] And a party having such deed is presumed to enter under it.[4] (*b*) But an unrecorded deed of

[1] Morris *v.* Hayes, 2 Jones, Law, 93.
[2] Ibid.
[3] Warner *v.* Cochran, 10 Fost. 379; Gardner *v.* Heartt, 2 Barb. 165. See Rogers *v.* White, 1 Sneed, 68.
[4] M'Grady *v.* Miller, 14 Verm. 128.

(Browning *v.* Beston, Plow. 142.) Or a devisee, against an abator. (2 Mod. 7.) Or a lessee for years. (4 Bac. Abr. *Leases*, M.) In Maine, an heir or devisee may bring trespass before entry. Dexter *v.* Sullivan, 34 N. H. 478.

(*a*) Title may be shown in a corporation by *vote*, sufficient for legal possession. Vassalborough *v.* Somerset, &c. 43 Maine, 337.

(*b*) The burden of proof is held to be upon the party claiming under a deed, which is referred to and excepted in the plaintiff's grant, to prove its application to the land entered upon by the plaintiff. Thus, in an action of trespass, the plaintiff declared on a grant from the State of land described by metes and bounds, with the exception of 250 acres previously granted. Held, that it was incumbent on the defendant to show, that the trespass was committed on the part previously granted. McCormick *v.* Munroe, 1 Jones, Law, 13.

In an action of trespass brought by an owner of land against a railroad corporation, for entering upon his land and there constructing their road; the burden of proving that the land is covered by the authorized location of their road is upon the defendants. Hazen *v.* Boston, &c. 2 Gray, 574.

A deed described the land as *lot No.* 6, the extent of which lot was doubtful, but the plaintiff, claiming under such deed, showed an entry upon what he claimed by definite boundaries, as part of that lot. Held, an action of trespass was maintainable against one without title, who interfered with the plaintiff's possession, whether the land were actually part of this lot or not. Poor *v.* Gibson, 32 N. H. 415.

In trover, for personal property conveyed by a deed which was not properly registered, proof of the delivery of the property is competent, inde-

wild land is not of itself sufficient evidence of possession by the grantee, to entitle him to maintain trespass.[1] Nor, it is held, a deed, more especially of mere release and quitclaim, without proof of actual possession by the grantor, or of any entry by the grantee.[2] (*a*)

[1] Estes *v.* Cook, 22 Pick. 295.

[2] Marr *v.* Boothby, 1 App. 150; Gardner *v.* Heart, 1 Comst. 528.

---

pendently of any question about the admissibility of the deed. Grady *v.* Sharron, 6 Yerg. 320.

(*a*) Though *an instrument not under seal* cannot convey the legal title to land, yet, in an action of trespass, it may be competent evidence to show a license or authority from the owner of the land to the defendant to enter thereon. Floyd *v.* Ricks, 14 Ark. 286.

But a promise under seal, to make a title in fee-simple at some future time to land, provided the passage of an act of Congress can be obtained to authorize such conveyance, is not evidence to show title in the defendant in trespass. James *v.* Tait, 8 Port. 476.

Where the defendant went into possession of land under a parol contract of purchase, and, not having paid the purchase-money according to the contract, the owner of the land sold and deeded it to the plaintiff; it was held, that this did not constitute the defendant a tenant to the plaintiff, nor give the plaintiff any possession of the land, so as to enable him to maintain trespass against the defendant for an injury done to the plaintiff. Ripley *v.* Yale, 16 Verm. 257.

Where a father conveyed slaves to his son by deed ; in trover by the father agaiust the son, it was held competent to prove a parol agreement, made at the time of the conveyance, that the father should retain possession of the slaves during his life. Strong *v.* Strong, 6 Ala. 345.

One who has made and left shingles on vacant land may maintain trespass against one who carries them away, though under a license from a party receiving a grant of the land after the making and before the removal of the shingles. Reader *v.* Moody, 3 Jones, Law, 372.

In an action of trespass *quare clausum*, a party has a right to show such evidence of title as he possesses, in order to obtain a decision upon the proper construction of a deed, under which he claims a right by license from the grantees to enter upon the lands and do the acts complained of. Lonk *v.* Woods, 15 Ill. 256.

In an action of trespass to try title, it is held that extrinsic evidence is not admissible to invalidate a grant, by showing that it has been obtained by fraud or mistake, or that an undue priority has been given to it. Mounce *v.* Ingram, 1 Brev. 55.

21. Where a man enters into possession of land, it is presumed that he enters in his own right; and, if he enters under a deed, his acts are taken to be the acts of an owner, and not of a trespasser.[1] But where the plaintiff, who was in possession of premises sold under execution to the defendant, brought an action of trespass against the defendant, for an entry before he had received a deed from the sheriff; held, while the sheriff's deed related back to the sale *as to the title*, it did not relate back so as to justify a breach of the plaintiff's possession, and the defendant was therefore liable for the trespass.[2] (*a*)

22. In this connection, it becomes necessary to speak of the common transaction of *a sale of personal property*, as affecting the legal and constructive possession of the thing sold, in the absence of any actual change of possession. In the Law of Sales, this is a fruitful and important topic, but

[1] M'Grady *v.* Miller, 14 Verm. 128. [2] Presnell *v.* Ramsour, 8 Ired. 505.

But the contrary and better doctrine is laid down, that the defendant may impeach a conveyance under which the plaintiff claims, by showing that it was obtained by duress or fraud, or that the consideration of it was the compounding a felony; and, if there be evidence to support either of these objections, the jury are to judge of the sufficiency of the evidence. Price *v.* M'Gee, 1 Brev. 373.

The lands of A. and B. being separated by a crooked fence, A. showed to B. the two extreme points of a division line, and declared that the boundary line between them was straight, and consented to its being so run. B. caused a straight line to be run between the two points, and erected another fence thereon, which included some land which had been in the possession of A. and his ancestors for more than twenty-five years. While the surveyor was running the straight line, A. made no objection to it; but, before the fence was erected, he gave notice to B. to desist, and forbade the erection of it, and, after it was put up, caused it to be pulled down; on which B. brought an action of trespass against him. Held, the parol declarations or admissions of A. were not sufficient to change the possession, and that B. could not therefore maintain trespass. Dunham *v.* Stuyvesant, 11 Johns. 569.

(*a*) A person claiming land as a preëmptor cannot maintain replevin for timber cut thereon before his right has been proved. Bower *v.* Higbee, 9 Mis. 259.

the plan of the present work does not require or permit us to do more than state the general principles pertaining to it, with the citation of a few illustrative leading cases. It will be seen that some of these cases arise between the parties to the sale, and not between one of them and a third person.

23. Sale of a chattel, without actual delivery, gives the vendee a constructive possession, sufficient to maintain trespass against one who takes the chattel without right.[1] (*a*) It is said, "If the intention of the parties to pass the property, whether absolute or special, in certain ascertained chattels, is established, and they are placed in the hands of a depositary, no matter whether such depositary be a common carrier, or shipmaster, employed by the consignor, or a third person, and the chattels are so placed on account of the person who is to have that property, and the depositary assents, it is enough, and it matters not by what documents this is effected; nor is it material, whether the person who is to have the property be a factor or not."[2] And even such constructive delivery is not in all cases requisite. Thus, where the owner of a chattel sold it to the plaintiff on Saturday night, and the plaintiff used due diligence to obtain possession of it on Sunday, but a creditor of such owner took it on that day and secreted it, and caused it to be attached on Monday on a writ against the owner; it was held that the plaintiff might maintain trespass against the creditor and the attaching officer.[3] So, in trespass, three defendants, who were execution creditors, pleaded, first, not guilty, and, secondly, not possessed; and the other defendants, who were bailiffs of the County Court, pleaded, first, not guilty; secondly, not possessed; thirdly,

[1] Parsons *v.* Dickinson, 11 Pick. 352.
[2] Per Parke, B., Bryans *v.* Nix, 4 M. & W. 775.
[3] Parsons *v.* Dickinson, 11 Pick. 352.

(*a*) The same principle has been applied to a *gift*. If goods given at one place are, at the time of the gift, in another place, and afterwards converted by a stranger before the donee can take possession of them, an action by the donee will lie for the conversion. Collis *v.* Bowen, 8 Blackf. 262.

no notice of action; fourthly, that the action was not commenced within three calendar months. It appeared that R. had made a deed of assignment to the plaintiff of the goods in a certain house, to hold upon trust, to permit and suffer R. to hold the goods and premises, until demand of payment of money which should become due, and with further trusts to sell if the money should not be paid. The execution creditors obtained judgment against R. in the County Court, execution issued, and the goods mentioned in the assignment were seized. The plaintiff proved the seizure and sale, by the production of the writ, with the levy indorsed by the bailiff. The jury found that the assignment was not *bonâ fide*, that the bailiffs had been indemnified by the other defendants, and that the bailiffs acted *bonâ fide*, believing that they were acting under the authority of the County Courts Act. A verdict was entered for the plaintiff on the first issue, for all the defendants on the second, and for the defendants who were bailiffs on the third and fourth issues. Held, that a right to the present possession of the goods passed under the assignment, sufficient to entitle the plaintiff to maintain trespass.[1] So the purchaser of a chattel at a sale by auction may, upon offering to comply with the terms of the sale, and a refusal by the vendor to make delivery, maintain trover therefor.[2]

24. More especially, as has been suggested, where a sale is accompanied or followed by a *constructive delivery*, the buyer acquires a possession sufficient to maintain an action against one who takes or withholds the property. Such delivery generally consists in the delivery to the purchaser of some written voucher or evidence of title, which by the agreement of parties or the usage of trade denotes a complete and executed transfer of the property. Thus a party, to whom the property is to be delivered by the terms of a bill of lading, has the legal title, and may maintain replevin.[3] So where

[1] White *v.* Morris, 11 Eng. L. & Eq. 515.

[2] Simmons *v* Anderson, 7 Rich. 67.

[3] Powell *v.* Bradlee, 9 Gill & Johns. 220.

goods are shipped to a person, for the special purpose of placing funds in his hands to meet a bill drawn by the shipper upon him; he may maintain trover, although no bill of lading is executed, but merely a receipt signed by the mate of the vessel, acknowledging the shipment of the goods, to be delivered to the plaintiff. Thus a manufacturer at Newcastle consigned goods to the plaintiffs, his factors in London, specifically to meet a bill drawn upon them, transmitting to them a receipt, signed by the mate of the vessel, acknowledging the goods to have been received on board, to be delivered to the plaintiffs. Held, that the plaintiffs had a sufficient property in the goods, and right to the possession, to entitle them to maintain trover against a wrongdoer, the consignor not having repudiated the contract upon which they were sent.[1] So W., possessed of a Stockton wharfinger's receipt for goods about to be shipped to London, assigned the receipt to the plaintiff, together with an order to the defendant, a London wharfinger, to deliver the goods to the plaintiff. The defendant, on sight of the order, before the goods arrived, promised to deliver them to the plaintiff on their arrival. Held, that the plaintiff might maintain trover against him, on his refusal to deliver after arrival.[2] So, a vendor having ascertained, whilst the goods were in the hands of a wharfinger, that the purchaser to whom they had been originally consigned had stopped payment, indorsed the bill of lading to the plaintiff, and directed him to take possession of the goods, and he accordingly demanded them of the wharfinger. Held, the plaintiff had a sufficient special property in the goods to enable him to maintain trover, on the ground, that the right of stoppage *in transitu* by the vendor was not at an end when the plaintiff made the demand.[3]

25. But, in case of sale, although a *right of property* may be acquired by the contract itself and other accompanying

[1] Evans v. Nichol, 3 Man. & G. 614; 4 Scott, N. R. 43.

[2] Holl v. Griffin, 10 Bing. 246.

[3] Morrison v. Gray, 9 Moore, 484; 2 Bing. 260.

acts; it is often held that the *right of possession*, necessary to maintain an action, is not acquired without *payment* or tender of the price.[1] Thus A., a hop-merchant, on several days in August, sold to B., by contract, various parcels of hops. Part of them were weighed, and an account of the weights, together with samples, delivered to the vendee. The usual time of payment in the trade was the second Saturday subsequent to the purchase. B. did not pay for the hops at the usual time, whereupon A. gave notice, that, unless they were paid for by a certain day, they would be resold. The hops were not paid for, and A. resold a part, with the consent of B., who afterwards became bankrupt, and then A. sold the residue without the assent of B. or his assignees. Account sales were delivered to B., in which he was charged warehouse rent from the 30th of August. The assignees demanded the hops of A., and tendered the warehouse rent, charges, &c.; and, A. having refused to deliver them, brought trover. The jury found that the defendant had not rescinded the sale. Held, the action could not be maintained, the plaintiffs not having a right of possession until they paid or tendered the price.[2] So a quantity of hops was purchased from the defendants in April, 1831, the invoice of which contained the words "on rent." The hops remained in the seller's warehouse, and a bill accepted by the buyer was afterwards given them at their request, which they indorsed on getting it discounted. During the running of that bill, a part of the hops was delivered, in pursuance of the buyer's order to his sub-purchaser, who paid the warehouse rent charged by the sellers. Afterwards, and before the bill became due, the original buyer became bankrupt, and it was dishonored at maturity. Held, that, though the sellers might not have a right, while the bill remained outstanding, to part with the hops remaining in their possession, the assignee of the original buyer could not maintain trover for them, without actual payment of the price agreed on, as well as of the warehouse rent, he having only the right of

[1] Bloxham *v.* Morley, 7 Dow. & R. 407

[2] Bloxham *v.* Sanders, 4 B. & C. 941.

property, without that of possession.[1] So the defendant agreed to sell to the plaintiff certain apples, to be taken and paid for by the latter on a given day. In the interim, the apples were deposited in a kiln within a *hoast-house*, the key of the kiln being delivered to the plaintiff, that of the *hoast-house* being retained by the defendant. The plaintiff making default, the defendant resold the apples. Held, that the plaintiff had not such a possession as to entitle him to maintain trover against the defendant, for reselling before the lapse of a reasonable time.[2] So A., being possessed of an old vessel, sent her to B.'s yard to be repaired. B. agreed to find timber for the repairs, and materials were accordingly supplied by B. and other persons to the amount of £200. The vessel was repaired in B.'s yard with these materials, but no work was done upon her by either B. or the other creditors. On the vessel's being advertised for sale, B. and the other persons insisted that she should not be removed until they were paid. A.'s agent assented, and said that they should be paid out of the purchase-money, and signed an authority to the auctioneer to that effect. The sale then proceeded, and the vessel was knocked down to the plaintiff for £300. Immediately after the sale, B. and the other creditors applied to the plaintiff for payment, and he promised that he would, on a certain day, bring the purchase-money for the auctioneer to pay the creditors with, but failed to do so. Held, that the agreement for payment of the repairs out of the purchase-money, of which the plaintiff was cognizant, and to which he assented, precluded him from maintaining trover until such payment was made.[3] So A., the owner of flour, delivered it to a forwarder at Rochester, and took a receipt, expressing that the flour was to be sent to the defendant at Albany; he being the factor to whom A. usually consigned flour for sale, and A. being indebted to him for advances on previous consignments. A. on the same day drew upon the defendant against the flour, and procured

[1] Miles v. Gorton, 4 Tyr. 295.

[2] Milgate v. Kebble, 3 Scott, N. R. 358.

[3] Norris v. Williams, 1 Cr. & M. 842.

the plaintiffs, a bank at Rochester, to discount the draft, on delivering to the bank the forwarder's receipt, and agreeing that the bank might hold it as security for the acceptance of the draft. The defendant refused to accept the draft, but subsequently received the flour and converted it to his own use, having notice of the transaction with the plaintiffs. Held, the defendant was liable in trover.[1] So, where one sold to the plaintiff a quantity of hops, to be paid for on delivery, and sent them to the defendants, who were forwarders and warehousemen, to be delivered to the plaintiff on payment; held, the title did not pass before payment, and the plaintiff, having neglected to make payment and receive the hops, for an unreasonable time after being notified of their arrival, could not maintain trover against the defendants, who shipped them to another market, in accordance with the orders of the vendor.[2]

25 *a*. And, on the other hand, the fact of payment is often relied upon, as effecting a change of possessory title. Thus, where A. agrees to sell horses to B., at a certain price, and B. pays the price, which A. accepts, and agrees to deliver up the horses; the sale is complete, and B., after demand and refusal, can maintain trover for the horses.[3] So also the payment of *earnest*, more especially if accompanied by a tender of the whole price. Thus in an old case, the plaintiff agreed to exchange The Folly, his own vessel, for The Roker, the defendant's, and to give twenty-five guineas to boot; and, if The Folly was lost in the voyage she was then upon, thirty guineas. The plaintiff also paid a guinea as earnest. The defendant wrote to excuse himself, that he could not make the exchange, because he had sold the vessel. The plaintiff then tendered twenty-four guineas, deducting one for earnest; but the defendant refused them. Afterwards, in another voyage, The Folly being lost, the plaintiff brought trover for the value. Held, the action would lie; for the delivery was complete by payment of the ear-

[1] The Bank, &c. *v*. Jones, 4 Comst. 497.

[2] Conway *v*. Bush, 4 Barb. 564.

[3] Miller *v*. Koger, 9 Humph. 231.

nest, and the defendant's detention of the vessel afterward was tortious.[1]

25 *b*. But, after delivery, non-payment of the price will not revest a title in the vendor. Thus, where the consignor of goods abroad advised the consignee by letter that he had chartered a certain ship on his account, and inclosed him an invoice of the goods laden on board, which were therein expressed to be for account and risk of the consignee, and also a bill of lading in the usual form, expressing the delivery to be made to order, &c., he paying freight for the said goods according to charter-party; and the letter of advice also informed the consignee, that the consignor had drawn bills on him at three months for the value of the cargo: held, the invoice and bill of lading sent to the consignee, and the delivery of the goods to the captain, vested the property in the consignee, subject only to be divested by the consignor's right to stop the goods *in transitu* in case of the insolvency of the consignee. And, the consignor's agent having obtained possession of the cargo under another bill of lading, and having refused to deliver it up, unless the consignee would make immediate payment, which he declined doing, but offered his acceptances at three months in the manner before stipulated; held, the consignee might maintain trover against such agent, without having tendered payment of the freight either to him or to the captain, the defendant having possessed himself of the goods wrongfully.[2]

26. The principle, that payment is essential to a complete right of property and possession in the vendee, is held more especially applicable, where a sale is by its express terms not to be complete until payment of the price. Thus where a verbal condition is made, that property delivered to a vendee shall not vest in him until the price is paid, the vendor may bring trover, if the property is attached and sold by an officer on an execution against the vendee.[3] So where the defendant acknowledged in writing, that he had received a

[1] James *v*. Price, Lofft, 219.
[2] Walley *v*. Montgomery, 3 E. 585.
[3] Bennett *v*. Sims, 1 Rice, 421.

pair of oxen from the plaintiff, for the purpose of enabling him to perform certain work, which he had contracted to do for the plaintiff, and the writing contained a condition, that, when the job was completed, or at any time, if the plaintiff should choose, he should have the right to take the oxen, by paying the defendant for what he had done towards the work, and, on completion of the work, and on settling therefor, the oxen, with other property delivered on the same terms, were to be "turned in" in payment for the work; it was held, that the payment to the defendant was a condition precedent to the right of the plaintiff to take the oxen, and, without such payment, he could not maintain trover, though the defendant had sold them before the work was complete.[1] So, where A. purchased land, under an agreement with his vendor that no timber should be cut until the land was paid for, and afterwards A. sold the timber to B., and transferred his interest in the land to C., with notice of the sale of the timber; held, B. could maintain case against C. for cutting the timber.[2]

26 *a*. But on a contract for the sale of a chattel *on credit*, time, without express stipulation, is not of the essence of the contract; and the vendee, on tender of the price, though after the expiration of the period of credit, may maintain trover against the vendor to recover such chattel. The vendor cannot rescind the contract on non-payment at the day.[3]

27. Questions often arise in reference to property and possession, where a sale is indeterminate as to the precise number or quantity of goods sold, for want of selection or appropriation from a bulk, mass, or larger number of distinct but similar articles. So also, where the specific articles designed to be sold are not distinctly identified. Or where the contract is in its form or nature rather *executory* than executed; including contracts of *manufacture*. Thus an order, signed by A., for the delivery by the defendants, wharfingers,

[1] Walker *v*. M'Naughton, 16 Verm. 388.

[2] Lillibridge *v*. Sartwell, 8 Barr, 523.

[3] Martindale *v*. Smith, 1 Gale & Dav. 1.

of twenty sacks of flour to the plaintiff, was lodged with and accepted by them in the usual course of business; they at the same time declaring they had but five sacks to spare, which the party might have, and which he received accordingly. On application for the rest, they declined to deliver it. In this action, of trover, it did not appear that the plaintiff knew that A. had any other flour in the defendants' possession, and the defendants did not produce any delivery orders, by which any such flour had been previously appropriated by A. Held, the action was maintainable, as the defendants had not limited their acceptance to any minor quantity of flour, or alleged that they must select the sacks to be delivered to the plaintiff.[1] So the defendant sold to the plaintiff 625 bags of corn, which was a portion of a larger quantity which the defendant had previously purchased, and which was to be delivered to the defendant at the railroad depot in Charleston; and the defendant gave to the plaintiff the following delivery order: "Mr. C. D., Agent, Railroad Company: Sir, please deliver to (the plaintiff) 625 bags of corn, consigned to me, and oblige (the defendant). P. S. I am not certain that all the corn has arrived at the depot, but when it comes let (the plaintiff) have it. January 25, 1847." When the corn had arrived, the plaintiff tendered to the defendant the purchase-money, and demanded the corn, but the defendant refused to let him have it. Held, that the order sufficiently identified the corn, as being the first 625 bags that should arrive, and transferred to the plaintiff the right of property therein, and gave him such constructive possession as would enable him to maintain trover therefor, on demand and refusal.[2] But, where ten sacks of salt are bought with the funds of the plaintiff, and at the same time five with the funds of another person, and all are delivered, without any distinguishing marks, to the latter, from whom the defendant receives them and converts them to his own use; trover does not lie.[3]

27 *a*. And in general trover does not lie to recover goods

[1] Gillett *v*. Hill, 4 Tyr. 290.

[2] Sahlman *v*. Mills, 3 Strobh. 384.

[3] Hill *v*. Robison, 3 Jones, Law, 501.

due under an executory contract.[1] Thus an agreement to purchase property for another, no funds being furnished, and no general agency existing, vests no title in such other person, and, if he takes the property forcibly, he is liable in trover.[2] So, where the plaintiff and A. entered into an agreement, which stated that the plaintiff had bought of A. a certain quantity of timber, which the plaintiff was to pay for at the measurement in the city of New York, when it was delivered; and the plaintiff also agreed that the amount of the timber should be indorsed on notes which he held against A.; held, this agreement was executory, and did not vest the property in the timber in the plaintiff, who, therefore, could not maintain trover against a third person for the conversion of it.[3] So the defendants contracted to sell to K. fifty hogsheads of sugar, called double loaves, at 100*s.* per cwt., to be delivered free on board a British ship. K. sold to the plaintiff by the same description, and the defendants assented to the re-sale, the sugar not having been delivered or weighed. Held, the plaintiff could not recover for it in trover.[4] So, where the defendant agrees generally to make three lumber wagons for the plaintiff within a given time, and deliver them, and he completes but does not deliver them; no title passes, and replevin will not lie, but the remedy is a suit on the contract.[5]

27 *b.* But, where an unfinished sleigh was in the shop of a painter, who was to finish it by a time specified; and the owner of the sleigh went to the shop with the plaintiff, and there sold the sleigh to the plaintiff at a price agreed upon; and no payment was made, nor the sleigh then actually delivered to the plaintiff, but it was agreed that it should be when finished, and the painter, who was present, was directed and agreed so to deliver it; held, the plaintiff might maintain trespass against a sheriff, who attached and took away the sleigh before it was finished, on a writ against the vendor.[6]

1 Wood *v.* Atkinson, 2 Murph. 87.
2 Paige *v.* Hammond, 26 Verm. 375.
3 M'Donald *v.* Hewett, 15 Johns. 349.
4 Austin *v.* Cravan, 4 Taunt. 644
5 Updike *v.* Henry, 14 Hill, 378.
6 Willard *v.* Lull, 17 Verm. 412.

So A. and B. entered into a contract in writing, that A. would deliver to B., at his factory, from time to time, as might be required to keep the factory in operation, a specified quantity of wool; that B. would manufacture the wool into cassimeres, and deliver the cassimeres so manufactured to A. at the factory, from time to time, as they should be finished and ready for market; that A. should send the cassimeres to market and have them sold, and pay to B., for manufacturing, the balance of money obtained for them, after deducting 44 cents for every pound of wool so delivered by A., and the interest and cost of freight; that A. should pay to B. one third of the money received in advance for the cassimeres, for the purpose of defraying the expense of manufacturing; that A., before sending the cassimeres to market, might take one ninth of the number of yards at 90 cents per yard; and that B. would also manufacture for A. another lot of wool of about 5,000 pounds, upon receiving notice within two weeks that A. so desired. Held, the property in the cloth was in A., and he had the right to the possession of it as fast as it was manufactured, and might sustain trover against B. and one to whom B. had sold a portion of the cloth, to recover for the cloth so sold.[1]

28. As a necessary result of the principles already stated, it may be added, that a *conditional* or *qualified* sale and delivery will not divest the seller of his possession, so as to prevent his maintaining a possessory action against a party who interferes with the property. More especially where payment has not been made. Thus the plaintiffs, machinists in Connecticut, contracted to furnish B. with a paper-making machine, to be put up by them in B.'s mill in Worcester; and, if it worked to B.'s satisfaction, he was to pay for it, otherwise the plaintiffs were to take it away. It weighed about eight tons, and B. was to cart it from Connecticut to Worcester. The plaintiffs accordingly set it up, in a new mill adapted purposely to the dimensions and structure of the machine, and, before the setting up of the machine was

[1] Buckmaster v. Mower, 21 Verm. 204.

completed, and while some of its essential parts were wanting, it was put in operation for experiment, but did not work advantageously and to the satisfaction of B.; and on the same day on which this trial was made it was attached as the property of B. Held, that the property had not been transferred to B., and that the plaintiffs had sufficient possession to maintain trespass against the attaching officer.[1]

29. The question of the right of possession also arises, in case of transfers *for security of debts.* Thus, where goods are assigned as security for an advance of money, upon trust to permit the assignor to remain in possession until default in payment at the time stipulated, and then to sell them; the assignee has sufficient possession to maintain trespass against a wrongdoer.[2] So an indenture was executed between A. and B., setting forth that, B. having become surety for A. for £600, due from A. to C., in consideration of C.'s forbearing proceedings against A., A., for the purpose of securing B., in case he should be required to pay C., had executed a bond to B., conditioned for the payment to B., his executors, &c., of £600 on a certain day; and that, for the better securing B., A. had agreed to grant, &c., his household goods and effects, &c., to B.; and that A., in consideration of B.'s having become such surety, granted unto B. his said goods and effects, &c., but to be void on payment to C. of £600, with interest, on a given day; with a covenant by A. to pay the £600 and interest to C., and to indemnify B., his executors, &c., from the payment thereof, a covenant by A. for quiet enjoyment by B. in case of default, a covenant to insure, and a power of sale for payment to C. of the £600 and interest. Held, that B. might maintain trespass against the sheriff for seizing these goods under a *fi. fa.* against A., notwithstanding that up to the time of the seizure they remained in A.'s possession.[3] But where A., being indebted to B., by a *bonâ fide* bill of sale conveyed to him all his stock in trade, household furniture, &c., with a covenant to

[1] Phelps *v.* Willard, 16 Pick. 29.
[2] White *v.* Morris, 11 Com. Bench, 1015.
[3] Watson *v.* Macquire, 5 Com. Bench, 836.

pay the debt on demand, and a proviso for redemption on payment of the debt and interest on demand, and also that the assignor should continue in possession until default; the goods having before any demand been seized under a *fi. fa.* against A.; held, B. had not a sufficient right of immediate possession to maintain trover.[1]

30. A purchase of property *by an agent*, more especially if made in the name of the principal, will give to the latter a possession sufficient to maintain an action for the wrongful taking of the property. Thus, by an agreement between a father and his son, the plaintiff, the father was to carry on business in the name and on the account of the son, and as his agent, and the son was to give to the father one half of the profits as a compensation for his services; but the business did not yield any profits, and no settlement of accounts was ever made between them. A former, separate creditor of the father having attached certain property, purchased by the father in the name of the son under this agreement, it was held that trover might be maintained by the son against the attaching officer.[2] (*a*) Though it is also said, "It is not true, that in cases of special property the party must once have had possession in order to maintain trover; for a factor, to whom goods have been consigned, and who has never received them, may maintain such an action."[3] So, where the owner of goods delivers them to his agent to keep, and they are taken from the agent by third persons, the owner may maintain trespass.[4] Thus, where A. owned lumber in and about a mill, and mortgaged it to the plaintiff and

[1] Bradley *v.* Copley, 1 Com. Bench, 685.

[2] Blanchard *v.* Coolidge, 22 Pick. 151.

[3] Per Eyre, C. J., Fowler *v.* Down, 1 B. & P. 47.

[4] Thorp *v.* Burling, 11 Johns. 285.

(*a*) On the other hand, a servant or agent may maintain an action on the ground of possession, though he has no right of property. Thus a master of a fly-boat, who is hired by a canal company at weekly wages, may maintain trespass for cutting a rope fastened to the vessel, whereby it was being towed along an inland navigation, although the vessel and the rope were the property of the company. Moore *v.* Robinson, 2 B. & Ad. 817.

B., who had possession and charge of it, and the plaintiff went to the mill to take possession, and desired B. to take possession for him, and to take charge of it as he had done before, to which B. made no objection; and a son of the mortgagor, as his agent, accompanied the plaintiff for the purpose of giving him possession; held, the plaintiff might maintain trespass against the defendants, who showed no title.[1] So the gratuitous lender of a chattel may maintain trespass against the officer and plaintiff, in a suit against the borrower, for an attachment of such chattel.[2] So a servant, put into the occupation of a cottage, with less wages on that account, does not occupy it as a tenant, but the master may properly declare on it as his own occupation, in an action on the case, for a disturbance of a right of way over the defendant's close to such cottage. And it matters not that the cottage was divided into two parts, one of which only was in the occupation of such servant, the other being occupied by a tenant paying rent.[3] So one claiming land under color of title, who puts a servant into a house upon the land, with the privilege of getting fire-wood therefrom, is, as against a wrongdoer, in possession of the whole tract, and may maintain trespass for the cutting of timber thereon.[4]

30 *a*. But where the plaintiff, a prisoner, assigned all his effects under the insolvent debtor's act, June 17th; and his wife continued to reside in his house, retaining some of the furniture; and, on the 9th of July, the wife having been absent for two days, and no one being in the house, the defendant committed a trespass in an attempt to distrain for rent; held, the wife had not a sufficient possession to enable the plaintiff to sue in trespass.[5]

31. In general, *possession* and *change of possession* are questions of fact for the jury. But where, in trespass against a constable and others, for taking a horse alleged to belong to the plantiff, by virtue of an execution against A., the plaintiff's brother, it appeared in evidence that the horse be-

[1] Morse *v.* Pike, 15 N. H. 529.
[2] Overby *v.* Magee, 15 Ark. 459.
[3] Bertie *v.* Beaumont, 16 E. 33.
[4] Lamb *v.* Swain, 3 Jones, Law, 370.
[5] Topham *v.* Dent, 6 Bing. 515.

longed to A., who sold him to the plaintiff, before the execution, for a full price; that the plaintiff and A. lived together; and that after the sale the plaintiff kept the horse in the same stable in which A. had kept him; and there was no evidence of any actual change of possession; held, it was error for the Court to leave it to the jury to say, from the evidence, whether or not the possession was changed.[1]

32. Title *by execution* may also be the foundation of an action founded on legal possession. Thus, in trespass *quare clausum*, if the land was purchased by the plaintiff at sheriff's sale, and was vacant at the time of the sale, and when the sheriff's deed was executed; he may recover without taking actual possession.[2] So the purchaser of an equity of redemption, sold on execution, which had been attached on the writ, takes a right of immediate possession, which enables him to maintain trespass *quare clausum* against a party, claiming under a conveyance made by the debtor since the attachment.[3]

33. In accordance with the general rule, that possession raises a presumption of title; where goods are taken upon execution while in the actual possession of the defendant in the execution, and are replevied by a person claiming to be the owner, the *onus* of proving that they are his property rests upon the plaintiff. Otherwise, if the goods were not in possession of the defendant. And the plaintiff in replevin has a right to go to the jury upon the question as to the actual possession.[4] But, in reference to real property, a plaintiff in trespass to try title, who claims under a sale by the sheriff, must show a title in the execution debtor; and the judgment sale and conveyance by the sheriff, with proof that the party was in possession, and was the reputed owner at the time of the sale, are not sufficient to put the defendant to show a better title. But any evidence, which would have protected such party in a suit against him for the recovery of the land; as, for instance, proof of adverse possession

[1] Hoffner *v.* Clark, 5 Whart. 545.
[2] Raub *v.* Heath, 8 Blackf. 575.
[3] Abbott *v.* Sturtevant, 30 Maine, 40.
[4] Merritt *v.* Lyon, 3 Barb. 110.

for the time required by the statute of limitations; will sustain the action.[1] (*a*)

34. With regard to mere constructive possession, either by deed or otherwise, it is an important qualification to the right of action thereby acquired, that prior constructive possession must yield to subsequent actual adverse possession.[2] (*b*) Thus, where the plaintiff entered under claim of title upon a tract

[1] Sims *v.* Randal, 1 Brev. 85.

[2] Davis *v.* White, 1 Williams, 751.

(*a*) An authenticated copy of the judgment, and the original execution, are admissible evidence. Stevelie *v.* Laury, 2 Brev. 135.

But the sheriff's return to the execution cannot be received in evidence to contradict his deed, by showing that there has been no sale; and evidence that the purchase-money had not been paid is also inadmissible. Hairston *v.* Hairston, 1 Brev. 305.

But, in an action of trespass to try title, a subsequent purchaser at sheriff's sale may show, that a prior sheriff's sale was fraudulent and void, although there had been no proceeding in equity setting aside such prior sale. Martin *v.* Ranlett, 5 Rich. 541.

The action of trespass to try titles cannot be sustained, on a sheriff's deed bearing date subsequently to the commencement of the action, although the sale was previous to that period. Bank, &c. *v.* South Carolina, &c. 3 Strobh. 190.

But, under a plea of *liberum tenementum*, in trespass *quare clausum*, the plaintiff, who claimed title under a decree of sale as purchaser thereunder, was allowed to prove the decree and sale, which were prior to the trespass for which the action was brought, although the ratification of the sale and the deed to the plaintiff were subsequent to such trespass. Hunter *v.* Hatton, 4 Gill. 115.

(*b*) Where each of the parties, in an action of trespass *quare clausum fregit*, claimed title when the acts complained of were done; and the defendant further claimed, that, if the legal title was in the plaintiff, he, having disseized the plaintiff, was then in exclusive possession; whereupon the Court charged the jury, that, if the plaintiff had been disseized, and was not in possession when the acts were done, he could not maintain this action; and further, that, if the plaintiff had title at the time, his having been previously disseized and dispossessed thereof by the defendant would not prevent his recovery in this action, provided he had, previous to such acts of trespass, regained and retaken possession, so that he was in possession at the time the acts of trespass were committed; that, although a simple reëntry would not revest the possession in him, yet if, as he claimed, he went upon the land, and as owner thereof retook possession and remained there

of land on which was a house which had never been occupied, nailed up the windows, and put into it some old boards; and, a year afterwards, the defendant entered, tore off the boards, and rented the house, and finally moved the house off; held, the plaintiff had not such a possession, without reëntry, as would give him an action of trespass against the defendant.[1] So purchasers of land cannot, by any act of their own, gain such possession, as will enable them to maintain trespass against those in the adverse possession of the premises.[2] Thus a town, having no title to land besides a survey thereof, and an entry thereon under a claim of title, conveyed the land to the plaintiff by deed of warranty, and the plaintiff sued the defendant for a subsequent trespass upon the land. Held, the action could not be maintained, if the defendant, prior to the entry and deed, had possession, claiming title.[3] So an action of trespass *quare clausum*, to recover mesne profits, will not lie in favor of a disseizee, unless he has regained the possession *by entry*.[4] So the plaintiff, who had built a chapel, conveyed it to the defendant by a deed, the validity of which was questionable. The defendant took possession, and gave the key to a gardener, who, with his permission, lent it to the plaintiff to preach in the chapel. The plaintiff thereupon locked the chapel, and refused to redeliver the key. Held, that he had not sufficient possession to maintain trespass, the defendant

[1] Patterson *v.* Bodenhammer, 11 Ired. 4.

[2] Sigerson *v.* Hornsby, 14 Mis. 71.

[3] Williston *v.* Morse, 10 Met. 17.

[4] Fry *v.* The Branch Bank, &c. 16 Ala. 282.

---

for some two or three days, cutting and carrying away the wood and timber, keeping the defendant out of the possession, and forbidding him from entering upon the same; such a retaking of possession would enable him to maintain this action for any act of trespass committed by the defendant at any time thereafter: it was held, that, taking the whole charge together, it did not dispense with possession by the plaintiff at the time of the alleged trespasses; nor assert that the acts of the plaintiff constituted, as *matter of law*, a retaking of the possession by him; consequently, that, after a verdict for the plaintiff, a new trial ought not to be granted for a misdirection. Payne *v.* Clark, 20 Conn. 30.

having broken open the chapel.[1] And a similar principle has been applied in a case of personal property. Thus goods are sold by the defendant to the plaintiff, to be paid for by instalments, the balance to be paid before removal. The defendant allows the plaintiff to place the goods under lock and key upon the defendant's premises, and delivers the key to the plaintiff, but retains the key of the external enclosure. The balance being unpaid, the plaintiff has not such a possession, as will entitle him to maintain trover against the defendant, upon a wrongful removal and sale of the goods.[2]

35. In further illustration of the general proposition, that possession rather than title is the legal foundation of an action for tort, it may be added; that, while damages for a wrongful entry on land by *a disseizor* may be recovered, although the owner has not regained possession when the suit is brought;[3] the owner of land cannot maintain such action against a disseizor in actual possession, after a mere formal entry, and more especially pending a writ of entry against the disseizor.[4] Nor, after an ouster, can the plaintiff recover damages for subsequent trespasses, without a reëntry; but, after reëntry, he may lay his action with a *continuando*, and recover for mesne profits as well as damages for the ouster,[5] together with damages for a subsequent entry by the defendant.[6] So, where a remainder-man enters upon a party, who is in possession by intrusion; trespass lies against the intruder, although he retain the actual possession.[7] So, if a disseizee lawfully enters upon the land and exercises acts of ownership thereon, he thereby regains the possession, sufficiently to entitle him to maintain an action of trespass against the disseizor for his subsequent entry.[8] And an entry upon the land, measuring the lines, asserting thereupon

[1] Revett *v.* Brown, 5 Bing. 7; 2 Moo. & P. 12.

[2] Milgate *v.* Kebble, 3 M. & Gr. 100.

[3] Gilchrist *v.* McLaughlin, 7 Ired. 310.

[4] Chadbourne *v.* Straw, 9 Shep. 450. See Pratt *v.* Battels, 2 Wms. 685; Holcomb *v.* Rowlins, Cro. Eliz. 540; Monckton *v.* Pashley, 2 Ld. Ray. 974; 2 Salk. 638; Case *v.* Shepherd, 2 Johns. Cas. 27; Shields *v.* Henderson, 1 Lit. 239; King *v.* Baker, 29 Penn. 200.

[5] Stean *v.* Anderson, 4 Har. 209.

[6] Cutting *v.* Cox, 19 Verm. 517; King *v.* Baker, 25 Penn. 186.

[7] Butcher *v.* Butcher, 1 M. & Ry. 220.

[8] Putney *v.* Dresser, 2 Met. 583.

his claim of title, and directing his agent to cut the grass, with notice to the disseizor or trespasser, constitutes a sufficient reëntry by the owner, to enable him to recover damages, in an action of trespass, for the value of the grass which the disseizor subsequently cut upon the land.[1] (*a*) So any acts of ownership on the land, as ploughing it, or the like, or a formal declaration of the intention accompanying the entry, will maintain an action of trespass.[2] (*b*) And the levy of an execution on land which is not the judgment debtor's, even though followed by acts of constructive possession, does not work such a disseizin of the true owner, as will prevent his maintaining an action of trespass, without reëntry, against the judgment creditor or those acting under him. Thus, where the land was part of a large unenclosed meadow, and the judgment creditor entered thereon two or three times for the purpose of showing the grass for sale, but took no actual possession; and afterwards advertised a sale of the grass in a public newspaper, as grass growing on his land, and caused the same to be sold at auction, at a distance from the land; and the purchaser thereof cut and carried it away, the true owner of the land having no actual notice of the proceedings: held, the owner might maintain trespass against the purchaser of the grass.[3] (*c*)

1 Cutting *v*. Cox, 19 Verm. 517.
2 Byrum *v*. Carter, 4 Ired. 310.
3 Blood *v*. Wood, 1 Met. 528.

(*a*) But, where the defendant was owner in fee of land of which the plaintiff in replevin had disseized him, and had sown wheat thereon, and after the disseizin the defendant reëntered, and was in the actual and lawful possession of the land and the wheat as his own property; held, the plaintiff had no right to immediate possession of the wheat, and could not maintain replevin. Hooser *v*. Hays, 10 B. Mon. 72.

(*b*) But although such entry be made, yet, if the wrongdoer continue his possession, the deed of the owner, not being made on the land, and such adverse possession continuing, is not valid to pass a title. 4 Ired. 310.

(*c*) The plaintiff recovered judgment, in a case of unlawful detainer, against B., for a tract of land in the possession of B.'s tenant, the defendant, and the sheriff delivered the plaintiff constructive possession on a

36. Where the owner of land has been disseized for six years, and has brought a writ of entry, and the disseizor has put in his claim for improvements made by him, and the amount has been found by the jury, and the owner has elected to retain it and pay for the improvements; the disseizor should not be made accountable for timber trees cut upon the land during the disseizin by another without his consent or connivance; and, if the timber thus cut has come into possession of the owner, and is afterwards taken from him by the disseizor, he may maintain trespass against the disseizor for such taking during the pendency of the writ of entry.[1]

[1] Brown *v.* Ware, 25 Maine, 411.

---

writ of *habere facias*, since which the plaintiff's tenant had farmed the land. B. afterwards obtained a *supersedeas* of the judgment, and the defendant refused to deliver the landlord's share of the crop to the plaintiff, but delivered it to B., notwithstanding he had, previously to the *supersedeas*, and on the plaintiff's request, promised the plaintiff to deliver it to him. Held, the plaintiff could not maintain trespass against the defendant therefor, and the execution of the writ of *habere facias* gave the plaintiff no possession as against the defendant. Kretzer *v.* Wysong, 5 Gratt. 9.

CHAPTER XIX.

NUISANCE.

1. For the reasons already explained, (*ante*, p. 535,) first in order among injuries to property, we proceed to consider that of *Nuisance*. Much that would be appropriate to this title has already been stated, in the chapter (chapter 3) relating to the necessary elements of actions in general, or the essential ingredients of those wrongs, for which actions may be maintained. (*a*)

(*a*) It will be seen at once, that this preliminary inquiry must necessarily involve many consideratious more specially applicable to the present title, *cause of action* and *nuisance* or *injury* being almost equivalent or synonymous expressions.

Nuisance, in its largest sense, signifies "anything that worketh hurt, inconvenience, or damage." 3 Bl. Comm. 215.

"All the acts put forth by man, which tend directly to create evil consequences to the community at large, may be deemed nuisances, where they are of such magnitude as to require the interposition of the Courts. 2 Bish. on Crim. L. § 848.

The word is sometimes used as equivalent to *tort*, and applied as well to wrongs against the person or personal property, as against real estate. 3 Stark. Ev. 979. While by other writers it is restricted to acts "injuriously affecting the *lands, tenements, or hereditaments* of an individual." 2 Greenl. Ev. § 465.

2. One prominent characteristic of a *nuisance*, technically so called, is, that it is to some extent an *undefined* injury. Thus it is *indirect* or *remote*, as distinguished from an immediate invasion by one man of another's property; and for this reason the proper subject of an action on the case, which is a remedy appropriate to the misuse of a party's own right or property, to the damage of his neighbor; and not of trespass or trover, which lies for an unlawful taking or conversion of the property of another. And for another reason, the injury of nuisance is of a more comprehensive or miscellaneous character than any other; namely, that it relates to rights not in their nature specific, definable, or tangible, but incident to or growing out of corporeal property, and, in part on account of this incorporeal character, varying with the diverse circumstances of individual cases. Hence the origin of the legal phrase — action on the case; which means an action not falling within the ancient and technical formulas, but adapted to the particular case which arises, and which otherwise would be without remedy. (*a*) Thus it is

---

(*a*) "The action on the case is so termed, as distinguishing the remedy from the *brevia formata*. In its most comprehensive signification, it includes assumpsit as well as an action in form *ex delicto;* but at the present time, when an action on the case is mentioned, it is usually understood to mean an action in form *ex delicto*." 1 Chit. Pl. 135.

"At a very early period specific forms of actions were provided for such injuries, as had then most usually occurred; and Bracton, observing on the original writs on which our actions are founded, declares them to be fixed and immutable, unless by authority of parliament." 3 Bl. Comm. 117. But, to meet "like case falling under like law, and requiring like remedy," but not coming within the established forms, an ancient statute (Westminster 2d, 13 Edw. I. c. 24) authorized the clerks in chancery to make a writ or "adjourn the plaintiffs until the next parliament; and by consent of men learned in the law, a writ shall be made." 2 Bl. R. 1113; 3 Woode. 168; Webb's case, 8 Co. 45 *b*.

With reference to the distinction between a nuisance and other wrongs to property, as connected with *the remedy;* it may be added, and will be more fully stated hereafter, that an injunction in equity, which partakes more of the character of the action on the case than any other action at

said, "Actions on the case are founded on the common law, or upon acts of parliament, and lie generally to recover damages for torts, not committed with force actual or implied, or having been occasioned by force, where the matter affected was not tangible or the injury was not immediate but consequential, or where the interest in the property was only in reversion. Torts of this nature are to the absolute or relative rights of persons or to personal property in possession or reversion, or to real property, corporeal or incorporeal, in possession or reversion."[1]

3. In reference to the general question, what constitutes a nuisance, technically so called; a precise definition is of course impracticable, and the law is best explained by the particular instances of annoyance or injury, which have been adjudged to be, or not to be, nuisances. The following criterion has been suggested by high authority: "Is the inconvenience more than fanciful, or one of mere delicacy or fastidiousness; as an inconvenience materially interfering with the ordinary comfort physically of human existence, not merely according to elegant or dainty modes and habits of living, but according to plain, sober, and simple notions among the English people,"[2]

[1] 1 Chit. Pl. 135.

[2] Per Knight Bruce, V. C., Walter *v.* Telfe, 4 DeG. & S. 315.

---

law, is a familiar process to prevent or restrain nuisances; while it is very rarely allowed for a mere trespass. This difference is usually predicated upon the ground, that a nuisance is ordinarily continuous, while a trespass commonly consists of a single act.

A court has no authority to enjoin a trespasser without color of right. Lutheran Church *v.* Maschop, 2 Stockt. 57.

An injunction ought not to be granted in aid of an action of trespass, unless it appear that the injury will be irreparable, and cannot be compensated in damages. Waldron *v.* Marsh, 5 Cal. 119.

It is not sufficient that the affidavit alleges that the injury would be irreparable; it must be shown to the Court how and why it would be so; especially where no action has ever determined the plaintiff's rights. Ibid.

A prayer for an injunction, to restrain a trespass which does not appear to cause irreparable injury, is fatally defective. Bolster *v.* Catterlin, 10 Ind. 117.

4. As has been already, in other connections, explained, one of the characteristics of nuisance, as distinguished from trespass or conversion, is, that it consists in a use of one's own property, which involves injury to the property or other right or interest of his neighbor. And the principle is laid down, that, if one carry on a lawful business in such a manner as to prove a nuisance to his neighbor, he is answerable for the damages.[1] But it is also said, that which is authorized by an act of the legislature cannot be a nuisance.[2] Neither an injunction nor an action will lie, to redress a consequential injury, necessarily resulting from the lawful exercise of a right granted by the sovereign power of the State, or authorized by competent municipal authority.[3] Thus it is held, partly upon this ground, that a railroad in the streets of a city or village is not *per se* a nuisance.[4] (*a*) And a railroad company, authorized to lay rails in the public streets, will not be liable for accidents resulting therefrom, unless guilty of negligence in the laying down.[5] So, where commission-

[1] Fish *v.* Dodge, 4 Denio, 311.

[2] Per Hand, J., Trustees, &c. *v.* Utica, &c. 6 Barb. 313; Stoughton *v.* State, 5 Wis. 291; Hatch *v.* Vermont, &c., 2 Wms. 142.

[3] Williams *v.* The New York, &c. 18 Barb. 222.

[4] Ibid.

[5] Mazetti *v.* New York, &c. 3 E. D. Smith, 98.

(*a*) It is said, in a very recent case, "The public have a right to the maintenance of streets and roads as common highways, subject to restriction by the legislative power of the Commonwealth. There is no longer any reason for controversy as to the right of the legislature to grant the use of them to companies proposing to facilitate the transit of the public along them. This is settled definitively in the cases of The Philadelphia and Trenton Railroad Company, 5 Wharton, 25, and Commonwealth *v.* The Erie and Northeast Railroad Company, 3 Casey, 339." Per Thompson, J., Musser *v.* The Fairmount, &c., Am. Law Reg. March, 1859, p. 285.

But in the same case it was decided, that where a statute, incorporating a City Passenger Railway, required the previous consent of the city councils to use or occupy the streets, and the councils by an ordinance disapproved the statute and declined to permit such use; the privilege was thereby nullified, the power designated by the act being exhausted, and not subject to be exercised by a subsequent conditional approval of the councils. Musser *v.* The Fairmount, &c. Am. Law Reg. March, 1859, p. 284. (This principle has also been recognized in a very recent case in Massachusetts, which, however, has not been formally reported.)

ers, appointed under an act of the legislature to drain swamp lands, are acting in good faith, and are not violating the plain and manifest intent of the statute, a Court would not be justified in restraining their proceedings by injunction.[1] And where a railroad corporation was authorized by the municipal authorities of a city to build a tunnel through the city, a preliminary injunction was refused to an owner of adjoining land, on the allegation by him that it was a nuisance.[2] So it has been held, that equity will not enjoin a turnpike company from taking the complainant's land for their road, where the only question involved is the constitutionality of the act incorporating the company; but will leave the party to his remedy at law.[3] Nor will the Court restrain the erection and continuance of a lamp-post and lamp in front of or near a dwelling-house, upon the ground that it is a nuisance to the owner or inhabitants, unless the fact that it is so is clearly established by proofs. Whether such an erection shall be permitted or continued, rests in the discretion of the corporation of the city having jurisdiction of the subject, and, when no special injury is shown, the Court has no right to restrain the exercise of this discretion.[4]

4 *a*. But the *abuse* of a corporate charter for purposes which it does not contemplate will subject the corporation to an injunction as for a nuisance. Thus a railway company became, by conveyance from a canal company, the owner of a canal, with lands, acquired from several owners for the formation of a reservoir, from which to supply water to the canal; the rights of fishing and sporting over the reservoir, but no other use, being reserved to the former owners. The company projected and held a regatta with aquatic sports on the reservoir, ran cheap trains, and thereby congregated a large concourse of persons, who trespassed on the park surrounding the mansion-house of the plaintiff,

[1] Hartwell *v.* Armstrong, 19 Barb. 166.

[2] Hodgkinson *v.* Long Island, &c. 4 Edw. Ch. 411.

[3] Troth *v.* Troth, 4 Halst. Ch. 237.

[4] Parsons *v.* Travis, 1 Duer, 439.

and adjoining the reservoir, and injured her right of fishing and sporting over the greater part of the reservoir. Notwithstanding her remonstrances, the company announced a second regatta. Upon motion on her behalf, in the suit by her against the company, the latter undertaking not to hold another regatta for a limited period, the Court permitted the plaintiff to try her right at law against the company. On a trial at law, the jury, not agreeing, were discharged; but, on a second trial, a verdict was given for the plaintiff, with nominal damages. The undertaking having expired, the company announced another regatta on the reservoir. The plaintiff again moved an injunction. Held, that the regatta was a nuisance to the plaintiff's property, and an injunction was granted to restrain the defendants from holding the regatta; and the Court directed an issue, to try whether the company could use the reservoir for any other purpose than to supply their canal with water.[1] So it is held, that a citizen of New York, owning property in Ohio, has a right to come into the Circuit Court of the United States, and enjoin a railway company, incorporated under the laws of the latter State, from doing acts which would produce an irreparable injury to his property situated there. Thus a person owning a tannery, saw-mill, flouring-mill, a store and warehouses, a wharf and water-lots, on a river navigable for steamboats, schooners, and other vessels, and on which a commerce is carried on with different ports, shipments of flour and lumber from his mills and leather from his tannery being constantly made; and who owns stock in a plank-road, which pays a profit by the transportation of produce to and from the place where his property is situated; may enjoin a railway company from materially obstructing the navigation of the bay into which the river discharges.[2] So where a railroad company have voluntarily, and for their own profit, so constructed their road as necessarily to injure a person's property, though in a proper manner and place,

[1] Bostock *v.* North Staffordshire, &c. 19 Eng. Law & Eq. 307.

[2] Works *v.* Junction Railroad, 5 McLean, 425.

there being no remedy given by their charter, they are liable therefor.[1] And it is held, that though the grantee of a franchise for private emolument, as a railroad company, may be vested with the sovereign power to take private property for public use, on making compensation, it is not clothed with the sovereign's immunity from resulting damages. But this power leaves their common-law liability, for injuries done in the exercise of their authority, precisely where it would have stood, if the land had been acquired in the ordinary way.[2]

4 *b*. And it is to be further observed, that, while acts done under authority of law are *primâ facie* not to be treated as nuisances, so, on the other hand, a prohibition by public authority makes the thing prohibited *primâ facie* actionable. Thus, where a city, by its charter, has power to remove all nuisances, the action of the common council, in declaring a certain house to be a nuisance, because its dilapidated condition endangers the lives of passers-by, is *primâ facie* evidence of the fact, and throws the burden of disproving it on the party complaining of the act of the city, in directing the building to be taken down.[3] So the mayor, councilmen, and constable of a town being sued individually, in an action of trespass, for pulling down the plaintiff's house, justified under an ordinance of the corporation, declaring the house a nuisance, it being unoccupied by the plaintiff or a tenant, but used by others in such manner as to endanger the town by fire, and also to make it offensive to the citizens and endanger their lives, and providing, if the plaintiff did not, within a specified time after notice, abate the nuisance, the constable should proceed to do so. On demurrer, held, the justification was sufficient.[4] And chancery has jurisdiction to enjoin and abate a public nuisance, caused by the obstruction of a highway; though the town, within which the nuisance is erected, has been invested by act of the legislature with power to abate nuisances within its limits;

[1] Evansville, &c. *v*. Dick, 9 Ind. 433.

[2] Tinsman *v*. Belvidere, &c. 2 Dutch. 148.

[3] Montgomery *v*. Hutchinson, 13 Ala. 573.

[4] Harvey *v*. Dewoody, 18 Ark. 252.

unless there be an express provision to the contrary.[1] And an act of assembly, legalizing, for the time being, erections already existing in a borough, and being then nuisances, may be afterwards repealed by the assembly.[2] (*a*) So, where the board of health of a city adjudge certain premises to be a nuisance, and an ordinance of the corporation is thereupon passed directing its abatement; in an action of trespass against the corporation, for the act of an agent in carrying the ordinance into effect, the plaintiff is not at liberty to show that the nuisance did not in fact exist at the time of the adjudication; or, on the part of the board of health, any irregularity or non-compliance with the requirements of the statute in such case.[3]

5. We have already (chapter 2) briefly considered the general proposition, that for *a public nuisance* a private

[1] Hoole *v.* Attorney-General, 22 Ala. 190.

[2] Reading *v.* The Commonwealth, 11 Penn. 196.

[3] Van Wormer *v.* The Mayor, &c. 15 Wend. 262.

(*a*) Similar questions often arise upon *indictment.* Thus, where one act gave a company power to make a railway, and another, unqualified power to use locomotive steam-engines thereon, and the railway was constructed in some parts within five yards of a highway; upon an indictment for a nuisance, alleging that horses passing along the highway were terrified by the engines; it was held, that the proceedings complained of must have been sanctioned by statute, and the benefit derived by the public from the railway showed the reasonableness of the privilege granted. Pease's case, 4 B. & Ad. 30.

But where the defendant, proprietor of a colliery, without authority of parliament, made a railway from his colliery to a seaport town, upon the turnpike road, which in some places it narrowed so that there was not room for two carriages to pass, although he gave the public, for a toll, the use of the railway; held, indictable. Morris's case, 1 B. & Ad. 441.

So it is an indictable nuisance, for a gas company to open trenches in the public streets of a populous town, for the purpose of laying their pipes, although they use reasonable dispatch in laying down the pipes and restoring the road. Regina *v.* Sheffield, &c. 22 Eng. L. & Eq. 200.

And it is no defence to an indictment for exercising a noxious trade in a public place, that the selectmen have not assigned a place for the exercise of the trade, as they may do by statute. The State *v.* Hart, 34 Maine, 36.

action cannot be sustained, without proving special and peculiar damage to the plaintiff. As to the nature and degree of such damage, it has been held, that being delayed four hours by an obstruction in a highway, and thereby prevented from performing the same journey as many times in a day as if the obstruction had not existed, is a sufficient injury to maintain an action against the obstructor.[1] So a declaration is sufficient, that the plaintiff, before and at the time of committing the grievance, was navigating his barges, laden with goods, along a public navigable creek, and the defendant wrongfully moored a barge across, and kept the same so moored, from thence hitherto, and thereby obstructed the public navigable creek, and prevented the plaintiff from navigating his barges so laden, *per quod* the plaintiff was obliged to convey his goods a great distance over land, and thereby put to trouble and expense.[2]

5 *a.* So equity will interfere, by injunction, to restrain a public nuisance, which causes special damage to the property of individuals.[3] Thus parties, suffering special damage in the value and use of their property, may have an injunction, to restrain the owner of an adjoining house from its contemplated use as a brothel.[4] But simply cutting off the facilities of a party, for making a new entrance to his lot from a public street, is not sufficient actual damage to justify a private action.[5] And it may be added, in illustration of the general rule, that *an injunction* to prevent a public nuisance is never granted on the application of a private individual, unless the apprehended nuisance would be specially dangerous to himself or injurious to his property,—an injury

[1] Greasly *v.* Codling, 2 Bing. 263. See Cole *v.* Sproul, 35 Maine, 161; Hatch *v.* Vermont, &c. 2 Wms. 142; Bruning *v.* New Orleans, &c. 12 La. An. 541; Hubert *v.* Groves, 1 Esp. 148; Lansing *v.* Wiswall, 5 Denio, 213; Paine *v.* Patrick, Carth. 191; Mayor, &c. *v.* Henley, 1 Bing. N. 222; Pierce *v.* Dart, 7 Cow. 609; Wilkes *v.* Hungerford, &c. 2 Bing. N. C. 281; Mayor, &c. *v.* Furze, 3 Hill, 612; Baxter *v.* Winooski, &c. 22 Verm. 114; Quincy, &c. *v.* Newcomb, 7 Met. 276; Hughes *v.* Heiser, 1 Bin. 463; Pittsburgh *v.* Scott, 1 Barr. 309; Barr *v.* Stevens, 1 Bibb. 293; O'Brien *v.* Norwich, &c. 17 Conn. 372; Dougherty *v.* Bunting, 1 Sandf. 1; Dobson *v.* Blackmore, 9 Qu. B. 991; Seeley *v.* Bishop, 19 Conn. 128.

[2] Rose *v.* Miles, 4 M. & S. 101.

[3] Hamilton *v.* Whitridge, 11 Md. 128.

[4] Ibid.

[5] McLauchlin *v.* Charlotte, &c. 5 Rich. 583.

distinct from that which he suffers in common with the rest of the public.[1] Thus, where a bill in equity was brought by an individual against a railroad company, alleging, that the defendants were engaged in extending their road across a certain cove, which is an arm of the sea, in which the tide ebbs and flows, communicating with the ocean through a navigable river; that the waters of the cove are navigable, and from time immemorial have been used and enjoyed as such; and that the plaintiff, and all other persons, have been accustomed to pass and repass, at their pleasure, up and down the cove, into the river, to the ocean or elsewhere, in boats, schooners, or other vessels, without molestation or obstruction; and that by means of the road so extended, the navigation of the cove will be greatly obstructed, and rendered almost wholly useless: — it was held, that the case stated was that of a public nuisance. And, although the bill stated, also, that the plaintiff resided near the head of the cove; that the right to navigate the cove was a common right, the enjoyment of which was valuable to him in respect to trade and commerce, the building and launching of vessels, and for agricultural purposes and fisheries; and that he was in danger of being deprived of his lawful right to navigate the cove; — it was held, that the injury complained of was not one peculiar to the plaintiff, but common to him and all others having occasion to use the cove for such purposes.[2] (*a*)

6. Upon the question, what constitutes a nuisance, it may be further remarked, that everything which is indictable as

[1] Smith *v.* Lockwood, 13 Barb. 209.

[2] O'Brien *v.* Norwich, &c. 17 Conn. 372.

(*a*) On the other hand, in an indictment for nuisance, the objection may be taken, that the injury is merely private and not public. Thus, where a tinman was indicted for the noise made by him in carrying on his trade, and it appeared that it only affected the inhabitants of three sets of chambers in Clifford's Inn, and that the noise might be partly excluded by shutting the windows; it was held that an indictment would not lie, the annoyance, if anything, being but a private nuisance. Lloyd's case, 4 Esp. 200.

such may properly come under this general description, although most public nuisances, for the very reason that they are public, cannot be made the ground of an action for damages. But, inasmuch as they are sometimes liable to abatement or injunction, and even to an action for damages, by individuals, it is unnecessary to discriminate precisely between the two classes of nuisance. In general it may be said, that any injury to lands or houses, which renders them useless or even uncomfortable for habitation, is a nuisance. Thus, in regard to offensive odors, it is said, the neighborhood has a right to pure and fresh air. And a smell need not be *unwholesome*, if it is offensive, and renders the enjoyment of life and property uncomfortable; as by giving many persons headaches.[1] So, with reference to nuisances in violation of *decency*, that, whatever place becomes the habitation of civilized men, there the laws of decency must be enforced.[2] (*a*) Thus a distillery, with sties in which large

[1] Neil's case, 2 C. & P. 485; White's case, 1 Burr. 333; Howard *v.* Lee, 3 Sandf. 281.

[2] Per M'Donald, C. B., Crunden's case, 2 Camp. 89. See Crane *v.* State, 3 Ind. 193.

(*a*) The following establishments or occupations have been held public nuisances: —

A smith's forge. Bradley *v.* Gill, Lutw. 69.

A privy. Styan *v.* Hutchinson, 2 Selw. 1047.

A pig-sty. Aldred's case, 9 Co. 59.

A lime-kiln. Ibid.

A tobacco-mill. Jones *v.* Powell, Hutt. 136.

Making candles by boiling stinking stuff. Tohayle's case, Cro. Car. 510.

A manufactory for spirit of sulphur, vitriol, and aquafortis. White's case, 1 Burr. 333.

A tannery. Pappineau's case, 2 Str. 686.

Conveying gas into a river, thus destroying the fish, and making the water unfit to drink. Medley's case, 6 C. & P. 292.

Exposing one who has the small-pox in public. Vantandillo's case, 4 M. & S. 73.

A common provision dealer, selling unwholesome food, or mixing noxious ingredients with it. Dixon's case, 3 M. & S. 11.

Common stages for rope-dancers. Hawk. b. 1, c. 75, § 6.

Pigeon-shooting. Moore's case, 3 B. & Ad. 184.

quantities of hogs are kept, the offal from which renders the waters of a creek unwholesome, and the vapors from which render a dwelling uninhabitable, is a nuisance.[1] So it is a nuisance to throw, from day to day, into water used for the ordinary purposes of life, any substance that renders it less pure, and excites disgust in those who use it.[2] And a soap-boiling establishment in the midst of a densely populated city is a nuisance, against which a perpetual injunction will be issued.[3] So, although a stable in a town is not, like a slaughter-pen or a hog-sty, necessarily or *primâ facie* a nuisance, yet, if it be so built, so kept, or so used, as to destroy the comfort of persons owning and occupying adjoining premises, and impair their value as places of habitation, or if the adjacent proprietors are annoyed by it in any manner which could be avoided, it becomes an actionable nuisance.[4] So a livery stable, in a city, erected within sixty-five feet of a hotel, is *primâ facie* a nuisance, and may be restrained by injunction. And the answer of the defendant, admitting the facts charged in the bill, as to the distance and relative situation of the stable from the tavern, but

[1] Smith *v.* M'Conathy, 11 Mis. 517.
[2] Lewis *v.* Stein, 16 Ala. 214.
[3] Brady *v.* Weeks, 3 Barb. 157.
[4] Dargan *v.* Waddill, 9 Ired. 244.

It has been held no offence against the law, to utter loud cries and exclamations in the public streets, to the great disturbance of divers citizens; such acts, if an offence at all, constitute a nuisance, and must be alleged to be to the great damage and common nuisance of all the citizens. Commonwealth *v.* Smith, 6 Cush. 80. (Infra, § 9.) But, if a count charges a person with "openly and publicly speaking with a loud voice in the hearing of the citizens, &c., wicked, scandalous, and infamous words, representing men and women in obscene and indecent attitudes, with the intention to debase, debauch, and corrupt the morals of the youth and others," without averring that the offence was a common nuisance; it is good, such offence being a misdemeanor at common law; and the precise words and attitudes need not be described. And a person who collects together a large crowd in the public highways and streets of a city, by means of "violent and indecent language addressed to persons passing along the highway," thereby obstructing the free passage of the street, is indictable for committing a common nuisance. Barker *v.* The Commonwealth, 19 Penn. 412.

denying that a livery stable is a nuisance, is mere matter of opinion, and not sufficient to authorize the dissolution of the injunction, before the final hearing. Nor will the Court discharge the *ad interim* interdict, so far as to permit the experiment to be made, whether a livery stable could be erected and constructed in such a manner as not to be a nuisance.[1] So a powder-magazine, erected in a populous part of a city, in which large quantities of gunpowder are stored, is *per se* a nuisance.[2] So the occupation of a building in a city as a *slaughter-house* is *primâ facie* a nuisance to persons residing in the neighborhood; and may be restrained by injunction, notwithstanding the denial by the defendant, that it is a nuisance.[3] So a melting-house in a city, for the purpose of trying animal fat from the slaughter-houses, is presumptively a nuisance to the inhabitants in its vicinity; and a general denial that it is a nuisance or offensive will not justify the dissolution of a preliminary injunction.[4] So a dwelling-house cut up into small apartments, inhabited by a crowd of poor people, in a filthy condition, and calculated to breed disease, is a public nuisance, and may be abated by individuals residing in the neighborhood, by tearing it down, especially during the prevalence of a disease like the Asiatic cholera.[5] So, under a power to do all acts, make all regulations, and pass all ordinances which they shall deem necessary for the preservation of health and the suppression of disease, and to carry into effect and execute the powers granted by the charter, a municipal corporation has power to pass an ordinance, prohibiting the depositing of dead animals, decayed vegetables, &c., in any public street, or upon any lot, &c., and imposing a penalty for the violation of such ordinance.[6] (*a*) But a person sick of an infectious

[1] Coker *v.* Birge, 10 Geo. 336.
[2] Cheatham *v.* Shearon, 1 Swan. 213.
[3] Brady *v.* Weeks, 3 Barb. 157.
[4] Peck *v.* Elder, 3 Sandf. 126.
[5] Meeker *v.* Van Rensselaer, 15 Wend. 397.
[6] City, &c. *v.* Collins, 12 Barb. 559.

(*a*) In all the class of cases above referred to, as will be presently seen, (§ 17,) although obviously *public* nuisances, a court of equity may inter-

or contagious disease, in his own house, or in suitable apartments at a public hotel or boarding-house, is not a nuisance. And, under the provision of a city charter, authorizing the common council to make and publish ordinances, by-laws, &c., for the purpose of abating and removing nuisances, they have no power to direct the removal of a person, sick of a contagious or infectious disease, from one place to another, without his consent.[1] And more especially where a vessel was wrecked thirteen miles from Charleston, and the cholera had made its appearance among the passengers, and the city authorities, in order to prevent the spread of the infection, ordered the destruction of the vessel and cargo; it was held a violation of the authority of the corporation, — the nuisance existing beyond their corporate limits; and they were held liable in trespass.[2] So health officers have no authority to take exclusive control and possession of a ship, though infected with a contagious disease; and a city is not responsible for such an unauthorized act of its officers, though through want of ordinary care the vessel is destroyed.[3]

7. It has been suggested that erections of every kind, adapted to *sports and amusements*, having no useful end, and notoriously fitted up and continued for the profit of the owner, are regarded by the common law as nuisances.[4] And upon this ground, a *bowling-alley*, kept for *gain or hire*, is held a public nuisance at common law, though gambling be expressly prohibited.[5] And, under a village charter, authorizing the trustees to pass by-laws relating to nui-

[1] Boom *v.* The City of Utica, 2 Barb. 104.

[2] Jarvis *v.* Pinckney, Riley, 123.

[3] Mitchell *v.* Rockland, 41 Maine, 363.

[4] Per Cowen, J., Tanner *v* The Trustees, &c. 5 Hill, 121. See Hackney *v.* State, 8 Ind. 494.

[5] Tanner *v.* The Trustees, &c. 5 Hill, 121.

pose by injunction. And, as will be explained, to entitle parties to such an injunction, it is not necessary that they should reside on the premises affected by the nuisance. It suffices that the nuisance is calculated to diminish the value of their property, by preventing good tenants from occupying it, or by destroying its value for building lots.

sances, they have power to make a by-law prohibiting the keeping of bowling-alleys for hire.[1]

8. A nuisance may also consist in *the obstruction of a highway*, more especially if accompanied with noise and disorder, and tending to the interruption of regular business. A temporary occupation of a part of a street or highway, by persons engaged in building, or in receiving or delivering goods from stores or warehouses or the like, is allowed from the necessity of the case; but a systematic and continued encroachment upon a street, though for the purpose of carrying on a lawful business, is unjustifiable.[2] Thus, where the defendants, proprietors of a distillery, in Brooklyn, were in the habit of delivering their grains, remaining after distillation, to those who came for them, by passing them through pipes to the public streets opposite to their distillery, where they were received into casks standing in wagons and carts; and the teams and carriages of the purchasers were accustomed to collect there in great numbers, to receive and take away the article; and, in consequence of their remaining there to await their turns, and of the strife among the drivers for priority, and of their disorderly conduct, the street was obstructed and rendered inconvenient to those passing thereon; held, a nuisance. So, although the teams were not owned by the defendants, or under their control, the defendants having, by the manner of conducting their business, invited those assemblages, at the point where the article was delivered. And proof of strife and collision among the drivers, while awaiting their turns, is competent evidence towards establishing the fact of the obstruction.[3] So, if the property of a person is endangered by a *moving building*, he may use all the force necessary to defend it. But a mere prospect of future injury will not justify the destruction of the building, unless it be a common nuisance. Where there is time and opportunity for the interposition of an adequate legal remedy, which may

[1] Ibid. See The People *v.* Sergeant, 8 Cow. 139; Hall's case, 1 Mod. 76.

[2] The People *v.* Cunningham, 1 Denio, 524.

[3] Ibid.

be effectual, the law will not justify a summary resort to force.[1]

9. Although *noise* may amount to a nuisance, and is also actionable, yet it must be a very special case in which real estate can be injured by a mere noise, so as to sustain an action for the injury.[2] (Supra, § 6, n.) But to justify such an action, it is not necessary that the plaintiff should be driven from his dwelling; it is enough that the enjoyment of life and property be rendered uncomfortable; as by the business of finishing steam-boilers, in a compact part of a city, whereby the occupant of an adjoining dwelling is annoyed by the noise and dust.[3] So a railroad is not *per se* a nuisance, and, although persons residing on the street may be subjected to some inconvenience from the noise and smoke and frequency of passing trains, yet it must be a very special and peculiar case in which real estate can be injured by mere noise, or the usual concomitants attending the passage of a railroad train.[4] The fact of nuisance must be determined by a jury.[5] So, although the noise of a steam-engine, under some circumstances, may become a private nuisance; the use of a steam-engine is not *primâ facie* a nuisance, on account of the danger to life from explosion.[6] And no action lies, for keeping pointers so near the plaintiff's house, that his family were disturbed and kept awake in the night.[7]

10. In conformity with the general law of nuisance, no man has the right to suffer to run at large *animals of a dangerous kind*, either to the person or property of another; and, if he does, he is responsible for all damages, which result from the acts of such animals.[8] Thus a *furious dog*, more especially if accustomed to bite mankind, is a common nui-

[1] Graves *v.* Shattuck, 35 N. H. 257.
[2] Per Hand, J., Trustees, &c. *v.* Utica, &c. 6 Barb. 313.
[3] Fish *v.* Dodge, 4 Denio, 311.
[4] Williams *v.* New York, &c. 18 Barb. 222.
[5] Bell *v.* Ohio, &c. 25 Penn. 161.
[6] Davidson *v.* Isham, 1 Stockt. 186.
[7] Street *v.* Tugwell, 2 Selw. 1047.
[8] McManus *v.* Finan, 4 Iowa, 283.

sance, and may be killed by any one. (*a*) In an action to recover damages for killing such a dog, the defendant need not prove that he was obliged to kill him in self-defence.[1] And this, whether he is permitted to run at large by his owner, or escapes through negligent keeping; the owner having notice of his vicious disposition.[2] And any person is justified in killing a dog, which has been bitten by another mad animal.[3] So one may kill the dog of another, if he cannot otherwise protect his property from injury by him. Hence where, in trespass for killing the plaintiff's dog, there was evidence tending to show that the dog was vicious, known to be so by the owner, and in the act, at the time he was killed, of doing injury to the defendant's property, in his garden; it was held error to instruct the jury to find for the plaintiff, leaving to them to fix only the amount of damages.[4] So the inhabitant of a dwelling-house may lawfully kill the dog of another, where such dog is in the habit of haunting his house, and by barking and howling, by day and by night,

1 Brown *v.* Carpenter, 26 Verm. 638; Dunlap *v.* Snyder, 17 Barb. 561.

2 Putman *v.* Paine, 13 Johns. 312.

3 Ibid.

4 King *v.* Kline, 6 Barr, 18.

(*a*) Barrington *v.* Turner, 3 Lev. 28. It has been held, however, that, if a justification be pleaded for the destruction of a dog, it must be shown that at the time he was either in the act of destroying the defendant's property, or that it was absolutely necessary for the preservation of his property. Janson *v.* Brown, 1 Camp. 41; Wells *v.* Head, 4 C. & P. 568

The defendant's merely having put up a notice, that all dogs trespassing on his land would be shot, is not a sufficient justification. Corner *v.* Champneys, 2 Marsh. 584. But the servant of the owner of an ancient park may justify shooting a dog that is chasing the deer, though not absolutely necessary for the preservation of the deer, and although the dog were not chasing the deer at the moment of shooting; if the chasing and shooting were all one transaction. Protheroe *v.* Mathews, 5 C. & P. 581.

If the defendant justify shooting the plaintiff's dog by pleading that he attacked him, and that "he was accustomed to attack and bite mankind;" the plaintiff may offer evidence of the general quietness of the dog. Clark *v.* Webster, 1 C. & P. 104. See Arnold *v.* Norton, 25 Conn. 92.

Suffering fierce and dangerous animals, as a fierce bull-dog, which is used to bite people, to go at large, is an indictable offence. 4 Burn's Just. 578.

disturbs the peace and quiet of his family, if the dog cannot be otherwise prevented from annoying him; although a wanton destruction of the animal is not justifiable.[1] (*a*) So, although a man may keep a dog for the necessary defence of his house, garden, or fields, and may cautiously use him for that purpose in the night-time; yet, if he permit a mischievous dog to be at large on his premises, and a person is bitten by him in the day-time, the owner is liable in damages, though the person be at the time trespassing on the grounds of the owner, by hunting in his woods without license.[2] And the owner of one animal is liable for injuries done by it to another animal belonging to the plaintiff. Thus a dog, accustomed to attack and bite other dogs without being incited, though not trained to the habit, is a vicious animal, and the owner will be liable for the damage done by him to other dogs lawfully and peaceably on the premises where he is.[3] Though it is not a rule, that when

[1] Brill *v.* Flagler, 23 Wend. 354.
[2] Loomis *v.* Terry, 17 Wend. 496.
[3] Wheeler *v.* Brant, 23 Barb. 324.

(*a*) It has been held, that, in an action to recover damages for the killing of a dog, the opinion of a witness as to his value is inadmissible, there being no standard market value for such property. After hearing the evidence of the peculiar qualities and properties of the animal, it is for the jury to judge of the value. Dunlap *v.* Snyder, 17 Barb. 561; *contra*, Brill *v.* Flagler, 23 Wend. 354.

If, in such an action, proof of the good qualities of the dog is admitted, the defendant may show, by way of rebuttal, and in mitigation of damages, that the dog was worthless, and in the habit of worrying and killing sheep, although such facts were not set up in the answer. Ibid.

An indictment for malicious mischief will lie for killing a dog. But, to support such indictment, it must be shown that the killing was from malice against the master. It is not sufficient that it was the result of passion, excited against the animal, by an injury he had done to the defendant's property. The State *v.* Latham, 13 Ired. 33.

A person may follow a fox with hounds over the grounds of another, if he does no more than is necessary to kill the fox. Gundry *v.* Feltham, 1 T. R. 334.

Because they are *noisome* animals. Nicholas *v.* Badger, 3 T. R. 259.

Exercising unruly horses, in an improper place, is a nuisance. Michael *v.* Alestree, 2 Lev. 172.

two dogs fight, and one is killed, the owner of the latter can have satisfaction for his loss from the owner of the other.[1] So the owner of a bull is liable to an action, if the bull break from his enclosure and fatally gore a horse of his neighbor.[2] (*a*)

11. But, although an injury done by a dog or other animal is generally treated as technically a *nuisance*, yet it is to be observed, that in many cases such an injury, like other wrongs against person or property, is a *trespass*, and the proper subject of an action of trespass, rather than an action on the case. The distinction upon this subject is made, that, if a person cause an injury with his dog, the remedy is trespass; but, if the dog do an injury of his own accord, in the absence of his owner, the remedy is case.[3] This, however, is not the limit of the liability as for a trespass. Thus trespass is held to lie against the owner of a dog which has worried and killed the plaintiff's sheep, although the owner were not present.[4] And the broad distinction upon the subject is no doubt accurately stated by an approved writer, as follows: "The owner of domestic and other animals not necessarily inclined to commit mischief, as dogs, horses, and oxen, is not liable for any injury committed by them to the person or personal property, unless it can be shown that he previously had notice of the animals' vicious propensity, or that the injury was attributable to some other neglect on his part; it being in general necessary in an action for an injury committed by such animals to allege and prove the *scienter;* and though notice can be proved, yet the action must be *case*,

1 Wiley *v.* Slater, 22 Barb. 506.
2 Dolph *v.* Ferris, 7 W. & S. 367.
3 Dilts *v.* Kinney, 3 Green, 130.
4 Paff *v.* Slack, 7 Barr, 254; Campbell *v.* Brown, 19 Penn. 359.

(*a*) In an action of trespass under the statute of Pennsylvania, the defendant is liable for injuries done to a flock of sheep by fright, as well as for the sheep killed by the dog. But, if the action be either in trespass under the statute, or in case at common law, the defendant is not liable for damages, unless it be shown that he knew his dog had worried and killed sheep before. And the jury must determine the question of *scienter*. Campbell *v.* Brown, 19 Penn. 359.

and not *trespass.* But if the owner himself acted illegally, he may be liable, even as a trespasser, as where a person in company with his dog trespassed in a close through which there was no footpath, and the dog, without his concurrence, killed the plaintiff's deer; and if a person let loose or permit a dangerous animal to go at large, and mischief ensue, he is liable as a trespasser, the law in such cases presuming notice to the defendant of the mischievous propensity of such animal. And with respect to animals *mansuetæ naturæ*, as cows and sheep, as their propensity to rove is notorious, the owner is bound at all events to confine them on his own land; and if they escape and commit a trespass on the land of another, unless through the defect of fences which the latter ought to repair, the owner is liable to an action of trespass, though he had no notice, in fact, of such propensity. But for damage by animals, &c., *feræ naturæ* escaping from the land of one person to that of another, as by rabbits, pigeons, &c., no action can be supported, because the instant they escaped from the land of the owner, his property in them was determined. And a person cannot be liable for the act of cattle, unless he were the general owner, or he actually put them into the place where the injury was committed; and if a servant or a stranger, without the concurrence of the owner, chase or put his cattle into another's land, such owner is not liable, but the action must be against the servant or stranger."[1] And, in a very late case in Pennsylvania, it is said, "the law seems to be settled, that the owner of beasts prone to commit trespasses is liable for injuries resulting from such propensity, such as breaking into enclosures, and consuming and destroying grain, grass, herbage, &c.[2] So where a bull broke into an enclosure and gored a horse, that he died.[3] So, too, in case of a horse permitted to run in the streets of a city, which, in its gambols, kicked and injured a person;[4] *and that the remedy is in trespass.* The property in the animal raises the duty, on the part of

[1] 1 Chit. Pl. 71.

[2] 3 Bl. Com. 211; Bac. Abr. tit. Trespass, G. 2.

[3] Dolph *v.* Ferris, 7 W. & S. 369.

[4] Goodman *v.* Gay, 3 Harris, 194.

the owner, to guard against its mischievous propensities, and failing in this, it holds him answerable for its injurious acts, without regard to the degree of care bestowed in controlling it. *Sic utere tuo ut non alienum lædas* applies to all such cases. *It is not a question of negligence or want of due care* on the part of the owner."[1] (*a*)

[1] Per Thompson, J., Russell *v.* Cottom, Am. Law Reg. May, 1859, p. 406.

(*a*) We have already considered (chap. 17) the rights and remedies of the owner of animals, in case of their being *distrained* or *impounded*. It may be further remarked in the present connection, that the frequent cases of injuries done by animals upon or near the highway, or in consequence of defective fences, are also usually treated as *trespasses* and the subjects of an action of trespass, and not an action on the case. It is the ancient doctrine, as stated in the text, (p. 648,) that a party is not liable for any injury done on the lands of another by animals *feræ naturæ*, over which he has no control; such as rabbits which escape from his lands. Boulston's case, 5 Co. 104 *b*.

But it is now held, that at common law every unwarrantable entry by a person *or his cattle* upon the land of another is a trespass, though the cattle come from the highway, and the land be unfenced; and though the owner exercised care and prudence to keep them in his own enclosure. Otherwise, it is said, if cattle driven along a highway escape into an adjoining field, against the owner's will. More especially in the absence of any public regulation as to fences, or as to cattle's running at large. The Tonawanda, &c. *v.* Munger, 5 Denio, 255; Wells *v.* Howett, 19 Johns. 385; *contra*, Cleveland, &c. *v.* Elliott, 4 Ohio, (N. S.) 474.

So it is not a trespass, for cattle used by a person in making a road, to stray upon adjoining unfenced land, against the will of their owner. Nor where they are necessarily driven upon adjoining land. Cool *v.* Crommet, 1 Shep. 250.

But the owner of a cow, accustomed to hook, the vicious propensity being known to him, is liable for damage done by her, although it be done in the highway, against his land, and while going to her usual watering-place. Coggswell *v.* Baldwin, 15 Verm. 404.

And trespass is held to lie for the entry of cattle on land, though the owner had no notice of their mischievous propensity. Page *v.* Hollingsworth, 7 Ind. 317.

In an action of trespass *quare clausum* for damages done by the defendant's sheep, a town by-law, authorizing cattle and sheep to run at large upon the highways and common lands of the town, even if such a by-law were a

12. It is held, that the owner of a domestic animal is not liable for the injuries which it may have committed, unless

sufficient authority for the defendant to allow his sheep to run at large on the highways, furnishes no excuse for suffering them to break through the plaintiff's fence and depasture his meadow. And, in an action for such an injury, and for that alone, the giving of the by-law in evidence, unaccompanied by any other proof, will not constitute a defence. White *v.* Scott, 4 Barb. 56.

Where A.'s sheep escaped from his land into B.'s land, through the insufficiency of a fence which B. was bound to repair, and thence passed into another adjoining lot of B., which was surrounded by a sufficient fence, and committed damage; it was held, that B. could not maintain trespass therefor against A. Page *v.* Olcott, 13 N. H. 399.

He who has the care and custody of sheep, for the purpose of depasturing them, is liable for damage done by them, in the same manner and to the same extent as the owner. Barnum *v.* Vandusen, 16 Conn. 200.

And, on the other hand, upon a full examination of the somewhat contradictory authorities, it has been very recently decided, in Pennsylvania, that the owner of cattle is not liable in trespass — and it is doubted whether he would be liable in case — for any injury to land committed by them while in the custody of an *agister*. Rossell *v.* Cottom, Am. Law Reg. May, 1859, p. 405.

One cannot justify the killing of his neighbor's stock, under the Missouri "inclosure" act, (Revised Statutes, 1845,) without showing himself exactly within its protection. Early *v.* Fleming, 16 Mis. 154.

In an action of trover for a ram, the defence was, that it was taken going at large, contrary to the statute, and that the defendant selected this ram, claiming him to be forfeited. To prove the fact of the selection, the defendant relied upon evidence introduced by the plaintiff, showing that the defendant secretly removed the ram in question several miles off, and that he afterwards brought him back in the night, and kept him awhile privately confined in his barn, in his cellar, and in his office, and then killed him. Held, that these acts did not conduce to show a selection of this ram, or an intention of selecting him, from others, as the subject of the forfeiture. Watson *v.* Watson, 14 Conn. 188.

In an action for trespass by cattle, it is a *matter of defence*, and *to be shown by the defendant*, that the fence which the plaintiff was bound to keep in repair was defective. Colden *v.* Eldred, 15 Johns. 220.

Where beasts, *damage feasant*, have been distrained or even impounded, the distrainor may relinquish the proceedings by distress, before satisfaction for the damage, and bring an action of trespass. Ibid.

A., the owner of a field, leased eight acres of it to B., the whole being under a common enclosure, without any division fence. A. turned his stock

he had *notice* of its vicious propensity, or that it was accustomed to do mischief.[1] And the question of *scienter* is for the jury.[2] Hence in an old case it was decided, that a declaration, in an action on the case for an injury done by the defendant's dog, must state, that he knew that the dog was of a mischievous nature, or had done mischief before. The allegation, that the dog was a mongrel mastiff, *very fierce*, and not muzzled, and that he *furiously and violently attacked, and grievously bit and wounded* the plaintiff, &c., is not sufficient.[3] So a declaration, that a fox-hound belonging to the defendant went into the plaintiff's field, and worried his sheep, but not averring that the dog was of vicious propensities, known to the defendant, and that he negligently allowed it to be at large, (see § 13,) is insufficient. Blame can only attach to the owner of a dog, when, after having ascertained that the animal has pro-

[1] Vrooman *v.* Sawyer, 13 Johns. 339; Lyke *v.* Van Leuren, 4 Denio, 127; 1 Comst. 515. But see Arnold *v.* Norton, 25 Conn. 92.

[2] Campbell *v.* Brown, 19 Penn. 359.

[3] Mason *v.* Keeling, 12 Mod. 332.

---

upon the ground possessed by himself, and they went thence to the land occupied by B., and consumed his crop. Held, that A., having leased the land to B., had no right to prevent him from reaping the full benefit thereof, and that the removal of the enclosure, so as to let in his stock, was an actionable injury. Also, that trespass *vi et armis* was the appropriate and only remedy. Also, that B. was not bound to erect a division fence, nor to aver in his declaration that A. was bound to do so. Henly *v.* Neal, 2 Humph. 551.

A person finding horses trespassing on his land may turn them into the highway, and is not liable, though they may be lost in consequence. Humphrey *v.* Douglass, 10 Verm. 71.

So, though they escape from the enclosures of the owner, through the insufficiency of a division fence, which it was his duty in common with another to maintain, the latter may lawfully turn them from his enclosure into the highway. Humphrey *v.* Douglass, 11 Verm. 22.

The defendant, A., by virtue of the charter of a turnpike company, had the right to enter the enclosed field of B., the plaintiff, for the purpose of procuring materials to construct such turnpike; and, in so doing, left down the fences of the plaintiff, whereby cattle entered and destroyed his crop. Held, A. was liable, although the plaintiff's fence was not as high in other places as was required by statute. Crawford *v.* Maxwell, 3 Humph. 476.

pensities not generally belonging to his race, he omits to take proper precautions to protect the public against the ill consequences of those anomalous habits.[1] And the same rule applies, where the defendant's swine tore and fatally injured a cow with a calf newly brought forth; though the swine were trespassing upon the plaintiff's land, when they committed the injury:[2] unless the declaration is for breaking and entering the close, and the killing of the animal alleged in aggravation; in which case the defendant would be liable.[3] So an action on the case will not lie for keeping a mad bull, without saying *scienter*.[4] And a father is not liable, for injury occasioned by his minor daughter's wilfully setting his dog upon a neighbor's swine, without proof that he knew that his dog was accustomed to do mischief.[5] (*a*)

13. One who knowingly keeps an animal, accustomed to attack and bite mankind, is *primâ facie* liable in an action on the case to any person attacked and injured by such animal, without any averment of *negligence* or *default* in securing or taking care of it, (see p. 651). The gist of the action is the keeping of the animal after knowledge of its mischievous propensities. And an allegation of duty in the defendant, to use due and reasonable care and precaution in keeping the animal, is an immaterial allegation.[6] So it is doubted whether it would be a defence, even that the injury was occasioned solely by the wilfulness of the plaintiff, after

[1] Fleeming *v.* Orr, 29 Eng. L. & Eq. 16.
[2] Lyke *v.* Van Leuren, 4 Denio, 127.
[3] Van Leuren *v.* Van Lyke, 1 Comst. 515.
[4] Buxentine *v.* Sharp, 3 Salk. 12.
[5] Tifft *v.* Tifft, 4 Denio, 175.
[6] Card *v.* Case, 5 Com. B. 622.

(*a*) But, in an action for trespass in killing a dog, where the defence was, that the dog was ferocious and in the habit of attacking individuals, it was held not necessary to prove a *scienter* as to the plaintiff, to support the defence. Maxwell *v.* Palmerton, 21 Wend. 407.

So the owner of a horse, who suffers it to go at large in the streets of a populous city, is answerable for an injury done by it to any person, without proof that the owner knew that the horse was vicious. Goodman *v.* Gay, 15 Penn. 188.

warning.[1] And it has been held, that an action on the case lies for knowingly keeping a dog used to bite, though the damage happened by accidentally treading on him.[2] So where the owner of a dog, which had bitten other persons, had notice of the fact, and afterwards suffered him to be at large, when he bit the plaintiff; it was held, that evidence was not admissible that the dog was generally inoffensive.[3]

14. In an action for an injury alleged to be done by a ferocious and mischievous dog of the defendant, known by him to be of that character, the plea of not guilty puts the *scienter* in issue, as well as the character of the dog.[4] Proof that the dog is of a furious disposition, and has bitten cattle, is no evidence of the *scienter;* but a promise by the owner, on being informed of the injury, to make compensation, is some, though very slight evidence of it.[5]

15. With regard to the proper *parties* in the action for a nuisance, it has been held in the State of New York, where the subject is regulated by express statute, that, in the common-law action by *writ of nuisance*, as retained and regulated by the Revised Statutes, it seems the declaration must show, that the plaintiff has *a freehold estate* in the premises affected by the nuisance, this being a real action. But, in an action on the case for damages, it is enough that the plaintiff is in *possession.* And, where the plaintiff commenced his action by writ of nuisance pursuant to the statute, and the formal commencement of the declaration was appropriate to that action, and referred to the writ; but the declaration contained no averment that the plaintiff had a freehold estate, but showed a good cause of action on the case, and concluded thus, "to the nuisance of said dwelling-house and premises of the plaintiff and to his damage five thousand dollars;" held a good declaration in an action on the case, although it showed no ground of recovery in the action of

[1] May *v.* Burdett, 9 Ad. & Ell. N. S. 101; Popplewell *v.* Pierce, 10 Cush. 509.

[2] Smith *v.* Pelah, 2 Stra. 1264.

[3] Buckley *v.* Leonard, 4 Denio, 500.

[4] Thomas *v.* Morgan, 1 Gale, 172; Card *v.* Case, 5 Com. B. 622.

[5] 1 Gale, 172.

nuisance proper.[1] (a) But it is also held in the same State, that, under the statute which abolishes the writ of nuisance, but enacts that such injuries shall be the subject of an action, like other injuries, in such actions, the plaintiff must aver all that was before requisite to sustain an action of that nature; that he is tenant of the freehold injured, and that the defendant was tenant of the freehold of the land whereon the nuisance was erected.[2] (b)

15 a. With regard to the party *liable* for a nuisance, it is held, that one who demises premises, for carrying on a business necessarily injurious to the adjacent proprietors, is liable as the author of the nuisance.[3] And a distinction has been suggested in the State of New York, between the writ of

[1] Cornes v. Harris, 1 Comst. 223.
[2] Ellsworth v. Putnam, 16 Barb. 565.
[3] Fish v. Dodge, 4 Denio, 311. See Brady v. Weeks, 3 Barb. 157.

(a) A. conveyed a lot of land to B., who at the same time mortgaged it back. B. quitclaimed to C., who made a sealed lease to D. and E., and their assigns, of the right and privilege of digging a well in the land, and of conducting water therefrom to their houses. About the same time, A., after entry for foreclosure, but before foreclosing his mortgage, undertook to confirm the lease by an instrument under seal, but not acknowledged, and afterwards quitclaimed the land to C. and F., with a covenant against all claiming under him or his heirs. C. afterwards conveyed all his interest in the land to D., who had meanwhile also become the owner of E.'s house. Held, D. had sufficient title in the well, to enable him to maintain an action on the case, for a corruption of the water therein by means of a cesspool sunk in the ground near by, no plea in abatement having been filed to the nonjoinder of E. or of F., and that it was immaterial whether B. had released his equity of redemption to A. before A. confirmed the lease. Call v. Buttrick, 4 Cush. 345.

(b) It has been made a question, whether the alienee of a house can maintain an action for continuance of a nuisance, without notice to remove it Penruddock's case, 5 Co. 101 *a;* Cotterell v. Griffiths, 4 Esp. C. 69; Chandler v. Thompson, 3 Camp. 82; Willes, 583; Jenk. 260, pl. 57.

A devisee can maintain an action for the continuance of a nuisance erected in the lifetime of the testator. Some v. Barwish, Cro. Jac. 231.

A reversioner may sue, where his reversionary interest is injured. Jackson v. Pesked, 1 M. & S. 234; Biddlesford v. Onslow, 3 Lev. 209. As by tending to alter the evidence of title. Alston v. Scales, 9 Bing. 3.

nuisance and the modern action on the case for damages, similar to that already mentioned in relation to the plaintiff in the suit. It is there held, that the writ of nuisance is an obsolete proceeding, not to be encouraged; and the Court will not, therefore, in such a proceeding, relax the strictness of the ancient practice.[1] Hence the writ of nuisance must be brought against the party by whom the nuisance was erected; or, if he has transferred the land to another, then against both of these parties. But an action of nuisance against the alienee alone, for keeping up and continuing a nuisance erected by his grantor, was unknown to the common law, and is not authorized by the Revised Statutes.[2](a)

16. But, in general, every injury caused by the continuance of a nuisance is in law a new nuisance, and affords a new and distinct ground of action, with a liability to increased damages. Thus a purchaser may maintain an action for the continuance of a nuisance erected before his purchase, and an heir for the continuance of one erected in the time of his ancestor.[3] And this principle more especially applies, where the plaintiff derives his title from the defendant who created the nuisance before, but continues it after, the transfer to the plaintiff. Thus the defendant had, more than twenty years before the action, constructed a sewer or watercourse through property of his own, and then occupied

[1] Kintz v. McNeal, 1 Denio, 436.
[2] Brown v. Wordworth, 5 Barb. 550.
[3] Per Beardsley, J., Vedder v. Vedder, 1 Denio, 257; Brady v. Weeks, 3 Barb. 157; New Jersey, &c. v. Wright, 1 Zabr. 469; 2 Wheat. Selw. 1141.

(a) An infant only a year or two old, upon whose lands a nuisance is erected, cannot be made criminally answerable for it. Nor a *feme covert*, upon whose lands her husband erects a nuisanee. To maintain such indictment, it is not enough merely to show ownership of the lands on which the nuisance exists; but it must appear that the defendant either erected or continued it, or in some way sanctioned its erection or continuance. And where, on the trial of an indictment for a nuisanee upon the defendants' land, they admitted the title in fee to be in a third person, as trustee for them, and that they were *cestuis que trust*, &c.; held, not an admission of their being owners of the land, or that they had any estate in it. The People v. Townsend, 3 Hill, 479.

by him. In 1845, the defendant let a house, shop, and cellar to the plaintiff, which the defendant down to that time also occupied with the property. In 1851, the sewer or water-course burst, and thereby the plaintiff's cellar and goods were damaged; and the plaintiff thereupon brought an action against the defendant for negligently and improperly making and constructing the sewer, and keeping and continuing the same negligently and improperly made and constructed, and so causing the damage. The jury found that the sewer was not originally constructed with proper care, and it was proved that it had been continued in the same state. Held, upon the letting of the premises to the plaintiff, a duty arose, on the part of the defendant, to take care that that which was before rightful did not become wrongful to the plaintiff, because that would be in derogation of the defendant's own demise to the plaintiff; and, upon this ground, as also upon the principle *sic utere tuo ut alienum non lædas*, the action was maintainable.[1] So, if one erect a nuisance on his own land, to the injury of the land of another, and then convey the premises to a purchaser with warranty; he nevertheless remains liable in an action for the subsequent continuance of the nuisance.[2]

16 *a*. And this consideration of course affects the amount of damages in such action. The rule of damages is the injury actually sustained at the commencement of the suit; and a party cannot recover in this action, for permanent or prospective injury.[3] (*a*) Thus, in an action by a reversioner,

[1] Alston *v*. Grant, 24 Eng. L. & Eq. 122.

[2] Waggoner *v*. Jermaine, 3 Denio, 306.

[3] Thayer *v*. Brooks, 17 Ohio, 489.

(*a*) Evidence cannot be given of injuries other than those alleged. Smith *v*. McConathy, 11 Mis. 517.

The gist of the action in nuisance is the damage, and therefore evidence may be given of consequential damages; not so in trespass, which is one entire act. Case of Farmers of Hempstead Water, 12 Mod. 519.

In an action for a nuisance caused by the discharge of impure water from the brewery of the defendant into the plaintiff's clay-pits, through a drain which the defendant dug from his premises to the plaintiff's; the water hav-

for damages done to the reversion by cutting off the eaves of a building belonging to him, and by erecting a wall with a drip over his premises; as there may be repeated actions for continuing the nuisance, evidence of a diminution in the salable value of the premises is not admissible.[1]

16 *b*. And an action lies for the continuance of a nuisance, though the plaintiff have accepted money paid into court in full satisfaction of the original erection.[2] So parties who cause a nuisance, by acts done on the land of a stranger, are liable for its continuance; notwithstanding the defence, that they cannot lawfully enter, to abate the nuisance, without rendering themselves liable to an action by the owner of the land.[3] So the rule applies as against a mere *lessee*. Thus, where the plaintiff had recovered from a tenant for years, who afterwards underlet the premises on which the nuisance was erected to a sub-tenant, and an action for the continuance of the nuisance was brought against the former tenant; it was held, that the action was maintainable, for the defendant had transferred the premises with the original wrong, and by his demise had affirmed the continuance of it.[4] So, where a tenant for years erects a nuisance, for which damages are recovered, and assigns the term, and the nuisance is continued; an action will lie either against the tenant for years, or his assignee. But there shall be only one satisfaction.[5]

16 *c*. The qualification, however, is usually annexed to the liability in question, that a person, who continues a nuisance erected by another, is liable therefor at the suit of any party damaged thereby, *if notified to remove it*. But, it is held, the

[1] Bathishill *v*. Reed, 37 Eng. L. & Eq. 317.

[2] Holmes *v*. Wilson, 10 Ad. & Ell. 503.

[3] Smith *v*. Elliott, 9 Barr, 345.

[4] Rosewell *v*. Prior, Salk. 460.

[5] Ibid. 12 Mod. 635.

ing been complained of as a nuisance, and the Board of Health having ordered that the plaintiff fill up one of the pits; the expense of such filling up may be included in the damages. Shaw *v*. Cummiskey, 7 Pick. 76. See Carhart *v*. The Auburn, &c. 22 Barb. 297; Roush *v*. Walter, 10 Watts, 86; Commrs. &c. *v*. Wood, 10 Penn. 93.

absence of proof of a request to discontinue it must be objected to specifically at the trial, or it will not be available on appeal.[1]

17. *Courts of equity* have concurrent jurisdiction with courts of law in cases of private nuisance; as in case of nuisance to a neighboring trade or tenement.[2] But it is not every case of nuisance which will authorize the exercise of the jurisdiction. It rests upon the principle of a clear and undoubted right to the enjoyment of the subject in question, and will only be exercised in a case of strong and imperious necessity, or where the rights of the party have been established at law; more especially, the court will not interfere, when an erection has a tendency to promote the public convenience.[3] This jurisdiction is said to be of recent origin, and always exercised sparingly and with great caution.[4] (*a*)

[1] Brown *v.* Cayuga, &c. 2 Kern. 486; Snow *v.* Cowles, 6 Fost. 275.

[2] Gilbert *v.* Mickle, 4 Sandf. Ch. 357; Norris *v.* Hill, 1 Mann. 202.

[3] Fisk *v.* Wilber, 7 Barb. 395; Middleton *v.* Franklin, 3 Cal. 238; Harrison *v.* Brooks, 20 Geo. 537; Dumesnil *v.* Dupont, 18 B. Mon. 800.

[4] Simpson *v.* Justice, 8 Ired. Eq. 115.

(*a*) Where a party does not take an injunction in the first instance, but permits the other party to go on erecting the building and fixtures from which a nuisance is anticipated, if, at the hearing, he prays for a perpetual injunction, he must do so on the ground, that, in the mean time, the fact of nuisance has been established by an action at law, or, at all events, he must support his application by strong and unanswerable proof of nuisance. Simpson *v.* Justice, 8 Ired. Eq. 115.

A plaintiff complained of works intended to be executed by the defendants, churchwardens of his parish, which he alleged, in the way in which it was proposed to execute them, constituted a nuisance. Much negotiation took place, in the course of which the defendants showed a continued acquiescence in the suggestions made by the plaintiff as to the mode of executing the works, and suspended their execution. While these negotiations were still going on, and before any works were commenced, the plaintiff filed his bill for an injunction, and obtained special leave to give notice of motion, and served the notice of motion. On the day following the service of the notice of motion, the defendants, in order to avoid litigation, passed a resolution at a vestry, at which the plaintiff was present, that the work should be wholly abandoned. After that, the plaintiff brought on his motion. Held, without going into the question whether there would be any nuisance,

18. The law not only allows an action for damages in case of nuisance, but also provides the remedy of *abatement* or compulsory discontinuance of the nuisance itself. It is the prevailing doctrine, that a public nuisance may be abated by any one; (*a*) a private nuisance, by any one whose prop-

---

that, under the circumstances, the motion was useless and improper, and it was refused, with costs. Woodman *v.* Robinson, 15 Eng. Law & Eq. 146.

Where the defendant, as mayor of New York, and head of its police, after many complaints made to him against the complainant's establishment, as being a mock auction store, under the statute making it the duty of such police to caution strangers against mock auctioneers, caused a placard to be displayed in front of the defendant's store, as follows, "Strangers, beware of mock auctions;" held, a proper case for the granting of an injunction, although the placard might be libellous; but, as the defendant had acted *bonâ fide*, and was in the proper discharge of his duty, the complainant must be left to his remedy by law. Gilbert *v.* Mickle, 4 Sandf. Ch. 357.

Judge Story remarks: "The interference of courts of equity by way of injunction is undoubtedly founded upon the ground of restraining irreparable mischief, or of suppressing oppressive and interminable litigation, or of preventing multiplicity of suits. It is not every case which will furnish a right of action against a party for a nuisance, which will justify the interposition of courts of equity to redress the injury, or to remove the annoyance. But there must be such an injury as, from its nature is not susceptible of being adequately compensated by damages at law, or such as, from its continuance or permanent mischief, must occasion a constantly-recurring grievance, which cannot be otherwise prevented, but by an injunction." Such are cases of loss of health, trade, or means of subsistence, or permanent ruin of property; darkening windows; obstructing watercourses; abuse of the powers of a corporation; interference with a ferry. 2 Story's Eq. 238, §§ 925–927.

And in a late case, where property was appropriated to public use under a corporate charter alleged to be invalid, it is said, "The injury complained of, as impending over his property, is its permanent occupation and appropriation to a continuing public use, which requires the divestiture of his whole right, its transfer to the company in full property, and his inheritance to be destroyed as effectively as if he had never been its proprietor. No damages can restore him to his former condition; its value to him is not money, which money can replace; nor can there be any specific compensation or equivalent; his objects in making his establishment were not profit, but repose, seclusion, and a resting-place for himself and family." Bonaparte *v.* Camden, &c. 1 Baldw. 231.

(*a*) But in a recent English case, the well-established limitation of *the*

erty is injured; and entry for such purpose is justifiable:[1] though a nuisance cannot at common law be abated by a judgment in an action on the case; there must, for that purpose, be either an *assize* or a *quod permittat*.[2] And an action on the case for a nuisance is not abated or barred by a subsequent abatement of the nuisance by the plaintiff.[3] (*a*)

18 *a*. With regard, however, to the extent and limitations of the right in question, it is said: "Nuisances by an act of commission are committed in defiance of those whom such nuisances injure, and the injured party may abate them, without notice to the party who committed them; but there

[1] Lancaster, &c. *v*. Rogers, 2 Barr, 114; State *v*. Dibble, 4 Jones, Law, 107. See Stiles *v*. Laird, 5 Cal. 120; Harvey *v*. Dewoody, 18 Ark. 252.

[2] Kendrick *v*. Bartland, 2 Mod. 253.

[3] Call *v*. Buttrick, 4 Cush. 345.

---

right of action has been also applied to the remedy of abatement. It is said, "the ordinary remedy for a public nuisance is itself public, — that of indictment, — and each individual who is only injured as one of the public, can no more proceed to abate than he can bring an action." Mayor, &c. *v*. Brooke, 7 Qu. B. 377.

And the same principle has been applied to the remedy by *mandamus*, Reading *v*. Com. 11 Penn. 196.

(*a*) In an action for a nuisance, if it be laid as continuing after it has been abated, yet the plaintiff shall recover damages for the injury he sustained previous to the abatement. Kendrick *v*. Bartland, 2 Mod. 253.

Under a provision in the charter of a municipal corporation, authorizing it to pass and enact by-laws and ordinances, to *abate and remove* nuisances, it has no power to pass an ordinance to *prevent* nuisances, or to impose penalties for the creation thereof. City, &c. *v*. Collins, 12 Barb. 559.

The acts of a board of health of a city, in directing the abatement of nuisances, cannot be shown by parol evidence, but only by written minutes of the proceedings or written orders of the board. Meeker *v*. Van Rensselaer, 15 Wend. 397.

Keeping a nuisance is a criminal offence at common law, as well as by the Indiana statute. But an action of debt does not lie for keeping a nuisance within a city, in favor of such city. Indianapolis *v*. Blythe, 2 Cart. 75.

The right of abating or indicting a public nuisance is not affected by a statute imposing a penalty for the offence, unless negative words are added, evincing an intent to exclude common-law remedies. Rennick *v*. Morris, 7 Hill, 575.

is no decided case which sanctions the abatement by an individual of nuisances from omissions, except that of cutting the branches of trees which overhang a public road, or the private property of the person who cuts them. The permitting these branches to extend so far beyond the soil of the owner of the trees is an unequivocal act of negligence, which distinguishes this case from most of the other cases that have occurred. The security of lives and property may sometimes require so speedy a remedy, as not to allow time to call on the person on whose property the mischief has arisen, to remedy it; in such cases an individual would be justified in abating a nuisance from omission without notice. In all other cases of such nuisances, persons should not take the law into their own hands, but follow the advice of Lord Hale, and appeal to a court of justice."[1] So it is held, that so much only of the thing as causes the nuisance should be removed. Thus, if a house be built too high, only so much of it as is too high should be pulled down.[2] And, in general, where it is the wrongful use of a building that constitutes a nuisance, the remedy is to stop such use, not tear down or demolish the building.[3] So, although it is often held that *public nuisances* may be abated by the mere act of individuals;[4] yet it is held that a citizen has no right to abate a public nuisance, if such abatement involve a breach of the peace.[5] And, with regard to the kind of nuisance subject to abatement; it is doubted whether an individual has the right, upon his own mere motion, to abate as a nuisance *a few loads of ashes* laid in the vicinity of his dwelling.[6] But a statute, authorizing commissioners of highways to order the removal of *fences*, by the erection of which the highway has been encroached upon, does not abrogate the common-law remedy of abatement of nuisances by the mere act of individuals, or abolish the proceeding by indictment; but

[1] Per Best, J., Lonsdale *v.* Nelson, 2 B. & C. 311.

[2] Baten's case, 9 Co. 53; Trahern's case, Godb. 233. See Dubost *v.* Beresford, 2 Camp. 511.

[3] Barclay *v.* Commonwealth, 25 Penn. 503.

[4] Wetmore *v.* Tracy, 14 Wend. 250.

[5] Day *v.* Day, 4 Md. 262.

[6] Rogers *v.* Rogers, 14 Wend. 131.

is merely cumulative, and seemingly intended to provide a remedy in doubtful or questionable cases.[1] (*a*)

[1] Wetmore *v.* Tracy, 14 Wend. 250.

(*a*) A very noted and important case relating to this subject recently arose in Massachusetts; the decision of which has not yet been authentically reported, but is doubtless stated with substantial correctness in the following newspaper abstract: —

John Brown *v.* Stephen Perkins and Wife. — This was an action for breaking and entering the plaintiff's shop and destroying various articles of property. The defendants insist that it was justifiable by law, on the ground that the shop was a place used for the sale of spirituous liquors, and was so declared to be a nuisance; that they bad a right to abate the nuisance, and for that purpose to break and enter the shop, as the evidence shows that it was done.

2d. That the shop contained spirituous liquors kept for sale; that the so keeping them was a nuisance by statute; that they had a right to enter by force and destroy them; that they entered for that purpose and destroyed such articles, and did no more damage than was necessary for that purpose.

The Court are of opinion that spirituous liquors are not of themselves a common nuisance, but the act of keeping them for sale by statute creates them a nuisance, and the only mode in which they can be lawfully destroyed is the one prescribed by law — by warrant, bringing them before a magistrate and giving the owner of the property an opportunity to defend his right to it. Therefore, it is not lawful for any person to destroy them by any abatement of a common nuisance, consequently not to use force for that purpose.

2d. That it is not lawful by the common law for any and all persons to abate a common nuisance, merely because it is a common nuisance, though it may have been sometimes stated in terms so general as to give countenance to this supposition; that this right and power is never intrusted to individuals in general without process of law, by way of vindicating the public right, but solely for the relief of a party whose right is obstructed by such nuisance.

3d. If such were intended to be made the law by force of the statute, it would be contrary to the provisions of the Constitution, which direct that no man's property can be taken from him without compensation, except by the judgment of his peers or the law of the land; and no person can be twice punished for the same offence. And it is clear that, under the statute, spirituous liquors are property, and entitled to protection as such. The power of abatement of a public or common nuisance does not place the penal law of the Commonwealth in private hands.

4th. The true theory of abatement of a nuisance is, that an individual

19. It has been questioned whether any length of time will enable a party to *prescribe* for a nuisance.[1] (*a*) Thus

[1] Lewis *v.* Stein, 16 Ala. 214.

citizen may abate a private nuisance injurious to him, when he could also bring an action; and also when a common nuisance obstructs his individual right, he may remove it to enable him to enjoy that right, and he cannot be called in question for so doing. As in case of the obstruction across a highway, and an unauthorized bridge across a navigable water, which he was accustomed to use, he may remove it, by way of abatement. But this would not justify strangers being inhabitants of other parts of the Commonwealth, having no such occasion to use it, to do the same.

Some of the earlier cases, in laying down the general proposition that private subjects may abate a common nuisance, did not perhaps remark this distinction; but we think, upon the authority of modern laws, where the distinctions are here accurately made, and upon principle, this is the true rule of law.

5th. That as it is the use of a building, or of keeping spirituous liquors in it, which in general constitutes the nuisance, the abatement consists in putting a stop to such use.

6th. That the keeping of a building for the sale of intoxicating liquors, if a nuisance at all, is exclusively a common nuisance; and the fact that the husbands, wives, and children of any persons do frequent such a place and get intoxicating liquors there, does not make it a special nuisance or injury to their private rights so as to authorize and justify such person in breaking the shop where it is thus sold and destroying the liquor therein found and the vessels in which it may be kept. But it can only be prevented as a public or common nuisance in the mode prescribed by law.

(*a*) No grant, license, or authority to erect or continue a nuisance can be presumed from length of time, in opposition to repeated intermediate expressions of the legislative will, prohibiting its erection. Lewis *v.* Stein, 16 Ala. 214.

A party cannot defend *an indictment* for nuisance, by showing its continued existence for such a length of time as would establish a prescription against individuals. The People *v.* Cunningham, 1 Denio, 524; State *v.* Phipps, 4 Ind. 515.

It has been ruled, that one cannot be indicted for continuing a noxious trade which has been carried on in the same place for nearly fifty years. Neville's case, Peake, 93.

But a distinction has been made in this respect between an indictment and an action. 1 Russ. (by Grea.) 320.

And it has been held, that, though twenty years' user may bind the right

damages may be recovered for any injuries caused within six years, by an erection which amounts to a nuisance,

---

of an individual, the public are not thus barred. Weld *v.* Hornby, 7 E. 199; 3 Camp. 227.

Even though such user be an ancient custom of a town; as, to place a wood-stack in the street before a house, leaving sufficient room for passengers. Fowler *v.* Sanders, Cro. Jac. 446.

But, upon an indictment for obstructing a highway with bags of clothes, it appearing that the place had been used as a market for clothes for over twenty years, and that these bags were put there for sale; Lord Ellenborough said, that, as it appeared to all the world that there was such a market, he could not hold one to be criminal, who came there under the belief that it was a legal fair. Smith's case, 4 Esp. 111.

In a late case, in Massachusetts, being an indictment for carrying on an offensive trade, after the making of roads and erection of buildings in the immediate neighborhood; the following remarks were made in reference to the attempted defence of prescription: —

"It derives more countenance from a case in which it is reported to have been said by Abbott, C. J., that if a noxious trade be already established in a place remote from habitations and public roads, and persons afterwards come and build houses, and a public road is made near to it, the trade, though otherwise a nuisance, may be continued with impunity, because it was legal at its commencement. Rex *v.* Cross, 2 Car. & P. 484.

"If the opinion was in fact ever expressed by the chief justice, it was a mere *obiter dictum;* it could not have been a deliberately formed opinion, for nothing of that kind was requisite to the decision of the question before the Court. But with whatever degree of confidence such an opinion may have been expressed, it seems to be very clear that, upon well-settled principles, it cannot be maintained. No person can lawfully exercise an absolute dominion over the land of which he is the owner. His use and enjoyment of it must have reference to the rights of others, and be subordinate to general laws, which are established for the benefit of all. Under the limitations to which he is thus subjected, it is certainly doubtful whether a proprietor can be justified in making such an appropriation of his estate as will debar others, or the public at large, from the lawful and proper enjoyment of contiguous territory. Without, however, relying upon this consideration, there are other conclusive objections to the proposition asserted as the ground of defence.

"In the first place, the defendant did nothing to acquire the peculiar right upon which he insists. The right acquired by prescription must be by means of adverse and exclusive enjoyment. When the defendant erected his slaughter-house, and commenced the prosecution of his business,

although such erection may have been maintained more than six but less than twenty years.[1] So, to an action for a noisy nuisance near the plaintiff's dwelling-house, which he was possessed of for a term of years, the defendants pleaded that they had been possessed of certain workshops, in which the noise was made, ten years before the plaintiff was possessed of the term in his house, and that they had always during that time made the noise in question, which was necessary for carrying on their trade. Held, a bad plea.[2] So, in an action for annoying the plaintiff in the enjoyment of his house, by causing offensive smells to arise near, in, and about it; enjoyment as of right for twenty years was pleaded of a *mixen* on the defendant's land, contiguous and near the house, whereby, during all that time,

[1] Delaware, &c. v. Wright, 1 New Jersey, 469.

[2] Elliotson v. Feltham, 2 Bing. N. R. 134.

---

he did not interfere with any one, or cause inconvenience either to individuals or the public at large. His acts were therefore strictly legal; because, in the then condition of things, his business could have no tendency to affect the health of the community, or to render the enjoyment of life and property uncomfortable. There was no adverse occupation or possession, to be defended by him or resisted by others. He could therefore gain nothing by prescription.

"But even if the prosecution and continuance of his business for more than twenty years could be regarded as the assertion and maintenance of a claim adverse to the law and the public right, it could be so considered only upon the ground that it was, during all that time, a nuisance subject to be suppressed and abated, and of this he could not avail himself in defence of the present indictment. No length of time will legitimate a nuisance. Easements may be created in lands, and the rights of individuals may be wholly changed by adverse use and enjoyment; but lapse of time does not equally affect the rights of the State." Per Merrick, J., Commonwealth v. Upton, 6 Gray, 475.

On a bill by an individual, complaining of injury to his property and the health of himself and family, by chemical works on lands adjoining the lands on which he resides, and which he alleges to be a nuisance, an injunction should not be allowed, unless a clear case of nuisance and irreparable injury be made out; nor if the complainant has resided three years and a half in the place, after the works have been in operation, before filing his bill. Tichenor v. Wilson, 4 Halst. Ch. 197.

offensive smells necessarily arose therefrom. On a traverse of the right, the defendant prevailed, but judgment was rendered for the plaintiff *non obstante*, &c., because the plea did not show a right to cause offensive smells in the plaintiff's premises, nor that any smells had really been used to pass beyond the defendant's own land.[1] So a soap factory, in the compact part of a city, where it had been carried on for a long period, was held to be a nuisance and restrained by injunction; upon the ground, that such trade, though long established, must give way and recede with the advance of the population.[2] But, on the trial of an indictment for establishing a noxious trade, near certain dwellings, &c., the defendant was allowed to prove, in bar of the prosecution, under the general issue, that the dwelling-house, in the vicinity of the place, &c., was built after the establishment of the alleged nuisance.[3] (*a*)

[1] Flight *v.* Thomas, 10 Ad. & Ell. 590.

[2] Howard *v.* Lee, 3 Sandf. 281.

[3] Ellis *v.* State, 7 Blackf. 534.

(*a*) In case of indictment, where the business complained of has been long carried on, but in a less annoying manner or extent; it has been sometimes held, even admitting the general validity of a prescriptive right, that the defendant cannot avail himself of this defence; more especially if he has not adopted improvements in the mode of conducting the business, which would render it less annoying. Watt's case, Moo. & M. 281.

Thus, where the defendant set up the business of a melter of tallow in the neighborhood of other manufactories, which emitted disagreeable and noxious smells, it was held that he was not indictable, unless the annoyance was thereby much increased. Neville's case, Peake, 91.

The language, upon this subject, of the learned English judge already referred to, (p. 664, n.) is as follows: "If a noxious trade is already established in a place remote from habitations and public roads, and persons afterwards come and build houses within the reach of its noxious effects; or if a public road be made so near it, that the carrying on of the trade becomes a nuisance to the persons using the road; in those cases the party is entitled to continue his trade." Per Abbott, C. J., Cross's case, 2 C. & P. 483.

CHAPTER XX.

NUISANCE. — WATERCOURSE, ETC.

1. Having considered the injury termed *Nuisance*, generally, we now proceed to a consideration of those special violations of the right of property, which, according to the established, technical rules of law, appropriately fall under this head. It has been already suggested, (p. 630,) that an injury to any *incorporeal* right is a nuisance, not a trespass; the subject of an action on the case, not of an action of trespass. And this rule is not modified by the further inquiry, which is the turning-point in cases of corporeal property, whether such right is *directly* or *consequentially* invaded. Thus *a right of way* is an incorporeal right, and therefore the obstruction of a way, though a direct or immediate injury, is a nuisance, not a trespass; while, on the other hand, a right to *ancient lights* being also incorporeal, an obstruction of such lights, though caused by an erection upon the land of the party liable for the obstruction, is also a nuisance. (*a*) And, in regard to incorporeal rights, not per-

(*a*) Osborne *v.* Butcher, 2 Dutch. 308. It seems, one in the actual use of tangible property may maintain *trespass* for a direct injury to it, though his right to use it be incorporeal merely; *e. g.* a franchise. In general, however, where an incorporeal right has been interfered with, the appropriate remedy is by *action on the case.* Per Cowen, J., The Seneca, &c. *v.* The Auburn, &c. 5 Hill, 170.

taining to real estate, but purely personal; such as a patent or copyright, (see chap. 22,) which, in the nature of things, cannot be otherwise invaded than by the exercise of some other real or pretended privilege of the same description; any injury to such rights, being both consequential and also committed against this peculiar kind of property, is for a double reason a nuisance. A *watercourse* — the subject of injuries which we propose now to consider — may perhaps be regarded as an intermediate kind of property, an immediate injury to which is a trespass, if the owner also owns the soil beneath, but not if his interest is merely in the water;[1] while the class of injuries for which actions are far most frequently brought, such as the diminution, obstruction or diversion of the water by acts not applied directly to the subject of injury itself, are nuisances. (*a*) So, in other points of view, it will be seen that the dividing line between nuisance and trespass, or between the action on the case and the action of trespass, in reference to watercourses, cannot be drawn with perfect precision. Thus, although a privilege to build a dam on the land of another, and divert the water for the use of the grantee, is a franchise;[2] (*b*) and an injury

[1] 1 Chit. Pl. 176; Griffiths *v.* Marson, 6 Price, 1.

[2] Conwell *v.* Brookhart, 4 B. Mon. 580.

(*a*) The declaration, in an action on the case, alleged, that the plaintiff was owner of a mill a short distance from one occupied by the defendant on the same stream, and that the defendant "wilfully, and with intent to injure the plaintiff," frequently shut down his gates, so as to accumulate a large head of water, and then raised them, by which means an immense volume of water ran with great force against the plaintiff's dam, and swept it away. Held, that trespass and not case was the proper remedy. Kelly *v.* Lett, 13 Ired. 50.

(*b*) A right to flow land, by means of a pond created by a dam attached to an ancient mill-site, is *a prescriptive right in a que estate.* Sargent *v.* Gutterson, 13 N. H. 467.

An action by a mill-owner for an obstruction of the stream below his mill and close, whereby the water was prevented from passing off from the wheel of his mill, along the stream, in the usual course and as of right it ought to pass; is an action respecting an easement on real estate. Cary *v.* Daniels, 5 Met. 236; acc. Soule *v.* Russell, 13 Met. 436.

caused to the land of one man, by the erection of a dam on the land of another, is a nuisance; yet an injury done to that dam itself, being a tangible and corporeal article of property, is a trespass.[1] (*a*) In general, however, as has been remarked, the right to a watercourse is *incorporeal*, and an injury done to a watercourse is not *immediate*, but the result of the improper use of his own property by the party causing such injury; and therefore the subject may most properly be considered in the present connection.

2. Like *light* and *air*, water is a subject of merely *qualified ownership*. Lord Coke says,[2] the word "land comprehendeth any ground, soil, or earth whatsoever, as meadows, pastures, woods, moors, *waters*," &c. But the well-established doctrine now is, that water is neither *land* nor a *tenement*, and is not demandable in a suit, except as so many acres of land covered with water. It is a movable, wandering thing, and must of necessity continue common by the law of nature. The air which hovers over one's land, and the light which shines upon it, are as much land as water is.[3] But the right to water is also said to be a right *running with the land*, and a corporeal privilege bestowed upon the occupier or appropriator of the soil; and, as such, has none of the characteristics of mere personalty; and it has been sometimes held to exist without private ownership of the soil, upon the ground of prior location upon the land, or prior appropriation and use of the water.[4]

[1] Conwell *v.* Brookhart, 4 B. Mon. 580. See Fiske *v.* Framingham, &c. 12 Pick. 68.

[2] Co. Litt. 4 a.

[3] 1 Hill. on R. Prop. (3d ed.) 3; Mitchell *v.* Warner, 5 Conn. 497; Co. Litt. 4 a.

[4] Hill *v.* Newman, 5 Cal. 445.

So is an action by an owner of salt meadow, situate above a mill-dam on a navigable stream, against the owner of such dam, for obstructing the natural ebb of the tide and thereby injuring the grass on such meadow. Turner *v.* Blodgett, 5 Met. 240, n.

(*a*) Where the plaintiffs, employed as contractors, to complete a navigable canal, had erected a dam composed of piles and earth, with the consent of the owner of the soil; held, they might maintain trespass against the defendant for breaking and destroying it, but not case. Dyson *v.* Collick 1 D. & Ry. 225.

3. In general, the owner of land upon a river not navigable, or above tide-water, owns to the centre of the stream, subject to the public right of passage, as upon a highway.[1] (a) But, to constitute a watercourse from one tract of land into another, there must be something more than a mere *surface drainage*, over the entire face of the first tract on to the second, occasioned by unusual freshets or other extraordinary causes.[2] And a declaration, alleging that a brook run through the plaintiff's land in its natural channel, and across the defendant's land, and that the defendant obstructed the same, is not supported by proof of a right of mere surface drainage, from the plaintiff's land over the defendant's land, without any regular stream, channel, or banks.[3] (b) So, if

[1] 3 Hill. on R. Prop. 87; 3 Kent, 431.

[2] Luther *v.* Winnisimmet Co. 9 Cush. 171.

[3] Ashley *v.* Wolcott, 11 Cush. 192.

(a) A stream far above tide-water, never declared a public highway by statute, nor capable, in its natural state, of bearing up a stick of timber or log, is not a navigable stream, but merely private property; and, if the owner of the land on each side has built a dam across it, which would be endangered by floating logs down the stream, when swollen by freshets, and any one threatens to do so, the owner of the land is entitled to an injunction. Curtis *v.* Keesler, 14 Barb. 511. See Treat *v.* Lord, 42 Maine, 552; Glover *v.* Powell, 2 Stockt. 211; Beach *v.* Schoff, 28 Penn. 195; American &c. *v.* Amsden, 6 Cal. 443; Porter *v.* Allen, 8 Ind. 1.

(b) A special verdict found, that a pit in the plaintiff's close, adjoining a close of the defendant in and since 1796, had been principally supplied with water, coming from the defendant's close through an agricultural tile drain for the better cultivation of the land, and which water flowed thence into a ditch, and then into the pit; that the drain came from a hillside through the defendant's close, through a wet, boggy soil, and not from any ascertained source, and that it aided in effecting the general surface drainage of the defendant's close; that the defendant, for the purpose of more effectually draining and cultivating his close, deepened the course of an old drain, and, by making a communication between it and the drain which fed the plaintiff's pit, drew the water from the pit; and that the immediate object was to get a better fall of water from the defendant's close, which previously had been so wet and boggy as to be comparatively unproductive. Held, that, under the above circumstances, no grant of the flow of water to the plaintiff was to be presumed, and that the plaintiff had no right of action

water raised by a steam-engine from a mine, or flowing from the eaves of houses, is thrown upon adjoining land used by the owner; such use gives no claim to have the privilege continued.[1]

3 *a.* But where land-owners have agreed to have a watercourse made through their respective lands for the purpose of supplying a town with water; an injunction lies against one of them who diverts the stream into its old channel.[2] So, several proprietors of contiguous land on a stream having contributed jointly to the erection of a dam, and changed

[1] Arkwright *v.* Gell, Gale & What. 182.

[2] Duke *v.* Elgin, 7 Eng. L. & Eq. 39.

against the defendant for the diversion of the water. Greatrex *v.* Hayward, 20 Eng. L. & Eq. 377.

Outside the defendant's land was a wet, springy spot, at which, at most seasons of the year, some water rose to the surface and flowed down the slope of the land. In wet seasons a great body of water flowed down, and after a long drought there was scarcely any, and sometimes none. There was no regularly-formed ditch or channel for the water, the place where it flowed being constantly trodden in with cattle. The water, which was not absorbed, (and all was not absorbed except in times of drought,) ran into an old watercourse of the plaintiff. The water had so flowed for more than twenty years. The defendant, for the purpose of supplying some of his property with water and draining his land, diverted the water in question from the plaintiff's reservoir. At a certain other spot in the defendant's land there had always been, as far back as any one could recollect, water rising to the surface; there had generally been a regular drinking-place for cattle, formed with stones, and the overflow of the water went down a ditch and thence into a watercourse, to the plaintiff's reservoir. The defendant carried a drain under the spot in question, and conveyed away the water to another portion of his property, so that the water ceased to rise to the surface and flow into the plaintiff's reservoir. Held, that in neither case was the plaintiff entitled to the benefit of the flow of the water, and that the defendant was not liable for the diversion. Rawstron *v.* Taylor, 23 Eng. L. & Eq. 428.

One of the accompaniments of a *river*, technically so called, is a *bank*. It is said, "The banks of a river are those elevations of land which confine the waters when they rise out of the bed; and the bed is that soil so usually covered by water, as to be distinguishable from the banks, by the character of the soil or vegetation, or both, produced by the common presence and action of flowing water." Per Curtis, J., Howard *v.* Ingersoll, 13 How. 426.

the course of the creek, in part at least, by conducting it in a raceway across their lots; the law secures to each the right to a just and reasonable participation in the use of the water, and the rights of the parties are liable to be changed in the same way and under the same circumstances as in regard to a natural stream.[1] And, after an artificial vent has been substituted for the natural channel of a water-course, it is the duty of the party who obstructed the natural channel to keep such vent in repair.[2]

4. Every proprietor of land, on the bank of a fresh water river, has a right to the use of the water, as it *was wont to run* (*ut currerè solebat*), without diminution or alteration; (*a*) and no owner has, in general, a right to use it, to the prejudice of other owners above or below him, by throwing it back upon the former, or subtracting it from the latter.[3] (*b*)

[1] Townsend *v.* McDonald, 14 Barb. 460.

[2] Brisbane *v.* O'Neall, 3 Strobh. 348.

[3] 2 Hill. on R. Prop. 98.

(*a*) The water-power, belonging to a riparian proprietor, is said to be the difference of level between the surface where the stream in its natural state first touches his land, and the surface where it leaves it. M'Calmont *v.* Whitaker, 3 Rawle, 84.

(*b*) Although, in actions relating to watercourses, the conflicting rights of owners above and below are ordinarily brought in question; yet the general rules upon this subject equally apply to *opposite* proprietors. In this, as in the other case, each owner is entitled to the natural use of *the whole water*, and has a remedy against the other for any diversion or diminution of it. Curtis *v.* Jackson, 13 Mass. 507; Wetmore *v.* White, 2 Caines's Cas. in Er. 87; Canal, &c. *v.* Havens, 11 Ill. 554; Moffatt *v.* Bremer, 1 Greene, 348.

The plaintiff and defendant owned different mills on one dam. The plaintiff brings an action against the defendant, for opening a canal into the pond above, for a supply of water to work his mill. The water thus withdrawn was returned to the stream immediately below the dam, and was less in quantity than the defendant would have used at his mill on the dam. By means of a reservoir higher up, the defendant also increased the quantity of water in the stream. Held, both parties were entitled, *per my et per tout*, to their share of the whole stream on its arrival at the dam; and therefore, notwithstanding the above defences, the action was sustained. Webb *v.* Portland, &c. 3 Sumn. 169.

Where the plaintiff, who had no title to the land, beyond the centre of the channel, erected a dam across the stream, and upon the defendants' land,

The riparian proprietor has, annexed to his lands, (*a*) *the general flow of the stream*, so far as it has not been already acquired by some prior and legally operative appropriation.[1] "*Primâ facie*, the proprietor of each bank of a stream is the proprietor of half the land covered by the stream, but there is no property in the water. Every proprietor has an equal right to use the water which flows in the stream, and consequently no proprietor can have the right to use the water to the prejudice of any other proprietor. Without the consent of the other proprietors who may be affected by his operations, the proprietor can neither diminish the quantity of water which would otherwise descend to the proprietors be-

[1] Buddington *v.* Bradley, 10 Conn. 213.

---

and so continued it for many years, and until the defendants removed the dam; held, the erection of the dam partly upon the defendants' land, and thus diverting half of the water, was an injury for which the defendants might maintain an action, and therefore might lawfully remove the obstruction. Adams *v.* Barney, 25 Verm. 225.

(*a*) The right does not depend upon *a personal grant* or long acquiescence on the part of the riparian proprietors, above and below, but arises *ex jure naturæ*, and is an incident of property. Dickenson *v.* The Grand, &c. 9 Eng. L. & Eq. 513.

In an old case, it is said, "In this action there was no need that it should be an ancient mill; for if one erect a new mill on his freehold, and another diverts the watercourse of that mill, as it passes by his land, still, if the water used to follow this course, an action on the case lies against him; for he cannot use his land or the water which passes through his land to the damage of the other." Per Doddridge, J., Rutland *v.* Bowler, Palm. 290.

And no allegation is necessary, that the plaintiff's mill is more ancient than the defendant's. Beavers *v.* Trimmer, 1 Dutch. 97.

In an action for damages to the plaintiff's mill-privilege by the diversion of the water, it is not necessary to aver the manner or the means of the diversion. It is sufficient to aver injury to the privilege, without alleging the existence of a mill. Stein *v.* Ashby, 24 Ala. 521.

But the right of the plaintiff must be accurately stated; and, where it was averred that the plaintiff was entitled to all the water which should rise above a certain mark in a dam, and the evidence showed that he was only entitled to that part of such water which should remain after a prior use by the defendant; held, a fatal variance. Wilbur *v.* Brown, 3 Denio, 356.

low, nor throw the water back upon the proprietors above."[1] Thus the owner of land, over which a stream of water runs, has a right to such use only of the water, as will not materially *reduce its quantity* or *corrupt its quality*, to the injury of the proprietors below.[2] Use of a stream by one riparian proprietor, if it essentially impair the use below, is said to be unreasonable and unlawful, unless altogether indispensable to any beneficial use at every point of the stream.[3] And on the other hand, a land-owner has a right, even without resorting to a prescription, to have the water from his land flow through the natural channels and drains convenient to it. And, when another cuts him off from such right by an embankment, he has a right to remove such embankment.[4]

5. A distinction has been made between the title to streams above ground and *subterraneous* streams; and it has been held, that independently of a claim by prescription, a party, having the benefit of a stream of the latter description, cannot maintain an action for its subtraction or diversion by another owner, enjoying the like benefit.[5] In reference to a claim of this nature, it is remarked in a leading case: "We think that it rather falls within that principle, which gives to the owner of the soil all that lies beneath his surface; that the land immediately below is his property, whether it is solid rock or porous ground, or venous earth, or part soil, part water; that the person who owns the surface may dig therein, and apply all that is there found to his own purposes at his free will and pleasure; and that, if in the exercise of such right, he intercepts or drains off the water collected from underground springs in his neighbor's well, this inconvenience to his neighbor falls within the description of *damnum absque injuria*."[6] But the contrary doctrine has also been held, that, where a spring is supplied by a subterraneous stream, an

[1] Per Sir J. Leach, V. C., Wright *v.* Howard, 1 Sim. & Stu. 203; Mason *v.* Hill, 3 B. & Ad. 312.

[2] Wheatley *v.* Chrisman, 24 Penn. 298.

[3] Snow *v.* Parsons, 2 Wms. 459.

[4] Overton *v.* Sawyer, 1 Jones, Law, 308.

[5] Acton *v.* Blundell, 12 Mees. & W. 324; Roath *v.* Driscoll, 20 Conn. 533; Chatfield *v.* Wilson, 2 Wms. 49. See Chasemore *v.* Richards, 2 H. & N. 168.

[6] Per Tindal, C. J., Acton *v.* Bell, 12 Mees. & W. 324.

owner of the land above the spring cannot divert the stream to the injury of those who use the spring, or on whose land the stream comes to the surface as a spring, more especially where the underground flow of water is so well defined as to be a constant stream.[1] So, where the water from a spring flows in a gully or natural channel to a stream upon which the plaintiff has a mill, and the spring is cut off at its source, and the water received into a tank as it rises from the ground, by the license of the owner of the soil on which the spring rose; an action lies against the party thus abstracting the water.[2] (*a*)

[1] Smith *v.* Adams, 6 Paige, 435; Wheatley *v.* Beaugh, 25 Penn. 528; Whetstone *v.* Bowser, 29 Penn. R. 59. See Arbuckle *v.* Ward, 3 Wms. 43.

[2] Dudden *v.* Guardians, &c. 38 Eng. L. & Eq. 526.

(*a*) In reference to *subterraneous water*, generally, — including *streams*, *aqueducts*, *springs*, and *wells*, — the law can hardly be considered as perfectly settled.

It is held, that the owner of a farm may dig a ditch to drain his land, or open and work a quarry upon it, even if by so doing he intercept one of the underground sources of a spring on his neighbor's land, which supplies a small stream of water flowing through the land of each, and thereby diminish the supply of water, to the injury of the adjoining proprietor. Ellis *v.* Duncan, 21 Barb. 230.

So, where a spring is produced by percolations through the land of the owner above, and in the use of the land for mining the spring is destroyed, he is not liable, unless guilty of negligence or malice. 25 Penn. 528.

And one in possession of land, containing a spring, may use it for culinary purposes and watering cattle, even by artificial means; as, for instance, by an aqueduct leading to his house and barn. Wadsworth *v.* Tillotson, 15 Conn. 366.

In Pennsylvania, the owner of land adjoining a navigable river owns to low-water mark, subject to the public right of navigation to high-water mark, and such ownership gives him title to a spring situated between high and low-water mark, subject only to the public easement. Lehigh, &c. *v.* Trone, 28 Penn. 206.

A bill in equity is held to lie, for the diversion of water from a spring and watercourse, by digging a deep well and fountain. Dexter *v.* Providence, &c. 1 Story, R. 387.

So an action lies in favor of a riparian proprietor, either upon a special statute or an express agreement, for the abstraction of water which never

6. As already stated, every proprietor of land on the bank of a natural stream has a right to use the water, provided he so uses it as not to work any material injury to the proprietors above or below him; and may begin to exercise that right whenever he will.[1] It has indeed been sometimes laid down, that by *the first occupancy* of a stream

[1] Sampson *v.* Hoddinott, 19 Com. B. 590; 38 Eng. L. & Eq. 241.

made part of the river, but has been prevented from doing so in its natural course by the digging of a well; whether the water was part of a subterraneous stream, or percolated through the strata, and though no actual injury be sustained. Dickinson *v.* The Grand, &c. 9 Eng. L. & Eq. 513.

But the owner of land may dig a well on any part of it, though he thereby diminishes the water in his neighbor's well, unless the latter has gained an adverse right by grant or prescription, or unless the act is done merely with a malicious intent. Greenleaf *v.* Francis, 18 Pick. 117. It is said: "The proprietor, in the absence of any agreement subjecting his estate to another, may consult his own convenience in his operations above or below the surface of his ground. He may obstruct the light and air above, and cut off the springs of water below the surface. The proprietor must, at his peril, so place his house and make his excavations below it, as to obtain water, air, and light, even if his neighbor should exercise his full rights of dominion upon his adjoining estate. Now the case finds, that the defendant dug his well in that part of his own ground where it would be most convenient for him. It was a lawful act, and although it may have been prejudicial to the plaintiff it is *damnum absque injuria.*" Per Putnam J., 18 Pick. 117; acc. Chasemore *v.* Richards, 29 Law Times, 230.

As to liability for corrupting the subterraneous currents that supply a well, by means of noxious matter placed upon one's own land, see Brown *v.* Illius, 25 Conn. 583.

The adverse or exclusive use of water, flowing through *an aqueduct*, by the owners and occupants of a house, for twenty years, furnishes presumptive evidence of a grant from the owner of the land through which it is brought. Watkins *v.* Peck, 13 N. H. 360.

The owner of two adjoining messuages and lots, one occupied and the other leased by him, constructed *a drain* from one through the other into a common sewer, and suffered his tenants to use it more than ten years. He afterwards sold the lots to different persons at the same time, not mentioning in the deeds any right of *drain.* Held, one purchaser might close up the drain of the other's lot which passed over his land, if by reasonable labor and expense another might be made elsewhere. Johnson *v.* Jordan, 2 Met. 234.

a party acquires a *property in the current.*[1] And this has been recognized in some American cases as the common-law doctrine.[2] But, as may be gathered from the general course of authorities cited in this chapter, the well-established doctrine now is, that running water cannot be appropriated by mere prior occupancy, but only by express grant, general consent, or continued use.[3] (*a*) Thus one, who erects

[1] 2 Bl. Comm. 403.

[2] Hatch *v.* Dwight, 17 Mass. 289; Martin *v.* Bigelow, 2 Aik. 184.

[3] Tyler *v.* Wilkinson, 4 Mas. 400.

(*a*) With a general similarity between the elements of light and air on the one hand and running water on the other, as the subjects of qualified ownership; the marked distinction has been pointed out, that the former *have no owner*, until appropriated, while the latter, as incident to the land over and through which it flows, belongs, in a qualified sense, to the owners of such land, and cannot therefore be appropriated by one to the exclusion of others. Per Story, J., Tyler *v.* Wilkinson, 4 Mas. 400.

It is said: "Water flowing is *publici juris*. By the Roman law, running water, light, and air, were considered some of those things which were *res communes*, and which were defined as things, the property of which belongs to no person but the use to all." Per Tindal, C. J., Liggins *v.* Inge, 7 Bing. 692. See Dilling *v.* Murray, 6 Ind. 324.

The following accurate distinctions and lucid illustrations are found in a late case in Massachusetts: "The erection of a mill on one proprietor's land may raise and set the water back to such a distance as to prevent the proprietor above from having sufficient fall to erect a mill on his land. In such case, the proprietor who first erects his dam for such a purpose has a right to maintain it, as against the proprietors above and below; and to this extent, prior occupancy gives a prior title to such use. For the same reason, the proprietor below cannot erect a dam in such a manner as to raise the water and obstruct the wheels of the first occupant. Such appears to be the nature and extent of the prior and exclusive right, which one proprietor acquires by a prior reasonable appropriation of the use of the water in its fall; and it results, not from any originally superior legal right, but from a legitimate exercise of his own common right. But such appropriation of the stream to mill purposes gives the proprietor a prior and exclusive right to such use only so far as it is actual. If, therefore, he has erected his dam and mill, with its wasteways, sluices, and other fixtures necessary to command the use of the water to a certain extent, and there is a surplus remaining, the proprietor below may have the benefit of that surplus. If he erects a dam and mills for the purpose of using and employing such surplus, he is, as to such part of the stream, the first occupant, and makes the first appro-

a mill and dam upon a stream, does not, by the mere prior occupation, unaccompanied with such a length of time that a grant may be presumed, gain an exclusive right, and cannot maintain an action against a person erecting a mill and dam above his, by which the water is in part diverted, and he is in some degree injured.[1] (*a*)

[1] Platt *v.* Johnson, 15 Johns. 213.

---

priation. As to that, therefore, his right is prior and exclusive." Per Shaw, C. J., Cary *v.* Daniels, 8 Met. 466.

Possession or actual appropriation must be the test of priority in all claims to the use of water, wherever such claims are not dependent on the ownership of the land through which the water flows. Such appropriation cannot be constructive, and the erection of a dam across a natural watercourse is an actual appropriation of the water at that point, but not below it, although the water flowing over the dam is brought back into the watercourse by means of canals made by the owners of the dam. Kelly *v.* Natoma, &c. 6 Cal. 105.

(*a*) A. erected a mill in 1823, on his own land, the former owner of which had, for twenty years before 1818, appropriated the water of a stream, running through it, to the purposes of watering his cattle and irrigating his land. In 1818, B. had erected a mill near the same stream, and the owner and occupier of A.'s land then gave a parol license to B. to make a dam at a particular spot, and take what water he pleased from that point, which water was so taken, and returned by pipes into the stream, above the spot where A.'s mill was afterwards erected. In 1818, B., without license, conveyed part of the water, which had before flowed into the stream from certain springs, into a reservoir for the use of his mill. In 1828, A. appropriated to the use of his mill all the surplus water which flowed through and over the dam, and which was not conducted into the reservoir. In 1829, A. demolished the dam erected by B., and gave him notice not to divert the water. B. then erected a new dam lower down the stream, and by means of it diverted from A.'s mills, at some times, all the water before appropriated by A.; at others, a part of it; and the water, when returned into the stream, was in a heated state. Held, on special verdict, 1st. That, whether the right to the use of flowing water be in the first occupant, or in the possessor of the land through which it flows, A. was entitled to the surplus water; for he was the first occupant of that, and also owner and occupier of the land through which it flowed, and might maintain an action for the injury sustained by the abstraction or spoiling of such surplus water.

6 *a*. But, on the other hand, any proprietor may, as soon as he is injured by the diversion of the water from its natural course, maintain an action against the party so diverting it, although the defendant first appropriated the water to his own use; unless he has had twenty years' undisturbed enjoyment of it in the altered course.[1] So where the plaintiff, a riparian proprietor, had used the water for more than fifteen years — the period requisite to give a prescriptive right — for a mill, by conducting it through a raceway into a reservoir, and thence to the mill; and the defendant, an owner above, afterwards obstructed the natural flow of the water, the plaintiff having a short time before given up his reservoir, in consequence of which he required more water, and but for which he would have suffered no injury; it was held, that an action might be sustained; that the plaintiff had a right to the flow of the water, not by his artificial channel, or into his reservoir, but within its banks, through his lands, as it was wont; and that his mode of using the water was immaterial, except as affecting the damages.[2] So where A., an owner upon a stream, diverted the water upon a channel, through the banks of which the water percolated, and passed into the soil of B.; and B. afterwards erected a house, the foundation of which being sunk below

[1] Mason *v*. Hill, 3 Barn. & Ad. 304.

[2] Buddington *v*. Bradley, 10 Conn. 213.

2d. That A. was in like manner entitled to recover in respect of the water diverted by B. at his new dam; because the license granted to B. by the former occupier was, to take the water at one particular point, and not at the place where his dam was made; and further, because, if the license had been general to take at any place, it would have been revocable, except as to such places where it had been acted on, and expense incurred; and it was revoked before the last dam was erected.

3d. That A. was entitled to recover for the water diverted from the springs, and collected in a reservoir in 1818; for the possessor of land, through which a natural stream flows, has a right to the advantage of that stream flowing in its natural course, and to use it when he pleases for his own purposes; no adverse right having been acquired by actual grant, or by twenty years' enjoyment. Mason *v*. Hill, 5 B. & Ad. 1.

the soil, the water became injurious; held, A. could not longer justify filling his channel.[1] So where the defendant, an owner above, by a wear or dam diverted the water; and, about ten years afterwards, the plaintiff, the adjoining owner below, made a channel in his own land, contiguous to the stream, for some purpose of manufacturing not previously carried on; the defendant was held to have acquired no right against the plaintiff by his use of the water.[2] So it is no defence to an action, that the interruption would have caused the plaintiff no injury, if he had continued to use the water as he had formerly done. As, for example, where the plaintiff had lowered his *hammer-wheel*.[3]

7. It is the prevailing rule, that a riparian proprietor is entitled to *nominal damages* for a diversion of the water from his mill, without any proof of actual damage.[4] That the wrongful diversion of a stream of water implies some damage;[5] inasmuch as a repetition of the injury might establish an adverse right.[6] More especially a diversion of a large portion of the water of a natural watercourse, by a proprietor of land through which the watercourse runs, renders him liable to an action on the case by a proprietor of land below, from which the water is thus diverted; although the latter thereby sustains no present actual damage.[7] So, in an action for turning the course of an ancient stream, so that it no longer flowed on the lands of the plaintiff, it is *an intendment of law* that the plaintiff, by the loss of the water, was thereby injured; and evidence that, in consequence thereof, he was compelled to haul water from a distance, to supply the uses of the stream, is proper and admissible, to give the jury certain data upon which they may estimate the real damages; and it is not claiming

[1] Cooper *v.* Barber, 3 Taunt. 99.

[2] Mason *v.* Hill, 3 B. & Ad. 304.

[3] King *v.* Tiffany, 9 Conn. 162. See Stein *v.* Burden, 29 Ala. 127; Bowen *v.* Hill, 1 Bing. N. 549; Parker *v.* Griswold, 17 Conn. 288.

[4] Stein *v.* Burden, 24 Ala. 130; Butman *v.* Hussey, 3 Fairf. 407; Bolivar, &c. *v.* Neponset, &c. 16 Pick. 247; Plumleigh *v.* Dawson, 1 Gilm. 544; Hendrick *v.* Cook, 4 Geo. 241. See Mason *v.* Hill, 1 B. & Ad. 1.

[5] Chatfield *v.* Wilson, 1 Williams, 630.

[6] Steen *v.* Ashby, 24 Ala. 521; Tillotson *v.* Smith, 32 N. H. 90.

[7] Newhall *v.* Ireson, 8 Cush. 595.

damages for a distinct injury, not necessarily resulting from the nuisance.[1]

7 *a*. But on the other hand it has been held, that the owner of a mill is not entitled to damages for a mere theoretical injury to his mill, occasioned by another mill on the same stream, though for any actual perceptible injury he is entitled to recover.[2] And the same rule has been applied to an action, brought by a lower riparian proprietor against an upper one, for a diversion of part of the water of a natural watercourse flowing through their lands.[3] (*a*) And the owner of a lower water privilege has no right of action against the owner of an upper privilege, for a diversion of the water, where, on account of the rights of an intervening proprietor, he is not entitled to use the water so diverted.[4] And, in general, any diversion of running water, not injuriously affecting other proprietors, is allowable.[5]

8. With regard to the nature and amount of the injury, it is held, that any benefit derived by the plaintiff from the act complained of may be taken into consideration.[6] And only the direct and immediate damage can be allowed. Thus a railroad corporation, building a bridge across a

[1] Hart *v.* Evans, 8 Barr, 13.

[2] Thompson *v.* Crocker, 9 Pick. 59; M'Elroy *v.* Goble, 6 Ohio, 187. See Burden *v.* The Mayor, &c. 21 Ala. 309.

[3] Elliot *v.* Fitchburg Railroad Co. 10 Cush. 191.

[4] Olney *v.* Fenner, 2 R. I. 211.

[5] Ford *v.* Whitlock, 1 Williams, 265.

[6] Addison *v.* Hack, 2 Gill, 221.

(*a*) It is somewhat difficult to extract from the decided cases any settled rule upon this subject. On the one hand, we find the phrases, *sensibly injurious — public convenience and general good — useless and unproductive — fair proportion — partial loss — unrestricted use — destructive;* importing that a mere violation of a party's right is not sufficient to maintain the action; while other expressions regard *the right* as the only essential point of inquiry.

A question has been made, in regard to the word *unappreciable*, whether it properly means "so inconsiderable as to be incapable of value or price." Embrey *v.* Owen, 4 Eng. L. & Eq. 466.

As affecting the question of damage, the capacity of the stream, the adaptation of machinery to it, and all attendant circumstances, are to be taken into view. Dilling *v.* Murray, 6 Ind. 324.

stream, are liable for the damage thereby occasioned to the owner of a saw-mill above, by the obstruction of the stream, so as to prevent the water from passing off from his mill as freely as it had previously; but are not liable for the damage suffered by him, by being impeded and put to increased expense in getting logs up the stream to his mill, whether the stream be navigable for boats and rafts or not.[1]

9. With regard to the question, what is *a justifiable use of water*, in reference to the rights of other owners; it is held, that a person owning an upper mill has a legal right to use the water, and may apply it to work his mill, subject to such reasonable limitations as the rights of the mill-owner lower down the stream require him to observe; but if, by an unreasonable use, the lower mills are essentially impaired in their usefulness, the law will interpose and limit the common right; so that the owners of the lower mills shall enjoy a fair participation in the use of the stream. And the Court cannot lay down any rule which shall limit the precise boundaries of the rights of such owners, in all cases; but the question of reasonable use of the water by the mill-owner above, depending as it must on the ever-varying circumstances of each particular case, must be determined by the jury;[2] with suitable reference to the existence and wants of other mills.[3] To justify an action, the injury must be real, material, and substantial.[4]

9 *a*. With more particular reference to an ordinary and important use of the watercourse alone; it has been held, that the owner of land, adjoining an ancient brook, may lawfully divert the water, for the purpose of *irrigating his close;* although a close adjoining the brook below becomes less productive by that means.[5] It is said, " A man owning a close on an ancient brook may lawfully use the water thereof for the purposes of husbandry, as watering his cattle or irrigating his close; and he may do this, either by dipping

[1] Blood *v.* Nashua, &c. 2 Gray, 137.
[2] Thomas *v.* Brackney, 17 Barb. (N. Y.) 654.
[3] Parker *v.* Hotchkiss, 25 Conn. 321.
[4] M'Elroy *v.* Goble, 6 Ohio, N. S. 187.
[5] Weston *v.* Alden, 8 Mass. 136; Perkins *v.* Dow, 1 Root, 535; Anthony *v.* Lapham, 5 Pick. 175.

water from the brook and pouring it upon his land, or by making small sluices for the same purpose; and, if the owner of a close below is damaged thereby, it is *damnum absque injuriâ*."[1] So where, in an action on the case, founded on an irrigation, against a riparian proprietor above, by a mill-owner below, it appeared that the irrigation was not continuous, but intermittent, when the river was full, and that the working of the mill was not thereby affected, nor the water diminished perceptibly to the eye; it was held, that the action would not lie.[2] So it has been held, that a riparian proprietor has the right to use the water which flows from or through his lands, for all ordinary purposes and for the gratification of natural wants, even though he consume *the entire stream*.[3]

9 *b*. But a party cannot, by irrigation, lawfully diminish the quantity of water which has been accustomed to flow to a mill of forty years' standing, so as to impede its operation.[4] And the more recent doctrine is, that the owner of land, through which a natural stream flows, cannot divert the water for the purposes of irrigation, without returning the surplus into the natural channel, and thereby deprive the owner of land below of his privilege to use the water in the same manner.[5] (*a*) And the still more rigid rule has

[1] Weston *v.* Alden, 8 Mass. 136.
[2] Embrey *v.* Owen, 4 Eng. L. & Eq. 466.
[3] Stein *v.* Burden, 29 Ala. 127.
[4] Cook *v.* Hull, 3 Pick. 269.
[5] Anthony *v.* Lapham, 5 Pick. 175.

(*a*) The plaintiff had immemorially enjoyed the benefit of irrigating certain meadows with the water of the Yeo, subject to the right of the occupier of a mill to detain the water for the use of his mill; and, although the natural flow of the river was prevented by the exercise of the miller's right, the water came down at such times, that the plaintiff was enabled to irrigate his meadows effectually. But, of late, the defendant had, for the purpose of irrigating his own adjacent land, from time to time diverted the water after it had passed the mill, and before it reached the plaintiff's meadows; and, although it did not appear that the quantity of water which ultimately reached the plaintiff's meadows was thereby sensibly diminished, yet the effect was that the water was detained by the process of irrigation, and did not arrive till so late in the day, that the plaintiff was deprived of the power

been sometimes laid down, that, if the supply of water is no greater than the riparian proprietors need for the natural uses, none of them can subtract it for the purposes of irrigation *or manufacturing*.[1] And, in illustration and justification of this doctrine, it is said, "These wants are either natural or artificial. Natural are such as are absolutely necessary to be supplied in order to his existence. Artificial, such only, as by supplying them, his comfort and prosperity are increased. To quench thirst, and for household purposes, water is absolutely indispensable. In civilized life, water for cattle is also necessary. These wants must be supplied, or both man and beast will perish. The supply of a man's artificial wants is not essential to his existence — he could live if water was not employed in irrigating lands, or in propelling his machinery. So of manufactures, they promote the prosperity and comfort of mankind, but cannot be considered absolutely necessary to his existence. An individual owning a spring on his land, from which water flows in a current through his neighbor's land, would have a right to use the whole of it, if necessary, to satisfy his natural wants. If he desires to use it for irrigation or manufactures, and there be a lower proprietor to whom its use is essential to supply his natural wants, or for his stock, he must use the water so as to leave enough for such lower proprietor. Where the stream is small, and does not supply water more than sufficient to answer the natural wants of the different proprietors living on it, none of the proprietors can use the water for either irrigation or manufactures."[2]

9 *c*. So it has been held, in an action of the case for divert-

[1] Evans *v*. Merriweather, 3 Scam. 494.

[2] Evans *v*. Merriweather, 3 Scam. 496.

to use it fully. Held, this detention of the water by the defendant was a use of it, which was in its character necessarily injurious to the natural rights of the plaintiff as a riparian proprietor, and a ground of action; and this without proof of actual damage to the plaintiff's reversionary interest, the law inferring damage from an obstruction of his right. Sampson *v*. Hoddinott, 19 Com. B. 590; 38 Eng. L. & Eq. 241.

ing a watercourse, that, if one has *ancient pits* in his land, which are replenished by a rivulet, he may *cleanse* them, but cannot *change* or *enlarge* them.[1] (*a*) So, the right to divert is contingent, and ceases, when the water cannot be restored to its natural channel; although these facts might reduce the damages.[2] (*b*) So, although the owner of a superior estate may improve his lands, though he thereby throw increased waters on his inferiors, *through the natural channels*, he cannot dig new channels therefor, and the lower owner may lawfully erect an impediment to the increased flow, but to no more.[3] And, in general, an upper proprietor of a more ancient mill has not a right, as against a more recent mill-owner below, to use the water as his own convenience or interest may dictate; but is bound to use it in a reasonable and proper manner. Thus a jury may find the constant use of the water entirely by night, and a detention of it during the day, to be an improper and unreasonable use, and, if so, an action lies, although such use is in good faith, and with no design to injure the rights of others.[4] (*c*) And the reasonableness of the detention of water, as to time, is a question for the jury.[5] So an

[1] Brown *v.* Best, 1 Wils. 174.
[2] Stein *v.* Burden, 29 Ala. 127.
[3] Kauffman *v.* Griesemer, 26 Penn. 407.
[4] Barrett *v.* Parsons, 10 Cush. 367; Merrit *v.* Brickenhoff, 17 Johns. 306.
[5] Hetrich *v.* Deachler, 6 Barr, 32.

(*a*) In trespass *quare clausum*, the defendant pleaded a general right to enter the plaintiff's land to cleanse a watercourse, which was the trespass complained of. Held, this plea was not supported by evidence of the particular right to use the watercourse and cleanse it, so as to drain the defendant's meadows. Darlington *v.* Painter, 7 Barr, 473.

(*b*) Hence, if water be diverted for artificial use, in quantity sufficient to affect injuriously the rights of the proprietor below, and be not returned to its channel before it reach the lands of such proprietor; it is no answer to an action, that the water would have continued to flow back into the stream, had not a stranger, by his unauthorized interference, rendered the means provided unavailing for that purpose.

(*c*) But where the owner of an upper mill *necessarily* detains water in his dam for several days for the purpose of working his mill, he is not liable therefor to a lower proprietor. Whaler *v.* Ahl, 29 Penn. 98.

action lies, if the owner of the mill above shuts down the gate, and detains the water for an unreasonable time, or lets it out in such unreasonable quantities as to prevent the owner of the mill below from using it, or in any way deprives him of the reasonable and fair participation in the benefits of the stream.[1] And the owner of a mill built after and above another is liable in damages, if he so uses the water that the lower mill is rendered less profitable than before; though it be by reason of improved machinery in the upper mill.[2] So the owner of a mill, who is entitled to use only the surplus water not required by another mill, is bound to shut his gate when there is not a sufficiency of water for both. But, if the other mill-owner in such case undertakes himself to prevent the passage of the water to the mill first mentioned, he will be liable to an action, if he does not remove the obstruction as soon as the deficiency of water ceases.[3] And, where the defendant was owner of an existing mill-dam, and the plaintiff rightfully erected a mill-dam above it on the same stream; it was held, that the defendant had no right to increase the height of his dam to a level with the plaintiff's wheel, and thereby to obstruct the wheel by back-water.[4] (*a*)

9 *d.* So the owner of land through which a stream passes has no right to make such use of it, as to send it down to an owner below, *poisoned or corrupted.* Thus the water may be used in connection with a tanyard or bark-mill, if so

[1] Merrit *v.* Brickenhoff, 17 Johns. 306.

[2] Wentworth *v.* Poor, 38 Maine, 243.

[3] Sumner *v.* Foster, 7 Pick. 32.

[4] Sumner *v.* Tilestone, 7 Pick. 198.

(*a*) But, where the plaintiff erected a dam across the outlet of a pond, and acquired a right by prescription to use the water; it was held, that the erection of a new dam by the defendants, higher than the old one, was not in itself an infringement of the plaintiff's rights; for the plaintiff had a right to adapt and use the new dam to the height of the old one; but that the defendants were entitled, as against the plaintiff, to use the water, when raised by means of the new dam above the top of the old dam, provided they did not thereby in any manner prejudice the rights of the plaintiff. Rogers *v.* Bruce, 17 Pick. 184.

much only be taken away as is necessary for this purpose; but the residue cannot legally be soiled by admixture with foreign substances, to the injury of another proprietor. So an action lies against a glover, who sets up a lime-pit so near the water as to corrupt it.[1] (*a*)

10. It will be presently seen, that in many of the United States express statutes have been enacted, in virtue of which the water of a stream may be applied to mill purposes, without subjecting the party making such a use of the water to a common-law action for damages; such statutes themselves providing a remedy more precisely adapted to the nature of the injury. (*Infra*, § 19.) But, where the proprietor of land, through which a stream flows, has actually built or is building a mill thereon, a proprietor below cannot, without a right acquired by grant, prescription, or actual use, erect a new dam or raise an old one, so as to destroy the upper mill privilege, simply under a liability to pay damages, pursuant to the statutes for the regulation of mills; nor do those statutes apply to such a case.[2] And no person can avail himself of the statutory privileges of a mill-owner, merely by erecting a dam, unless a mill is built in connection with the dam, or he has an intent forthwith to erect such mill. Otherwise he is liable at common law only for flowing.[3] So when a mill is disused and removed, and not replaced.[4] Nor does a statute, authorizing a proprietor of land, through which a natural watercourse runs, to lay a pipe or culvert,

1 Bealey *v.* Shaw, 6 E. 208; Howell *v.* M'Coy, 3 Rawle, 256; Aldred's case, 9 Co. 57 *b*; Magor *v.* Chadwick, 11 Ad. & Ell. 571; Stonehemer *v.* Farrar, 6 Ad. & Ell. N. S. 730.

2 Bigelow *v.* Newell, 10 Pick. 348.

3 Fitch *v.* Stevens, 4 Met. 426.

4 Baird *v.* Hunter, 12 Pick. 556.

(*a*) Erecting a cesspool near a well, Norton *v.* Scholefield, 9 M. & W. 565; the precipitation of minerals, Wright *v.* Williams, 1 M. & W. 77; and the corrupting of the atmosphere by the use of a watercourse, Story *v.* Hammond, 4 Ohio, 833; have all been held actionable injuries.

So it is held that an action lies by any party injured, against any party instrumental in causing the injury, and for any mode of corrupting the water. Carhart *v.* Auburn, &c. 22 Barb. 297.

from such watercourse, across a highway, to his mill, protect him from an action by a proprietor below, from whose land the water is thus diverted.[1]

11. In considering the general question, what is a lawful and justifiable use of the water of a stream; we have of course constantly referred to *dams*, without which this most important aid to human industry would be comparatively unavailable. It remains, however, to speak more particularly of the relative rights and liabilities of different proprietors, in reference to this single incident of watercourses and mills.

11 *a*. As a watercourse cannot be applied to its most valuable uses without the aid of a dam, every owner has the right to erect such dam; and neither the loss of water by evaporation from a pond thereby raised, nor the occasional increase or diminution of the quantity of water, or the acceleration or retardation of the current below, constitutes any legal ground of action against him. But the question turns upon the nature and extent of the injury.[2] Thus A., the owner of land and mills, on a stream above the land and more ancient mill of B. on the same stream, increased the height of his dam, and kept back the water only so long as was necessary to fill his pond; whereby B.'s mill was temporarily stopped. Held, that this was not an unreasonable use of the stream, and B. had no cause of action.[3] But, on the other hand, a proprietor of land upon a stream will not be debarred of his natural rights in the water, by authorizing a dam above his land. Thus B. built a dam on land of A., by his verbal permission, and subsequently a mill below; and A.'s grantee subsequently built a mill between the dam and the lower mill. Held, the ownership of the soil gave A.'s grantee no right to use the water to the detriment of the lower owner, who had the same right to the use of the stream as if no dam existed.[4]

[1] Newhall *v.* Ireson, 8 Cush. 595.

[2] Tyler *v.* Wilkinson, 4 Mas. 401; Palmer *v.* Mulligan, 3 Caines, 307. See Eddy *v.* Simpson, 3 Cal. 249.

[3] Pitts *v.* Lancaster Mills, 13 Met. 156.

[4] Pitman *v.* Poor, 38 Maine, 237.

11 *b.* And the grant of a right to make a dam will be strictly construed in favor of the party whose rights are thereby affected. Thus, under a grant of a mill, "also the mill-yard and all other appurtenances and privileges, roads and appendages belonging to said mill, with the right of digging, damming, and flowing for the accommodation of said mill," the grantee has not a right to erect a trough on the grantor's adjoining land, to conduct the water to the mill, no such trough having existed at the time of the grant, and the place where it was erected not having ever been flowed by the mill-dam.[1] (*a*)

11 *c.* And, although a mere *verbal license* is sufficient to justify the erection of a dam upon land of the licensor; yet, after the revocation of such license, the dam becomes a nuisance, and a bill in equity lies for its abatement. Thus S. gave to J. an oral license to erect and continue a mill-dam on S.'s land, and to dig a ditch through said land, to convey water to a mill that J. was about to build on his own land. J. erected the dam and dug the ditch, and afterwards erected the mill, and continued them during the life of S. After S. had granted the license, he conveyed his land to M., without any reservation. J. continued the dam and ditch, after the decease of S., for the purpose of working the mill, and M. requested him to remove the dam and fill up the ditch, and, upon J.'s refusal so to do, attempted to remove the dam, and tore down a part of it, when J. forcibly interposed, prevented M. from proceeding further, and repaired the injury. M. thereupon filed a bill in equity, praying that J. might

[1] Miller *v.* Bristol, 12 Pick. 550.

(*a*) A. owned an island, formed by a river and branch, and B. a mill, supplied by the branch with water. In the natural channel of the branch, there was a waste weir. A. agreed with B. that the branch should be closed, and a race through the island substituted for it; but not that there should be a waste weir in the new race. B. constructed such race; and the defendants, a railroad corporation, to protect their land from being flowed therefrom, closed the weir. Held, that B. had no right to the weir, and the defendants had a right to close it. Packer *v.* Rochester, &c. 17 N. Y. 283.

be enjoined and prohibited from any longer continuing the dam, which was alleged to be a nuisance, and that the same might be abated. On an issue framed and submitted to a jury, they found that the dam was a nuisance. Held, M. was entitled to these decrees, but that J. was not responsible for any acts done in pursuance of the license before it was countermanded, and therefore not liable to pay any expenses incurred by M. in removing the old dam; but that he was liable for building a new dam or repairing the old one after the license was countermanded, and that M. was entitled to have the same abated at the expense of J.[1]

11 *d*. But a license to erect a dam on land of the licensee cannot be thus revoked, more especially after the lapse of twenty years. Thus the owner of a mill privilege gave the owner of lands flowed thereby an oral license, to erect a dam on the land of the licensee, and also to dig a ditch across the land of the licensor, to drain the water from part of the licensee's land; and under this license the dam was erected and the ditch dug. Held, the licensor could revoke the license to dig the ditch, even after the expiration of twenty years, but not the license to build the dam; and, the licensor having undertaken to revoke the whole license, and after notice to the licensee made an incision in the dam, that the licensee was justified in making a ditch on his own land to draw off the water so thrown upon it; although he thereby diverted the water from the licensee's mill-pond also.[2]

12. The rights and liabilities of *opposite* owners upon a watercourse are often brought in question in reference to the erection of dams, (p. 672, n.) Thus where a dam, owned by the proprietor of land on one side of a river, is joined to the opposite shore by consent of the owner of land there, that owner may so far interfere with the dam, as to enjoy his own rights on that shore, but he cannot appropriate to his own use the materials of the dam.[3]

[1] Stevens *v*. Stevens, 11 Met. 251.
[2] Morse *v*. Copeland, 2 Gray, 302.
[3] Trask *v*. Ford, 39 Maine, 437.

13. Where there are mills on both sides of a watercourse, and the owner on one side has the exclusive right to use the whole of the water, when there is not enough for both; he has not a right to erect a permanent dam to turn the water to his mill, but must rely on his legal remedy, if his right be infringed by the owners on the other side.[1]

14. The defendant, owning the land on one side of and under a stream to the middle thereof, and also on both sides and under the stream at a place below, builds a mill at the place last mentioned, the dam of which causes the water of the stream to flow back to a dam and mill erected by the defendant at the place first mentioned, so as to prevent the plaintiff's mill from being wrought. Held, the defendant was not answerable to the plaintiff in damages.[2]

15. If the plaintiff owns a mill on one side of a river, and the defendant on the other, with a dam in common; and each is entitled to the water, alternately, six months in the year; each has a right to repair his own flume at any time of the year; more especially where each has a right to the surplus water not required by the other's mill. And if the defendant uses ordinary diligence in making the repairs, he will not be responsible for an accidental damage to the plaintiff. Thus where, in order to prevent great injury to both parties from an accident occasioned by him in making repairs, but without negligence on his part, he found it necessary to raise the waste gate and remove the flash boards of the plaintiff; it was held, that he was not liable for the damage.[3] (*a*)

16. Where a stream, by the act or neglect of the owner, is made to *overflow adjoining land;* this is an actionable

[1] Curtis *v.* Jackson, 13 Mass. 507.
[2] Jewell *v.* Gardiner, 12 Mass. 311.
[3] Boynton *v.* Rees, 9 Pick. 528.

(*a*) The degree of care, which a party who constructs a dam across a stream, is bound to use, is in proportion to the extent of the injury which will be likely to result to third persons, provided it should prove insufficient. Per Walworth, Ch., Mayor, &c. *v.* Bailey, 2 Denio, 433.

injury.[1] (a) Thus the owner of a superior estate may improve his lands, though he thereby throw increased waters on his inferiors, through the natural channels; but he cannot dig new channels therefor. The lower owner may lawfully erect an impediment to the increased flow, but to no more.[2] So the owner of a mill is liable to an action, if he cause the water upon a stream to be accumulated during the wet season, and draw it off in the summer, so as to cause a greater flow than usual, by means of which the banks of the proprietor below are washed away, his land drowned, and his grass depreciated; although the damage done thereby is

[1] Gilbert's case, Godb. 59; Brent v. Haddon, Cro. Jac. 556; Lev. 193; Neil, Bart. &c. v. Earl, &c. 3 Bligh, 414.

[2] Kaufman v. Griesemer, 26 Penn. 407.

(a) An agreement not to claim damages for flowing one's land, if the other party will erect a dam and mill, is not the conferring of any right, interest, or easement in land, but only a waiver of a claim for pecuniary damages, and need not be in writing. French v. Owen, 2 Wis. 250; Smith v. Goulding, 6 Cush. 154; Seymour v. Carter, 2 Met. 520.

But the permanent right to flow land by backwater, derived from grant or prescription, is an easement or incorporeal hereditament. Morgan v. Mason, 20 Ohio, 401; Pearson v. Tenny, 3 Dane, 14; Hazard v. Robinson, 3 Mas. 272.

One *tenant in common* has no right, by means of a dam erected on other lands of which he is sole seized, to flow the land owned in common, without the consent of his co-tenants, nor can he, by grant of the land of which he is so sole seized, convey such right of flowage to his grantee. Hutchinson v. Chase, 39 Maine, 508.

Where the owner of land through which there is a ditch, whether natural or artificial, which drains the upper part of the land, sells the upper part, including a portion of the ditch, he has no right to stop or obstruct the ditch below, so as to throw the water back upon the upper part. Shaw v. Etheridge, 3 Jones, Law, 300.

In case of two adjoining fields of unequal height, the owner of the lower one is obliged to receive the water falling from the upper; and, if the former dam up the water by building upon his own land, he cannot recover from the latter for the consequent injury to his own property. Laumier v. Francis, 23 Mis. 181.

One obstructing *a gutter* with building materials is liable for damage caused by the overflow of the water from very heavy rains into another's cellar. Ball v. Armstrong, 10 Ind. 181.

small.[1] And, on the other hand, a man has no right to erect a mill-dam on his own land, so as to throw the water back to his neighbor's line in the ordinary stage of the stream, and thus cause his neighbor's land to be overflowed by the natural swelling of the stream at certain seasons of the year.[2] And the causing of backwater, or increasing the quantity of water on the land of an upper proprietor, is an actionable injury, though he has erected no mill, and suffers no actual damage.[3]

17. If one having the right to maintain a dam to a certain height raise it, and thereby raise the water, so as to break the bank and overflow the land of a riparian proprietor, he cannot enter upon the land so overflowed, and erect an embankment upon the outer margin of it, for the purpose of preventing the escape of the water in that direction.[4] Nor can A. justify the obstructing of water so as to flood the land of B., upon the ground that C. changed the channel and thereby caused the water to flow on the land of A.[5] But, when a drain is made to discharge itself upon private land without the owner's consent, and he has not acquiesced for twenty years, he is not liable to an action at law, nor to the process prescribed by the mill act, for raising a mill-dam on his land, and thereby obstructing the drain and flowing the cellars connected with it.[6]

18. In regard to the amount of *damages* for flowage, (see § 7,) the general rule is adopted, that the plaintiff is entitled to *substantial compensation*; and, in case of trivial injury, or even without any actual injury, to merely nominal damages.[7] But flowage for a day or an hour is sufficient to maintain an action.[8] And it has been held, that, if the right of the plaintiff to damages, for overflowing his land, has been established by a former suit, he is entitled, in a subsequent one, to such

[1] Gerrish *v.* New Market, &c. 10 Fost. 478.

[2] McCoy *v.* Danley, 20 Penn. 85.

[3] Merritt *v.* Parker, 1 Coxe, 460.

[4] Fessenden *v.* Morrison, 19 N. H. 226.

[5] Amick *v.* Tharp, 13 Gratt. 564.

[6] Cotton *v.* Pocasset Man. Co. 13 Met. 429.

[7] Kemmerer *v.* Edleman, 23 Penn. 143; Wright *v.* Stowe, 4 Jones, 516; Lawrence *v.* The Great, &c. 16 Q. B. 643; Sackrider *v.* Beers, 10 Johns. 241. See Cooper *v.* Hall, 5 Ohio, 322.

[8] Cory *v.* Silcox, 6 Ind. 39.

damages, as will *punish* the defendant and compel him to abate the nuisance.[1]

18 *a*. But, in a complaint for flowing land, the inquiry is to be restricted to damage arising *immediately* from the dam complained of.[2] (*a*) The rule of damages is held to be the difference between the value of the plaintiff's premises before the injury, and the value immediately after the injury, taking into account only the damages which have resulted from the defendant's acts; or the loss arising to the proprietor from the direct injury done to his estate, as a whole, by flowing, deducting therefrom any benefit which may arise from the same cause, but not benefits which he may derive, in common with the owners of other lands similarly situated, by reason of the erection of a mill.[3] Nor any benefit that such flowing may cause to another part of his land.[4] Or to the public.[5]

19. In some of the United States, as has been already stated, (§ 10,) the subject of mills is regulated by express statutes. These chiefly relate to flowage; and their general purport is, to authorize the erection of dams, which overflow adjoining lands, and to provide a special remedy for the recovery of damages thereby caused. It is foreign from the plan of the present work to state in detail these statutory

[1] M'Coy *v*. Danley, 20 Penn. 85.

[2] Underwood *v*. North Wayne, &c. 38 Maine, 75.

[3] Chase *v*. The New York, &c. 24 Barb. 273; Brower *v*. Merrill, 3 Chand. 46. See Merritt *v*. Brinckerhoff, 17 Johns. 306; Platt *v*. Root, 15, 213.

[4] Gerrish *v*. New Market, &c. 10 Fost. 478.

[5] Engard *v*. Frazier, 7 Ind. 294.

(*a*) In an action for damages occasioned by the filling up by the defendants of their land, lying adjacent to that of the plaintiff, whereby the free flow of water off the plaintiff's land, as formerly existing, had been obstructed; instructions to the jury were held correct, that they should take into consideration the evidence on both sides bearing on this point, and, if they were satisfied that the filling up had actually benefited the plaintiff's estate in any particular, they would in assessing the damages make an allowance for such benefit, and give the plaintiff such sum in damages as they found upon the evidence would fully indemnify and compensate him for all the damage he had actually sustained. Luther *v*. Winnisimmet Co. 9 Cush. 171.

provisions. In general, they are substantially similar to those in Massachusetts, which may be referred to in connection with such points as have been made the subject of judicial construction. (*a*) It will be seen that the most frequent question has been, whether a particular injury, arising from the erection of a dam or mill, should be redressed by the special statutory complaint, or by the common-law action on the case. (*b*)

(*a*) By the Rev. Stats. of Massachusetts, ch. 116, any person may erect and maintain a water-mill and a dam to raise water for working it, upon and across any stream, &c.; but no such dam shall be erected to the injury of any mill lawfully existing on the same stream, nor of any mill-site on the same stream on which a mill or mill-dam shall have been lawfully erected and used, unless the right to maintain a mill on such last-mentioned site shall have been lost, &c. And any person, whose land is overflowed or otherwise injured by such dam may obtain compensation therefor upon his complaint pursuant to the statute.

(*b*) In this point of view, such statutes are held not open to the objection of *unconstitutionality*, because they merely *substitute* one process for another. Sowell *v.* Flagg, 11 Mass. 364.

They are designed to provide for the case, where the absolute right of each proprietor to use his own land and water privileges at pleasure cannot be fully enjoyed, and one must of necessity in some degree yield to the other. Fiske *v.* Framingham, &c. 12 Pick. 68.

Upon the general subject of the right of the State to interfere with private watercourses, the following remarks are found in a late American case: "It is not easy to understand how a man can be said to have a property in water, light, or air, of so fixed and positive a character as to deprive the sovereign power of the right to control it for the public good and the general convenience. Such a right exists as to individuals, and it cannot be interfered with by them. But the state, by virtue of her right of eminent domain, has the paramount right to control and dispose of everything, within her limits, which is not absolute and exclusive private property, to the promotion of the public good, and even to take private property for the same purpose, on rendering just compensation. The doctrine that the rule of the common law is not applicable to our large public rivers used for navigation, — that the rights of the owners of the lands bounded by such streams are subordinate to the right and power of the state to use and appropriate them to the public good in promotion of navigation, and that such rivers, whether tide-waters or not, are, as to the jurisdiction and power of the state, to be considered as navigable rivers, — is supported by sound rea-

19 *a*. Where a dam above has been erected for mill purposes, the owner below has no right to flow out such dam, even before a mill has been erected or commenced thereon, unless the design of building a mill has been abandoned. And the erection of a dam on a mill privilege, available for mill purposes, is *primâ facie* evidence that the dam is intended for such purposes, although the dam is weak or slightly built.[1] But where the plaintiff, being the owner of land bordering on a stream, began to erect a mill-dam thereon, none having existed there previously; and, before it was finished, the defendant began and completed a mill-dam below, whereby the plaintiff's mill privilege was destroyed; it was held, that the erection of the dam by the defendant was lawful, and the plaintiff could not maintain an action on the case for the injury, but his remedy was by complaint under the statute.[2] And a complaint under the statute is the proper remedy, where the owner of a mill erects a dam, across the outlet of a pond, which flows into the stream on which his mill is situated, for the purpose of creating a reservoir for the use of his mill, and land is flowed by means of such dam.[3] And where land is flowed during the existence of such a statute, a right of action becomes vested by virtue of the statute, which is not affected by its

[1] Mowry *v*. Sheldon, 2 R. I. 369.
[2] Baird *v*. Wells, 22 Pick. 312.
[3] Shaw *v*. Wells, 5 Cush. 537.

---

son, and should be established as the law of the land. Whilst the right of property exists in the individual, in relation to the streams of water exclusively his own, such as springs or small watercourses in the interior of his lands, and bounded by them on both sides, and whilst it may exist in reference to public rivers, as against the interference of private individuals, it cannot be admitted to prevail, as to public rivers and highways used for navigation, against the paramount jurisdiction of the state. The state, having the power to improve the navigation of her rivers, may judge of the expediency of doing so, and may execute, and provide for executing, such works of public improvement." Commissioners of Homochitto River *v*. Withers, 29 Miss. 21. See Minturn *v*. Lisle, 4 Cal. 180.

The reasons of the mill acts are said to be now obsolete. Jordan *v*. Woodward, 40 Maine, 317.

subsequent repeal, although prior to the institution of a suit; and an action at common law cannot therefore be sustained.[1] So, if an owner of land flowed sells and conveys the land before he has proceeded against the mill-owner for damages, he may afterwards maintain a complaint on the statute.[2] So, after a verdict for annual damages allowed and recorded, he may maintain an action under the statute against the owner or occupant of the mill, for the sum due and unpaid for the three years next preceding the commencement of such action, although the mill and dam are destroyed; provided the owner has not abandoned his mill privilege.[3]

19 *b*. But a complaint for flowing land, by means of a mill-dam, should allege that the dam was erected across a stream of water *not navigable*.[4] The mill act, of Massachusetts, does not apply to tide mills.[5] (*a*) Nor do statutes, in relation to the right of erecting mills, etc., justify their erection, so as to interrupt a public easement in a river.[6] And, being designed to provide for the most beneficial occupation and enjoyment of *natural* streams and watercourses, the statutes in question do not authorize the mill-owner to make *a canal* or *artificial stream* in such manner as to lead the water into the lands of another person. The remedy, therefore, of the party whose land is thus flowed, is by an action at common law. So, although made in virtue of a contract between the owner of the mill and the owner of the land.[7]

[1] Stephens *v.* Marshall, 3 Chand. 222. See chap. 3, § 30.

[2] Walker *v.* Oxford, &c. 10 Met. 203.

[3] Fuller *v.* French, 10 Met. 359.

[4] Bryant *v.* Glidden, 36 Maine, 36.

[5] Murdock *v.* Stickney, 8 Cush. 113.

[6] Treat *v.* Lord, 42 Maine, 552.

[7] Fiske *v.* Framingham Man. Co. 12 Pick. 68.

(*a*) A dam erected below a *steam-mill*, for the purpose of floating timber to the mill, and not for the purpose of driving the machinery of the mill, by which water is ponded back upon the land of another, does not come within the meaning of the act, requiring the proprietor of land overflowed first to apply by petition to the County Court. Bryan *v.* Burnett, 2 Jones, Law, 305.

To entitle a defendant to the process of complaint and take away the common-law remedy, it is necessary that the mill as well as the dam should be in the State. Wooster *v.* Great Falls, &c. 39 Maine, 246.

Thus a mill-owner, who erects a reservoir dam on his own land, across a natural stream other than the stream on which his mill is situated, and constructs an artificial channel from the reservoir to his mill-pond, for the purpose of conducting water from the reservoir to his mill, and also to enable him to use the reservoir for the purpose of holding the surplus water of the mill-pond; is liable to an action on the case, for the flowing, thereby occasioned, of the land of another person, situated above the reservoir, on the stream across which the reservoir dam is built.[1] So an action at common law lies, for damages caused by flowing land, by a dam that has been connected with a mill, if the defendant has abandoned the intention of again using the dam and water as a mill-power; and the jury may decide whether he has abandoned such intention.[2] So the remedy for a town against a mill-owner, who overflows a road which the town is by law obliged to repair, and does repair, is by an action on the case.[3] (*a*) So, upon a statutory complaint, a party cannot recover damages arising from offensive smells proceeding from the flowed land, when the water is drawn off, whereby his contiguous land is rendered less valuable for building lots. The statute affords to a mill-owner no warrant or excuse for causing or continuing a nuisance on his own land or the land of another.[4] So, the verdict of a sheriff's jury, in a complaint under the statute, having restricted a mill-owner from keeping up his dam, and flowing the land above, certain months in the year, he is liable in an action at common law for flowing the land during those months; although he causes such flowing through a canal cut by him by the side of the stream, after the verdict, instead of causing the

[1] Bates *v.* Weymouth, &c. 8 Cush. 548.

[2] Hodges *v.* Hodges, 5 Met. 205.

[3] Andover *v.* Sutton, 12 Met. 182.

[4] Eames *v.* New England, &c. 10 Met. 570.

(*a*) In such action, the town is entitled to recover the expense incurred in repairing the road, with interest from the time of demanding payment from the mill-owner, but not the costs of an indictment against the town for not seasonably repairing the road.

water to flow back in the natural stream, as it flowed before the verdict; and though the flowing was occasioned by a different structure from that which existed at the former trial; and though the new channel was of greater capacity, and would carry off the water more freely and fully from the plaintiff's land, than the old channel, and was kept open during the months specified in the verdict; and since the verdict the defendant had added a large amount of machinery to his mills.[1]

20. The right to use running water is *an easement*, and, like other easements, may be acquired as an adverse and exclusive privilege, varying from the natural and original title, by *prescription.* Thus it was formerly held, that, in an action on the case for diverting a watercourse, the *antiquity* of the mill must be set forth. And, if the declaration be for the diverting the water *ab antiquo et solitu cursu*, this amounts to a prescription, which must be proved at the trial, or the plaintiff would be nonsuited.[2] And it is now held, that twenty years' enjoyment or use of the water of a stream, in a particular manner, gives the right to its continued use in the same mode.[3] But the use of the water of a running stream for nine years confers no right.[4] So a right to a *spring* may be gained by continued use;[5] and, in an action against another for polluting a spring rising in his land and flowing through the plaintiff's, a use by the latter, and those under whom he claims, for twenty years, both supports the right and aggravates the damages for injury to the water.[6] So, where a mill-owner has in fact exercised the right of keeping up his dam, and *flowing* the land of another person, for twenty years, without payment of damages and without any claim or assertion by the land-owner of the right to damages; it is evidence of a right to flow without payment of damages, and will be a bar to such a claim.[7]

[1] Hill *v.* Sayles, 4 Cush. 549; 12 Met. 142.

[2] Heblethwaite *v.* Palmes, 3 Mod. 52.

[3] Olney *v.* Fenner, 2 R. I. 211. See Carlyon *v.* Lovering, 40 Eng. L. & Eq. 448; Murgatroyd *v.* Robinson, Ib. 219.

[4] Steen *v.* Ashby, 24 Ala. 521.

[5] Arbuckle *v.* Ward, 3 Wms. 43.

[6] Jate *v.* Parrish, 7 Mon. 325.

[7] Williams *v.* Nelson, 23 Pick. 141.

20 *a*. But, as already suggested, the distinction is well established, that, where an action is brought for diverting a stream from a mill, and the plaintiff *prescribes* for a water-course, there he must show that the mill was an ancient mill; but where the stream is his own, and he claims it as flowing over his own land, there he may maintain an action without showing that it was from an ancient mill.[1]

20 *b*. And it is to be further observed, that, although by usage one may acquire a right to use the water in a manner not justified by his natural right, such acquired right has no operation against the natural rights of a land-owner higher up the stream, unless the user by which it was acquired affects the use that the latter has made of the stream, or his power to use it, so as to raise the presumption of a grant, and render the tenement above a *servient* tenement.[2] In other words, a right to flow the lands of another, founded upon an exclusive and uninterrupted enjoyment for twenty years, cannot be acquired, unless the enjoyment be *adverse*. The uninterrupted enjoyment is *primâ facie* evidence that it is adverse, but such conclusion may be rebutted by proof, that it was commenced and continued *without claim of right*.[3] (*a*) Hence, in an action for flowing lands, the de-

[1] Palms *v*. Heblethwaite, Skin. 65.

[2] Sampson *v*. Hoddinott, 19 Com. B. 590.

[3] Hart *v*. Vose, 19 Wend. 365; Felton *v*. Simpson, 11 Ired. 84. See Davis *v*. Brigham, 29 Maine, 391.

(*a*) The plaintiff erected a mill in 1799, and the defendant, who owned a mill lower down on the same stream, was in the habit of raising his dam by means of flash boards, when the water in the stream was low, but, within twenty years after the erection of the plaintiff's mill, had been frequently ordered to take down the flash boards, and always acquiesced, claiming no right to keep them up to the injury of the plaintiff; and afterwards admitted that he had no right to keep them up. Held, this evidence was sufficient to defeat any claim of prescription on the part of the defendant, or to rebut the presumption of a grant. Sumner *v*. Tileston, 7 Pick. 198.

But a prescriptive right may be derived from a perpetual gift, and continued use under such gift. Arbuckle *v*. Ward, 3 Wms. 43.

After the death of the owner of a spring, from which the plaintiff had been accustomed to draw water to his house under an agreement, the widow sold the land on which the spring was, reserving the right to draw water from it

fendant must allege in his plea, not only that the use was uninterrupted, but that it was adverse.[1] So it has been held, that a right by prescription to flow land to a given height, by means of a mill-dam, cannot be sustained, unless the flowing *had caused damage* to the owner of the land.[2] And that the owner of a dam does not begin to gain a prescriptive right to maintain such dam, until damage accrues from maintaining it.[3] So, that there must have been *an actual occupation* of the flow of water upon the land above; not merely an uninterrupted flow through such land.[4] And also an occupation *by the defendant*, or those under whom he claims.[5] And, with reference to the rights of an owner *above* the party claiming by prescription, it has been held, that the constant use by a riparian proprietor, for fifty years, of the waters of a stream for the purposes of a mill, does not deprive a riparian proprietor above of the right to make a reasonable use of the waters of the stream for like purposes, although he thereby necessarily disturbs the natural flow of the water to the lower mill.[6]

21. The use of a watercourse, moreover, in order to be justified by prescription, must be *reasonable*, for the party's own benefit or convenience, not malicious, or uncertain.[7] And further, it must be substantially the same with that to which the prescription applies. The flow must remain the same as to quantity and rapidity.[8] Thus, in an action

[1] Colvin v. Burnet, 17 Wend. 564.

[2] Wentworth v. Sanford, &c. 33 Maine, 547; Parker v. Hotchkiss, 25 Conn. 321.

[3] Burleigh v. Lambert, 34 Maine, 322.

[4] Hoy v. Sterrett, 2 Watts, 327.

[5] Benson v. Soule, 32 Maine, 39.

[6] Thurber v. Martin, 2 Gray, 394.

[7] Twiss v. Baldwin, 9 Conn. 291. See Ford v. Whitlock, 1 Williams, 255.

[8] Darlington v. Painter, 7 Barr, 473; Arbuckle v. Ward, 3 Wms. 43; Postlethwaite v. Paine, 8 Ind. 104.

---

to her own house. Held, this reservation did not interrupt the prescriptive right, which the plaintiff was acquiring by his user. Ib.

A., owner of a spring, agreed that B.'s grantor should forever have the use of the spring, by bearing one third of the expenses of bringing the water to their respective houses. Under this agreement, B. and his grantor used the water for more than fifteen years, without interruption. Held, B. had acquired a prescriptive right, though A. continued to use the water jointly with B. Ib.

for diverting a watercourse, it was held, that, if one has ancient pits in his lands, which are replenished by a rivulet, he may cleanse them, but cannot change or enlarge them.[1] The extent of the right may be proved by the contract in which the use originated. And such contract, if clearly proved, and if the use conform to it, is as effectual as a deed.[2] So where a grant to flow land of an adjoining owner depends on presumption, the extent of the grant is measured by the extent of land actually flooded, and not by the height of the dam. And, if repairs to a dam flood the land, to a greater extent than it has been flooded for a period of twenty-one years, the owner is liable, though the dam may not have been made any higher.[3] So one cannot justify the use of a lath-mill under a prescription for a saw-mill.[4] So, where the defence to an action for the obstruction of a watercourse, by the erection of a dam below the plaintiff's works, and thereby setting the water back upon them, was a right in the defendant, acquired by prescription, to raise the water in the manner and to the height complained of; and it appeared that the defendant at first erected a temporary wooden dam, by which the water was raised to that height; but he afterwards, for his convenience in erecting a permanent stone dam, discharged the water, for some time, through a waste-way, in consequence of which the water was so lowered as not to flow up to the plaintiff's works; and then, when the permanent dam was completed, the water was raised again by means thereof, to the height complained of, and was so continued: it was held, that the period of user, by virtue of which the prescriptive right claimed by the defendant could be acquired, did not commence until the water was permanently raised by the stone dam, after its completion.[5] So where the defendants had, for thirty years or more, used the water from a river, and built a dam across it, and taken the water by an artificial channel, for several rods by the side and within the limits of the highway; and rebuilt said dam,

[1] Wolferstan v. Bishop, &c. 2 Wils. 174; S. P. Brown v. Best, 1 Wils. 174.

[2] Arbuckle v. Ward, 3 Wms. 43.

[3] Mertz v. Dorney, 25 Penn. 519.

[4] Simpson v. Seaney, 8 Greenl. 138.

[5] Branch v. Doane, 18 Conn. 233.

and constructed one of stone, higher and tighter than any dam previously built; and damages resulted from its use to the highway, which were unknown before the construction of the stone dam: it was held, that, as the water had been used, after the erection of the stone dam, but a short time, there was no ground to presume a grant from the town to use the water, as it had been used from the erection of that dam until the suit was brought.[1] (*a*)

21 *a*. But, in many cases, the rule, as to the precise identity of the use with the prescription, has been less rigidly en-

[1] Shrewsbury *v.* Brown, 25 Verm. 197.

(*a*) To an action for polluting a stream, and impregnating it with noxious substances, whereby the plaintiff's cattle were unable to drink the water, the defendant pleaded an immemorial right to use the water of the stream for the purposes of his trade of a tanner and fellmonger, and returning it polluted to the stream when so used, and also a prescriptive right for twenty and forty years, respectively. The plaintiff new assigned "that he sued not only for the grievances in the pleas admitted and attempted to be justified, but for that the defendant committed the grievances over and above what the defences justified." At the trial it appeared, that the defendant and his father and grandfather had for a long series of years carried on the business of tanners at the place in question, using the water of the stream as they wanted it; but that, within the last twelve years, the tannery premises had been considerably enlarged, and the business (and consequently the pollution of the stream) increased fourfold. Without leaving anything to the jury, the judge ruled, that the defendant was entitled to a verdict on all the issues except the first and second. Held, whether the pleas were to be understood as claiming an immemorial or a prescriptive right, not limited to the purposes of the tannery, or the more limited right to use the water for the purposes of the business as carried on more than twenty years ago, the verdict was not warranted by the evidence, and that the new assignment was well pleaded. Moore *v.* Webb, 19 Com. B. 673.

The owner of land bordering on a stream, whether navigable or not, may maintain an action of tort against a town, laying out a highway and bridge across the stream, to recover any special damage occasioned to his land, by the bridge being so built, or afterwards altered, by a third person, for his own benefit, with the permission or assent of the town, as to obstruct the course of the stream more than it would otherwise be obstructed; although the bridge was built over a tide-mill, the owners of which have acquired a prescriptive right to obstruct the water to a less degree. Lawrence *v.* Fairhaven, 5 Gray, 110.

forced. It is said, "If such an objection as this were allowed to prevail, any right, however ancient, might be lost by the most minute alteration in the mode of enjoyment, — the making straight a crooked line or footpath would have this result."[1] "The owner is not bound to use the water in the same precise manner, or apply it to the same mill; if he were, that would stop all improvements in machinery."[2] Thus the occupier of a mill may maintain an action for forcing back water and injuring his mill, although he has not enjoyed it precisely in the same state for twenty years; and therefore it was held to be no defence to such an action, that the occupier had, within a few years, erected in his mill a wheel of different dimensions, but requiring less water than the old one, although the declaration stated the plaintiff to be possessed of a mill, without alleging it to be an ancient mill.[3] So a prescription is valid, though the dam has not through the whole period been maintained upon the same spot, if it has been upon one mill-site.[4] And it is held, that, although the height, to which an owner below may raise the water, must be measured by the use; the time for which he may keep it up is not thus limited.[5] And that a prescriptive right may be acquired to the flow of the water in a particular, artificial channel, even though it is neither actually used, nor necessary for the mill erected.[6] So, where a mill-owner has acquired a prescriptive right to keep up a dam constantly, which, in its usual operation, would raise the water to a certain height; although, from the leaky condition of the dam, or the rude construction of the machinery in his mill, or the lavish use of the stream, the water has not been usually and constantly kept up to such height, yet, if he repair the dam, without so changing it as to raise the water higher than the old dam, when tight, would raise it, or if he use the water in a different manner and thereby keep up the water

[1] Per Tindal, C. J., Hall v. Swift, 6 Scott, 167.

[2] Per Abbott, J., Saunders v. Newman, 1 Barn. & Ald. 258.

[3] Saunders v. Newman, 1 Barn. & Ald. 258. See Hurd v. Curtis, 7 Met. 94; Adams v. Warren, 23 Verm. 395; Olmsted v. Loomis, 6 Barb. 152; Cromwell v. Selden, 3 Comst. 253.

[4] Stackpole v. Curtis, 32 Maine, 383.

[5] Alder v. Savill, 5 Taun. 454.

[6] Tyler v. Wilkinson, 4 Mas. 405.

more constantly than before; this is not a new use of the stream, for which a land-owner can claim damages, but is a use conformable to the mill-owner's prescriptive right.[1] So, in case of the change of one ancient pond into three new ones, it is said, "the use of the old pond was discontinued, only because the plaintiff obtained the same or a greater advantage, from the use of the three new ones. He did not thereby abandon his right, he only exercised it in a different spot; and a substitution of that nature is not an abandonment. The declaration means no more than this, that the plaintiff has a right to the overflow of water, either in one pond or in three ponds."[2] So the owner of one mill privilege brought an action against the owner of another below him, on the same stream, for an injury to his privilege, caused by the defendants erecting a new dam higher than his old one. On the trial, the Court instructed the jury, that, if the plaintiff's wheels had not been obstructed within twenty years before, as since the erection of the new dam of the defendant, and if such obstruction was caused by the defendant's dam, then the law was for the plaintiff. Held, that the instruction was erroneous, as the fact, that the plaintiff's wheels were obstructed more after the erection of the new dam than before, was not conclusive of the question, whether the new dam exceeded the height of the defendant's old dam, especially where it appeared in evidence that other causes existed, other than the height of the dam, to raise the water higher than before.[3] So the acquisition of a right to flow for one purpose — as for working mills, is not prevented or defeated by the existence, at the same time, of the right in another person to flow for another purpose — as for floating timber.[4] And where one, having by deed a right to maintain a dam and use a watercourse for irrigation, uses it more than twenty-one years for the further purpose of watering cattle; he acquires a right by prescription to the latter use.[5]

[1] Cowell v. Thayer, 5 Met. 253.

[2] Per Park, B., Hale v. Oldroyd, 14 M. & W. 789.

[3] Manier v. Myers, 6 B. Mon. 132.

[4] Davis v. Brigham, 29 Maine, 391.

[5] Wheatley v. Chrisman, 24 Penn. 298.

And where the plaintiffs had for more than twenty years, by means of a canal, adversely diverted and used the water of a stream, subject to a reservation, in favor of the owners of the meadow through which the canal was cut, of the right to turn the water down the natural channel, for six weeks in each year, for the purpose of getting hay more conveniently, and digging clay; it was held, that such reservation did not prevent the plaintiffs from acquiring the right to divert the water, by an actual use and diversion, substantially general and continuous; but operated only as a limitation of the right acquired.[1]

22. While long-continued use may establish a title, such title may be lost by *disuse* or *abandonment.* It is held, that the owner of a mill-privilege on which a mill has formerly stood, but on which no mill is actually standing, is entitled to an action against one, who, by erecting a dam below, renders the site useless for the purpose of erecting a mill; unless the owner has abandoned it evidently with an intent to leave it unoccupied.[2] And that where a mill-owner has acquired a right to flow the land of another without payment of damages; the mere non-user of the mill for a period less than twenty years is not alone sufficient evidence of an abandonment of such right.[3] So it is held, that a mere non-user, by a riparian proprietor, of his full water privileges for twenty years, does not deprive him of the right to use them; there must have been a use by another, adverse to this right, for the whole of such a period, to destroy the right.[4]

22 *a.* But it is the prevailing rule that, if the owner of a mill-privilege ceases to use it for an unreasonable length of time, the privilege is thereby lost; and the entire and continued disuse of such privilege for twenty years is strong *primâ facie* evidence of a non-user for an unreasonable length of time, and, unless rebutted by clear and satisfactory proof, is conclusive.[5] So an express declaration by the

[1] Bolivar, &c. *v.* Neponset Man. Co. 16 Pick. 241.

[2] Hatch *v.* Dwight, 17 Mass. 289.

[3] Williams *v.* Nelson, 23 Pick. 141.

[4] Townsend *v.* McDonald, 2 Kern. 381.

[5] French *v.* Braintree, &c. 23 Pick. 216; 34 Maine, 394.

owner of a mill-privilege, that it is no longer his intention to keep up the mill, accompanied with corresponding acts, such as removing the dam and mill, giving notice of such intention to those whose lands he has flowed, and to whom he has paid damages, and the like, will be deemed an abandonment and extinguishment of the privilege.[1] And the proprietor of a dam, having represented that he intended to abandon it for mill purposes, is estopped to deny that such was his intent, as against one who has been influenced by his representations to build a dam below, which flows back upon the dam above.[2] So, although twenty years have not elapsed after a mill-privilege and dam have ceased to be used as such, when a new dam is erected below, in such a situation as to overflow and destroy the privilege above; if the owner of the latter make no objection to the erection of such new dam during the twenty years from the destruction of his dam, he may be presumed to have abandoned his privilege. And the acceptance, within twenty years, of a deed granting a mill-site, and reciting the existence of another mill-site above it, does not estop the grantee to assert the abandonment by non-user of the upper site, unless the deed shows that the upper site had a right of priority in the use of the water.[3] So, when a mill is disused and removed and not replaced, the dam ceases to be a mill-dam under the protection of the mill acts, and the remedy for the owner of land which is flowed by it is an action at common law. In such case, the plaintiff can recover only for the injury caused by the dam since it ceased to be under the protection of the mill acts.[4] (*a*)

[1] French *v.* Braintree, &c. 23 Pick. 216.

[2] Mowry *v.* Sheldon, 2 R. I. 369.

[3] Farrar *v.* Cooper, 34 Maine, 394.

[4] Baird *v.* Hunter, 12 Pick. 556.

(*a*) Where a mill-owner, who has a grant of a right to flow certain lands, suffers his mill and dam to go to decay, and ceases to flow the land, and a highway is then made across the land; he cannot, by afterwards granting his mill privilege and right to flow, authorize his grantee to overflow such highway by means of a new mill-dam on the site of the old one; and his

23. As in other cases of nuisance, in addition to the ordinary remedy of an action on the case, a party injured may sometimes resort to *a bill in equity.* Thus equity will entertain a bill for injunction by a riparian proprietor, whose title is clear, to restrain the diversion of water from his mill, without requiring him first to establish his right at law; on the ground that he cannot obtain full reparation in an action at law for damages, and that the injury may involve the necessity of a multiplicity of suits.[1] So the Maryland high court of chancery has power to prohibit by injunction the obstruction of watercourses, the diversion of streams from mills, the back flowage upon them, and injuries of the like kind, which, from their nature, cannot be adequately compensated by damages at law.[2]

23 *a.* So chancery has power to issue a decree and perpetual injunction, for the requisite abatement of a milldam, which has been erected to such a height as to overflow the complainant's *mining claim.*[3] But it is also held, that a court of equity will not, at the suit of an individual, interpose an injunction to prevent the erection of an embankment across a stream, or other obstruction thereto, not amounting to a public nuisance.[4] So an injunction was refused, where one owner of a water privilege alleged that another was using more than his share of the water, on the ground that the right had not been determined at law, and that a remedy existed by action.[5] (*a*) And where the rem-

[1] Burden *v.* Stein, 27 Ala. 104. See Sprague *v.* Rhodes, 4 R. I. 301.

[2] Lamborn *v.* The Covington Co. 2 Md. Ch. Decis. 409.

[3] Ramsay *v.* Chandler, 3 Cal. 90.

[4] Gilbert *v.* Morris, &c. 4 Halst. Ch. 495.

[5] Jordan *v.* Woodward, 38 Maine, 423.

---

grantee, if he so overflow the highway, is punishable for a nuisance. Commonwealth *v.* Fisher, 6 Met. 433.

(*a*) A bill in equity will not lie on behalf of a mill-owner, to restrain a riparian proprietor, bordering upon a pond above, on the same mill stream, from *cutting ice* in such pond, the rights of the parties not having been determined at law. Cummings *v.* Barrett, 10 Cush. 186.

An injunction will not be allowed, to prevent the obstruction of a right to

edy at law is complete and adequate, an injunction will not be granted.[1]

24. As in other cases of nuisance, the proprietor of a watercourse may sometimes resort to the remedy of *abatement* by his own act. Thus one owning an ancient mill may lawfully go upon the land of another, and remove an obstruction erected across the stream, for the purpose of irrigating the land, by which the mill is prevented from working.[2] So, where one is the owner of an ancient mill, to which there has been attached a raceway, being an artificial canal for conducting off the water, and without the free and unobstructed current of which the mill could not be worked; and such canal has, from time immemorial, passed through the land of another; and there is no grant or contract regulating the rights of the parties: the owner of the mill has a right to enter upon the land through which the raceway passes, and to clear out the obstructions therefrom in the mode, if any, hitherto practised for clearing out the raceway; otherwise, in the usual and ordinary mode of cleansing such canals; doing no unnecessary damage. And the right or duty of the mill-owner, in cleansing such raceway, to place on the adjoining banks, or to carry off, the materials taken out, may depend on the nature of the materials and other circumstances in the particular case.[3]

24 *a*. But a claim of a right to enter upon the land of another, to repair a mill-dam and embankment necessary to the working of a mill, and originally erected with the consent of the owner of the soil, cannot be maintained, but by showing a grant or prescription.[4] And where a party claiming by prescription merely uses his prescriptive right in excess; the proprietor injured thereby can justify only an

[1] Winnipiseogee, &c. *v.* Worster, 9 Fost. 433.

[2] Colburn *v.* Richards, 13 Mass 420; Hodges *v.* Raymond, 9 Mass. 316.

[3] Prescott *v.* White, 21 Pick. 341.

[4] Cook *v.* Stearns, 11 Mass. 533.

allow water, falling from the eaves of a man's house, to run upon his neighbor's land, unless such obstruction would inflict an important and irreparable injury. Cherry *v.* Stein, 11 Md. 1.

abatement or removal of the unauthorized part of the obstruction. Thus the plaintiff, who had a right to irrigate his meadow by placing a dam of loose stones across a small stream, and occasionally a board or fender, fastened the board by means of two stakes, which had never been done by his predecessors. The defendant, who had rights on the same stream, removed the stakes and board. Held, that the defendant had no right to remove the board as well as the stakes, on the ground that the stakes gave the board a character of permanency incompatible with her own rights.[1] And, in general, in abating an obstruction to a watercourse, a party must proceed in a reasonable manner, with reference to the damage thereby occasioned, though not necessarily in the manner most convenient to the other party.[2]

25. With reference to *the parties*, by and against whom legal proceedings may be instituted in relation to watercourses; it is held that the general rule as to diversion applies to *the government* and its grantees, as well as to individuals.[3]

26. As in other cases of nuisance, the party obstructing a watercourse, as by erecting a dam, or making it higher and lighter than it had been, so that it overflows the plaintiff's land, is not exonerated, by conveying the land to another, more especially if with warranty, from damages arising therefrom after the conveyance. Nor is he entitled to notice to abate before action brought.[4] But a purchaser of mills is not liable for continuing a nuisance, which was commenced by his grantor, until after notice and request to remove.[5] (*a*)

[1] Greenslade *v.* Halliday, 6 Bing. 379. Acc. Moffett *v.* Brewer, 1 Iowa, 348.

[2] Great Falls Co. *v.* Worster, 15 N. H. 412.

[3] Hendricks *v.* Johnson, 6 Port. 472.

[4] Curtice *v.* Thompson, 19 N. H. 471; Waggoner *v.* Jermaine, 3 Denio, 306; Branch *v.* Doane, 17 Conn. 402.

[5] Snow *v.* Cowles, 2 Fost. 296; Woodman *v.* Tufts, 9 N. H. 88.

(*a*) A purchaser of a mill-dam, so constructed as to divert the water when the gates are closed, will be liable without notice, for diverting the water by keeping the gates closed, if his grantor has kept the gates open. 2 Fost. 296.

27. The grantee of land, having a mill and dam erected thereon, who has given his grantor a bond of defeasance which is not recorded, is the owner of such mill and dam, and liable to a complaint for flowing.[1] So also the lessor for years of a dam, which is used to raise a head of water to drive a mill subsequently erected by the lessee, and who retains an interest in the water raised by the dam.[2]

28. An action on the case for flowing is *local*, and must be brought in the county where the land lies. Thus, where the plaintiff 's land was situated in one county, and the defendant's dam, which caused it to be flowed, was erected in another county, an action cannot be brought in the latter county.[3] But where, in an action on the case for damage to the plaintiff's mill, situated in the county where the action was brought, occasioned by a dam erected by the defendants on the same stream, and alleged under a *videlicet* to be in the same county, the proof was, that the dam was in another county; held, the variance was immaterial.[4]

29. A general allegation in a complaint for the diversion of water, that the plaintiffs were entitled to all the water flowing into the canon at the head of their ditch, entitles them to prove a diversion of water from the smaller branches of the canon, supplying water to that point.[5]

30. In an action on the case for obstructing a watercourse, the plaintiff need not set out in his declaration the license or privilege, under which the defendant claims a right to divert a portion of the water.[6]

31. Where a declaration alleged, that the defendant caused water to overflow the plaintiff's meadow, and thereby rendered it spongy and impassable, and he was deprived of the use of his meadow; it was held that evidence was admissible, to show that his muck-bed in the meadow was made inaccessible by the flowage.[7]

1 Hennessey *v.* Andrews, 6 Cush. 170.
2 Sampson *v.* Bradford, 6 Cush. 303.
3 Worster *v.* Winnipiseogee, &c. 5 Fost. 525.
4 Thompson *v.* Crocker, 9 Pick. 59.
5 Priest *v.* Union, &c. 6 Cal. 170.
6 Whetstone *v.* Bowser, 29 Penn. 59.
7 Johnson *v.* Atlantic, &c. 35 N. H. 569.

32. In an action for obstructing a watercourse, the verdict only establishes conclusively that the obstructions then existing are illegal and unauthorized, and does not prevent the defendant from exercising any previous rights.[1]

[1] Whetstone *v.* Bowser, 29 Penn. 59.

CPSIA information can be obtained
at www.ICGtesting.com
Printed in the USA
BVHW041348270622
640732BV00001B/199